STAR TREK VOYAGER®
C O M P A N I O N

STAR TREK VOYAGER®
C O M P A N I O N

Paul Ruditis

P O C K E T   B O O K S

New York   London   Toronto   Sydney

An *Original* Publication of POCKET BOOKS

Pocket Books, a division of Simon & Schuster, Inc.
1230 Avenue of the Americas, New York, NY 10020

ISBN: 0-7434-1751-8

First Pocket Books trade paperback printing May 2003

10   9   8   7   6   5   4   3

Design by Richard Oriolo

For information regarding special discounts for bulk purchases,
please contact Simon & Schuster Special Sales at 1-800-456-6798
or business@simonandschuster.com

Printed in the U.S.A.

FOR DAD

who introduced me to "Star Track," [sic] in my childhood and convinced Mom that it was the Muppets

on Sesame Street *that were causing the nightmares and certainly not the Mugato.*

CONTENTS

ACKNOWLEDGMENTS

It takes many people to put together a work of this magnitude. To everyone involved directly and indirectly, I wish to bestow a multitude of thanks.

One man started it all. Gene Roddenberry, along with the original team involved in the creation of *Star Trek,* produced a vision of the future that is still *Star Trek*'s touchstone today. And to those who continued that vision with *Star Trek: Voyager*, my thanks for all their time and hard work, especially: Rick Berman, Michael Piller, Jeri Taylor, Brannon Braga, Kenneth Biller, Kate Mulgrew, Robert Beltran, Roxann Dawson, Jennifer Lien, Robert Duncan McNeill, Ethan Phillips, Robert Picardo, Tim Russ, Jeri Ryan, and Garrett Wang. The directors, writers, production crew, guest actors, and the collective of personnel—who helped bring the show to the screen one hundred and seventy-two times—are the unsung heroes of the show. Please take a moment to look through the production credits at the end of this book, as *all* the people listed contributed so much of themselves turning the idea into reality.

To everyone at Paramount Pictures who contributed to the series and—more specifically—to this book, I would like to let them know they made all this possible. Candice Clark, in Media Relations, set up the interviews; and the former V.P. of Advertising & Promotion, Gary Holland, and his staff in Domestic Television provided invaluable help with the episode summaries.

For the hardworking publishing teams of past and present at Viacom Consumer Products, you deserve an extra special note of appreciation. Pam Newton and Paula Block, your guidance, inspiration, and most important, your patience were key to making this book a reality.

To everyone at Pocket Books—most notably, in the *Star Trek* department— I wish to express my gratitude to all, especially to my editor, Margaret Clark, and the book's designer, Richard Oriolo.

And finally, to my ever-present personal support group headed up by my mom, Barbara, and my sister, Michele, "thank you" just doesn't seem to be enough, but you have that and more. To all my close friends, thanks for sticking by me no matter what, with an extra nod of appreciation to Chris Van Note-Burman—the friend I know will always be by my side, figuratively, if not literally (and to her husband, Dave, for putting up with the marathon phone calls).

Finally, to my dad, Frank, the one to whom this book is dedicated. I thank you for your inspiration.

PAUL RUDITIS
Burbank, CA

C O M P A N I O N

The crew of the *U.S.S. Voyager*: Clockwise from top: Garrett Wang as Ensign Harry Kim; Jennifer Lien as Kes; Robert Duncan McNeill as Lieutenant Tom Paris; Robert Picardo as the Doctor; Roxann Dawson as Lieutenant B'Elanna Torres; Tim Russ as Lieutenant Tuvok; Kate Mulgrew as Captain Kathryn Janeway; Robert Beltran as Commander Chakotay; Ethan Phillips as Neelix.

SEASON ONE

"For I dipt into the future, far as human eye could see;

Saw the vision of the world, and all the wonder that would be . . ."

From "Locksley Hall" by Alfred, Lord Tennyson
Inscribed on the Commemoration Plaque of the *U.S.S. Voyager*

On Monday night, January 16, 1995, the United Paramount Network signed on with the newest installment of the *Star Trek* series, *Star Trek: Voyager.* The fledgling UPN chose the familiar *Star Trek* name as the flagship of its programming to entice stations across the country to carry what was intended to become the sixth major television network. Likewise, *Star Trek: Voyager* chose UPN to be the first network to carry the historic series since the original *Star Trek* ran on NBC. Its immediate predecessors, *Star Trek: The Next Generation* and *Star Trek: Deep Space Nine,* initially aired in first-run syndication.

But the story of *Star Trek: Voyager* is not about what network it aired on, or even how it came to be. It is the story of a makeshift family lost on the other side of the galaxy, thousands of light years from home, of a woman in command of a combined crew of Starfleet heroes and Maquis rebels. And it is also the story of strange new worlds and new civilizations explored in a region that was truly where no one had gone before. Yet it is the combination of the fantastical storytelling mixed in with the realities of television production that made *Star Trek: Voyager* the show that launched a network.

Following on the heels of *The Next Generation* and airing simultaneously along with *Deep Space Nine, Voyager* sought to stand apart from its predecessors by setting a different stage for storytelling. More than just putting another group of people on a ship visiting familiar territory or choosing a central location around which the stories would revolve, the new series needed a hook, something that brought it back to the heart of *Star Trek* and exploration. Co-creators Rick Berman, Michael Piller and Jeri Taylor met the challenge head on by sending the crew farther than any other Federation starship had explored—to the uncharted regions of the Delta Quadrant.

What follows is one of the many drafts of the *Star Trek: Voyager* bible, which served as the framework from which the series would evolve. Though some of the concepts would change as the realities of production set in, it is from these pages that the series was born. Through these many drafts, *Voyager* was shaped and molded into the fourth television series of the entertainment monolith known as *Star Trek.*

STAR TREK: VOYAGER BIBLE

Star Trek: Voyager is set in the same time frame as "The Next Generation and "Deep Space Nine." It chronicles the adventures of a Starfleet vessel which must find its way back to Federation space from a distant part of the galaxy.

THE BACKSTORY

The Cardassian War is over, but the conflict refuses to die. Cardassians within the Demilitarized Zone continue to harass Federation outposts, and while Starfleet responds to any significant aggression, some colonists have decided to take matters into their own hands. This group of resistance fighters calls itself the Maquis—and they are becoming more than a nuisance. The Federation considers them outlaws.

The Starfleet ship *Voyager* is dispatched to search for a Maquis ship which has disappeared in an unusual region of space known as the "Badlands." But *Voyager* finds itself swept up in a strange and terrifying phenomenon which ultimately deposits the ship at the far reaches of the galaxy—so far that, even at warp speeds, it would take nearly seventy years to return.

They also find the Maquis ship there, and, in an uneasy liaison, the crews of the two ships agree to band together in order to maximize their chances of surviving and returning to Federation space.

But the Maquis ship is destroyed and its crew must come aboard *Voyager*. The two ships' captains negotiate for key positions: the Maquis insist on certain pivotal roles for their senior staff. An agreement is struck, and the ship sets out, manned by this unusual mix of Starfleet and renegade officers—some of whom get along, and some of whom don't.

Their quest is to find a "shortcut" home, a wormhole or other phenomenon that will transport them over the huge distance in minutes. But the *Voyager* captain also insists that—even though they are seventy years from Starfleet Command—they behave as a Starfleet crew. They will continue to go boldly, to explore, study, and investigate, so that when they do return, they will have amassed a vast wealth of knowledge about a heretofore unexplored region of space.

THE *STARSHIP VOYAGER*

It is smaller, sleeker, and more advanced than the *Enterprise*. It holds a crew of some two hundred, and does not have families on board.

Details of the ship will be provided as it is designed.

THE MAQUIS

The Cardassians and the Federation may consider the Maquis outlaws, but in their own minds they are freedom fighters. They are idealistic nonconformists who believe passionately that they are taking the only course of action they can to protect themselves and their loved ones from continued Cardassian aggression.

Some are Starfleet officers who have resigned their commissions or dropped out of the Academy. Some have been asked to leave Starfleet. But most share a common trait: they are not comfortable living under the strict rules of conduct demanded by Starfleet. They are independent, free-thinking individuals with perhaps a few more rough edges than we might see in a typical Starfleet crew.

In addition to the two regular characters that are Maquis (Chakotay and B'Elanna), we assume that some twenty more have come on board and can be used from time to time in stories.

CONTINUING CHARACTERS

ELIZABETH JANEWAY

A human, Janeway is by no means the only female captain in Starfleet. But it is generally acknowledged that she is among the best—male or female. She embodies all that is exemplary about Starfleet officers: intelligent, thoughtful, perspicacious, sensitive to the feelings of others, tough when she has to be, and not afraid to take chances. She has a gift for doing the completely unexpected which has bailed her out of more than one scrape.

The daughter of a mathematician mother and an astrophysicist father, Janeway was on a track for a career in science. Her natural leadership abilities manifested themselves quickly, however, and she was rapidly promoted to ever-more-responsible positions. And because of her hands-on experience in various science posts, she brings to her captaincy a greater familiarity with technology and science than any captain we've yet experienced.

Her relationship with her mother, a Starfleet theoretical mathematician, was particularly close, and she used to enjoy talking with her, discussing esoteric issues of math as well as down-to-earth issues of life. Her mother was her role model, and bequeathed Janeway with warmth, sensitivity, intellectual curiosity, and likability. She misses her mother's presence in her life.

Janeway was in the midst of a relationship with a man when *Voyager* took its unscheduled leap to the edge of the galaxy. The last conversation she had with him took place on a monitor, and it was a rushed, harried chat. She never realized it was to be the last. Although she keeps up a positive front about finding a quick way home, she realizes that she may never reach Federation space in her lifetime, and that her lover, after an appropriate mourning period, will move on and undoubtedly find someone else. These thoughts, held at bay during the day, tend to surface in the middle of the night when it's hard to sleep.

Janeway is respected and loved by the members of her crew, but what about the renegades? Their captain, Chakotay, has agreed to the position of First Officer, and must now report to a Starfleet officer. Chakotay himself develops a strong bond with Janeway. He had known of her, heard of her diplomatic and tactical exploits, and realizes that if they were to be dumped at the ends of the galaxy with any Captain—they're lucky it was this one.

Tom Paris has been given his chance at redemption by Captain Janeway, and he's determined to prove to her that it was a good idea. But B'Elanna maintains a distance between herself and the Captain. She won't be won over so easily.

TOM PARIS

Paris's career in Starfleet was expected to be exemplary. He descended from a proud lineage of Starfleet legends; his great-grandfather, grandmother, father, and aunt were all admirals. Everyone assumed that Tom, who was bright, capable, and charming, would achieve those same heights. No one knew that Tom felt a tremendous pressure to live up to the name his family had carved—and had grave doubts whether that was possible.

He fared well enough at Starfleet Academy—his grades, while not dazzling, were decent. He played on the Parises Squares team and participated in various activities. His greatest skill was as a pilot, and he often said he'd rather pilot a ship than sit in the captain's chair. After graduation, he joined a unit of Starfleet's S.A.V. division (Small Attack Vessel), where his piloting skills would be put to good use.

But there was an accident during a war games demonstration, a pilot was killed—and Tom Paris, fearing his reputation might suffer and derail his career, lied and placed the blame on the dead man. The fault was actually his, and had he simply owned up to that, he would

have been disciplined. But he was young, and was terrified of bringing disgrace onto his illustrious family.

That mistake cost him dearly. When the lie was revealed, he was discharged. His worst fears had been realized—he had sullied the family name. He sank into a severe depression, wandering the next few years aimlessly, piloting freighters and tankers just to be behind the controls of a ship again—the only place he felt even vaguely alive. At one point he landed in a port where he fell into a game of Dabo with some members of the Maquis, and at the end of a long night he ended up joining them. They offered him the one thing he wanted most: to pilot a sleek starship in situations which require extraordinary prowess. He wasn't much interested in their cause—but it did provide a fight which took his mind off the fight with his own soul. He was with them barely a month when he was captured, and in his mind that was another "failure."

When Captain Janeway contacts him in prison, it is with the gift of a new chance at life, and he has always credited her for that opportunity. He would stop a phaser blast for her, and is determined to make her glad she gave him a chance. He of all the crew is not dismayed by the cruel fate which has befallen them: what does it matter that they're at the ends of the galaxy? He's flying a ship and having adventures—that's just what he wants to be doing, and it doesn't matter particularly to him where it happens.

He has an affection for B'Elanna, seeing in her a soul at war and reminding him of himself. And, like B'Elanna, he is drawn toward the rock-like steadiness of Tuvok.

CHAKOTAY

The First Officer is a complex—some would say difficult—man. His background is unique: he spans two cultures, one foot in each, belonging to both and yet to neither.

In the twenty-second century, a group of Indian traditionalists became dissatisfied with the "homogenization" of humans that was occurring on Earth. Strongly motivated to preserve their cultural identity, they relocated to a remote planet near what has now become known as the Demilitarized Zone.

Chakotay is a member of that Indian nation, but was always what his people call a "contrary;" he had a mind of his own, an individualistic rather than communal way of thinking. Though proud of his heritage and his traditions, he was not satisfied to ignore the galaxy around him—a galaxy teeming with diverse life-forms and amazing technology. He broke from his people, educated himself in the ways of the twenty-fourth century, and attended Starfleet Academy.

But he was "contrary" at the Academy, also, and found he had difficulty adhering to the rigid codes and rules. He was commissioned and posted to the *Merrimac* just after the end of the Cardassian wars. When he learned that his people were becoming victims of attack by Cardassians, he left Starfleet to defend them, joining the then-infant group, Maquis.

Chakotay never gave up his practice of traditional rituals, and he preserves them aboard *Voyager*. In his quarters is an Indian altar and other traditional fetishes. One wall contains a version of traditional mural art. He visits the Holodeck where he has a "habak" program for the celebration of his people's ceremonial cycle.

As an adolescent, Chakotay pursued a vision quest, and in doing so obtained a "spirit guide"—a timber wolf—which appears to him now in dreams and visions, and often guides him in his decision-making process.

He has a reverence for all living things, and when he eats he offers thanks to the earth for providing food; he will not eat meat; he takes no drugs or alcohol.

As a leader he is steady, fearless, and capable of inspiring absolute devotion. Though he comes onto *Voyager* more by necessity than choice, he quickly wins the respect of even the most die-hard Starfleet veterans. He strikes an immediate and powerful bond with Janeway, and an unusual one with Kim, who through Chakotay's example begins to question his own homogenization and the loss of his traditional values.

TUVOK

The Vulcan Tactical/Security Officer is getting on in years—he's 160 (about 60 in human terms), but is as fit as people half his age. He is a powerful combination of maturity, wisdom, experience—and vitality. His Vulcan equanimity and patience serve him well in his role as the ship's peacekeeper, but it is his unofficial role which most binds him to the other crew members. His grandfatherly presence is comforting to many particularly the young and headstrong B'Elanna, and his age is seen as a virtue; many of the crew turn to him for advice and counsel, and are rarely disappointed.

Tuvok has lived long, but he has also lived well, tasting of most of life's experiences. He married young, had four children (three of whom are Starfleet), and outlived his wife of ninety years. He has grandchildren for whom he feels such devotion that at times it threatens to shatter his Vulcan emotional control. It is this loss—not to see them grow and flourish—that he feels most keenly.

He has worked with Janeway for some time; they know each other well and have achieved the kind of comfortable relationship that comes with time and experience. She turns to him as a strong shoulder; she is the person he turns to when *he* needs one.

But it is with B'Elanna that Tuvok has the most intense relationship. His calm, logical demeanor is comforting to her—and reassuring that one's volatile instincts can be contained. Without Tuvok, B'Elanna's journey would be a much rougher one.

HARRY KIM

Kim, the Ops/Communication officer, is a human of Asian descent, and had the happiest day of his life when he reported to duty aboard *Voyager*. He knew his parents were proud—though he was a bit embarrassed by their hugs and kisses as they said good-bye—and that meant a lot to him. As the only child of a couple which had tried for years to conceive, he was their great pride, their golden child. He grew up with love, warmth, and support, and an assumption that he would excel at whatever he chose. More than anything, he wanted to fulfill that expectation, to repay his parents for their undying devotion to him. And he had always done that, through his shining academic career and his graduation with honors from the Academy.

After *Voyager* was swept to the far reaches of the galaxy, when he realized he would never see his parents again and they would believe him dead, his greatest regret was for the pain they would feel.

But if Harry was raised with love and care, he was also raised in a somewhat sheltered way. He had no worries, no cares, and whatever minor annoyances life might have brought were deflected from him by his parents. So Harry has some growing up to do. Having never experienced adversity, he has fewer of the tools for coping than some of the others. Though he tries to keep such thoughts from surfacing, he's scared. He's over his head in this mission; he thought he'd be gone a month and then go home to share his adventures with his folks. But what has happened is unthinkable, and often he has the sensation that it's just a bad dream, that he will wake up in his bedroom at home, to the sound of his mother singing in the garden and his father hammering copper plate for sculptures.

He goes about his duties with diligence—it's comforting, somehow, to have a job to do—but more than anyone else, Harry is suffering.

The others know this, and in their varying ways, try to give the young man a helping hand. Their methods range from Chakotay's stern insistence on duty to Janeway's comforting maternal presence, but among the crew there is no one who doesn't like Harry Kim.

B'ELANNA TORRES

The Chief Engineer has a facade that's worked well for her: tough, knowledgeable, able to take care of herself, bothered by nothing. In fact, beneath the surface, there dwells a person confused and at war with herself. B'Elanna has a mixed heritage—Klingon and human—that she deplores. Her Klingon side is disturbing to her; she makes every effort to suppress it, preferring to develop her human side. She distrusts the feelings her Klingon blood produces, and wishes that, like Tuvok, she could achieve total control of them.

B'Elanna's attitude stems from a complex mix of factors: Her Klingon mother and her human father separated when she was young and vulnerable, and she grew up not knowing her father. Consequently, he was transformed by her into a fantasy image: the perfect daddy-prince, an idealized figure who stood for all that was good and valuable.

She and her mother lived, not on the Klingon Home World, but on a remote colony which was largely human, and where the young child inevitably grew up feeling like the "other." As she grew older, the feelings began to solidify: being Klingon was equated with alienation and loss, and being human represented everything that was desirable.

The turning of her back on her Klingon side was epitomized when she was accepted at Starfleet Academy, where she excelled in the sciences. But even then she struggled with the structure and discipline demanded of the students. After graduation she joined the Starfleet Engineering Corps, but her conflict with the Starfleet way of life continued. Her brief career was stormy; she was at odds with her colleagues over almost every aspect of Starfleet life. She quit, with great regret, once again feeling that she didn't fit in—and blamed this, once more, on her Klingon side.

As a member of the Maquis, B'Elanna had finally found an outlet for many of her frustrations—a tangible enemy against whom she could fight. She was a courageous soldier, and either didn't realize or didn't acknowledge the fact that warring on the Cardassians, allowed her Klingon warrior's blood to course freely and unashamedly.

Now, on *Voyager*, that foe has been taken away, and her own inner frustrations are thrown into marked relief. Without an enemy, B'Elanna is forced to deal with angry parts of herself that no longer have an appropriate outlet. It is through Tuvok's calm counsel that she is learning to accept herself.

B'Elanna has grown into a fetching young beauty with an incandescent sexuality. She turns many heads, but the person she has designs on is Tom Paris, who won't clutter their professional relationship by having an affair with another officer.

DOC ZIMMERMAN

Doc is not really a person, but a holographic figure—an E.M.P. to be precise: Experimental Medical Program. When the ship's doctor is unavailable, or needs added assistance, he can call on the E.M.P. The holo-doctor appears as a human male and has been programmed with the most up-to-date medical knowledge; he is capable of treating any disease or injury.

Doc identifies himself as E.M.P. 1, Zimmerman—Zimmerman being the programmer who created him in his own image. He has awareness that he is a hologram, and is fully aware of his limitations. He had no personality when we first met him, and was as dry and dull as an automaton. Subsequently, he has undergone a number of personality changes depending on the person who is programming him. The crew is never sure who they're going to get when they call up Doc Zimmerman.

NEELIX and KES

Neelix is an alien male unlike any we've ever seen, in that he comes from the part of the galaxy that has been heretofore unexplored. He's a strange one—small, scraggly, toothless, and cunning. He's part scavenger, trader, con man, procurer, and sage. His life has not been an easy one, but he has toughed it out—surviving by his wits and instincts in a dangerous part of space.

Neelix has developed the capacity to be all things to all people. You want a guide? I'm a guide. You want a weapon? I'm an arms trader. You want a cook? I'm a gourmet chief. He's the ultimate in flexibility and a Jack of many, many trades.

Kes is his Ocampa lover. She is delicate, beautiful, young—and has a life span of only nine years. Neelix adores her, is protective of her, is insanely jealous of her. Kes, doesn't give him any reason for those feelings; she loves Neelix and is loyal to him. But she is inquisitive and eager to absorb knowledge about this starship and its fascinating crew. She is an innocent who sees humanity through a fresh perspective, and the crew of *Voyager* never cease to fascinate her.

Neelix is the "cook" in the officers' mess. It's a job he wangled to get himself and Kes a comfortable life on this luxurious starship. Because of the huge power drain that replicators place on the ship's systems, the crew must, for the first time in years, eat real food. Neelix knows where to find it, and how to prepare it, and before long, he's invaluable. He also enjoys being right in the heart of things—and where else is that but in the officers' mess? He knows when to listen, when to keep quiet, and when to speak up . . . and the crew find that he can be a valuable repository of information.

Kes helps him cook and serve, but she'd much rather be roaming the ship, getting to know the people; Neelix can never seem to find her when he needs her, and he's always sure she's standing up in a closet with a sailor.

Their relationship is offbeat, wry, and funny and allows us insights into a uniquely alien relationship. Neelix and Kes, a truly odd couple, become oblique commentators on the human condition.

"When Voyager came around and we knew we were going to place the next series back on a starship we wanted to do it in a way that was not going to be that redundant when it came to The Next Generation. So we had a certain amount of conflict on the ship because of the Maquis. We had a different dynamic because we were not speaking everyday to Starfleet and because we had a female captain. Those were the major differences that set this show apart from the others. . . . It had the core belief of what Star Trek was all about, both in terms of the excitement and the action and in terms of the provocative elements of ideas that Star Trek has always been known to present to the audience."

—RICK BERMAN

From the bible, the series would grow. Though rumors of *Voyager* coming come early circulated around the fifth season, the basic premise would remain the same throughout the seven-year life of the show. Uneasiness between the Starfleet and Maquis crews diminished relatively early in the run as the crew learned to embrace the adventure, although there would be occasional tensions through the seventh season. Most of the larger changes from bible to reality came in the form of the characters.

"We didn't want to just create a captain and cast it with a female. We wanted to create a female captain who was a captain that was somewhat more nurturing and a little bit less swashbuckling than someone like Captain Kirk, a little bit less sullen than someone like Captain Sisko, and a little bit more approachable than Captain Picard. And Kate, I think, remarkably delivers a feminine nurturing side and at the same time, a sense of strength and confidence. And that's just what we were looking for and I think that we've gotten it in spades."

—RICK BERMAN

Much of the character of Janeway (Kate Mulgrew) remains the same as what was laid out in the bible. The "intelligent, thoughtful, perspicacious, sensitive to the feelings of others, tough when she has to be, and not afraid to take chances," captain is perfectly embodied in Kate Mulgrew. However, glimpses into her past relationship with her mother fall by the wayside in favor of exploring her feelings for her father, who would become a Starfleet admiral by the time the pilot was shot. This relationship is deeply examined in "Coda," when an alien takes the form of her father to convince her that she has died. Another powerful relationship that stays the same from bible to series was that with her fiancé Mark, "her lover, [who] after an appropriate mourning period will move on and undoubtedly find someone else." The repercussions of Mark's marrying another woman are felt by Janeway in the fourth season episode "Hunters."

The redemption Tom Paris (Robert Duncan McNeill) seeks in the bible comes fairly early in the series, if not by the end of the pilot episode, "Caretaker." Though at times he backslides into his old ways, by the time of "Threshold" he has largely come to terms with himself and how he fits into the crew. The writers are, however, able to get some play out of the backstory in the second season when Paris's apparent descent into his old ways serves as the perfect ruse to sniff out the traitorous Crewman Jonas, who had been sending secret messages to Seska.

Born of a "group of Indian traditionalists," Chakotay (Robert Beltran) is another character who remains fairly true to his "contrary" description in the bible. Though some of his traditional rituals and "habak" program are not seen as described, many of his beliefs would be explored in the early seasons through the use of the vision quest and his animal guide, noted in the bible to be a timber wolf, but never named onscreen.

The character who changes the most from page to screen is Tuvok (Tim Russ). With the hiring of an actor years younger than the envisioned character, many changes were required beyond those related to his age. A younger Tuvok would not have the "grandfatherly presence" that was "comforting to many" so the role needed to be reimagined to take that character from someone envisioned as the "ship's peacekeeper," whose logical nature often kept him at a distance from the crew. His kinship to Janeway does evolve as noted in the bible, but his relationship with B'Elanna does not. However his "calm, logical demeanor" does have an impact on B'Elanna ("Random Thoughts").

Harry Kim (Garrett Wang), was the most fully realized Alpha Quadrant character in the crew. Much of his personality was defined by his relationship to his parents, a trait that would continue throughout the series. Kim serves as the character who longs for home. The young, eager officer matures as the series develops, occasionally in concert with Paris, the result of the hurdles he has to overcome, from various mental and physical strains to death on two occasions.

The half-Klingon, half-human B'Elanna Torres (Roxann Dawson) also remains as originally envisioned. Her duality of nature serves as the genesis for many episodes that focus on her character, most notably "Faces," in which she is quite literally split in two. Though she never comes to idolize the father who abandoned her as a child, she does eventually come to terms with her relationships with her mother and father in "Barge of the Dead" and "Lineage" respectively. Although Torres and Kim do seem to share a flirtation in the early seasons, a different relationship hinted at as early as the bible is that of her romance with Tom Paris. The pair eventually wed in "Drive."

The character description for the Doctor (Robert Picardo) led to a little behind-the-scenes confusion in the first season. Based on the fact that the bible refers to him as "Doc Zimmerman," an early press release from the studio also referred to him by that name, leading the audience to believe that, indeed, was to become his moniker. In actuality, the plan for the Doctor changed and his search for a name ultimately goes unfulfilled throughout the series. Also of note is that the name of the system itself—Experimental Medical Program (EMP)—is changed early on to Emergency Medical Hologram (EMH).

Neelix (Ethan Phillips) and Kes (Jennifer Lien) are also fairly well fleshed out by this draft of the bible. The pair become "oblique commentators on the human condition" in two distinctly different ways. In the early seasons, Neelix questions the logic behind some of the captain's more exploratory motives, but he does it with his own unique brand of cheer, ultimately becoming one of her staunchest supporters. Meanwhile, Kes views her new friends as if through the eyes of an excited child, eager to learn more about humanity.

The one character who goes unmentioned in the bible is, quite understandably, the one whom the producers did not create until later in the series. Seven of Nine (Jeri Ryan), ultimately serves as a true mirror of the human condition. Her striving to recover her humanity serves to show how difficult it is to be human and to lead a righteous life.

In this first season of *Voyager* the crew encounters the great unknown with the spirit of excitement of adventure found in early *Star Trek*. They visit strange new worlds, as in "Time and Again" and "Ex Post Facto." Meet new life-forms who come in a variety of guises from presumed spatial anomalies ("The Cloud") to holograms ("Heroes and Demons") to friends—the Ocampa and Talaxians—to enemies—the Kazon and Vidiians. They will grow into one crew—a Starfleet crew—overcoming their differences. And, first and foremost, they will work together to find their way home.

I think that Captain Janeway and her crew represent the very best of what Roddenberry envisioned the future has in stone for us. In terms of their principles, in terms of their lack of pettiness, in terms of their sense of exploration and the betterment of the human species.

—RICK BERMAN

CARETAKER

EPISODES #101/102
TELEPLAY BY MICHAEL PILLER & JERI TAYLOR
STORY BY RICK BERMAN & MICHAEL PILLER & JERI TAYLOR
DIRECTED BY WINRICH KOLBE

GUEST STARS

CARETAKER/BANJO MAN	BASIL LANGTON
JABIN	GAVIN O'HERLIHY
AUNT ADAH	ANGELA PATON
and	
QUARK	ARMIN SHIMERMAN

CO-STARS

LT. STADI	ALICIA COPPOLA
OCAMPA DOCTOR	BRUCE FRENCH
OCAMPA NURSE	JENNIFER PARSONS
TOSCAT	DAVID SELBURG
HUMAN DOCTOR	JEFF McCARTHY
MARK	STAN IVAR
ROLLINS	SCOTT MacDONALD
CAREY	JOSH CLARK
GUL EVEK	RICHARD POE
FARMER'S DAUGHTER	KEELY SIMS
DAGGIN	ERIC DAVID JOHNSON
COMPUTER VOICE	MAJEL BARRETT

EPISODE #101

STARDATE 48315.6

Unhappy with a new treaty, Federation Colonists along the Cardassian border have banded togeth-

Captain Kathryn Janeway takes command of the *Starship Voyager.* ROBBIE ROBINSON

er. Calling themselves "The Maquis," they continue to fight the Cardassians. Some consider them heroes, but to the governments of the Federation and Cardassia, they are outlaws.

Lieutenant Tuvok, of the *Starship Voyager,* has infiltrated the crew of a Maquis ship led by Chakotay, a former Starfleet officer. As a member of the Maquis crew, Tuvok helps them evade a Cardassian ship then, along with his crewmates, disappears in an area of space know as the Badlands.

Tuvok's commanding officer, Captain Janeway, leads a mission to find the Vulcan lieutenant, enlisting the aid of Starfleet prisoner Tom Paris, a former Maquis, to guide her ship through the Badlands. His presence aboard *Voyager* is unwelcome to many of the ship's crew, Paris befriends Ensign Harry Kim, a recent graduate of Starfleet Academy. To his credit, the young crewman is able to look beyond Paris's past, which includes being drummed out of Starfleet.

Once they are in the Badlands, a coherent tetrion beam of unknown origin scans *Voyager.* The beam is followed by a displacement wave that sends the ship to the Delta Quadrant over 70,000 light years from Federation space. Their destination is a huge alien Array that has also captured the missing Maquis ship.

The journey has inflicted severe damage to *Voyager* and caused numerous casualties and fatalities among the crew. The ship's doctor is killed and replaced by *Voyager's* Emergency Medical Hologram (EMH), which was developed to supplement the medical staff during emergencies. As such, he was only intended for short-term use. Before the EMH can treat the surviving members of the crew, they are transported away from the ship to what appears to be a farmland setting. In actuality, the scene is a holographic projection, inside the alien Array.

Janeway refuses to accept the bucolic setting as reality, and soon the holographic façade is dropped. The crew is taken prisoner and subjected to painful experiments, but eventually, the crews of *Voyager* and the Maquis vessel are returned to their respective ships minus Harry Kim and B'Elanna Torres, a half-Klingon, half-human engineer from the Maquis vessel.

After forming an uneasy alliance with Chakotay, Captain Janeway leads an away team back to the Array where they confront its only apparent inhabitant, an old man playing a banjo. The man, who speaks for the alien entity that controls the Array, refuses to answer their questions, claiming he does not have the time to help them. He returns the away team to *Voyager* without

Back on *Voyager* the crew traces energy pulses from the Array that are being sent from the fifth planet of a neighboring star system. With her options limited, Janeway decides that the planet may provide some answers and promises Tuvok that she will do what she can to get her entire crew back home.

Enroute to the planet, *Voyager* and the Maquis ship come across a debris field, where the crews encounter a Talaxian scavenger named Neelix who surprises them by recounting exactly what has befallen their ships. He explains that the "Caretaker," who controls the Array, has been abducting ships for months and confirms their suspicions by suggesting that the missing crew members may have been sent to the Ocampa, a race that lives below the surface of the fifth planet. Neelix agrees to serve as their guide in exchange for water, a precious commodity in the sector.

As Kim and Torres continue their treatment at the medical facility, they learn that an environmental disaster forced the Ocampa to move underground where they have lived for over 500 generations. During that time, the Caretaker has provided for all their needs.

An away team beams down to the planet's surface. Neelix introduces Janeway to the Kazon-Ogla, one sect of a savage alien race that has taken possession of the surface, which is rich in cormaline deposits. Janeway asks Maje Jabin, the Kazon-Ogla leader, if he can help them, but he refuses.

Neelix suggests that Jabin trade Kes, an Ocampa woman he is holding captive, for some of *Voyager*'s water. But the Kazon are more interested in forcibly obtaining

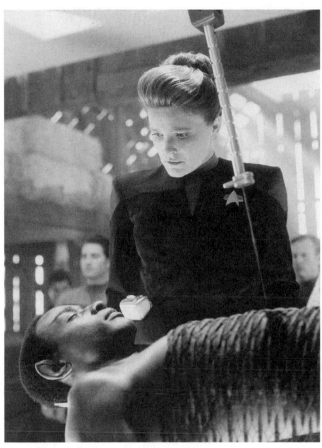
Janeway finds her missing security officer captive in the Delta Quadrant. ROBBIE ROBINSON

telling them that he has sent Kim and Torres to a medical facility. It is in an underground city, on another world which is suffering from an unknown malady.

Starfleet and Maquis officers combine forces to search for their abducted crew members in the underground Ocampa city. ROBBIE ROBINSON

Voyager's technology. Producing a phaser, Neelix takes Jabin captive and forces the Kazon to release his love, Kes. The away team, along with Kes and Neelix, beam back to *Voyager*, Kes agrees to lead Janeway and the others through the tunnels to the underground city to search for the missing pair.

Two miles beneath the surface, Kim and Torres persuade an Ocampa woman to show them a route that could lead to the surface. As the Array increases the rate of the energy pulses that power the city, the pair begin the journey, narrowly missing the search party from *Voyager*. Tuvok theorizes that the increased activity of the Array may indicate that the Caretaker is dying, and intends to give the Ocampa a surplus of power that will sustain them after he is gone.

To protect the Ocampa, the Array begins firing a weapon at the planet to seal all the energy conduits. Paris, Neelix, and Kes split from the rest of the team and find Kim and Torres in one of the tunnels leading to the planet's surface. Paris and Neelix see to it that the others are beamed to the ship, then go back for Janeway, Chakotay, and Tuvok. Chakotay's skepticism about Paris's loyalty is erased when Paris saves his life.

Returning to the Array, Janeway again encounters the old man, who explains that he was trying to find a compatible species with which he could procreate and leave someone to care for the Ocampa after he dies. Janeway tries to convince the Caretaker to send *Voyager* and the Maquis ship back home, but he refuses, explaining that he intends to destroy the Array so it will not fall into Kazon hands. The Caretaker dies before he can carry out his plan, leaving Janeway to decide whether to use the Array to get home or to destroy it to protect the Ocampa. She chooses what seems to be the only moral option, stranding both crews and making a mortal enemy of the Kazon.

With Chakotay's ship destroyed in the battle with the Kazon, Janeway asks the Maquis to join her crew. She also allows Neelix and Kes to stay aboard. With Chakotay serving as her first officer, Paris reinstated as a Starfleet lieutenant, and Torres and Kim cured by the EMH, Janeway sets course for home.

SENSOR READINGS: The *U.S.S. Voyager* NCC-74656 is an *Intrepid*-class starship with a sustainable cruise velocity of warp factor 9.975. With fifteen decks and an original crew complement of 141 the ship is equipped with bio-neural circuitry: gel packs containing synthetic neural cells that organize information more efficiently and speed up response time. The ship uses variable geometry warp nacelles—a design configuration by which the wings and nacelles fold upward when the ship goes to warp. According to the staff's internal technical manual, written by Rick Sternbach and Michael Okuda, this design indicates that "warp fields may no longer have a negative impact on habitable worlds, as established in ["Force of Nature"] *TNG*." ▪ Tricobalt devices are used to destroy the Caretaker's Array. ▪ At maximum warp it will take the ship seventy-five years to get back to the Alpha Quadrant. Janeway orders the away team to arm themselves with compression phaser rifles. ▪ There are fourteen varieties of tomato soup available from *Voyager*'s replicators.

DAMAGE REPORT: There is a hull breach on Deck 14 and a warp core microfracture that nearly leads to a core breach The magnetic constrictors must be locked down to bring the reaction rate down before the crew can seal the breach. ▪ The Maquis ship, which is powered by a thirty-nine-year-old rebuilt engine, is destroyed when Chakotay takes it on a kamikaze run against one of the Kazon ships.

SHUTTLE TRACKER: Stadi pilots Shuttlecraft 71325 when transporting Paris to *Voyager*. Neelix's ship is stored in the Shuttlebay, which is in the aft section of the ship.

DELTA QUADRANT: The Caretaker is a sporocystian life-form who was a member of a race of explorers. Their technology proved to be too advanced for the Ocampa homeworld, causing an environmental disaster that removed all neucleogenic particles from the atmosphere and making it unable to produce rain. The Caretaker and a female of this life-form were left behind to care for the Ocampa, but the female abandoned the system years ago. The Caretaker uses a coherent tetrion beam followed by a massive displacement wave with a polarized magnetic variation to bring ships to the Delta Quadrant. When the Caretaker dies, his remains are stored aboard *Voyager*.

The Ocampa have lived underground for five hundred generations on the fifth planet in a G-type star system. Their average life span is nine years, and they can speak telepathically. According to legend, they once possessed extraordinary mental abilities that have been rendered dormant due to their reliance on the Caretaker to supply all their needs. There is a movement among some Ocampa to return to their independent lifestyle.

The Kazon-Ogla sect, led by Maje Jabin, mine cormaline deposits that are in high demand in the sector. They are unfamiliar with transporter and replicator technology.

Janeway and Chakotay question a holographic representation of the Caretaker, whom they come to know as "Banjo Man." ROBBIE ROBINSON

ALPHA QUADRANT: Gul Evek is the Cardassian who chases the Maquis into the Badlands. ▪ While *Voyager* is stationed at Deep Space 9, Quark and Morn appear in Quark's bar.

PERSONAL LOGS: Captain Kathryn Janeway once served under Admiral Paris (Tom's father) as science officer on the *Al-Batani* during the Arias expedition. She is currently involved with a man named Mark who lives on Earth and is looking after her dog, who is due to give birth in seven weeks. Despite Starfleet protocol, she does not like being called "sir," preferring to be referred to as "Captain" (or Ma'am in a crunch). ▪ Chakotay, a Native American, is the leader of the Maquis crew. Formerly a Starfleet officer, he resigned his commission to defend his home against the Cardassians. Janeway names him first officer, her own having died, when the two crews merge. ▪ Tuvok is *Voyager*'s chief of security. Janeway relies heavily on the counsel he regularly provides her. She spoke with his family before leaving on the rescue mission into the Badlands. ▪ Thomas Eugene Paris was being held at the Federation Penal Settlement in Auckland, New Zealand, when Captain Janeway asked him to join her

crew as an "observer" on the mission into the Badlands. Paris was forced out of Starfleet after admitting to falsifying reports in an accident caused by his own pilot error that resulted in the deaths of three officers. It is implied that the accident occurred while Paris was stationed on Caldik Prime. Paris then joined the Maquis and was arrested on his first assignment. During his time in the Maquis, Paris and Chakotay met but did not get along. When Janeway merges the two crews, Paris is given a field commission of lieutenant and stationed at the conn. ▪ B'Elanna Torres is a half-Klingon, half-human Maquis engineer. During her second year at Starfleet Academy, she and the administration made what she calls a "mutual decision" that she should leave the school. ▪ Ensign Harry Kim recently graduated from Starfleet Academy and is on his first assignment on a starship. He is assigned to the ops position. An only child, he played clarinet in the Julliard Youth Symphony, but he left his instrument behind when accepting his position on *Voyager*. On Deep Space 9 he is nearly conned by Quark into purchasing a selection of lobi crystals until Paris comes to his rescue, beginning what will soon become a trusted friendship. ▪ Kim first activates the Emergency Medical Hologram after the medical staff is killed. The Doctor's program is intended only as a short-term medical supplement although he is capable of treating any injury or disease. ▪ Neelix, a Talaxian, is found scavenging in a debris field. Due to his knowledge of the sector, the captain accepts his offer to come aboard as a guide, supply officer, and cook. ▪ Kes, a member of the Ocampa race and is the object of Neelix's affection, has been held prisoner and abused by the Kazon.

Of the *Voyager* crewmen named in the episode, only Ensign Rollins in security and Lieutenant Carey in engineering survive the abduction by the Caretaker. Among the crewmen killed are Lieutenant Commander Cavit, the human first officer, and Stadi, the Betazoid conn officer. Fatalities also include the unnamed human doctor, the Vulcan nurse, and the unseen chief engineer.

CREW COMPLEMENT: Stadi lists *Voyager*'s crew complement as 141, though it is unclear whether she includes Paris or Tuvok in that number. The number of Maquis who join the crew is not provided; however, in the seventh-season episode "Repression," Crewman Chell will state that almost one quarter of the crew is Maquis (and this is following a considerable number of deaths among the Maquis crewmen). The combined crew complement is not spoken of until "The 37's," where it is said that there are 152 crewmen (the number is also repeated in "Persistence of Vision").

EPISODE LOGS: Location shooting for the Ocampa settlement was filmed at the Los Angeles Convention Center. Due to a change of hairstyle for Janeway, many scenes filmed at the center needed to be reshot when it was again made available to the production. ▪ Tom Paris's middle name "Eugene" was chosen in honor of *Star Trek* creator Gene Roddenberry. ▪ The Doctor is listed as Zimmerman in this and all future scripts written in the first season because the character was originally intended to take on the name of his creator. ▪ The Caretaker's remains will be seen again in "Cold Fire," in which the crew meets his female counterpart. ▪ When Neelix first meets Tuvok, the security officer introduces himself as being Vulcan. Neelix misunderstands and believes that to be his name, beginning his longstanding affectionate reference to the security chief as "Mister Vulcan."

PARALLAX

EPISODE #103

TELEPLAY BY: **BRANNON BRAGA**
STORY BY: **JIM TROMBETTA**
DIRECTED BY: **KIM FRIEDMAN**

GUEST STARS

SESKA	**MARTHA HACKETT**
LT. CAREY	**JOSH CLARK**

CO-STAR

JARVIN	**JUSTIN WILLIAMS**

STARDATE 48439.7

Some strain begins to show early in the process of integrating the Maquis crew into the Starfleet vessel. When Torres ends a dispute in Engineering by breaking the nose of Starfleet Lieutenant Carey, Tuvok readies her court-martial while some of the

Captain Janeway knows her ship is the crew's only haven.
ROBBIE ROBINSON

In the meantime, only Kes shows concern over that fact that the EMH's holoprojectors are malfunctioning.

The tractor beam does not work, almost pulling *Voyager* into the singularity instead. At Neelix's suggestion, the ship heads for Ilidaria. En route, Janeway decides to learn more about Torres, but the conversation between them does not go well. After Torres leaves, the EMH reports that various crew members have suddenly become ill. Janeway hardly has time to discuss the situation before the ship jolts once again. They are back at the singularity.

Noting the peculiar effects of the singularity on the EMH, Torres comes up with an idea that may allow them to contact the crew of the trapped ship, which, in turn, may provide clues to their own predicament. Torres's plan works, but when they finally hear the message from the other ship, they discover that it is really a time-delayed reflection of their own hails.

Torres and Janeway realize that *Voyager* must return to the rupture in the event horizon that was created when the ship travelled through it. Otherwise, the singularity will crush them. Using a dekyon beam fired from a shuttlecraft piloted by the pair, they force the opening wide enough for *Voyager* to escape.

Because of her tempered initiative and creative approach to saving the ship, Torres is given the chief engineer's post, and a field commission of lieutenant.

Maquis prepare to mutiny. Chakotay puts a stop to both plans and surprises Torres by telling her that he intends to suggest her as the new chief engineer.

At the next senior staff meeting, Neelix and Kes interrupt, hoping to make themselves more useful to the crew. When Kes suggests a hydroponics bay for growing vegetables to cut down on the use of the replicators, Janeway agrees to the plan, placing her in charge of the project. With that new position filled, Janeway is surprised by Chakotay's suggestion of Torres as chief engineer, but agrees to place her under consideration. As the discussion turns to Paris working as a field medic under the EMH, *Voyager* is jolted by spatial distortions emanating from a Type-4 quantum singularity.

A ship trapped in the event horizon of the singularity hails *Voyager*, but the message is unclear. At Torres's suggestion, the crew prepares a subspace tractor beam to cut through the event horizon and rescue the ship. While the engineering crew works on the beam, Janeway has a tense discussion with Chakotay about the Maquis's place on the ship, with a particular emphasis on his role as first officer.

SENSOR READINGS: Replicators are down, and emergency rations are low. With adjustable environmental controls, Cargo Bay 2 was designed for organic storage and is determined to be the most suitable location for the new hydroponics bay (which will later come to be known as the airponics bay). ▪ Engine efficiency is down fourteen percent. Chakotay suggests they relocate all security personnel to Deck 7 so they can shut down power to Deck 9 and reroute it to propulsion. ▪ As an additional energy source, the crew has attempted to hook the holodeck reactors to the power grid, only to wind up blowing out half the relays. Kim says, "the holodeck's energy matrix isn't compatible with other power systems." (This will be overcome in future episodes.) ▪ *Voyager* is about 116 meters wide (allowing less than 2 meters clearance on either side through the 120-meter-wide diameter of the rupture). ▪ Early in the episode, Janeway had replaced the deceased transporter chief, but the crew is still missing an astrogation plotter, chief engineer, and medical support personnel.

DAMAGE REPORT: The encounter with the singularity results in a shield failure, a loss of power to the port

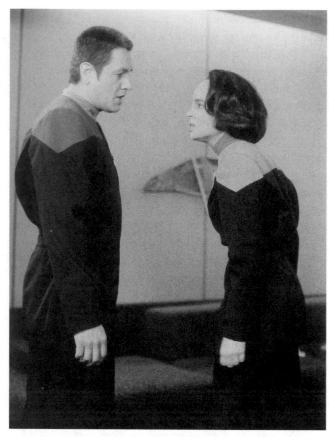

Chakotay insists that Torres apologize to Carey. ROBBIE ROBINSON

impulse engine forcing them to switch to auxiliary power, and a loss of hull integrity. ▪ Torres's first assignment as chief engineer is to get warp power back online.

SHUTTLE TRACKER: Janeway and Torres take an unnamed type-8 shuttlecraft to the rupture in the singularity.

DELTA QUADRANT: The crew encounters a highly localized disturbance in the space-time continuum: a type-4 quantum singularity. Neelix defines the singularity as a star that has collapsed in on itself and the event horizon as a very powerful energy field surrounding it. The singularity's gravimetric flux density is over two thousand percent. ▪ Unbeknownst to the crew, they become trapped in the singularity when responding to a distress call from themselves. As Janeway explains, "One of the more difficult concepts to grasp in temporal mechanics is that sometimes effect can precede cause. A reaction can be observed before the action which initiated it." At Torres's suggestion the crew unsuccessfully attempts to use a subspace tractor beam to rescue the "other ship." When Torres and Janeway realize that the spatial distortions are interfering with the EMH projector's phase

alignment, they devise a way to screen out the distortions by setting up a localized damping field. The same type of field can be used around the external sensors to allow them to communicate with the other ship. To locate the rupture they made when entering the singularity, they saturate the event horizon with warp particles that can escape through the rupture, allowing them to pinpoint the location. To generate the warp field necessary to emit the warp particles they take the main deflector offline and reroute the port and starboard plasma flow to the main deflector. To enlarge the rupture, they fire a dekyon beam at the breach from the shuttlecraft.

The singularity is less than three light years from the planet Ilidaria.

ALPHA QUADRANT: Striking a fellow officer is a court-martial offense.

PERSONAL LOGS: In command school, Janeway was taught that maneuvering a starship is a very delicate process. Over the years, she has learned that "sometimes you just have to punch your way through." ▪ Tuvok was able to provide the names of the entire Maquis crew to Janeway before *Voyager* began its mission. ▪ Torres is confined to quarters for breaking Lieutenant Carey's nose in three places during an argument. According to her records, she had four disciplinary hearings and one suspension before she left Starfleet Academy. Professor Chapman placed a letter in her permanent file stating that if she ever reapplied, he would support her. It also said that she was one of the most promising cadets he had ever met. ▪ The EMH was designed with information drawn from over two thousand medical reference sources and the experience of forty-seven individual medical officers. He can operate only in the confines of sickbay. The EMH channel is monitor input 47. Janeway says she will look into linking the Doctor's program into the ship's database so he will be aware of what is happening on the ship. The singularity has an effect on the EMH projectors, causing the Doctor to shrink in size at a rate of five centimeters every hour. ▪ Neelix begins to recount a story about a dangerous trade mission he conducted to the twin stars of Keloda before being interrupted. His *feragoit* goulash is apparently known across twelve star systems.

Lieutenant Carey is the senior Starfleet engineer onboard and next in line to become chief engineer when Torres is promoted over him.

MEDICAL REPORT: Numerous crew members—including Kim—are affected by the singularity and experience severe headaches, muscle spasms, and dizziness.

EPISODE LOGS: Seska, a Maquis crewmember, appears for the first time, prepared to mutiny to support Torres's side in the fight in engineering. In this episode she wears a blue uniform from the Science Department, but in later episodes she will be in a yellow operations uniform.

Paris and Janeway attempt to restore the timeline of an alien world without breaking the Prime Directive. ROBBIE ROBINSON

TIME AND AGAIN

EPISODE #104

TELEPLAY BY: DAVID KEMPER and MICHAEL PILLER

STORY BY: DAVID KEMPER

DIRECTED BY: LES LANDAU

GUEST STARS

MAKULL	NICOLAS SUROVY
TERLA	JOEL POLIS
LATIKA	BRADY BLUHM

CO-STARS

SHOPKEEPER	RYAN MacDONALD
OFFICER	STEVE VAUGHT
GUARD	JERRY SPICER

STARDATE UNKNOWN

At the end of their duty shift, as Paris pressures Kim to join him on a double date with the Delaney sisters, *Voyager* is shaken by a huge shockwave. Investigating its origins, the crew finds a nearby M-class planet where a cataclysmic explosion has recently extinguished all life.

Kes is drawn to the bridge by a dream that may be linked to the tragedy, although she remains silent as an away team beams down to the planet. There they find the remains of what appeared to be a pre-warp civilization destroyed by a chain reaction of polaric ion explosions that also fractured subspace. Before the full away team can safely beam back to the ship, Paris and Janeway are caught in a subspace fracture and transported back in time to the day before the explosion.

Surrounded by a civilization on the eve of destruction, Janeway orders Paris not to warn the populace about the approaching disaster, citing the Prime Directive. Searching for clues to get them back to *Voyager,* the pair heads for a polaric ion power station while an inquisitive boy follows them, suspecting that they are up to no good. While avoiding the child, they unintentionally become caught up in a clash between the local authorities and a group of protesters who rightly believe the power station is a danger to the environment.

Kes realizes that her latent Ocampan psychic abilities seem to have been sensitized by the explosion. She accompanies an away team as they attempt to track Janeway and Paris's movements in the past. Once they find their crewmates' subspace signal, the away team should be able to reopen a fracture and bring them into the correct timeline. They do manage to track a signal from a combadge, but instead of guiding them through subspace, it leads to the ruins of a house, signifying that Janeway and Paris may have been caught in the explosion.

In the past, Janeway attempts to explain that she and Paris are not spies from the government, when the boy, Latika, is found and brought in to blow their cover story. Since it appears that their presence on the planet may have resulted in the explosion, Janeway thinks they may have inadvertently broken the Prime Directive, making them responsible to set things right. However, the protestors' refusal to believe her is only strengthened when the away team is able to get a garbled communication to their captain. The protestors take away their combadges and continue with their plan to sabotage the power station.

A day in the future, the away team finds the flashpoint of the blast at the power station and uses a polaric beam to cut through subspace and find the missing crew members. When Janeway sees their polaric beam moments before the explosion's to take place, she realizes that it was not the protesters who caused the accident; it was the away team's rescue attempt. Using her phaser to blunt the impact of the beam, Janeway succeeds in sealing the opening and resetting time.

Janeway realizes that despite her best efforts they have already unwittingly broken the Prime Directive. ROBBIE ROBINSON

The crew is returned to *Voyager,* a few seconds before the shockwave hit the ship, entirely unaware of the experience except for Kes, who finds herself strangely relieved that a nearby planet is teeming with life.

SENSOR READINGS: The polaric generator uses the same polaric energy that destroyed the planet. When directed at intense levels, it can open a subspace fracture. The device burns itself out in thirty seconds, and the damage to subspace renders it useless for more than one attempt in any given location. ▪ Combadges are designed to self-activate when the casing is destroyed, to help locate injured victims.

DAMAGE REPORT: The shockwave causes a minor hull breach on Deck 3. The damage is erased when the timeline is reset.

DELTA QUADRANT: Density patterns on the surface of the devastated M-Class planet in a red dwarf system show artificial waterways and a global aqueduct system. ▪ The

inhabitants are unnamed, and Janeway uses the cover story that the Continental Transport brought her and Paris from the Kalto Province. A pre-warp civilization with no satellites in orbit or spacecraft in the area, the world is powered by polaric energy, which is a source of much protest especially following an accident in the energy plant at Markov. ▪ The planet's timepieces are broken down into units of rotations, intervals, and fractions. Their unit of money is kelodas.

Neelix recounts the story of the Drakian Forest Dwellers, a tribe with paranormal abilities similar to what Kes experiences.

ALPHA QUADRANT: The Chalok IV incident, in which a Romulan research colony was destroyed during the tests of a polaric device, led to the Polaric Test Ban Treaty of 2268. ▪ The Standard 15-501 Crew Personnel Report is usually transmitted to Starfleet medical by an alien world's government so that there is a record of the physiological makeup of crew members from new species. Customarily it is the ship doctor's responsibility to update the medical database on additions to the crew.

PERSONAL LOGS: Janeway and Paris trade their Starfleet uniforms for native clothing. ▪ Admiral Paris used to have annual discussions with Tom on the importance of the Prime Directive (discussions that Tom largely ignored). ▪ Kim is reluctant to accompany Paris on a date with the Delaney sisters, citing the fact that he has "a girl back at home." Paris counters by claiming that he has five women waiting at home for him. ▪ To date, no one has updated the medical database to inform the Doctor that Kes, Neelix, and the Maquis are on board, even though he has met some of these people on previous occasions. ▪ Kes has always believed the stories that her ancestors had extraordinary mental powers and begins to experience some of those abilities for the first time. The Doctor suggests that the reawakening of her mental capabilities may be due to the biological adjustments the body makes for the requirements of life in space.

The Delaney sisters work in Stellar Cartography.

MEDICAL REPORT: Janeway receives a head wound during the protest at the polaric energy plant and Paris is later shot by Terla. The injuries are erased when the timeline resets.

EPISODE LOGS: This episode marks the first mention of the Delaney sisters, who become an ongoing potential romantic pairing for Paris and Kim, though it is not specified which of the unnamed twins in intended for which man. The sisters will not be given first names until later episodes and will be seen only once, in the fifth season episode, "Thirty Days."

PHAGE

EPISODE #105
TELEPLAY BY: **SKYE DENT and BRANNON BRAGA**
STORY BY: **TIMOTHY DeHAAS**
DIRECTED BY: **WINRICH KOLBE**

GUEST STARS

DERETH	**CULLY FREDRICKSEN**
MOTURA	**STEPHEN B. RAPPAPORT**
SESKA	**MARTHA HACKETT**

CO-STAR

COMPUTER VOICE	**MAJEL BARRETT**

STARDATE 48532.4

About to partake of an unpleasant breakfast of Ration Pack Number 5, Captain Janeway is even less pleased to find that Neelix has turned her private dining room into a makeshift galley for the crew. Before she can fully discuss the protocols involved in obtaining permission before redesigning parts of the ship, she and Neelix are called to the bridge. *Voyager* is approaching a planetoid that appears to be rich in raw dilithium, a resource for which the energy-low ship is in desperate need.

During an away team survey of the planetoid, an unidentified alien attacks Neelix, leaving him for dead. Chakotay and Kim beam him to sickbay, where the Doctor reports that his lungs have been removed. Out of options for replacing the missing organs, the Doctor fits Neelix with a set of holographic lungs that were created by using a blueprint provided by the transporter's identification matrix. The experimental lungs will require him to remain confined in an isotropic restraint in sickbay for the rest of his life.

Janeway leads an away team back to the planetoid, where they discover a medical lab filled with harvested organs. Unfortunately, Neelix's lungs are not among them. Minutes later, an alien ship speeds away from the planet. As soon as the away team returns to the ship, Janeway sets a pursuit course.

In sickbay, a despondent Neelix is having difficulty

Vidiian scanners reveal that the Doctor does not physically exist. ROBBIE ROBINSON

Kes offers to donate her lung to Neelix out of love and appreciation for all that he has done for her. ROBBIE ROBINSON

The Doctor lists *Voyager*'s weight as 700,000 tons. ▪ Neelix turns the captain's private dining room (Cabin 125-Alpha, Deck 2) into a galley. To do so, he completely reroutes the power conduits. ▪ The ship continues to suffer a power shortage. Torres intends to modify the auxiliary impulse reactor to convert it into a crude dilithium refinery (a solution that ignores Starfleet protocols). ▪ A Vidiian dampening field bleeds energy directly from their warp nacelles. The crew compensates for the drain with a KLS stabilizer. ▪ To locate the Vidiian ship in the mirrored cavern of the asteroid, they reduce phaser level to a minimum setting and send out a continuous beam reflecting off the bulkheads until it encounters a nonreflective material. ▪ There is no counselor onboard. ▪ Type-3 phasers are issued to the security team. ▪ The design specifications for a cytoplasmic stimulator are in the ship's medical database, allowing Paris to replicate the device. ▪ Ration Pack 5 is stewed tomatoes with dehydrated eggs.

DELTA QUADRANT: According to Neelix, the rogue planetoid is an extremely rich source of raw dilithium. The ship's sensors indicate that the strongest readings come from ten to twenty kilometers inside the planetoid in a series of caves that have an oxygen-nitrogen atmosphere. The readings prove false when Kim uses a geo-stratal analysis on the rocks in the caves and finds no dilithium formations.

The Vidiians, who read as class-3 humanoid organisms, suffer from the Phage, a disease that first attacked them over two millennia ago. The Phage literally consumes their bodies, killing thousands of Vidiians each day. They harvest bodies to replace their own diseased tissues, since their immuno-technology cannot keep up with the Phage's, highly adaptive properties. The *honatta* is responsible for finding organs, and uses a device that is both a sophisticated medical scanner and a surgical instrument that employs an neural resonator to stun the victim while a quantum imaging scanner conducts a micro-cellular analysis of the entire body. More precise than a tricorder, it can read everything about a victim's body, down to the DNA sequencing. Before the Phage, the Vidiian Sodality were educators and explorers—a people whose greatest achievements were artisitc.

The Talaxian respiratory system is directly linked to multiple points along the spinal column, making it too difficult to replicate artificial lungs.

Neelix claims to know of a few Yallitaian engineers who would give all three of their spinal columns to know the location of the planet supposedly rich in dilithium.

adjusting to his situation and grows paranoid over what he perceives as Paris's interest in Kes. The EMH, still serving as the ship's only doctor, admits to Kes that he is also having a difficult time adjusting to the demands of a full-time physician. Kes's intelligent, soothing advice leads the Doctor to think that the young woman might make a good medical assistant.

The vessel's ion trail leads *Voyager* inside an alien-made asteroid. Deft piloting by Paris, combined with some technological investigation by the bridge crew, guides them to the alien ship. When confronted, the aliens, members of the Vidiian Sodality, defend their actions by recounting the battle that their species has fought for two millennia against the Phage, a gruesome disease that destroys their genetic codes and cellular structure. Unable to defeat the Phage, they have learned to survive by scavenging organs from the bodies of healthier species in order to replace their own diseased tissues. In rare cases they have been forced to remove organs from living donors. Unfortunately, Neelix's lungs have already been transplanted into one of the Vidiian's bodies. Unwilling to sentence the Vidiian to death to regain Neelix's lungs, Janeway reluctantly releases the scavengers.

Grateful to the captain for sparing them, the Vidiians use their superior medical technology to enable Kes to donate one of her own lungs to Neelix. After the successful procedure, the Doctor tells Kes that Janeway has granted permission for her to begin training as a medical assistant.

IN THE WORDS OF THE DOCTOR

"I'm a doctor, not a bricklayer."

Leonard McCoy "The Devil in the Dark"

Among the more famous quotes in *Star Trek* history have been Dr. Leonard "Bones" McCoy's gruff retorts when asked to perform duties outside of his defined medical obligations. Beginning with his original rejoinder in "The Corbomite Maneuver" ("What am I, a doctor or a moon-shuttle commander?") the writers later streamlined the dialogue with the more familiar "I'm a doctor, not a *fill in the blank*." Though Bashir did mimic the quote on a couple of occasions on *Deep Space Nine*, the mantle was eventually passed to *Voyager*'s Emergency Medical Hologram, who embraced it and made it his own.

ROBBIE ROBINSON

"I'm a doctor, Mr. Neelix, not a decorator." ("Phage")

"I'm a doctor, not a bartender." ("Twisted")

"I am a doctor, not a voyeur." ("Parturition")

"I'm a doctor, not a performer." ("Investigations")

"I'm a doctor, not a counterinsurgent." ("Basics Part II")

"I'm a doctor, not a database." ("Future's End Part II")

"I'm a doctor, not a peeping tom." ("Drone")

"I'm a doctor, not a battery." ("Gravity")

"I'm a doctor, not a dragon slayer. ("Bliss")

"I'm a doctor, not a zookeeper." ("Lifeline")

"I'm a doctor, not an engineer." ("Flesh and Blood, Part I")

Variations on the theme

DOCTOR: I shouldn't have to remind you, I'm a doctor . . .

TORRES: . . . not an engineer. Right. ("Prototype")

EMH DIAGNOSTIC (ZIMMERMAN HOLOGRAM): I have pointed out over and over again, I am a diagnostic tool, not an engineer. ("The Swarm")

EMH-2: I'm a doctor, not a commando. ("Message in a Bottle")

PARIS: I am a pilot, Harry, not a doctor. ("Message in a Bottle")

U.S.S. ENTERPRISE-E EMH: I'm a doctor, not a doorstop. (*Star Trek: First Contact*)

"I loved my 'Bonesisms,'—'I'm a doctor, not a blank.' I ad-libbed in my audition. And, you know, ad-libbing in a network audition is never a really smart thing to do, but I closed my audition and, I think my last scripted line was 'I believe someone has failed to terminate my program.' And then I took a long deadpan look around the room at the very people I was reading for and said 'I'm a doctor, not a night-light.' "

—**Robert Picardo**

PERSONAL LOGS: Tuvok has observed the captain over the past four years, leading him to be able to anticipate her actions. ▪ The magnetic containment field that creates the illusion of the Doctor's body can be manipulated to allow matter to pass through it or be stopped. He is capable of learning, as he is programmed with the ability to accumulate and process data. ▪ Neelix has been studying tricorder operations and Torres brought him up to date on dilithium geophysics as part of his self-initiated week-long training for his first away mission. ▪ Kes accepts the Doctor's offer to begin training as a medical assistant.

MEDICAL REPORT: A blood-gas infuser is used to keep Neelix's oxygen levels steady, but the infuser is only good for an hour. The Doctor uses Neelix's transporter identification matrix to create holographic lungs. Neelix must remain motionless in an isotropic restraint to keep the holographic lungs perfectly aligned to his internal physiology.

EPISODE LOGS: The Doctor sneers at Neelix's request for him to sing, though in later episodes the Doctor will pursue singing as a hobby. The Doctor will also attempt to fill the position of counselor in "Retrospect"; however, it will lead to disastrous results. ▪ In the shooting script, the "Vidiian Sodality" was originally named the "Vaphoran Sodality."

THE CLOUD

EPISODE #106

TELEPLAY BY: **TOM SZOLLOSI** and **MICHAEL PILLER**

STORY BY: **BRANNON BRAGA**

DIRECTED BY: **DAVID LIVINGSTON**

GUEST STARS

RICKY	**ANGELA DOHRMANN**
SANDRINE	**JUDY GEESON**
GAUNT GARY	**LARRY A. HANKIN**
GIGOLO	**LUIGI AMODEO**

STARDATE 48546.2

Concerned about the low morale and her own inability to mingle with her crew, Janeway hopes to raise spirits with the exploration of a nebula emitting a high level of omicron particles, which could prove useful for the ship's dwindling energy reserves. Chakotay suggests that the captain may improve her own mood with the help of an animal guide, an ancient Native American tradition in which she can seek counsel from a

An awkward moment between the captain and her bridge officers as they try to figure out the protocols of their relationship. ROBBIE ROBINSON

creature believed to accompany her throughout life. Janeway accepts the invitation for a later time as they reach the nebula.

Shortly after *Voyager* enters the cloudlike formation, it encounters an energy barrier that brings the ship to a dead stop. The ship breaks through the barrier and continues its penetration of the nebula's inner reaches, where it is bombarded by unidentified globules that pass right through the shields and attach themselves to the hull. With the globules draining the ship's energy reserves, Janeway orders the crew to leave the nebula. Reversing course, they are unable to break through the now-strengthened energy barrier, and the crew is forced to use one of their few remaining photon torpedoes to blast their way out.

While Torres examines one of the energy-draining globules, Paris invites Kim to the holodeck, where he has created a touch of home in the form of a holographic re-creation of Paris's favorite hangout back on Earth, a bar called Sandrine's.

Torres interrupts Janeway's first attempt to contact an animal guide with the surprising discovery she and the Doctor made regarding the globules. Torres explains that the globules are organic elements of a much larger life-form. The "nebula" they thought they were investigating is actually a living entity, and the phenomena they encountered were part of the life-form's natural defense systems. Concerned that the encounter may have caused the entity serious injury, Janeway proposes returning and repairing the harm they have done.

Once they are back inside the life-form, the crew prepares to irradiate the wound with a nucleonic beam. The attempt is interrupted when the entity's natural defense systems again attack the ship, forcing it away from the wound. Although the ship sustains minor damage, the crew is able to return to the wound by riding the energy currents Chakotay believes make up the entity's circulatory system.

At the energy barrier, the Doctor suggests a method of "suturing" the wound, which they manage to do after distracting the entity's defense systems with a micro-probe. Just before the wound heals, *Voyager* escapes from the cloud and sets course for a planet where they will be able to replenish their depleted energy reserves. The threat over, Kim invites the captain to Sandrine's, where she surprises the crew with her pool-playing expertise.

SENSOR READINGS: *Voyager's* complement of photon torpedoes stands at thirty-seven after one is launched to break free of the nebula. ■ To initiate emergency shutdown of all thrusters, deuterium must be vented out into

The Doctor provides unexpected assistance in dealing with the spatial anomaly. ROBBIE ROBINSON

space. ■ Releasing positive ions through the nacelles repels the dust in the life-form without harming the creature. The ship serves as an energy conduit to seal the creature's wounds, when it fires a nucleonic beam along the edge of the wound to promote regeneration. ■ Holodeck Program Paris 3 recreates Chez Sandrine (commonly known as "Sandrine's"), a bar outside Marseilles, France. The simulation is programmed to include a pool table and some of the best pool hustlers in Earth history. ■ Holographic wine served at the bar cannot cause heartburn.

DAMAGE REPORT: The ship loses the rear driver coil assembly, inertial dampers go offline, there are electro-plasma leaks on Deck 14, and the optical data network shuts down. Over twenty percent of their energy reserve is depleted by the encounter.

DELTA QUADRANT: The unnamed life-form carries high levels of omicron particles that the crew would like to add to antimatter reserves. The creature is seven astronomical units in diameter, containing intermittent gamma and thermal emissions and hydrogen, helium, hydroxyl radicals, with some local dust particles. When Torres examines one of the globules attached to the ship, she finds neucleogenic peptide bonds, which lead her and the Doctor to realize they are dealing with a life-form and not a nebula.

Neelix is aware of a planet fourteen light years away from their position that may have a compatible energy source.

ALPHA QUADRANT: Pickpockets are in practice in Marseilles, France, but they are only show for the tourists. ▪ In the language of Chakotay's tribe a *nuanka* is a period of mourning. He believes the crew is experiencing this natural response to suddenly being so far from home. His people also believe that the bear is a very powerful animal with a great *pokattah,* though he does not define the term.

PERSONAL LOGS: At the Academy, students are taught that captains must maintain a certain emotional distance from their crew. Janeway has always felt comfortable with that distance, but present circumstances are changing her opinion. Janeway expresses a love of coffee and shows that she is a bit of a pool shark. When Chakotay attempts to introduce Janeway to an animal guide, he tells her to remember a place where she was the most content and peaceful she has ever been. Her memory takes her to a familiar beach, but Chakotay does not allow her to reveal its location. Janeway's animal guide is a lizard, but she is interrupted before she has a chance to speak with it ▪ Chakotay's animal guide is female, but he would offend it if he spoke its name. His medicine bundle consists of a blackbird's wing, a stone from a river, and an *akoonah.* The *akoonah* is a piece of technology that facilitates the search for an animal guide without relying on the psychoactive herbs his ancestors once used. Chakotay had never shown his medicine bundle to anyone before Janeway, though he had introduced Torres to an animal guide on a previous occasion. She is the only person Chakotay knows who tried to kill her guide. ▪ Paris learned how to override door locks while he was in prison. He says that he includes a woman named Ricky in all his holoprograms. Similar to Janeway, Paris likes dogs and says that he always had one. ▪ Kim's Starfleet Academy roommate was James Mooney MacAllister. Because his roommate liked to stay up all night studying, Kim began sleeping with an eye mask that he continues to wear to this day. He claims that he remembers being in his mother's womb. Kim gets acid heartburn when

he drinks wine too late at night. ▪ The Doctor refers to his programmer as a man at the Jupiter Station Hologramming Center named Zimmerman, who looks a lot like him. He communicates with the bridge via the main viewscreen and is programmed to say "Please state the nature of the medical emergency" when activated but cannot change his programming. Torres offers to help him adapt the programming. ▪ Neelix names himself morale officer.

EPISODE LOGS: When Torres suggests that the Doctor alter his own program, he sarcastically asks her the point of such an endeavor and if he could then "create a family or "raise an army." The Doctor will go on to create a holo-family in the episode "Real Life," and Torres will lend a hand, altering the program to create a more realistic representation of domestic life. And, though he does not "raise" the army, he does take control of a holographic revolution in the seventh season episodes "Flesh and Blood Parts I&II." ▪ This is the first mention of the name Zimmerman as the creator of the EMH. The real Zimmerman (and a holographic representation) will be seen in future episodes of *Voyager,* as well as the *Deep Space Nine* episode "Dr. Bashir, I Presume." ▪ The real Sandrine's will be seen in an altered reality of Earth in "Non Sequitur."

EYE OF THE NEEDLE

EPISODE #107
TELEPLAY BY BILL DIAL and JERI TAYLOR
STORY BY HILARY J. BADER
DIRECTED BY WINRICH KOLBE

GUEST STARS

TELEK	VAUGHN ARMSTRONG
LT. BAXTER	TOM VIRTUE

STARDATE 48579.4

When Ensign Kim finds a wormhole that might lead to the Alpha Quadrant, the crew believes they may have found a shortcut home. Although the opening to the tunnel through space proves too small for *Voyager* to fly through, its size will allow for a microprobe to investigate where it leads.

To the crew's disappointment, the probe gets stuck in a gravitational eddy, but readings indicate someone is scanning the probe on the other side of the wormhole. In

Janeway welcomes the Romulan, Telek, to the Delta Quadrant. ROBBIE ROBINSON

the hopes of initiating contact, the crew transmits a series of subharmonic pulses through the probe as a signal. Before long, they receive a subspace response from the Alpha Quadrant.

In the meantime, Kes begins her training as a medical assistant. Surprised by how rudely the crew treats the Doctor because he is "only a hologram," she asks the captain if anything can be done to remedy the situation. After some consideration, Janeway tells the Doctor that she intends to give him control over his own deactivation sequence and asks him to come up with a list of other suggestions that could help in integrating himself into the crew.

When *Voyager* finally succeeds in achieving audio contact they are surprised to find it is coming from a Romulan vessel. The captain of that ship, a scientist named Telek, is suspicious of the communication from a Starfleet vessel claiming to be in the Delta Quadrant, thinking they must be Federation spies. Once they establish a visual link and the two captains can communicate eye-to-eye, Telek becomes more sympathetic to their plight, saying he will consider relaying messages to the crew's families back home.

Anxious to explore any avenue that will facilitate their return, Torres tells the captain that she might be able to piggyback a transporter beam onto the visual link allowing the crew to beam to the Romulan ship. After several test objects safely complete the journey Telek refuses to allow the crew beam over as the Romulan government would never allow Starfleet officers onboard his ship. However, Telek allows himself to be transported to *Voyager* and says if the transfer is successful he will arrange for a troop ship to be made available to them.

Regrettably, Tuvok discovers they have actually beamed the Romulan scientist from twenty years in the past, due to a time rift in the wormhole. Knowing that transporting the crew back in time or alerting Starfleet to abort their original mission would cause irreparable damage to the timeline, Janeway asks the Romulan to relay the crew's messages to their families in the future, after *Voyager* has been pulled into the Delta Quadrant. He agrees and returns to his ship. Unfortunately, through a database check, Tuvok discovers that the Romulan died four years before *Voyager* left the Alpha Quadrant, making it unlikely that he had the opportunity to pass along

CONTACT WITH THE ALPHA QUADRANT: SEASON 1

"This is my idea of home, Harry . . . my little piece of Earth here in the Delta Quadrant."

Tom Paris (regarding Sandrine's) "The Cloud"

From the moment Janeway first alerted her newly combined crew to the fact that she intended to destroy the Caretaker's Array, leaving them stranded in the Delta Quadrant, her people began to long for home. They wondered if their last memories of familiar places would be of a Cardassian ship, the Badlands, or a space station named Deep Space 9 with its Ferengi bartender. However, they quickly discover that, even 70,000 light-years away they can still find home, through holodeck recreations, unexpected Delta Quadrant encounters, and even, remarkably enough, actual contact.

What quickly becomes an integral part of taking their minds off their distance is the use of the holodeck. Paris is the first to take a crack at designing a retreat for the crew that reminds them of home. His choice, Chez Sandrine, is a bar that he recalls from his early days at the Academy, when he was stationed outside of Marseilles, France ("The Cloud"). He populates Sandrine's with a host of Alpha Quadrant characters including: Ricky, whom he includes in all his programs; the Gigolo, born of a French father and Daliwakan mother; Gaunt Gary, a pool hustler from 1953 New York; and the lecherous Sandrine herself. Sandrine's will be seen in a number of future episodes and is last used in "The Swarm." However, it will be referred to in "Worst Case Scenario."

A surprise encounter with the captain's personal hero, Amelia Earhart. ROBBIE ROBINSON

"I think initially the writers felt like it was a great holodeck [location]—a relaxed sort of cozy atmosphere to create for our series regulars to go hang out and let their hair down. There was something that was just a little too dark and moody. It didn't have enough fun to it. Something about a bar didn't seem like quite the right atmosphere for us. Sandrine's, it was fine [but] I was not heartbroken when they moved on to trying other things."

—Robert Duncan McNeill

For more personal relaxation with a touch of home instead of a crew retreat, Kim escapes to a holonovel of the epic *Beowulf* ("Heroes and Demons"), which is set in sixth-century Denmark. However, Kim's time in that holoprogram as the

---

the letters to home. However, the crew holds out hope that Telek may have passed the task onto someone else.

SENSOR READINGS: The crew launches a microprobe into the wormhole, which acts as a booster for the communication signal. The microprobe is smaller than the 30-centimeter opening of the wormhole. Kim attempts to determine where the wormhole leads by extrapolating the verteron exit vector, but cannot do so because of the strange phase variance in the radiation stream (which later turns out to be a temporal shift). ▪ The phase amplitude of the visual link with the Romulans is within a few megahertz of meeting transporter protocols. This enables the crew to piggyback a transporter beam onto the visual link as a means of transferring the crew (after substantially reconfiguring the matter transmission rate). ▪ The transporter test cylinder is a standard Starfleet mechanism with a varietal molecular matrix that simulates most known organic and inorganic compounds. It is not classified and Telek notes that the Romulans have a similar device on their ship even twenty years in the past.

DELTA QUADRANT: The wormhole originally shows up on subspace scanners as a grouping of verteron emana-

hero Beowulf proves to be anything but relaxing when the ship makes contact with an alien life-form that takes over the Grendel character and abducts Kim, Chakotay, and Tuvok.

Janeway too will find solace in Earth literature, choosing an Edwardian holonovel set in ancient England ("Cathexis"). In the story, she plays the governess, Mrs. Davenport, charged with the care and education of Henry and Beatrice, the children of Lord Burleigh. The storyline, slightly reminiscent of Henry James' *The Turn of the Screw*, will be revisited in "Learning Curve" and finally "Persistence of Vision" when, following an alien encounter, Janeway will decide to take a break.

The Doctor also intends to use the holodeck for relaxation, but a kinoplastic radiation surge causes a feedback loop in his program. As a result, a holographic version of Alpha Quadrant resident Reg Barclay (of *TNG*) tries to convince the Doctor that he is, in fact, the real Dr. Zimmerman and currently on Jupiter Station and not the *Starship Voyager*.

The holodeck will also be used for more practical Starfleet purposes when Tuvok trains a team of Maquis crew members in a defense simulation ("Learning Curve"). Tuvok programs the simulation to include Ferengi and Romulans, with a ship from the latter race seen on the viewscreen.

In the real world, the *Voyager* crew first makes contact with the Alpha Quadrant as early as "Eye of the Needle." Unfortunately, the meeting takes place with a Romulan from twenty years in the past, whom the crew contacts through a miniature wormhole with a temporal shift. Though the Romulan promises to deliver messages to the families of the crew after they are abducted to the Delta Quadrant, he dies four years before their disappearance.

Several times over the course of the series, Janeway will contemplate giving up on the trek home and allowing the crew to set up their own little corner of the Alpha Quadrant on the nearest M-class planet. This is first considered in "The 37's," in which the crew meets descendants of abductees from Earth, circa 1937. The descendants live rather comfortably on a planet quite reminiscent of Earth and honor a group of the original abductees—known as the "37's" who are actually in suspended animation. When the 37's are awakened, famed aviatrix Amelia Earhart is found to be among them. Janeway makes the decision on whether or not to stay on this new Earth an individual one for her crew, and she is pleased when every one of them chooses to continue the journey home.

"It had marvelous resonance for Janway. Amelia Earhart was her hero. She was well versed in the life of Amelia Earhart. Janeways' a little bit of a historian and to actually confront her . . . was I think . . . a kind of epiphany for Janeway . . . to meet her and to share their humanity and the same essential struggle. I think that's what Janeway came away with, that the heart of an aeronautical heroine remains the same centuries later. It's the same drive and impulse to explore and to confront dilemmas with great courage and humanity. And I think that was reflected in those scenes between Earhart and Janeway."

—Kate Mulgrew

tions and tunneling secondary particles. The aperture is only 30 centimeters in diameter, and the wormhole itself seems to be in an advanced state of decay, signifying that it has probably been collapsing for centuries.

ALPHA QUADRANT: The other end of the wormhole opens in Sector 1385, in an area with no known shipping lanes. Due to a temporal shift it leads into the past to the year 2351. ▪ The Romulan originally claims to be captain of the cargo vessel *Talvath*. The comlink signature of the transmission indicates that the message is coming from a Romulan ship that, given the precise calibration of the

signal, Tuvok reports to be a science vessel. The Romulans use a signal amplifier with reconfigured protocols to penetrate the radiation stream of the wormhole providing a visual link. The captain of the vessel is Telek R'Mor, of the Romulan Astrophysics Academy. He died in the year 2367.

PERSONAL LOGS: Torres's father left her for Earth when she was five, and she hasn't seen him since. She believes that her mother lives on Qo'noS, but she is unsure, since they did not get along. She considers the Maquis to be her only family and feels no one is waiting for her back

Upon further study, Tuvok realizes the flaw in their plan to return home. ROBBIE ROBINSON

father is explored in "Lineage"—although she will be depicted in flashbacks as a twelve-year-old, apparently contradicting her statement that she last saw him when she was five. One possible explanation for this apparent age discrepancy can be the different rate at which Klingon children seem to mature from human children (as seen with the rapid maturation rate of Worf's son Alexander in *TNG* and *DS9*). ▪ The Doctor's search for a name continues through the seventh season and will go unresolved in the present timeline. ▪ Neelix does not appear in this episode though there was originally a scene in the shooting script where Kes spoke with him before going to the captain to discuss the Doctor's situation. ▪ The shooting script also opened with the introduction of Janeway's Edwardian holonovel, which was cut and later used in the opening teaser for "Cathexis."

home. ▪ Before being pulled into the Delta Quadrant, Harry Kim always called his family once a week, even on training missions. ▪ The EMH program is fully integrated into the sickbay system and at present cannot be downloaded. Janeway tells the Doctor that he should be considered a full-fledged member of the crew. She intends to give him control over his deactivation sequence and asks for a list of other requests he may have. The Doctor also asks Kes to help him in search of a name. ▪ Kes has begun her training as a medical assistant and already studied all the materials the Doctor has given her. The Doctor thinks that she may have an eidetic memory.

Lieutenant Baxter's need for strenuous exercise results in him continually reporting to sickbay. ▪ The Doctor was preparing a culture to test Lieutenant Hargrove for the Arethian flu when Ensign Kyoto deactivated him.

EPISODE LOGS: The year, as established in this episode, is 2371. ▪ The messages sent to the crew's families obviously do not make it to Starfleet, since the ship is listed as lost, as they find out in "Message in a Bottle." ▪ Torres's relationship with her mother will be more fully examined in "Barge of the Dead," while her relationship with her

EX POST FACTO

EPISODE #108

TELEPLAY BY **EVAN CARLOS SOMERS** and **MICHAEL PILLER**

STORY BY **EVAN CARLOS SOMERS**

DIRECTED BY **LeVAR BURTON**

GUEST STARS

LIDELL REN	**ROBIN McKEE**
MINISTER KRAY	**FRANCIS GUINAN**
BANEAN DOCTOR	**AARON LUSTIG**
TOLAN REN	**RAY REINHARDT**

CO-STAR

NUMIRI CAPTAIN	**HENRY BROWN**

STARDATE UNKNOWN

The Doctor and Kes are discussing possible names for the undesignated EMH when Ensign Kim is beamed into sickbay, dehydrated and barely able to speak. As the Doctor works, Kim weakly recounts his story to Janeway and Tuvok. On a planet Paris and he were visiting, Paris has been found guilty of the murder of a Banean native—Tolen Ren—who was helping them repair the ship's damaged collimator. It is believed that Paris killed the scientist after being caught in a passionate embrace with Ren's wife Lidell. As his punishment, Paris has been sentenced to relive the crime from his victim's perspective every fourteen hours, thanks to memory engrams implanted in his brain by a Banean doctor.

Paris and Lidell share an embrace in the doctored image seen through the murder victim's eyes. ROBBIE ROBINSON

When Janeway orders *Voyager* to the Banean homeworld to retrieve Paris, Neelix warns her that they are likely to be approached by a Numiri patrol vessel. The Numiri are at war with the Baneans and can be expected to give them a difficult time. When a Numiri vessel does stop *Voyager*, the alien captain only offers a warning before allowing the ship to proceed. Janeway continues to the planet, where she meets with the Banean minister and learns that the evidence—the murder as seen through Ren's own eyes—proves Paris's guilt, though he strongly denies any wrongdoing. As Janeway and Tuvok talk with him, Paris enters another cycle reliving the murder and loses consciousness. The Baneans grant Janeway permission to take Paris back to the ship for a medical evaluation, as the memories should not have provoked such a strong physical response.

The Doctor reports that the neurological implant is causing serious brain damage to Paris, due to the differences in human physiology from Banean. Tuvok launches his own investigation into the murder and interviews Ren's wife, who says she saw Paris kill her husband. Later, Paris suggests that she may have spiked his cup of tea the night of the murder, but there was no evidence of narcotics in his system. The conversation is interrupted by a Numiri attack that the *Voyager* crew successfully fends off.

Tuvok performs a Vulcan mind-meld with Paris to experience his visions of the murder. Emerging from the experience, Tuvok declares that he is convinced of Paris's innocence and that he knows why the Numiri chose to attack *Voyager*.

After tricking the Numiri into confirming his suspicions, Tuvok gathers the key players in the murder mystery. He deduces that a Banean traitor altered Ren's memory engrams in an attempt to use Paris's brain to send secret data to the enemy since the flashbacks include equations taken from the scientist's weapons research. Tuvok exposes the Banean doctor who implanted the engrams as both Lidell's secret lover and Ren's killer. A grateful Paris later thanks Tuvok for saving his life, telling the solitary Vulcan that he has made a friend.

SENSOR READINGS: Kim and Professor Ren work together to repair *Voyager*'s damaged collimator by focusing on the navigational beam specifications and rewriting baseline code algorithms. ▪ To enact the Maquis trick of "playing dead," the crew blows out the dorsal phase emitter, vents a couple of LN-2 exhaust conduits along the dorsal emitters, and takes the engines offline. ▪ When setting up the Numiri, Janeway claims that Paris's shuttle has forty-one tons of thalmerite explosives onboard. ▪ An autonomic response analysis (ARA) is used to prove whether Paris is telling the truth.

SHUTTLE TRACKER: Kim's unseen shuttle has damage to various subsystems following his encounter with the Baneans.

DELTA QUADRANT: The Baneans have the capability of isolating memory engrams in the brain. They take them from the victim's final moments of life and use them in the trial, where an artificial life-form serves as a host to the engrams and testifies to their content. If the accused is found guilty, the engrams are transplanted into the perpetrator's brain. Before the neuro-implants were developed, the Banean punishment for murder was lethal injection. ▪ Tolen Ren had developed four generations of navigational arrays for Banean ships and invented the Banean warship technology. He was stabbed through the intercostal space between the eighth and ninth ribs, where the Banean heart is located. ▪ The Baneans are at war with the Numiri, though they once coexisted on the same planet.

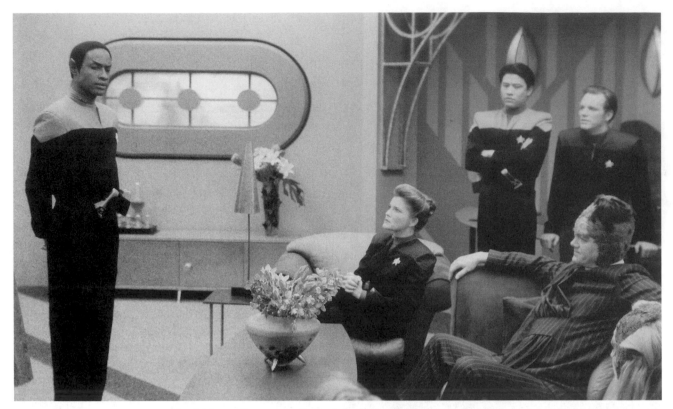
Tuvok informs the suspects that he has solved the crime. ROBBIE ROBINSON

The Numiri are a covert society with directed energy weapons comparable to *Voyager*'s and regenerative shielding that may give them an advantage in a firefight. A standard Numiri tactic is to lock a tractor beam onto ships they intend to board.

ALPHA QUADRANT: Humans gave up smoking centuries ago.

PERSONAL LOGS: Tuvok has been married for sixty-seven years. ▪ The memory engrams implanted in Paris's brain would force him to relive the last moments of Professor Ren's life every fourteen hours for the rest of his natural life. ▪ Kim was interrogated by the Baneans for two days straight, left dehydrated and exhausted. ▪ The Doctor asked Janeway to give him a name since he did not believe that a hologram could name itself. He is programmed with over five million possible treatments with contingency and adaptive programs. Although he believes that this means he has no independent decision-making capabilities, Kes believes otherwise and suggests that he use a name from his database. His program has the names of Starfleet doctors, their patients, and medical personnel in both historic and literary context.

EMANATIONS
EPISODE #109
Written by: BRANNON BRAGA
Directed by: DAVID LIVINGSTON

GUEST STARS

DOCTOR NERIA	**JERRY HARDIN**
HATIL GARAN	**JEFREY ALAN CHANDLER**
PTERA	**CECILE CALLAN**
SESKA	**MARTHA HACKETT**
HATIL'S WIFE	**ROBIN GROVES**

CO-STAR

ALIEN #1	**JOHN CIRIGLIANO**

STARDATE 48623.5

Believing they have found a new element in an asteroid belt surrounding a Class-D planet, Chakotay, Kim, and Torres stumble upon what appears to be an alien burial ground while investigating the find. The element their scanners picked up is emanating from the deceased bodies as a by-product of their decomposition process. While they view the site, a dimensional distortion forms in their vicinity. Chakotay orders an emergency beam out, but *Voyager* is able to retrieve only

Kim emerges from a burial pod that the Vhnori believe came from the Next Emanation. ROBBIE ROBINSON

Chakotay, Torres, and the body of a recently deceased woman. When Tuvok scans the asteroid, there is no sign of Ensign Kim.

Kim has been transported to another dimension after having switched places with the corpse; he finds himself trapped inside a ceremonial burial pod on an alien planet. After he is freed from the pod, Kim is told that he is on the Vhnori home world. The Vhnori believe that he has come from the Next Emanation, or afterlife, and they are disturbed when he reveals that he has just come from a chamber that contained Vhnori bodies.

On *Voyager,* the Doctor is able to revive the dead woman, named Ptera. She becomes hysterical when she realizes that she is not in the Next Emanation. Later, she reveals that her people believe that when they die, the vacuoles take their bodies to another plane of reality. To learn that the distortions merely take their bodies to a barren asteroid is difficult for her to accept. Not long after, a vacuole forms on the ship and deposits a second corpse, and still later, a third.

After hearing Kim's story about the bodies on the asteroid, a Vhnori man named Hatil—who was about to move on to the Next Emanation to ease his family's burden in caring for him—begins to question his own beliefs.

Unable to cope with the facts that contradict her beliefs, Ptera asks to be sent home, even if that means dying a second time. Seeing this as a possible means of rescuing Kim, the crew attempts to beam her into a forming vacuole, but the procedure does not work, and when they retrieve her, Ptera is dead. The situation is worsened by the fact that the vacuoles that continue to form on the ship are damaging the warp core. If the crew does not find Kim soon, they will have to leave him behind.

On the Vhnori world, Kim finds a way to escape. Taking Hatil's place in a burial pod, Kim is transferred to *Voyager* when the next vacuole appears. Although the process of transference was fatal, the Doctor is able to revive him. Captain Janeway informs the ensign that they may have found evidence of what could be a Vhnori afterlife and tells him to take a few days off to think about his experience.

SENSOR READINGS: Janeway instructs the away team to set their tricorders for passive scans only, so as to not to desecrate the bodies. Chakotay instead prefers not to use scanning devices at all. • When Seska attempts to retrieve the missing Kim, Janeway orders her to initiate Emergency Transport Procedure 21-Alpha ▪ Tuvok has the Vhnori bodies taken to the ship's morgue. ▪ The subspace vacuoles disrupt the warp core's magnetic interlock. Torres develops a dampening field to protect the warp core from the vacuoles.

DELTA QUADRANT: The Vhnori are class-5 humanoids who believe that after death they evolve to a higher level of consciousness and move on to the Next Emanation, where their departed loved ones are waiting for them. The dying wrap themselves in a ceremonial shroud before taking part in the Transference Ritual. The ritual involves placing the person in a cenotaph, which terminates the Vhnori's life just before the appearance of a spectral rupture. The ruptures are naturally occurring subspace vacuoles that appear every six hours at the transference facility that Kim was taken to. Doctor Neria is the Chief Thanatologist of the complex. There are thousands of such sites on the Vhnori world. ▪ In reality, the vacuoles deposit the bodies in the ring system of a Class-D planet in the Delta Quadrant. As the bodies' tissues decay, the cell membrane breaks down into a bio-polymer resin which is then excreted by the epidermal layer. The crew sees this as a new element with an unusually large atomic mass, containing over 550 nucleons. The bodies release

The Vhnori celebrants prepare to send their loved one to the Next Emanation. ROBBIE ROBINSON

a neural energy with a frequency identical to the ambient radiation in the asteroid field. Readings indicate the energy is unusually dynamic with a great deal of variation in the pattern complexity and quantum density, leading Janeway and Kim to hypothesize that it could reflect a form of afterlife.

The Ocampa are buried when they die, believing that the *comra* (soul) is released into an afterlife.

ALPHA QUADRANT: There are 246 elements known to Federation science. ▪ Klingons believe in an afterlife, but when they die their bodies are disposed of by the most efficient means possible.

PERSONAL LOGS: The first time Chakotay went on a tomb excavation on Ktaria VII, he took a memento that he later realized was a sacred stone and thus he had desecrated a grave.

Seska is stationed in Transporter Room 3.

MEDICAL REPORT: Kim dies in the Tranference Ritual and is revived by the Doctor using two cc's of cordrazine. ▪ The Doctor uses two cc's of netinaline to wake Ptera.

PRIME FACTORS

EPISODE #110
TELEPLAY BY **MICHAEL PERRICONE & GREG ELLIOT**
STORY BY **DAVID R. GEORGE III & ERIC A. STILLWELL**
DIRECTED BY **LES LANDAU**

GUEST STARS

GATH	RONALD GUTTMAN
EUDANA	YVONNE SUHOR
JARET	ANDREW HILL NEWMAN
SESKA	MARTHA HACKETT
CAREY	JOSH CLARK

STARDATE 48642.5

The crew beams aboard Gath Labin, a representative from the planet Sikaris, with an offer that may go a long way to strengthen the crew's growing bonds. He invites them to vacation on his homeworld, a planet with a reputation for its hospitable inhabitants. Janeway accepts the offer to visit Sikaris, where the residents welcome her crew with open arms.

While Kim visits with a woman named Eudana, he learns that her people place a high value on storytelling and that new stories are a precious commodity. Excited by the opportunity to hear Kim's stories, Eudana uses a spatial trajector to take them to Alastria, a planet 40,000 light-years away. Realizing that the space-folding device could bring the crew much closer to home, Kim rushes to tell the captain about his discovery. Janeway, in turn, asks Gath about using the trajector, but he refuses, citing the Sikarian canon of laws, which strictly forbids sharing technology with other species.

While speaking with the senior staff, Janeway remarks on how frustrating it is to be on the receiving end of another race's version of the Prime Directive, but realizes that she must respect their laws. However, Tuvok believes that the Sikarians may be willing to make a trade for the technology, leading Kim to suggest that the ship's library would make for a tantalizing offer.

Gath is intrigued but puts off a response citing that he will have to discuss it with the other magistrates. Later, Gath's associate, Jaret Otel, makes his own secret offer for the technology in exchange for the stories, citing that Gath has no intention of pursuing the deal.

After Kim tells Janeway about the offer, she approaches Gath one last time. Realizing that Gath is interested only in serving his own needs, Janeway returns to *Voyager* and orders the crew back to the ship. Although Janeway opts to reject Otel's offer, Seska, Carey, and Torres plan to follow through and deliver a download of *Voyager's* library. Tuvok stops them and beams himself to the planet to carry out the deal.

Tuvok returns with the matrix for the trajector, but when the engineering crew secretly tries to use it, they nearly cause a warp core breach, as it is incompatible with Federation technology. Although they can easily erase the evidence of their attempt, Torres prefers to accept the responsibility as chief engineer and admits the act to the captain. Janeway warns Torres against any future transgressions, but is more concerned by Tuvok's participation. The Vulcan says that he was willing to sacrifice his own career so that the crew could return home without forcing Janeway to compromise her own ethics. Although touched by Tuvok's sacrifice, Janeway tells him that she relies on his advice as her moral compass and orders him never to go behind her back again.

Gath offers Janeway to have a dress made of fabric spun from the petals of a flower that blooms only in moonlight. ROBBIE ROBINSON

Tuvok believes that he is acting in the captain's interests. DANNY FELD

SENSOR READINGS: Torres performs a routine maintenance check on the shock attenuation cylinders and determines that they will have to be replaced in another two thousand hours. ▪ The crew stocks their food stores with some of Sikaris's huge variety of edible plants.

DELTA QUADRANT: The Sikarians are known for their incredible hospitality; however, Gath's behavior proves that their motivation for generosity is selfish in nature. They value stories as an important part of their culture. ▪ The Sikarian Canon of Laws determines their entire system of values and is similar in concept to the Prime Directive. The Laws forbid the sharing of technology with alien races, for fear it would be abused. ▪ The atmospheric sensor works on a principle of nonlinear resonance, adjusting the dynamic variables in the atmosphere. ▪ The spatial trajector can fold space, transporting people and objects to distances as great as 40,000 light-years away. The folding of space leaves a subspace residue in which a neutrino dispersion pattern can be detected. The trajector operates within a neutrino envelope. The trajector field is ten orders of magnitude larger than anything the crew had ever created. To get a field that size the planet acts as an amplifier since Sikaris has a mantle of tetrahedral quartz twenty kilometers thick. The crystalline structure of the mantle acts to focus and amplify the trajector field, meaning that once *Voyager* leaves orbit, they will lose the ability to traject. When they enact the trajector, the plasma manifold becomes unstable because it is being bombarded by antineutrons that serve as a catalyst for the space-folding process. The warp core heats to a temperature of fifty million Kelvin and nearly breaches.

Alastria is a planet in a binary star system 40,000 light-years away from Sikaris. The dawn zephyr brings the Erosene winds, known as the "passion winds." They come just before sunrise and are known to cause a feeling of euphoria.

PERSONAL LOGS: Paris and Kim recently had a double date with the Delaney sisters in a recreation of Venice on the holodeck. The date ended poorly, when Kim fell out of his gondola. ▪ Torres expresses an interest in Ensign Murphy.

Seska claims that her brother's birthday is in four days and she had promised to meet him on Nivoch. ▪ Lieutenant Carey has a wife and two young sons. ▪ One of the Delaney sisters is named Jenny.

EPISODE LOGS: Torres's actions result in the second time she is threatened with being thrown in the brig. The first time was in "Parallax," in which Tuvok wanted to place her in the brig for breaking Lieutenant Carey's nose. ▪ Gath tells Janeway that word has spread about her crew being lost and searching their way home. In future episodes, Kazon will spread news of their travels with a more negative slant.

STATE OF FLUX

EPISODE #111
TELEPLAY BY **CHRIS ABBOTT**
STORY BY **PAUL ROBERT COYLE**
DIRECTED BY **ROBERT SCHEERER**

GUEST STARS	
SESKA	**MARTHA HACKETT**
CAREY	**JOSH CLARK**
CULLUH	**ANTHONY DeLONGIS**

CO-STAR	
COMPUTER VOICE	**MAJEL BARETT**

STARDATE 48658.2

While an away team is on an uninhabited planet gathering food supplies, *Voyager* picks up a Kazon ship on its scanners. Janeway orders the team back to the ship, but Chakotay reports that Seska is missing. The ensign was last seen near a cave that may be blocking their scans for her. While the rest of the team beams to safety, Chakotay locates the cave and finds

Seska and an injured Chakotay flee from the cave where they encountered Kazon soldiers. ROBBIE ROBINSON

Seska hiding from a pair of Kazon. They manage to beam up to the ship, but not before Chakotay is hit by Kazon fire.

While Chakotay recuperates from his injury, *Voyager* receives a distress call from a Kazon-Nistrim ship. As there are no other ships in the area, Janeway decides to offer aid. The crew finds that the ship has been badly damaged by an explosion that appears to have involved Federation technology. They are curious as to the origins of the technology, but the crew is unable to remove it from the ship for examination due to the intense levels of radiation. They do find one survivor, whom they beam over for treatment in the hopes that he can explain the origin of the technology.

Tuvok believes the most likely explanation for the Kazon-Nistrim having access to Federation technology is that someone onboard *Voyager* has covertly given it to them. He suspects Seska, due to the fact that she was found near the Kazon on the planet. Chakotay, who is Seska's former lover, staunchly defends her, even when she makes an unauthorized trip to the damaged Kazon ship in an attempt to retrieve the Federation equipment. Tuvok thinks she may be trying to destroy evidence, but Chakotay feels she is trying to clear her name. Before they

can find out the truth, Seska is injured and beamed directly to sickbay.

Voyager is hailed by another Kazon-Nistrim ship inquiring about the damaged vessel. Janeway allows First Maje Culluh to beam aboard and check on the status of the injured Kazon, but he instead kills the recovering patient. After the captain orders Cullah off the ship, the Doctor and Kes inform her that while treating Seska they found her blood seems to indicate that she is Cardassian, not Bajoran as she appears.

Chakotay still refuses to believe that Seska is a spy. After the Federation technology is recovered from the damaged Kazon vessel, Chakotay confronts Seska about her altered blood chemistry, which she claims is the result of a bone marrow transplant she received from a Cardassian woman. Nevertheless, Chakotay, denying his personal feelings for her, joins forces with Tuvok to lay a trap.

Seska is caught altering the database inventory and admits to the accusations. Revealing that she is indeed Cardassian, Seska blames Janeway and her Federation rules for trapping them all in the Delta Quadrant. As a means of forging an alliance with the powerful Kazon, Seska gave them the plans for a Starfleet replicator, a bit

Seska fails to retrieve Starfleet technology from the damaged Kazon ship. ROBBIE ROBINSON

er system in sickbay to input her security code into the inventory manifest in order to frame herself. ▪ The pattern buffer relays in *Voyager*'s food replicators are composed of bio-neural fibers. According to Torres, no other Federation ship employs this technology signifying that it must have come from *Voyager*.

DELTA QUADRANT: The Kazon-Nistrim, led by First Maje Culluh, is one of the most violent sects in the entire Kazon Collective. ▪ The first Kazon ship *Voyager* comes across uses masking circuitry as a rudimentary type of cloaking device. The circuitry is hardly effective as the ship has a reflection when the sun hits it at a certain angle and a lateral EM scan allows *Voyager* to pick up their ion trail. A polaron burst places the Kazon ship in view for a moment. Later, after sending a distress signal, the Kazon ship shows fluctuating nucleonic patterns that could indicate a reactive breakdown onboard. The ship's automatic containment systems were activated when nucleonic radiation entered the bridge. ▪ The injured Kazon's body has been altered and fused with inorganic matter. The Doctor needs to do a complete pyrocyte replacement to keep the Kazon alive. Kes runs a cytological screening of the crew to look for a blood type match for the Kazon so they can completely replace his blood. The injured Kazon is killed when a nerve toxin is injected into his system. ▪ The Kazon ship was damaged because they did not use enough shield casing on the replicator, and once the radiation leaked out, a cascade was inevitable.

Neelix directs the away team to dig for *leola* root to add to the ship's stores. He considers the horrible-tasting food the best source of vitamins and minerals in the quadrant and will make many future dishes with it as the base ingredient.

ALPHA QUADRANT: Starfleet security has documented several incidents in which Cardassians have used cosmetic alterations for the purpose of infiltrating an enemy. ▪ Orkett's disease is a terminal virus that affected thousands of Bajoran children during the Cardassian Occupation.

PERSONAL LOGS: Prior to joining *Voyager*, Chakotay was involved in a relationship with Seska until they decided that it would be best not to continue. While they were together, he told her about his animal guide. His favorite soup is mushroom. ▪ Tuvok uses Vulcan logic to beat Chakotay in a game of gin. ▪ According to Torres, she does not exaggerate when it comes to engineering work and that when she says "tomorrow," she means "tomorrow." ▪ The Doctor's program includes the complete Bajoran medical text on Orkett's disease.

of "minor technology" that destroyed the other vessel. Before Seska can be taken into custody, she beams herself over to Culluh's vessel. With more Kazon ships approaching then *Voyager* can handle alone, Janeway orders the crew to leave the region, noting that they will have to wait for another day to settle up with Seska.

SENSOR READINGS: The residue from the explosion on the Kazon ship has a .41 percent trace of neosorium composite. Torres knows only the Federation to use neosorium technology. ▪ Seska's communication to the Kazon was masked by a test of the dorsal emitters a week prior to the investigation. The entire engineering team was working on the test while the communication was sent from Lieutenant Carey's workstation. ▪ Seska tries to use a localized subspace bubble to get herself safely through the intense levels of nucleonic radiation and retrieve the Federation technology, but the attempt is unsuccessful. Later, the engineering team successfully follows Lieutenant Carey's suggestion to use an expander to manipulate the force field and rotate it and the radiation inside it away from the console. ▪ Seska uses the comput-

With other crew members creating a diversion, Seska and Jackson break into the kitchen and loot the food reserves in order to make mushroom soup for Chakotay. As a result, Chakotay revokes the guilty parties' (and his own) replicator privileges for two days. Until she was injured, Seska had managed to avoid providing a blood sample for the ship's medical records. Her Cardassian physiology is revealed when Kes and the Doctor discover that her blood chemistry is lacking all common Bajoran blood factors. Her cover story was that she had Okrett's disease as a child and received a bone marrow transplant from a Cardassian woman named Kattell. Seska initiates Command XJL to transport her from sickbay to the Kazon ship. ▪ Lieutenant Carey, who has had a distinguished Starfleet career, is restricted to quarters during the investigation.

CREW COMPLEMENT: Seska defects to the Kazon.

EPISODE LOGS: Tuvok notes that one of the possible explanations for the Kazon having access to Federation technology is that there could be another Federation ship brought to the Delta Quadrant prior to their arrival. Although Janeway has no knowledge of other missing ships, three Alpha Quadrant ships are later discovered: The Hansen family ship, the *Raven* ("The Raven"), the Ferengi shuttle ("False Profits") and the *U.S.S. Equinox* ("Equinox"). ▪ At some point in this episode, on Stardate 48671, Seska accesses Tuvok's security training program "Insurrection: Alpha," and reprograms it with booby traps. The events of this reprogramming will be played out in "Worst Case Scenario."

Freya sacrifices her own life to save the Doctor. ROBBIE ROBINSON

HEROES AND DEMONS

EPISODE #112
WRITTEN BY **NAREN SHANKAR**
DIRECTED BY **LES LANDAU**

GUEST STARS

FREYA	MARJORIE MONAGHAN
UNFERTH	CHRISTOPHER NEAME
KING HROTHGAR	MICHAEL KEENAN

CO-STAR

COMPUTER VOICE	MAJEL BARRETT

STARDATE 48693.2

 After beaming aboard photonic matter samples from a nearby protostar, Janeway intends to assign Kim to assist in its analysis, until she discovers that the ensign is missing. Since he was scheduled for time in Holodeck 2, Chakotay and Tuvok investigate and find that Kim's program, a holonovel based on the ancient English epic *Beowulf*, is still running. Unable to shut down the program, they enter the holodeck to search for the ensign.

They encounter a holographic character named Freya, who reveals that Beowulf, whom Chakotay and Tuvok assume is Kim, has been killed. When she takes them to meet her father, King Hrothgar, they learn that the monster Grendel was responsible for Beowulf's death.

The two officers report to Janeway, who tells them to send their tricorder scans to the bridge, while Torres runs a diagnostic on the holodeck's imaging control systems. The data from the tricorders reveal that some of the photonic material they beamed aboard seems to have infiltrated the holodeck. Before they can fully discuss the implications, Chakotay and Tuvok encounter Grendel and disappear as well.

HOLODECK MALFUNCTIONS

"Holodecks are a pointless endeavor . . . fulfilling some human need to fantasize. I have no such need."

Seven of Nine, "One"

A ship lost thousands of light-years from home. A crew consumed with thoughts of family, friends, and familiar surroundings. From the very inception of the series, the holodeck was intended to serve as an important morale booster for the crew. What better way to combat homesickness than with a simulation of home? However, since holodecks first made their appearance in the *TNG* episode "Encounter at Farpoint" their uses for relaxation have given way to adventure with the dreaded holodeck malfunction.

The holodeck malfunction is a storytelling device in which the writers take a simple program and add some form of danger or dramatic situation from which the crew needs to escape, usually with the safety protocols going offline. Add to that mix a holographic character in your cast, and the storytelling possibilities become endless.

"HEROES AND DEMONS" When the *Voyager* crew accidentally abducts photonic energy life-forms, the beings take over the holodeck and retaliate by abducting members of the crew. While Kim is running the *Beowulf* holonovel, the energy beings use the Grendel character to turn Kim, Chakotay, and Tuvok into energy and transport them to their "ship." The Doctor, being made of energy and the only inorganic being on *Voyager* that can safely enter the holodeck, returns the abducted life-form in exchange for the missing crewmen.

"PROJECTIONS" While the Doctor enjoys a holonovel, a kinoplastic radiation surge from a spatial anomaly affects the holodeck's imaging system. The resulting feedback loop between the holodeck computer and the Doctor's program causes him to question the nature of his existence by convincing him that he is Dr. Lewis Zimmerman, a real man and not a hologram.

"WORST CASE SCENARIO" Torres comes across Tuvok's unfinished security training program on dealing with a potential Maquis mutiny. Paris and Tuvok are assigned to finish the story for the crew's entertainment, but their lives are put in jeopardy when they discover that, prior to leaving *Voyager*, Seska reprogrammed the storyline to be lethal for the participants. Following a torturous game of cat and mouse, Tuvok reprograms a phaser to malfunction, killing the holographic Seska and ending the program safely.

"THE KILLING GAME PARTS I&II" The Hirogen take over the ship and force most of the crew to unknowingly participate in holoexercises allowing the Hirogen to enjoy the thrill of the hunt while keeping an almost endless supply of prey. Eventually, with Kim's forced expansion of the holoprojectors through several decks, an explosion allows the characters to escape the holodeck and overrun the ship. With both crews suffering heavy losses, a truce is called and Janeway supplies the Hirogen with a holomatrix so they can continue to pursue a variety of prey without causing the extinction of their own race.

"BRIDE OF CHAOTICA!" *Voyager* intersects a layer of subspace inhabited by photonic life-forms who enter the holodeck believing the Captain

DANNY FELD

Proton program to be real. Soon, a holographic war is waged between Dr. Chaotica and his minions and the transdimensional aliens. With holodeck controls offline and the crew unable to shut down the program, Captain Janeway and members of the senior staff must play out the events of the program to a conclusion so they can free the alien lifeforms.

"SPIRIT FOLK" Running the Fair Haven program continuously results in damaged subroutines in all the character files. As their perceptual filters malfunction the townspeople begin to become aware of the *Voyager* crew's ability to alter their reality and dub them "spirit folk." After they take Paris, Kim, and the Doctor hostage, Janeway is forced to tell the residents a partial truth so the crew can continue to visit the town.

"FLESH AND BLOOD PARTS I&II" Using holotechnology obtained from *Voyager* the Hirogen program holograms to be worthy prey. Eventually the holograms prove to be too worthy as they adapt to the programming and turn into hunters hoping to secure their freedom. At first the Doctor takes their side, but soon he and Torres become hostages who ultimately negotiate a peaceful solution for all but one rogue character.

Holo-Related Malfunctions

"ALTER EGO" A lonely alien woman masquerades as a holodeck character so that she can spend time with the crew, leading both Kim and Tuvok to grow closer to the character. She ultimately takes control of the ship in the hopes that Tuvok will stay with her.

"DARKLING" The Doctor's program develops a "Jekyll and Hyde" type of instability when he adds new personality subroutines from historical characters in the holodeck.

"REVULSION" A psychotic alien hologram named Dejaren takes out his hatred of organics on Torres.

"CONCERNING FLIGHT" After the theft of the ship's main computer processor, the Leonardo da Vinci holocharacter is downloaded into the stolen Doctor's mobile emitter and allowed to roam freely on a alien planet.

"LIVING WITNESS" The Doctor's backup program is found on a planet seven hundred years after an encounter with *Voyager* altered the world's history.

"LATENT IMAGE" The Doctor's program is affected when he wrestles with the guilt of having chosen to save Kim's life over that of another crew member.

"TINKER, TENOR, DOCTOR, SPY" After alien observers tap into the Doctor's daydreams and believe him to be the ship's Emergency Command Hologram, they plan an attack based on the information they have acquired.

"FAIR HAVEN" Captain Janeway falls in love with a holographic character from Paris' Fair Haven program.

"INSIDE MAN" A counterfeit hologram of Lieutenant Barclay is sent to *Voyager* by a group of Alpha Quadrant Ferengi trying to lure the ship into a trap so they can obtain Seven's nanoprobes.

"BODY AND SOUL" To save the Doctor from being decompiled by an alien crew, his program is downloaded into Seven of Nine's body.

"SHATTERED" As *Voyager* is split into numerous time periods, Chakotay and Janeway must play along with the characters in the Captain Proton program to inject a serum into the holodeck's gel packs.

"HUMAN ERROR" Seven of Nine becomes addicted to her "second life" on the holodeck.

The captain knows she must use all of her guile to get *Voyager* home. ROBBIE ROBINSON

Torres uncovers a malfunction in the holodeck's matter conversion nodes that seems to occur whenever Grendel appears, leading them to the conclusion that the missing crewmen have been converted into energy. Since the Doctor is already energy, he is the only one who can safely investigate the holoprogram and is sent on his first "away mission."

Kes suggests that the Doctor should give himself a name to reflect the importance of such an important milestone. He chooses a name from his medical texts, Schweitzer. When he is transferred to the holodeck, the Doctor first encounters Freya, and tells her that he has come to find Grendel. When he finally meets the creature, he discovers that it is a photonic energy formation. Under attack, the Doctor is beamed back to sickbay.

Based on their findings, Janeway speculates that they are dealing with photonic life-forms that have reacted to the unintentional capture of their species by taking counter measures—kidnapping crew members from the holodeck and converting them to energy—in essence, holding them hostage.

The Doctor suggests that he return to the holodeck and release the remaining sample of photonic matter to Grendel, in the hopes that the beings will return the crew. The plan works, and Kim, Tuvok, and Chakotay return safely, although Freya is killed while attempting to defend her beloved Schweitzer. When Janeway asks the Doctor for a name to attach to the commendation she is noting for his first away mission, he claims that he had chosen one, but decided against it as it is now associated with the painful memory of Freya's death.

SENSOR READINGS: Janeway and Torres conduct experiments on photonic energy hoping to boost efficiency of the power converters by fifteen or twenty percent. ▪ The crew believes that the holodeck's matter conversion nodes turned the missing crewmen into energy since the holodeck is an outgrowth of replicator and transporter technology.

DAMAGE REPORT: The life-form causes a hull breach that is contained. Due to the presence of the photonic life-form the holodeck's manual overrides, command system, and safety programs malfunction.

SHUTTLE TRACKER: While searching for Kim, Tuvok notes that *all* shuttles are accounted for in the shuttlebay, indicating that there are a number of shuttles.

DELTA QUADRANT: Janeway believes that the energy lattice may be the equivalent of the photonic life-forms' ship. There are three distinct bio-electrical patterns in the lattice (the missing crewmen).

ALPHA QUADRANT: There are no demons in Vulcan literature. ▪ The Vok'sha of Rakella Prime believe that hate is a beast who lives inside the stomach. Their greatest hero is a man who ate stones for twenty-three days to kill the beast and became a saint.

PERSONAL LOGS: The Doctor's first away mission turns into first contact. On the mission in the holodeck, the Doctor becomes romantically involved with Freya, one of the holographic characters. To transfer him to the holodeck the crew has to modify his data stream protocols and imaging systems. Torres gives him complete control over his magnetic containment field so he can make himself solid or allow matter to pass through him. Contact with the photonic energy disrupts his magnetic cohesion, resulting in the loss of his right arm (which Paris replaces). The captain places a special commendation in the logs for exemplary performance by the chief medical officer during his first away mission. ▪ Continuing her medical studies, Kes has finished studying the protein synthesis text and is ready to move on to learning how to operate the base pair sequencer.

EPISODE LOGS: Neelix does not appear in this episode. Kim appears only in the penultimate scene with just one line of dialogue.

CATHEXIS

EPISODE #113

TELEPLAY BY **BRANNON BRAGA**

STORY BY **BRANNON BRAGA & JOE MENOSKY**

DIRECTED BY **KIM FRIEDMAN**

GUEST STARS

LT. DURST	**BRIAN MARKINSON**
LORD BURLEIGH	**MICHAEL CUMPSTY**
MRS. TEMPLETON	**CAROLYN SEYMOUR**

CO-STAR

COMPUTER VOICE	**MAJEL BARRETT**

STARDATE 48734.2

Janeway's attempt to relax with a new holonovel is interrupted by the return of a badly damaged shuttlecraft manned by an unresponsive Tuvok and Chakotay. The two injured officers are beamed to sickbay where Janeway learns that something has drained all the bio-neural energy from the Chakotay's brain. Torres places a Native American medicine wheel near Chakotay's bed, in the hopes that it will help him "find his way home" from his illness.

Tuvok reveals that an unidentified ship emerged from a dark matter nebula and attacked them. Janeway orders *Voyager* to the nebula to investigate, but before they reach it, the ship changes course twice. The navigational computer shows Paris made the changes, but he denies the charge. A short time later, Torres initiates a warp core shutdown, but like Paris, she cannot remember anything. When the Doctor examines the pair, he discovers that a strange brainwave pattern was superimposed on their own during the tampering incidents, possibly indicating that an alien entity momentarily seized control of their minds. As a precaution, Janeway transfers the ship's command codes to the Doctor, as he is the only member of the crew that would be unsusceptible to mind control.

When Kes tells Janeway that she has been sensing an alien presence on the ship, Tuvok suggests that he per-

Trained in native American psycho-spiritual beliefs, the Doctor corrects Torres's placements of stones on the medicine wheel. ROBBIE ROBINSON

form a mind-meld with her to help focus her telepathic abilities. But a short time later, the two are found unconscious in a turbolift. When someone disables the Doctor's program, the command codes revert to Janeway, who decides to divide them between herself and Tuvok. The unseen force tries to take over Janeway, but the crew incapacitates her. It jumps to Kim, and then Lieutenant Durst, before Tuvok finally stuns everyone on the bridge.

Under increasing suspicion, Tuvok forcibly takes command of the ship and orders it into the nebula, where he cryptically says that his race, the Komar, await. As they enter the nebula, something makes Torres eject the warp core, leading the crew to believe there is another presence on the ship. Janeway reasons that it must be Chakotay.

Realizing that the Komar want to extract their neural energy, the crew manages to overpower Tuvok. The lifeform leaves his body to join the other energy beings in the nebula. *Voyager* needs to leave the area, but since the possessed Tuvok plotted the course in, they are uncertain how to escape the nebula.

In sickbay, Neelix is compelled to rearrange the markers on Chakotay's medicine wheel. Janeway realizes Chakotay has drawn them a map showing them the correct course out of the nebula. Later, the reestablished Doctor reintegrates Chakotay's displaced neural energy with his body and he is revived at last.

SENSOR READINGS: Helm control is temporarily transferred to ops. ▪ Navigational control is on Deck 12, Section B-7. ▪ Sickbay visual relay 16 gives the bridge

Under alien control, Tuvok threatens the bridge crew. ROBBIE ROBINSON

trail in his multiphasic scan on the Alpha-K band. The ion trail Tuvok created leaves no sign of subspace distortion in its wake, suggesting that the fake ship has no engines. ▪ Tuvok orders all security personnel to Condition 4 during the intruder alert.

DAMAGE REPORT: Under attack by the Komar, shields fail and Janeway reroutes all power, including life support, to the thrusters to escape the dark matter nebula. ▪ The electromagnetic energy in the nebula blinds ship's sensors.

SHUTTLE TRACKER: Tuvok and Chakotay's unseen shuttle is badly damaged by the Komar.

DELTA QUADRANT: The Komar are picked up on sensors as energy pulses that are highly coherent with a biomatrix. They are trianic-based energy beings. The collective neural energy of the crew has the ability to sustain the Komar for years.

ALPHA QUADRANT: Chakotay's tribe believes that the medicine wheel is a representation of both the universe inside and outside the mind, and that each is a reflection of the other. When a person is sleeping or on a vision quest, it is said that his soul is walking the wheel. If the person is in a coma or near death, it is believed that he is lost. In that case, someone would place stones on the wheel as signposts, pointing the persons way back. Torres places the coyote stone at the crossroads of the fifth and sixth realms, diverting Chakotay's soul to the Mountains of the Antelope Women, a very attractive locale.

The Vulcan neck pinch is characterized by marks on the neck and shoulder of the victim. There is an extreme trauma to the trapezius nerve bundle, rupturing nerve fibers.

PERSONAL LOGS: Janeway takes two lumps of sugar in her tea. ▪ Paris is made temporary medic when the Doctor and Kes are incapacitated. As a child of nine, Paris caught a really bad cold. His doctor at the time, Doc Brown, not only treated him, but also whipped up a pot of garlic soup and brought it over. Paris used to read holocomics. ▪ The medical treatments known by the Doctor include those based on psycho-spiritual beliefs. ▪ Kes senses Chakotay's presence on the ship in a manner different from the experience she had a week before where she had sensed Lieutenant Hargrove's presence in sickbay although he had left hours earlier.

MEDICAL REPORT: All bio-neural energy had been

access to view Chakotay's medicine wheel in sickbay. ▪ The captain transfers command codes to the Doctor using Authorization Janeway 841-Alpha-65. ▪ A forensic sweep of navigational control finds traces of Paris's DNA on the console. ▪ The most thorough scanning device onboard is a magneton scanner. Torres creates a magneton flash to scan the entire ship at once. The process requires reconfiguring every sensor array on the ship to emit a single burst to illuminate the anomalous energy. The high-intensity burst causes dizziness and disorientation among the crew for several seconds. ▪ Under Chakotay's influence, Torres initiates a warp core shutdown, crashes the main computer, and locks out the bridge. When the warp core goes offline, it takes at least two hours to regenerate the dilithium matrix. Later Torres ejects the warp core, although it takes a command code to do so. ▪ While possessed, Tuvok uses a phaser set on wide dispersal to stun the crew. ▪ Torres uses a parity trace scan on the shuttle's sensor logs and determines that they were erased before the sensor matrix was overloaded to make that appear the cause of the damage. ▪ Janeway concludes that Tuvok is lying when she determines that he is tracking a fake ion

extracted from Chakotay's brain, leaving him brain dead. The process used to reintegrate his consciousness involved three neural transceivers, two cortical stimulators, and fifty gigaquads of computer memory. ▪ Tuvok's Vulcan neck pinch on Kes puts her in a coma.

EPISODE LOGS: Tuvok now wears the pips of a lieutenant, as opposed to the lieutenant commander pips he had been wearing. No formal explanation is provided for this change in costume and correction of rank; however, Tuvok will be promoted to lieutenant commander in "Revulsion." ▪ Janeway's holonovel scene was originally the opening for "Eye of the Needle." In the original scene, the program was interrupted when Kim came to the holodeck to tell the Captain he may have found a wormhole. In this episode, the scene is interrupted when Kim, via the com system, alerts the captain of the returning shuttle. ▪ Lieutenant Durst is introduced and will have a crucial role to play in next episode, "Faces." ▪ The Vulcan neck pinch is more commonly referred to as the Vulcan nerve pinch.

The Klingon Torres lashes out at her captor after he murders Lieutenant Durst and steals the man's face. ROBBIE ROBINSON

FACES

EPISODE #114

TELEPLAY BY KENNETH BILLER

STORY BY JONATHAN GLASSNER and KENNETH BILLER

DIRECTED BY WINRICH KOLBE

GUEST STARS

LT. DURST/SULAN	BRIAN MARKINSON
VIDIIAN GUARD #1	ROB LaBELLE
TALAXIAN	BARTON TINAPP

STARDATE 48784.2

In an underground lab, a Vidiian scientist named Sulan has extracted Torres's Klingon genetic material to create an entirely Klingon version of her. By injecting the pure subject with the deadly Phage disease, he plans to test his theory that the Klingon genetic structure has Phage-resistant nucleotide sequences that could lead to a cure for his people. But his interest in Torres is more than purely scientific, a fact the Klingon woman soon realizes.

Trapped in another Vidiian cell, Paris and Lieutenant Durst are stunned when a new prisoner is brought in. She is an all-human version of Torres—the other "half" of Torres that was left after Sulan removed the Klingon genetic material. When the guards return and forcibly remove Durst from the cell, Paris tries unsuccessfully to help his friend, while all the human Torres can do is cringe in fear.

In an attempt to find the missing away team, Chakotay, Kim, and Tuvok beam down to the planet to investigate. Chakotay traces the missing crew members to the caves, but cannot break through the Vidiian forcefield to find them.

The Klingon B'Elanna is horrified to see Sulan wearing Durst's face. He has killed the lieutenant and grafted the dead man's face over his own diseased features in the hopes that B'Elanna will find him more attractive. Instead, her anger helps her break the bonds restraining her. She attacks Sulan and escapes the lab.

Paris and the human B'Elanna are sent out on a labor detail, but when she claims to be too exhausted to work, she is sent back to the barracks where she plans to use the Vidiians' technology to contact *Voyager*. Her work is thwarted when the guards discover the attempt. Luckily, her Klingon counterpart finds her and helps bring her to safety. Despite much tension between the human and Klingon, the two women acknowledge that each has unique qualities that contribute to the whole that is B'Elanna. Together they go to the lab where the Klingon Torres was being held in the hopes that they can use the technology there to bring down the force field, allowing *Voyager* to beam them up. While the human Torres works, she accidentally trips an alarm that brings Sulan back to his lab.

Disguised as a Vidiian, Chakotay is beamed through a small opening in the forcefield and he rescues Paris

THE VIDIIANS

"Please understand that this disease has been killing my people for hundreds of years. Trying to stop it has become an obsession. And many of our politicians and scientists have never developed compassion for the people who keep us alive."

Denara Pel, "Lifesigns"

The Vidiians are introduced in "Phage" and quickly become one of the most popular new races of *Voyager* aliens. A true *Star Trek* villain, the Vidiians are not purely evil; rather, they are victims of circumstance. Infected with the deadly Phage disease, this once proud race of educators and explorers is forced to rely on any means necessary to survive. In the *Star Trek* tradition, they hold a mirror to humanity and ask the question how far would one go when faced with extinction? From a storytelling standpoint, each episode in which the Vidiians appear also allows the writers to further explore the show's main cast of characters.

That was a great concept for an alien species. Very rarely do you stumble on something that has real resonance. The Vidiians started off with "What if the Black Plague had never gone away? How would humanity have been changed if the entire world had to live with the Black Plague? How would culture have changed? How would we be?" And that led to these people who were highly advanced, enlightened people who just had a horrible disease. And then it led to great-looking aliens, really creepy. That was a great Star Trek villain, because they're creepy and frightening and have a unique, scary M.O. but they also have a deeper philosophical underpinning to them. That's what makes for a good old-fashioned Star Trek villain.

—Brannon Braga

For much of "Phage" we know very little about the aliens, least of all their name. The episode is more of a chase show, while focusing on Neelix's character and exploring the possibility of his spending the rest of his life hooked up to a machine. This serves as one of the few times in the course of the series in which his character is engaged in dramatic pathos rather than comic relief. When the crew finally comes face-to-face with the aliens, they learn the atrocities are motivated by a warped sense of logical motivation, but that's not enough to redeem their acts. In the end, one of the pair does show a redeeming side by offering the expertise that will save Neelix, but that appears to be a rare act among their people. In later episodes, the Vidiians will prove to be a much greater threat.

In "Faces," the actions of the chief surgeon of the Vidiian Sodality, Sulan, are based on his desire to help his people. However, this is at the expense of harming or killing another, Torres, whom he splits into two parts. He cavalierly comments that he might have been in error to leave her memory and consciousness intact. Even worse, he is deluded enough to think that killing a fellow crew member and using his face will make the Klingon Torres admire him. One can conjecture that the psychosis has driven him to no longer care for his victims. In the end, he proves that Klingon DNA does have

before reuniting with the two halves of Torres. Just as they are about to beam back up to the ship, Sulan fires and the Klingon Torres takes the deadly hit to save her human self. On *Voyager* the Doctor is able to use her Klingon DNA to restore Torres back to her original self, with a greater appreciation of her Klingon characteristics.

SENSOR READINGS: *Voyager* has completed a two-day survey of the Avery system and returned to the third planet to retrieve the away team that was inspecting magnesite formations. The dense magnesite formations block

the ship's scanners. Kim modifies subspace transponders to be deployed at regular intervals along the second away team's path as a means of maintaining a signal link and transporter lock with the ship.

DELTA QUADRANT: The cave walls function as movable, disguised force fields. The energy configuration of the force field matrix leads the crew to realize that they are dealing with the Vidiians. The force fields, which surround an area 600 kilometers in circumference, have been reconfigured to repulse phaser fire since *Voyager's*

Phage resistant properties, which allows Torres to later help Danara Pel. The Vidiian science created a perfect story device in which Torres is split into human and Klingon halves, thus allowing for the exploration of her character in further detail and for her to begin learning to accept her Klingon heritage.

Dr. Danara Pel is introduced in "Lifesigns" and will be the only Vidiian character the crew encounters who has only the best intentions at heart. It is in this episode that the audience gets to see the more "human" side of the aliens by seeing the ravages of the disease through her eyes rather than the crew's. Danara is a purely noble character and she serves as the catalyst for the Doctor's first story of real romance.

It is in the follow up episodes "Deadlock" and "Resolutions" that the Vidiians become a true threat to the *Voyager* crew. In the earlier episodes, their acts were somewhat balanced by their motivation. However, in these episodes, they serve solely as villains, intent on harvesting the crew's organs. When the Vidiians board the undamaged *Voyager* in "Deadlock," they do so with cold, heartless precision, attacking the crew and preparing them for harvesting. The horrific action leads one of the two Janeways to destroy her ship and sacrifice her crew in order to

ROBBIE ROBINSON

save the duplicate *Voyager*. These events are followed up on when, in "Resolutions," Tuvok must make the almost emotional decision to contact the Vidiians in hope for a cure for Janeway and Chakotay's illness. In the end, the Vidiians use the request as an opportunity to attack *Voyager*, but Danara Pel comes to the rescue for the crew and provides an antibody to the disease.

In "Fury" Kes returns to *Voyager*, jumping back to an earlier conflict with the Vidiians, although little use is made of the alien threat beyond its ability to endanger the ship. With "Resolutions," the *Voyager* crew has what appears to be their last actual encounter with the alien race, however, they will been seen again in the illusory threat of Janeway's death in "Coda." The final notable mention of the Vidiians comes in "Think Tank," when Janeway learns that they have been cured of the dreaded disease by Kurros and his "think tank."

I loved the Vidiians. I think they, for me, were the most interesting [aliens]. The Vidiians are organ thieves, but they are not cruel. It is simply their biological imperative to do this. It is essential that they do this in order to propagate their race. For us it is so horrific. I think it is just another fascinating example of what each species may in fact need in order to stabilize their own people and how, to them, that is ethically correct. How then does Janeway even talk to these people? And I loved that, because there is poignancy to that.

—Kate Mulgrew

first encounter with them. Deep-level scans of the Vidiians' forcefield reveal microfissures—minuscule openings that develop briefly each time the field matrix remodulates. The crew uses a tightly focused transporter beam to send Chakotay through one of the fissures. ▪ Sulan is chief surgeon of the Vidiian Sodality. He reconstitutes Torres's genome by a procedure that stimulates her cell division. He then extracts her Klingon genetic material, converts it from matter to energy via the genetron and rematerializes her as both fully Klingon and fully human. ▪ One of the early stages of the Phage is

excruciating joint pain. Some have been known to die from the agony alone. ▪ The Vidiians use captured slaves to dig their tunnels before harvesting them for organs. The Talaxian prisoner tells Paris that, of the twenty-three people on his ship, he is the only one left alive.

ALPHA QUADRANT: Torres informs Sulan that Klingon females are not only known for their physical strength, but their sexual prowess as well.

PERSONAL LOGS: As a child, Paris used to wear hats to

Paris attempts to calm the frightened human Torres. ROBBIE ROBINSON

cover the haircuts his father made him get the first day of every summer. ▪ Torres also used to use hats and scarves to hide her Klingon ridges when she was a child. She grew up in a colony of Kessik IV where she and her mother were the only Klingons at a time when relations with the Federation were strained. After her father left when she was five, Torres cried herself to sleep every night for months and believed that he left because she looked Klingon.

Lieutenant Ayala is stationed at ops.

MEDICAL REPORT: Torres's Klingon genetic structure is proven to have Phage-resistant nucleotide sequences when her body successfully fights off the disease. The human Torres's cells ability to synthesize proteins is severely compromised proving she needs the Klingon genes to survive. The Doctor uses the counterpart's tissues to replicate Klingon DNA.

CREW COMPLEMENT: Lieutenant Peter Durst is killed by the Vidiians. His organs are harvested and will be used to save over a dozen Vidiian lives.

JETREL

EPISODE #115
TELEPLAY BY **JACK KLEIN & KAREN KLEIN**
and **KENNETH BILLER**
STORY BY **JAMES THOMTON & SCOTT NIMERFRO**
DIRECTED BY **KIM FRIEDMAN**

GUEST STARS

JETREL	JAMES SLOYAN
GAUNT GARY	LARRY HANKIN

CO-STAR

COMPUTER VOICE	MAJEL BARRETT

STARDATE 48832.1

Neelix is alarmed when a Haakonian named Ma'Bor Jetrel contacts *Voyager* and asks to meet with him. The Haakonians had fought a long, destructive war against his people fifteen years earlier, and Jetrel is the scientist who helped them conquer Talax by developing the metreon cascade. The superweapon was responsible for killing over 300,000 Talaxians,

The inventor of the metreon cascade, Dr. Ma'Bor Jetrel.
ROBBIE ROBINSON

including Neelix's family, on Talax's moon Rinax. Jetrel claims that he is examining Talaxians like Neelix who helped evacuate survivors from Rinax, in the process exposing themselves to high concentrations of metreon isotopes. Although he considers Jetrel a monster, Neelix agrees to be examined after some gentle prodding by Janeway and Kes. The diagnosis is grim; Neelix is told that he has the fatal blood disease.

Jetrel persuades Janeway to make a detour to the Talaxian system, citing that the ship's transporter system may be useful in finding a cure for the disease by retrieving samples of the metreon cloud still surrounding Rinax. Janeway agrees, but Neelix remains bitter. He angrily condemns Jetrel for the devastation he had caused, only to learn that the scientist also has the disease and does not have long to live.

The ship's arrival at Rinax opens old wounds for Neelix. He confesses to Kes that he has lied for years about being part of the Talaxian defense forces. Instead of reporting for duty, he spent the war in hiding. Kes reasons that much of the hatred Neelix feels toward the doctor is actually anger he is afraid to direct at himself. That

may be true, he concedes, but he still refuses to forgive Jetrel for the deaths on Rinax.

Later, Neelix seeks out Jetrel, only to find him covertly conducting experiments in the lab on the isotope samples beamed aboard from the metreon cloud surrounding Rinax. Suspecting the worst of Jetrel, Neelix tries to notify Janeway, but the scientist renders him unconscious.

In the transporter room, the captain confronts Jetrel, who finally admits to his true plan. Pleading with Janeway, he explains that he has found a way to bring back the deceased Talaxian victims of Rinax. He believes that he can use the transporter to regenerate their disassociated remains, and confesses he came to *Voyager* as a pretext to use the ship's transporter; Neelix was falsely diagnosed and is fine.

Although the odds are slim that Jetrel's theory could work, Neelix asks that the captain allow the scientist to proceed. Taking Neelix's very personal request to heart, Janeway allows Jetrel to move forward, but the experiment fails. The scientist collapses, knowing that he will never be able to redeem himself. While Jetrel lies dying in sickbay, Neelix pays a last visit to him and tells him that he is forgiven, allowing the Haakonian to die with some semblance of peace.

DELTA QUADRANT: The Talaxians were conquered by the Haakonian Order following a war that had lasted a decade. The day after Doctor Ma'Bor Jetrel's metreon cascade was deployed, Talax surrendered unconditionally. One of the side effects of the cascade is the degenerative blood disease known as metremia, which causes the body's atomic structure to undergo fission. It mirrors the way the cascade vaporized its victims through biomolecular disintegration. This cover story is used to hide the fact that Dr. Jetrel has been working on a way to rebuild the atomic structure into regenerative fusion to restore the people vaporized by the metreon cascade. The electrostatic properties of the metreon cloud are such that the disassembled bio-matter has been held in a state of animated suspension. Jetrel has used medical records to identify the genetic coding of a specific victim as a test case. Once they input the victim's DNA sequence they plan to isolate his atomic fragments with the transporters targeting scanner and rematerialize him. The procedure is unsuccessful. ▪ Previous to the metreon cascade the colony of Rinax had the most temperate climate in the entire Talaxian system. ▪ During wartime, the Talaxian punishment for refusing military service was death. ▪ According to Neelix, the two-tailed talchoks of Rinax are a particularly nasty little vermin with sharp claws and dripping fangs.

Neelix would prefer that the Doctor, rather than the Haakonian, Jetrel, examine him. ROBBIE ROBINSON

LEARNING CURVE

EPISODE #116

WRITTEN BY **RONALD WILKERSON &
JEAN LOUISE MATTHIAS**

DIRECTED BY **DAVID LIVINGSTON**

GUEST STARS

KENNETH DALBY	ARMAND SCHULTZ
CHELL	DEREK McGRATH
GERRON	KENNY MORRISON
MARIAH HENLEY	CATHERINE MacNEAL

CO-STARS

HENRY	THOMAS DEKKER
BEATRICE	LINDSEY HAUN
COMPUTER VOICE	MAJEL BARRETT

STARDATE 48846.5

When Maquis crewman Dalby accidentally disrupts power to the ship's energy grid while making an unauthorized repair, Janeway realizes that she cannot expect Starfleet behavior from people who never went to the academy. To bring the Maquis officers up to speed on Starfleet protocols, Janeway asks Chakotay to choose four members of his former Maquis crew for a Starfleet training session to be led by Tuvok. Predictably, the Maquis recruits, including Dalby, balk at Tuvok's by-the-book discipline until Chakotay forcefully gets the point across that this is not a voluntary exercise.

Dalby complains to Torres about Tuvok's tough tactics, but Torres suggests that Dalby is afraid he can't cut it. The conversation is abruptly halted, however, when one of the ship's bio-neural gel packs malfunctions—the second of the packs to fail in only a short time. At a loss for any mechanical fix, Torres takes the pack to sickbay, asking the Doctor to examine the biological component. A medical scan reveals that the gel pack has an infection and must be "cured" before it spreads to the rest of the ship's systems.

Tuvok's rigorous training sessions seem to have little effect on the Maquis, as they are easily discouraged. Sensing that his duties as morale officer may be needed, Neelix manages to get Tuvok to confess that he cannot understand why his techniques, honed through years of instructing cadets at the Academy, are not working. Neelix suggests that Tuvok may need to be more flexible in his approach, since the Maquis are not Starfleet cadets and should not be treated as such.

When their conversation moves to the kitchen, Tuvok realizes the bacterial spores from Neelix's home-

PESONAL LOGS: To self-terminate his program, the Doctor tells the computer to "Override Command 1-EMH-Alpha and end program" (in later episodes he will simply say "Computer, deactivate EMH."). ▪ Neelix originally claimed that he was a hero in the battle of Pyrithian Gorge. He later admits to that being a lie as he never joined the military, instead hiding himself on Talax. ▪ Until Kes met Neelix, she had not believed anyone could live beyond nine years.

EPISODE LOGS: When Neelix is speaking of his family, he refers to his mother, father, and little brothers; however, he does not mention his favorite sister Alixia, or any of his other sisters who were also on Rinax, as we learn later in "Rise!" In later episodes all mention of his brothers will be dropped.

Crewmen Chell and Henley succeed in convincing Tuvok to make a decision based on emotions. ROBBIE ROBINSON

made cheese may be the cause of the gel pack infection. The mess hall's ventilation ducts are absorbing the bacteria and carrying it to the rest of the ship. The Doctor finds that Tuvok's hunch is correct, and the bacterium carries a virus affecting the gel packs.

Not long after, Tuvok and his students find themselves trapped in a cargo bay when another system falls victim to the virus. When the crew heats the gel packs with a plasma burst to kill the infection, noxious vapors leak into the cargo bay, where Tuvok and his recruits are stranded. Nearly overcome by the fumes, Tuvok helps three of the four cadets escape through a Jefferies tube and is prepared to leave one behind, as the young man is unconscious and it would be unsafe to go back in for him. However, Dalby challenges the reason with emotion, forcing Tuvok to reevaluate the logic and go back for the crewman. As the toxic gas ultimately overcomes him, the other Maquis cadets band together and come to their rescue. Dalby notes that if Tuvok can break the rules—sometimes—then maybe they could learn to follow protocol under his tutelage after all.

SENSOR READINGS: The disruption of power from energy grid Beta 4 results in power fluctuations on Deck 6 that affect the holodeck, among other areas. ∎ The gel packs run half the critical systems on the ship and are almost impossible to damage. After the first bio-neural gel pack is replaced, there are only forty-seven left. Torres suggests they switch some of the systems to conventional isolinear circuits. A virus infects the biological components of the gel packs systematically attacking every cell in the gel pack's biological matrix. The virus was carried in bacteria absorbed into the ventilation system when Neelix makes brill cheese from the schplict he purchased from the Napinne. To prevent the infection from spreading through the gel packs, Torres takes the forward systems offline, resulting in the loss of replicators and the rerouting of primary systems. To cure the virus, the crew super heats the gel pack system to raise its temperature by infusing the gel pack circuits with a high energy burst from a symmetrical warp field. To generate that heat they have to invert the warp field toward the ship by bringing warp engines to eighty percent while they are standing still so they can initiate the plasma burst. Before they implement the burst, the bio-neural network fails sequentially leaving every system on the main grid inoperative. ∎ An EPS conduit bursts in the cargo bay, filling it with plasma gas, which becomes poisonous within min-

Torres examines one of the ship's damaged bio-neural gel packs.
ROBBIE ROBINSON

utes. ▪ While training the Maquis cadets, Tuvok increases the gravity on Deck 13 by ten percent. • It takes over 50 Jefferies tubes to get from Deck 11 to Deck 13 by way of the mess hall on Deck 2. ▪ To degauss the entire transporter room with a microresonator takes about 26.3 hours. To do the same with a magneton scanner takes about five minutes. ▪ Janeway's holonovel is program Janeway Lambda 1.

ALPHA QUADRANT: The wearing of headbands and jewelry are in violation of Starfleet dress code. ▪ According to Chell, the Ferengi have been known to deceive ships by pretending to be damaged in order to trap them.

PERSONAL LOGS: Tuvok taught thousands of students at Starfleet Academy for sixteen years. His training program for the Maquis adheres to the standards established for Starfleet cadets including physical training, academic studies, and tactical simulations on the holodeck. Neelix notices that something is wrong with the Vulcan when he sees him in the mess hall with no cup of tea and no padd, and he is sitting on the opposite side of the table from where he usually sits. ▪ At the request of the crew, the

Doctor is trying to become more sensitive to his patients' needs (he practices his bedside manner on a gel pack).

Among the Maquis crew, Chakotay chooses Crewmen Kenneth Dalby, Mariah Henley, Gerron, and Chell for Starfleet training. In addition to performing unauthorized repairs, Dalby has been caught tampering with ship's systems to increase a friend's replicator rations and has missed three of his last ten duty shifts. He lived a hard life on the Bajoran frontier, where he fell for a woman who "taught him about love." Three Cardassians raped and killed that woman, causing Dalby to join the Maquis to seek revenge. He has command experience and is protective of Gerron. ▪ Chakotay chose Gerron for the training in the hopes that the young Bajoran would learn new skills and set some goals that might help in making him feel better about himself. ▪ The Bolian Crewman Chell's report indicates he is talkative, disruptive, and unreliable.

EPISODE LOGS: Of the remaining 47 gel packs, it is unknown how many are used to replace the malfunctioning ones. ▪ This was the final episode to air in the first season of *Voyager*. The following episodes were filmed during season one, but held for airing in season two.

PROJECTIONS

EPISODE #117

WRITTEN BY **BRANNON BRAGA**

DIRECTED BY **JONATHAN FRAKES**

SPECIAL GUEST STAR

BARCLAY	DWIGHT SCHULTZ

CO-STAR

COMPUTER VOICE	MAJEL BARRETT

STARDATE 48892.1

A shipwide emergency automatically activates the Emergency Medical Hologram. When the Doctor asks the computer to scan for signs of the crew, he learns they were all forced to abandon ship. Moments later Torres surprises him by entering sickbay through one of the Jefferies tubes. She explains that she and the captain stayed behind to stop a warp core breach caused by a Kazon attack. The internal sensors were damaged in the attack, which would explain why the computer told him he was alone on the ship. The remaining crew

since he believes the ship to be real. Barclay tells the Doctor that he must end the simulation before radiation from the accident kills him, and the only way to do so is by destroying *Voyager*.

At first, the Doctor flatly refuses. However, Barclay's arguments are persuasive, as he points out that the Doctor is free to move about the ship without being confined to holoemitters. Swayed by the logic, the Doctor considers destroying *Voyager*'s warp core until Chakotay appears and orders the Doctor to lower his weapon.

Chakotay explains that there has been an accident on *Voyager* that affected the imaging system while the Doctor was in the holodeck. Chakotay says that Barclay himself is a simulation, and that if the Doctor listens to him, he will destroy his own program. The Doctor is not sure who to believe but delays acting on Barclay's advice long enough to prove that Chakotay's story is true. The problem is finally solved and the Doctor is returned to sickbay, where, for the first time, he questions the meaning of his own existence.

SENSOR READINGS: *Voyager* encounters a subspace anomaly that emits a kinoplasmic radiation surge, causing a feedback loop between the holodeck computer and the Doctor's program. The entire situation is a holographic simulation generated by the EMH's codes, subroutines, and memory circuits. The holomemory core that is the central memory nexus for all holographic systems aboard

The Doctor does not know what is real: Is he a hologram or is he really Lewis Zimmerman, as his wife, Kes, insists? ROBBIE ROBINSON

escaped in lifepods, though the Kazon ship intercepted them. Informed that the injured captain needs his assistance, the Doctor is sent to the bridge, courtesy of new holoemitters installed in various parts of the ship.

Finding the captain unconscious, the Doctor attempts to scan her. He discovers that all the medical tricorders, both those on the bridge and the ones in sickbay, are malfunctioning and not reading any life-forms. After reviving Janeway, the Doctor is transferred to the mess hall to assist Neelix, who is engaged in battle with a Kazon soldier. After the scuffle, the holographic doctor is astonished to learn that he is bleeding. When queried, the computer insists that he is actually Dr. Lewis Zimmerman, the human who created *Voyager*'s EMH. Stranger still, when the captain tells the computer to shut down all of the ship's holographic systems, Janeway, Neelix, Torres, and the Kazon soldier vanish, but the Doctor remains intact.

Lieutenant Reginald Barclay appears and introduces himself as Zimmerman's assistant. Barclay also claims that the Doctor is Zimmerman, who is really at Jupiter Station running a holodeck program on a holographic *U.S.S. Voyager*. A radiation surge caused the holodeck to malfunction and must be affecting the Doctor's memory,

The Doctor remembers his real identity. ROBBIE ROBINSON

the ship is located in engineering. Chakotay is projected into the simulation from the holodeck control station in engineering. ▪ Auto initiation of the EMH occurs when a ship-wide Red Alert goes into effect. ▪ The Doctor can transfer bridge logs to the workstation in his office. ▪ An emergency medical kit is stored on the bridge behind the tactical console. ▪ To get from the bridge to sickbay, the holographic Torres has to crawl through thirty-one Jefferies tubes on five decks. ▪ According to the holographic Barclay, a sustained phaser burst set on full power can punch through the outer duranium shielding on the warp core and cause a breach. ▪ Holographic Janeway informs the Doctor that bypassing a power relay is similar to a coronary bypass.

DELTA QUADRANT: In the simulation, two Kazon *Predator*-class warships attack *Voyager.* ▪ Nonduran tomato paste leaves nasty stains in clothing.

ALPHA QUADRANT: Dr. Lewis Zimmerman, the holo-engineer who created the EMH on Jupiter Station is seen to resemble his creation. ▪ Lieutenant Reg Barclay was part of the original engineering team that designed the EMH. He was in charge of testing the EMH's interpersonal skills. ▪ Holo-transference dementia syndrome (HDTS) refers to a person believing himself to be a part of the holodeck simulation.

PERSONAL LOGS: The Doctor was first activated on Stardate 48308.2 (six months earlier). His program is formally designated as EMH Program AK-1 Diagnostic and Surgical Subroutine Omega 323. In the simulation, the Doctor sees the bridge, mess hall, engineering, and other parts of the ship for the first time. He is not programmed to feel pain, bleed, or experience hunger. The pain that he does feel is caused by the feedback loop eradicating his memory circuits. He thinks Kes is beautiful. ▪ Regarding the simulation, Kes asks the Doctor not to tell Neelix that they were "married," since the Talaxian tends to get jealous.

EPISODE LOGS: The episode flashes back to "Caretaker." At one point the Doctor tells holographic Janeway that the crew is about to meet an entity known as the Caretaker or "banjo-man." The term "banjo-man" was used only in the stage directions of the shooting script—none of the characters referred to it in the dialogue. The Doctor refers to the date of his activation as Stardate 48308.2. This is roughly consistent with "Caretaker," as the first Stardate mentioned in that episode is 48315.6, which is almost three days after the Doctor is activated.

▪ In the holosimulation, the crew has been working on a remote holoprojection system by setting holographic emitters on critical decks (Decks 1-5, engineering, mess hall, and cargo bay). This will later be attempted in reality in "Persistence of Vision." ▪ In the simulation, Dr. Lewis Zimmerman is married, and his wife is Kes. In future episodes, Zimmerman is single. ▪ It can be assumed that Barclay took a leave of absence from the *U.S.S. Enterprise* for his work on the development of the EMH system since he is back on the ship during the events of the *Star Trek: First Contact.* The real Reg Barclay (and another holographic simulation of him) will appear in future episodes.

ELOGIUM

EPISODE #118

TELEPLAY BY KENNETH BILLER and JERI TAYLOR

STORY BY JIMMY DIGGS & STEVE J. KAY

DIRECTED BY WINRICH KOLBE

GUEST STARS

SAMANTHA WILDMAN	NANCY HOWER

CO-STARS

CREW MEMBER	GARY O'BRIEN
CREW MEMBER	TERRY CORRELL

STARDATE 48921.3

*V*oyager encounters a swarm of space-dwelling life-forms that the crew opts to study from a distance. But after the creatures draw *Voyager* into their midst, their unusual energy patterns create problems for many of the ship's systems and cause some very strange symptoms in Kes. The young Ocampan cannot stop eating strange foods, and Neelix has to physically force her to go to sickbay.

As the crew tries to figure out how to move away from the life-forms without harming them, the Doctor examines Kes and discovers that they are wreaking havoc within her body. The activity of the life-forms is prematurely pushing her into the phase of life in which Ocampan women become fertile, known as the *elogium*. The process should only occur once in her life, meaning if Kes ever wants to have a child, she must do so immediately.

Janeway and Chakotay discuss the implications of having children aboard *Voyager,* while Kes asks Neelix to father her child. Neelix's initial hesitation causes Kes to question whether he really wants a baby with her. Later,

Neelix consults Tuvok on the realities of parenthood and eventually decides that he is ready to have a child.

Anxious to escape the life-forms, the crew projects an inverted magnetic pulse toward them in an attempt to break free of the swarm. The plan works until some of the life-forms attach themselves to the nacelles, causing a massive energy drain to the ship. Suddenly, an even larger version of the creatures appears and blocks *Voyager*'s path. Bewildered at first, the crew realizes that it is a mate for the swarm and that it thinks *Voyager* is a rival. Every aggressive move they make is met by a stronger counter-move from the creature.

Finally, Chakotay suggests the ship act submissively by mimicking the actions of the smaller life-forms by rolling over and, as Kim adds, venting plasma residue to turn the ship blue. The plan works and the swarm moves away with the larger creature.

Kes ultimately decides against having a baby, but is relieved by the Doctor's belief that her *elogium* may have been a false alarm brought on by the electrophoretic field created by the swarm. If that proves to be true, she should have another chance at having a child. Ironically, Janeway learns that Ensign Wildman is pregnant, effectively putting an end to the captain's internal struggle on whether or not *Voyager* should be a generational ship.

SENSOR READINGS: When the crew realizes they are dealing with life-forms, Janeway moves the ship into bio-scanner range ■ Torres modifies the main deflector to create an inverted magnetic pulse to repel the creatures. ■ Power is released from the impulse capacitance cells straight into the driver coils in an attempt to generate a short engine burst at impulse. ■ The crew launches a class-4 probe to distract the larger life-form.

DAMAGE REPORT: Their proximity to the space dwelling life-forms results in a huge fluctuation in the EPS grids that affects the impulse engines. After the life-forms attach to the warp nacelles, there is a massive drain in all ship's systems.

DELTA QUADRANT: The *elogium* is the time of change in an Ocampa woman. Usually occurring between the ages of four and five, it is the period of time in which a woman's body prepares for fertilization. It only occurs once in a lifetime. One of the early stages of the *elogium* is the formation of the *mitral sac* on the woman's back. This is where the child will be carried. The *ipasaphor* forms on the hands and makes the mating bond possible. Once the *ipasaphor* develops, the woman has fifty hours to begin the mating process. The *rolisisin* is a massaging

Kes knows *she* is ready to participate in the mating bond.
DANNY FELD

of the feet until the tongue begins to swell. This is usually performed by one of the woman's parents, as they use this time to help the young woman adapt to her new role in adulthood. Afterward the mating bond begins and will last for six days.

The swarm of space-faring life-forms originally appears on scanners as a magnetic disturbance. They emit an EM resonance field, creating their own magnetic wake that pulls *Voyager* into the swarm. Their internal energy patterns appear to be consistent with discrete energy processes. The swarm is dense with approximately two thousand life-forms. To propel themselves they flagellate like protozoa and can achieve speeds of over three thousand km per second. They do not appear to have a digestive system of any kind, but they do have an extremely porous outer covering. This leads the crew to hypothesize that the life-forms absorb nutrients directly from space, making them capable of metabolizing inorganic matter. Since the particle density in this area of space is not very high, it might explain why they move so fast. The larger creature emits an electrically charged plasma stream with almost the same subspace signature as

Neelix doesn't share Kes's desire to proceed with the ritual.
DANNY FELD

they are going to need a replacement crew in about half the time, making *Voyager* a generational ship. ▪ Tuvok has three sons and one daughter. He admits that his children are in his thoughts. ▪ Neelix's nickname for Kes is "sweeting." ▪ Kes experiences increased electrophoretic activity in her nervous system, causing a premature occurrence of the *elogium*. Her body temperature increases by more than 3.9 degrees, and her pulse and blood pressure are incredibly high. Normally, she would ask the captain to take the place of her parents in performing the *rolisisin,* but since Janeway is busy, Kes chooses the Doctor instead. Since the activity of the swarm caused the premature *elogium*, the Doctor believes that Kes may go through the process again at the proper time.

Ensign Wildman works at the bridge science station. She and her husband, who is stationed on Deep Space 9, had been trying to have a child before she left on her mission. She has just discovered that she is pregnant.

EPISODE LOGS: The hydroponics bay's name has been changed to airponics bay. ▪ Janeway's comment about Mark giving her up for dead is prophetic, as it will be learned in "Hunters" that he has done just that. ▪ Kes changes and leaves *Voyager* before she is old enough to experience the true *elogium*. When she returns in "Fury," she is childless. ▪ It seems odd that Wildman would just discover that she is pregnant by her husband six months into their mission. We will later learn that the father is Ktarian, which could account for the difference in prenatal development.

the warp nacelles. The smaller creatures are attracted to the subspace emissions.

ALPHA QUADRANT: Wildman indicates that the crew's original mission into the Badlands was only supposed to last two to three weeks. ▪ When Chakotay suggests establishing rules about fraternization, Janeway reminds him that Starfleet has always been reluctant to regulate people's personal lives.

Klingon place *targ* scoops on the front of their ground assault vehicles that emit a high frequency tone that disperses *targ* herds in their path. ▪ In the Gree, stimulating follicles on the proboscis results in a swelling of the auricular canal. ▪ Among the warlike Breen, pregnancy at a young age is a common event. Conversely, among the Scathos any woman who conceives a child before her fourth decade is summarily executed.

PERSONAL LOGS: Janeway says that, as captain, the idea of "pairing off" is a luxury that she does not have—though she intends to get the ship home before Mark gives her up for dead. On the subject, Chakotay points out that if it does take seventy-five years to get home,

TWISTED

EPISODE #118

TELEPLAY BY **KENNETH BILLER**

STORY BY **ARNOLD RUDNICK & RICH HOSEK**

DIRECTED BY **KIM FRIEDMAN**

GUEST STARS

SANDRINE	JUDY GEESON
GAUNT GARY	LARRY A. HANKIN
LT. BAXTER	TOM VIRTUE

CO-STAR

CREW MEMBER	TERRY CORRELL

STARDATE UNKNOWN

During a surprise birthday party for Kes at Sandrine's, *Voyager* encounters a spatial distortion wave that surrounds the ship and disables its

The Doctor tries to allay Kes's fears as they watch over the unconscious captain. ROBBIE ROBINSON

main systems, including communications and warp drive. Unable to reach the senior staff in the holodeck, Tuvok sends Kim from the bridge to report to the captain directly. In the meantime, Janeway orders the rest of the staff to their duty stations for the emergency. Unfortunately, Janeway cannot find her way to the bridge, Torres is unable to locate engineering, and everyone else in the crew is just as confused.

Back at Sandrine's, Janeway calls an impromptu senior staff meeting to discuss their situation. It appears that the distortion wave is somehow changing the layout of the ship, moving rooms, halls, and entire decks in the process. Janeway assigns teams to investigate. Paris and Torres team up to find engineering and attempt a site-to-site transport to the bridge, while Chakotay, Neelix, Janeway, and Kim pair off to locate the bridge by way of the halls and Jefferies tubes. Kes stays behind in the holodeck with the Doctor so she can try to send him back to sickbay.

Paris and Torres manage to reach their goal, but the others are not as lucky. Chakotay finds Tuvok but loses Neelix in the process. Meanwhile, in the Jefferies tube, Janeway is nearly dragged into the distortion by an unseen electromagnetic force. Kim rescues Janeway and gets her back to Sandrine's, where she loses consciousness.

Shortly after, Chakotay and Tuvok wind their way back to the holodeck, while Torres and Paris are beamed there instead of the bridge. With Neelix still missing, the spatial distortion continues to squeeze the ship. Tuvok estimates that the unstoppable ring will crush the vessel in little more than an hour.

Chakotay takes command and orders Torres and Kim back to engineering. There they trigger a warp shock pulse to save the ship. However, instead of dispersing the spatial ring, it pulls it in even faster, surrounding engineering and eventually the sanctuary in Sandrine's.

Lacking other options, Tuvok advises the crew to do nothing and allow the anomaly to twist its way through the bar. Uncertain of what to expect, the senior staff takes a moment to reflect on the friendships that they have formed, as it may be their last chance. Once the wave passes, Janeway regains consciousness and explains that the distortion was trying to communicate with them. The ring leaves the ship undamaged and moves out into space. In its wake, the crew discovers that it left twenty million gigaquads of new information in the ship's computer and downloaded *Voyager*'s entire database in what Janeway believes was its way of saying "hello."

SENSOR READINGS: The bridge is located on Deck 1, Holodeck 2 is on Deck 6, and engineering is on Deck 11.

Tuvok prepares for the distortion ring to pass through him.
ROBBIE ROBINSON

DELTA QUADRANT: The spatial distortion wave generates intense pulses of EM radiation. It penetrates the shields, coming into direct contact with the ship.

PERSONAL LOGS: Janeway tells Kim that he has far exceeded her expectations. ▪ Paris gives Kes a locket for her birthday. It cost him two weeks' replicator rations. ▪ Neelix believes his tracking skills to be legendary throughout the quadrant. ▪ Kes celebrates her second birthday, and the crew throws her a surprise party in Sandrine's. Neelix makes her a Jibelian fudge cake with seven layers of Jibelian fudge and icing made of pureed *l'maki* nuts (her favorite). She asks Neelix to provide a picture of himself for her locket. Her quarters are on Deck 8.

Baxter is in security. He continues his exercise routine as mentioned in "Eye of the Needle," though it is assumed he is approaching it less strenuously, as ordered by the Doctor. ▪ Lieutenant Ayala is left in command of the bridge when Tuvok goes to find the senior staff. ▪ Hargrove and Ayala's quarters are on Deck 7, Nicoletti is on Deck 4, and Kyoto is believed to be on Deck 6.

An emergency access conduit leads directly from Deck 6 to Deck 1 opening in a cargo hold directly behind the bridge. There is a gym on board. ▪ A site-to-site transport can be conducted from engineering. ▪ Before going off duty, Kim completes a sensor diagnostic and recalibrates the accelerometer relays. ▪ The senior staff collects tricorder data tracking the changes in the ship. They feed that data into the ship's central database to extrapolate a schematic of the ship. ▪ Torres and Kim unsuccessfully attempt a warp shock pulse to counter the implosion. To create a shock pulse of the necessary magnitude they have to raise the pressure of the warp core to fifty-three megapascals, which results in subatomic particle showers all over the ship.

DAMAGE REPORT: The distortion ring affects all major systems and collapses the warp field, knocking the engines offline. The encounter ends with no harm to the crew or damage to the hull or ship's systems.

THE 37's
EPISODE #120
WRITTEN BY **JERI TAYLOR & BRANNON BRAGA**
DIRECTED BY **JAMES L. CONWAY**

GUEST STARS

EVANSVILLE	**JOHN RUBINSTEIN**
NOONAN	**DAVID GRAF**
HAYES	**MEL WINKLER**
NOGAMI	**JAMES SAITO**
and	
AMELIA EARHART	**SHARON LAWRENCE**

STARDATE 48975.1

When *Voyager*'s scanners show a reading of rusted iron in the vicinity, the crew is surprised to follow its trail to a 1936 Ford pickup truck floating in space. Curious, they beam the truck into a cargo bay for closer inspection. When Paris, who has a fascination for ancient Earth vehicles, gets in and starts the engine, he discovers that the truck's AM radio is picking up an old-

Earhart's copilot, Fred Noonan, rejects Janeway's story that he is in the future. ROBBIE ROBINSON

fashioned SOS distress call. Kim traces the signal to the third planet in a nearby star system, and Janeway orders the crew to lay in a course in the hopes that whatever brought the truck from Earth is still around to send them back.

An unusual amount of interference in the upper atmosphere prevents them from beaming down or taking a shuttle, so Janeway tells Paris to land *Voyager* on the planet's surface, where she sends two teams to investigate. The captain's team follows the SOS to the cockpit of an airplane that was built during the same era as the truck, while Chakotay's team comes across a mine shaft with odd energy readings. Janeway joins him, finding a chamber with eight humans in cryostasis units. All are dressed in 1930s attire, and one unit holds famed aviatrix Amelia Earhart, who disappeared with her navigator Fred Noonan on July 2, 1937.

After Janeway revives the people from suspended animation they demand to know where they are and how they got there. When she explains that they were probably abducted by aliens four hundred years earlier, a sus-

picious Noonan and the others take the crew hostage. Hoping to convince them of the truth, Janeway gets Earhart to venture outside the chamber to see *Voyager*, but they come out right in the middle of a firefight between Chakotay's security team and unknown aliens.

Janeway quells the attack and learns the snipers are two humans who have mistaken the crew for the Briori, an alien race that abducted over three hundred people from Earth in 1937, brought them to the planet and turned them into slaves. Their descendant, Evansville, explains that the slaves revolted, killed the Briori, took their weapons and technology and built a new civilization. Now, fifteen generations later, there are over one hundred thousand of them living in three cities about fifty miles from the stasis chambers. The Briori never returned to the planet, and the ship that abducted the humans was destroyed in the fighting. The survivors believed that the people in Earhart's group were dead, and left them in their cryostasis units for centuries.

The colonists offer "the 37's" and *Voyager's* crew the

LANDING *VOYAGER*

"Captain, I think I should tell you, I've never actually landed a starship before."
"That's all right, Lieutenant. Neither have I."

Paris and Janeway, "The 37's"

The possibility of actually landing a starship had been a question looming since the early days of *Star Trek*. The special effects required for such an endeavor whenever the crew visited a planet proved too cost prohibitive for a weekly TV show. As a result, the idea of the transporters was introduced. Later, shuttlecraft were added; however, even shuttlecraft have rarely been seen actually landing. Instead, the descent from the clouds is followed by a shot of the shuttle already on the ground—usually following a crash. Now, with advances in technology the post-production team can land a starship on screen without breaking the budget.

According to the show's internal technical manual, "The structural strain of landing would be absorbed by ground Hover Footpad System, a set of four stabilization pads which work in concert with the warp engines to suspend the ship over the terrain." It should also be noted that the landing procedure requires a significant output of energy. The process by which the ship prepares to land and lift off again follows:

Setting Down

The captain orders the conn officer and bridge crew to prepare the ship for landing, then alerts engineering. The chief engineer is ordered to take the warp core offline, vent all plasma from the nacelles, and stand by to engage atmospheric thrusters.

Meanwhile, the tactical officer alerts all decks that they are preparing to land, places the ship on Blue Alert, and orders the crew to report to Code Blue stations.

The conn officer plots a descent course, places atmospheric controls at standby, brings landing mechanisms online, and puts inertial dampers at maximum.

At this point the captain orders the conn officer to commence landing.

The conn officer puts the ship on the glide trajectory, first reducing speed to 10,000 kph.

When the ship is within 20 kilometers of the landing site, the captain orders the landing struts extended and locked.

---

opportunity to remain with them, since the technology that could return them to Earth was destroyed long ago. Although Neelix and Chakotay know they want to continue toward home with Janeway, she can't be so sure about the other crew members. Ultimately, Amelia Earhart and the other 37's decide to stay with their "ancestors," but to Janeway's relief, the entire *Voyager* crew opts to leave with her.

SENSOR READINGS: Sensors pick up high levels of ferric oxide—corroded iron particles (rust). Traces of hydrocarbons are also present: benzene, ethylene, and octane (gasoline: a liquid fuel used centuries ago). ▪ The SOS—an ancient Earth distress call—is sent on AM radio frequency, which is not one of the standard frequencies monitored on *Voyager*, since messages on the channel only travel at the speed of light and are too slow for interstellar communications. ▪ The trinimbic interference from the planet's upper atmosphere blocks sensor readings. It is also impossible to transport through the interference or to safely navigate a shuttle through the currents. Due to these factors, Janeway decides to land *Voyager*. Turbulence during the landing causes EM discharges in the lateral relays. Kim reroutes the ODN conduit. ▪ Warp 9.9 is equivalent to about 4 billion miles per second. ▪ Janeway indicates that universal translators are built into the combadges, "allowing people of different languages to speak to one another" (although this does not explain

This is followed by an order to prepare to release inertial dampers and adjust them to match the planet's gravity. The ops officer then adjusts environmental controls accordingly.

Upon landing engines are disengaged and thruster exhaust is secured.

Lifting Off

The captain orders all stations to prepare for departure, and the tactical officer places the ship on Code Blue status once again.

The chief engineer brings the antigrav thrusters online.

The conn officer puts inertial dampers on flight configuration and places the impulse drive on stand by.

Once all stations report ready the captain orders lift off.

Episodes in which *Voyager* lands:

"THE 37'S" The crew finds an ancient Earth pickup truck floating in space and follows an SOS signal to a planet. The trinimbic interference in the atmosphere blocks sensor readings and transporter signal. Since a shuttlecraft cannot safely navigate the currents in the atmosphere, Janeway decides to land the ship.

"BASICS, PARTS I&II" The Kazon take over the ship and land it on a planet in the Hanon system, marooning the crew. Later, Paris and a group of Talaxians retake the ship and presumably land it to rescue the crew (although the actual landing goes unseen).

"DEMON" With the ship low on power, Paris and Kim take a shuttle to a Demon-class planet with a toxic atmosphere. When the ship loses communication with the pair, rather than risk another shuttle in their rescue, Janeway lands the ship.

"DRAGON'S TEETH" Under attack by the Turei, *Voyager* hides under the radiogenically charged atmosphere of a planet and sets down for repairs.

"NIGHTINGALE" As the episode opens, *Voyager* has landed on a planet to conduct some much-needed maintenance.

---

how the crew can communicate with aliens on occasions when the combadges are taken from them). ▪ The alcohol level in Noonan's body is so high that it initially inhibits the repair of his circulatory system.

DELTA QUADRANT: The distress call comes from a continent in the northern hemisphere of a class-L planet with an oxygen-argon atmosphere (third planet in the star system). A high concentration of trianium particles leads the crew to the cryostasis chamber. Both the chamber and the distress signal are run off fusion-based generators. ▪ There are no signs of any wormholes or temporal anomalies in the area. ▪ The eight 37's are: Amelia Earhart (American aviator), Fred Noonan (Earhart's copilot), Nogami (Japanese officer), Jack Hayes (African-American farmer), "an Indian woman in a sari, a Scandinavian fisherman in turtleneck and watch cap, and a young (twenties) couple whose red hair and freckles might suggest that they're Irish." (The description of the unnamed 37's comes from the shooting script).

ALPHA QUADRANT: War and poverty no longer exist on Earth ▪ Mars was colonized by people from Earth in 2103. ▪ Paris notes that hovercars were in existence in the twenty-first century.

PERSONAL LOGS: Janeway can differentiate horse manure from other types of manure by its smell. Neither

Janeway considers staying in the Delta Quadrant. ROBBIE ROBINSON

Janeway nor Paris has ever landed a starship before. ▪ When Chakotay reminisces about Earth, he remembers sunrise over the Arizona desert and swimming in the Gulf of Mexico. ▪ Paris's interest in antique vehicles will later be broadened into an interest in twentieth century history). ▪ Kes covers her ears with her hair to appear human when they revive the 37's.

Jarvin is involved with a young woman in quantum mechanics. ▪ Walter Baxter is known for his sense of adventure.

CREW COMPLEMENT: This is the first mention of the combined crew complement. Janeway notes: "There are a hundred and fifty-two men and women on this ship."

CAPTAIN KATHRYN JANEWAY

HIS [TOM PARIS'S] POV—STARFLEET BOOTS

Tilting up to reveal KATHRYN JANEWAY, a charismatic woman in her early forties, in uniform. She has a warm thoughtful face and remarkably attentive eyes that suggest a deep awareness of all that is going on around her . . .

—Kathryn Janeway's first appearance "Caretaker"

In filming, camera angles can often be broken down by their very basic purposes. Scenes filmed from a high angle—with the camera pointing down at the actors—imply weakness and vulnerability, as conveyed by the fact that the audience is effectively looking down on the characters. With a camera placed at a low angle, the reverse is true. The camera sees the character standing tall and proud—a traditional pose of strength. From her first appearance on the screen, taken directly from its description on the page, Janeway stands tall, with hands firmly on hips, and is visually shown to be a captain of strength, poise, and power.

ROBBIE ROBINSON

Her actions in the pilot, "Caretaker" established her as more than just the standard Starfleet captain. With Tuvok—her security chief and friend—missing, she took her new ship and untried crew on a dangerous rescue mission, choosing a convicted felon to lead them through a treacherous part of space. There was no typical *Star Trek* debate of "the needs of the many outweigh the needs of the few." Her confidant was in trouble and she did what it took to save him. This act of rescuing a crewman in the face of daunting odds was mirrored several times over the series, for example her retrieval of Seven of Nine from the Borg in "Dark Frontier."

Later in the pilot, her forward thinking was also in evidence with her immediate decision to team with the Maquis. Originally distrusting them as the enemy, Janeway realized that the only way they could survive was to join together as one ship— a Starfleet ship—serving as a single crew under her strong leadership as they grew together over their seven-year journey home.

Kate Mulgrew: She's put all of her emotional efforts and conviction into these people and that they have experienced together an intimacy and a profundity that one seldom encounters in life and she would prize and value this above all other things. She is if nothing else, fiercely loyal.

As the crew grew and bonded, Janeway developed close relationships with all the members of her senior staff. In Chakotay, she found a new confidant, whose counsel she eventually learned to trust as much as Tuvok—himself an old and valued friend. As Chakotay noted in "Lifesigns," Paris became Janeway's "personal reclamation project" as she guided him into a shining example of a Starfleet officer. She also shepherded Kim through his growth into a mature officer and the Doctor into his role as a sentient being. With Neelix, she found a useful resource that evolved into a trusted counselor, ambassador, and friend.

PETER IOVINO

Ethan Phillips: The captain has always been someone whom Neelix has had the greatest devotion to. I think it's evident in many of our scenes together that he has profound respect for her that sometimes even borders on adoration. He's very grateful for the position she has given him on her ship. He came from being an itinerant street person—or space person—to having a position of some authority on a cutting edge vessel. He also really admires her strength and her ability to combine a feminine emotional nurturing side with the steeliness that she needs.

Garett Wang: I think that Kim holds the captain in very high regard and I think the captain, in essence, became somewhat of a surrogate mother or an aunt—you know, that's a better way to look at it—sort of like his favorite aunt. Someone who looked after him from day one and has always had his best interests in mind. Especially since for the first three or four seasons Kim had no contact with his parents. He had nobody to really talk to except for Paris. And Janeway sort of stepped into that role.

Because Janeway is a female captain, it is too obvious to note that she had a "mothering" relationship with her crew. Though she did step into this role with Kim, it is often the other female characters that Janeway interacted with most in this manner. In the first three seasons, Janeway and Kes fell into the mother/daughter relationship most prominently. Kes's natural eagerness, coming from her young age, was expressed through the childlike wonder in which she looked at the captain with respect and admiration. Though Torres had somewhat of a less familial relationship with the captain, there were definite moments in their relationship where they shared this bond. This was exemplified most prominently in the episode "Barge of the Dead" where Janeway was often confused with Torres's own mother in the young Klingon's mind. And, of course, Seven of Nine quickly became the rebellious daughter that Janeway found both the most troubling and rewarding to raise, as seen in numerous episodes.

But there was another relationship that Janeway also developed during the journey—the one with *Voyager*. Having just met prior to the events of "Caretaker," Janeway quickly developed a bond with her ship and eventually addressed it from time to time as if it were a living being. Though her love for her ship momentarily evolved into obsession in "Year of Hell," she generally managed to respect *Voyager*, as she knew its survival was the only chance for getting the crew home safely. Beyond that, she felt strongly about the idea of home that *Voyager* represented to the crew. Even when faced with the option of a new—though fraudulent—Alpha Quadrant ship in "Hope and Fear," she still did not hurry to abandon the only home they had known in the Delta Quadrant.

Kate Mulgrew: The writers have colored the relationship with wonderful subtleties. I often talk to the ship. My deepest personal references are to the ship in the form of my captain's log. Although it will be filed and reported in the archives, it is essentially to the ship itself. I do have a very visceral relationship with Voyager, no question about it. And I'd save her beyond myself without blinking.

Beyond her close relationships with her crew, Janeway had a few opportunities to explore more personal connections, though sadly without lasting results. The most tragic element of Janeway's love life was obviously the fact that her trip to the Delta Quadrant lost her the man she was to marry. Though she initially held out hope that her fiancé, Mark, would not give up on her, she eventually discovered in "Hunters" that he had found someone else, forcing her to move on as well.

As noted various times in the journey, as captain, it was inappropriate for Janeway to mingle with members of her crew. This had been the most obvious stumbling block in her exploring the obvious chemistry with her own first officer. Though the gradually growing bond between Janeway and Chakotay was addressed in "Resolutions," their relationship was never entirely resolved. Feelings persisted throughout their journey with even the future Janeway's act of changing time in "Endgame" based partially on her still lingering feelings of regret over the loss of Chakotay. But with her ship traveling light-years through space, Janeway had little opportunity for love. It seems, however, that when she did find someone to share her feelings with he turned out to be either duplicitous, as in "Counterpoint," or not even real as in "Fair Haven."

Kate Mulgrew: This is a fully fleshed woman with vigorous passions, who has probably said to herself on many occasions, this may never come to pass. Rather than jeopardize her judgment and therefore her ship, she would not fraternize with the crew. But in her darkest hours her isolation has been an ongoing dilemma. Not because of her gender, I think she has given up intimacy in order to be a scientist, captain, and to see her crew home. I hope that I've brought all of those forces to bear with her captaincy.

Throughout the seven seasons, Janeway's actions proudly portrayed the first fully fleshed-out female captain in *Star Trek* series history. Though she did experience momentary regret over stranding her crew in "Night," she was a person who rarely looked back. Ever moving forward toward home, Janeway is a "tough cookie" much in the same vein of the classic female film stars like Katherine Hepburn. Kate Mulgrew brought a stately elegance to Janeway, and gave her a commanding presence that never left in question who was in command of the ship.

Brannon Braga: To a degree Janeway evolved along with the actress and we started to play to her strengths. Kate has a very wry sense of humor and she's something of a brazen personality and that's what Janeway kind of eventually became. She always had the big plan . . . The big wacky plan . . . The I Love Lucy of the Delta Quadrant. I think Janeway will be remembered as being unique because she was a woman and because we had to strike a balance between making her as strong as any man without losing her feminine qualities. I think both were revealed in an interesting way.
Kate Mulgrew: First of all, all of my senses were assaulted in that first season and I was truly shot out of a cannon both creatively and constitutionally. And I had no time to think about who Janeway was to Mulgrew or Mulgrew to Janeway. And of course with the passage of time comes relaxation, and with relaxation comes confidence. Out of which is born a marriage between the actress and the character so that I now would say that I have full and unparalleled possession of this woman.

SEASON TWO

Filming for the first season of *Star Trek: Voyager* began in September of 1994, the premier episode did not air until January 1995. The series' production schedule allowed for episodes to be filmed during the first season that could be held for the second season, specifically episodes seventeen through twenty. The second season of *Voyager* opened with "The 37's" on August 28, 1995.

From a production standpoint, the second season differs from the first in a variety of ways. Most notably, it consists of a full slate of twenty-six episodes, as a typical television season generally averages twenty-two episodes. Even more unusual is that a number of episodes air out of production order with airdates determined by dramatic story development and postproduction considerations. For the purpose of this book, the episodes are listed according to their production number. The season would, once again, wrap with several completed episodes unaired, and destined to be carried over to season three.

The sophomore season of *Star Trek: Voyager* picks up where it left off. Maquis tensions are starting to abate as the crew continues to bond. The Kazon with Seska's help, are attempting to take over *Voyager,* and the starship is exploring strange new worlds, as the captain looks for a way home. Janeway's attempts to forge alliances are thwarted by the Kazon who have said *Voyager* is a ship bent on destruction.

"I think, the beauty of long lived television series is that the characters become much richer because they develop a longer and longer backstory. When we first created these characters we didn't know all that much about them. We created them, we hired actors to play them and together the actors and the writers have worked on starting to build these characters."

—RICK BERMAN

Though each episode of *Voyager* is intended to be a stand-alone, which would be easier to schedule when in the repeated airings of syndication, subtle story arcs would be forever a part of the series. The tempered feelings between captain and first officer, integration of the Maquis crew, and, later, the return of Seven of Nine's humanity are some themes carried out across episodes and years, but as individual stories as opposed to being continued episodically. The second season brings one of the few continued major story arcs of the series with the revelation of Crewman Jonas's secretly aiding Seska and the Kazon from "Alliances" through "Lifesigns" and "Investigations." The season of *Voyager* also ends in a more dramatic fashion with the first cliff-hanger episode of the series.

INITIATIONS

EPISODE #121

WRITTEN BY KENNETH BILLER
DIRECTED BY WINRICH KOLBE

GUEST STARS

KAR	ARON EISENBERG
RAZIK	PATRICK KILPATRICK
HALIZ	TIM deZARN

CO-STAR

COMPUTER VOICE	MAJEL BARRETT

STARDATE 49005.3

Chakotay faces down the Kazon maje. DANNY FELD

Chakotay borrows a shuttlecraft to perform a solitary ritual commemorating his father's death. His vessel inadvertently drifts across the ever-changing border of Kazon-Ogla space. The shuttle is fired upon by Kar, a Kazon youth who attempts to earn his warrior name by killing the Federation trespasser. Defending himself, Chakotay destroys Kar's ship, but beams the boy aboard before it explodes. When Chakotay tries to return Kar to his people, the first officer is taken hostage.

The Kazon view Kar's inability to kill Chakotay as a failure. The young man blames Chakotay for his fate. Dying in battle would have been honorable and far preferable to Kar, who faces a shamed future in which he may never win his warrior name. The Kazon first maje, Razik, tells Chakotay that he will free him, but only if he agrees to kill Kar as he should have in battle. Chakotay refuses, overpowers Razik, and demands the return of his shuttlecraft. Facing certain death himself, Kar leaves with Chakotay. With their shuttle damaged by Kazon fire, the pair is forced to beam down to a nearby moon that serves as a training base for the Kazon-Ogla. Back on *Voyager*, the crew, which has been looking for its missing first offi-

cer, finds debris from Chakotay's destroyed shuttlecraft and continues their search, hoping that he is safe.

Kar helps Chakotay negotiate the surface of the moon, which is riddled with booby traps that are part of the Ogla training. Taking shelter in a cave, Kar waits until Chakotay falls asleep and then raises his weapon, but finds himself unable to murder Chakotay or to steal the much sought-after Federation technology.

Unable to get a clear scan for life-forms on the fortified moon, Janeway leads an away team to search for the missing officer. Razik and his crew shortly join Janeway and offer to lead her to Chakotay and Kar. Instead, the Kazon manage to temporarily trap the Federation team behind a force field and set off to search on their own without interference. As the Kazon search party is almost upon them, Chakotay comes up with a plan to help Kar win his name, but Kar comes up with an alternative. Realizing that Chakotay is not his enemy—Razik is—Kar kills the Ogla leader, making Razik's second in command first maje. Kar is pronounced a warrior and given the name Jal Karden. Although Karden warns Chakotay that he will not hesitate to kill him the next time they meet, when the first officer continues the interrupted memorial for his father, he includes a prayer for the Kazon.

SENSOR READINGS: Chakotay tells Paris to have the Doctor prepare for a Code White resuscitation, showing that Federation technology can resuscitate someone who has been brain dead for two minutes. ▪ While he holds him in custody, Chakotay places Kar in a Federation form of handcuffs.

SHUTTLE TRACKER: Destroyed. The shuttle Chakotay takes to conduct his private memorial is destroyed by the Kazon.

DELTA QUADRANT: The Kazon-Ogla were the sect of Kazon encountered by *Voyager* when they first arrived in the Alpha Quadrant. At the time, the sect was led by First Maje Jabin. During the current encounter, the sect is led by First Maje Razik, who is killed. At that point it is taken over by Haliz. Kar refers to the Nistrim ("State of Flux") and Relora sects of the Kazon. Both the Kazon territorial claims and the number of Kazon sects change every day. At last count, there were eighteen Kazon sects. The Kazon fought for their independence from the Trabe twenty-six years ago. At that time, the two races shared a home-world. ▪ Kazon children begin combat training as soon as they are old enough to protect their siblings. A Kazon youth earns his name in battle from which he is expected to emerge victorious or to die nobly. The Ogla name is created by lengthening the child's name and adding *jal*. ▪ Kazon shuttles are composed of a polyduranide alloy that is not used in Federation spacecraft. Kazon ships are less maneuverable at lower speeds. ▪ The moon, Talok, is a Kazon-Ogla training facility where live ammunition is used. Among the "booby traps" on the moon are proton beams, bio-magnetic traps, and disruptor snares. Due to radiothermic interference surrounding the moon, *Voyager* is unable to contact crew members on the surface until Torres sets up a dampening field. A soil analaysis indicates that the surface will not support landing *Voyager*. ▪ A *goven* is a Kazon outcast. It is customary to cut a finger off a *goven* at each sect he visits. A kiss from the first maje is a sign of disrespect.

ALPHA QUADRANT: In Chakotay's tribe, the *pakra* is a solitary ritual commemorating the anniversary of someone's death. It is known as the "Day of Memories."

PERSONAL LOGS: Chakotay's father's name was Kolopak. Chakotay considers his own name a gift from

The crew must trust the duplicitous Kazon in order to rescue Chakotay. ROBBIE ROBINSON

his tribe. ▪ Paris is left in command of the ship when Janeway, Chakotay, and Tuvok are on the moon. ▪ Neelix feels underutilized and is offended when he is not invited to the holodeck defense simulations. Janeway promises that he will be included in the next simulation. Neelix sold the Ogla a few Plaxan sensors a few years ago.

Lieutenant Ayala has sons in the Alpha Quadrant.

EPISODE LOGS: Chakotay's medicine bundle must have been found in the shuttlecraft's debris field because it was returned to him. ▪ Aron Eisenberg is more familiar to the *Star Trek* audience as Nog, a recurring character on *Deep Space Nine.* ▪ The location shoot was filmed at Vasquez Rocks, a familiar *Star Trek* location.

NON SEQUITUR

EPISODE #122
WRITTEN BY BRANNON BRAGA
DIRECTED BY DAVID LIVINGSTON

GUEST STARS

COSIMO	LOUIS GIAMBALVO
LIBBY	JENNIFER GATTI
ADMIRAL STRICKLER	JACK SHEARER
LIEUTENANT LASCA	MARK KIELY

CO-STAR

COMPUTER VOICE	MAJEL BARRETT

STARDATE 49011

Harry is surprised when he wakes up in twenty-fourth-century San Francisco, although no one else seems surprised to see him there—not his girlfriend Libby, nor a local coffee shop owner named Cosimo, nor his friend Lieutenant Lasca, a fellow design specialist at Starfleet Headquarters. As the strange morning continues, Kim finds himself in a meeting with high-ranking officers who want to hear Kim and Lasca's proposal for a new runabout.

Feigning illness, Kim leaves the meeting and tries to figure out how he got to Earth and why no one knows he was lost in the Delta Quadrant along with the rest of *Voyager*'s crew. A check of classified Starfleet records reveals that he never served on *Voyager,* although the ship has been reported missing in the Badlands. His request to be stationed on the ship was denied and the operations position was filled by a friend. He also discovers that Paris is not on *Voyager.* But he has been paroled from the penal settlement and lives in Marseilles.

Harry remembers the life he has left behind. ROBBIE ROBINSON

Harry locates his friend at the real Sandrine's, but to Kim's chagrin, Paris does not know him. Since Kim never went to Deep Space 9 to board *Voyager,* he never met Paris at Quark's. As a result, Paris was the unwitting victim of Quark's scam for selling Lobi crystals, and his actions got him thrown into the brig and removed from *Voyager*'s mission into the Badlands.

Paris is intrigued by Kim's story. He explains that his last recollection is being in a shuttlecraft heading back to *Voyager.* Kim begs Paris to accompany him to Starfleet Headquarters, where they can run a computer simulation and learn what happened. But this Paris, who never found the redemption that being a part of *Voyager*'s crew provided, refuses Kim's request for help.

When Kim arrives home, Lasca and Starfleet Security are waiting for him. After his unauthorized review of classified Starfleet files and his meeting with Paris, a known Maquis sympathizer, they suspect he may be a spy. Until the matter can be settled, an electronic anklet is placed on Kim to monitor his whereabouts.

Later, Cosimo reveals to Kim that he was sent to keep watch over the ensign after his shuttlecraft intersected one of his species' "time-streams." The incident scrambled the timeline and sent Kim back to the life he would have known if he had not joined the *Voyager* crew. Although he is tempted to remain on Earth, Kim asks Cosimo to tell him where to find the time-stream that could take him back. After saying goodbye to Libby, Kim makes a run for it, only to be apprehended by a Starfleet security guard. Thankfully, Paris arrives on the scene and helps him escape.

Even in this alternate reality, Paris rises to his nobler instincts. ROBBIE ROBINSON

Needing a ship to re-create the shuttle accident that will allow him to ride the time-stream back to *Voyager*, Kim steals the prototype runabout at Starfleet Headquarters. With Paris at the helm, he re-creates the conditions of the incident that sent him to Earth and finds himself back on his original shuttlecraft, where he is safely beamed back to *Voyager* moments before the vessel explodes.

SENSOR READINGS: Kim was on the *Shuttlecraft Drake* travelling at 140,000 kph, running a polaron scan with the beam sweeping at a radius of a quarter million kilometers when his shuttle encountered the alien time stream. An emergency transport was in progress when he jumped to an alternate reality. When he returns to his reality, the crew ties the transporter directly into the ship's main deflector to extend the signal.

SHUTTLE TRACKER: Destroyed. When the *Shuttlecraft Drake* encounters the time stream, it suffers a hull breach and explodes.

DELTA QUADRANT: Cosimo belongs to a race of unnamed aliens who live within a temporal inversion fold in the space-time matrix.

ALPHA QUADRANT: Starfleet's last recorded contact with *Voyager* was on Stardate 48307.5. ▪ In the alternate reality, Harry's request to serve aboard *Voyager* was denied, he requested a transfer to the Starfleet Engineering Corps where he was placed as a starship design specialist. At some point, he received the Cochrane Medal of Excellence for Ourstanding Advances in Warp Theory. Harry's best friend, Danny Byrd, took the ops position on *Voyager* in his place. As a design specialist, Harry was developing a new runabout with Lieutenant Lasca. The *Runabout Yellowstone* was equipped with tetreon plasma warp nacelles and designed for a variety of mission profiles. ▪ Information related to the disappearance of the *U.S.S. Voyager* is classified for Security Level 3 or above. The memorial for *Voyager* was held two months prior to the events in the alternate reality (however, in "Message in a Bottle," viewers will learn that some time would pass before the ship was formally declared lost).

PERSONAL LOGS: Harry Kim graduated from Starfleet Academy on Stardate 47918, eight months prior to the events of the alternate reality situation. He and his girlfriend, Libby, met when he sat in her seat at the Ktarean music festival. It took Harry three weeks to ask her out.

CONTACT WITH THE ALPHA QUADRANT SEASON 2

"This can't be a dream. Everything's just a little too real . . . a little too clear. So what does that leave? A holodeck . . . an hallucination . . . some kind of trick?"

Harry Kim, "Non Sequitur"

Over the course of seven seasons, glimpses of home come to the crew in the forms listed above, as well as temporal distortions, alien re-creations, and even actual trips to the Alpha Quadrant. Season two brings many familiar visitors to the Delta Quadrant, both real and imagined. It also includes the most extensive trip home, to date.

In "Non Sequitur," Kim awakens to find himself back in San Francisco, in bed beside his girlfriend, now fiancée. Realizing that he has not simply traveled back in time, Kim attempts to figure out how he has been transported into this reality. Eventually Cosimo, the coffee shop owner, explains that he is a member of an alien race whose time-stream Harry intersected, sending him to an alternate timeline in which he never served on *Voyager*. With the help of the alternate Paris, he re-creates the accident that brought him to the Alpha Quadrant and returns to his timeline.

"I think Kim definitely thinks about Libby and that's still his girlfriend, but he realizes that the reality of the situation is that they may not get home for another fifty years, who knows. But definitely the thought of Libby is always in the back of his mind."

—Garrett Wang

Commander William Riker of the *Starship Enterprise* is whisked to *Voyager* courtesy of Q. ROBBIE ROBINSON

Kim is not the only crew member to return home during the second season. In "Death Wish" Q sends the ship to Earth for a brief moment in an attempt to get Janeway to side with him in the hearing against his fellow Q. It is unclear if the rest of the crew is aware of the fact that Earth is briefly out the ship's windows. The other Q, later known as Quinn, also transports *Voyager* to other destinations, one of which is the branch of a Christmas tree that may or may not be back on Earth. Later, in the transwarp experiment in "Threshold." Paris claims that he was everywhere at once, including various destinations in the Alpha Quadrant.

In addition to visiting the Alpha Quadrant, the crew has numerous visitors from home as well. Again in "Death Wish" Q brings Sir Isaac Newton, a spotlight operator named Maury Ginsberg, and Commander William Riker of the *Enterprise* as witnesses in the hearing. However, all memory of their trip to the Delta Quadrant is wiped from their minds when they are sent home. A more inanimate visitor from the Alpha Quadrant comes in the Cardassian-designed (and Maquis-conscripted) weapon of "Dreadnought." In this case, the device made its way to the Delta Quadrant in the same manner as *Voyager*, with the help of the Caretaker.

Other visitors from home come in the form of hallucinations or flashbacks. In "Persistence of Vision," an alien, presumably a member of the Botha, inflicts visions of loved ones on the crew as a part of an attempt to take over the ship. The visions include Janeway's fiancé, Mark; Paris's father, Admiral Paris; Tuvok's wife, T'Pel; and Kim's girlfriend. Chakotay later is visited with memories of his father and their trip to the Central American rainforest when he was a teen in "Tattoo." Also in that episode, Chakotay meets descendants of the ancient alien race that genetically bonded with his own ancestors thousands of years ago.

A brief simulation of home can be found in "Parturition," in which Paris includes Jem'Hadar ships in a shuttlecraft training exercise for Kes. A larger, more impressive re-creation can be found in "Lifesigns" in which the Doctor takes Danara Pel to Mars on a holographic date in a convertible while "I Only Have Eyes for You" plays on the car radio. But the most interesting re-creation, by far, would have to be the first-ever visit to the Q Continuum, which is perceived as an Earth-style road with an old shack, humans in twentieth-century dress, with a scarecrow in Starfleet uniform, and a pinball machine.

He tells her that while he was on *Voyager* he thought of her every nanosecond of every day, and woke up every night calling her name. In the alternate reality they became engaged. Also in the alternate reality, Harry's office at Starfleet Headquarters is in the Main Complex, Level 6 Subsection 47. ▪ Paris was originally convicted of treason and, in the alternate reality, paroled on Stardate 48702.

While Kim is reading off the crew complement, he lists the following names: Orlando, Parsons, Peterson, Platt, and Porter. Parsons is the only other crew member to be mentioned in other episodes; however, some of the others may have died when the ship was pulled into the Delta Quadrant.

EPISODE LOGS: The Doctor, Neelix, and Kes do not appear in this episode. ▪ The San Francisco street scenes were filmed on Paramount's New York Street backlot. The red brick streets were painted onto the regular blacktop and washed away after filming concluded. ▪ The scene with the spacedock doors is a recycled clip from the TNG episode "Relics."

Neelix and Paris risk their own safety to save an alien baby.
DANNY FELD

PARTURITION

EPISODE #123

WRITTEN BY **TOM SZOLLOSI**

DIRECTED BY **JONATHAN FRAKES**

CO-STAR

COMPUTER VOICE	**MAJEL BARRETT**

STARDATE 49068.5*

A jealous Neelix notices Paris's crush on Kes and instigates a fight in the mess hall. Despite the friction between them, Janeway assigns the pair to a mission to replenish food supplies. They take a shuttle down to a planet surrounded by trigemic vapors that obscure *Voyager*'s scans for food and life. The Doctor reports that the vapors can also cause severe skin irritation, and he prescribes a sealant to protect them.

As they approach the planet, electromagnetic disturbances in the atmosphere cause the shuttlecraft to lose power and force the pair to make an emergency landing. Tracking the shuttle, *Voyager*'s crew launches a search

*The stardate listed was taken from the shooting script and is not mentioned in the aired episode.

and rescue mission. Due to the atmospheric disturbances, they cannot beam down to investigate, or even scan for life-forms from their present position. The only solution is to bring the ship into the planet's atmosphere. Meanwhile, Kes's anger over the fight about her is tempered by her concern for the missing pair. She realizes that Paris is interested in her, just as Neelix believed.

The shuttlecraft is damaged and the trigemic vapors seep in. Neelix and Paris must seek refuge in a cave where they will be safer. Sealing themselves into the cave, they wait for their rescue, which, unbeknownst to them, is being hampered by an attack from an unknown alien vessel. Tuvok comes up with a plan to disable the alien ship's weapons systems so *Voyager* can proceed.

In the cave, Paris and Neelix cautiously explore their environment. They find footprints leading to a nest of eggs. As they watch, a repto-humanoid creature hatches from one of the eggs. With the baby's mother nowhere in sight, Neelix decides it is their responsibility to care for it. When the baby's heartbeat begins to weaken, Paris realizes that by sealing the cave, they have cut off the supply of vapors the newborn needs to survive. Opening the entrance, they manage to get some of the nutrients from the air into the baby's system, and it grows stronger.

Bonding over their concern for the creature, Paris and Neelix resolve their differences as they await rescue. There is only a limited window of opportunity for *Voyager* to beam them aboard, but when the ship is able to contact the pair, Paris and Neelix delay beaming up for

Janeway orders Paris and Neelix to set aside their personal problems.
DANNY FELD

the sake of the baby. Soon, one of the aliens arrives, and the pair assumes it is the baby's mother. As Paris and Neelix watch, she retrieves the newborn. Seeing that the baby is safe, the away team returns to *Voyager* and a waiting Kes, who is surprised to learn that the former enemies are getting along.

SENSOR READINGS: Food reserves are down thirty percent of capacity, since the crew has not had the opportunity to restock the food stores in weeks. Unfortunately, the planet does not provide any supplies.

DAMAGE REPORT: Under attack from the alien ship, *Voyager* suffers minor damage to the port nacelle and switches to the lateral thrusters. ▪ The unnamed shuttle crash lands on the planet after its vector controls malfunction—the result of a reaction in the driver coil assembly to the EM anomalies in the atmosphere. After losing impulse drive, Neelix shuts off the deuterium flow so Paris can dump the fuel. Paris then sets the DCA pulse to neutral, engages thrusters, and sends out an EMS pulse that is picked up by *Voyager*.

SHUTTLE TRACKER: Possibly Lost. It is unclear whether the shuttle is retrieved when the pair is rescued, as

Voyager only has a limited window of opportunity to remain in the planet's atmosphere and no mention is made of tractoring or beaming the shuttle up to the ship during that time.

DELTA QUADRANT: The unnamed M-class planet shows high amino acid and protein levels. The *Voyager* crew incorrectly concludes that this means the planet supports plant life. Instead, the elements exist only in the trigemic vapors on the planet which serve as a nutritional source for the hatchlings of a repto-humanoid race. The high levels of trigemic vapors can cause severe humanoid skin irritations and the Doctor develops a batch of dermal osmotic sealant to combat the problem. The electromagnetic (EM) disturbances in the atmosphere interfere with transporters and communication. The disturbances clear, allowing for a window of entry every thirty hours. ▪ Garnesite is a rock that provides continued warmth when heated.

The unknown alien race leaves its hatchlings unattended on the planet, where they are born and nursed by the trigemic vapors. The aliens have the skeletal system of a humanoid, are cold blooded with a reptilian epidermis, and have a brain significantly larger than most reptilian species. Their ship's weapons are comparable to *Voyager's*; however, the ship has a vulnerability in the shield configuration that is caused by a slight phase retraction when auxiliary power is transferred to the aft weapons system. *Voyager* fires a covariant phaser pulse into their aft control systems to disable their entire weapons array.

Alfarian hair pasta is made from the follicles of a mature Alfarian. The hair is harvested during the early fall shedding season and known to be high in protein. ▪ Neelix has been waiting for a special occasion to open his bottle of Potuk cold fowl. The drink is made from the glandular secretions of an adult dunghill bird found only on Potuk III. It is very rare—with only twenty-seven bottles in existence—and has a very smoky flavor, going well with strong meaty dishes, although Neelix prefers other serving options.

PERSONAL LOGS: Paris finally admits to himself that he has feelings for Kes but has no intention of acting on them. When he was a child, he and his mother rescued a fallen baby bird by feeding it through an eyedropper. ▪ After saving a week's worth of replicator rations, Kim replicates a clarinet for himself so he can resume practicing. ▪ When activated, the Emergency Medical Program establishes comlinks with all key areas of the ship. The Doctor has been using this advantage to eavesdrop on what is occurring throughout the ship until he is ordered by the captain to stop this practice. The Doctor can quote autopsy reports from duels as far back as 1538 A.D. ▪ Neelix refers to himself as having been a junk dealer before joining the *Voyager* crew. Ensign Baytart has taken him through the basics of shuttle operations. ▪ Paris is teaching Kes how to pilot a shuttlecraft. The Ocampa choose a mate for life. According to Kes, they have no concept of distrust, envy, or betrayal.

EPISODE LOGS: The crew nicknames the world "Planet Hell" due to its similarities to primordial Earth. The nickname "Planet Hell" is an inside joke, as that is the unofficial name for the generic cave set that is redressed and reused for most cave settings on the show (a tradition that goes back to TNG days). ▪ The attacking ships seen in the shuttlecraft simulation are Jem'Hadar fighters.

Paris is mesmerized by his vision. ROBBIE ROBINSON

PERSISTENCE OF VISION

EPISODE #124

WRITTEN BY JERI TAYLOR

DIRECTED BY JAMES L. CONWAY

GUEST STARS

LORD BURLEIGH	MICHAEL CUMPSTY
MRS. TEMPLETON	CAROLYN SEYMOUR
MARK	STAN IVAR
ADMIRAL PARIS	WARREN MUNSON
BEATRICE	LINDSEY HAUN
HENRY	THOMAS DEKKER
BOTHAN	PATRICK KERR
T'PEL	MARVA HICKS

CO-STAR

COMPUTER VOICE	MAJEL BARRETT

STARDATE UNKNOWN

As the crew readies themselves for a potentially dangerous encounter with a race known as the Botha, the Doctor orders an exhausted Captain Janeway to take some R&R in the holodeck. Janeway tries to get into her favorite holonovel, but before long, she is called back to the bridge for first contact with the alien race. The Botha representative gives the crew a cold reception, but sets up a rendezvous to determine whether or not his people will allow *Voyager* to pass through their space.

Later, Janeway experiences visions of elements from her holonovel, including one of the characters, a little girl named Beatrice. Unable to attribute Beatrice's appearance to experiments the crew is performing on *Voyager*'s imaging systems to project the Doctor into various parts of the ship, Janeway wonders if she is seeing things. When Kes also sees Beatrice, they begin to believe that there may be more to the visions than originally thought. Later, after Janeway hears the voice of her fiancée Mark in her quarters, another holonovel character, Mrs. Templeton, attacks her with a knife.

Janeway relieves herself from duty and places Chakotay in charge of meeting with the Botha while she undergoes medical testing. Once again, the alien representative is hostile, and this time, his ship engages the crew in battle. With *Voyager* in trouble, Janeway races to the bridge, where she is stunned to see that it is Mark attacking the ship.

At least, that is how it looks to her. But on the same viewscreen, Paris sees his disparaging father, Admiral Paris; Kim sees his girlfriend, Libby; and Tuvok sees his wife, T'Pel. Torres contacts Janeway and reports that the crew seems to have fallen under some kind of psychoactive trance, the result of a bio-electric field emanating from the Botha ship. But even as she begins working on a way to block the field, she falls prey to its spell, imagining a romantic encounter with Chakotay. Janeway leaves the hallucinating bridge crew behind to race for engineering, but Mark stops her, asking questions about her loyalty to their relationship. This time, Janeway is unable to break free of the hallucination.

Tuvok gives himself over to the dream. ROBBIE ROBINSON

As more and more of the crew lose themselves to their dreams, it is up to Kes, whose telepathic abilities allow her to resist the field, and the Doctor to block the mysterious force disabling the ship. Kes manages to complete Torres's work and restore the crew to normal, revealing the alien intruder in the process. A telepathic Botha confesses to having caused the disturbance, but he disappears before they can learn any more from him. As they continue on their way, the crew reflects uneasily about what lurks in the subconscious corridors of their minds.

SENSOR READINGS: Torres and Kim work on setting up holo-emitters in key areas such as engineering and the bridge to expand the Doctor's mobility. They found several holoprojectors in storage and are reconfiguring them one-by-one. ▪ Janeway notes that there was a problem with one of the deflector shields. ▪ Janeway places the bridge controls on security lockout before she succumbs to the hallucinations, which are caused by a massive bioelectric energy field emanating from the Botha ships on a delta wave frequency. The field permeates the hull with

its psionic properties resulting in a psychoactive effect. In an unsuccessful effort to block the effects of the field the crew remodulates shields on a rotating basis while Torres sets up a resonance burst from the warp core as a more permanent solution. When Torres is overcome by the hallucinations, Kes must finish the job by sequencing the magnetic plasma constriction using a formula of $T = C_1/\text{Theta} \times P_E$. The Doctor consults Starfleet's interactive database to walk her through the operation. First Kes activates the command module and selects magnetic plasma sequencing. Then she raises the core temperature to three million kelvins and activates the warp field to emit the burst, successfully reviving the crew. ▪ According to Torres—in her hallucination—it would take an escape pod a week to travel the distance *Voyager* had covered in a day.

DELTA QUADRANT: According to Neelix's sources from the planet Mithren, there are numerous rumors of ships entering Botha space, never to be heard from again. The Botha protect their territory fiercely, though some believe that they do not have a legitimate claim to the area. It is unclear whether the alien that attacked the ship is working alone, or even a member of the Botha.

During Torres's hallucination, it is revealed that *Voyager* passed an M-class planet the day prior to the events of the episode.

ALPHA QUADRANT: Starfleet regulations direct that the chief medical officer outranks the captain in health matters.

PERSONAL LOGS: Janeway's last shore leave was two months ago. She has made a habit of skipping meals and has not partaken in her holonovel in weeks. The Doctor notes that she is under stress and orders her to rest (after noting it is probably the first time a hologram has given an order to a captain). Coffee ice cream is an indulgence of hers. Her boyfriend Mark referred to her as "Kath." ▪ Tuvok used to play his lute for his wife T'Pel. ▪ Kes has been doing some mental exercises with Tuvok to develop her telepathic abilities.

TATTOO

EPISODE #125

TELEPLAY BY **MICHAEL PILLER**

STORY BY **LARRY BRODY**

DIRECTED BY **ALEXANDER SINGER**

GUEST STARS

KOLOPAK	HENRY DARROW
ALIEN	RICHARD FANCY
YOUNG CHAKOTAY	DOUGLAS SPAIN
SAMANTHA WILDMAN	NANCY HOWER
CHIEF	RICHARD CHAVES

CO-STARS

ANTONIO	JOSEPH PALMAS
COMPUTER VOICE	MAJEL BARRETT

STARDATE UNKNOWN

While mining polyferranide deposits on an alien moon, Chakotay is surprised to discover a symbol scrawled in the ground that is similar to one he observed as a teen on Earth. He'd seen it while on a journey with his father, Kolopak, to discover descendants of their ancient ancestors. Back on *Voyager* Janeway informs him that they have picked up a warp signature leading away from the moon. Intrigued, Chakotay asks that they follow the trail hoping that it may provide

A reluctant Chakotay accompanied his father on a quest to find descendents of the ancient Rubber Tree People. DANNY FELD

answers or at least lead to the minerals that the ship needs for repairs.

Meanwhile, Kes chides the Doctor for his lack of compassion toward the discomforts experienced by pregnant Ensign Wildman. When Kes notes that he would have a better understanding of his patients if he had ever been sick, the Doctor takes it as a challenge and programs himself with a twenty-nine-hour Levodian flu. The purpose of the exercise is to show the crew how mature adults should behave when they are ill.

Voyager follows the trail to what appears to be an uninhabited planet. As Chakotay's away team prepares to land their shuttlecraft, he remembers back to when, at age fifteen, he disappointed his father by not embracing the traditions of his tribe. Before he can absorb the implications, the team lands and a native hawk attacks Neelix, who is beamed back to sickbay. There a noticeably irritable Doctor—who is not reacting well to his illness—cares for him.

When Tuvok finds what appears to be an abandoned village, Chakotay advises Tuvok and Torres to lay down their weapons in a gesture of trust. A violent storm kicks

TRIBAL HISTORY

*A-koo-chee-moya . . . I pray on this day of memories to speak to my father, the one whom the wind called Kolopak.
Though I am far from his bones, perhaps there is a spirit in these unnamed skies who will find him and
honor him with my song . . . A-koo-chee-moya*

Chakotay "Initiations"

Chakotay is a Native American and a descendent of the Ancient Rubber Tree people, though his tribe goes unnamed throughout the series. His tribe left Earth a few hundred years ago and settled on a planet that was later turned over to the Cardassians following the Federation-Cardassian treaty that established new boundaries between the two entities. A *contrary*, Chakotay broke from his people's teachings to explore more modern twenty-fourth-century ideas.

After his father died fighting to protect the tribal lands from the Cardassians, Chakotay took up the banner and joined the Maquis to fight in his father's place. He now wears the tattoo on his forehead to honor his father who, in turn wore it to honor their ancestors. Chakotay was not interested in learning the history of his people as a youth, he was prepared to embrace the experience when he later encountered the life-form that his people know as the "Sky Spirits" ("Tattoo").

Forty-five thousand years ago, the alien race of Sky Spirits first visited Earth and met a small group of nomadic hunters who were Chakotay's ancestors, and became known as the Rubber Tree People. At the time they had no spoken language and no culture but they had mastered the use of fire and stone weapons. They also had a respect for the land, and for other living creatures, that deeply impressed the Sky Spirits. The Spirits decided to give them an inheritance in the form of genetic bonding, so they might thrive and protect their world. From that time forward the Sky Spirits referred to Chakotay's people as the Inheritors.

On subsequent visits, the Spirits found that their genetic gift brought about a spirit of curiosity and adventure. It impelled the Inheritors to migrate away from the cold climate to a new, unpeopled land, taking them almost a thousand generations to cross the planet. Hundreds of thousands of them flourished in their new land, and their civilization had a profound influence. But after new people came, with weapons and disease, the Inheritors who survived were forced to scatter and seek refuge in other societies. Twelve generations ago, when the Spirits returned, they found no sign of the Inheritors' existence.

The descendents of the Sky Spirits believed that the Inheritors had been annihilated and their world had been ravaged by those with no respect for life or land. Chakotay informs the alien that the society has changed and ancestors of the Inheritors, or Rubber Tree People, did survive. Chakotay, himself, traveled to the Central American rain forest to find the homeland of the descendants of the Rubber Tree People. The secretive people of that tribe never left the jungle and rarely intermarried with other tribes. They had chosen to live like that for centuries, which is why Chakotay's group had traveled into the rain forest on foot. In that way they honored their ancestors beliefs.

At the time, Chakotay did not share his father's appreciation of the land, which Kolopak said the Sky Spirits honored

up, forcing Tuvok and Torres to beam back to the ship. But Chakotay is left behind, knocked unconscious by a falling tree.

After twenty-nine hours, the Doctor's condition worsens. He is concerned that the flu has not worked its way out of his system. Then Kes reveals that she altered the program so that he would understand what it was like to be an unwilling patient.

Janeway is frustrated after several unsuccessful attempts to find Chakotay. It's as if something on the planet is trying to prevent them from transporting. As they

try to bring *Voyager* down into the planet's atmosphere, the ship is engulfed in a cyclone that seems to have been generated to ward off intruders.

When Chakotay revives, he finds the planet's inhabitants who, surprisingly, speak the language of his ancestors. They recognize the symbol tattooed on Chakotay's forehead, which he wears to honor his father. The inhabitants say their people met his ancestors when they visited Earth some 45,000 years earlier.

Chakotay realizes that these are the "Sky Spirits" of his people's lore. The aliens tell Chakotay that they

above all else. Later, Chakotay embraced his father's teachings that said a man does not own the land—he does not own anything but the courage and loyalty in his heart. Though Chakotay did return to his people after his father's death, he was never able to make contact with his father in his vision quests until after his experience meeting the descendants of the Sky Spirits.

Tribal Terms and Customs

NUANKA: a period of mourning. ("The Cloud")

ANIMAL GUIDE: Chakotay's people believe that an animal guide accompanies them throughout life and serves as a counselor to whom they can speak when troubled. He likens the idea to what Carl Jung thought he invented when he came up with his active imagination technique in 1932. Animal guides are different for every person, and would be offended if the person even spoke its name. The specific type animal guise chosen for the guide does not serve to define who the person is. Instead, it is merely the animal that chooses to be with the person. ("The Cloud")

MEDICINE BUNDLE: used as an aid in the vision quest and the search for one's animal guide. Chakotay's medicine bundle consists of a blackbird's wing, a stone from a river, and an akoonah. ("The Cloud")

AKOONAH: A device that facilitates a vision quest, in the place of the psychoactive herbs used in the past. ("The Cloud")

CHAMOZI: a blessing to the land in the form of an ancient healing symbol. ("Tattoo")

MEDICINE WHEEL: a talisman that represents both the universe outside and the universe inside the mind. It is believed that each is a reflection of the other. When a person is sleeping or on a vision quest, it is said his soul is walking the wheel. If he is in a coma or near death, it is said that he has gotten lost. Stones placed on the wheel are used as signposts to help point the way back. ("Cathexis")

PAKRA: a solitary ritual in which Chakotay commemorates the anniversary of father's death. ("Initiations")

The *chamozi*—a native American symbol found in Chakotay's medicine bundle.
DOUG DREXLER

"OM-NAH-HOO-PEZ NYEETZ": The phonetic spelling of the blessing, "Peace in your heart, fortune in your steps." ("Innocence")

"EVEN THE EAGLE MUST KNOW WHEN TO SLEEP": A tribal proverb. ("The 37's")

attacked *Voyager* and its crew with storms because they feared they were enemies who would try to destroy them. Chakotay assures them that humans have evolved since those ancient days and mean them no harm. The storms vanish, and the ship is safe. After the aliens give Chakotay some of the minerals that *Voyager* needs, they bid him farewell, leaving Chakotay with a stronger connection to his people and his father.

SENSOR READINGS: *Voyager* requires polyferranide to seal the warp core and prevent the nacelles from burning

themselves up. ▪ It takes at least twenty minutes to augment the engines with power from the auxiliary fusion reactors and only results in an eight percent boost in power.

SHUTTLE TRACKER: Inertial dampeners go offline in the shuttle that is used to search for the polyferranide deposits.

DELTA QUADRANT: There is a high concentration of polyferranide ten kilometers below the planet's surface. A

Chakotay finds familiar images on a planet in the Delta Quadrant.
ROBBIE ROBINSON

of his people. ▪ Tuvok was formerly a breeder of prize Vulcan orchids. ▪ Neelix also breeds orchids. ▪ The Doctor had previously altered his program so that he no longer says, "Please state the nature of the medical emergency" when activated. Regretting the decision, he reinstates the greeting because he does not know how to start a conversation.

Ensign Wildman is experiencing back pain because her unborn baby is pressing on her sciatic nerve. To relieve the pain the Doctor suggests that she sit with her feet up while on duty. This is her first pregnancy.

EPISODE LOGS: The fact that both Tuvok and Neelix breed orchids will play an important part in the episode "Tuvix." ▪ It is assumed that the Captain Sulu who sponsored Chakotay at the Academy is either Hikaru Sulu who served under Captain Kirk on the *Enterprise* or Demora Sulu who served on the *U.S.S. Enterprise* NCC-1701-B.

problem with the crust reactivity needs to be solved before excavation or it might contaminate the entire yield. The aliens eventually permit the crew to remove some of the deposits, but not all that they need to replenish the supplies. ▪ The aliens possess a cloaking device that hides their colony from ship's sensors and weather-altering technology that serves as a defense mechanism.

ALPHA QUADRANT: Starfleet protocol demands that an away team remain armed and ready to defend themselves until contact is made.

PERSONAL LOGS: According to his father, Chakotay was born upside down, which led him to believe that his son would be a *contrary*. At fifteen Chakotay accompanied his father on a journey through the Central American rainforest on Earth to discover his roots. On the journey, Chakotay informed his father that he would be leaving their colony along the Cardassian border because he was accepted to Starfleet Academy. Captain Sulu sponsored Chakotay's application to the Academy under the false impression that Chakotay's father approved of the endeavor. Chakotay does not speak the ancient language

COLD FIRE

EPISODE #126
TELEPLAY BY **BRANNON BRAGA**
STORY BY **ANTHONY WILLIAMS**
DIRECTED BY **CLIFF BOLE**

GUEST STAR	
TANIS	GARY GRAHAM

CO-STARS	
GIRL	LINDSAY RIDGEWAY
OCAMPA	NORMAN LARGE
NARRATOR	MAJEL BARRETT

STARDATE 49164.8*	

Kes and the Doctor notice a peculiar change in the remains of the Caretaker—the alien who trapped *Voyager* in the Delta Quadrant. They seem to be resonating in response to an unusual energy source. Remembering the dying Caretaker had mentioned a female of its kind, Janeway wonders if she could be nearby, hoping that the alien could return the crew home. As a precaution, Tuvok develops a toxin that could debilitate the female life-form if she poses a threat. Using the Caretaker's remains in a makeshift compass, the crew follows the energy trail to a space station inhabited by Ocampa.

*The stardate listed was taken from the shooting script and is not mentioned in the aired episode.

Kes explores her powers to give life. ROBBIE ROBINSON

After a hostile reception in which the ship is fired upon, Kes agrees to act as the crew's liaison to her people. When the Ocampa leader, Tanis, boards *Voyager,* Kes assures him that the crew bears no hostile intent, contrary to the negative rumors that have preceded them. In a private meeting Tanis tells Kes that the female Caretaker, Suspiria, is nearby. She has aided his group of Ocampa for three hundred years and has taught them how to develop their psychokinetic skill, showing Kes a sample of the powerful abilities she has yet to tap. Later, Tanis communicates with Suspiria, who demands that he deliver *Voyager* to her.

As Tanis leads the crew to Suspiria, he tutors Kes on her mental skills. Eager to show her mentor the new abilities, she meets with Tuvok for her regularly scheduled lessons. The presentation nearly ends in disaster when Kes tries to boil water with her mind and, to her horror, inadvertently boils Tuvok's blood instead. He collapses, writhing in agony.

Fortunately, Tuvok recovers from the near-fatal incident. Kes realizes the full potential of her mental powers when her mind causes the plants in the Airponics Bay to burn and eventually wither and die. Tanis urges Kes to leave *Voyager* and live on the Ocampa space station,

where he says she will be embraced by Suspiria and surrounded by her own people.

As Kes considers Tanis's offer, Suspiria boards the ship and attempts to destroy *Voyager* in retaliation for what she believes to be the crew's part in the Caretaker's death. Suspiria attacks several officers and is about to complete her mission of revenge when Kes becomes aware of the plot. Kes attacks Tanis with her expanded psychic abilities, and Tanis's pain temporarily incapacitates Suspiria. Janeway is then able to fire the toxin, subduing her. Realizing she may have been mistaken, Suspiria takes Tanis and leaves the ship without sending the crew home.

SENSOR READINGS: The odd activity of the Caretaker's remains leads Tuvok to suggest they place it in a Level 3 Biohazard Containment Field. Torres creates a hexiprismatic field surrounding the remains so it can act as a compass that will lead them to the other life-form. The Doctor runs a microcellular analysis of the remains and discovers a critical enzyme in the cellular structure. An energy weapon is developed that will break down that enzyme and cause temporary paralysis in similar sporocystian life-forms.

Linking minds, Tuvok tutors Kes in controlling her mental powers.
ROBBIE ROBINSON

DAMAGE REPORT: Suspiria's attack on the ship causes the hull integrity to fail.

DELTA QUADRANT: There is no record of an Ocampan ever leaving the home world, which led Kes to believe she was the first. There are over two thousand Ocampa on the space station, which is over three hundred years old and one-tenth the size of the Caretaker's array. The Ocampa can contact Suspiria directly and do not consider her a "Caretaker" although they are dependant on her in many ways. Three Ocampa generations ago, Suspiria helped them develop technology that would extend their lifespan. Tanis is fourteen while his father lived to be twenty. The oldest known Ocampa on the home world only lived to be nine.

Suspiria and the Caretaker are members of a race known as the Nacene. She lives in Exosia, a region of pure thought and energy. Although the Ocampa consider it to be a place of the mind, Tanis admits that the *Voyager* crew would call it a subspace layer. Ship's scanners read Suspiria as a plasmatic field when she enters the ship.

PERSONAL LOGS: Tuvok continues to instruct Kes in the use of her mental abilities. When Kes tries to show him what she has learned from Tanis, she accidentally puts Tuvok's cell membrane through hyperthermal induction resulting in a thirty-seven degree rise in his blood temperature in seconds putting him in shock. The Doctor restricts him to light duty for the next three days, but

Tuvok refuses, citing the Vulcan healing abilities. ▪ Neelix gets a haircut, presumably from the ship's barber. ▪ In her exercises with Tuvok, Kes is able to pick out Neelix's thoughts from the rest of the crew and read his mind. Tuvok attributes this to their close bond. Her classes with Tuvok are at 1500 hours and recently have been running over, causing her to be late for her duty shift in sickbay. In the session before they encountered the Ocampa space station, Tuvok taught her a sensory focus exercise, worked on her precognitive skills, and showed her how to self-induce a hypergogic mental state. Tanis helps her further expand her mind by teaching her the psychokinetic manipulation of matter.

EPISODE LOGS: It has been ten months since *Voyager* was pulled into the Delta Quadrant. ▪ Tanis informs Janeway that *Voyager* has a reputation of being a "ship of death" that killed the Caretaker, declared war on the Kazon, and raided planets for their resources. The crew will encounter these rumors, spread by the Kazon, in future episodes. ▪ Tanis tells Kes that her abilities will eventually cause her to become a danger to the ship, which is shown to be true in "The Gift."

MANEUVERS

EPISODE #127
WRITTEN BY **KENNETH BILLER**
DIRECTED BY **DAVID LIVINGSTON**

GUEST STARS	
SESKA	MARTHA HACKETT
CULLUH	ANTHONY DeLONGIS
HARON	TERRY LESTER
SURAT	JOHN GEGENHUBER

CO-STAR	
COMPUTER VOICE	MAJEL BARRETT

STARDATE 49208.5

To the surprise of the *Voyager* crew, sensors pick up a transmission with a Federation signal. In the hopes that the Federation launched a probe in search of their missing ship, Janeway lays in a course toward the signal. Although the crew is careful when they arrive at the source of the signal, a Kazon Raider ambushes them, allowing a smaller vessel to penetrate *Voyager*'s shields.

Chakotay knows they will need a few surprises to stop Seska. ROBBIE ROBINSON

Intruders gain access to the starship, steal a transporter module and beam away to their own ship. When contacted by the raiding party, Janeway informs the Kazon leader, Culluh, that the module cannot be integrated into the Kazon technology. Culluh is unconcerned by the captain's words and reveals that he has joined forces with Seska, the Cardassian spy who was *Voyager*'s crew member.

Tuvok points out that, due to their alliance with Seska, the Kazon now have an adviser with Maquis, Cardassian, *and* Starfleet tactical experience and suggests that they use Chakotay's intimate knowledge of Seska to balance the odds. Although they suspect another trap, Janeway has Paris follow the Kazon ship's warp trail, determined to retrieve the missing technology so it cannot be used to upset the balance of power in the quadrant. Chakotay tells Torres he feels responsible for Seska's actions because he recruited her into the Maquis, and later he decides to leave *Voyager* to go after the device on his own.

Culluh does plan to use the stolen module to persuade rival sects to help him conquer the Federation ship, but his first attempt to join with the Relora fails. Seska manages to turn the situation around by using the trans-porter technology to beam the Relora maje and his aide into space killing them. She is then able to manipulate Culluh into agreeing with her plan to have the majes from weaker sects join them. Together, she believes, they will have enough strength to take over *Voyager*.

When Chakotay reaches the Kazon ship, he is unable to retrieve the transporter module. Improvising a plan, he beams undetected from the cockpit of his shuttlecraft to the Kazon bridge. There, he manages to destroy the stolen module before surrendering to Seska. He is then tortured for *Voyager*'s command codes, which he refuses to reveal.

When *Voyager* arrives on the scene, the Kazon majes gathered order Culluh to use the command codes to obliterate the starship, but it soon becomes obvious that he does not have them. Seska's quick thinking prevents *Voyager* from beaming Chakotay off the Kazon ship, so Janeway transports the Kazon majes instead. They agree to release Chakotay and his shuttlecraft in return for their freedom. Later Chakotay is shocked when he receives a message from Seska, informing him that while he was unconscious, she extracted some of his DNA and impregnated herself with his child.

Seska suggests using an alternate form of persuasion. BRYON J. COHEN

SENSOR READINGS: The carrier wave frequency that Seska uses as a trap corresponds with standard Starfleet security codes and was not scheduled for implementation until Stardate 48423 (a month after *Voyager* left DS9). The beacon was placed in an ionized hydrogen cloud that interferes with sensors. ▪ The Kazon steal a transporter module from Transporter Room 2 that Seska successfully helps them integrate into their systems. The stolen module contains a quantum resonance oscillator. ▪ Torres suggests transporting Chakotay from the Kazon ship while *Voyager* is at warp by synchronizing the transporter's annular confinement beam to the Kazon ship's warp core frequency. The maneuver is a direct violation of Starfleet safety protocols because, at a relative speed of two billion kilometers per second, they would risk scrambling the transporter signal and killing Chakotay. Torres has performed the maneuver on at least one prior occasion. ▪ *Voyager*'s transporter renders the Kazon weapons inoperable when the majes are beamed to the ship.

SHUTTLE TRACKER: Chakotay's shuttle shows up as intermittent EM readings on the Kazon scanners. The abnormal fluctuations are energy spikes from maneuver-

ing thrusters because the shuttle is running shadow maneuvers. The Kazon resonate a coherent polaron pulse off the shuttle's hull and initiate a continuous stream of pulses from the lateral deflectors to locate the shuttle. After sending out a message beacon, Chakotay wipes the shuttle's computer core so the Kazon cannot take the technology.

DAMAGE REPORT: The Kazon vessel pierces *Voyager*'s hull on Deck 4 in Cargo Bay 2, causing a power loss on the deck and destabilizing the warp core. With the low power, it would be difficult to dislodge the ship without losing structural integrity. They reroute additional power to the containment field and tow the shuttle out with one of their own.

DELTA QUADRANT: Jal Sankur is credited with uniting the Kazon sects to overthrow the Trabe. The current first majes of the Kazon sects are: Jal Culluh of the Nistrim; Jal Surat of the Mostral; Jal Loran of the Hobii; and Jal Valek of the Oglamar. Seska and Cullah execute Jal Haron of the Kazon-Relora and his aide by transporting them into space. Haron wore a green band on his uniform that signified he was the first maje of the Relora sect. The Kazon-Relora and Kazon-Ogla are the strongest Kazon sects.

ALPHA QUADRANT: While in the Maquis, Seska once disabled the computer core of a Cardassian ship orbiting Bajor by modifying an antiproton beam to penetrate its shields and hull. The maneuver needed to be conducted at close range. Chakotay unsuccessfully attempts the same maneuver to retrieve the stolen equipment.

PERSONAL LOGS: Chakotay overrides the ship's lockout commands when he steals the shuttle. Janeway puts him on report. Though the concept of being on report may not mean anything so far from the Federation, it does mean something to Chakotay. ▪ Torres previously considered Seska to be her best friend.

EPISODE LOGS: Seska is in the process of restoring her Cardassian physiology. In future episodes she will be seen as both Cardassian and Bajoran depending on the story-line. ▪ Cargo Bay 2 was previously turned into the airponics bay, although it is back to being a cargo bay in this episode. This could be because Kes incinerated all the plants in airponics in the preceding episode and has not yet restocked. ▪ Kes does not appear in this episode.

Torres is captured by Mokra soldiers. ROBBIE ROBINSON

RESISTANCE

EPISODE #128

TELEPLAY BY **LISA KLINK**

STORY BY **MICHAEL JAN FRIEDMAN & KEVIN J. RYAN**

DIRECTED BY **WINRICH KOLBE**

GUEST STARS

AUGRIS	ALAN SCARFE
DAROD	TOM TODOROFF
GUARD #1	GLENN MORSHOWER

SPECIAL GUEST STAR

CAYLEM	JOEL GREY

STARDATE UNKNOWN

In search of tellerium to power the ship, Janeway, Tuvok, Neelix, and Torres transport to an Alsaurian city occupied by the hostile Mokra. Tipped off to the crew's presence, Mokra soldiers capture Tuvok and Torres. Neelix manages to beam back to *Voyager* with the tellerium, and the captain is secreted away by Caylem, an eccentric man.

On the ship, Chakotay contacts Augris, the Mokra magistrate, to request the return of the missing crew members, but when the effort fails to produce results, he begins formulating a rescue plan. In Caylem's home, Janeway learns that Torres and Tuvok have been taken to the Mokra's impenetrable prison. Hoping to find his missing wife, Caylem asks Janeway—whom he believes to be his daughter—if he can accompany her there. Janeway refuses, but the point becomes moot when Mokra soldiers arrive, looking for her. The pair slip out of Caylem's shelter seconds before the soldiers burst in.

Janeway and Caylem approach Darod, the resistance member who provided the tellerium, and ask for help in obtaining weapons so they can break into the prison. Darod agrees, but only after warning Janeway that her companion is a lunatic who will probably get her killed. Unable to shake Caylem, Janeway continues to the meeting.

When Janeway realizes that the exchange is a trap, she must forego weapons and resort to using her feminine wiles to overtake two guards protecting the prison's access tunnels. Janeway sneaks into the prison, leaving

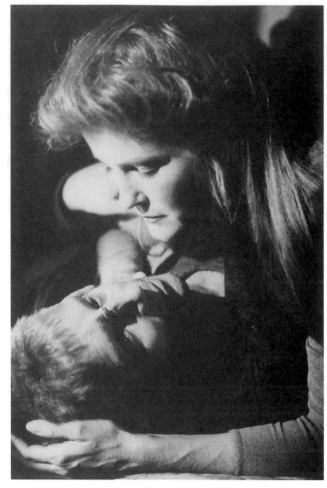
Janeway comforts a dying Caylem. ROBBIE ROBINSON

Caylem behind, unable to get past the security force field. Meanwhile, *Voyager* comes under hostile fire by the Mokra, and the ship is ordered to leave the area immediately.

Janeway disconnects the power to the security net, which frees Tuvok and Torres. But before the captain connects with her missing crewmen, she finds Darod, and then unexpectedly comes across Caylem. The old man claims he could not leave his daughter to conduct the search for his wife alone. Unfortunately, they are discovered by Augris, who reveals that Caylem's wife and daughter—both members of the resistance—are dead. Caylem fatally stabs the magistrate and takes a phaser shot in return. As Caylem dies, Janeway plays the role of his daughter and assures him that both she and her mother forgive him for having been too fearful to join the resistance years earlier. Seconds later, Paris arrives and the entire away team beams back to the ship. In her ready room, Janeway reflects on the events that lead to the death of her temporary adoptive father and the gift he gave her, his wife's necklace.

SENSOR READINGS: The ship requires tellerium for the warp core because the antimatter reaction rate is down to twelve percent. If it drops below nine, the plasma injectors will lock up and the crew will never be able to reinitialize the nacelles. To save power they take all systems offline, including shields, and reduce life support to minimum. ▪ Kim modifies the main deflector to send out dozens of radion beams to penetrate the prison shields while planning to use one of the beams to carry the transporter signal. Since the prison's sensor net will be unable to determine which of the beams carries the signal, the away team will have extra time to attempt a rescue. The Mokra fire on the ship before they are able to carry out the plan. ▪ The crew hides behind an ion storm to keep the ship off the Mokra's sensors.

DAMAGE REPORT: Following the attack by the Mokra, the ship's main deflector goes offline and there is minor damage to Deck 14.

DELTA QUADRANT: The Alsaurian Resistance is fighting against the Mokra Order. The Mokra prison has metaphasic forcefields, detection grids, physical barriers, and numerous guards. Previous to the encounter with the *Voyager* crew, no one had ever escaped from the prison. There are access tunnels on the north side of the prison and the detention level is subterranean. The Mokra possess weapons that can fire at spacefaring vessels from the planet and have eighty-five phased ion canons targeted on *Voyager*.

ALPHA QUADRANT: Vulcans are capable of suppressing certain levels of physical pain; beyond that, they must simply endure the experience.

PERSONAL LOGS: Janeway impersonates a prostitute to gain access to the prison. In the end, she keeps Caylem's wife's necklace. ▪ Tuvok and Torres are held prisoner in the Mokra prison where Tuvok is tortured by the Mokra.

EPISODE LOGS: Again, *Voyager*'s reputation has preceded them, as Augris claims that he knows they have been making more enemies than friends and that many think their story about being from the Alpha Quadrant is a lie. ▪ Kes and the Doctor do not appear in this episode.

PROTOTYPE

EPISODE #129

WRITTEN BY **NICHOLAS COREA**

DIRECTED BY **JONATHAN FRAKES**

CO-STARS

3947/CRAVIC 122	**RICK WORTHY**
6263/PROTOTYPE	**HUGH HODGIN**

STARDATE UNKNOWN

When the crew beams a deactivated robot on board, Torres works feverishly to revive the mysterious mechanical being. After exploring many dead ends, the chief engineer finally finds an appropriate power source and is delighted when the sentient artificial life-form is reactivated.

The robot introduces itself as Automated Personnel Unit 3947, one of a nearly extinct line of workers created by the Pralor, a species of extinct humanoids. Concerned over the potential extinction of its own mechanical race, 3947 asks Torres to build a prototype power module to help with the construction of additional units, but Janeway points out that giving the robotic species the

Cravic Automated Personnel Unit 3947. ROBBIE ROBINSON

power to "procreate" would be a violation of the Prime Directive. The unit refuses to accept that answer and kidnaps Torres, beaming them both to the ship that has come to retrieve him.

The crew is unable to penetrate the subspace defense shield surrounding the Pralor vessel which is populated entirely by robots. When *Voyager* fires on the alien ship, the robots respond by launching a violent attack that threatens to destroy the starship. Unable to contact her crew because 3947 deactivated her combadge, Torres realizes that the only way to save her friends is to agree to build the desired prototype.

While the crew plots her rescue, Torres learns that the robots have been unable to produce their own prototype because each power module has an individual energy code that can be used only in the specific unit. She sets out to design a standardized module that can power any unit and would allow for mass production of the robots.

A second alien vessel, manned by similar robots, begins firing on the Pralor vessel, insisting that *Voyager* will not be harmed as long as they stay out of the battle. Seeing this as the diversion they need, Janeway mounts a rescue mission, having Paris take a shuttlecraft through the Pralor ship's shielding to retrieve Torres.

Completing her work, Torres discovers that the builders of the attacking robots, the Cravics, used the machines to fight their war against the Pralor builders. All of the warring robots were programmed for victory, and when the Pralor and Cravic humanoids called a truce, the robots terminated them and continued their battle. The new prototype that Torres has created will allow the Pralor robots to win their war against the Cravic robots. Horrified, Torres destroys the prototype just before Paris beams her away from the Pralor ship, leaving the robots to continue their war.

SENSOR READINGS: Janeway tells Tuvok to load Torpedo Bays 1 through 4. It is unclear how many torpedoes are fired, but at least one weapon's discharge is seen and additional shots do shake the robots' ship. ▪ Before Torres can repair the robot, she uses an EPS charge to keep it running for at least eighteen hours. Torres replaces the robot's plasma with reconstituted warp plasma. She modifies a series of anodyne relays and attaches them directly to the robot's power module to act as a regulator that will make the warp plasma compatible with the robot's energy matrix. ▪ At optimal efficiency, *Voyager*'s engines are more powerful than the Pralor ship's weapons.

DAMAGE REPORT: Following the encounter with the Pralor vessel, *Voyager*'s aft shields are nonfunctional and

Torres and 3947 watch over the new unit they are creating. ROBBIE ROBINSON

propulsion systems are offline. There is a hull breach on Deck 6, artificial gravity is lost on Deck 8, environmental control systems are failing, oxygen levels on Decks 3 through 7 drop to critical, and those decks are also without power. The robots' sensors indicate that it will take *Voyager* 140 hours (five days) to repair the damage, though Chakotay estimates six days. The priority repair is the dilithium matrix that has destabilized, since they cannot get engines running.

DELTA QUADRANT: Automated Personnel Unit 3947 reported that he had been in service 1,314,807 hours and 33 minutes. He was activated by a Builder from the Pralor home world, where thousands of units were built as service units. He has no organic components of any kind. His head contains a programming center, but there are no detectable pathways for transmitting information. The energy module powers the entire mechanism and runs on superconducting plasma: a type of chromo-dynamic module powered by a tripolymer plasma. However, the plasma is contaminated and decaying. Each unit's power module has a slightly different energy signature so it cannot be used in any other module. The Builders did this to make sure the robots did not procreate. 3947 emits a

chromo-dynamic energy discharge to disable Torres and the transporter operator. ▪ The Pralor ship has a subspace defense field that *Voyager*'s transporter targeting scanners cannot penetrate or scan through to determine the ship's weapons strength. The Pralor ship fires quantum resonance charges.

ALPHA QUADRANT: A blood transfusion from a Vulcan to a Bolian would kill the unfortunate Bolian. However, there have been instances when artificial blood was unavailable and blood cells were genetically altered for interspecies transfusions.

MEDICAL REPORT: Torres is injured in the Cravic attack on the Pralor vessel ▪ During the Pralor attack, injuries are reported all over the ship.

EPISODE LOGS: As a possible diversion, Chakotay recounts a story from his time in the Maquis, when Torres linked a holoemitter to the deflector array and projected another ship into space. They do not use the diversion in this episode, but they do use a similar defense in "Basics." ▪ The Pralor and Cravic robots and ships are of the same design, but painted differently. The Pralor are silver, while the Cravic are gold. ▪ Following back to back episodes in which she did not appear, Kes shows up in the last scene of this episode with only two lines of dialogue.

DEATH WISH

EPISODE #130
TELEPLAY BY **MICHAEL PILLER**
STORY BY **SHAWN PILLER**
DIRECTED BY **JAMES L. CONWAY**

GUEST STARS

QUINN	GERRIT GRAHAM
ISAAC NEWTON	PETER DENNIS
MAURY GINSBERG*	MAURY GINSBERG
and	
Q	JOHN DE LANCIE

SPECIAL APPEARANCE BY

WILL RIKER	JONATHAN FRAKES

A battle of wills among the Q. ROBBIE ROBINSON

STARDATE 49301.2

During an attempt to beam aboard a comet sample, the crew inadvertently brings aboard a member of the Q Continuum, who was imprisoned inside the comet. The released Q expresses his gratitude at being rescued, then bids the crew farewell. He intends to commit suicide, but unfortunately he makes all the male members of *Voyager* disappear instead. When Janeway orders him to return her crew, he sheepishly informs her that he does not know how. Luckily, the better known Q, who has bedeviled the officers of the *U.S.S. Enterprise* for years, appears and returns the missing crewmen.

Q tells Janeway that the escaped Q has been locked up for the past three hundred years due to his repeated suicide attempts. The former prisoner Q demands asylum and attempts to press the point by haphazardly tossing the ship around space and time in an attempt to lose the other Q. Janeway calls a halt to the dangerous game of hide-and-seek, agreeing to hold a hearing to consider the request for asylum. The terms are set: if the captain rules in the Continuum's favor, the escaped prisoner must return to confinement. If she does not, the freed Q will be granted mortality so he can fulfill his death wish.

The escaped Q asks Tuvok to represent him at the

*The duplication of Maury Ginsberg's name in the cast list is not a mistake. According to the *Star Trek Encyclopedia,* by Michael Okuda and Denise Okuda, everyone liked the actor's name so much that Michael Piller changed the character's name to match.

hearing, where he explains he wants to end the tedium of immortality. The prosecuting Q counters by explaining that a suicide could have unpredictable consequences for the Continuum, which has never known anything but immortality. A courtroom drama ensues when Q calls himself to the stand along with other witnesses—including the *Enterprise's* William Riker—whose lives were profoundly changed by the escaped Q's influence.

Q tries to sway Janeway's ruling by promising to send the crew back to Earth if the decision is in his favor. Determined to render a just verdict, Janeway, Tuvok, and the two Qs visit a manifestation of the Q Continuum to see what life is like there. The court adjourns to a desert road stop—a metaphorical representation of the boredom experienced by the suicidal Q. The morning following the visit, Janeway grants the freed Q's request for asylum, and urges him to explore the mysteries of mortal life. Within hours, the escaped Q commits suicide, using a rare poison that does not exist on the ship. Q confesses that he secured the poison for his friend because the events of the trial forced him to rethink the sedate life of the Continuum.

SENSOR READINGS: Torres sets up a class-3 containment field for the core sample they beam aboard. The "core sample" is actually the imprisoned member of the Q, who easily passes through the field. ▪ *Voyager* is sent to the beginning of the cosmos, shrunken to a subatomic particle, and hung from a Christmas tree in Q's flight from

The character Q first appeared in the *TNG* pilot "Encounter at Farpoint" and became an occasional annoyance to the *Enterprise* crew. Following a single guest appearance on *DS9*, the irrepressible guest soon made his presence known to the *Voyager* crew. Since his inception, Q (both the individual and other members of his singularly named race) has always displayed a way with words, a quick wit, and a knack for stating what was on the minds of the audience.

"Death Wish"

Q: Oh, well I guess that's what we get for having a woman in the captain's seat. You, know I was betting that Riker would get this command.

Q (AFTER Q2 MAKES ALL THE MEN DISAPPEAR): Say, is this a ship of the Valkyries, or have you human women finally done away with your men altogether?

Q (TO CHAKOTAY): Facial art. Ooh . . . how very wilderness of you.

Q (TO JANEWAY IN SHOOTING SCRIPT—CUT FROM SHOW): We really have to do something with your hair.

Q (TO JANEWAY): Did anyone ever tell you you're angry when you're beautiful?

Q (TO JANEWAY): A hearing? You would have me put his future into your delicate little hands? Oh, so touchably soft. What is your secret, dear?

Q: My, my, now I guess we get to find out whether the pants . . . (looks at Janeway's posterior) . . . really fit.

All the Q have played the role of the scarecrow in this representation of the Continuum. ROBBIE ROBINSON

Q. The formation of the cosmos is noted as a large buildup of baryonic particles. ▪ Replicators will not produce fatal poisons, and the Doctor does not keep them in storage.

DELTA QUADRANT: The imprisoned Q (known as Q2 in the script) has been trapped inside the comet for over three hundred years. Apparently, the Q call up their powers in different ways—Q2 waves his right hand, while the original Q just snaps his fingers. ▪ Q2 says that the Q are not omnipotent, although their evolutionary progress as compared to humans makes them appear that way. He

believes that as they evolved, they sacrificed many things such as manners, mortality, a sense of purpose, a desire to change, and a capacity to grow. Q2's suicide will prove to have numerous consequences for the Continuum, since it marks the first time the Q have dealt with the unknown since the new era began. It is noted that the Q have executed members of their own race on prior occasions (such as Amanda Rogers's parents in the *TNG* episode "True Q"). Janeway and Tuvok are the only visitors ever to have come to the Continuum. It is presented to them in a manner they can understand, a shack by the side of a desert road. The road takes the Q to the rest of the uni-

Q: Without Q, there would have been no William T. Riker at all. And I would have lost at least a dozen really good opportunities to insult him over the years.

Q: Forget Mark. I know how to show a girl a good time. How would you like a ticker-tape parade down Sri Lanka Boulevard? The captain that brought *Voyager* back, a celebrated hero. I never did anything like that for Jean-Luc. But I feel very close to you. I'm not sure why. Maybe it's because you have such authority, and yet manage to preserve your femininity so well.

Q: *Au revoir*, madame captain. We will meet again.

"The Q and the Grey"

Q: I have no intention of getting between those Starfleet issue sheets. They give me a terrible rash.

Q: Oh, Kathy, don't be such a prude. Admit it . . . it *has* been a while.

Q (RE: CHAKOTAY): I was wondering, Kathy, what could anyone possibly see in this big oaf, anyway? Is it the tattoo? Because mine's bigger.

Q (TO NEELIX): You, bar rodent.

FEMALE Q (RE: JANEWAY): What *are* you doing with that dog? (BEAT) I'm not talking about the puppy.

FEMALE Q: The Vulcan talent for stating the obvious never ceases to amaze me.

FEMALE Q (SUZIE PLAKSON IS BEST KNOWN TO THE *STAR TREK* AUDIENCE AS WORF'S HALF-KLINGON MATE, AND ALEXANDER'S MOTHER ON *TNG*): You know, I've always liked Klingon females. You've got such . . . spunk.

"Q2"

Q (TO HIS SON): If the Continuum's told you once, they've told you a thousand times: don't provoke the Borg.

JANEWAY: I'm not a parent.

Q: Maybe not in the biological sense, but you're certainly a "mommy" to this crew. Just look how quickly you housebroke that Borg drone.

Q2: Kirk may have been a lowly human, but at least he had *pizazz*.

Q2: Scan, scan, scan . . . that's all you people ever do! I've been through every deck on this ship and do you know what I've seen? Bipeds pushing buttons, bipeds running diagnostics, bipeds replacing relays . . . When are you going to do something *interesting*?

Q2 (TO JANEWAY): I like you, Aunt Kathy. You've got gumption.

---

verse then it leads them back in an endless circle. ▪ Q2 uses Nogatch hemlock to commit suicide.

ALPHA QUADRANT: Q calls Maury Ginsberg, Isaac Newton, and William Riker as witnesses. Maury Ginsberg was a light operator who saved the festival at Woodstock when he noticed an unplugged cable. Q2 had given him a ride to the festival. Isaac Newton was credited with developing his theory of gravity when Q2 shook an apple tree, resulting in an apple falling on the theorist's head. Q2 was also responsible for rescuing an ancestor of William Riker's named Colonel Thaddeus Riker, after he

was wounded at Pine Mountain in 1864. They used to call him "Old Iron Boots." He was in command of the 102nd New York, during General Sherman's march on Atlanta. ▪ When the captain of a Starfleet vessel receives an official request for asylum, there is a clear procedure to follow, which includes holding a hearing to determine facts. ▪ In many cultures known to the Federation, suicide is acceptable. The double effect principle on assisted suicide that dates back to the Bolian Middle Ages, states that "an action that has the principal effect of relieving suffering may be ethically justified even though the same action has the secondary effect of possibly causing death."

The Q Continuum, as humans can perceive it. ROBBIE ROBINSON

ALLIANCES

EPISODE #131

WRITTEN BY **JERI TAYLOR**

DIRECTED BY **LES LANDAU**

GUEST STARS

MABUS	CHARLES O. LUCIA
CULLUH	ANTHONY DeLONGIS
SESKA	MARTHA HACKETT
JONAS	RAPHAEL SBARGE
TERSA	LARRY CEDAR
SURAT	JOHN GEGENHUBER
HOGAN	SIMON BILLIG

CO-STAR

RETTIK	MIRRON E. WILLIS

STARDATE 49337.4

After a series of Kazon assaults on *Voyager* badly damage the ship and cause the deaths of three crew members, Chakotay urges Janeway to loosen her strict adherence to Federation rules and start thinking more like the Maquis. He suggests forming an alliance with several factions of the Kazon—an option the captain rejects until Tuvok convinces her that such an arrangement could bring stability to the quadrant.

While Neelix visits a Kazon-Pommar contact on the planet Sobras to feel him out about the viability of such an alliance, Janeway meets with Seska and Maje Culluh of the Kazon-Nistrim. The talks seem to go well until Culluh stubbornly refuses to allow a woman to dictate the terms of an alliance, leading Janeway to end the talks. On Sobras, Neelix is taken prisoner by the Kazon for no apparent reason. He meets Mabus, a fellow prisoner and a Trabe leader, who assures Neelix that escape is not far off. Trabe supporters liberate the prisoners.

Since Neelix was not at the rendezvous point, the crew sets a course for Sobras to retrieve him. En route, they spot an armada of Kazon ships closing in on their position. Apprehension turns to relief when the crew realizes these are actually Trabe ships and Neelix is aboard one of them. Mabus explains that the Trabe once held the Kazon as slaves, until the Kazon rose up forcing them into exile. Despite the animosity between Trabe and Kazon forces, Janeway and Mabus form an alliance. Mabus, however, has a bolder plan and suggests they call for a conference to unite the warring factions in the quadrant.

Seska persuades Culluh to attend the meeting as his first step toward destroying the Trabe and seizing *Voyager.* When Cullah lashes out at Seska because of her improp-

---

Vulcans who reach a certain infirmity with age practice ritual suicide. ▪ According to Q, one of Q2's self-destructive stunts created a misunderstanding that ignited the hundred year war between the Romulans and the Vulcans. ▪ Q claims that humans are not supposed to be in the Delta Quadrant for another hundred years.

PERSONAL LOGS: Janeway's grandfather used to make her Welsh rarebit. After bringing herself up to date on Q's history with the *Enterprise* she notes that his one redeeming virtue is that he has never been a liar.

CREW COMPLEMENT: Q2 takes the name Quinn and is added to the crew manifest as a passenger. He is on the manifest only a short time before he commits suicide.

EPISODE LOGS: The repercussions of Quinn's suicide will be seen in "The Q and the Grey." ▪ The script originally opened with a scene in Kim's quarters with him playing the clarinet. The scene is later used in "The Thaw."

Janeway realizes Mabus is the saboteur when he tries to convince her to leave the meeting. ROBBIE ROBINSON

er tone, she warns him not to hurt their unborn child, a child she had previously told Chakotay was his. To calm the maje, she reminds him that they have a contact aboard *Voyager,* a former Maquis crewmate of hers named Jonas.

Having been tipped off that someone may try to sabotage the conference, Janeway and Tuvok proceed with caution to the meeting, which brings many of the first majes of the Kazon sects together. In the middle of the meeting a Trabe ship appears and opens fire on the room. *Voyager* drives off the Trabe vessel, and Janeway, stunned by the ambush, orders Mabus off her ship. But the damage has been done. The Kazon are furious, and the crew is more vulnerable than ever.

SENSOR READINGS: After the failed meeting with the Kazon, Janeway takes stock of the ship's situation and orders continual diagnostics on all ships systems. Tuvok schedules additional battle drills. Neelix reports that food supplies are in good shape and they should not have to stop for several weeks. There is a reasonable supply of antimatter for the propulsion system and they should have maximum performance from warp and impulse engines.

SHUTTLE TRACKER: Although it is not mentioned in the episode, it is assumed that the shuttle *Neelix* took to the planet Sobras was retrieved following his imprisonment by the Kazon.

DAMAGE REPORT: Following the fourth Kazon attack in two weeks, damage to *Voyager* is extensive. All engines are offline, and shields are down, as are all weapons arrays. Torres has to shut down the warp engines to avoid a breach and the impulse engines are gone. There is a hull breach on Deck 4 and the navigational deflector has sustained massive damage. It is necessary to repair the deflector before they can achieve more than thruster power.

DELTA QUADRANT: According to Neelix, everything the Kazon have (including their ships) was stolen from the Trabe. Mabus, a Trabe governor, was eight years old when the Kazon rebelled against the Trabe. At that time, the Kazon lived in restricted areas that Trabe children were not allowed to go near. They lived in poverty and filth and were persecuted by the Trabe police. At first, Mabus admits the Trabe brought it on themselves. They treated the Kazon like animals, fenced them in, and encouraged

The Kazon eventually rose up against their Trabe oppressors.
ROBBIE ROBINSON

ALPHA QUADRANT: Tuvok speaks of his past when ". . . a great visionary named Spock recommended an alliance between the Federation and the Klingon Empire." (*Star Trek VI: The Undiscovered Country*). At the time, Tuvok spoke against such a coalition but he now acknowledges that it brought stability to the Alpha Quadrant. ▪ Janeway notes that ". . . it's always been Starfleet's policy to deal with new species on the basis of openness and trust, until proven otherwise."

PERSONAL LOGS: Chakotay had met the late Crewmen Bendera in a bar fight in a mining community on Telfas Prime. ▪ Tuvok is unaccustomed to the captain visiting his quarters, noting that she only comes there when troubled. He replicates hot Vulcan spice tea for Janeway. He refers to the hybrid orchid he grew in his quarters. ▪ Crewman Bendera once saved Torres's life along the Cardassian boarder.

MEDICAL REPORT: A dozen crew members have sustained serious injuries in the Kazon attacks.

CREW COMPLEMENT: Maquis Crewman Bendera dies in a Kazon attack. His memorial service is held in the mess hall, which is emptied of tables. According to Chakotay two unnamed crew members died in previous attacks by the Kazon.

EPISODE LOGS: This is the first episode in the Crewman Jonas-traitor arc. ▪ Kes is seen in this episode; however, she has no dialogue.

them to fight amongst themselves so they would not turn on the Trabe. Then they sat by while the Kazon turned into a violent, angry army that realized the Trabe were their true enemies. Since the exile of the Trabe, the Kazon have refused to allow them to find a new home. Every time they try to settle somewhere, the Kazon attack and drive them away. Before the uprising, the Trabe were a highly evolved species. Their society produced scholars and artists who were widely admired, and their technology was among the finest in the quadrant. No one knew how the Kazon were being treated because the Trabe were rich and powerful, which allowed them to manipulate information about the conditions on their planet. No one wanted to risk offending them and losing opportunities for trade.

The first majes of the Kazon Order who attend the meeting are Minnis of the Pommar, Surat of the Mostral, Loran of the Hobii, Valek of the Oglamar, and Culluh of the Nistrim. The Kazon-Pommar inhabit the planet Sobras.

THRESHOLD
EPISODE #132
TELEPLAY BY BRANNON BRAGA
STORY BY MICHAEL De LUCA
DIRECTED BY ALEXANDER SINGER

GUEST STARS	
JONAS	RAPHAEL SBARGE

CO-STARS	
RETTIK	MIRRON E. WILLIS
COMPUTER VOICE	MAJEL BARRETT

STARDATE 49373.4

After a month of experiments, Paris, Torres, and Kim believe that they have found a way to cross the warp 10 threshold with the help of a newly

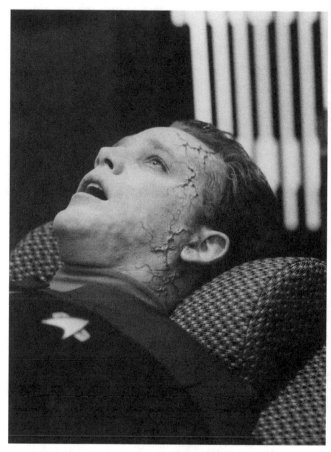

Paris suffers the early stages of his mutation. ROBBIE ROBINSON

matic changes in Paris's biochemistry—his organs are mutating, and his cell membranes are deteriorating rapidly. Despite the Doctor's best efforts, Paris dies.

Hours later, as the crew mourns, Paris spontaneously begins breathing again. When the Doctor examines him, he is amazed to find that the revived lieutenant now has two hearts. A series of accelerated mutations leave Paris radically transformed and subject to bouts of paranoia and violence. The Doctor determines the only way to save him is to destroy the mutant DNA with highly focused antiproton radiation from the warp core, but the procedure is interrupted when Paris breaks out of confinement.

Paris kidnaps Janeway and takes her to the *Cochrane*, launching them both on another transwarp journey. The crew eventually locates Paris and Janeway, only to find that they have mutated into amphibian creatures and mated, producing three offspring, that Chakotay decides to leave behind. Once Paris and Janeway are brought back to *Voyager*, the Doctor is able to perform the procedure to eliminate the mutant DNA from their bodies and return them to normal. After the experience, Paris realizes that he needs to stop worrying about what other people may think of his shortcomings and work on his own feelings of self-esteem.

discovered type of dilithium that remains stable at higher warp frequencies. Following a series of holodeck simulations to reach warp 10, the team irons out the technical glitches and prepares to send Paris out on a real flight.

The night before his historic journey, Paris is surprised in his quarters by a visit from the captain. Janeway informs him that, according to the Doctor, there is a imbalance in his brain that means he may not survive the flight. Therefore she is assigning Ensign Kim. After an impassioned plea from Paris, Janeway relents and allows him to take the flight. The next day, the entire crew waits as Paris takes the *Shuttlecraft Cochrane* to warp 10, crosses the transwarp threshold, and abruptly vanishes.

Moments later, the *Cochrane* appears beside *Voyager* and they beam a sleeping Paris to sickbay. He appears no worse for wear, weakened but exhilarated by the experience, which he likens to "being everywhere at once." As Torres and Janeway discuss the potential of the data obtained in Paris's brief flight, Crewman Jonas eavesdrops on the conversation. Later, the duplicitous Jonas sends information on Paris' flight to the Kazon.

Not long after his trip, Paris collapses in the mess hall. After he is rushed to sickbay, the Doctor tracks dra-

SENSOR READINGS: During the survey of an asteroid field in the previous month the crew discovered a new form of dilithium that remains stable at a much higher warp frequency. The finding inspired the transwarp testing. They theorize that if a person could reach warp 10, that person would be traveling at infinite velocity and would occupy every point in the universe simultaneously, meaning a person could go anyplace in the wink of an eye—time and distance would have no meaning. The holodeck transwarp simulations fail because the subspace torque rips a nacelle off the shuttle every time they get close to reaching the warp 10 threshold. In actuality, the shuttle is ripped from the nacelle because it is moving at a higher rate of speed. The hull of the shuttle is made of tritanium alloy that depolarized and created a velocity differential causing the fuselage to travel at a faster rate of speed than the nacelles. They set up a depolarization matrix around the fuselage to remedy the problem. In the shuttle, warp 7 is noted as critical velocity. At warp 10 the shuttle disappears from sensors. There is no sign of the shuttle for five parsecs. A quantum surge off the port bow indicates the shuttle is coming out of subspace. The shuttle logs' data describes every cubic centimeter in the sector with over five billion gigaquads of information and are transferred to stellar cartography for analysis and for

Chakotay tries to figure out how he will word his report on the altered Janeway and Paris. ROBBIE ROBINSON

the crew to make a starchart. ▪ When Paris falls ill, Torres requests a medical team to the mess hall, implying that Kes is not the only person working with the Doctor. ▪ When Jonas contacts Rettick to give him the data on their transwarp flight, he can stay in contact with the Kazon for only 30 seconds before security will pick up the transmission. ▪ Tuvok places the ship on a level-3 security alert after Paris breaks out. ▪ The computer reports that if *Voyager* continues to travel at warp 9.97, there will be a structural failure in 45 seconds.

DAMAGE REPORT: Paris uses a phaser on the port plasma conduit resulting in power failures all over the ship. They cannot get power to the internal sensors in order to track him or to use the tractor beam to bring his shuttle in.

SHUTTLE TRACKER: The *Shuttlecraft Cochrane* is the second shuttle in the series. It is a sleeker form of the type-9 shuttle. Though the actual craft is not damaged, a holographic simulation of the ship is destroyed numerous times in the test flights.

DELTA QUADRANT: After three days searching for the captain and Paris, they are found on the fourth planet in

an uninhabited star system. The shuttle is located in one of the jungles near the equator.

PERSONAL LOGS: When Paris was a child, his father, teachers, and friends all expected him to do something important with his life. He feels that he has been a disappointment to them, and the transwarp flight will be a chance for redemption. In the end, Janeway puts him in for a commendation. Paris lost his virginity at age seventeen in his bedroom while his parents were away for the weekend. His father thought that crying was a sign of weakness. Tom disagrees with that belief and claims that he does not trust people who do not cry. ▪ The Doctor is not programmed to cry. ▪ Neelix served for two years as an engineer's assistant aboard a Trabalian freighter and considers himself to be well versed in warp theory. Neelix recounts the story of a time when he lost a warp nacelle going through a dark matter nebula. As the ship went through the nebula, it sent out a dark matter bow wave. Eventually, so much pressure built up that it tore the nacelle from its housing.

MEDICAL REPORT: The transwarp experiment affects Paris in such a way that his DNA rewrites itself, and the

Doctor believes it changes him into a future stage in human evolution (ultimately doing the same to Janeway). The mutations are unlike anything in Starfleet medical records. His internal organs are rearranged, some having atrophied and been absorbed into his body. At least three other organs appear to have no identifiable function at all. To cure Paris and Janeway the Doctor has to destroy all the new DNA in their bodies with highly focused antiproton radiation, so their cells will have to use the original coding as a blueprint. The warp core is the only place on the ship that generates antiprotons. The procedure calls for them to first place Paris in an isotropic restraint and then infuse it with a controlled two-second antiproton burst. To do this they take the warp engines offline and bleed off .057 A.M.U. of antiproton radiation, shunting it through the interface. The two-second burst does not work and when they try to increase to a five-second burst, he escapes. The process later restores Paris and Janeway, but it is unclear how the full treatment was administered. Paris and Janeway are held in sickbay under observation for three days.

EPISODE LOGS: The *Shuttlecraft Cochrane* was named after Zephram Cochrane, the human who discovered warp drive. In the shooting script, the shuttle was originally named the *Drake;* however, that shuttle was destroyed in "Non Sequitur."

Tuvok questions his prime suspect, Suder. ROBBIE ROBINSON

MELD

EPISODE #133

TELEPLAY BY **MICHAEL PILLER**

STORY BY **MICHAEL SUSSMAN**

DIRECTED BY **CLIFF BOLE**

SPECIAL GUEST STAR

SUDER	BRAD DOURIF

GUEST STARS

RICKY	ANGELA DOHRMANN
HOGAN	SIMON BILLIG

CO-STAR

COMPUTER VOICE	MAJEL BARRETT

STARDATE UNKNOWN

When the body of Crewman Darwin is found in engineering, it is assumed his death was accidental until the Doctor determines that Darwin was, in fact, murdered. Tuvok launches an immediate investi-gation and a check of engineering logs places a Maquis named Suder at the scene of the crime. At first, Suder denies being involved, but when DNA evidence implicates him, Suder confesses. The only motivation that Suder can supply Tuvok to explain his actions is that he did not like the way Darwin looked at him.

Unwilling to accept such a senseless motive for such a serious crime, Tuvok interrogates Suder in great detail, ultimately securing his permission to perform a Vulcan mind-meld, which Tuvok hopes will help him understand Suder's motivations for the illogical crime. He also believes that some of his own Vulcan self-discipline will affect the confessed killer, allowing him to better control his violent nature.

Tuvok briefs Janeway on his mind-meld with Suder, and they discuss punishment options. Although the crewman is willing to be put to death for his crime, executions are not part of Federation practices. Since it would be almost as unacceptable to lock him away in the brig for the rest of the journey, Janeway suggests they confine him to quarters, install maximum security containment around his room, and begin efforts at rehabilitation. Throughout the discussion, Janeway notices Tuvok growing increasingly agitated. The Vulcan admits that although Suder seems calmer since the meld, he finds himself somewhat disconcerted. Later, an encounter with the playful Neelix so enrages Tuvok that he strangles the cook/morale officer. Fortunately, the event occurs in a holodeck simulation.

TUVOK'S MIND-MELDS

"Tuvok, no more mind-melds without my permission, understood?"

Kathryn Janeway, "Meld"

My mind to your mind . . . my thoughts to your thoughts . . .

Upon the utterance of those words, the Vulcan ritual telepathically linking two minds has been used in a variety of ways in *Star Trek* history. First used by Spock, in *Star Trek,* as a means of determining the truth, the mind-meld has grown to serve a variety of purposes. Throughout this series Tuvok uses the meld a number of times on several members of the *Voyager* crew.

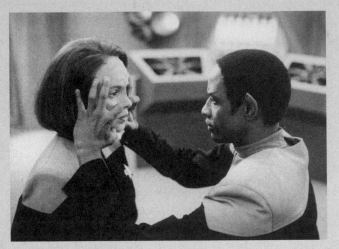

ROBBIE ROBINSON

JANEWAY

- On two occasions, Janeway melds with Tuvok, serving as his *pyllora* (guide), in the hopes of bringing out a repressed memory before it does permanent brain damage. In the end, the meld reveals an alien parasite living in the implanted memory in his brain. ("Flashback")
- Tuvok uses his meld as a conduit to link Seven and Janeway in a "bridging of the minds" to allow the captain to visit Unimatrix Zero. ("Unimatrix Zero")

CHAKOTAY

- Under mental programming from a former Maquis member, Tuvok melds with Chakotay and various Maquis, implanting instructions for them to take over the ship. ("Repression")

PARIS

- A mind-meld is performed to determine whether or not Paris is telling the truth about his innocence in the death of Tolan Ren. In the meld, Tuvok notices a series of numbers as part of the memory and finds an important clue to the setup. ("Ex Post Facto")

TORRES

- Similar to his link with Paris, Tuvok melds with Torres to determine the solution to a crime. He promises the reluctant Torres that the meld will focus only on the events leading to the crime for which she is accused. In the meld, he is able

Meanwhile, the events of the Suder investigation are consuming Tuvok to the point that he is unaware of another security problem onboard. In the Sandrine's holo-program Paris has been running a betting pool with the crew putting up their replicator rations. Paris has been skimming ten percent off the top. Chakotay discovers the inappropriate gaming and puts an end to it after confiscating all of the bet rations and placing Paris on report.

Once again, Tuvok meets with Suder, who unsettles the Vulcan with his comments about the seductive lure of violence, which Tuvok now fully understands. Fearful of his own impulses, Tuvok seals himself in his quarters and tells Janeway he is no longer fit for duty.

Concerned, Janeway sends Tuvok to sickbay, where he begins treatments to control his violent tendencies. That evening, Tuvok disables the force field holding him and breaks out of sickbay determined to execute Suder, but his rational instincts prevent him from completing the act of murder. After Tuvok collapses, Suder summons help, and Tuvok is returned to sickbay, where he successfully completes his rehabilitation.

SENSOR READINGS: There is an issue with the warp drive when the manifolds refuse to fire up due to a problem in EPS Conduit 141. Ensign Suder was monitoring the EPS flow and the CCF. He used a two-kilo coil-to determine that her feelings of anger may have been transferred to the alien, Guilli ("Random Thoughts")

- Under mental programming from a former Maquis member, Tuvok melds with Torres and various Maquis, implanting instructions for them to take over the ship. ("Repression")

KES

- Tuvok first suggests a mind-meld with Kes to expand her telepathic abilities. ("Cathexis") Later, he uses an exercise reminiscent of a mind-meld while helping Kes expand her telepathic abilities. ("Cold Fire")
- Tuvok uses a meld as a means of trying to communicate with Kes when she is possessed by the warlord Tieran. ("Warlord")
- As Kes's body begins to destabilize, Tuvok initiates a mind-meld to slow the process. He manages to delay the transformation slightly, but is overwhelmed by the link. ("The Gift")

SEVEN OF NINE

- When the personalities of numerous people whom Seven had assimilated begin to reassert themselves, Tuvok must meld with her to help her own self resurface. ("Infinite Regress")
- Tuvok uses his meld as a conduit to link Seven and Janeway in a "bridging of the minds" to allow the captain to visit Unimatrix Zero. ("Unimatrix Zero")

SUDER

- Tuvok melds on two occasions with the Betazoid murderer in an attempt to discern his motivation for the inexplicable crime. As a result of the meld, Suder gains Tuvok's interest in horticulture, while the Vulcan begins to feel Suder's drive toward violence. In the end, Tuvok stops short of using the mind-meld to kill Suder. ("Meld")

TABOR, JOR, AND YOSA

- Under mental programming from a former Maquis member Tuvok melds with these and other Maquis crewmen, implanting instructions for them to take over the ship. ("Repression")

GUILL

- Tuvok melds with this member of the Mari race and determines that he was involved in the trafficking of illegal violent thoughts that led to the death of a Mari woman named Talli. ("Random Thoughts")

NOSS

- After being trapped with the alien woman, Tuvok shares a meld with her so that she fully understands the depth of his feelings for her, which he can not properly explain with words. ("Gravity")

spanner to deliver the fatal blow to Crewman Darwin. Suder then hid the spanner behind a comline access panel on Deck 7. ▪ When Suder is confined to quarters in place of the brig, Tuvok is told to work with Kim to install maximum security containment on the room. ▪ Tuvok places a Level 1 security seal on his own quarters then tells the computer to delete security clearance Tuvok 1494-Lambda.

ALPHA QUADRANT: The Vulcan holiday, *Kal Rekk,* is a "Day of Atonement," celebrated with solitude and silence. The holiday is two weeks away. In the past it was observed with the Vulcan *Rumarie,* an ancient pagan fes-

tival full of barely clothed Vulcan men and women covered in slippery Rillan grease chasing one another. The festival has not been observed for a millennium. ▪ Under Starfleet Directive 101, Suder does not have to answer any questions while he is a suspect in the murder. When he insists on confessing, Tuvok suggests he obtain counsel. ▪ Tuvok refers to Cardassian pinochle but the card game is not actually played.

PERSONAL LOGS: As a Vulcan, Tuvok has internal processes that allow him to control violent instincts. He believes that through the meld it is likely that Suder will gain, at least for a time, some of Tuvok's self-discipline to

Driven mad by his link with Suder, Tuvok destroys his quarters. BRYON J. COHEN

better control his own violent nature. Tuvok has studied violence for over one hundred years and is trained in the martial arts of many Alpha Quadrant cultures, knowing of at least ninety-four ways to kill someone without using a weapon. In an unseen rage, Tuvok destroys his quarters. ■ The Doctor is programmed with the medical knowledge of every world in the Federation. ■ Neelix believes that it is part of his duty as morale officer to know of all the native holidays of the crew.

While working as a Maquis, Crewman Suder seemed to enjoy the battles a little too much, according to Chakotay and Torres. A Betazoid, Suder claims that he cannot feel his own emotions, much less the emotions of others. Suder's genetic profile reveals that his neurogenetic markers are normal and there is no tendency toward bipolar disorder. ■ Crewman Frank Darwin's training instructor recommended him as an officer candidate. He turned it down for a position on *Voyager*. The Doctor's postmortem reveals that ninety-eight percent of Darwin's body suffered third-degree plasma burns. If the circuit had not failed, he would have been vaporized. It was made to appear that Darwin had entered the conduit to repair a faulty circuit when the accident occurred, but he has a contusion that is the result of a hard blow to the back of the skull. The time of death is listed as 2214

hours. He is survived by three sisters back in the Alpha Quadrant. ■ Jones, Lewis, and Rodgers are among the crew members participating in Paris's game in Sandrine's.

MEDICAL REPORT: After Tuvok's mind-meld the levels of neuro-peptides in his limbic system are down fifteen percent and there is a definite neurochemical imbalance in the mesio-frontal cortex, which is where the Vulcan psycho-suppression systems are located. This may be the result of an incompatibility with the Betazoid telepathic neural center. The Doctor immediately follows the recommended course of treatment, which consists of the following: First they take away his ability to control his violence, which is done in short bursts over a period of time in the hope it will provide a shock to his system. If it works, his mind's neural controls will take over again. They temporarily remove his emotional suppression abilities and he feels emotion. They also disable his telepathic abilities so he cannot affect Kes.

CREW COMPLEMENT: Crewman Darwin dies.

EPISODE LOGS: The holocharacter Ricky, whom Paris once claimed appears in all his holoprograms ("The Cloud"), appears in this episode. This is the last time she will be seen in one of his holoprograms. ▪ Paris's "gambling operation" is presumably the first step in Janeway and Tuvok's plan to discredit Paris in the hope they can discover who on the ship is providing information to the Kazon. As will be learned later, Chakotay is not aware of the trap that later reveals Crewman Jonas to be a traitor ("Investigations"). ▪ A scene with Chakotay "dressing down" Tuvok for being unaware of the gambling operation was cut from the episode.

DREADNOUGHT

EPISODE #134
WRITTEN BY GARY HOLLAND
DIRECTED BY LeVAR BURTON

GUEST STARS

JONAS	RAPHAEL SBARGE
WILDMAN	NANCY HOWER
LORRUM	MICHAEL SPOUND
KELLAN	DAN KERN

CO-STAR

COMPUTER VOICE	MAJEL BARRETT

STARDATE 49447

In the middle of the Delta Quadrant the crew is shocked to discover a Cardassian-designed weapon packing a warhead capable of wreaking mass destruction. Even more surprising is that some of the crew is already familiar with the device. During a briefing that the increasingly troublesome Paris is late to, Chakotay and Torres recount the story of when they encountered the missile, dubbed "Dreadnought," in the Alpha Quadrant. Torres had reprogrammed it to assault the Cardassian fuel depot on Aschelan V, but the weapon went astray and was lost in the Badlands. Now *Voyager*'s scanners report that Dreadnought is inexplicably headed straight for a heavily populated planet in the Delta Quradrant.

As Jonas, the traitor in *Voyager*'s crew, informs the Kazon about this superweapon, Janeway warns an official on the planet Rakosa about the approaching missile. Torres beams onto Dreadnought, where she manages to convince the device's sophisticated computer system to stand down from its attack plans by informing the machine that it is not headed for its intended target. After she beams back to the ship, Torres learns that Dreadnought has inexplicably resumed its deadly course for Rakosa.

Torres boards the Dreadnought weapon. ROBBIE ROBINSON

The computer informs Torres that it does not believe her story that it is in the Delta Quadrant. It still thinks Rakosa is the Cardassian target in the Alpha Quadrant, and that Torres has been coerced by the Cardassians into logging false information into its navigational sensor array. Attempts to disable the missile from *Voyager* backfire when Dreadnought blows out many of the starship's main systems.

With two million lives at stake on Rakosa, Torres manages to beam back onto Dreadnought as the Rakosan fleet approaches to intercept the missile. This time, Dreadnought perceives Torres to be a threat, assuming that she has switched sides and aligned with the Cardassians, and terminates life support within missile.

Under fierce fire from Dreadnought, the Rakosan ships retreat. As a last ditch effort, Janeway orders her crew to abandon ship as she initiates *Voyager*'s self-destruct sequence in an attempt to destroy the missile in the explosion. As the minutes count down to *Voyager*'s destruction, Torres manages to initiate an old Cardassian program in Dreadnought's systems as she struggles to

It's man against machine as Torres tries to incapacitate the Cardassian weapon. ROBBIE ROBINSON

maintain consciousness. The two programs immediately begin to "quarrel" over the missile's target, distracting it from her attempts to breach Dreadnought's containment field and detonate the warhead. When *Voyager*'s sensors convey Torres's success, Tuvok, who stayed behind with his captain, beams Torres back to the starship just as Dreadnought explodes.

SENSOR READINGS: *Voyager* is equipped with type-6 photon torpedoes, which were not standard weapons used on Starfleet ships when Torres reprogrammed the Dreadnought two years ago. Two torpedoes are fired at the Dreadnought. ▪ The captain initiates *Voyager*'s self-destruct sequence using authorization Janeway Pi-110 and sets the warp core to overload in twenty minutes. ▪ All escape pods are launched and need to be retrieved after the self-destruct is aborted.

DAMAGE REPORT: The Dreadnought's attack on *Voyager* leaves the ship with damage on Decks 3 and 4 and EPS relays burned out all over the ship. There is no response from the warp or impulse drives and even the maneuvering thrusters are out.

DELTA QUADRANT: First Minister Kellen tells Janeway that the Rakosans are not a warlike race and have not devoted their resources to building weapons like the ones *Voyager* possesses. The Rakosan fleet sent to intercept the Dreadnought consists of fifteen small ships. Dreadnought's targeting parameters confuse the planet Rakosa V with the Alpha Quadrant planet Achelon V due to its size, radiothermic signature, atmospheric composition, and additional factors.

ALPHA QUADRANT: Originally, the Cardassians sent the missile to destroy a Maquis munitions base. It is a self-guided, tactical missile, carrying a charge of a thousand kilos of matter and another thousand of antimatter (enough to destroy a small moon). It also has one of the most sophisticated computer systems Torres has ever seen. The Cardassians made the missile adaptable, evasive, and armed with its own defensive weaponry. It passed through all the Maquis defenses and worked the way it was supposed to, except it did not explode because the Cardassians armed the warhead with an old kinetic detonator. As a result the missile skipped off into the atmosphere and went into orbit around the Maquis base. Torres got inside it and reprogrammed the computer giving it a new mission to destroy the Cardassian fuel depot on Aschelan V. Dreadnought never made it out of the Badlands because it was intercepted by the same coherent tetryon beam that brought *Voyager* to the Delta Quadrant. Dreadnought is programmed to deflect its image up to 100,000 kilometers from its true location. It masks its warp field with a randomized EM field but Torres modifies *Voyager*'s navigational sensors to cut through the field. Dreadnought conducts a self-diagnostic every fourteen hours and access to primary navigational systems is denied at Stage 3 alert status. Torres had reprogrammed Dreadnought's computer to speak with her voice. The only vulnerability Torres remembers was in the thoron shock emitter. She believed if they could get it to fire at full power that would destabilize the reactor core for thirty seconds. A single sustained tachyon beam is fired to penetrate the core but Dreadnought sends a plasma burst back along the beam into *Voyager*'s main power system. Torres's tactical subroutine instructed Dreadnought to prepare responses for thirty-nine potential Cardassian threats. The possibility of her capture and coercion was number seven. If it were not destroyed Dreadnought could have provided *Voyager* with replacement parts that would have augmented the ship for years.

Dreadnought refers to the Cardassian-Federation alliance as described in the treaty of 2367, noting that it is a treaty rejected by the Maquis. (The treaty between the Federation and Cardassians was actually signed in 2366.)

The name Cameron is derived from the ancient Celtic term for "one whose nose is bent," while Frederick bears a close resemblance to a rather impolite term on the Bolian homeworld. The Vulcan name Sural was also the name of a dictator on Sakura Prime, famed for beheading his rivals and his parents.

PERSONAL LOGS: Janeway cites "captain's prerogative" when she decides to remain on the bridge after setting *Voyager*'s self-destruct sequence. Tuvok remains with her in case she becomes incapacitated before intercepting Dreadnought. ▪ Torres had not known Chakotay well when they first encountered Dreadnought. When she reprogrammed it without his permission, he told her that she "hurt him" since he thought he had earned her trust and loyalty. She was last on the Dreadnought on Stardate 47582. Torres is "slightly singed" in Dreadnought's explosion and suffering from oxygen depravation. ▪ Paris shows up late (and disheveled) for a briefing. He also has an argument with Lt. Rollins over his conn report not being up to Starfleet protocol. ▪ The Doctor has reviewed historical, literary, and anthropological databases from over five hundred worlds, and has yet to find a suitable name. He is hurt by the fact that Kes never suggested he take her father's name. ▪ Kes's father was Benaren. She considers him to be the greatest inspiration in her life. Her uncle's name was Elrem, and she once knew a boy named Tarrik.

Ensign Wildman believes that she is carrying a boy. Her Ktarian husband's name goes back five generations (Wildman will actually have a baby girl in "Deadlock") ▪ Jonas makes contact with the Kazon regarding Dreadnought. His new control (contact) is named Lorrum. Jonas has a communications scrambler that also tells him when someone is about to make a subspace transmission so he will not be caught.

EPISODE LOGS: The Caretaker's coherent tetryon beam was ultimately responsible for bringing *Voyager*, the Maquis ship, Dreadnought, and the *U.S.S. Equinox* ("Equinox") to the Delta Quadrant. ▪ Kellen has also heard the rumors the Kazon had been spreading about *Voyager* being a ship of destruction.

INVESTIGATIONS

EPISODE #135
TELEPLAY BY **JERI TAYLOR**
STORY BY **JEFF SCHNAUFER & ED BOND**
DIRECTED BY **LES LANDAU**

GUEST STARS

JONAS	RAPHAEL SBARGE
SESKA	MARTHA HACKETT
LAXETH	JERRY SROKA
HOGAN	SIMON BILLIG

CO-STAR

COMPUTER VOICE	MAJEL BARRETT

STARDATE 49485.2

As part of his duties as *Voyager*'s morale officer, Neelix begins an onboard news program entitled "A Briefing with Neelix." After Kim suggests that the show could use more substance, Neelix begins to rethink the concept. When he hears a rumor that someone is leaving the ship to join a Talaxian convoy, he passes the news along to Janeway and Tuvok. The pair admits to Neelix that Tom Paris has requested the transfer. Neelix uses his show to bid a fond farewell to his friend while Paris leaves the ship.

As Janeway ponders Paris's replacement, Neelix busies himself by covering an accident in engineering

Neelix tries to convince Paris to stay aboard *Voyager*. ROBBIE ROBINSON

Neelix defends himself against the traitor Jonas. ROBBIE ROBINSON

that leaves three crew members, including Crewman Jonas, nursing minor wounds. With the warp engines shut down, Neelix informs the captain that they can find the substance necessary for repairs on a class-M planet in a yellow dwarf system called Hemikek. A short time later, *Voyager* is contacted by the Talaxian vessel and notified that it has been attacked by the Kazon-Nistrim, who have taken Paris hostage.

Seska welcomes Paris aboard the Kazon vessel and tries convincing him to join forces with the Nistrim sect. Back on *Voyager*, Neelix wonders how the Kazon knew that Paris was aboard the Talaxian ship. Following his new career as an investigative journalist, Neelix pokes around engineering, where he finds suspicious gaps in the subspace communications logs. Fearful of exposure, Jonas prepares to kill the Talaxian with a plasma torch, but the Doctor appears on a nearby companel, interrupting before any harm is done.

Neelix tells Tuvok his suspicions that a crew member has been making covert transmissions to the Kazon. Ignoring the security chief's order not to investigate further, Neelix finds evidence that Paris is the traitor, and transmits his findings on his daily briefing. Janeway con-

fides to Neelix that Paris's recent departure was a ruse to flush out a suspected spy on board. She asks the Talaxian for assistance in exposing the traitor.

On the Kazon ship, Paris finds evidence that proves Jonas is the turncoat. When Seska discovers him accessing the files, Paris manages to escape in a stolen Kazon shuttlecraft. At the same time, on *Voyager*, Neelix realizes that Jonas is the guilty party, and when the two men come to blows in engineering, Jonas plunges to his death. The Kazon retreat, and Paris returns to the ship a hero.

SENSOR READINGS: Operations detects a minute increase in the engine core temperature of which Torres is already aware. There is a slight imbalance in the magnetic constrictors, causing the plasma stream to overheat. When the magnetic constrictors lose alignment, the plasma stream gets too hot and starts to infect the injector valves, forcing them to close, allowing antimatter to seep into the warp core. The crew tries adjusting the power transfer conduits with no effect. To contain the reaction in the core PTC temperature cannot go above 3.2 million kelvins. Plasma must be vented through the nacelles, but at a temperature of over 3 million kelvins this will fry the warp coils (although that is preferred to a core breach). They reinforce the structural field around the power transfer conduits and then vent the plasma. The plasma burst irradiates the engine nacelles and burns away the inner layer of the warp coils rendering the warp engines useless until they can be rebuilt. (This is all a result of Jonas's sabotage.) The warp coils are made from a substance known as verterium cortenide, which is a densified composite material composed of polysilicate verterium and monocrystal cortenum. ▪ Usually it is possible to recover data from the communication logs unless extraordinary measures were taken to erase it. Hogan assists Neelix in trying to recover the missing logs by running a signal modulation analysis of the file. To do this a security authorization is required, and Hogan enters his engineering authorization Omega-47, which Neelix will later use to access the files in Paris's quarters. Hogan cannot recover the logs because the messages were sent without using any of the antenna arrays. Instead, they were sent through the ship's power grid and encoded in the waste energy from the propulsion systems, which is almost indistinguishable from galactic background noise. To determine who sent the messages, Hogan looks for signal correlation traces that would indicate a comlink to the EPS conduits and show a location of origin. The source of the comlink is on Deck 4, Section 3C. In researching the missing files, Neelix checks every log system they have, including subcom logs, sensor logs, power allocation logs, warp maintenance logs, and environmental control logs.

DELTA QUADRANT: Neelix directs the crew to a yellow dwarf system called Hemikek under the belief that they should be able to find the necessary materials to rebuild the warp coils on the planet Hemikek IV, where the mining rights belong to a consortium of nonaggressive people. The Kazon, with the help of Seska, have anticipated their need and set up an ambush including ground forces on the planet.

Neelix's friend, Laxeth, is the communications master of the Talaxian convoy that Paris joins.

PERSONAL LOGS: Janeway and Tuvok admit to knowing there was a spy onboard; Chakotay was insulted at being kept in the dark. ▪ Paris's quarters are located on Deck 4, Section 3C. ▪ "A Briefing with Neelix" is intended to be a morale boost for the crew and originally consists of little more than gossip and entertainment. The Doctor is asked to host a segment called "Hints for Heathful Living," although Neelix never has the time to include the segment on his first shows.

Hamilton and Ensign Pablo Baytart are seen as possible replacements for Paris when he leaves the ship. Ensign Baytart is also a juggler who performs on the first installment of "A Briefing with Neelix," though he is not actually seen.

CREW COMPLEMENT: Jonas dies in his fight with Neelix.

EPISODE LOGS: In the episode chronology, this episode should follow "Lifesigns" as the set up for the Jonas's sabotage and the Kazon trap is laid in that episode. ▪ Seska notes that her child is due in one month, meaning that a Cardassian pregnancy lasts for a shorter term than a human/Ktarean pregnancy, since Ensign Wildman has been pregnant for a considerably longer time than Seska. ▪ When Neelix goes over the com logs, he notes that in the past month the crew has been in contact with the Mithren and the Katati. The Mithren were first mentioned in "Persistence of Vision" as the race among which Neelix had friends and the crew intended to leave their Botha prisoner with before he disappeared. ▪ The unidentified crewman who Kim is speaking to in the teaser was played by Prince (now King) Abdullah of Jordan, in an uncredited, nondialogue, role.

LIFESIGNS

EPISODE #136

WRITTEN BY **KENNETH BILLER**

DIRECTED BY **CLIFF BOLE**

GUEST STARS

DANARA PEL	SUSAN DIOL
JONAS	RAPHAEL SBARGE
SESKA	MARTHA HACKETT
LORRUM	MICHAEL SPOUND

CO-STAR

GIGOLO	RICK GIANASI

STARDATE 49504.3

The crew answers a distress call from a small spacecraft and beams its occupant into sickbay. The deathly ill Vidiian female is suffering from the phage, which has ravaged her people. In an effort to postpone her oncoming death the Doctor puts her decaying body into stasis and transfers her synaptic patterns into

The Doctor and Danara Pel enjoy the view of Utopia Planitia. ROBBIE ROBINSON

sickbay's holobuffer. He then creates a holographic body that reflects the way the female would look if she were not afflicted with the phage.

The astonished patient revives and introduces herself as Dr. Danara Pel. She is grateful for what the Doctor has done for her, even though he admits it is just a temporary fix, since she cannot survive long in this form. The Doctor tells her that he still has hopes of treating her ravaged physical body.

Embittered by her own harrowing experience as a prisoner of the Vidiians, Torres first balks at the Doctor's request that she donate some of her brain tissue to help Danara, since Klingon DNA is resistant to the phage. But after Danara has a chance to show Torres that all Vidiians are not like her former captors, she relents, and allows for her donated tissue to be grafted onto the Vidiian's brain. Because it will take several days before they know if the graft works, the Doctor and Danara begin spending time together.

The Doctor is confused by his affection for Danara, but Kes urges him to tell her how he feels. Yet when the Doctor blurts out his interest in her, she says she would prefer to keep their relationship strictly professional. While the disappointed Doctor seeks Paris's dating advice, Kes gets Danara to admit she really does like the

Doctor. Later, Paris tells the Doctor he knows the perfect romantic getaway to impress Danara, and using Paris's holodeck program they have a lovely date on Mars in a '57 Chevy.

As one relationship grows, another deteriorates. Paris's ability to get his job done and connect with his fellow crew members has been compromised by his recent behavior. Chakotay attempts to address the destructive attitude, but Paris reacts by lashing out and the captain sends him to the brig.

Not long after, the Doctor is shocked to discover that Danara's brain is rejecting the graft. He does not understand what could have gone wrong until she admits to sabotaging the treatment because she does not want to return to her diseased body although the alternative is death. The Doctor convinces her that he will love her no matter what she looks like, and convinces her to survive and go on caring for her sick compatriots. As *Voyager* heads for her home, she returns to her body and shares a tender dance with the Doctor in Sandrine's bar.

SENSOR READINGS: It will take *Voyager* about twenty-two days to travel ten light-years to be in the vicinity of Danara's planet.

Torres refuses to help Danara, citing the Vidiian experiment that split her into two separate entities. ROBBIE ROBINSON

DELTA QUADRANT: Dr. Danara Pel has an implant in her parietal lobe that is a very complex web of bio-neural circuitry and nanofibers. The device stores her synaptic patterns, processes them, and transmits neural-electrical impulses to the rest of her systems. The Doctor compares it to a neuro-cortical stimulator, designed to supplement the higher brain functions. The implant itself is functioning, but it is connected to mostly dead nerve cells that, if left untreated, will leave her brain dead in a matter of minutes. The Doctor transfers her synaptic patterns into the holobuffer before they degrade. He creates a model of healthy a Vidiian that will aid in treating Pel. He uses the undamaged chromosomes in her cerebellum to re-create her original DNA code then programs the computer to project a holographic template based on that genome. To conclude the procedure, he uses transporter records to re-create her clothing. Danara was first diagnosed with the phage when she was seven. Her area of medical specialty is hematology. She was returning to her home from treating an outbreak of the phage on Fina Prime. The Doctor's plan for treatment relies on the information

learned when Torres was taken hostage by the Vidiians ("Faces"). He plans to drill an opening into Torres's skull precisely two millimeters in diameter, and use a neuralyte probe to extract a sample of her parietal lobe, weighing approximately one gram. Once he finishes ingrafting the Klingon neural tissue to Danara's cerebral cortex, all he has to do is create an axonal pathway between that tissue and her basal ganglia. The exact procedure was developed by Dr. Leonard McCoy in the year 2253. Danara's body rejects the graft because of elevated levels of nytoxinol in her body. She injected herself with the nytoxinol because she wanted to remain in holographic form. Cervaline is used to reduce the rate of tissue rejection. ▪ Among Vidiians, congregating in groups is strictly regulated, as it is considered to be a threat to public health.

PERSONAL LOGS: As part of the ongoing undercover operation to uncover the traitor on board, Paris is late for duty four times in one week. He has a confrontation with Chakotay in the mess hall and on the bridge, with the latter encounter becoming physical when he pushes Chakotay to the ground. As a result of his actions, the captain has him sent to the brig. Paris tells the Doctor about the time he was dumped by his first love, Susie Crabtree, back in his first year at Starfleet Academy. In reaction to the breakup he claims to have broken out in hives and been unable to get out of bed for a week. The Doctor tells Danara that Paris is an automobile aficionado. ▪ The Doctor is equipped with the collective medical knowledge of more than three thousand cultures and his program contains over 50 million gigaquads of data. Since he was activated on Stardate 48308, he has performed three hundred forty-seven medical exams, healed eleven compound fractures, performed three appendectomies, and cured Neelix of an acute case of hiccups. The Doctor makes his first personal log entry on Stardate 49504.3. Dancing is not part of his programming until he downloads a dancing subroutine. Kes notes that since the Doctor's programming is adaptive, it is possible for him to fall in love. It is also possible that he and Danara make love in this episode because in a future episode ("Message in a Bottle") he tells the EMH-2 that he has previously fallen in love and engaged in sexual relations. Danara gives the Doctor the name Shmullus, after an uncle who used to make her laugh.

When Paris is late for duty, his position at conn is filled by Mr. Grimes. ▪ Kes reports that only two crewmen had been in sickbay on the day they check to see if Danara's graft was effective, Crewman Foster came in for some analgesic, and Ensign Wildman was there for her regular prenatal visit.

EPISODE LOGS: "Investigations" was shot prior to "Lifesigns" but was aired after to maintain story continuity. ▪ The name "Danara" is actually spelled "Denara" in the script for this episode; however, in future episodes (and the *Star Trek Encyclopedia*) it is spelled with an "a." ▪ Seska convinces Jonas to cause an accident to destroy the warp coils as the Kazon are planning to ambush *Voyager* on Hemikek IV. The events of the sabotage are played out in "Investigations."

Janeway fights to save her vessel. ROBBIE ROBINSON

DEADLOCK

EPISODE #137

WRITTEN BY: BRANNON BRAGA

DIRECTED BY: DAVID LIVINGSTON

GUEST STARS

ENSIGN WILDMAN	NANCY HOWER
HOGAN	SIMON BILLIG

CO-STARS

VIDIIAN SURGEON	BOB CLENDENIN
VIDIIAN COMMANDER	RAY PROSCIA
VIDIIAN #2	KEYTHE FARLEY
VIDIIAN #1	CHRIS JOHNSTON
COMPUTER VOICE	MAJEL BARRETT

STARDATE 49548.7

As *Voyager* enters a plasma cloud to evade approaching Vidiian ships, Ensign Wildman goes into labor and delivers a baby girl. But when the crew emerges from the cloud, an odd series of events occur when the warp engines stall, the antimatter supplies drain, and proton bursts emanating from an unknown source cause a hull breach on Deck 15. Subsequently, Kim is sucked into space while trying to fix the hull breach, Kes vanishes in a mysterious void, and Wildman's baby dies.

As the hull breach widens, the ship is forced to run on emergency power. When another proton burst, causes a new breach to form on Deck 1, Chakotay is forced to order everyone off the bridge. As the captain reluctantly abandons her post, she sees a mirror image of her crew overlaid onto the partially destroyed bridge.

At the same time, another Janeway sees an image of her battered self walk across the undamaged bridge. Assuming it is a spatial fluctuation caused by their pas-

sage through the plasma cloud, Janeway visits Wildman in sickbay and admires her newborn baby, who appears to be fine. While in sickbay, the captain also checks in on a mysterious patient who just appeared on Deck 15. It is an identical version of their own Kes.

This newly arrived Kes reports the same series of odd occurrences, which leads Janeway to speculate that there is another *Voyager* nearby. Apparently, a divergence field had caused every particle of matter on the ship to duplicate in the instant they passed through the field. The two ships are to be linked by the antimatter in the warp drive, but there isn't enough antimatter to sustain both vessels. Janeway alerts the other *Voyager* crew, and after an attempted merger of the ships fails, goes over to the other ship utilizing the void Kes previously disappeared into.

The two Janeways meet and strategize their options. The captain of the more heavily damaged *Voyager* proposes the self-destruction of her ship and crew to save the other. With the Vidiians closing in, the two captains know they must act quickly or both ships and crews will be destroyed. Meanwhile, the Vidiians board the undamaged *Voyager*.

Desperate to steal healthy organs to help battle the phage, the Vidiians begin attacking crew members. Realizing that the odds are against her, the Janeway of the undamaged *Voyager* alters the plan and sets her own ship on self-destruct, ordering the duplicate Kim to take Wildman's baby through the void. The Vidiians are destroyed when the duplicate *Voyager* explodes, while Kim, the baby and the other *Voyager* crew are saved, but left with tremendous repairs needing to be done to the ship.

SENSOR READINGS: The thermal array in the mess hall kitchen overloads and vaporizes a pot roast. It needs a new set of anodyne relays, which Wildman intends to get from storage. The mess hall replicator has been having a problem making anything with a large amount of cellulose, due to a malfunction in the power grid. Neelix has been using the replicator to supplement his cooking because vegetable yields from the airponics bay have been low. ▪ The undamaged *Voyager* crew analyzes the sensor logs from their trip through the plasma cloud but cannot find anything unusual, they run a quantum-level analysis and discover that the subspace turbulence they had encountered was a divergence field. Mass, energy output, bio-signatures—everything—was duplicated in the instant they left the cloud. As an explanation, Janeway refers to an experiment she witnessed at Kent State when quantum theorists duplicated a single particle of matter using a divergence of subspace fields (or a spatial scission). They theorize that if the same forces were at work inside the plasma cloud, they might have duplicated every particle of matter on *Voyager,* except for the antimatter. In that Kent State experiment, she continues, they were able to duplicate normal matter, but when they tried to duplicate antimatter particles, the experiment failed. This leads them to realize that both ships' engines have been trying to draw power from a single source of antimatter. At first the crew has trouble contacting the other *Voyager* crew to inform them of the findings because the molecular signatures of the two ships are slightly out of phase. However, if they recalibrate their carrier waves at the same time, to match phase variance, they could connect. To inform the other ship to do this, Torres sends a rotating band pulse on all subspace bands just to get their attention. She then uses the emergency encryption code for a short message telling the other *Voyager* to lock onto a frequency of twelve gigahertz. Once communication is

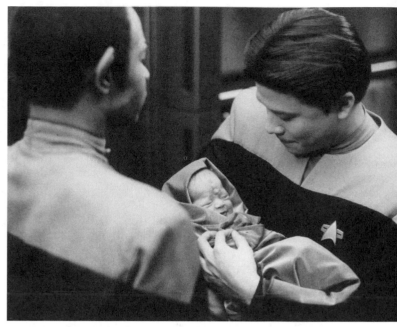

The only two survivors from the duplicate *Voyager*. ROBBIE ROBINSON

established, the two ships attempt to re-create the subspace divergence field they passed through and depolarize it by sending out a massive resonance pulse from their deflector dishes at exactly the same time, hoping it will merge the ships. They have to abort the merge when the plasma flow becomes too turbulent, and the divergence fields are so chaotic they threaten to destroy both ships.

DAMAGE REPORT: The surviving *Voyager* is badly damaged. There is a major coolant leak in the mess hall. The hull breach on Deck 15 widens to include Deck 14, Section 12. There are 632 microfractures along the hull's infrastructure. All primary systems are offline and they are running on emergency power only. The antimatter supply drops to eighteen percent, and continues to fall. Warp coils in both nacelles fuse and are inoperative. The environmental control systems are failing. Fifteen crew members are seriously wounded with plasma burns, twenty-seven experience other injuries, and Ensign Kim and Samantha Wildman's baby do not survive (although their doppelgangers come over to the ship before the other *Voyager* is destroyed). The Doctor sets up triage facilities in sickbay and Holodeck 2. A hull breach on Deck 1 forces the crew to abandon the bridge. They use engineering as a temporary bridge and it is estimated that they can return to the actual bridge in three days.

DELTA QUADRANT: A large plasma drift extends almost half the length of the sector the ship is traveling through.

Voyager enters the field to avoid twenty Vidiian ships and a G-type star system with two planets showing Vidiian lifesigns since interference from the plasma should block them from the Vidiian's sensors. More than 347 Vidiians eventually board the undamaged Voyager and begin harvesting organs from the crew, leading Janeway to destroy the ship. Vidiian ships are armed with hyperthermic charges.

PERSONAL LOGS: When Janeway was twelve years old, she walked home—a distance of over seven kilometers—in a thunderstorm because she lost a tennis match. She has been making a blanket for Wildman's baby. ▪ Chakotay's father had a saying: "Home is wherever you happen to be." ▪ Tuvok's wife was in labor for ninety-six hours during the birth of his fourth child. ▪ After Kes disappears from the damaged Voyager, Paris is told to assist the Doctor. ▪ The Doctor now has a backup power supply and claims he is programmed to be heroic when the need arises. ▪ According to the Vidiians, Kes (and presumably all Ocampa) has an extremely high rate of tissue regeneration.

Ensign Samantha Wildman goes into labor, which lasts at least seven hours. During the delivery, the baby shifts position and her exo-cranial ridges lodge in the uterine wall. This is a rare complication, but has been known to happen in human-Ktarian pregnancies. The Doctor cannot reposition the baby, since her spinal column is too fragile and he does not want to risk nerve damage. If they had not delivered the baby immediately, her ridges could have perforated the uterus and caused internal bleeding. To deliver the baby safely, they initiate a fetal transport. Wildman is surprised to have a girl, as she was expecting a boy. The baby's incisors will erupt in three to four weeks. Since Wildman does not have the scales of a Ktarean, she and the Doctor will need to discuss breast-feeding options. On the original Voyager medical systems were heavily damaged, and the osmotic pressure therapy they used on the baby did not work, resulting in her death. Kim brings the surviving baby with him when he crosses over.

INNOCENCE

EPISODE #138

TELEPLAY BY: **LISA KLINK**

STORY BY: **ANTHONY WILLIAMS**

DIRECTED BY: **JAMES L. CONWAY**

GUEST STARS

ALCIA	MARNIE McPHAIL
TRESSA	TIFFANY TAUBMAN
ELANI	SARAH RAYNE
CORIN	TAHJ D. MOWRY

CO-STAR

ENSIGN BENNET	RICHARD GARON

STARDATE 49578.2*

While entering the atmosphere of an uninhabited moon, the shuttle piloted by Tuvok and Ensign Bennet is rocked by electrodynamic turbulence. Bennet is killed in the shuttle crash. Tuvok leaves the damaged craft, and realizes he is not alone on the moon as three frightened children venture out from hiding. The children tell him that their ship crashed too, killing the people who were looking after them.

In the meantime, Voyager welcomes Alcia, the first prelate of Drayan II, a planet known for deeply valuing its privacy. Despite the natives' preference for seclusion, Janeway hopes to develop a relationship with them so she can negotiate for some of the polyferranide deposits available on the Drayan's moons. The initially warm visit is interrupted when Alcia receives an emergency message, calling her away. Before she goes, she brusquely asks the crew to leave the area.

As Tuvok tries to repair his damaged shuttlecraft, the children—Tressa, Elani, and Corin—express their fears of being killed in the night by a creature they call the Morrok. They are even more frightened when a Drayan search party arrives, the children tell Tuvok that the Drayans sent them to the moon to die.

With Tuvok's help, the children elude the search team. Later, Alcia informs Janeway that they have found Tuvok's crashed shuttle on the moon, which they consider sacred ground. She orders Janeway to remove her surviving crew member immediately.

The next morning, hysterical Tressa claims that Elani and Corin have vanished. In a nearby cave, Tuvok finds their clothes, but not the children. During a break in the atmospheric turbulence, Tuvok manages to send a brief

*The stardate listed was taken from the shooting script, as it is not mentioned in the aired episode.

Tuvok tries to work while under prying eyes. DANNY FELD

message to *Voyager*. Unable to transport him to the ship, Janeway and Paris are forced to take a shuttlecraft to rescue him. Immediately after the shuttle leaves *Voyager*, a Drayan shuttle begins pursuit in an attempt to keep them from landing on the sacred site.

As the Drayan search party surrounds Tuvok and Tressa, Janeway and Paris arrive. Tuvok refuses to let the Drayans take the child, but he is stunned when Alcia reveals that Tressa is actually 96 years old. Among the Drayans, the aging process is reversed, and Tressa was not brought there to be killed, but to die a natural death. After the miscommunications are cleared up and Alcia learns how calming Tuvok had been for the children, she allows him to stay with Tressa to comfort her in her final moments. Despite their initial conflict, it turns out that the *Voyager* crew has made new friends in the Drayans.

SENSOR READINGS: The warp core is designed to operate for up to three years before refueling (a fact that will come into play in "Demon"). The reaction chamber is equipped with a compositor that allows the crew to recrystallize the dilithium. ▪ According to the Doctor, sickbay's research abilities are the most advanced in Starfleet—at least they were at the time the ship was launched. ▪ Tuvok places a stasis field around Ensign Bennet's body to protect it from harm. ▪ The away teams are searching for polyferranide, which is the same material they were searching for in "Tattoo." At that time, they did receive some of the material, but not as much as they needed. Presumably they make a trade for the remaining quantity when the relations with the Drayans improve. There is a vein of polyferranide three kilometers long on one of the Drayan moons.

SHUTTLE TRACKER: The crash landing finds Tuvok's shuttle nearly destroyed, however it is salvageable. Janeway and Paris take a type-9 shuttle—presumably the *Cochrane*—to rescue him.

DELTA QUADRANT: According to Neelix, no one has had contact with the Drayans in decades. Their ancestors were brilliant scientists and engineers who were continually developing more efficient machines until the technology became more important than the people. Alcia believes that the society would have self-destructed if it were not for the Reformation. Her great-grandfather helped them eschew technology and, since that time, they have remained isolated to avoid the influence of those who might lead them back down the wrong path. They believe that physical matter is only an illusion and the body is not the true self, only a representation. Their connection to a "higher plane" is more important than their attachment to this brief existence, however real it may seem. ▪ "May this day find you at peace, and leave you with hope," is a traditional Drayan blessing from the ancient scrolls. ▪ Though she appears to be a child to the *Voyager* crew, Tressa is ninety-six. At her age, people become easily confused. Near the end of life, Drayans reach a stage of complete innocence and free themselves from all responsibilities to this life, so they can leave it peacefully. It is a normal biological process that begins the day they are created. The energy contained within their bodies remains cohesive for a limited number of years, and then it is released. They believe the moon (known as the *crysata*, or sacred ground) is where the very first spark of life was created and they are all compelled by a powerful instinct to return there at the end, to complete the cycle and rejoin the infinite energy. The attendants would have helped prepare her for her death if they had not died in the shuttle crash. ▪ There is electrodynamic

"FALOR'S JOURNEY"

*I have never understood the practice in some cultures of describing ferocious creatures
in an attempt to lull children to sleep.*

Tuvok, "Innocence"

In contrast to some of the Brothers' Grimm more horrific tales, "Falor's Journey" is a Vulcan tale of enlightenment, consisting of 347 verses. What follows is the abridged version Tuvok shares with the "children" to calm their nerves so they will sleep.

"Falor was a prosperous merchant,
who went on a journey to gain greater awareness.
Through storms he crossed the Voroth Sea
To reach the clouded shores of Raal
Where old T'Para offered truth.
He traveled through the windswept hills
And crossed the barren Fire Plains
To find the silent monks of Kir.
Still unfulfilled, he journeyed home
Told stories of the lessons learned
And gained true wisdom by the giving."

Tuvok recounts "Falor's Journey" to pacify the "children." DANNY FELD

---

turbulence in the ionosphere surrounding the Drayan moon. A thermal inversion gradient causes unusually strong and unpredictable currents in the upper levels of the atmosphere. Those currents cause Tuvok's shuttle to crash and interfere with *Voyager*'s transporter and communications. The Drayans use some kind of dielectric field to protect their shuttles from the turbulence. Paris generates the same kind of field with the shuttle's warp coils so he and Janeway can fly through the turbulence.

ALPHA QUADRANT: The Federation consists of over 150 different worlds that have agreed to share their knowledge and resources in peaceful cooperation. ▪ Starfleet rations are concentrated, vitamin-enriched nutritional supplements. ▪ Vulcan children learn to detach themselves from their emotions at an early age. Vulcans believe that a person's *katra*, or soul, continues to exist after the body dies. When Tuvok was younger, he accepted it without question. In recent years, he has experienced doubts, though he does believe there is more within than science has yet explained. Vulcans consider death to be the com-

pletion of a journey. The Vulcan lute is a five-stringed instrument, tuned on a diatonic scale. ▪ In the language of Chakotay's ancestors, the phrase "Peace in your heart, fortune in your steps," (pronounced Om-NAH-hoo-pez NYEETZ) is a traditional greeting.

PERSONAL LOGS: On Chakotay's initial first contact assignment his ship was sent to make contact with the Tarkannans. He studied all the information they had and pestered the captain into letting him be part of the diplomatic team. When he came face-to-face with the Tarkannan delegation, he made the traditional gesture for hello, not realizing that males and females of their race use different styles of movement, and accidentally propositioned the ambassador. ▪ Tuvok's children had already mastered several states of heightened awareness by the time they were the young age he believes the Drayan children to be. Tuvok used to play his lute and sing "Falor's Journey" to his four children when they could not sleep. His youngest son was particularly fond of the song. Tuvok can go several days without rest if

Minister Alcia reveals the significance of the Drayan moon.
ROBBIE ROBINSON

necessary. ▪ Kes has been coaching the Doctor on his diplomatic skills, which he proudly uses on the first prelate.

CREW COMPLEMENT: Ensign Bennet dies in the shuttle-craft.

THE THAW

EPISODE #139
TELEPLAY BY: **JOE MENOSKY**
STORY BY: **RICHARD GADAS**
DIRECTED BY: **MARVIN V. RUSH**

GUEST STARS

VIORSA	**THOMAS KOPACHE**
SPECTRE	**CAREL STRUYCKEN**
LITTLE WOMAN	**PATTY MALONEY**
KOHL PHYSICIAN	**TONY CARLIN**
KOHL PROGRAMMER	**SHANNON O'HURLEY**

SPECIAL GUEST STAR

THE CLOWN	**MICHAEL McKEAN**

STARDATE UNKNOWN

When *Voyager* comes across a planet that suffered an environmental catastrophe nineteen years earlier, the crew is surprised to pick up a hail from the deserted world. It turns out that the automated message came from the Kohl settlement, where a handful of members survived by going into artificial hibernation. The crew beams the hibernation pods aboard and finds two humanoids dead and three in deep stasis, their minds connected to a sensory system that is controlled by a computer. The Doctor reveals that the deceased pair died from heart failure, brought on by mental stress, which, he says could be evidence of extreme fear.

Hoping to learn how to revive the survivors, Kim and Torres enter the now vacant pods and are attached to the computer, which allows them to enter the colonists' dream state. They are thrown into an environment that resembles a bizarre carnival run by a malevolent Clown, whose followers quickly drag Kim to a guillotine.

Although the Clown spares Kim, the pair suddenly understands how the Kohl could literally be frightened to death in the surprisingly realistic situation. Because the Clown's survival depends on the colonist's minds remaining linked to the sensory system, the Kohl—and now Kim and Torres—cannot awaken because the Clown will not allow it. The computer has manifested the worst fears of their subconscious minds into the persona of the Clown, thus making them prisoners to that fear.

The Clown allows Torres to leave so she can warn the captain that if the hibernation pods are deactivated, everyone will die. While Janeway contemplates how to negotiate with the Clown, he begins a cruel game of mental torment on Kim. Since the Clown can read the minds of

Kes and Janeway hope they can rescue the Khol. ROBBIE ROBINSON

humanoids attached to the pods, the Doctor is sent to discuss the release of the hostages, but the Clown refuses to cooperate, especially since he cannot read the negotiator's mind. When Viorsa, one of the hostages, provides a clue to the Doctor to help them escape, Janeway mounts a rescue mission to free Kim and the Kohl settlers.

Unfortunately, the Clown catches on to Torres's attempts to disable his program. Infuriated, he puts Viorsa in the guillotine, where the frightened man succumbs to heart failure. To prevent more deaths, Janeway orders Torres to stop.

The captain comes up with a final offer for the Clown to trade the current captives for Janeway herself. He agrees, only to discover that his prize is actually a holographic image. Since it takes a few minutes before the Clown is able to read the participant's mind through the interface the settlers and Kim are freed before he is onto the ruse. With no one alive left to torment, fear is conquered and the Clown disappears forever.

SENSOR READINGS: According to Kim, the cargo bay has bad acoustics, and the fluid conduits running between the walls of the crew quarters conduct sound.

DELTA QUADRANT: The planet Kohl was once a major trading spot. EM signature indicates that a major solar flare occurred nineteen years ago radically changing the weather patterns and causing a glacial freeze. The planet was also hit by magnetic storms and extreme levels of radiation. The glaciers are now receding, and the biosphere is recovering. There is evidence of advanced technology: warp reactors, subspace transmitters, and nonfunctional communications satellites in orbit. Indications are that any attempt at an evacuation at the time of the solar flares would have been prevented by the atmospheric disturbances. The estimated population was approximately 400,000. Originally, five inhabitants managed to survive in a state of artificial hibernation programmed to end in fifteen years by which time the ecorecovery would have begun. They would attempt to rebuild their settlement. In the stasis unit their brains are interconnected in a complex sensory system controlled by a computer. Their minds are active, and encephalographic readings suggest they are dreaming. There is interactivity between their minds and the computer as it scans their brain functions and sends a data stream back to them. The computer uses bio-neural feedback from the participants' brains to create the environment. The system was sup-

Kim faces down his own fear. ROBBIE ROBINSON

posed to bring them out of hibernation four years ago, but the decision was not left entirely to the computer. The programmers wanted the people in the system to decide for themselves when it would be safe to come out. This was accomplished by a subroutine that periodically displayed atmospheric conditions to them. The optronic pathways control the basic elements of the environment. When Torres interrupts the optronic pathways, she disassembles the entire world and its characters, piece by piece, until the Clown realizes their plan. A holographic image of Captain Janeway is sent by the same technique they used to send the Doctor. The hologram is programmed to respond as Kathryn Janeway would while the captain is on the system, but not in stasis. They modify the pods so that she can be connected to the system without having to enter the environment, allowing the Clown to sense her brain activity without putting her in actual jeopardy.

ALPHA QUADRANT: Chulak of Romulus was defeated at Galorndon Core. ▪ Roller coasters are still in existence in the Alpha Quadrant.

PERSONAL LOGS: According to the Clown, Kim has a mind full of technical and operational thoughts and ideas

and he still misses his girlfriend, Libby, very much. Kim does not like being helpless and hates being considered the baby of the crew. When he was nine, his parents took him on a humanitarian mission to a colony that had suffered a radiation disaster. He wandered off by himself when they visited a hospital and saw people who were sick and dying. The image of an operation on a young girl still haunts him. He can never hit that G sharp on his clarinet in the Mozart concerto. Kim has been working with Lieutenant Susan Nicoletti on a new orchestral program for the holodeck.

Ensign Baytart's quarters are next to Kim's. ▪ Lieutenant Nicoletti plays the oboe, and Paris has apparently been "chasing after" her for six months.

EPISODE LOGS: The first half of the show teaser, in which Harry plays the clarinet in his quarters, was originally the teaser for "Death Wish," but it was cut from that episode.

TUVIX

EPISODE #140
TELEPLAY BY: KENNETH BILLER
STORY BY: ANDREW SHEPARD PRICE & MARK GABERMAN
DIRECTED BY: CLIFF BOLE

GUEST STARS

TUVIX	TOM WRIGHT
HOGAN	SIMON BILLIG

CO-STAR

SWINN	BAHNI TURPIN

STARDATE 49655.2

The hybrid Tuvix believes he possesses the best qualities of Tuvok and Neelix. DANNY FELD

On an away mission to locate nutritional supplements, Tuvok and Neelix find a promising native orchid. Later, when the crew beams them back to *Voyager* with samples of the flower, the pair never arrives. Instead, a single entity appears on the transporter platform. The Doctor confirms that this strange, but oddly familiar alien is actually a fusion of Tuvok and Neelix. With all the memories and abilities of the pair, the new crew member decides to name himself "Tuvix."

The senior officers meet and conclude that the symbiogenetic properties of the orchids the pair carried during transport caused the merger of their biological matter on a molecular level, creating Tuvix. After the meeting, Tuvix attempts to adjust to his new identity and find his own place on the ship, while Kes tries to adjust to him. Although she is drawn to Tuvix, she misses Neelix deeply and is unsettled by the amalgam's affection for her.

After Paris and Torres gather more samples of the alien orchid, they confirm the method of Tuvix's creation by beaming together new plant hybrids, but are unsuccessful in their attempts to reverse the process. The Doctor admits he is not optimistic about bringing Tuvok and Neelix back as separate individuals. On hearing this, Kes mourns the loss of two men who meant so much to her.

Kes tells Janeway that despite Tuvix's wonderful qualities, she is not ready to let go of Neelix. Two weeks pass, and Tuvix settles into life aboard the ship. In time, Kes reaches out to him and apologizes for being distant. Just as it looks as if everyone has adjusted to *Voyager*'s new crew member, the Doctor announces that he has devised a way to restore him to his two original components. There is just one problem—Tuvix does not want to die— even if it means allowing the other two men to live.

Tuvix argues that he has a right to life, and that restoring Tuvok and Neelix amounts to his execution, while Janeway counters that her two merged crewmen have the same rights. The Doctor refuses to take Tuvix's life against his will, so in the end, Janeway is forced to take responsibility for performing the procedure. Tuvok and Neelix are fully restored, but Janeway's relief is tempered by the weight of her decision to end Tuvix's life.

SENSOR READINGS: There is a minor glitch in the transporter's molecular imaging scanners. They try narrowing the annular confinement beam to correct it. After Kim runs a diagnostic on the bio-filters and transporter logs they confirm that the glitch did not interfere with the beam out. ▪ Among the flowers grown in the airponics bay are prize-winning chrysanthemums and garden variety clematises. ▪ Tuvix attempts to conduct a field test of the aft sensor array. ▪ Sickbay is on Deck 5.

DELTA QUADRANT: Initial scans of the planet show a variety of flower that may prove to be a valuable nutritional supplement. According to Paris, the weather on the planet gets nasty at night.

ALPHA QUADRANT: A traditional Vulcan funeral dirge

begins with the line, "Oh, starless night of boundless black . . ." Neelix says that it is the most cheerful song he could find in the Vulcan database.

PERSONAL LOGS: Janeway prefers Tuvix's cooking to Neelix's. ▪ Tuvok appreciates nature, causing Neelix to call him a nature lover. Tuvok wrote letters to Janeway when he was temporarily assigned to Jupiter Station. Janeway has always found his writing to be concise, efficient, and thoughtful. ▪ Tuvix continues to carry Tuvok's rank of lieutenant. He accidentally refers to Kes as "sweeting," which is Neelix's nickname for her. ▪ On Wednesdays, Neelix cooks Kes's favorite meal, Trellian crepes. ▪ Kes lights two Ocampan prayer tapers, one for Neelix and one for Tuvok. ▪ The Doctor is programmed to do no harm and cannot perform the separation on an unwilling Tuvix.

MEDICAL REPORT: Tuvix is formed when all of Tuvok and Neelix's biological matter merges on a molecular level. All vital signs are stable, and he has the memories of both men, but a single consciousness. Initial microcellular scans show no cause or method of separation. Kes performs a full bio-spectral analysis in the science lab while the Doctor examines the genetic data. A biochemical analysis shows that the orchid contains the same elements as many plants—chloroplasts, lysosomal enzymes, cytoplasmic proteins—but it is the presence of lysosomal enzymes that could be evidence of symbiogenesis, which provides the explanation for their situation. Symbiogenesis is a rare reproductive process where symbiogenetic organisms merge with a second, hybrid, species. For example, Andorian amoebas are able to merge with other single-cell organisms to form a third unique species. Neelix and Tuvok were broken down to a microcellular level during transport, and enzymes that cause symbiogenesis interacted with their DNA while they were in the matter stream. The Doctor initially makes over one hundred attempts to reverse the symbiogenesis using the medical transporter. With each attempt there is complete cellular collapse since the genetic codes of the test flowers were so scrambled that the targeting scanners couldn't recognize the original patterns. Eventually, the Doctor develops a radioisotope that attaches itself to the DNA of one of the merged species, but not the other. To reverse the process of symbiogenesis they must beam out the selected DNA and segregate the two merged species. To do this they have to modify the molecular imaging scanners, and compensate for the higher levels of radiation.

EPISODE LOGS: Tuvok's and Neelix's appreciation for orchids was first introduced in "Tattoo." ▪ The events of this story take place over a two-week period.

Tuvix asks Kes to speak with the captain on his behalf. ROBBIE ROBINSON

RESOLUTIONS

EPISODE #141

WRITTEN BY: JERI TAYLOR

DIRECTED BY: ALEXANDER SINGER

GUEST STARS	
DANARA PEL	SUSAN DIOL
HOGAN	SIMON BILLIG
SWINN	BAHNI TURPIN

STARDATE 49690.1

During an away mission on an uninhabited planet, an insect bites Janeway and Chakotay, infecting them with a virus. After working nonstop for a month, the Doctor is unable find a cure, and the two offi-

The captain and her first officer go through their supplies.
ROBBIE ROBINSON

to rendezvous with a Vidiian convoy, in the hopes that the aliens' advanced medical knowledge might include a cure for the virus. Tuvok refuses, since Janeway has forbidden the crew to contact the Vidiians.

On the planet, Janeway works to develop a cure for the virus, while Chakotay tries to make their lives comfortable. Realizing that their regular command structure is inappropriate for the current conditions, Janeway asks Chakotay to refer to her by her first name. Uncomfortable with the request, Chakotay eventually does accept it and their relationship takes a new turn. Kathryn is equally uncomfortable with the gifts of a bathtub and other items that Chakotay builds for her, since they signify that the pair may be on the planet for a long time. After a violent plasma storm strikes the planet and her research equipment is destroyed, she must come to grips with the fact that they are unlikely to ever leave the world. As a result, she shifts from trying to examine one of the local primate life-forms to an attempt at befriending the animal.

With the *Voyager* crew's morale worsening every day, Kes helps Tuvok realize that sometime a captain must disobey an order for the welfare of his crew. He contacts the Vidiians and asks them to put *Voyager* in touch with the Vidiian physician Danara Pel. She quickly responds with an offer to share the cure to the mysterious virus. They arrange a rendezvous for the next day.

As Janeway and Chakotay continue to draw closer, responding to the intimacy of their situation, *Voyager* goes to meet the Vidiians who use the opportunity to set

cers resign themselves to remaining on the planet, which has an environment that blocks the progression of the terminal disease. After supplies are beamed to them from *Voyager,* Janeway places Tuvok in command of the ship and gives the crew orders to proceed to the Alpha Quadrant.

The decision to leave the captain and first officer behind weighs heavily on the crew, and they urge Tuvok

Chakotay and Janeway take shelter from the plasma storm. ROBBIE ROBINSON

a trap for them. In the midst of the attack, Pel contacts the Doctor and offers him the serum, expressing her own surprise at the violence. Tuvok is able to drop the shields long enough for them to beam it onboard and to eject an antimatter container from the ship. Then they fire a torpedo at the container and the resulting explosion incapacitates the Vidiian ships long enough for *Voyager* to escape. Tuvok retrieves the captain and Chakotay.

SENSOR READINGS: Among the items left on the planet with Janeway and Chakotay are a modular shelter, weapons, tricorders, a replicator, petri dishes, protein analyzers, DNA sequencers, and other items for research and survival. When they leave the planet, they do not take the shelter. *Voyager* can stay in contact with them for approximately thirty-six hours after leaving orbit. ▪ A total of three torpedoes are fired during the conflict with the Vidiians. Two torpedoes are fired from aft torpedo bays at the Vidiian ships, and one is fired at the antimatter container dropped from the ship (the resulting explosion disables all three Vidiian ships). ▪ An osteogenic stimulator is used to set a broken arm. ▪ After they return to *Voyager*, Janeway asks Chakotay to see if the problem with the prefire chamber temperature has been fixed in their absence.

SHUTTLE TRACKER: An unseen type-9 shuttle is also left on the planet with Janeway and Chakotay. Although no mention is made of it being retrieved, it can be assumed it was.

DELTA QUADRANT: Janeway and Chakotay are infected by the virus when bitten by a burrowing insect. Something in the planet's environment shields them from the effects of the virus. The Vidiians possess an antiviral agent that will counteract the virus. ▪ The planet's plasma storm is not recognized by their tricorders.

PERSONAL LOGS: Janeway and Chakotay were left in stasis on the planet for seventeen days, while the Doctor worked on a cure. Janeway hates to cook, believes she looks better in beige than gray, and considers taking baths to be her favorite way of relaxing. When she was young, her parents took the family on backpacking trips as a way of keeping a connection to their pioneer roots. She also grew up around farmers because her parents insisted she and her sisters learn some basic gardening skills. At the time, she hated both the camping and farming, but now she finds gardening to be very satisfying. ▪ Chakotay cooks, and constructs a bathtub and a headboard for Janeway. His father had him build log cabins when he

was growing. His people have a saying: "Even the eagle must know when to sleep." ▪ Kim is temporarily relieved of duty for arguing with Tuvok on the bridge. ▪ The Doctor does not deactivate himself for a month while looking for a cure to the virus. Danara Pel refers to him by the name, Shmullus, which she gave him when they met. ▪ Kes's father died just after she had turned one year old. Kes equates her relationship with Tuvok to that of her relationship with her father.

EPISODE LOGS: The time frame for this episode takes place over two months.

BASICS, PART I

EPISODE #142
WRITTEN BY: MICHAEL PILLER
DIRECTED BY: WINRICH KOLBE

SPECIAL GUEST STAR

ENSIGN SUDER	BRAD DOURIF

GUEST STAR

CULLUH	ANTHONY DeLONGIS
TEIRNA	JOHN GEGENHUBER
SESKA	MARTHA HACKETT
KOLOPAK	HENRY DARROW

CO-STARS

KAZON #1	SCOTT HAVEN
COMPUTER VOICE	MAJEL BARRETT

STARDATE UNKNOWN

While Tuvok works to rehabilitate the unstable Crewman Suder, Chakotay receives a desperate subspace message from Seska. She has given birth to the child that was fathered with his stolen DNA, and she claims that Maje Culluh is going to take her son away.

Chakotay is torn. Knowing Seska is untrustworthy, he fears she could be leading *Voyager* into a trap. But the spirit of his father helps him realize that if it is truly his child, he owes the baby his help. They set out to find Seska, and en route, *Voyager* receives a distress call from a Kazon shuttle manned by Teirna, one of Seska's aides. The injured Kazon reports that Culluh killed Seska when he found out the child was not his own. Teirna managed to survive by bribing a guard and stealing a shuttle.

Voyager heads for the Gema IV colony, where, according to Teirna, Culluh has sent Chakotay's son to be

Chakotay suspects that Teirna knows more about the attacks than he is telling. ROBBIE ROBINSON

raised as a servant. Along the way, the starship experiences several small Kazon attacks that focus on the secondary command processors on Deck 12. Although the damage is relatively minor, the pattern of the attacks does raise their suspicions. When Janeway tells Paris to alter their course, the ship is suddenly confronted with eight large Kazon vessels, clearly attempting to coerce them into a different direction. Unwilling to be manipulated, Janeway decides to intercept the lead Kazon vessel.

Using some deception of its own, *Voyager* manages to send most of the vessels at different targets, leaving only the lead vessel to fight. As the battle intensifies, Teirna deliberately triggers a massive explosion using chemicals smuggled aboard in his own body, sacrificing his life to damage the ship. The tactic also serves to destroy *Voyager*'s decoy, and three of the previously distracted Kazon vessels return to attack. Paris quickly boards a shuttlecraft to seek help from a neighboring Talaxian colony, but his ship is hit by Kazon fire, and *Voyager* loses contact with him.

As Kazon intruders board the crippled starship, Janeway attempts to initiate the self-destruct sequence.

But the damage to the secondary command processors renders the sequence inoperative, revealing the plot behind the earlier attacks. With no other options, the captain is forced to surrender. A victorious Culluh and Seska, who is still very much alive, take command of the ship while the Doctor secretly deactivates himself for twelve hours. The Kazon then strand the crew on a primitive planet and depart, unaware that the Doctor has reactivated himself and he is not alone. In their earlier search of the ship, the Kazon overlooked the fact that Suder is still on board.

SENSOR READINGS: *Voyager* can stay in communications range with the Talaxian mining colony on Prema II for about forty hours at the average speed of warp 2. In preparation for an encounter with the Kazon, Tuvok recommends a full diagnostic of their tactical array prior to the start of the mission. Janeway orders the crew to cut power to all systems to minimum requirements so they do not show up on scanners. In anticipation of a trap the crew programs the deflector grid to use a method of echo displacement to fool the Kazon scanners into seeing multiple decoy images like these. They also install holoemitters along the hull, with parabolic mirrors to enlarge the images as they are reflected into space so they can project holographic ships. The process uses up a lot of the power reserves. ■ The crew fires a minimum of three photon torpedoes during the encounter, further decreasing their supply. ■ An Autonomic Response Analysis (ARA) is a form of "lie detector" that depends on making a baseline comparison with the known response for a given species. It cannot be used with any of the new species of the Delta Quadrant because there is no record from which to make the comparison. ■ The Doctor orders forty milligrams of pulmozine to combat the noxious gases inhaled by Teirna.

DAMAGE REPORT: Four preliminary Kazon attacks focus on *Voyager*'s starboard ventral section, affecting secondary command systems. With these systems offline Janeway is unable to set the ship's auto-destruct sequence. Damage to the ship is extensive and includes the following: EPS power supplies and isolinear controllers are offline, Deck 12 is a shambles, and minor damage is reported on Deck 14. Following the massive discharge on Deck 8 caused by the explosion, they lose a primary plasma conduit and experience power failures all over ship. They lose power to the new holodeck grid and the reactant injector controls are damaged. Starboard targeting scanners are offline, and they are unable to go to warp because the containment field generator has been

The Kazon take over *Voyager*. ROBBIE ROBINSON

damaged. Fires are detected on Decks 12 and 15, Sections A4 through C18. Navigational array is offline, and power to forward phasers is lost. The driver coil assembly is destroyed and impulse engines are offline. The ship is boarded through the shuttlebays.

SHUTTLE TRACKER: The type-9 shuttle Paris takes to get reinforcements is presumed destroyed by the Kazon, but the report will later prove to be unfounded.

DELTA QUADRANT: The molecular variance residual on Teirna's shuttle is evidence of disruptive blasts with a Kazon signature. There were toxic nitrogen tetroxide fumes in the cabin. Cullah intends to raise the newborn child to become a Nistrim *askara*. The word *askara* goes undefined, but it can be assumed that it is some form of leader. To get to the Gema IV Colony, Teirna suggests they avoid the Tenarus cluster, as the Kazon-Nistrim fleet is stationed in that location. Teirna shows signs of polycythemia, a blood disorder, which is actually the result of

the chemicals in his bloodstream that will serve as the explosive.

The crew is left behind on a planet in the Hanon system that, at first glance, appears to be a class-M planet in a Pliocene stage of evolution (similar to Earth several million years ago). The planet is seismically active and inhabited by humanoids in an early stage of development.

PERSONAL LOGS: An ancestor of Chakotay's was conceived from a rape by white conquerors. His name was Ce Acatl, and he became a great leader of their people. ∎ The Doctor sets his medical holographic automatic recall for twelve hours so he can hide from the Kazon.

Suder's secured quarters are on Deck 8. His previous mind-meld with Tuvok led to his interest in horticulture. Suder cross-breeds orchids to create a new breed, which he names the Tuvok orchid. He asks permission to turn his quarters into an airponics laboratory and has discussed the matter with Kes, who he said is interested in the development.

COMMANDER CHAKOTAY

INT. MAQUIS SHIP—CLOSE ON A TATTOOED FACE of an intense Native American man in his late thirties. This is CHAKOTAY. Suddenly an explosion illuminates his face.

—Chakotay's first appearance in "Caretaker"

It is said that one can tell a lot about a person by the way he functions under pressure. In the opening scenes of "Caretaker," the intense Native American man was functioning under the immense pressure of being overwhelmed by a far superior Cardassian ship that his Maquis crew was trying to outrun and outgun. The odds against them, Chakotay coolly took suggestions from his trusted bridge crew, finally settling on Torres's suggestion to drop their weapons and route all available power to the impulse engines. Commanding and powerful, his somewhat informal demeanor made it clear from his first scenes that Chakotay was a different kind of officer from the clean-cut Starfleet mold. Yet, there was definitely a formal training behind this captain, as came to light later in the show.

Chakotay was one of the few Maquis characters who did receive training at Starfleet Academy, which was a prerequisite to accepting him in the position of first officer aboard a starship. When Janeway offered to combine the crews, Chakotay knew that alone—and without their ship—the Maquis did not have a chance in the Delta Quadrant. Without appearing weak, he put aside his feelings about the Starfleet organization he once abandoned to ensure that his own crew would be safe. Stepping down to accept an inferior position, he proudly made the decision to serve under Janeway.

Though the tensions between Starfleet and Maquis crewmen diminished rather quickly, Chakotay continued to assume a protective position over his original crew even through the seventh season as seen in "Repression." However he never let those feelings get in the way of the merging of the two crews. Personally, his own feelings toward Starfleet evolved to the point where Chakotay had fully accepted the principles of a Starfleet officer in "Equinox." At that time he convinced the captain that *her* behavior did not reflect Starfleet's training and beliefs.

Of the senior staff, Chakotay was, naturally, closest to his fellow Maquis, Torres, and he shared some powerful moments with her throughout the seasons. At various times he was at odds with both Paris and Tuvok because of his history with the conn officer and the security chief's infiltration of his Maquis crew. However, he did make amends with both men and often teamed with Tuvok when challenging the captain. Throughout the various episodes, Chakotay interacted with the rest of the senior staff largely in the traditional role of the first officer as the one responsible for handing out duty assignments. But, without the burden of command, Chakotay often let down his guard to connect with his crewmates on a more personal level.

Ethan Phillips: Chakotay always has a bemused attitude around Neelix. Although I have to say that he is the one who convinced Neelix not to kill himself ("Mortal Coil"). Chakotay is the one that convinced him to stay alive and

ROBBIE ROBINSON

help Naomi, so Neelix owes him his life in that way. The fact that Chakotay took the time and saw that as something important . . . of course he would, he's a noble character.

The one area of Chakotay's life that had been most difficult was definitely his romantic entanglements. These troubles begin early on in the series with the already concluded affair between himself and Seska. Although the relationship was over by the time the events of the series aired, their bond was the cause for much tension between the characters, and ultimately between the crew and the Kazon. The scenes in which he agonized over the child he believed to be his own showed great depth for his character and reflected his upbringing. His string of romantic misfortunes continued as he often fell for the wrong women—a former Borg who ultimately used him ("Unity"), a member of an enemy race in disguise ("In The Flesh"), and a woman who was forced to forget everything about their relationship ('Unforgettable").

It was his hardly explored feelings for the captain that were most telling in his development. The chemistry between Chakotay and Janeway was unmistakable, yet it would have been inappropriate for them to act on it. In "Resolutions" it was ultimately his decision—out of respect—not to pursue her even though the feelings would not diminish. As the series continued, the couple shared dinners and even experienced feelings of jealousy with regards to other suitors. However, Chakotay's promise not to confuse their professional relationship held true to the end, when he began an affair with another crew member, Seven of Nine.

The most explored facet of Chakotay's personality was obviously his Native American heritage. Though his tribal ancestry was never specified we did learn much about his background in episodes like "Initiations," "Basics" and especially "Tattoo." These episodes also highlighted his formerly troubled relationship with his father which ultimately led him to make his decision to leave Starfleet and fight for the Maquis.

ROBBIE ROBINSON

Brannon Braga: My only real big regret is the first officer. He suffered from first officer's syndrome, which is what Riker had. He's sitting next to the captain and when you're sitting next to the captain you don't do much because you're not the captain. There's nothing worse than being second-in-command. It's better to be an ensign on a television show.

As Chakotay, Robert Beltran was second-in-command of the ship and the series itself. The noble character did have many adventures in which he could shine as both a hero and a fighter. The intensity Beltran brought to his character and the series was highlighted in such episodes as "Nemesis" and "Memorial," wherein Chakotay's Maquis warrior background played an integral role. It was, however, the slightly less intense episode "Shattered" that truly highlighted how his character had grown over the course of the series. Evolving from a rebellious enemy to the captain's most trusted advisor, Chakotay exemplified the true personification of character growth.

SEASON THREE

The third season of *Star Trek: Voyager* opens with the crew bidding a fond farewell to the Kazon. As with the first season's production schedule, several episodes (143–146) that were shot during season two were held over for airing in season three. Beyond the departure of the Kazon, "Basics, Part II" also represents the last episode written by one of the three series creators, Michael Piller. The co-executive producer moved into the role of creative consultant to allow time for his work on the script for *Star Trek: Insurrection,* as well as developing his own, non–*Star Trek* projects.

Voyager would now turn its focus toward single-episode villains and new and different alien races. The crew finds their way back to Earth, albeit Earth of 1996, in "Future's End" (Parts I & II). This is the first of the two-part episodes produced to air during the all-important sweeps ratings period, soon to become an annual event on *Voyager,* and eventually leading to the two-hour movie nights in future seasons.

"Voyager *started its turnaround for us, personally and creatively, when we did the very first two-parter because we said to ourselves let's start having fun. What's fun to write is fun to watch and we've been toiling with the Maquis storyline and we've been having these angst-ridden characters deal with being lost and it's not much fun to write anymore and we felt that it couldn't possibly be all that fun to watch. Let's let it all hang out and do something insane . . . What seemed more insane back then—but if you hear about it now it sounds ridiculously antiquated—*Voyager *in 1996! And we conceived of big action sequences and big concepts with an epic villain. Henry Starling was our first great Voyager villain. It sounds like a pat on the back, but I think we created great single individual villains and that was the first one, played by Ed Begley Jr. And we crafted big action set pieces like the chase between a Mack truck, a shuttlecraft, and a Volkswagon van. Things that we never would have thought of even attempting on* The Next Generation *or in the early days of* Voyager. *It's crazy, but we did it and we pulled it off and it was a charming, fun episode."*
—BRANNON BRAGA

The new season marks the celebration of thirty years of *Star Trek*. In honoring the milestone anniversary of the *Star Trek* franchise, both *Voyager* and *Deep Space Nine* developed special episodes featuring the crew of the original series *Starship Enterprise*. Using the film *Star Trek VI: The Undiscovered Country* as a jumping-off point for the story, Sulu (George Takei) and Janice Rand (Grace Lee Whitney) make an appearance in the episode "Flashback." The episode reveals that Tuvok served on the *U.S.S. Excelsior* during the historic period prior to the Federation-Klingon peace treaty.

"It was a rush. It was a great honor and fun to work with George Takei in "Flashback." I really appreciated the clever aspect of the storyline being placed inside a part of the ship from a certain angle that we never saw in the original film. Being able to play that out and being tied to that story so directly was great."

—TIM RUSS

And finally, season three witnesses something the audience had been expecting since learning that *Voyager* would be lost in the Delta Quadrant: the Borg. Eventually, *Voyager* would grow to embrace the Borg as the prime villains of the series, but things start out slowly in this season before escalating to the point where they are ultimately responsible for the crew getting home.

BASICS, PART II

EPISODE #146

WRITTEN BY: MICHAEL PILLER

DIRECTED BY: WINRICH KOLBE

SPECIAL GUEST STAR

ENSIGN SUDER	BRAD DOURIF

GUEST STARS

CULLUH	ANTHONY De LONGIS
SESKA	MARTHA HACKETT
ENSIGN WILDMAN	NANCY HOWER
HOGAN	SIMON BILLIG
KAZON	SCOTT HAVEN
PRIMITIVE ALIEN	DAVID COWGILL
PRIMITIVE ALIEN	MICHAEL BAILEY SMITH
KAZON	JOHN KENTON SHULL

CO-STARS

PAXIM	RUSS FEGA
NARRATOR/COMPUTER VOICE	MAJEL BARRETT

STARDATE 50032.7

Stranded by the Kazon on a desolate planet ravaged by earthquakes and vicious cave creatures, the crew seeks food and shelter. Early on they learn of the dangers of the planet when Hogan turns up missing with only his bloodied clothing left behind. At the

Suder realizes that he may be forced to kill. ROBBIE ROBINSON

same time, Paris, who managed to flee *Voyager* in a shuttle before the Kazon seized the ship, solicits help from the Talaxians.

On *Voyager,* the Doctor surprises Seska when he reveals that her newborn baby is not Chakotay's child after all—he's Culluh's. After she leaves sickbay, the Doctor discovers that he is not the only member of the crew left on the ship, as Crewman Suder, the sociopath whom Tuvok has been attempting to rehabilitate, is still aboard. The two join forces against the Kazon, but as they plot strategy, Suder expresses regret over the fact that he will probably need to kill Kazon to wrest control of *Voyager,* and he is afraid of returning to his violent ways.

On the planet, primitive humanoid natives kidnap Kes and Neelix. Chakotay and a rescue party free them, but during their getaway, they are forced to take cover in one of the dangerous caves. Another crewman is lost to the enormous eel-like creature that lives inside, before the rest of the team escapes, sealing off the opening as they exit.

As Paris heads back to *Voyager* with reinforcements, he sends a message to the Doctor, asking him to disable the secondary phaser couplings. Suder has been sabotaging *Voyager*'s systems from within, using an old Maquis trick to avoid detection, but the former Maquis Seska figures out that there is a saboteur aboard and confronts the Doctor. He claims that he is the only saboteur, and Seska disables his program before he can cripple the backup couplings, leaving Suder as the crew's last hope. After a prerecorded message from the Doctor gives him words of encouragement, Suder heroically disables the phasers before being killed by a Kazon.

Paris knocks out *Voyager*'s main phasers, and when Culluh tries to use the backup system, an overload caused by Suder's sabotage mortally wounds Seska and many of the Kazon on the bridge. Reaching for her son, Seska dies as Paris and the Talaxians board *Voyager.* Knowing he has lost, Culluh takes the baby with him and abandons ship. Paris regains control of the starship and goes back for the crew, who have in the meantime managed to survive a volcanic eruption while making friends with the natives. Later, Tuvok offers a Vulcan prayer of peace over Suder's body as Janeway sets a course for home.

SENSOR READINGS: The Doctor uses Emergency Medical Priority 114 to delete the signature of Suder's combadge from the system. ■ A portable thoron generator is used to treat radiation burns and can also be used to neutralize tricorder sensors. ■ The Kazon complete all repairs to *Voyager;* however, Suder sabotages the internal

Paris returns with Talaxian reinforcements. ROBBIE ROBINSON

scanner relays and the antimatter injector. Seska notes that there should have been a warning before the antimatter injector froze by either a drop in core temperature or a magnetic constriction alarm. Following Paris's plan, Suder has the computer block the discharge from the backup phaser power couplings. When Paris takes out the primary couplings, the backup couplings overload when the Kazon switch over to them. ■ The Doctor suggests five cc's of improvoline to calm Suder. ■ The Kazon use escape pods to leave the ship. ■ All of *Voyager*'s propulsion and navigational systems are functioning within normal parameters when the crew returns to the ship.

SHUTTLE TRACKER: Believed to be destroyed, Paris and his shuttle are fine, although the craft's stabilizer acceleration sensors are damaged.

DELTA QUADRANT: On the planet, the crew finds a nest with eggs and a cucumberlike vegetable that grows on a vine. Neelix prepares a beetle stew. Chakotay creates solar

THE KAZON

"Their biological and technological distinctiveness was unremarkable. They were unworthy of assimilation."
"I didn't realize the Borg were so discriminating."
"Why assimilate a species that would detract from perfection?"
Seven of Nine and Neelix, "Mortal Coil"

One of the few races actually rejected for assimilation by the Borg, the Kazon prove to be a surprising threat to the *Voyager* crew for much of their first two years in the Delta Quadrant. Though they even manage to take over the ship for a short time, the Kazon failed to take a hold on the audience and even those on the production staff. One possible reason for the lack of interest in the aliens is simply that they did not have the one quality indicative of all *Star Trek* aliens—a common goal.

The most popular aliens in the *Star Trek* universe all have well-developed extensive histories and a wealth of different character traits, but at the basis of each species is a single motivation, a shorthand by which they can be explained. The Klingons live for honor. The Vulcans strive for logic. The Romulans are secretive. The Borg assimilate. But the Kazon have no unifying theme. In fact, the entire identity of the Kazon sects is based on the fact that they are against one another, giving them the overtones of a gang.

Upon their first meeting in "Caretaker," *Voyager* starts off on bad footing with the Kazon-Ogla sect by stealing their Ocampa slave, Kes. Though the sect, led by Maje Jabin, has spacefaring vehicles with remarkable firepower, they also set up a mining facility on a planet without the ability to produce water, making the substance a valuable commodity. From the start, they are set up as a weak race in that they choose to suffer by remaining on a planet that is lacking in one of the basic requirements for life.

ROBBIE ROBINSON

Voyager's second encounter with the Kazon introduces new enemies in the form of Maje Culluh, of the Nistrim sect, and the revelation that the Cardassian, Seska, is onboard ("State of Flux"). Coupled with their first appearance, the Kazon's singular goal seems to be stealing *Voyager*'s technology. Seska gives a seemingly harmless replicator to the Kazon, leading to a horrendous accident destroying a Kazon ship. The duplicitous Seska is revealed; although, she manages to beam herself over to Culluh's vessel and escape.

Throughout the first two years of the series, the Kazon will do everything in their power to meet this goal of obtain-

stills, using the remains of Hogan's uniform, estimating that it will take a day for the stills to collect water. He also suggests they use hair as kindling to start fires and the crew fashions rudimentary weapons using what they find on the planet.

Eighty-nine Kazon are aboard *Voyager.* The Doctor notes that Seska's baby has Cardassian and Kazon DNA,

but no human DNA, which has a significantly different nucleotide sequence.

PERSONAL LOGS: Chakotay has never been good at starting fires and has never used a bow and arrow. ▪ Tuvok taught archery science for several years at the Vulcan Institute of Defensive Arts. ▪ The Doctor tells Seska that

ing technology. However, the goal itself is weak, since the audience knows they will not succeed in taking *Voyager* from its crew. This is coupled with the fact that there is no true nobility in theft. The Romulans, the Cardassians, and even the Borg may commit horrendous atrocities, but behind every action these villains take is some warped sense of their own noble cause. Their actions may be immoral, but they *believe* themselves to be in the right. The Kazon seem to be little more than thugs.

"Initiations" succeeds in building on the Kazon mythos and adding some depth to their character. Through their rite of passage in which a youth obtains his Kazon name, the child, Kar, explains that the Kazon once were slaves to the Trabe, until they rose up and rebelled twenty-six years ago. Now, the various sects of the Kazon, numbering around eighteen at the time, do battle with each other over their ever-changing borders. In a move that seems to emulate the motives of one of the more popular *Star Trek* races—the Klingons—Kar kills his leader/enemy, Maje Razik, to prove his worthiness to receive his Kazon name.

Though the Kazon demonstrate a misogynistic bent, Maje Culluh becomes the central Kazon villain when he follows Seska's plans and manages to obtain Federation technology ("Maneuvers"). Noting it was Jal Sankur who united the sects to overthrow the Trabe, Culluh plans to join together a band of the less powerful sects to take over *Voyager*. Thus, they begin to develop the Kazon's unifying theme.

The concept of uniting the sects continues in "Alliances," when, after repeated attacks, Janeway finally relents and agrees to consider siding with one or more of the sects in an attempt to obtain safe passage through the sector. Ultimately negotiations fail when Maje Culluh chooses to dictate terms rather than allow a woman to take control of the proceedings. As a result, Janeway ends the discussion and Seska warns Culluh that his attitudes toward women will ultimately be his undoing. Later, Janeway pursues a more palatable plan to unite the sects with their former oppressors, the Trabe. However, the Trabe prove to be just as untrustworthy as their former slaves and her actions ultimately make *Voyager* an even more mortal enemy of the Kazon.

Beginning with "Maneuvers," and culminating in "Investigations," the Kazon provide for one of the few concentrated story arcs of the series, with the traitorous Jonas reporting to Seska and various Kazon underlings. Again, Seska proves to be in charge of the operation, setting a trap against her former crewmates that ultimately fails. This arc provides one of the last examples of infighting among *Voyager*'s combined Federation/Maquis crew, but it still manages to forward the series attempt to evolve the Kazon.

With a common enemy in *Voyager* the Kazon eventually do unite and enact an attack plan that allows Culluh to take over the ship ("Basics, Part I"), and strand the crew on a hostile planet. The Kazon story arc comes to a natural conclusion once their goal is obtained. With the help of the Talaxians and Crewman Suder, the crew ultimately manages to take back the ship. With Seska dead, Culluh takes their child and leaves *Voyager* forever, as Janeway, the woman who led to his undoing, reclaims the bridge.

"I never cared much for the Kazon . . . They're just great big stupid giants."

—Kate Mulgrew

he does not have much experience lying, but his program is adaptive and he can learn. Obviously, he has already adapted, as he lies to her throughout the episode.

CREW COMPLEMENT: Hogan and an unnamed crewman are killed by the creature on the planet. Suder is killed by the Kazon.

EPISODE LOGS: Although Seska dies at the end of this episode, the character will return in "Worst Case Scenario" and "Shattered." ▪ Ensign Wildman's baby is featured in this episode; however, she remains unnamed.

SACRED GROUND

EPISODE #143
TELEPLAY BY: LISA KLINK
STORY BY: GEO CAMERON
DIRECTED BY: ROBERT DUNCAN McNEILL

GUEST STARS

GUIDE	BECKY ANN BAKER
OLD WOMAN	ESTELLE HARRIS
OLD MAN #2	KEENE CURTIS
OLD MAN #1	PARLEY BAER
THE MAGISTRATE	HARRY GROENER

STARDATE 50063.2

While touring the Nechani homeworld, Kes is rendered comatose by an energy field that protects one of the alien shrines. The local magistrate tells Janeway that Kes violated a holy place that only the Nechisti monks may enter after they have undergone a purification ritual to protect themselves from the energy field. When Neelix uncovers an ancient story of a king who went through the ritual to save his comatose son's life, Janeway requests permission to do the same.

The Nechisti Council, intrigued by the petition, approves Janeway's request. The Doctor implants a subdermal bioprobe to monitor her condition during the ritual in the hope that the information provided by the probe will lead to a cure for Kes. As a safety precaution, the probe also acts as a homing device; with only a tap, Janeway will be beamed back to the ship.

A guide meets Janeway at the sanctuary and leads her to a room where she finds three elderly people who admit they have been waiting there for as long as they can remember. With Kes's life in the balance, Janeway politely insists that the ritual begin. Taking Janeway from the

Kes looks forward to experiencing the Nechani temple. ROBBIE ROBINSON

waiting area, the guide hands her a rock and asks what she sees. Janeway says she sees a stone, and is told to keep looking. Hours and numerous grueling tests later, an exhausted Janeway is told to put her hand in a basket, where an unseen creature bites her.

On *Voyager,* the Doctor tracks the toxins from the bite as they course through Janeway's bloodstream, theorizing it might be the key to treating Kes. In a vision, Janeway asks the spirits to restore Kes's health, and her guide cryptically tells the captain that she already has what she needs to save Kes. Janeway returns to *Voyager,* where the Doctor prepares a cure from the toxins in Janeway's system. Yet when she applies it to Kes, her condition worsens. Baffled, Janeway confronts the guide. When Janeway realizes that her own impatience kept her from accepting the truth of the ritual, she is sent back to the waiting room.

The elderly council members chide Janeway, saying she has no faith in the spirits because she cannot scan them with her technology. They tell her that the only way to save Kes is to kill her by taking her back through the energy field. Janeway realizes that for this to work, she has to believe—if not in the spirits, then in her own faith that she can help Kes. Janeway carries her back into the shrine, where they are both hit by the mysterious energy and Kes is healed. On *Voyager* the Doctor explains that Janeway's altered biochemistry caused the healing; however, Janeway suspects that it may have been something a little more spiritual.

Janeway prepares herself for the ritual. ROBBIE ROBINSON

DELTA QUADRANT: While on the Nechani home world, the crew tours a sanctuary that honors the Nechani ancestral spirits. When Kes is injured, they are told that bringing scanning equipment to the sanctuary would show disrespect to the spirits. Later it is determined that there are 800 megajoules running through the shrine and the thoron radiation levels are off the scale. The Brothers of the Nechisti Order have devoted their lives to serving the Spirits. There is an agreement between the government and the Nechisti Council in which neither interferes with the other's practices. The shrine that injures Kes is the place where the monks go to receive the gift of purification or a cleansing of the soul. It is one of their most holy places. The Brothers prepare themselves with a sacred ritual during which they speak directly with the Ancestral Spirits. After that, they are able to enter the shrine safely. The energy field—an intense biogenic field—is a naturally occurring phenomenon. There is a story about a young prince who wandered into the shrine accidentally and went into a death sleep. Everyone said it

was the will of the Spirits. His father, King Nevad, refused to accept that, so he went through the ritual to seek an audience with the Spirits, and he pleaded for his son's life. The Spirits, in their infinite mercy, granted his request. Although Janeway forces herself to do more than necessary, the actual ritual involves being dressed in native robes and painting the face with markings before waiting with the Ancestral Spirits. The brothers believe that *nessets* are able to travel from their world into the spirit realm. And they serve as gatekeepers.

ALPHA QUADRANT: According to the Federation's cultural database, most traditional spirit quest ceremonies involve some kind of physical challenge, or test of endurance, to prove the mastery of spirit over body. The shamans of the Karis tribe on Delios VII practice a ritual that increases the electrical resistance of their skin. It protects them from plasma discharges in their sacred caves. ▪ It is standard procedure to carry arms on an away mission, but Janeway does not want to appear hostile and leaves her weapon behind.

PERSONAL LOGS: Janeway has always been driven to succeed, and as a child she worked out mathematical problems while other children played. She says that her sister is the artist in the family. ▪ Chakotay admits that he was disappointed when his mother explained the science behind the vision quest to him.

MEDICAL REPORT: In the early stages of her own ritual, Janeway's respiration and pulse remain steady, but there is a gradual buildup of lactic acid in her extensor muscles due to light strain. After the ritual becomes more intense there are significant increases in her respiration, neural peptides, and adenosine triphosphate levels, which suggests she is going through a grueling physical experience. She goes for over three days without sleep, but her vital signs remain normal, and she is fully conscious with complete motor control. Her entire biochemistry undergoes a series of unique interactions, forming an amino acid as a result of the breakdown of the *nesset*'s toxin in her bloodstream. ▪ As a result of the contact with the biogenic field, Kes's synaptic pathways undergo a severe neuroleptic shock that disrupts all cortical functions. The Doctor takes the information learned from Janeway's bioprobe and creates a program to analyze the immune mechanism and develop a treatment regimen, which ultimately fails. Later, he explains the cure when tricorder readings Commander Chakotay take at the shrine reveal traces of iridium ions. He believes they caused a temporary dielectric effect in the outer epidermal layers, which neutralized some of the biogenic energy enough to make the captain's altered biochemistry an effective defense. The metabolic treatment he administered protected Kes against the full impact of exposure to the field when the captain took her through. That exposure functioned like a natural cortical stimulator, and reactivated her synaptic pathways.

FALSE PROFITS

EPISODE #144

TELEPLAY BY: **JOE MENOSKY**

STORY BY: **GEORGE A. BROZAK**

DIRECTED BY: **CLIFF BOLE**

GUEST STARS	
ARRIDOR	**DAN SHOR**
KOL	**LESLIE JORDAN**
BARD	**MICHAEL ENSIGN**
KAFAR	**ROB LaBELLE**
SANDAL MAKER	**ALAN ALTSHULD**

CO-STAR	
MERCHANT	**JOHN WALTER DAVIS**

STARDATE 50074.3

After detecting evidence of an unstable wormhole in a nearby solar system, *Voyager*'s sensors find something even more unusual—evidence that a replicator from the Alpha Quadrant is in use on one of the planets. Janeway sends Paris and Chakotay down to the planet to investigate and they find a pair of Ferengi

Chakotay and Paris adorn themselves with native "lobes" before approaching the temple. B. D. MCLAUGHLIN

The Ferengi follow the Rules of Acquisition when arbitrating for their followers. B. D. MCLAUGHLIN

who are being worshiped as gods by the locals because of their advanced technology.

The crew learns that the Ferengi, Kol and Arridor, arrived in the Delta Quadrant seven years earlier, victims of an attempt to lay claim to an unreliable wormhole. With no way to return home, they settled on the primitive planet and took advantage of the population through the "Song of the Sages," a local myth predicting the arrival of Great Sages.

Unhappy about the exploitation of the unsophisticated people, Janeway beams the Ferengi aboard *Voyager*. The captain has the crew work on a way to draw the wormhole back to the area and the captain intends to use it to return *Voyager* and the two Ferengi back to the Alpha Quadrant. However, she reluctantly releases the pair after they persuade her that the sudden disappearance of Takar's "gods" would cause turmoil among the inhabitants.

Janeway realizes that the only way to get the Ferengi to leave the planet without causing chaos among the native population would be to persuade the Ferengi to leave on their own, after they have prepared the people for their departure. In an attempt to "out-Ferengi the

Ferengi," Janeway sends Neelix to the planet, disguised as the Ferengi grand proxy to inform the pair that they are being recalled by their leader, the grand nagus. The plan backfires when the Ferengi decide they would rather kill Neelix than give up their profits. To save himself, Neelix confesses his true identity.

After Chakotay and Paris have an opportunity to hear the final verse of the "Song of the Sages," a new plan is enacted. Drawing from the mythic prophecy that the gods will leave on "wings of fire" following the arrival of a "Holy Pilgrim," Neelix proclaims himself to be that pilgrim. *Voyager* fires three photon bursts to fulfill a line in the prophecy that says the gods will depart when three new stars appear in the sky.

Just as the crew's efforts to "attract" the wandering wormhole pay off, *Voyager* beams Kol and Arridor aboard, saving them and Neelix from the very literal "wings of fire." The Ferengi manage to escape in their shuttle and are pulled into wormhole, destabilizing the phenomenon before *Voyager* can follow. The crew may have saved a planet from exploitation, but they lost a chance to go home.

SENSOR READINGS: Neutrino scans are used to locate the wormhole. ▪ The crew launches a high resolution reconnaissance probe to gather information about the dress and appearance of the planet's population. ▪ The Ferengi reconfigured their matter/antimatter generator to produce an ionic disruption field around the temple square so they cannot be beamed away. Chakotay destroys the dampening field by firing a phaser at the generator.

DELTA QUADRANT: Based on the residual neutrino levels, the crew is able to estimate that the wormhole last appeared at least six months prior to their arrival. The dispersal pattern of the interstellar plasma shows that it is not fixed on this end, but rather seems to be traveling through space. A phase profile of the wormhole's neutrino emissions is run to confirm that it leads to the Alpha Quadrant. They detect a subspace instability at their current location that is a result of the wormhole's last appearance there. Bombarding the area of the subspace instability with verteron particles returns the wormhole to their location. The gravitational effects of the wormhole refract the tractor beam, making it impossible for *Voyager* to get a lock. The transporter targeting scanners are also out of phase, so they try setting the scanners to a narrow band subspace frequency. Ultimately, a graviton pulse from the Ferengi shuttle destabilizes the wormhole and knocks it off its axis, making it jump erratically on both ends.

The inhabited second planet in the solar system shows a class-M atmosphere and humanoid lifesigns. Metallurgic analysis indicates a preindustrial civilization similar to a bronze-age level of technology. Before the Ferengi came, their society was flourishing. ▪ The unit of money is a *frang*. ▪ Their holy icon is the Ferengi replicator. ▪ Artificial Ferengi ears are worn on necklaces. Fines are imposed if the talismans are not worn when visiting the temple.

ALPHA QUADRANT: According to Starfleet computer records, approximately seven years ago, the *U.S.S. Enterprise* NCC-1701-D hosted negotiations for ownership of the Barzan wormhole. Included among the bidding parties were two Ferengi, minor functionaries known as Arridor and Kol. The wormhole is fixed in the Alpha Quadrant, but in the Delta Quadrant, it jumps around and turned out to be worthless. The Ferengi, unaware of that fact, had attempted to secure the wormhole for themselves and were pulled into it and deposited in the Delta Quadrant. ▪ The Ferengi Rules of Acquisition unabridged and fully annotated edition includes all 47 Commentaries, all 900 Major and Minor Judgments, and all 10,000 Considered Opinions.

EPISODE LOGS: While Neelix was portraying the grand proxy, he stated that the 299th Rule of Acquisition is "Whenever you exploit someone, it never hurts to thank them. That way, it's easier to exploit them the next time." The rule does not really exist, and the Rules of Acquisition only go up to 285. ▪ Ethan Phillips previously played the Ferengi Dr. Farek in the *TNG* episode "Ménage à Troi." ▪ This episode follows the events played out in the *TNG* episode "The Price."

FLASHBACK

EPISODE #145

WRITTEN BY: BRANNON BRAGA
DIRECTED BY: DAVID LIVINGSTON

GUEST STARS

LT. COMMANDER RAND	GRACE LEE WHITNEY
VALTANE	JEREMY ROBERTS
EXCELSIOR HELMSMAN	BORIS KRUTONOG
KANG	MICHAEL ANSARA
and	
CAPTAIN SULU	GEORGE TAKEI

STARDATE 50126.4

As *Voyager* approaches a nebula rich in sirillium, Tuvok is plagued by visions of himself as a boy, trying to rescue a girl who is falling off a cliff—an event he does not recall experiencing. The Doctor suspects he is reliving a repressed memory, which can cause permanent brain damage in a Vulcan. The proper healing techniques call for the patient to mind-meld with a family member so the two can bring the memory into the Vulcan's conscious mind. Because of their long-standing friendship, Janeway agrees to meld with Tuvok, as she is the closest thing to a family member Tuvok has on board. Together, the pair journeys through his subconscious to relive the past.

The meld, though intended to take them back to his childhood to the time of the alleged encounter on the cliff, instead it takes Tuvok and Janeway back eighty years to the Vulcan's first assignment on the *Starship Excelsior*, then commanded by Captain Hikaru Sulu. As the pair tries to discover why they were taken to this memory, they have to participate in the events as they happened.

Captain Sulu, who served under the legendary James T. Kirk for many years, disobeys Starfleet orders in order to try and help Kirk and another old shipmate, Dr. McCoy, who have been imprisoned for the murder of the Klingon chancellor. On the way to assist them, the *Excelsior* passes through a nebula that looks similar to the one *Voyager* spotted prior to Tuvok's first flashback. Once again, Tuvok experiences the memory of the little girl falling, but this time he experiences erratic brain patterns that lead to convulsions.

On *Voyager,* the doctor revives Tuvok, and Janeway wonders what the little girl had to do with this period on the *Excelsior.* All Tuvok can recall is that the Klingons ambushed the starship in the nebula, forcing Sulu to abort the rescue mission.

Re-forming the mind-meld, Tuvok relives the Klingon attack. He recalls that during the battle he aided an injured crewman named Valtane, who died in Tuvok's arms. As he goes through this again, the Doctor notices that the Vulcan is again experiencing erratic brain patterns.

Unable to break the mind-meld between Tuvok and Janeway, the Doctor exposes Tuvok's brain to bursts of thoron radiation and in doing so, inadvertently discovers the truth. When Valtane died, a strange alien virus he had been carrying in his brain migrated to Tuvok's brain, camouflaging itself as a repressed memory. The Doctor increases the intensity of the radiation and is able to destroy the peculiar virus, leaving the minds of Tuvok and Janeway healthy. Afterward, the pair reflects on the earlier time in Starfleet history when space was still new for exploration, and, with a sense of nostalgia, Janeway admits that she now feels like she was a part of it too.

SENSOR READINGS: Engineering has been making adjustments to the plasma conduits to accommodate a new energy source and may have created a thermal surge in the galley systems. ▪ Sirillium is a highly combustible and versatile energy source. It can be useful as a warp plasma catalyst and can also be used to boost deflector shield efficiency. Torres intends to use the Bussard collectors to gather the sirillium. Janeway plans to convert Storage Bay 3 into a containment chamber so they can stockpile the sirillium. Storage Bay 3 was originally Neelix's pantry.

DELTA QUAQDRANT: *Voyager* encounters a class-17 nebula, detecting standard amounts of hydrogen and helium, and 7,000 parts per million of sirillium.

On Talax, it is traditional to share the history of a meal before you begin eating as a way of enhancing the

Tuvok relives his first Starfleet posting on the *Starship Excelsior,* under Captain Sulu. ROBBIE ROBINSON

culinary experience. Neelix's mother could make every course, and even every garnish, come alive by making it a character in a story.

ALPHA QUADRANT: The events of Tuvok's flashback occurred approximately eighty years earlier on Stardate 9521, while he was stationed under Captain Sulu on the *U.S.S. Excelsior* NCC-2000. This was at the time of the explosion of the Klingon moon, Praxis, which was the inciting incident that eventually led to the first Federation-Klingon Peace Treaty. Janeway claims that the portrait of Captain Sulu at Starfleet Headquarters looks nothing like the man. Tuvok explains that twenty-third-century holographic imaging resolution was less accurate than current standards. ▪ It took Janice Rand three years to be promoted from yeoman to ensign. ▪ The Azure nebula being surveyed by the *Excelsior* looks very similar to the one observed on *Voyager,* however, it is a class-11 nebula containing some sirillium but has few other similarities.

Tuvok's memory engrams in the dorsal region of the hippocampus are being disrupted by the virus, creating symptoms that resemble a Vulcan syndrome known as *t'lokan* schism. A repressed traumatic memory begins to resurface, a battle is waged between the Vulcan's con-

scious and the unconscious mind causing severe brain trauma. In extreme cases, the patient can literally lobotomize himself. There is no medical treatment for this condition. Vulcan psychocognitive research suggests that the patient initiate a mind-meld with a family member and the pair attempt to bring the repressed memory into the conscious mind. In advanced stages of *t'lokan* schism, memories and thought processes become distorted and confused. The family member, in this case Janeway, will act as a *pyllora,* or guide and counselor. She will help reconstruct the memory in its entirety and help the subject to objectify the experience. By processing the experience, rather than repressing it, he can begin to overcome fear, anger, and the other emotional responses, and to reintegrate the memory into the conscious mind. ▪ The Vulcan *keethera,* which translates to "Structure of Harmony," is a special set of building blocks used as a meditational aid. It helps to focus thought and refine mental control.

The Bolian tongue has a cartilaginous lining that protects it against even the most corrosive acid.

PERSONAL LOGS: Janeway considers herself to be the closest thing to family that Tuvok has aboard *Voyager.* She was under the incorrect belief that his first Starfleet post-

Through a Vulcan technique, Janeway becomes incorporated as part of Tuvok's memory. ROBBIE ROBINSON

MEDICAL REPORT: After Tuvok's first flashback episode his heart rate accelerates to 300 beats per minute and his adrenaline levels rise by 113 percent, with his neuroelectrical readings nearly jumping off the scale. The Doctor gives him a neurocortical monitor in order to record a complete encephalographic profile and alert sickbay if he has another traumatic experience. The monitor is worn on the back of his neck on the parietal bone. Tuvok spends fourteen hours in meditation.

EPISODE LOGS: Although this episode retells events from *Star Trek VI: The Undiscovered Country,* from the point-of-view of virus-created memory, it should be no surprise that upon review of the film, Tuvok is never actually seen on the bridge of the *Excelsior.* However, the writers did use a portion of the film as part of the Vulcan's memory. In the scene where the *Excelsior* is struck by the Praxis shock wave, Sulu's cup of tea falls to the deck and shatters. In the episode, we see Tuvok bring his captain that cup of tea.

THE CHUTE

EPISODE #147

TELEPLAY BY: KENNETH BILLER

STORY BY: CLAYVON C. HARRIS

DIRECTED BY: LES LANDAU

GUEST STARS

ZIO	DON McMANUS
LIRIA	ROBERT PINE
VEL	JAMES PARKS
PIT	ED TROTTA
RIB	BEANS MOROCCO

CO-STAR

PIRI	ROSEMARY MORGAN

STARDATE 50156.2

During shore leave on Akritiri, Paris and Kim are falsely accused of a terrorist bombing and sent to prison. Paris is already in the nightmarish alien jail when Kim arrives via a long metal chute. As if confinement in the brutal hellhole was not bad enough, Paris explains that the clamp every prisoner wears seems to affect the wearer's nervous system and cannot be removed.

Akritirian Ambassador Liria informs Janeway, that Paris and Kim have been imprisoned for a bombing that killed forty-seven people. The only "proof" of the crime is

ing was aboard the *Starship Wyoming.* ▪ Tuvok's first actual deep space assignment was aboard the *Starship Excelsior,* where her as one of several junior science officers. He was twenty-nine years old, and his father was also in Starfleet, stationed on the *Yorktown.* He joined Starfleet under pressure from his parents, but resigned his commission once his first assignment was complete because he considered the experience to be unpleasant. He left Starfleet for fifty years, during which time he returned to Vulcan and spent several years in seclusion, immersing himself in the Kolinahr, a rigorous discipline intended to purge all emotions. Six years into his studies, he began the *Pon farr* and took a mate (his wife, T'Pel), postponing his studies to raise his family. The experience helped him to better understand his parents, and their decision to send him to the Academy. Realizing that there were many things he could learn from humans and other species, he rejoined Starfleet to expand his knowledge of the galaxy.

Ensign Golwat is a female Bolian crew member.

Kim vows to protect his friend. ROBBIE ROBINSON

traces of trilithium found on their clothes. Although trilithium can be made from the dilithium *Voyager* uses to power its engines, Janeway emphatically denies that her people were involved. Under attack from the Akritirians, Janeway departs the area determined to find the real bombers.

Back in the prison, Paris and Kim plot an escape through the chute, which is protected by a deadly forcefield. But before they can enact the plan, a brutal inmate stabs Paris, critically wounding him. With no medical assistance available, Kim makes a deal with another inmate named Zio. In exchange for some supplies to clean up Paris's wound Kim agrees to take Zio with him when he disables the forcefield.

After deactivating the forcefield Kim and Zio climb to the top of the chute, where they find that the opening is actually a docking port leading into space. What they had thought was an underground jail is actually a large isolated space station. With Paris close to death, Kim tries to talk some of the inmates into cooperating in a prison break, but the idea seems so ridiculous to them that they will not hear it. Later, when a delirious Paris disables the tool that Kim had used to neutralize the forcefield, Kim comes close to killing his friend, but regains his senses just in time.

Janeway is able to track down and capture the real bombers, a young brother and sister, but she is shocked when Liria refuses to trade them for her people. Realizing that she cannot negotiate with their illogical criminal jus-

Janeway leads the away team in retrieving her missing crew members. ROBBIE ROBINSON

tice system, in which a conviction is never overturned, Janeway decides it would be easier to deal with the bombers. In exchange for their freedom, the pair leads Janeway and an away team to the prison in Neelix's shuttle, where they extricate their officers and escape.

SENSOR READINGS: Tuvok conducts a full sensor sweep of the planet Akritiria, including a multispectral subsurface scan, but cannot detect Paris's or Kim's lifesigns or combadges. ▪ Both dilithium and paralithium can be easily converted into trilithium. Paralithium is used as a fuel for some ion-based propulsion systems. ▪ Neelix's vessel is still in the shuttle bay. Tuvok notes that although it has limited combat capabilities, it can outmaneuver Akritirian ships.

DELTA QUADRANT: Paris and Kim are convicted of the terrorist bombing at the Laktivia Recreational Facility (or Laktivia Canteen), which resulted in the death of forty-seven off-duty patrollers. The explosion was the result of a trilithium-based bomb. Liria accused the *Voyager* crew of working in league with the Open Sky Terrorists. The Akritirians are armed with pulse guns. ▪ Inmates of the prison believe they are 300 meters underground, but they are really in space. Paris counts around fifty prisoners. The clamp is an implant fixed to the back of a prisoner's head and designed to stimulate the production of acetylcholine in the hypothalamus. Acetylcholine is a brain chemical common to the neural structures of most humanoids that helps stimulate one's aggressive tendencies. The device also kills the prisoner if he attempts to remove it. Zio has been in the prison for six years. ▪ There is no source of trilithium in the sector.

As his cover story, Neelix claims that he has mistaken the prison for the Heva VII refueling port.

PERSONAL LOGS: The second Delaney sister, Megan, receives a first name in this episode. (Jenny was named in "Prime Factors").

EPISODE LOGS: To give this episode a different look, the majority of the camera work in the prison was done with handheld cameras.

REMEMBER

EPISODE #148
TELEPLAY BY: LISA KLINK
STORY BY: BRANNON BRAGA & JOE MENOSKY
DIRECTED BY: WINRICH KOLBE

GUEST STARS

JOR BREL	EUGENE ROCHE
DATHAN	CHARLES ESTEN
JESSEN	ATHENA MASSEY
KORENNA MIRELL	EVE H. BRENNER

SPECIAL GUEST STAR

JARETH	BRUCE DAVISON

CO-STARS

WOMAN	NANCY KAINE
GIRL	TINA REDDINGTON
COMPUTER VOICE	MAJEL BARRETT

STARDATE 50203.1

As *Voyager* transports a group of Enarans to their home world, Torres begins having intense dreams. Every night she envisions herself as Korenna, an Enaran woman who is in love with a man named Dathan, much to the chagrin of her father Jareth, a community leader.

Torres relives the life of Korenna. ROBBIE ROBINSON

Janeway is surprised when she telepathically receives the knowledge to play an Enaran instrument. B. D. MCLAUGHLIN

Torres shares her unsettling visions with Chakotay, noting that each new dream seems to advance Korenna's story. Chakotay wonders if there might be a connection between the dreams and the presence of the telepathic Enarans. Later, Torres passes out while having a waking vision of Korenna's life.

When she awakens in sickbay, the Doctor tells Torres that she is not dreaming, as she believed. Instead she is experiencing actual memories that have been specifically implanted in her mind. In her next vision, Korenna realizes that her father is forcibly "resettling" people like Dathan, who are known as Regressives because they reject modern technology. Korenna's face is accidentally scarred by a Regressive attempting to flee Jareth's soldiers. When Torres awakens, she goes to the quarters of an old Enaran woman named Mirell, who has a scar like the one Torres saw in the dream. Mirell admits she is Korenna, and that she planted her memories in Torres's mind so the truth about the fate of the Regressives will not be forgotten when she dies.

Mirell telepathically gives Torres the last part of the story allowing her to relive the night Dathan told Korenna that the Regressives were being killed, not relocated. Dathan urges Korenna to run away with him, but Jareth interrupts, forcing Dathan to hide. Convinced by her father that Dathan does not really love her, Korenna betrays him by revealing him in his hiding place. Soon after, Jareth has him executed, as Korenna joins the cheering Enaran mob. The final image Torres sees is herself as a slightly older Korenna telling the revised history to a group of children, teaching them the lie. When Torres wakes up, Korenna Mirell is dead.

As the Enarans prepare a farewell toast to the crew, Torres bursts in and proclaims the group as murderers. She accuses the Enarans of whitewashing their past and killing Mirell to continue the cover-up, but none of them are willing to listen to her. Finally, a young Enaran woman that Torres had befriended during the trip offers to telepathically link with Torres to receive Korenna's memories. Torres gratefully accepts, knowing that what happened to the Regressives will live on in the Enarans' memories.

SENSOR READINGS: In appreciation for the speedier transport to their home world, the Enarans share their energy conservation technology with the *Voyager* crew. The Enarans new components are slightly out of sync with *Voyager*'s EPS system resulting in a minor flow problem in the modified power relays. The engineering teams have to pull some longer shifts but they expect the modifications to be complete by the time they reach the Enaran homeworld. ▪ In light of Torres's experience, Janeway cancels the trade negotiations and the crew's shore leave.

DELTA QUADRANT: The Enaran passengers are being taken from a colony in the Fima system to their homeworld of Enara Prime. They are a telepathic race able to share their experiences with others through a telepathic link. The colors of the Enaran flag are blue and green. When dining, they use cushions or pillows in place of tables and chairs so when they are done eating they can just lie back and fall asleep. They prefer temperatures slightly chillier than humans and have molten seas on their home world. They are very hygienic, possessing cleansing marbles that sanitize hands. ▪ In Enaran history the Regressives were frowned upon and ultimately resettled because they eschewed all but the most primitive technology. In truth, the resettlement was mass murder. It was believed that the transports did not go anywhere; instead, the passengers were vaporized in a thermal sweep.

PERSONAL LOGS: Janeway has always regretted that she never learned to play a musical instrument. She experiences Brell's ability to play his musical instrument through a telepathic link. ▪ Torres once insisted on finishing a hoverball championship with a broken ankle. She is late for two duty shifts due to the intense dreaming she has been experiencing and is later told to take two days off to recuperate from the mental invasions. ▪ Kim is interested in Jessen, an Enaran woman who spent her life on the Fima Colony and ultimately the one Enaran woman willing to listen to Torres's story.

MEDICAL REPORT: Torres's cortical theta waves indicate she was experiencing implanted memories, and there is strong evidence of telepathic activity in her frontal lobe. The synaptic patterns of the implanted memories are not quite compatible with her neural pathways, resulting in some minor cortical damage, which the Doctor corrects. He gives her an inhibitor to control her theta wave activity and suppress the memories.

EPISODE LOGS: The Enaran colony is in the Fima system, not to be confused with the Fina system in which there is a Vidiian colony ("Lifesigns").

THE SWARM

EPISODE #149

WRITTEN BY: **MIKE SUSSMAN**

DIRECTED BY: **ALEXANDER SINGER**

GUEST STARS

DIVA	CAROLE DAVIS

CO-STARS

CHARDIS	STEVEN HOUSKA
COMPUTER VOICE	MAJEL BARRETT

STARDATE 50252.3

When Paris and Torres take a shuttle to investigate some intermittent sensor readings, an unknown pair of aliens beam aboard. Unable to communicate through the universal translators, the aliens fire a weapon at the pair before departing the shuttle. Although Paris sustains serious injuries from the charge, Torres recovers sufficiently to get them back to *Voyager.* The Doctor, who had been studying opera on the holodeck, is called to sickbay to care for the injured crewmen.

Neelix informs the captain that he does not know these aliens by name, only by reputation. They attack any outsider who enters their territory, leaving ships badly damaged and rarely with any survivors. Unfortunately, a route around their territory would take *Voyager* over fifteen months, so Janeway opts to stay on course, asking the crew for a plan to go through undetected.

In sickbay, the Doctor forgets how to perform the operation on Paris and is required to reconstruct his motor cortex because the EMH's memory circuits are degrading. The only way to help him is to reinitialize his program, but Torres reveals that if she does that, all of the memories the Doctor has acquired in the past two years would be lost, along with much of his personality.

At Kes's insistence, Torres transfers the Doctor's program to the EMH diagnostic system, a holodeck recreation of Jupiter Station, where his database originally had been written. There, they meet a holographic re-creation of Dr. Lewis Zimmerman, creator of the EMH. Zimmerman explains that the Doctor's "meltdown" is understandable, since his program was designed to run for only 1,500 hours. However, he is unable to come up with any solution beyond resetting the program.

The crew adjusts *Voyager*'s shields so that the ship can slip through the aliens' sensor net without being spotted. Once in their space, *Voyager*'s sensors pick up a mass of thousands of small alien vessels. As the crew proceeds, one of the tiny alien ships fires a polaron burst that makes the starship visible on the alien sensors. The small ships launch a pursuit and attach themselves to *Voyager* in an attempt to drain the starship's energy. Realizing that every vessel in the swarm is connected at some quantum level, the crew is able to create an explosive chain reaction that drives them off long enough to get through the territory.

With the Doctor's memory degradation worsening every minute, Kes persuades the Zimmerman program to graft its matrix onto the Doctor's. When the program is reinitialized, the Doctor is restored although he initially seems to have reverted to his original programming without knowledge of the previous two years. Then, as he treats Torres for a minor headache, he begins to hum the song he was performing earlier in the holodeck, showing that all has not been forgotten.

SENSOR READINGS: To get past the alien sensor net, the crew adjusts *Voyager*'s shields to refract the interlaced tachyon beams. They try to stay at warp 9.75 for as long as they can, but a resonant particle wave dampens the warp field and slows the ship. Torres tries realigning the dilithium matrix to compensate. Although she would

A member of the swarm materializes on the bridge. ROBBIE ROBINSON

prefer to shut down the warp core, she has to do the realignment while the ship is at warp.

DELTA QUADRANT: According to Neelix, no one knows the name of the alien race, how many of them there are, or what their culture is like. All that is known is that the aliens do not want anyone violating their territory and they have been known to kill those who do. The alien language is so unlike the crew's that the universal translators are ineffective. Kim remodulates the translators and is ultimately able to get some semblance of what the aliens are saying. Their borders are so large, with hundreds of sectors, that it will take over fifteen months at maximum warp for *Voyager* to go around, while it will take only four days at high warp to go through their space. ▪ The aliens have thousands of ships that swarm together. One of their ships fires a polaron burst to change *Voyager*'s shield polarity so it rotates at ninety-two gigahertz and is made visible to scanners. *Voyager*'s scans show no weapons signature on the alien ships however they do possess an interferometric pulse that knocks out *Voyger*'s shields.

Voyager comes across a disabled Mislen ship with only one surviving crew member. Before he dies, the crew member tells them his planet is five parsecs from their current location in a yellow dwarf system.

ALPHA QUADRANT: Encroaching on the territory of an alien species is prohibited by Starfleet regulations. ▪ The Zimmerman hologram suggests that Torres schedule the Doctor to have his memory circuits expanded during the ship's next maintenance layover at McKinley Station. Obviously, this is not an option.

PERSONAL LOGS: When Janeway was in high school, she sneaked out of her house on a few occasions, passing her parents' bedroom in the process. ▪ Torres and Paris are fired on by a type of neuro-electric weapon that affects their nervous systems. While Torres is only mildly affected, Paris requires a motor cortex reconstruction. ▪ The Doctor has recently begun a thorough study of opera and performs an aria from *La Boheme* entitled *"O Soave Fanciulla."* The Doctor has to scrub up for Paris's operation, though the process goes unseen. He suffers a level-4 memory fragmentation because his personality subroutine has grown to more than 15,000 gigaquads. Although

The EMH diagnostic program was designed to resemble its creator Dr. Zimmerman. ROBBIE ROBINSON

FUTURE'S END, PART I

EPISODE #150

WRITTEN BY: BRANNON BRAGA & JOE MENOSKY

DIRECTED BY: DAVID LIVINGSTON

GUEST STARS

RAIN ROBINSON	SARAH SILVERMAN
CAPTAIN BRAXTON	ALLAN G. ROYAL

SPECIAL GUEST STAR

HENRY STARLING	ED BEGLEY, JR.

CO-STARS

ENSIGN KAPLAN	SUSAN PATTERSON
POLICEMAN	BARRY WIGGINS
DUNBAR	CHRISTIAN R. CONRAD

STARDATE UNKNOWN

Voyager is fired upon by a twenty-ninth-century Federation timeship commanded by Captain Braxton, who has traveled through a spatial rift to destroy Janeway's ship. Braxton claims that *Voyager* is responsible for a temporal explosion that will obliterate Earth's solar system in his era. The crew's efforts to deflect Braxton's blasts damage his ship, and he is sucked through the rift, along with *Voyager*. The starship winds up in orbit around Earth in 1996, with Braxton and his timeship nowhere to be found.

Knowing Braxton's ship holds the key to returning to their own era, the crew begins their search, and an away team beams down to Los Angeles to investigate subspace readings that are out of place in the twentieth century. Meanwhile, at the Griffith Observatory, astronomer Rain Robinson picks up *Voyager's* warp emission on her instruments and reports the finding to computer mogul Henry Starling, who funds her lab. Against Starling's instructions, Rain transmits a greeting to *Voyager*, and the crew tracks her to the observatory.

While Paris and Tuvok head for the observatory, Chakotay and Janeway identify a homeless man as Captain Braxton. Through paranoid ramblings he explains that the time rift dropped him in 1967 and his ship crashed in a remote mountain range after he performed an emergency beam-out. A young Henry Starling found the timeship before him and utilized its technology to start a high-tech empire. Starling is now planning to use Braxton's vessel to travel to the future, and, according to Braxton, that will cause the explosion in the twenty-ninth century.

Fearing that Rain is a security risk, Starling sends a

Torres had programmed safety buffers, they are breaking down and his memory circuits are deteriorating. The Jupiter Station diagnostic program Alpha-1-1 contains a sophisticated diagnostic matrix specifically created for the emergency medical system. The diagnostic program's adaptive heuristic matrix is the same as the Doctor's, so they graft one onto the other (which means that there is no longer a diagnostic program for the EMH). It requires synchronous transfer of all the EMH databases and sub-routines and must be shut down for an undisclosed period of time to reinitialize.

Ensign Freddy Bristow has a crush on Torres, who once beat him in a parisses squares match.

EPISODE LOGS: Robert Picardo provides his own singing for this and many of the future episodes. ▪ Although this is the first holographic appearance of Dr. Zimmerman, a photo of the man was seen in "Projections." The actual Lewis Zimmerman (also played by Robert Picardo) was first seen in the *Deep Space Nine* episode "Dr. Bashir, I Presume." ▪ Paris and Torres begin a flirtation in this episode that will eventually lead to their marriage in "Drive."

Tuvok and Paris pose as lost tourists in order to delete all information pertaining to *Voyager*'s arrival. ROBBIE ROBINSON

henchman to silence her. Paris and Tuvok, however, manage to spirit her away before she can be harmed, but after they delete all traces of *Voyager* from her computer. When Rain questions what they are up to, Paris concocts a flawed cover story explaining that they are secret agents tracking a Soviet UFO spy operation.

Chakotay and Janeway break into Starling's office, where they discover Braxton's timeship just as Starling walks in and confronts them. Janeway warns Starling not to launch the ship, explaining that it will unleash disaster. Undaunted, Starling threatens to kill Chakotay and Janeway, but they are transported to *Voyager* just in the nick of time. They try to beam up the timeship, but Starling uses his stolen technology to adjust the transporter beam to access *Voyager*'s computer and study its systems. Minutes later, the captain learns that the Doctor is missing from sickbay and *Voyager*'s presence has been disclosed on the evening news.

SENSOR READINGS: *Voyager* was launched in the year 2371. ▪ The ship's emergency transporters have a range of only about ten kilometers. ▪ According to astrometric readings they have gone back in time to the year 1996. Since they are in a time with satellite technology, the crew maintains a high orbit and modulates the shields to

scatter Earth radar. ▪ Starling is able to use the transporter beam as a downlink and steals twenty percent of *Voyager*'s computer files, including the Doctor's program.

DAMAGE REPORT: A high energy polaron pulse fired from the deflector interferes with the subatomic disruptor fired from the Federation *Timeship Aeon*. The weapon takes helm control offline and starts to pull *Voyager*'s molecular structure apart. ▪ The trip through the temporal rift affects *Voyager*'s primary systems. Weapons are offline, three EPS conduits are blown, and the main transporter buffer crashes. Later damage includes inertial dampeners going offline, minor power fluctuations in the impulse drive and a few burned out circuits in the main computer core.

ALPHA QUADRANT: The *Aeon* is approximately six meters in length. The timeship's use of a gravitation matrix shows that distortion in the space-time continuum is artificial. The *Voyager* crew is blamed for a temporal explosion that destroys all of the Sol solar system in the twenty-ninth century since debris from their secondary hull was found. *Voyager* knocks the timeship's navigational system off course, which is why they ended up at

Both Janeway and Starling refuse to back down. ROBBIE ROBINSON

two different times in the past. ▪ On Earth, Braxton calls a police officer a "quasi-Cardassian totalitarian."

Henry Starling introduced the very first isograted circuit in 1969 leading Janeway to believe that he was responsible for Earth's computer age. ▪ Rain Robinson is an astronomer at the SETI (Search for Extra-Terrestrial Intelligence) lab under Starling's funding. She picked up a gamma emission that matched the frequency profile he gave her and is tracking the warp emissions from *Voyager*'s engines. ▪ Tuvok reports that the current thermal and ultraviolet radiation are at hazardous levels. After the Hermosa Quake in 2047 the region of Los Angeles the crew beamed to sank under 200 meters of water and became one of the world's largest coral reefs, home to thousands of different marine species.

PERSONAL LOGS: Janeway was on her high school tennis team. After nineteen years, she decided to take up the sport again, but lost her first marth in straight sets on the holodeck novice tennis program. She previously mentioned losing a tennis match at the age of twelve ("Deadlock"). Janeway claims that she is not aware of what any of her ancestors was doing around the turn of

the millennium, which will contradict the events portrayed in "11:59." ▪ One of Chakotay's ancestors was a schoolteacher in Arizona. ▪ Paris's appreciation for twentieth-century history comes heavily into play. Of special note is his interest in sci-fi B-movies, which will eventually lead to his Captain Proton holodeck adventures. ▪ Ensign Kim is left in charge of the bridge for the first time. ▪ Neelix and Kes monitor television transmissions and get hooked on a soap opera.

EPISODE LOGS: The cast goes on location to several areas of Los Angeles, most notably, the Santa Monica Pier and Griffith Observatory. ▪ In Rain's office there is a toy model of the *S.S. Botany Bay* as well as a photo depicting the launch of the ship. This was the sleeper ship that carried Khan Noonian Singh and his followers after the Eugenics Wars of the mid-1990s. However, no mention of the wars is made in this episode. ▪ Also on Rain's desk is a Talosian action figure based on the aliens from the original *Star Trek* series. ▪ When Janeway is trying to type on the computer keyboard, she compares the technology to being "like stone knives and bearskins." This is a direct reference to Spock's line from "City on the Edge of

Forever" in which he uses the same comparison to describe 1930's Earth radio equipment. Also similar to Spock, Tuvok uses a bandana to cover his ears and when asked about their unusual shape, he explains that they are a family trait.

FUTURE'S END, PART II

EPISODE #151

WRITTEN BY: BRANNON BRAGA & JOE MENOSKY

DIRECTED BY: CLIFF BOLE

GUEST STARS

RAIN ROBINSON	SARAH SILVERMAN
CAPTAIN BRAXTON	ALLAN G. ROYAL
BUTCH	BRENT HINKLEY
PORTER	CLAYTON MURRAY

SPECIAL GUEST STAR

HENRY STARLING	ED BEGLEY, JR.

CO-STARS

ENSIGN KAPLAN	SUSAN PATTERSON
DUNBAR	CHRISTIAN R. CONRAD
COMPUTER VOICE	MAJEL BARRETT

STARDATE 50312.5

Janeway's attempts to beam up twentieth-century computer mogul Henry Starling and the *Timeship Aeon* are stymied because *Voyager's* long-range transporters are not functioning. As an alternate plan astronomer Rain Robinson lures Starling to a meeting where the crew hopes to hijack him. Starling shows up with the Doctor, whom he has equipped with a twenty-ninth-century portable holoemitter that allows him to exist in environments without holographic emitters.

Having reconfigured the shields on a shuttlecraft to disguise it from twentieth-century radar, Chakotay and Torres try to beam Starling from the rendezvous to their shuttle but Starling has a twenty-ninth-century tricorder that interferes with the attempt. *Voyager* is able to redirect the transporter signal to beam him out of the shuttle's buffers and directly to the starship. Unfortunately, Starling's attempt to disrupt the beam-out damages the shuttle's controls. It goes down in the desert, where an extremist group takes Chakotay and Torres hostage. *Voyager* traces the crash site to Arizona, and the Doctor and Tuvok travel there to find them, while Paris re-

mains in Los Angeles with Rain, hoping to find the timeship.

On *Voyager,* Starling admits to Janeway that he intends to travel into the future to steal more advanced technology. Although Janeway thinks she has put an end to those plans, Starling's henchman, Dunbar, uses more scavenged twenty-ninth-century technology to transport Starling back to his office. Outside Starling's headquarters, Paris spots a truck that appears to be moving the timeship to another location. In Arizona, Tuvok and the Doctor manage to free Chakotay and Torres, and after they repair the shuttle, they join Paris and destroy the truck. Unable to find the remains of the timeship in the wreckage, they realize the truck was a ruse to allow Starling to launch the ship from his office.

After Paris bids a farewell to Rain, he and the away team return to *Voyager.* The crew hails Starling, who refuses to abort his mission, forcing Janeway to destroy the timeship. Seconds later, a time rift opens, and Braxton appears in his undamaged timeship. With his previous timeline altered by the destruction of Starling, this Braxton has come from the future to lead *Voyager* back to the twenty-fourth century, where it belongs. Back in the Delta Quadrant, the crew finds that even though they are no closer to home, they have gained one advantage from

Starling begins his flight, despite Janeway's warning that he will destroy the future. ROBBIE ROBINSON

"Mr. Leisure Suit" enjoys his newfound mobility. ROBBIE ROBINSON

their journey: The Doctor has retained the twenty-ninth-century portable holoemitter and is no longer confined to sickbay.

SENSOR READINGS: With *Voyager's* weapons offline, they can arm photon torpedoes, but cannot launch them because the launch activation sequencers do not respond to commands. Since there is no time to reroute fire command through the helm Janeway orders Kim to open the access portal to Torpedo Bay 1 so she can reconfigure the torpedo for manual launch. With the activation sequencers down she has to launch from inside the tube, which is dangerous due to the plasma exhaust from the torpedo.

SHUTTLE TRACKER: Torres uses interferometric dispersion to hide a type-9 shuttle from radar detection and configures the shuttle to disguise the visual profile to make them look like a twentieth-century aircraft. The interference from Starling's twenty-ninth-century tricorder disables the shuttle's aft thrusters, causing it to crash. The shuttle is retrieved.

ALPHA QUADRANT: Starling's office is equipped with a holographic simulator for testing new microchip designs. Emitters are placed throughout the room. He uses a tem-poral transponder, set to give off tachyon signals, tricking Paris into following the empty truck. SAT-COM 47 is the communications satellite used to locate and transport Starling back to Earth.

The *Timeship Aeon* has a hyper-impulse drive and travels via temporal inversion. The "new" Captain Braxton informs the crew that in his century, they can scan time in much the same way twenty-fourth-century sensors scan space. The Temporal Integrity Commission detected their vessel over twentieth-century Earth and he was sent to correct that anomaly. He cites the Temporal Prime Directive as the reason he cannot send the crew back to the Alpha Quadrant.

PERSONAL LOGS: Janeway is burned by the exhaust from the photon torpedo, but refuses to go to sickbay. ▪ Chakotay considers becoming an archeologist if they are stuck in the past. ▪ The Doctor refers to his recent program loss and notes that he is still in the process of retrieving his memory files ("The Swarm"). Starling reconfigures the Doctor's tactile response sensors to allow him to feel pain. Starling has him equipped with an autonomous self-sustaining mobile holoemitter that allows him to move freely. His program can now easily be downloaded back and forth from the ship's computer to the emitter.

EPISODE LOGS: The park in the opening scenes of the episode is on the Paramount Pictures lot. The studio's administrative offices can be seen in the background. In this scene, Tuvok eats a chili burrito, which would seem to contradict the previously established fact that Vulcans do not eat meat. However, being that it is set in California, it can be assumed that it is a vegetarian chili burrito and that part just went unsaid. ▪ The design Starling used for the Chronowerx logo is the same design as the twenty-ninth-century communicator worn by Braxton.

Kes fights against Tieran's intrusion within her mind. ROBBIE ROBINSON

WARLORD

EPISODE #152

TELEPLAY BY: **LISA KLINK**

STORY BY: **ANDREW SHEPARD PRICE & MARK GABERMAN**

DIRECTED BY: **DAVID LIVINGSTON**

GUEST STARS

ADIN	ANTHONY CRIVELLO
DEMMAS	BRAD GREENQUIST
NORI	GALYN GÖRG
RESH	CHARLES EMMETT
AMERON	KARL WIEDERGOTT
and	
TIERAN	LEIGH J. McCLOSKEY

CO-STAR

COMPUTER VOICE	MAJEL BARRETT

STARDATE 50348.1

The crew beams aboard three Ilarians named Tieran, Nori, and Adin, moments before their damaged ship explodes. Although the Doctor and Kes try to save him, Tieran dies as a result of the accident. Not long after, Neelix is shocked when Kes, who had been spending a lot of time with the surviving Ilarians, announces she would like to spend some time apart from him.

When *Voyager* arrives at Ilari, the local leader, known as the autarch, sends a representative to the ship instead of coming himself. Inexplicably, Kes pulls out a phaser, kills the representative and a *Voyager* crew member before escaping in a stolen shuttlecraft with Adin and Nori.

Kes takes the shuttle to an Ilarian military encampment and assumes command of the waiting troops. In the meantime, Demmas, the autarch's oldest son, is beamed aboard *Voyager* to investigate the situation. Immediately understanding what must have happened, he explains that Kes's body is now inhabited by Tieran, a former Ilarian ruler who was overthrown by Demmas's ancestor two hundred years ago. Since then, Tieran has lived on by transferring his mind to a series of host bodies. Janeway agrees to help stop Kes/Tieran, but before she can, the tyrant kills Demmas's father and appoints himself the new autarch.

Kes/Tieran makes contact with the autarch's youngest son, Ameron and easily poisons his thoughts against his brother, Demmas. With Ameron agreeing to cooperate with the new regime, the rebels maintain a stronghold on the planet. In the meantime, the Doctor designs a synaptic stimulator that will remove Tieran's neural pattern from Kes. Tuvok beams into the autarch's palace to attach the stimulator to Kes's skin, but is caught and imprisoned before he can proceed with the attempt. When Kes/Tieran interrogates Tuvok, the Vulcan is able to initiate a mind-meld and speak directly to Kes, who tells Tuvok she is fighting Tieran for control of her body.

Kes/Tieran orders *Voyager* to leave orbit, but the

stress of the mental battle between Kes and Tieran results in a paranoid Kes/Tieran killing Adin. To Nori's chagrin, Kes/Tieran announces she is marrying Ameron. Moments later, a coalition of *Voyager*'s crew and Demmas's forces burst into the palace. Paris releases Tuvok, while Neelix places the synaptic stimulator on Kes/Tieran. Tieran jumps to a new body—Ameron—but Kes places the device on him and Tieran is finally destroyed. Demmas, the rightful heir, becomes autarch, while Kes is left to deal with the painful memories of actions over which she had no control.

SENSOR READINGS: Kes/Tieran alters the hijacked shuttlecraft's shields so it scatters *Voyager*'s tractor beam and remodulates the shuttle's plasma injectors to hide the warp signature. ▪ Neelix's new holoresort is based on the Paxau Resort on Talax and modified by Paris, Kim, and Torres. Kim adds characters from Kim Sports Program Theta-2: the Gold Medal Volleyball team of 2216.

SHUTTLE TRACKER: It is presumed that the shuttle Kes/Tieran steals is later retrieved.

DELTA QUADRANT: Radiation inside the damaged alien vessel rose to toxic levels and their warp core was heavi-

Tuvok's thoughts reveal his presence in the royal chamber.
ROBBIE ROBINSON

ly damaged. ▪ The original host of Tieran is given 20 milligrams of lectrazine to restart his heart, but his biochemistry is incompatible. A cortical implant is automatically activated at the moment of the host's death. It enhances Tieran's neural pattern, and sends it out along the peripheral nerves. The actual transfer takes place through bioelectric microfibers located in the hand. When he comes into direct contact with Kes, Tieran's pattern is transferred through her nervous system and into her brain. ▪ Adin claims to be a very prominent physician and says Nori is cousin to the autarch. Tieran ruled Ilari over two centuries ago. He was a war hero who brought security and stability during a difficult time in their history. In peacetime, he began to treat his own subjects as enemies and became convinced everyone was a potential traitor. There was a rebellion led by one of Demmas's ancestors that laid siege to the Imperial hall for over a year, burning the surrounding city to the ground before Tieran was finally defeated. During his reign, he became obsessed with his own mortality and spent most of his time, and Ilari's resources, searching for ways to overcome death. A necklace is the symbol of the autarch. ▪ There are reports that Demmas's fleet of at least twenty ships is massing behind the fifth moon. The Imperial hall's detection grid makes a surprise attack difficult; however, during a maintenance cycle the system goes through every ten hours, there are a few seconds when it might be vulnerable to a narrow band EM pulse (Tieran is aware of the glitch).

PERSONAL LOGS: While probing his mind, Kes/Tieran suggests that Tuvok has feelings for her, but the Vulcan denies it. ▪ Neelix had very basic military training on Talax and participates in tactical exercises with the crew every month. ▪ Kes breaks up with Neelix, and although she is under the alien influence at the time, they do not get back together. While under Tieran's influence the one portion of Kes's personality that continues to surface is her love of flowers and gardens. In the end she notes that despite using all of Tuvok's meditation exercises, she is unable to get past the horrible memories she has of the experience.

CREW COMPLEMENT: Ensign Martin, the transporter room operator, is killed by Kes/Tieran.

KES

He [Jabin] glances into the crowd and standing in the back observing the chaos is KES. Kes is an Ocampa female (the same species as we have seen caring for Torres and Kim). She has a dazzling, ethereal beauty, waifish and fragile. But Kes is not frail: there is a dignity to her bearing, an alertness in her look, that suggests a being of powerful intelligence. . . .

—Kes's first appearance in "Caretaker"

The paradox of Kes's "fragile power" is the perfect description for this young character. Born of a race with a lifespan of only nine years, Kes lived a life with the child-like wonder of a two-year-old coupled with the maturity of someone well into adulthood. Though her experiences living in an underground environment may have been limiting, her need for exploration brought her to the surface and ultimately to the *Voyager* crew.

From the start, Kes's willingness to follow the captain of *Voyager* almost blindly served as an example of her eagerness to explore the universe around her and learn all that she could. This evidenced itself through the youthful way in which she looked up to Janeway and treated her with a reverence usually reserved for a mother. She showed a similar respect to both the Doctor and Tuvok as they took mentoring roles in her life, training her in medicine and the expansion of her mental abilities, respectively. She herself likened her relationships with Janeway and the Doctor to those with her parents. In fact, she chose the Doctor to perform a parental role in the rituals involved in her premature *elogium*—a role she admitted she would have asked the captain to perform.

Kes's relationship with Neelix fell very much into that of a traditional first love. Although he was her senior, Kes often took the dominant role, helping Neelix to see his mistakes and the other side of any given situation. Their bond was at its strongest when she prematurely experienced the *elogium* and asked Neelix to join with her in what could have been her only chance to have a child. However, like many first loves, Kes eventually grew beyond her relationship with Neelix and ended it, but the pair remained friends.

ROBBIE ROBINSON

Ethan Phillips: "Working on the scenes I got to do with Jennifer Lien was a highlight. Not to diminish anybody else's work but I think Jennifer had a really unguarded immediacy and power as an actress that I always found her a terrific partner to work with and that was always a highlight for me."

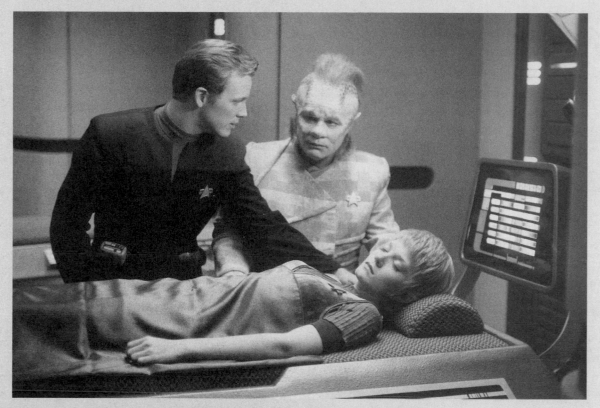

ROBBIE ROBINSON

Outside of her personal relationships with the crew, Kes had a number of experiences that she never could have imagined while living in the Caretaker's artificial environment. Free of the constrictions of Ocampa, the long-dormant mental abilities Kes always suspected her people to possess began to reveal themselves. Under Tuvok's tutelage, Kes began to explore powers that she never imagined. When the crew later came across a faction of Ocampans who had left their homeworld long ago, she began to get an idea of the potential of the power inside of her that could eventually endanger the ship. Ultimately, the prophecy did prove true and Kes was forced to leave.

Jennifer Lien struck the perfect balance of the mature child, keeping the quality evident in her interactions with the rest of the characters. Although "Before and After" gave a glance into a possible comfortable future for Kes, her ultimate fate would be quite different. With Lien's return for the episode "Fury" a different, darker Kes appeared, wanting to harm the people she used to call friends. However, it was a young Kes who came to the rescue and convinced her older self of the truth and sent her back home where she longed to be.

ALTERED STATES

Mister Neelix, just because a man changes his drink order doesn't mean he's possessed by an alien. You're acting a little paranoid . . . In fact, one could say that you're acting a little too paranoid.

The Doctor, "Cathexis"

The concept of alien possession is not new to *Star Trek: Voyager*. In fact, Starfleet crews were being possessed in various manners by alien beings all the way back in the original pilot episode of the classic *Star Trek* series, "The Cage." Through mental invasion, hallucinations, or simple impersonations, alien influences have used many ways to skew the *Voyager* crew's perception of reality many times in many ways.

"Ex Post Facto"—Through the use of neuro-implant, Paris is forced to relive the final moments of a Banean man's life every fourteen hours until he is cleared of the murder charges.

"Cathexis"—The Komar take over Tuvok's body and try to lead *Voyager* back to their space, where they plan to feed on the crew's collective neural energy for years. A disembodied Chakotay uses his own neural energy to take over the bodies of various crew members—Janeway, Paris, Torres, Kim, Lt. Durst, and Neelix—to protect the ship from the alien threat and lead them to safety.

"Projections"—A feedback loop between the holodeck computer and the Doctor's program nearly convinces him that he is the real Dr. Lewis Zimmerman.

"Persistence of Vision"—An undetermined alien race takes over the entire crew through hallucinations.

"The Thaw"—Kim is trapped by the Clown in a simulated world when he tries to rescue hibernating members of the Kohl settlement from the mental link to their stasis system.

"Flashback"—An alien virus embedded in a repressed

Janeway and Tuvok are aboard the *Starship Excelsior*, if only in Tuvok's memory. ROBBIE ROBINSON

memory in Tuvok's mind nearly kills him until a meld with Janeway forces the parasite to reveal itself.

"Remember"—An Enaran woman uses telepathic contact to make Torres relive events of her life so that Torres can spread the word about atrocities in the planet's past.

"Warlord"—Kes is taken over by the warlord Tieran and forced to start a coup on the planet Ilari.

"Coda"—An alien entity takes over Janeway's mind, trying to convince her that she is dead so that her spirit will travel to his matrix where she will "nourish him for a long, long time."

"Unity"—A Borg cooperative uses its neural-transponder to control Chakotay's actions, forcing him to reestablish their collective link.

"Darkling"—The additional personality subroutines the Doctor adapts from historical holographic characters in an effort to augment his program, cause him to develop a Hyde-like personality.

"Favorite Son"—Implanted with Taresian DNA Harry's biological imperatives force him to fire on a Nasari ship and drive him toward a seemingly familiar area of space.

"Scientific Method"—Unbeknownst to the crew, alien scientists are conducting experiments on them, causing the crew to exhibit unusual behavior, as well as experience physical changes.

"The Killing Game"—The Hirogen take over the ship and use subdermal transmitters to link half the crew's neocortexes to the holodeck, making them believe they are characters within various war game simulations.

"Waking Moments"—In order to defend themselves, an alien group traps the crew in their own dream world.

"Vis à Vis"—Paris and Janeway's bodies are taken over by an alien capable of selective DNA exchange.

"Demon"—An alien compound duplicates Paris's and Kim's bodies, gaining sentience for the first time. Later, much of the crew volunteers to donate DNA samples so the new race can propagate.

"In the Flesh"—Species 8472 impersonates various Starfleet personnel, including Starfleet Academy gardener Boothby, in a simulation to prepare for a possible invasion of the Alpha Quadrant.

"Infinite Regress"—Various personalities of people Seven helped assimilate as a Borg surface and take control of her body.

"The Fight"—Attempting to communicate with the *Voyager* crew, aliens from chaotic space channel themselves through Chakotay via hallucinations that utilize a formerly suppressed genetic disorder common among his family.

"Bliss"—*Voyager* is trapped in the body of a life-form that uses telepathy and psychogenic manipulation to sense victims' thoughts and desires to prey on them. In this case, it makes the crew believe they are home.

"Course: Oblivion"—A duplicate *Voyager* crew composed of the mimetic life-forms resulting from the DNA that the original crew donated while on the Demon-class planet.

"Warhead"—The Doctor's program is accessed and taken over by an alien weapon.

"Equinox, Part II"—Captain Ransom removes the Doctor's ethical subroutines, allowing a less moral personality to torture Seven for information.

"Tinker, Tenor, Doctor, Spy"—The Doctor lives out his daydreams—à la Walter Mitty—and an alien observer believes it to be real.

"Alice"—An alien ship named *Alice* uses a neurogenic interface between itself and Paris to cause him to become obsessed with the ship.

"Memorial"—The crew is forced to live false memories as the result of an alien memorial that sends neurogenic pulses through a synaptic transmitter so that crews on passing ships will experience the massacre of the Nakan people.

"Live Fast and Prosper"—Alien con artists steal the crews' identities forcing *Voyager* to track them and bring them to justice.

"Repression"—As a result of experiments on Tuvok's mind—prior to his being transported to the Delta Quadrant—subliminal directives from a former Maquis member are awakened in the security chief. The mental orders force him to perform mind-melds on some of the former Maquis on *Voyager* and implant instructions for them to take over the ship.

"Inside Man"—A fake hologram of Lieutenant Barclay is sent to *Voyager* by Ferengi hoping to lure the crew into a trap so the Ferengi can profit from taking Seven's Borg nanoprobes.

"Body and Soul"—To save the Doctor from being decompiled by an alien species who look at holograms as illegal beings—his program is downloaded into Seven's Borg implants and the Doctor takes control of her body.

"Workforce"—Most of the *Voyager* crew is kidnapped, and the memory centers in their brains are radically altered in order to make them competent workers on an alien world.

"Renaissance Man"—In order to save a Captain Janeway, the Doctor impersonates several members of the crew as he attempts to steal the warp core.

THE Q AND THE GREY

EPISODE #153

TELEPLAY BY: KENNETH BILLER
STORY BY: SHAWN PILLER
DIRECTED BY: CLIFF BOLE

GUEST STARS

Q FEMALE   SUZIE PLAKSON
Q COLONEL   HARVE PRESNELL
                  and
Q   JOHN DE LANCIE

STARDATE 50384.2

After the crew is witness to the rare sight of a supernova, Q shows up in Janeway's quarters, announcing that he would like the captain to bear his child. Naturally, Janeway refuses, but Q is persistent. Believing her to be playing hard to get, Q appears several more times, trying different methods of wooing her. Although Janeway finally admits she would like to have a child someday, she is firm that it would not be with him, much to the relief of a jealous female Q who shows up on the ship.

After the crew witnesses the third supernova in as many days, they suspect that Q may be behind the explosions. The shockwaves from the cosmic phenomena could damage *Voyager,* so Janeway urges Q to do something. In response, Q transports Janeway to the Q Continuum, which now resembles the Southern United States during the 1860s. He informs her that he chose this familiar representation because the Q are in the middle of their own civil war.

The conflict began with the death of Quinn, the Q that *Voyager* had assisted in gaining his mortality a year earlier. His suicide caused chaos in the Continuum. One side is fighting to revert to and preserve the status quo while the other side—Q's side—want to experience individualism. In this metaphorical version of the conflict, the individualists are represented as the America's Northern Union versus the status quo-seeking Southern Confederacy. The unusual frequency of supernovas are being caused by spatial disruptions within the Continuum. To end the war, Q has decided to create a new breed of Q by mating with Janeway to ensure that the child has qualities that are "the best humanity has to offer."

Janeway nurses Q after saving him from the burning mansion. DANNY FELD

Q offers up Janeway's peace plan. ROBBIE ROBINSON

Back on *Voyager,* Chakotay questions the female Q about the war, and they agree to join forces. She helps *Voyager* enter the Continuum, where Janeway is in the process of encouraging Q to mate with the female Q. While he considers the idea, Janeway visits the "Confederate" camp to discuss a cease-fire. She offers a truce on Q's behalf, but the Confederate colonel Q decides the quickest way to end the war would be the execution of Q and his ally, Janeway.

Facing a firing squad, Q proclaims Janeway's innocence and asks the colonel to set her free. The colonel disregards the plea, but the cavalry in the form of the *Voyager* crew and the female Q, comes to the rescue. Q decides Janeway is right and asks the female Q to conceive a child with him. They touch their fingertips together, accomplishing the act, and peace again reigns in the Continuum. Later, Q visits Janeway with his son, and asks the captain to be the boy's godmother.

SENSOR READINGS: The female Q suggests several modifications that allows *Voyager* to enter the Continuum, but the modifications require a complete reconfiguration of the shield array. To strengthen the shields so the ship can be taken into the supernova, the female Q has Torres take the warp drive offline, remodulate the shields to emit a beta-tachyon pulse and emit a series of focused antiproton beams to the shield bubble. Torres believes that would increase power to the shields by a factor of ten. ▪ The senior staff has regularly scheduled morning briefings.

DAMAGE REPORT: The subspace shockwave from the star collapses the warp field so *Voyager* cannot go to warp. After the additional shockwaves, there is hull damage on Decks 9 through 14, and minor injuries are reported on all decks. The shockwaves knock the ship sixteen billion kilometers from its previous location.

DELTA QUADRANT: According to Q, foreplay can last for decades. Q has been involved with the female Q for about four billion years. ▪ Quinn's suicide ("Deathwish") resulted in chaos and upheaval in the Continuum, according to Q, who subsequently took up the banner to protest for individuality and freedom. When others followed, a battle ensued between them and the forces maintaining the status quo. Q believes that mating with Janeway will create a new breed of Q, a "messiah" who will bring about a new peace, because the human DNA will add new blood to the Continuum and bring about change. Q says that the Q are way beyond sex and that it has never been done (which raises the question of how foreplay can last decades). He says that the Q did not come into existence; rather, they always existed. ▪ A star going supernova is an event that occurs only once every hundred years. The pressure of the edge of the supernova's shockwave is over 90 kilopascals. These supernovas are caused by spatial disruptions within the Continuum. Each time a star implodes, a negative density false vacuum is created that sucks the surrounding matter into the Continuum.

ALPHA QUADRANT: Only two other crews in the history of Starfleet have witnessed a supernova explosion; however, neither of the other crews was as close to the event as the *Voyager* crew—less than ten billion kilometers from the first supernova.

PERSONAL LOGS: At the opening of the episode, Janeway has been on the bridge for fourteen hours straight. ▪ Although he knows it is inappropriate, Chakotay admits to being jealous of Q's interest in the captain. ▪ Kes expresses an interest in learning more about stellar phenomena after witnessing the first supernova.

Janeway finds her crew members unconscious in the mess hall.
ROBBIE ROBINSON

MACROCOSM

EPISODE #154

WRITTEN BY: BRANNON BRAGA

DIRECTED BY: ALEXANDER SINGER

GUEST STARS

TAK TAK CONSUL	**ALBIE SELZNICK**

CO-STAR

GARAN MINER	**MICHAEL FISKE**

STARDATE 50425.1

Returning from a trade mission with the Tak Tak, Janeway and Neelix are surprised to find *Voyager* adrift in space with a bio-electric field blocking their scans. After landing their craft in the shuttlebay, the pair notes there are no crew members in sight and that many of the ship's systems are offline. While they are investigating the seemingly empty ship, their turbolift is halted by several life-forms, one of which pokes a hole in the door with a large stinger. The stinger sprays Neelix with a mucilaginous compound, but the pair are able to escape. Not long after, Neelix falls ill, and Janeway goes to find an emergency medkit. When she returns, her morale officer is gone.

Now on her own, Janeway arms herself with weapons and goes to the bridge, where she is stung by a smaller version of the bizarre life-forms who range in size from the dimensions of a fruit fly to an eagle. In the mess hall, she discovers unresponsive, ailing crew members and a giant flying creature that tries to attack her.

Fleeing to sickbay, Janeway finds the Doctor holed up with a phaser. He reports that the ship is infected by a strange alien macrovirus. He explains that while Janeway and Neelix were away from the ship, *Voyager* responded to a medical distress call from a mining colony stricken by a virus. When the Doctor returned from this, his first away mission, a few of the "bugs" migrated back to the ship along with him. Since then, the virus has spread throughout the ship's systems, to the crew. The Doctor has come up with an antigen but has not had the chance to test it, since the huge, mature versions of the virus are preventing him from leaving sickbay. Now infected herself, Janeway volunteers to test the antigen and is cured. But there is still the problem of distributing it to the ailing crew.

Janeway comes up with the idea of distributing the cure in gaseous form through the ship's environmental system. Using her arsenal, she blasts her way through the ship till she reaches the controls. But before she can disperse the antigen, *Voyager* is fired upon by the Tak Tak, who want to eliminate the virus by destroying the ship. Janeway tells them about the cure and asks them to stop shooting long enough for her to treat the crew. They give her an hour.

With the environmental controls now damaged by the attack, Janeway revises her plan, concentrating on the fact that the virus is attracted to infrared radiation. Setting a trap in the holodeck, she uses Neelix's resort program as bait. When the virus attacks the holocharacters, Janeway uses a hastily pieced together antigen bomb to destroy the virulent invaders.

SENSOR READINGS: One of the bio-neural gel packs in the mess hall is ruptured due to the virus. ▪ When environmental controls fail, heat from the warp plasma conduits cannot be vented, resulting in a temperature rise in the ship. ▪ Chakotay initiates a level-4 quarantine on Deck 2. ▪ The mess hall is on Deck 2, Section 13, and environmental control is on Deck 12. To get from the Jefferies tube by sickbay to Deck 12, the Doctor has to use Jefferies tube 11, take a left at Section 31, and straight down past the tractor beam emitter until he reaches Deck 10. He leaves the Jefferies tube at Section 3 and follows the corridor all the way around until he hits the shuttlebay. Then he crawls through Access Port 9, past three airlocks, and then two decks down. The environmental controls is at the end of the hall. ▪ There is a weapons locker on the second floor of engineering. ▪ The bridge computer shows lifesigns in the mess hall on Deck 2, the cargo bay on Deck 4, and the cargo bay on Deck 10. ▪ Janeway sets a tricorder to emit a thermal scattering signal to throw off the viruses. ▪ Following the incident, Janeway gives the entire crew an extended period of R & R.

DAMAGE REPORT: When Janeway and Neelix return to the ship, they find the main computer and com system offline. Main power is also failing and environmental controls go offline as systems start to shut down one by one. A torpedo destroys the secondary power couplings taking the environmental controls offline. Janeway's bomb results in heavy damage to Holodeck 2, but no hull breaches in evidence.

DELTA QUADRANT: Janeway and Neelix are on a three-day trade mission with the Tak Tak, who use gestures as their main form of communication. Janeway offends

The offended Tak Tak insists that Janeway refrain from further, however unintended, insults. ROBBIE ROBINSON

them by putting her hands on her hips—one of their worst insults. Neelix notes that a lot of their gestures seem ritualistic or even superstitious.

In the Garan mining colony the ambient temperature is sixteen degrees Celsius, cavern illumination is minimal, and the cave walls are composed of granite, with a mixture of pyroclastic inclusions. The Tak Tak "purify"—destroy—the Garan mining colony because they believe that is the only way to kill the virus.

The macrocosm virus emanates a bio-electric field. On a microscopic level, the virus uses a needlelike projection to penetrate a cell membrane. On the larger scale, it impales its victim in much the same way, infusing him with its own genetic code. Each virus emits a mucilaginous compound with high concentrations of amino acids, proteins and fragments of nonhumanoid DNA. The virus absorbs growth hormones into its protein structure, and uses them to increase its own mass and dimensions. It is attracted to infrared radiation—that information Janeway uses to lead them to the holodeck. The larger macroviruses are driven to assemble their host population—in this case, the crew—into groups for unknown reasons.

ALPHA QUADRANT: According to Starfleet guidelines for an away team, if there could be a "Medical Emergency on Alien Terrain," it is recommended that the away team keep an open com channel at all times. Away team guidelines also specifically forbid the transport of unknown infectious agents onto a starship without establishing containment and eradication protocols. ▪ Klingons usually do not experience nausea due to their redundant stomach.

PERSONAL LOGS: Janeway has studied chromolinguistics, American Sign Language, and the gestural idioms of the Leyron. She loves skiing, but passes up Chakotay's offer to join the crew on the Ktarian glaciers in the holodeck, saying she has had enough exercise for the time being. Instead, she relaxes by painting in her ready room while listening to jazz. ▪ Paris volunteers to help out in the kitchen while Neelix is away. ▪ The Doctor has been studying Starfleet guidelines for away team members and goes on his first real away mission to the Garan mining colony. He refers to the mobile emitter as both the autonomous emitter and the portable emitter. ▪ Janeway suggests promoting Neelix from morale officer to ambassador due to his flair for diplomacy (the promotion will be formalized in "Revulsion"). Neelix grew up near the Rinax marshlands where summers were the hottest in the sector averaging 50 degrees Celsius, ninety percent humidity, and the most vicious lavaflies ever seen (about six centimeters long). These conditions were largely a result of the three suns in the system.

MEDICAL REPORT: Janeway ruptures her dorsal extensor muscle and bruises two ribs. The Doctor has to perform minor surgery.

EPISODE LOGS: Ensign Wildman's baby is referred to, although she still does not have a name. ▪ When Janeway scans Neelix with her tricorder, she notes that he has fluid in his lungs, and he quickly corrects her, noting that he only has one lung. This was a result of his encounter with the Vidiians ("Phage") ▪ Neelix's talk show is now called "Good Morning, *Voyager.*" The program is set for automatic playback until it is shut off. Although the dialogue is unclear and the transmission is cut off, according to the shooting script, the episode running in Wildman's quarters promises to have Ensign Kaplan share her unique insights into the peculiar art of holographic taxonomy. The program continues with the "Galaxy Report," in which Neelix talks about some "interesting space anomalies in the coming weeks," including an inversion nebula, which plays a large part in the next episode, "Alter Ego."

ALTER EGO

EPISODE #155

WRITTEN BY: JOE MENOSKY

DIRECTED BY: ROBERT PICARDO

GUEST STARS

MARAYNA	SANDRA NELSON
ENSIGN VORIK	ALEXANDER ENBERG

CO-STARS

HOLOWOMAN	SHAY TODD
COMPUTER VOICE	MAJEL BARRETT

STARDATE 50460.3

The crew is mystified by the atypical behavior of an inversion nebula. While they study the unique phenomenon, Kim asks for Tuvok's help in suppressing his emotions because, he reluctantly confesses, he has fallen in love with a holodeck character named Marayna. After meeting with the character to assess the situation, Tuvok advises Kim to avoid further contact with her, since it is impossible to have a relationship with a computer subroutine.

On the bridge, the crew watches as a plasma strand ignites, but fails to create the expected chain reaction throughout the nebula. Sensors show a dampening effect of unknown origin between the strands. That night, despite his vow to avoid Marayna, Kim accompanies Paris to the holodeck to join in a luau hosted by Neelix. There he sees Marayna in conversation with Tuvok. Troubled, Kim leaves, while Tuvok continues to talk to Marayna. The Vulcan is surprised at the depth of her insight into his nature, and he admits that he understands why Kim finds her so compelling.

When *Voyager* attempts to resume its course, the propulsion system inexplicably goes offline. While the engineering staff explores the problem, Kim goes to the holodeck and finds Tuvok again visiting Marayna. He accuses the Vulcan of betraying his trust, and Tuvok opts to delete Marayna's program rather than jeopardize his relationship with Kim. He is surprised, later, when he finds Marayna in his quarters with the help of the Doctor's mobile emitter.

To Marayna's annoyance, Tuvok calls security, but she disappears when they arrive. The crew investigates the holodeck and discovers that someone outside the ship has created an uplink and tapped into its programs. Suddenly, activity in the nebula increases, threatening the safety of the ship.

Tracing the uplink back to its source, Tuvok beams

The holographic Marayna pleads with Tuvok to stay with her. ROBBIE ROBINSON

over to a space station located inside the nebula. There he meets the real Marayna, a lonely humanoid alien who controls the plasma activity for the benefit of her home world's inhabitants. She threatens to destroy *Voyager* if Tuvok refuses to stay with her, but he explains that their relationship would not be what she desires if he stayed only to save his ship. Accepting the logic of the situation, she allows him and *Voyager* to leave.

SENSOR READINGS: When attempting to diagnose the propulsion problem, the engineering team determines that the warp drive is functioning within established levels, matter/antimatter containment is at recommended field strength and the impulse engines are also within tolerance. This leads them to believe there is a computer malfunction so they run a level-4 diagnostic. In actuality, Marayna is emitting a subspace signal that acts as an uplink to the ship's computer. ▪ Kim's quarters are on Deck 3.

DAMAGE REPORT: The ignited plasma strands result in inertial dampeners going offline and a loss of shields.

DELTA QUADRANT: An inversion nebula has never been seen in the Alpha Quadrant. According to Federation astro-theorists, inversion nebulae are so unstable they are supposed to burn out within a few years, but this one appears centuries old. When a plasma strand ignites the temperature reaches 9,000 Kelvins and there is a subatomic cascade reaction. Marayna keeps the plasma fires from chain reacting by creating a dampening field around the plasma strands. She generates it to preserve the nebula so others from her home planet may enjoy its beauty.

ALPHA QUADRANT: *Kal-toh* is a Vulcan game that, according to the shooting script, is "vaguely spherical, about eight inches in diameter, but composed entirely of toothpick-sized metallic-crystal rods, connected to one another in a chaotic and haphazard fashion." Harry calls it Vulcan chess, but Tuvok says that *kal-toh* is to chess as chess is to tic-tac-toe. The game is about finding the seeds of order, even in the midst of profound chaos. ▪ *T'san s'at* is the Vulcan intellectual deconstruction of emotional patterns. According to Tuvok, Kim is experiencing *shon-ha'lock*, the engulfment. It is the most intense and psychologically perilous form of eros, which humans call "love at first sight." The cure for *shon-ha'lock* is logical deconstruction followed by a regimen of meditative suppression. In the holoresort, Tuvok says that Neelix functioned in Vulcan terms as the *soo-lak*, the third party who by his very lack of interest trivializes Kim's. Meanwhile, the arrival of Kes with Marayna precipitated the *k'oh-nar,*

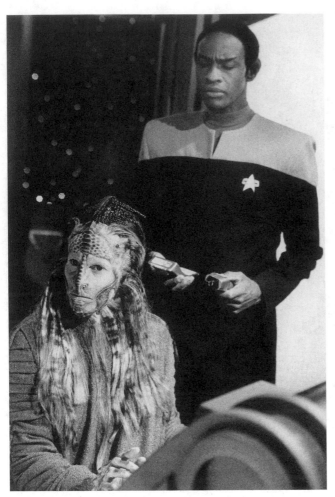

Tuvok discovers Marayna was living in a space station within the nebula. ROBBIE ROBINSON

FAIR TRADE

EPISODE # 156

TELEPLAY BY: ANDRE BORMANIS

STORY BY: RONALD WILKERSON & JEAN LOUIS MATTHIAS

DIRECTED BY: JESÚS SALVADOR TREVIÑO

GUEST STARS

WIXIBAN	JAMES NARDINI
BAHRAT	CARLOS CARRASCO
VORIK	ALEXANDER ENBERG
SUTOK	STEVE KEHELA
TOSIN	JAMES HORAN

CO-STAR

MAP VENDOR	ERIC SHARP

STARDATE: UNKNOWN

Neelix thinks he may be at the end of his usefulness to the crew when *Voyager* comes upon the Nekrit Expanse, a vast region of space that he knows little about. Since he is their expert on the Delta Quadrant, Neelix is determined to find a detailed map of the area. He suggests they stop at a space station located near the edge of the Expanse, where Janeway, Chakotay, and Paris negotiate for supplies. At the same time, Neelix reunites with Wixiban, an old Talaxian friend who went to prison for a crime that he and Neelix participated in years earlier.

Wix offers to help Neelix secure a map and pergium, a rare commodity required by engineering. The items can be obtained with the help of a trade negotiation in which Wix is already involved. Neelix borrows one of *Voyager*'s shuttles to deliver Wix's medical supplies, but when they arrive at the exchange site, a fight breaks out. Wix kills his contact, Sutok, with a Starfleet phaser from the shuttle.

Fleeing, Neelix realizes that the deal was not to bring medical aid, but to traffic in narcotics. Because he feels he is indebted to Wix, Neelix agrees to keep quiet about the murder. When Bahrat, the station manager, tells Janeway that a Federation weapon was involved in the slaying, an investigation is launched. Neelix's troubles deepen when Wix insists Neelix must steal warp plasma from *Voyager* to pay off the drug dealers, whose narcotics were stolen by Sutok's gang during the fight.

Later, Neelix meets with Wix and admits that he could not bring himself to steal from *Voyager*. At the same time, Bahrat arrests Paris and Chakotay for the murder. Unwilling to see his friends pay the price for a crime they did not commit, Neelix develops a new plan and trap for

the feeling of being completely exposed. ▪ Also according to Tuvok, Vulcans do not hydro-sail.

Chakotay notes that there is precedent for a hologram gaining sentience and taking over the ship, citing the Moriarty program on the *Enterprise*-D ("Ship in a Bottle" *TNG*) Kim says that he learned about the incident at Starfleet Academy.

PERSONAL LOGS: Tuvok took lessons in *kal-toh* from a master, starting at the age of five. ▪ Kim tries meditation to suppress his feelings for Marayna. ▪ For the luau, Paris replicates an exact re-creation of a 1963 Big Daddio Surf Special, a Hawaiian shirt he calls an American classic. He also tells Harry that "we've all fallen for a holodeck character before." ▪ Neelix has done a great deal of ethnographic research on the Polynesian cultures of Earth for the luau.

Ensign Vorik makes his first appearance, showing an attraction for Torres that will play an important catalyst for the events of "Blood Fever."

Old friends reunite. ROBBIE ROBINSON

Bahrat details the trading post's strict rules. ROBBIE ROBINSON

the top narcotics dealer, Tosin. The ploy works, and Tosin is arrested. Although Janeway is furious with Neelix for getting the crew involved in illicit activities, she understands that he was motivated by a misguided attempt to help them. Rather than putting him off the ship as he expected, she sentences him to two weeks scrubbing the exhaust manifolds.

SENSOR READINGS: Pergium is needed to regenerate the filters in the environmental control system. Neelix is able to obtain twenty kilograms of pergium, but not all that they need. Wix provides magnetic spindle bearings for reaction control assembly. ▪ The plasma flow in the warp manifold is constricted. The first thing Torres does in attempting to correct the problem is phase lock them to the dilithium matrix. She asks Vorik for a duotronic probe, but he suggests a gravitic caliper instead, citing that it is a more precise instrument. ▪ Neelix is having problems with the control interface on the mess hall food replicators. ▪ Starfleet standard issue L647X7 is the proper container for transporting a supply of biomimetic gel.

DELTA QUADRANT: The Nekrit Expanse is a vast territory of interstellar dust clouds thousands of light years wide. Plasma storms are a problem for navigation and, due to their instability, make the region too difficult to chart. ▪ Any transaction conducted on the Nekrit Supply Depot is subject to Manager Bahrat's approval, and he receives a twenty percent commission on all trade. The

punishment for trafficking in illicit substances is fifty years of cryostatic imprisonment. The Kolaati are arrested under Station Code 4279 Subsection Beta 325. Rhuludian crystals are an alien narcotic illegally sold on the station.

Wix has been stuck on the space station for three years. His ship was impounded and he cannot afford to give Bahrat what he wants to get it out. He and Neelix were involved in an incident with the Ubeans for which he spent a year in one of their prisons while Neelix remained free.

PERSONAL LOGS: Neelix has completed his study of Starship security protocols and feels fully qualified to serve in the capacity of a Starfleet security officer, junior grade. He has also been getting up to speed on the Federation warp propulsion. Neelix was a contraband smuggler before his position on *Voyager.* As punishment for his actions, he is told to report to deuterium maintenance at 0400 the following morning, where he will spend the next two weeks scrubbing the exhaust manifolds.

EPISODE LOGS: In the *Star Trek* episode "The Devil in the Dark," pergium was the material being mined at the Janus VI mining colony where the *Enterprise* was sent to investigate a number of mysterious deaths.

THE END OF THE AFFAIR: KES AND NEELIX

"Maybe I didn't realize a relationship could be any different. I've never been involved with anyone but you. It might be a good idea, for both of us, to spend some time apart . . . I'm sorry."

Kes, "Warlord"

He was her first love, but with those words, the relationship between Kes and Neelix came to an end. Though the pairing was established in the pilot, the full extent of the relationship went somewhat undefined as the series progressed. The surprise ending came while Kes was possessed by Tieran in "Warlord," and though her mind reverted to normal by the end of the episode, her relationship with Neelix did not.

"In 'Warlord,' when we broke up, there was not any kind of an acknowledgment by the writers of that. And I remember approaching them and saying I really think that they deserve their closure. And their feeling was 'No, let's just drop it, let's move on.' "

—Ethan Phillips

The courtship of Kes and Neelix provided much insight into both of their characters. From the moment Neelix tricked the *Voyager* crew into saving Kes, the pattern of their relationship was established. Neelix would do anything for her, and she would do the same in return; although it definitely was Kes who "wore the pants in the family." Though Neelix was much older, Kes was often the wiser, keeping her Talaxian on the straight and narrow while learning all that she could from him and her new friends on *Voyager.*

The largest hurdle in their pairing was Neelix's unchecked, and unjustified, jealousy. Hints of his possessiveness could be seen as early as "Parallax," when he shot a deathly glance at Paris for politely offering Kes his seat in a senior staff meeting. Although elements of his jealousy would be seen throughout the first season, it was in "Twisted" that they ran amuck. Following Paris's gift of a locket for Kes on her second birthday, Neelix's feelings of discomfort intensified as she innocently rattled off the locations of the quarters of various men in the crew. In "Parturition" the jealousy exploded as, shortly after Paris realized that he did have feelings for Kes, Neelix attacked him in the mess hall with a plate of Alfarian hair pasta, and a fight ensued. Forced to work together after crash landing on a planet the pair managed to settle their differences, which ultimately helped Neelix curb his feelings of jealousy.

ROBBIE ROBINSON

In spite of Neelix's bouts of envy, the pair did share a loving relationship and were there for each other in times of calm and crisis. Kes went so far as to donate her lung to Neelix so that he would not have to live in an isotropic restraint for the rest of his life ("Phage"). And Neelix was there for her when her body prematurely entered into the *elogium* and she needed to mate immediately if she was to ever have a child (*"Elogium"*). She asked Neelix to be the father of the child. Though he showed some initial reluctance, he ultimately decided that he was ready to be a father, although by that time Kes realized that she might not be ready to be a mother.

Neelix and his "sweeting," Kes, shared their first onscreen kiss inside what they believed to be a nebula in "The Cloud." Later, she tried to help him deal with his emotions after meeting Dr. Jetrel, the man responsible for inventing the weapon that killed his family during the Talaxian-Haakonian war ("Jetrel"). And in "Cold Fire," while performing mental exercises with Tuvok, she was able to pick out Neelix's thoughts from those of the rest of the crew, which Tuvok attributed to their close bond. In that same episode, when offered the chance to remain on the space station with the Ocampa, she asked Neelix to stay along with her.

One of the largest challenges in their relationship came when, due to a transporter accident, Neelix and Tuvok merged into one being ("Tuvix"). Although Kes eventually adjusted to the man who had Neelix's thoughts and feelings, she could not bring herself to ask the captain to spare Tuvix when the Doctor discovered a way to restore Neelix and Tuvok.

Though the pairing ended around the time of "Warlord," Kes and Neelix continued to have a bond, a fact they discussed over a bottle of moon-ripened Talaxian champagne in the mess hall moments before her newfound abilities forced her to leave the ship in "The Gift." Though their final scene together in that episode did provide the closure the characters were looking for, there still seemed to be a spark when, in the sixth-season episode "Fury," Kes returned on a mission of vengeance and appeared to experience a moment of solace with her former beau.

Much earlier than that the following scene was originally written for "Fair Trade," to help the pair move on. Regretfully, it had to be cut from the episode due to time constraints.

48. INT. SCIENCE LAB

KES is doing inventory on a carton of supplies when Neelix ENTERS. She glances at him, uncertain of what is to come. She has no way of knowing that he believes this is the last time he will ever see her.

KES

Hello, Neelix . . .

NEELIX

Kes . . . I wanted to clear the air
between us. It's very apparent
that our relationship has been
changing . . . that we aren't close
in the way we once were . . .

KES

I know. We seem to have . . .
drifted apart.

NEELIX

Maybe it's for the best. But I
want you to know . . . you've been
the finest friend anyone could
have. I'll always cherish that.

KES

Neelix . . . you sound as though
you're saying goodbye . . .
we'll always be friends, won't we?

NEELIX

Of course. Always.

Kes moves to him and gives him a quick kiss on the cheek—friendship only, nothing sensual. Neelix stands like a rock and then smiles sadly at her and EXITS. Kes looks after him, a bit puzzled.

BLOOD FEVER

EPISODE #157

WRITTEN BY: **LISA KLINK**

DIRECTED BY: **ANDREW ROBINSON**

GUEST STARS

VORIK	ALEXANDER ENBERG
ISHAN	BRUCE BOHNE
ENSIGN LANG	DEBORAH LEVIN

STARDATE 50537.2

Preparing for an away mission to an uninhabited planet that has a large reserve of gallicite, Torres is taken aback when Ensign Vorik, a Vulcan, asks her to be his mate. She declines, but Vorik grabs hold of her face and she dislocates his jaw in response. The Doctor concludes that Vorik is going through a Vulcan mating ritual known as the *Pon farr.* Although the ensign refuses to discuss the very personal experience, it is clear that if he does not mate, he may die. Seeing no other option, Vorik attempts to get through the difficult period by engaging in intensive meditation.

The away team begins the search for the gallicite, but Torres is strangely aggressive, at one point viciously biting Paris. After reluctantly interviewing Vorik about the encounter with Torres, Tuvok realizes that the young Vulcan initiated a telepathic mating bond with Torres when he touched her face. Now Torres is also experiencing *Pon farr.* Vorik is half-mad with his desire to mate with Torres, but he is forced to remain on *Voyager,* where the Doctor tries to help him by programming a holographic Vulcan female.

Back on the planet, Paris, Tuvok, and Chakotay locate Torres and explain to her what she is experiencing. As they try to convince her to leave the planet, a group of subterranean aliens surround the away team. A scuffle breaks out and the aliens disappear with Chakotay and Tuvok, leaving Paris and Torres alone. While searching for their missing crew members, Torres alludes to the idea of Paris mating with her, but he refuses to take advantage of her in her altered state.

Chakotay and Tuvok convince their alien captors, the Sakari, that they have no hostile intentions. The Sakari explain that they moved underground after unknown invaders attacked their ancestors. Since that time, they

The away team is surprised to find life on the planet. ROBBIE ROBINSON

have done everything in their power to remain hidden from passing ships. Chakotay offers to help the Sakari prevent future attacks in exchange for some gallicite. Elsewhere, Torres tries to seduce Paris, but he again rejects her advances. Not long after, Tuvok and Chakotay locate the pair. Observing that Torres is suffering from the advanced stages of the *Pon farr* Tuvok instructs Paris to ease the condition by allowing nature to take its course.

Suddenly, Vorik interrupts the pair. He challenges Paris for Torres, but Torres takes up the challenge herself and engages in the ritual battle, overcoming Vorik. The blood fever purged, the crew prepares to leave the sector as Chakotay finds evidence of the invaders that attacked the Sakari. He brings Janeway to witness the horrific find: a decayed skeleton. *Voyager* has had their first Delta Quadrant sighting of the Borg.

SENSOR READINGS: Gallicite is a very rare substance. Scans indicate a yield of nearly a kiloton on the planet, which would be enough to completely refit the warp coils. It is unclear exactly how much gallicite the crew receives from the Sakari, but the "generous supply" yields enough for Torres to have new warp coils by the end of the week.

SHUTTLE TRACKER: Before beaming down to the planet to claim Torres, Vorik disables the ship's communications, transporters, and shuttles.

DELTA QUADRANT: The Sakari colony is on the fourth planet in what the crew believes to be an uninhabited star system. The planet is full of seismic activity, and the Sakari possess technology that warns them of coming quakes.

ALPHA QUADRANT: The *Pon farr,* or blood fever, which occurs every seven years in a Vulcan's adult life, is when he or she experiences an instinctual urge to return to the homeworld and mate. This is accompanied by a neurochemical imbalance within the brain that can prove fatal if the drive to mate is not acted upon. There are three options that will cause the *Pon farr* to abate: taking a mate, performing ritual combat, or undergoing intensive meditation. *Kunat so'lik* is the Vulcan expression of desire to become someone's mate (similar to proposing marriage for humans). The *kunat Kal-if-fee* is the Vulcan ritual challenge.

In Klingon mating practices, fracturing a clavicle on the wedding night is considered a blessing on the marriage. Biting one's partner also has significance in Klingon

Paris refuses to act on Torres's advances. ROBBIE ROBINSON

mating rituals, though it is not specifically defined (but it is assumed to be the way of initiating physical relations).

PERSONAL LOGS: Tuvok has an artificial implant in his arm. It was necessary to replace the elbow joint after he was injured in a combat simulation. ▪ Paris has a lot of rock climbing experience. ▪ Neelix worked in a mining colony in one of his many pre-*Voyager* jobs. He falls in the cave and suffers a possible broken leg.

Ensign Vorik experiences *Pon farr* for the first time. He admits to having an arranged mate back on Vulcan, though he suspects she has probably been promised to another, as a respectable amount of time has passed since *Voyager* disappeared. Vorik spent several summers exploring the Osana caverns, which involved some quite treacherous climbing. ▪ Ensign Lang also works at ops.

CREW COMPLEMENT: According to Vorik, there are seventy-three male crew members onboard (it is assumed he is not including the Doctor in that number.)

EPISODE LOGS: The concept of *Pon farr* was first introduced in the *Star Trek* episode "Amok Time." ▪ The director of "Blood Fever," Andrew Robinson, may be more familiar to *Star Trek* fans from his role as Garak on *Deep Space Nine.* ▪ The aliens are the Sakari, not to be confused with the Sikarians from "Prime Factors."

CODA

EPISODE #158

WRITTEN BY: JERI TAYLOR
DIRECTED BY: NANCY MALONE

GUEST STARS

ADMIRAL JANEWAY   LEN CARIOU

CO-STAR

COMPUTER VOICE   MAJEL BARRETT

STARDATE 50518.6

When Chakotay and Janeway are forced to make an emergency landing, Chakotay suspects that Vidiians may be responsible for the damage to their shuttlecraft. A group of Vidiians arrives and attacks the pair, killing them. Then, suddenly, they are alive and back on the shuttlecraft, under attack by Vidiian warships. This time, the shuttle explodes before it can land. Seconds later, they are once again back at their stations in the shuttle.

Believing they are trapped in a time loop, the two officers manage to contact *Voyager* and this time elude the Vidiians. However, back on the ship, Chakotay refutes Janeway's claims about the temporal anomaly. The Doctor

Janeway experiences one of her many deaths. ROBBIE ROBINSON

diagnoses Janeway as suffering from the Vidiian phage and euthanizes her against her will, after which Janeway finds herself back on the shuttle with Chakotay. As they near a strange phenomenon in space, the shuttle explodes, and the next thing Janeway knows, she is back on the planet, watching Chakotay grieve over her dead body.

Returning to *Voyager* with Chakotay, Janeway discovers that the crew is unaware of her presence. In sickbay, the Doctor's attempts to revive her corpse are unsuccessful, but Janeway is able to get Kes to telepathically sense her presence. As the crew wonders if the captain is lost in an alternate dimension, Janeway is shocked to come face-to-face with her deceased father. Admiral Janeway tells her that she really did die in the shuttle crash, and tries to convince her she should accept that fact. Meanwhile, after days of unsuccessfully trying to reach Janeway, the crew accepts that their captain is dead and holds a memorial service.

Janeway tells her father that she is not ready to leave the crew yet. Suddenly, Janeway is in her corporeal body with the Doctor trying to revive her. Her father tells her it is a hallucination and urges her to give up. Janeway knows her real father would not push her in this way, and realizes that for some reason an alien has assumed her father's image to lure her to her death. Indeed, an alien presence has invaded her cerebral cortex, but now that she is aware of it, Janeway fights harder and regains consciousness on the planet's surface.

SENSOR READINGS: When the crew searches for Janeway's presence on the ship, Torres reconfigures the lateral sensor array to scan subspace. She has the forward array ready to scan for temporal phase shifting, chroniton particles, or field flux and activates the magneton scanner to see if it might pick up an anomalous presence. ∎ Janeway and Chakotay went to the planet to collect nitrogenase compound (though it is unclear why the captain and first officer chose to go by themselves on this mission).

SHUTTLE TRACKER: The *Shuttlecraft Sacajawea* is caught in a magnetic storm and crash lands on the second planet of a binary system. Attitude control and navigational systems are out. When hydrazine gas levels reach 112 parts per measure, the computer tells them to evacuate the ship, at which point where Janeway experiences her first death hallucination when she is physically attacked by a Vidiian. ∎ The shuttle is attacked two additional times in Janeway's hallucinations. In the first attack a Vidiian ship fires on the reactant injectors, which need to be shut down so they do not leak antimatter. The mag-

Janeway witnesses her own memorial as the life-form, impersonating her father, pleads with her to leave the ship. ROBBIE ROBINSON

netic fields fail and the gas flow separators go down, forcing them to dump the shuttle's warp core. In the second shuttle hallucination, Janeway and Chakotay use a tachyon burst to disperse the temporal field in which they believe themselves to be trapped. ▪ The crashed shuttle is retrieved.

DELTA QUADRANT: The unnamed alien entity inhabits Janeway's cerebral cortex. It tells her that its species comes to help the dying to make the crossing over to their Matrix an occasion of joy. It initially describes the Matrix as a place of wonder, but when Janeway proves uncooperative, it informs her that in the Matrix, Janeway will nourish the alien for a long, long time. It is unclear whether or not the alien entity is unique to the Delta Quadrant or is responsible for stories of near death experiences in the Alpha Quadrant as well.

PERSONAL LOGS: Neelix hosts a talent show for the crew and asks the captain if it could be a monthly event (and if she could keep Tuvok busy for the next one). ▪ Janeway danced the "Dying Swan" at the talent show, claiming it to have been the hit of the beginning ballet class when she was six years old. Her father, Admiral

Janeway, died over fifteen years ago when he drowned under the polar ice cap on Tau Ceti Prime. Janeway was so grief-stricken over her father's death that she fell into a terrible depression and spent months in bed, sleeping away the days, rather than confronting her feelings. During that time, there were several occasions when she woke up certain that her father was in the room until ultimately, her sister forced her into the real world again. Janeway's father/alien referred to her as "poor little bird." To revive her, the Doctor first uses cordrazine along with the cortical stimulator followed by synaptic stimulation and ultimately a thoron pulse. Since Janeway cheated death, she invites Chakotay to celebrate with a bottle of champagne and a moonlight sail on Lake George. ▪ Chakotay did not participate in the talent show, in which Tuvok read Vulcan poetry and Kim played his clarinet.

MEDICAL REPORT: In her hallucination, the Doctor tells Janeway that she has concomitant stress to the thalamus and is in the early stages of the phage. The injury is known to cause a kind of dementia that results in hallucinations. The Doctor fills the quarantined area of sickbay with neural toxin as a means of euthanizing Janeway.

EPISODE LOGS: In the hallucination, Kes senses Janeway's presence on the ship. It was established in "Cathexis" that she had this ability. ▪ Also in the hallucination, Torres suggests that Janeway may have phase shifted, which is a reference to what happened to Geordi LaForge and Ro Laren in the *TNG* episode "The Next Phase."

UNITY

EPISODE #159

WRITTEN BY: KENNETH BILLER
DIRECTED BY: ROBERT DUNCAN McNEILL

GUEST STARS

RILEY FRAZIER	LORI HALLIER
ORUM	IVAR BROGGER

CO-STAR

KAPLAN	SUSAN PATTERSON

STARDATE 50614.2

Lost while returning from a scouting mission, the shuttle manned by Chakotay and Ensign Kaplan picks up a Federation distress call from a planet. After launching a buoy to let *Voyager* know where they

are, they land the craft to render assistance, but are quickly attacked by a hostile group of humanoids. Kaplan is killed and Chakotay injured before help arrives in the form of another group, led by a human woman named Riley who gets Chakotay to safety. Riley explains she is part of a cooperative of different species that were kidnapped by aliens and left to fend for themselves. However, the other kidnapped aliens outside of the cooperative are not as friendly.

Back on *Voyager,* the crew finds a Borg cube adrift in space. When they board it, they discover the Borg crew is dead. An investigation reveals the ship ceased operation five years earlier. Finding a perfectly preserved Borg body, they bring it aboard for the Doctor to study.

On the planet, Chakotay discovers that Riley's story was only partially truthful and learns that she and the others were once Borg. Five years ago, their ship was damaged by an electrokinetic storm that severed their link to the Borg collective. Those that survived settled on the planet, but they quickly began fighting each other for the limited food and supplies. Riley is hoping Chakotay can help them. However, right now it is Chakotay who needs help. Badly injured from the attack, his only option is to temporarily join his mind with Riley and the rest of her small cooperative in a healing link. Afterward, his injuries are improved, and Chakotay feels far closer to the group, particularly Riley.

Tracking Chakotay's buoy, *Voyager* locates him and

The Doctor hopes a post-mortem on a Borg will aid the crew. ROBBIE ROBINSON

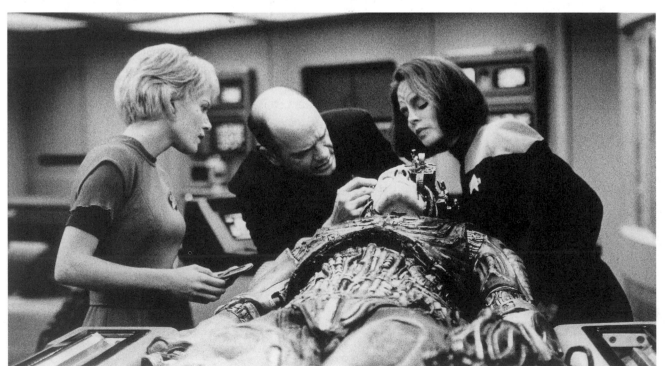

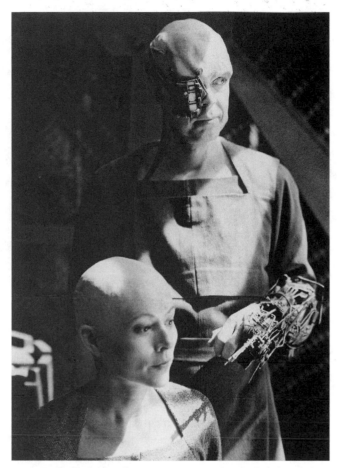

Desperate for peace, the Borg cooperative forces Chakotay to do their bidding. ROBBIE ROBINSON

beams the first officer and Riley up to the ship. Riley asks Janeway to help her use the generator on the dead Borg vessel to reestablish a neural link among all the former Borg on the planet. She believes this will stop the fighting and allow them to work together to build a true community. Janeway refuses, fearing that activating the Borg ship and creating a new collective could be dangerous to all. Riley returns to the planet, but she and her group use their former link with Chakotay to force him to assist in their plan. Chakotay takes a shuttle to the cube and does as they ask. As soon as the link is re-established, the new collective destroys the Borg cube and releases Chakotay from their link, thanking him and the *Voyager* crew for their coerced help.

SENSOR READINGS: Chakotay estimates that it will take sixty-seven years to get home from this point in *Voyager's* journey. ▪ Electrodynamic turbulence from the nebula interferers with *Voyager's* communications system. ▪ *Voyager's* warp plasma filters are due for a thorough cleaning.

SHUTTLE TRACKER: Destroyed. A type-9 shuttle is stripped by the former Borg. Though the ship goes unnamed, it is not the *Cochrane* (because that ship will be destroyed later). Later, another type-9 shuttle is seen while yet another shuttle of unspecified type is mentioned but goes unseen.

DELTA QUADRANT: Eighty thousand humanoid lifesigns are on the planet's western continent. Some rudimentary structures and technology exist, but no energy signature large enough to be a starship. There are three humans that Riley knows of, besides her, along with some Klingons, Cardassians, Romulans, and dozens of other species she has never seen before. Riley was assimilated at Wolf 359, where she was a science officer aboard the *Starship Roosevelt*. Five years ago, their Borg cube was damaged by an electrokinetic storm and their link to the collective was severed. After relocating to the planet, they found that resources were scarce, and it did not take long for the fighting to start. First a group of Klingons attacked the Cardassians, then the Farn raided the Parein. Eventually, anarchy reigned. ▪ The cooperative attaches a small neurotransmitter at the base of Chakotay's skull to link with him for healing purposes. The neural transponder they have built is only powerful enough to link a small group of people and the effect is only temporary. In order to reconnect the entire population permanently, they need a much bigger neural-electrical field generator, like that found on the Borg cube. ▪ Riley's favorite flowers are bluebonnets. She used to pick them with her grandfather.

If the crew can get the cube's Borg access nodes operational, they can tap into the main data systems. Scans of the Borg cube detect 1,100 corpses. The Borg collective consciousness allows them to transfer information instantaneously, to think with one mind, and it also has inherent medical applications. The Borg were connected by a continuous neuro-electric field that was capable of regenerating the damaged components of an injured Borg, and of healing both organic and inorganic body parts. In the autopsy of the Borg, the Doctor determines that the subject's pulmonary system exhibits evidence of extensive alveolar damage, as well as a slight swelling consistent with exposure to space. In addition, there are signs of severe cardiac depolarization, making it appear that he was electrocuted. The Doctor accesses an axonal amplifier and inadvertently activates a backup neuro-electric power cell. The autonomic response causes the drone to reset back to its original programming.

PERSONAL LOGS: Chakotay is a vegetarian. ▪ To help him out of his depression over Riley, Torres challenges Chakotay to a game of hoverball.

Mister McKenzie works at tactical.

CREW COMPLEMENT: Ensign Kaplan is killed by a rogue group of the former Borg.

EPISODE LOGS: The Battle of Wolf 359 that Riley refers to was the attack led by Captain Picard as Locutus of Borg ("The Best of Both Worlds" *TNG*). It is the same attack in which *DS9*'s Captain Sisko lost his wife, Jennifer. The Borg ship is believed to have been destroyed in the *DS9* episode "Emissary."

RISE!

EPISODE #160
TELEPLAY BY: **BRANNON BRAGA**
STORY BY: **JIMMY DIGGS**
DIRECTED BY: **ROBERT SCHEERER**

GUEST STARS

NEZU AMBASSADOR	**ALAN OPPENHEIMER**
LILLIAS	**LISA KAMINIR**
SKLAR	**KELLY CONNELL**
VATM	**TOM TOWLES**
HANJUAN	**GEOF PRYSIRR**

CO-STAR

GOTH	**GARY BULLOCK**

STARDATE UNKNOWN

As *Voyager* makes an unsuccessful attempt to destroy the asteroids threatening a Nezu planet, a distorted message comes from Vatm, an astrophysicist who has been analyzing the asteroid fragments on the surface below. Vatm wants to talk to the Nezu ambassador, who is currently aboard *Voyager,* claiming he has important information about the asteroids.

Unable to find the scientist's exact location due to interference in the ionosphere, Tuvok and a Nezu named Sklar take a shuttle to the surface along with Neelix, who sees the mission as a chance to log in more Starfleet training and try to win over the inflexible security chief. The same interference that has been blocking *Voyager*'s scans causes their shuttle to crash. Although they find Vatm, the crash has left them with no way to contact the ship. Neelix suggests they reactivate a mag-lev carriage that is tethered to an orbital space station. If they can rise above the atmospheric turbulence, they will be able to communicate with the ship. But as soon as they make the tether system operational, Vatm tries to leave by himself. Tuvok manages to stop him, and the group, along with two additional passengers, heads for the clouds.

Seeing no other option, Sklar grabs a phaser. DANNY FELD

The upward journey is uncomfortable and dangerous. Vatm refuses to say why he attempted to leave without them and sips at water to ease his discomfort. Later, he becomes delirious, insisting that something of great importance is on the roof of the carriage. Then he has a seizure and dies. Finding a poisonous substance in his water, Tuvok quickly concludes that the scientist was murdered.

Neelix insists they find out what is on the roof, and Tuvok reluctantly climbs up. He finds a data storage device that contains information about an alien vessel. After sneaking up behind the Vulcan, Sklar pushes Tuvok off the roof, but he survives by clinging to an induction coil on the bottom of the carriage. Neelix helps Tuvok back inside and in the ensuing struggle Sklar plunges to his death. Forced to reevaluate his treatment of Neelix, Tuvok begins to warm up to the Talaxian.

Finally, the group is able to contact *Voyager* and they are beamed aboard. The ship is in the midst of a confrontation with the Etanian Order, a group that has claimed the Nezu homeworld as their own. It turns out that the Etanians create "natural" disasters—like meteor showers—on the planets they covet, then take over when the residents evacuate. With the tactical information from the device Tuvok found, Janeway is able to disable the Etanian vessel. The crew realizes that Vatm knew there was a traitor among the Nezu, which turned out to be Sklar.

SENSOR READINGS: Tuvok injects the group with tri-ox compound to oxygenate their blood.

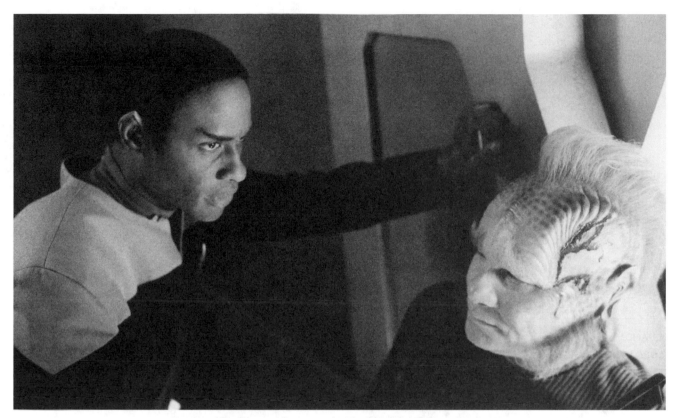

Tuvok and Neelix try to figure out the identity of the saboteur. DANNY FELD

DAMAGE REPORT: Structural integrity starts to fail due to the Etanian attack.

SHUTTLE TRACKER: Three shuttles are sent to search for Dr. Vatm. A layer of electrodynamic disturbance in the planet's atmosphere forces Tuvok and Neelix's shuttle down. It is unclear whether or not the shuttle is retrieved.

DELTA QUADRANT: The Nezu have five colonies on the planet. The asteroid debris lands on the largest continent approximately five hundred kilometers from the southern tip in an area that is not heavily populated known as the Central Desert. The next asteroid will hit in six hours on the same continent on the eastern coastal region, which is home to one of their largest colonies with over five thousand citizens. ▪ Mag-lev carriers are used to lift cargo to the orbital supply station using magnetic leverage to lift the carriage. The tether is over three hundred kilometers long, and it takes twelve hours to reach the top. The carriage was damaged on the last impact and the induction coils are offline and oxygen converters damaged. Neelix suggests they replace the coils with attitude control thrusters from the shuttle. They keep mag-lev velocity at forty-seven kilometers per hour. There is a gallicite excavation near the shuttle crash site.

According to *Voyager*'s sensors the asteroids appear to be made of a simple nickel-iron composition. Upon closer examination, Torres determines that the asteroid is composed of tryoxene, olivine, and triadium: an alloy that is present in the control node for an asteroid guidance system. ▪ The Etanian Order ship has a crew complement of at least 2,000. They remodulate their shields to fool *Voyager*'s sensors, making them read as if they are an asteroid. ▪ Tuvok determines that Vatm was poisoned when his cardiopulmonary tissues begin to deteriorate immediately. Acording to tricorder readings, his water supply was contaminated with a lydroxide corrosive, the coolant used in the tether couplings. Vatm's data storage device contains technical information about the Etanian ship including weapons, warp drive, and shield modulations.

PERSONAL LOGS: Tuvok's lungs are capable of respirations in an extremely thin atmosphere and he possesses physical strength above that of the average humanoid. ▪ Neelix claims that he spent two years on a mag-lev tether maintenance team on Rinax. In reality, his experience with the equipment is limited to building one-tenth scale models of mag-lev carriers. Neelix names the mag-lev carriage Alixia, after his favorite sister. He says that she was always taking him out to explore and she showed him the Caves of Touth, the equatorial dust shrouds, and even took him hunting for arctic spiders. Tuvok gives Neelix a special commendation for his endurance and bravery.

DARKLING

EPISODE #161
TELEPLAY BY: JOE MENOSKY
STORY BY: BRANNON BRAGA & JOE MENOSKY
DIRECTED BY: ALEX SINGER

GUEST STARS

ZAHIR	DAVID LEE SMITH
NAKAHN	STEPHEN DAVIES

CO-STARS

GHANDI	NOEL DE SOUZA
LORD BYRON	CHRISTOPHER CLARKE
ENSIGN	SUE HENLEY
COMPUTER VOICE	MAJEL BARRETT

STARDATE 50693.2

The crew visits an outpost of the Mikhal Travelers, a gypsylike band of space explorers who are willing to share their knowledge of the territory *Voyager* is about to enter. As Kes oversees the transfer of medical supplies to the group, she becomes infatuated with Zahir, a Mikhal pilot.

In the meantime, the Doctor is engaged in a new project to add personality routines of famous historical figures—such as Gandhi and Lord Byron—to his own program in order to enhance his performance. Torres expresses concern that the subroutines may interact unpredictably and offers to review his program.

As Kes grows increasingly fond of Zahir, the Doctor points out that she is neglecting her duties in sickbay. Later, Kes confides to Janeway that Zahir has asked her to leave *Voyager* and travel with him. As she ponders her decision, Zahir is seriously injured when a mysterious figure pushes him off a cliff. Shortly after, the cloaked man enters a local bar and reveals himself to be the Doctor.

The next day, a distraught Kes recounts Zahir's injuries to the Doctor, who seems genuinely surprised over the news of the attack. As he and Kes leave to attend to the injured Zahr, they are interrupted by Torres, who has found a potential problem with his program, she attempts to stop him from beaming to the planet. Later, Tuvok and Janeway find Torres collapsed on the floor of sickbay. The Doctor claims that she is in anaphylactic shock caused by something she ate, but after the pair leave, it becomes clear that he is the one who caused Torres's condition. The Doctor unsuccessfully tries to coerce her into removing his original "bland" personality from his unstable blend of subroutines that are rapidly destabilizing.

As Tuvok investigates the attack on Zahir, the Doctor attempts to adjust his program on his own. When Kes

Lord Byron and Gandhi are just two of the personalities the Doctor adds to his program. ROBBIE ROBINSON

interrupts him on the holodeck, he kidnaps her, taking her with him to the planet. The discovery of residual holographic signatures near the attack site alerts the crew that the Doctor is the culprit. Attempting to flee the planet, the Doctor forces Kes along the mountain path where he assaulted Zahir.

When the ship's scanners are finally able to locate the pair, Tuvok and Chakotay manage to trap the Doctor on the mountain. Refusing to give up, he throws himself and Kes over a cliff. Finally breaking through the scattering field the Doctor had set up to protect himself, *Voyager's* transporter beams them up before they hit bottom. Torres, now healed from the Doctor's evil machinations, is able to delete the dangerous subroutines, which restores the Doctor to normal. Realizing that it would be best to experience her life changes in familiar surroundings, Kes decides to remain on *Voyager* with her friends.

SENSOR READINGS: The asteroids of a nearby system are rich in vorilium, which *Voyager* needs.

DELTA QUADRANT: The Mikhal Travelers are a loosely governed race of explorers that have extensive knowledge of the territory ahead of *Voyager,* which they are willing to share. Their people have a saying: "My course is as elusive as a shadow across the sky." They live for the excitement of facing the challenge of space alone, and their ships are small, with only a pilot and a navigator. ▪ Zahir directs Tuvok on a course away from a plasma belt to avoid the Tarkan sentries. While the course would add several months to *Voyager's* direct course to the Alpha Quadrant, it would keep the ship safe. The Tarkan sentries are known to remove an entire crew, settle them on a moon somewhere, and take their ship as a trophy. ▪ Zahir invites Kes to explore the Sylleran Rift with him. Since his ship travels at high warp they could rendezvous with *Voyager* afterward. ▪ Zahir is found unconscious at the bottom of a ravine. He is taken to the emergency outpost facility with multiple fractures, skin lacerations, and damage to the left occipital nerve. The Doctor has Kes prepare a medkit, including an osteo-regenerator.

ALPHA QUADRANT: Among the historical figures included in the EMH Program 4C are Gandhi, Lord Byron, Socrates, and T'Pau of Vulcan (Leonardo da Vinci and Madame Curie are mentioned, but unseen). Lord Byron is described as a creative, poetic genius, but also emotionally intense and even unstable. T'Pau is described as a diplomat, a judge, a philosopher, and one of the most logical minds in Vulcan history. However, she was utterly ruthless in her application of that logic.

Kes grows closer to Zahir. ROBBIE ROBINSON

PERSONAL LOGS: Janeway considered herself the acknowledged master of the all-nighter in her Academy days. ▪ Torres gets sick from eating a small salad because Klingons lack an enzyme for metabolizing the planet's vegetation. The Doctor notes that he included that information on his away team preparatory report; however, he says it is the fifth time in as many weeks that the report has been ignored. The Doctor says he believes Torres went into anaphylactic shock in reaction to the salad. In reality the Doctor's dark side shot her full of cateline to simulate the reaction. The customary treatment for anaphylactic shock in a Klingon is ten cc's of alizine. ▪ The Doctor adjusts his program hoping to gain an improved bedside manner, a fresh perspective on diagnoses, and "more patience with his patients." By interviewing the historical personality programs in the database, he selects the character elements he finds admirable and merges them into his own program. Torres warns him that behavioral subroutines have a way of interacting with each other that is not always predictable. When his dark side emerges to torture Torres, he uses an intraspinal inhibitor to paralyze her from the waist down. He also blocks her speech center. ▪ Kes, now three years old, is behind in her work due to the time she is spending with Zahir.

EPISODE LOGS: The Leonardo da Vinci holocharacter mentioned, but not seen in this episode, will become a recurring character as a mentor to Janeway, beginning with "Scorpion" ▪ The holocharacters Socrates and T'Pau play *kal-toh,* which was first introduced in "Alter Ego." ▪ The Doctor mentions Kes's recent breakup with Neelix ("Warlord"). This is the first time in an episode that it has been confirmed that the breakup actually occurred and was not solely a result of Kes's possession at the time. ▪ The shooting script notes when the Doctor is in "evil" mode, by setting the character's name off in quotations marks, i.e., "Doctor."

FAVORITE SON

EPISODE #162

WRITTEN BY: LISA KLINK

DIRECTED BY: MARVIN RUSH

GUEST STARS

ELIANN	CARI SHAYNE
LYRIS	DEBORAH MAY
TAYMON	PATRICK FABIAN
RINNA	KELLI KIRKLAND
MALIA	KRISTANNA S. LOKEN

CO-STARS

ALBEN	CHRISTOPHER CARROLL
KIM'S MOTHER	IRENE TSU

STARDATE 50732.4

During an encounter between *Voyager* and a Nasari ship, Kim triggers an unwanted battle when he inexplicably fires on the ship. As they limp away from the confrontation, Janeway grills Kim, who says he just "knew" the Nasari posed a threat, despite their nonaggressive behavior. The captain suspends Kim from duty until she can investigate his hunch. That evening, Kim is stunned by the appearance of alien markings on his face following an intense dream.

The Doctor is unable to find an explanation for Kim's facial markings or the alteration in his blood chemistry, although Tuvok is able to confirm that the Nasari were about to fire on *Voyager.* When the captain questions Kim on how he knew, he thinks it may have something to do with the sense of déjà vu he has been experiencing since they entered this sector of space. Under a new attack from Nasari forces, Kim leads the crew to safety at the planet Taresia, which has a largely female populace. Surprisingly, an official of the planet welcomes Kim home.

Kim feels responsible for Torres's injuries. ROBBIE ROBINSON

The Taresians explain that Kim was conceived on their world, but his embryo was implanted in an Earth woman, to bring an infusion of new genetic material back to their race. As adults, Taresians like Kim are instinctively drawn back home. The women say the Nasari fired on *Voyager* because they detected Kim's presence. The Nasari have a long-standing feud with the Taresians and were trying to stop Kim from going home. Later, Janeway meets with the Nasari captain, who says he has no quarrel with *Voyager* but will attack the ship if they return with Kim on board, although he says Kim's return is unlikely. When *Voyager* returns to the planet, the crew now finds that they are not welcome.

Based on the growing suspicions the Doctor does further research and informs Janeway that Kim was not born with Taresian DNA. According to the Doctor's records and a check of transporter logs, it appears that he was deliberately infused with the DNA during an away mission. Apparently, the Taresians want to make him feel as if he belongs on their world.

After attending the wedding of Taymon, another

"returned" Taresian male, Kim decides he wants to go back to his ship. When he tries to leave, the Taresian women refuse to let him go. He races to Taymon's room, where he is stunned to find the young man is dead. Kim discovers that men do not voluntarily leave the planet; they are killed after the women extract enough genetic material to conceive children. The crew is able to beam up Kim and leave the area while the Nasari are busy in battle with the Taresians.

DAMAGE REPORT: Pressure builds in plasma Conduit G-6 until it blows, warp engines are down, and plasma injectors and propulsion are offline. Aft shield emitter is offline while phasers are operational, but torpedo launchers are not.

DELTA QUADRANT: After logging a trinary star system, *Voyager* enters the Nasari territory. Alben is captain of the *Voyager.* A tetyron surge indicates that the ship was charging weapons because the surge matched the energy signature of the beam field.

Taresia is the third planet in its star system. When *Voyager* returns to Taresia, sensors indicate that a network of satellites are generating a high-density polaron grid surrounding the planet that blocks communications and keeps the ship from approaching the planet. The crew generates a new shield configuration to get through the barrier. ▪ The Taresians claim that ninety percent of their population is female. Males of other species are transformed so they can provide suitable DNA to procreate. The Taresians must nucleate a large number of cells to collect enough genetic material for conception, which kills the male in the process. ▪ The Taresian phrase *lekaria san* means "pleasant dreams."

PERSONAL LOGS: Kim is temporarily suspended from duty due to his actions on the bridge (actions that were later determined to be out of his control). He was sick with the Mendakan pox when he was nine. His parents are practically tone deaf. They had been trying to have a baby for years when he was born, and they referred to him as the "miracle baby," spoiling him rotten in the process.

MEDICAL REPORT: When the Doctor checks Kim's previous microcellular scans, he finds no traces of the Taresian genetic fragments. The alien DNA continues to alter his genetic structure, and within a few days he will

Kim and Eliann participate in the unsuspecting Taymon's wedding ceremony. BRYON J. COHEN

be indistinguishable from a native Taresian. The Doctor believes that he was exposed to a retrovirus that was laced with the alien DNA. Typically, the transporter bio-filters would pick up the virus and eliminate it, but once the virus transferred the DNA into his cells, the damage would have been done. Since the transporter buffer performs its own version of a microcellular scan every time someone uses it, the Doctor reviews the logs and finds the first appearance of the alien genes in Kim's molecular pattern on Stardate 50698. Chakotay notes that that was the date of an away mission to a planet with vorillium. ▪ Torres's injuries resulting from the Nasari attack include second-degree burns on her lungs; the Doctor performs a pulmonary regeneration to heal the injuries before her neural tissues totally degenerate from oxygen depravation. She also has second and third degree burns to her body and several broken ribs. Torres notes that Kim's new spots make him look like a speckled *targ.*

EPISODE LOGS: In the preceding episode "Darkling," Zahir informs Janeway that there are asteroids with much needed vorilium in their path. An away team then collects vorillium (note the spelling difference) from a planet on a stardate that falls between the two episodes. It is unclear whether or not the writers were referring to the same substance; however, the *Star Trek Encyclopedia* does refer to them as two different materials.

BEFORE AND AFTER

EPISODE #163
WRITTEN BY: **KENNETH BILLER**
DIRECTED BY: **ALLAN KROEKER**

GUEST STARS

LINNIS	JESSICA COLLINS
BENAREN	MICHAEL L. MAGUIRE
ANDREW	CHRISTOPHER AGUILAR
YOUNG KES	JANNA MICHAELS

CO-STAR

MARTIS	RACHEL HARRIS

STARDATE UNKNOWN

Kes wakes to find herself in sickbay, on the verge of death. She hears the Doctor activate something he calls a bio-temporal chamber and Kes experiences a shift in perception. She finds herself with a boy—apparently her grandson, Andrew—who gives her a belated birthday gift. The Doctor then tells her he is going to put her into a bio-temporal chamber to prolong her life, since she is in the *morilogium,* the final phase of

the Ocampan life span. Confused, Kes experiences another shift.

Kes is now in her quarters, where Andrew is working on the present that he has already given her. Kes meets Linnis, her daughter, who is married to Harry Kim. Linnis's father is Tom Paris, who is also Kes's husband. Kes tries to take this all in and explain to her family what is happening to her, but to her frustration they attribute it to delusions caused by the *morilogium.* Once again Kes involuntarily shifts into another time.

In the mess hall Kes is now celebrating her ninth birthday with her family and friends. Andrew tells her he has not had a chance to begin working on her present. Bewildered, but with more facts at her disposal, Kes tells the Doctor that she seems to be experiencing life in reverse. Consulting her medical records, Kes learns she suffered from chroniton radiation poisoning in the past when *Voyager* was under attack by the Krenim. Kes reasons that the radiation exposure may explain her condition, but before they can do anything with the information, Kes experiences another jump.

This time Kes immediately goes to the Doctor, who confirms that the chroniton particles, reactivated in the future by the bio-temporal chamber, are moving her

In an alternate timeline, Paris helps his wife, Kes, review the forgotten events of her life. ROBBIE ROBINSON

Kes is finally able to understand and prevent her time jumps. ROBBIE ROBINSON

backward in time. To stop the jumps, they must purge her of the radiation—and the only way to do that is to find out the temporal variance of the Krenim torpedo that contaminated her.

Kes continues jumping back in time, to the birth of Linnis, and to the Krenim attack, when she was exposed to the radiation. Finding the torpedo, she notes the temporal variance, then jumps again to a year earlier, where she warns Janeway to avoid Krenim space and gives the Doctor the information to program a bio-temporal chamber that will purge her system. As the chroniton count begins to drop, Kes experiences several more jumps, eventually arriving at her moment of conception. Just as she ceases to exist, her body is purged and she awakens back in the period in which they were using the chamber to eliminate the chroniton particles.

SENSOR READINGS: During the "Year of Hell" one of the Krenim's chroniton torpedo fragments leaks radiation into the ship. Their torpedoes are able to penetrate *Voyager*'s shields because they are in a constant state of temporal flux. *Voyager* is finally able to defend themselves against the Krenim by remodulating the scanners through a parametric frequency to destroy the torpedo launchers before they fire.

SHUTTLE TRACKER: A type-9 shuttle is seen in the alternate future during the "Year of Hell."

DELTA QUADRANT: The *morilogium* is the final stage of the Ocampa life span. It comes on abruptly and progresses at a speed the Doctor has never seen before. Ocampa babies are born from the mother's back ("*Elogium*") and come out feet first. The average body temperature of an Ocampan is 16.3 degrees Centigrade.

BETA QUADRANT: Some species, including the Yattho of the Beta Quadrant, have been known to predict future events with uncanny accuracy.

PERSONAL LOGS: Most of the following information comes from the alternate future timeline and is not true at the end of the episode: Janeway, Torres, and nine others are killed in the first Krenim attack, resulting in Chakotay assuming the role of captain and Tuvok being promoted to commander. ▪ Paris and Torres are romantically involved by the time of the first Krenmin attack. ▪ Kim is the best man at Paris and Kes's wedding. ▪ The Doctor is offline for months due to the Krenim attacks. After he goes back online, he gives himself a full head of hair and decides to name himself Doctor Van Gogh. He comes up with the idea for a bio-temporal chamber on the day of Kes's ninth birthday. ▪ Neelix is made a security officer. ▪ Kes is one of the ship's doctors. Her mother's name is Martis. (Her father's name is Benaren ["Dreadnought"].)

MEDICAL REPORT: Kes is exposed to a bio-temporal field in an attempt to stop her aging process. The field reactivates the dormant chroniton particles in her cells, pushing Kes out of temporal sync with the rest of the crew. To purge her completely of the chroniton poisoning they need to know the precise temporal variance of the specific torpedo that contaminated the ship. Once Kes determines that the temporal variance is 1.47 microseconds, they set up a bio-temporal chamber and expose her to a precisely modulated field of antichroniton particles. She is restored to the normal timeline at an age of three years and two months old at the end of the episode.

EPISODE LOGS: The events of the Krenim attacks will eventually be played out in the fourth season two-parter "Year of Hell." The first attack is said to begin on Stardate 50973 (In the later episode, however, the first attack will actually occur around Stardate 51252.3). ▪ Ocampa babies are born with ears that resemble those of human babies. This is most likely due to restrictions associated with placing makeup on an infant.

REAL LIFE

EPISODE #164

TELEPLAY BY: **JERI TAYLOR**

STORY BY: **HARRY DOC KLOOR**

DIRECTED BY: **ANSON WILLIAMS**

GUEST STARS

CHARLENE	**WENDY SCHALL**
JEFFREY	**GLENN HARRIS**
BELLE	**LINDSEY HUAN**

CO-STARS

LARG	**STEPHEN RALSTON**
K'KATH	**CHAD HAYWOOD**

STARDATE 50836.2

When *Voyager* comes across a large debris field, the crew concludes that it is all that's left of the alien space station they were heading for. Finding a strange trail of plasma particles at the site, they set course to solve the mystery of what could have destroyed the station.

Meanwhile, in an effort to expand the horizons of his program, the Doctor creates a holofamily consisting of a wife named Charlene, a teenaged son named Jeffrey, and a young daughter named Belle. After he invites Kes and Torres to dine with his all-too-perfect family, the engineer offers to tweak the program to make it more realistic.

As *Voyager* follows the particle wake, an astral eddy—a tornado-like phenomenon—rips out of subspace and bears down on the ship. They come through the anomaly relatively unscathed, and Chakotay suggests that the next time an astral eddy appears, they capture some if its highly charged plasma particles. Paris suggests that taking a shuttle into the wake of an eddy might offer the best opportunity to capture the valuable plasma particles. When another one forms, Paris attempts the maneuver, only to be caught up in yet another eddy. The crew watches in horror as Paris disappears within the eye of the astral phenomenon.

Back in the holodeck, the Doctor is not pleased with the changes Torres has made to his program. Suddenly his wife's work conflicts with his idea of family unity, his son's Klingon friends appear to be leading the boy down the wrong path, and his daughter's incessant whining only exacerbates the situations.

The Doctor tries to talk things out with his rebellious son. The conversation turns into an argument that is interrupted when word arrives that Belle has been seriously injured in an accident. After hours of surgery, the Doctor realizes she is going to die and abruptly ends the program.

Trapped between space and subspace, in the spawning area of the eddies, Paris figures the only way out is the way he came in, inside a space tornado. As a huge storm crosses into space, *Voyager* manages to beam Paris aboard. In sickbay, Paris persuaders the Doctor to return to his holofamily program and face the pain that life sometimes delivers. The Doctor reactivates the program and then allows himself to witness Belle's death, to grieve and draw comfort from the new closeness the tragedy brings to the remaining members of his family.

DAMAGE REPORT: Propulsion and navigational control are offline and transporters also go offline for a time. There is a minor buckling of the hull on Deck 3.

SHUTTLE TRACKER: The *Shuttlecraft Cochrane*'s hull begins to buckle and breach, but it is ultimately beamed safely to the shuttlebay.

Torres and Kes convince the Doctor that the family he created is literally "too good to be true." ROBBIE ROBINSON

DELTA QUADRANT: *Voyager* has had long-range communications with the Vostigye and is traveling to rendezvous with them at one of their science stations. When the crew arrives, they find the station destroyed. There were sixty scientists onboard, but sensors detect no life-signs. The debris field encompasses nearly eighty cubic kilometers and is largely made up of baronite, sarium, and carbon-60 composites. Something ripped it apart, and energy decay readings indicate the damage occurred no more than an hour before *Voyager* arrived.

The crew follows a particle wake from the destroyed space station to discover an astral eddy that has formed at the confluence of space and subspace. The energy from the plasma in the eddies could give them extra power, allowing the crew to go off replicator rations for a while. After sending a probe into the anomaly they learn that it has a temperature gradient of nine million kelvins, massive discharges of plasmatic energy, and a perfectly calm "eye" in the center. Apparently some of the matter inside it is being exchanged between space and subspace. The eddies originate from an unstable interfold layer between space and subspace. It is possible to modify the Bussard

Paris tells the Doctor that he can't just turn away from the life he created, he has to experience it. ROBBIE ROBINSON

collectors to gather plasma particles, but *Voyager*'s energy emissions are so high they would corrupt the particles.

ALPHA QUADRANT: Every Klingon is given a *d'k tahg* knife in preparation for his Rite of Ascension. The Klingon dagger the *kut'luch,* is used in a ritual of violence, a first bloodletting in preparation for becoming a warrior. The term *Vulky* is apparently an insult among Klingon teens, used to describe something that could be considered Vulcan in nature.

PERSONAL LOGS: Torres is reading a Klingon romance novel entitled *Women Warriors at the River of Blood.* ■ Torres gives the Doctor little "tune-ups" on a regular basis, since he has been doing some tinkering with his system. She also adjusts the Doctor's holofamily (Family Program Beta-Rho) to be more realistic by adding some randomized behavioral algorithms to the program events so they will unfold due to probability. The Doctor's database contains what he believes is all he needs to know about pediatric care and child development.

MEDICAL REPORT: Paris is given a combination of hyronalin and lectrazine as a temporary protection against radiation from the eddy's plasma wake. He receives a mild concussion from the turbulence in the shuttle. ■ The Doctor works on a DNA probe to test Ensign Parsons's glial cells for a microbial infection.

EPISODE LOGS: The shooting script for this episode adds a new phrase to the *Star Trek* lexicon. Now, when the Doctor appears, the stage direction indicates that he "Zimmers in" (or, conversely "Zimmers out"). Obviously, this is taken from the EMH creator's name Zimmerman.

DISTANT ORIGIN
EPISODE #165
WRITTEN BY: BRANNON BRAGA & JOE MENOSKY
DIRECTED BY: DAVID LIVINGSTON

GUEST STARS

GEGEN	**HENRY WORONICZ**
VEER	**CHRISTOPHER LIAM**
	MOORE
HALUK	**MARSHALL R. TEAGUE**

SPECIAL GUEST STAR

MINISTER ODALA	**CONCETTA TOMEI**

CO-STARS

FROLA	**NINA MINTON**
COMPUTER VOICE	**MAJEL BARRETT**

STARDATE UNKNOWN

Professor Gegen and his assistant Veer find the remains of a Starfleet officer in a cave on an alien world. Gegen feels the evidence holds the key to the

Gegen contemplates the full ramifications of the discovery of Ensign Hogan's remains. ROBBIE ROBINSON

Chakotay agrees to help prove Gegen's theory to the Voth Ministry of Elders. ROBBIE ROBINSON

true origins of his race, the Voth, a saurian species that he suspects evolved in a distant part of the galaxy. The distant origin theory contradicts the doctrine of Chief Minister Odala and the powerful Voth elders, who believe the Voth were the first intelligent beings to evolve in the quadrant. The elders are unreceptive to his claims, but Gegen finds a clue on the uniform of the deceased: a microscopic identification code, presumably the name of a ship called *Voyager*.

Gegen and Veer trace *Voyager*'s path across the Delta Quadrant and finally find the ship itself. Thanks to their sophisticated cloaking technology, the Voth are able to transport onto the ship and observe the crew undetected. Eventually, *Voyager*'s sensors disclose the use of cloaking technology aboard the ship, and the crew finds Gegen and Veer. Frightened, Veer fires a tranquilizer dart at Chakotay, but is himself incapacitated by a phaser blast. Gegen transports back to his vessel with the unconscious Chakotay.

In sickbay, Veer goes into protective hiberation, while the Doctor discovers evidence that the alien has evolved from Earth's dinosaurs. On the Voth ship, after Chakotay regains consciousness, he and Gegen come to similar conclusions, reasoning that the Voth's ancestors survived

extinction, developed spacefaring technology, and left Earth. When Gegen is charged with heresy by the Voth elders, Chakotay is the best proof to Gegen's theories. But before he can take Chakotay to his supporters, *Voyager* is transported inside a massive Voth city-ship.

The Ministry of Elders holds the crew captive, vowing to kill them all unless Gegen returns to face the charges. Gegen agrees to confront his accusers, and Chakotay promises to help him, as his ship is also on trial. Odala accuses Gegen of being a destructive influence on Voth society and orders him to disavow his claims. But Gegen refuses to back down until Odala threatens to send *Voyager*'s crew to a detention colony and destroy their ship. To save them, Gegen retracts his theory, resigning himself to the fact that Voth's true heritage will remain a secret, at least for now.

SENSOR READINGS: Long-range scans indicate that if *Voyager* maintains its present course, it will enter a region of heavy tetryon radiation within two days. The alternative is a three-month detour. ▪ The crew can access the manual overrides from main engineering to restart the ship's systems. ▪ Starfleet uniforms contain a microscopic identification code indicating the name of the ship the

"As I recall, Tom, you're something of an aficionado of twentieth-century America."
"That's right."
"What will we need to pass as locals in this area?"
"Simple. Nice clothes, fast car, and lots of money."
Janeway and Paris, "Future's End, Part 1"

Through time and space, season three brings numerous glimpses of home to the *Voyager* crew. Brief Alpha Quadrant interactions and images fill the season along with one of the most ambitious visits home in the series. A two-part episode manages to bring *Voyager* back to Earth, but a few centuries before their time.

Star Trek history comes into play in season three when the crew meets up with a pair of Ferengi who were lost in the Delta Quadrant following their exploration of what was believed to be a stable Alpha Quadrant wormhole. The episode "False Profits" serves as a sequel to the *TNG* episode "The Price" and allows viewers to enjoy a little slice of the Ferengi culture on *Voyager*, and for Neelix the chance to don Ferengi guise and portray the grand proxy. History plays a role in the episode "Flashback," which honors thirty years of *Star Trek*. Due to an alien parasite inhabiting Tuvok's brain, he and Janeway travel back in time, in Tuvok's mind, to his days on the *U.S.S. Excelsior* under the command of Captain Sulu, formerly of the *Starship Enterprise*. The events are played out in accordance with the film

The crew beams down to an area of California that will eventually sink into the ocean during the Hermosa Quake of 2047. ROBBIE ROBINSON

Star Trek VI: The Undiscovered Country with familiar sets, scenes, and characters, including the aforementioned Sulu as well as Lieutenant Commander Janice Rand.

Another part of *Star Trek* history is seen in the form of the Borg. The alien race, first met on *The Next Generation* served as a looming threat to *Voyager* from the inception of the series, since the crew would have to journey through their space to get home. Before actually entering Borg space, the ship finds traces of the Borg's presence in "Blood Fever." Later Chakotay encounters a planet with Borg who have been severed from the collective. The group consists of a variety of alien races including Klingons, Cardassians, and Romulans, as well as at least four humans. Riley, a former science officer on the *U.S.S. Roosevelt* who was assimilated at the battle of Wolf 359, uses Chakotay to reestablish the Borg link to form a Borg cooperative on the planet.

The holodeck is also used to provide familiar images from home. Paris, Kim, and Torres add various Alpha Quadrant inhabitants to Neelix's Paxau resort holoprogram, including the Gold Medal women's volleyball team of 2216 ("Warlord"). Later, the Doctor fills the resort with historical Alpha Quadrant figures, including Gandhi, Lord Byron, Socrates, and T'Pau of Vulcan, when trying to broaden his programming ("Darkling"). Another historical holographic figure makes

crewman is stationed on. ▪ Tuvok erects a level-10 containment field around the bridge that prohibits the Voth scientists from transporting off the ship.

DELTA QUADRANT: The Voth live on city-ships. For mil-

lions of years, their people have believed that they were the first intelligent beings to evolve in this region of space, considering themselves "the first race." They share forty-seven genetic markers with humans and hundreds of other Earth species, dating back millions of years. The

his first appearance in "Scorpion" when the captain begins lessons with Leonardo da Vinci in art and philosophy.

"I think that Janeway's one flaw as a scientist was an inability to exercise her imagination sometimes as an artist. So who would she then appeal to who could help her in both regards? Well, da Vinci, who was both a scientist and an artist. So, really she was going to him for lessons in philosophy—to teach her the heart of an artist while honing the brain of a scientist. And he did indeed, in the end, give [her] the greatest gift of all, which was emotional flight and freedom."

—Kate Mulgrew

The Doctor also gets a lot of use out of the holodecks in season three beyond the historical figures he meets. It serves as a diagnostic device when his program begins to degrade in "The Swarm," providing a simulation of the Jupiter Station holoprogramming center with the Doctor's original programmer, Lewis Zimmerman. With another attempt at expanding his programming, the Doctor creates his own holofamily in an Earthlike setting ("Real Life"). Torres later changes the program to include a pair of Klingon teens and a Parisses Squares tournament. The Doctor also uses the holodeck to create a Vulcan woman to help Vorik cope with his case of *Pon farr.*

Visions of home also come in the form of alternate realities. Kim dreams of his mother in "Favorite Son," while infected with alien DNA of a race of women trying to convince him the Delta Quadrant is his home. Meanwhile, Janeway's vision of her deceased father comes from an alien trying to convince her to leave her own life and follow him into the next. And another visit to the Q Continuum is seen as the American Civil War as the Q wage a very dangerous conflict.

In a plotline with some similarities to the previous season's episode "Tattoo," Chakotay makes contact with an alien race that most likely had its beginnings on Earth. The Voth, who claim sovereignty over the sector, successfully manage to squelch all scientific evidence that one of their own scientists finds that may prove they are linked to the human race ("Distant Origin").

"['Distant Origin'] was one episode that was just about perfect. The acting, the effects, and the directing . . . It was a very complex [and] ambitious show that really turned out great."

—Brannon Braga

The crew's most involved visit to Earth comes as the result of an interaction with the future that leads them to the past ("Future's End"). Captain Braxton—from a future version of Starfleet—attacks *Voyager,* thrusting both starships back in time. *Voyager* discovers it is in Earth orbit, the year 1996. The captain leads an away team to Los Angeles in search of Braxton, hoping that he has the means to return them. The away team interacts with various locals, including an astronomer, Rain Robinson, and the entrepreneur, Henry Starling. *Voyager* manages to stop the threat to the future, and secure a return to their time. However, they cannot return to Earth citing the Temporal Prime Directive, so Captain Braxton instead returns the starship to the Delta Quadrant.

"I'd have to say that 'Future's End' was the most fun episode to shoot. Those were two great weeks. We were outside the studio. We were in the city. We were running around all over the place, different locations and that's just a blast because shooting inside a studio gets to be kind of boring sometimes. It was a great story. It was a great two-parter and it was just a lot of fun to shoot that episode."

—Tim Russ

closest link between them and humans can be found in Genus *Eryops* of the Devonian era. This creature lived over four hundred million years ago. The most highly evolved cold-blooded organism to develop from the *eryops* is Genus *Hadrosaur* of the Cretaceous era. The hadrosaur vanished when a mass extinction occurred at the end of the Cretaceous period. Janeway and the Doctor believe that some of the hadrosaurs may have escaped Earth on starships when a land mass they lived on was destroyed. The human cranial capacity is twenty-two percent smaller than the Voth, and humans lack a dilitus lobe that allows for the Voth's heightened sense of smell. The Voth can go into a protective hibernation in which their heart rate and body temperature drop and metabolism almost completely shuts down while the automatic nervous system remains fully functional. They also have tranquilizing darts they can fire from their wrists. ▪ Under the Voth Doctrine, nonindigenous beings have no rights. ▪ Their spatial displacement technology emits a type of cloak that causes their ships to go out of phase from their surroundings; the technology is also a personal cloaking device. The crew adjusts hand phasers to a dispersion frequency of 1.85 gigaghertz to disrupt their cloaking technology. The Voth also have transwarp abilities.

EPISODE LOGS: Gegen and Veer find Hogan's remains on Hanon IV ("Basics, Part II"), and they journey to the supply station at the edge of the Nekrit Expanse ("Fair Trade"). In their travels they obtain a tricorder, a combadge, and a canister of *Voyager*'s warp plasma, though it is unclear from where they obtain these items.

Torres realigns the Doctor's optical sensors so he can find an exit portal. ROBBIE ROBINSON

DISPLACED

EPISODE #166

WRITTEN BY: **LISA KLINK**

DIRECTED BY: **ALLAN KROEKER**

GUEST STARS

DAMMAR	**KENNETH TIGAR**
JARLATH	**MARK L. TAYLOR**
RISLAN	**JAMES NOAH**
TALEEN	**NANCY YOUNGBLUT**

CO-STARS

ENSIGN LANG	**DEBORAH LEVIN**
COMPUTER VOICE	**MAJEL BARRETT**

STARDATE 50912.4

A tense discussion between Paris and Torres is interrupted when a Nyrian named Dammar suddenly appears on *Voyager*, asking why he has been abducted. The crew, however, is not responsible for beaming him aboard, and they soon discover that Kes mysteriously vanished from the ship at the same instant Dammar arrived. Not long after, Kim disappears as another Nyrian turns up. Soon, Tuvok also vanishes.

After twenty-two Nyrians take the place of crew members, Janeway realizes that they are replacing her entire crew at nine-minute intervals.

Twelve hours later, the bizarre exchange has claimed half the crew. Rislan, a Nyrian astrophysicist, works with Torres to find the cause of the problem. But when Torres catches on to the fact that the Nyrians are responsible, Rislan sends her to an idyllic prison colony, where she finds her fellow abducted crew members.

On *Voyager*, Chakotay comes to the same conclusion, too late, that the Nyrians are trying to take control of the ship, and he too is transported to the colony, after downloading the Doctor into his mobile emitter. Taleen, a Nyrian spokeswoman, explains that her people steal ships by gradually replacing their crews because it is less violent than war. The prisoners are then relocated to surroundings that approximate their native environment.

As the crew tries to find a way out, they meet Jarlath, a prisoner from a neighboring environment, who reveals that different areas of the colony are connected by disguised portals. Torres reconfigures the Doctor's optical sensors so that he can detect the passages. He locates a

Taleen welcomes the *Voyager* crew to their new home. ROBBIE ROBINSON

portal that leads to a network of access tunnels, each, in turn, leading to a different biosphere. In the tunnel, Janeway finds a control panel that provides access to the translocation system that brought them to the colony.

The Nyrians detect the crew in the passages and send guards to capture them. Torres and Paris slip into an arctic environment and when the Nyrians, who are highly sensitive to cold, follow them, they are easily incapacitated. Meanwhile, Janeway takes control of the translocation system and beams Dammar and Rislan into the cold environment. Overwhelmed by the freezing temperatures, the Nyrians surrender *Voyager.* With the ship back in her control, Janeway leaves the Nyrians in a section of their own prison while she helps the other captives get back to their own homes.

SENSOR READINGS: When the Nyrians outnumber the crew almost two to one, Chakotay orders access to all systems restricted to authorized voiceprints only. He also seals off any part of the ship not in use (including Decks 11 through 15) and places security forcefields around sensitive areas like the warp core, the armory, and the tor-

pedo bays. ▪ From *Voyager*'s original position the nearest inhabited world is over ten light-years away.

DAMAGE REPORT: A circuit relay malfunction causes a problem with the internal sensors on Deck 4. During Chakotay's sabotage of the ship, the computer warns that disabling lateral EPS relays may disrupt computer functions throughout the ship (this can be done from a cargo bay).

DELTA QUADRANT: Nyrians prefer warm dark climates with low humidity. They claim to be from the third planet of the Nyrian system, a red giant star with a large cloud of interstellar dust just beyond the fifth planet (this may or may not be true). Torres detects a surge of polaron particles that create a spatial distortion field around Harry, but it collapses as soon as he vanishes. A tetryon scan shows neutrinos, ionized hydrogen, and theta-band radiation, making the effect look like a wormhole; however, the scan shows no quantum level fluctuations whatsoever, which would be impossible. ▪ The translocator has an extremely long range of over ten light-years. Janeway theorizes that great distances must limit its capacity, which is why the Nyrians could send only one person to *Voyager* at a time, and bring one of *Voyager*'s crew to their ship. There is a consistent interval of nine minutes and twenty seconds between the exchanges. ■ The Nyrians have data for ninety-four different environments on their ship and are holding thousands of prisoners in self-contained biospheres. The crew has been relocated to ten compounds spread over four square kilometers. The compounds have food dispensers programmed with selections from *Voyager*'s computer files and literature and entertainment downloaded from the ship's cultural database. Since the Nyrians downloaded *Voyager*'s cultural database, Janeway was able to tap into the translation algorithm.

Jarleth's people live in a desert environment. They were taken from their colony over nine years ago. ■ The previous residents of *Voyager*'s habitat were all killed by a plague. ■ The Argala habitat temperature is minus 20 degrees Celsius.

ALPHA QUADRANT: Klingons have much less tolerance for cold than do humans. Paris thought that was only true of Cardassians, but Torres says they just complain about it more.

PERSONAL LOGS: During the Rite of *tal'oth,* Tuvok survived in the Vulcan desert for four months, with a ritual blade as his only possession. ■ Paris claims he can give Torres orders because he is a bridge officer with two days more seniority than she. ■ The Doctor says he has never been completely cut off from the ship before and worries what might happen if the mobile emitter's power supply runs out. He is modified to function as a tricorder when his optical sensors are realigned to pick up the microwave signature of the portals. His mobile emitter can also be adjusted to inhibit his ability to speak.

As one of the few remaining crew members onboard, Ensign Lang is temporarily named security chief.

EPISODE LOGS: The bet Paris and Torres made in "Distant Origin" is honored in this episode when they get together to enjoy a Klingon martial arts program on the holodeck.

WORST CASE SCENARIO

EPISODE #167

WRITTEN BY: KENNETH BILLER

DIRECTED BY: ALEXANDER SINGER

GUEST STARS

SESKA   MARTHA HACKETT

CO-STAR

COMPUTER VOICE   MAJEL BARRETT

STARDATE 50953.4

After Janeway and Paris leave on an away mission, Chakotay leads a mutiny on *Voyager.* With Torres's help, he seizes control of the ship and vows that Federation principles will no longer stand in the way of getting the crew home. Just then, Paris walks in and asks Torres why she is late for their lunch date. Annoyed, Torres freezes the holodeck program she has been running. The whole mutiny scenario was part of a holonovel she discovered while purging the holodeck's backup database.

The identity of the holonovel's writer is unknown, but Paris is fascinated by the subject matter. He resets the program and replays the mutiny with slightly different plot twists. Just as the holonovel appears headed for an explosive climax, the program abruptly stops and Paris learns that the writer never completed the story.

The program is soon the talk of the ship, and Tuvok finally admits he is the author, but it was not meant as holonovel. He wrote it as a tactical training exercise when the Maquis and Starfleet crews first merged. Since the union went smoothly, Tuvok did not bother finishing the program. After Paris volunteers to complete the tale, Tuvok decides to collaborate with him. But when they reopen the narrative parameters file to write the final chapter, a holographic version of Seska appears. Before defecting to the Kazon, the real Seska discovered Tuvok's program and decided to finish it the way she thought it should play out. The holographic Seska tells Tuvok that she has sealed the holodeck and deactivated the safety protocols, so he and Paris are now in a life and death situation.

Although she gives them a brief head start, Tuvok and Paris find that Seska's scenario is quite deadly, to both them and the real *Voyager* crew. Seska has laid booby-trapped subroutines, which means that one wrong move could destroy the ship. Outside the holodeck, the crew discovers Seska's scheme and tries to find a way to help Paris and Tuvok.

In Seska's holonovel the Doctor is programmed to hurt, not heal. ROBBIE ROBINSON

As Seska prepares to execute Tuvok and Paris, the real Janeway works furiously to rewrite the program. Her efforts throw the program off just enough that Tuvok is able to rig a phaser rifle malfunction, which kills the holographic Seska, ending the program. Safely back from their ordeal, Tuvok and Paris congratulate Janeway on her literary skills, and the crew begins planning a new holoadventure.

SENSOR READINGS: Tuvok's security training program, "Insurrection Alpha," is accessed forty-seven times by thirty-three different crew members. Tuvok reinitiates the holographic program using Security Clearance Tuvok. When he reopens the narrative parameters on the file, Seska's program takes over, and the ship loses power in both transporter rooms, communications go down, and the holodeck system is completely scrambled. The holodeck is sealed, and safety protocols are off. Seska has laid booby-trapped subroutines everywhere, and if they try to open the holodeck doors, the power grid is rigged to explode. Janeway sends Tuvok and Paris a plasma

Long after her death Seska succeeds in taking over the ship, and threatening the lives of the crew. ROBBIE ROBINSON

extinguisher to put out a plasma fire in the program; however, the program reconfigures the subprocessors to counter every other change they make. When the holographic Seska orders the ship's self-destruct in the program, it initiates an overload in the holodeck power relays that would cause the whole system to blow, endangering the entire crew. ■ The brig has an electrostatic force field.

ALPHA QUADRANT: According to the "Dictates of Poetics" by T'Hain of Vulcan, a character's actions must flow inexorably from his or her established traits.

PERSONAL LOGS: Paris claims that he has always wanted to write a holonovel (and eventually becomes a holonovelist in the alternate future shown in the first part of "Endgame"). In the program he suffers a second-degree phaser burn. The reprogrammed holographic Doctor adds twenty cc's nitric acid to make the burn worse.

EPISODE LOGS: Although there are some minor inconsistencies, the holoprogram accurately reflects the early episodes of *Voyager* through some of the following inclusions: Seska is still in her Bajoran guise; Jonas is still alive (however, it is not Raphael Sbarge's voice when Jonas speaks over the com system); and both Kes and Janeway are wearing their hairstyles from that period. ■ In the current timeline, Paris says he thought he'd find Torres playing pool at Sandrine's, indicating that particular holoprogram is still in use, although it goes unseen. ■ In the tag at the end the crew suggests a follow-up story of either a Western or a detective story (or a biography of Neelix).

SCORPION, PART I

EPISODE #168

WRITTEN BY: BRANNON BRAGA & JOE MENOSKY

DIRECTED BY: DAVID LIVINGSTON

SPECIAL GUEST STAR

| LEONARDO DA VINCI | JOHN RHYS-DAVIES |

STARDATE 50984.3

Realizing they are about to enter Borg space, the crew attempts to plot a course through a corridor that seems devoid of Borg activity, which they dub the "Northwest Passage." The crew prepares the ship for possible encounters with the Borg while the Doctor and Kes research methods of fighting off Borg assimilation. As the pair works, recurring visions of dead Borg and the destruction of *Voyager* plague Kes.

Suddenly, scanners pick up an armada of Borg cubes racing toward *Voyager*. But, rather than attack, the cubes only pause briefly to scan the ship before continuing on their way as if they are fleeing from something. Not long after, Tuvok and Kim note that the power signatures of the same Borg cubes, which they have been tracking, have terminated. *Voyager* races to the last known coordinates of the cubes and find them destroyed. Tuvok finds an unknown weapons signature in the Borg debris, which raises the question: who could do this to the Borg?

Sensors pick up odd bio-readings from the outer hull of one of the cubes, and Janeway sends an away team to investigate. On the defunct vessel, the team finds a pile of Borg bodies, lying exactly as Kes had seen them in a premonition. When Kim senses an alien presence on the ship, Kes "sees" him screaming in agony. Janeway orders them back, but interference blocks the transporter beam. Torres is able to work through the interference and transports the team just as a fierce life-form attacks Kim. As *Voyager* races away, Kes informs Janeway that the alien, communicating telepathically, told her "the weak will perish."

In sickbay, Kim's body is infested with alien cells that entered his body in the attack. The Doctor devises a procedure to reprogram Borg nanoprobes to negate the damage. Meanwhile, Torres discovers that the alien life-form, known to the Borg as Species 8472, has taken over the "Northwest Passage," and Kes senses an invasion is planned. With their former plan no longer an option, Janeway faces a terrible choice: retreat into the Delta Quadrant and forget about getting home, or confront the Borg and risk assimilation.

After considerable thought, Janeway comes up with a third alternative. She will offer the Borg a way to defeat Species 8472 in exchange for safe passage through Borg space. Janeway is beamed aboard one of the cubes, where she presents her proposal. Suddenly, Species 8472's bioships begin firing at the Borg cubes, and at *Voyager*, which is locked in the grip of a Borg tractor beam. When more of the alien vessels appear they link together with an energy weapon powerful enough to destroy a planet. As the world explodes, the cube holding Janeway takes off, pulling *Voyager* in tow.

SENSOR READINGS: *Voyager* sent out a long-range probe two months earlier. It stops transmitting when it runs into the Borg. ■ Subspace turbulence prevents *Voyager* from creating a stable warp field. ■ The prepara-

Kim is entirely unaware that he is about to be assimilated. ROBBIE ROBINSON

tions for entering Borg space include placing the ship on full tactical alert. Tuvok reprograms the phaser banks to a rotating modulation, but suspects the Borg will adapt quickly. Kim configures the long-range sensors to scan for transwarp signatures as an early warning system. Chakotay also asks him to find a way to cut down the time it takes to seal off the decks and increase magnitude of the force fields. The Doctor has analyzed every square millimeter of the Borg corpse they recovered three months earlier ("Unity") and is closer to understanding how their assimilation technology works. Neelix is working on a plan to extend their food and replicator rations so the ship does not have to stop while in Borg space.

DELTA QUADRANT: Borg space includes thousands of solar systems. The "Northwest Passage" is filled with intense gravimetric distortions, originally believed to be caused by a string of quantum singularities. The crew eventually discovers that this is a result of Species 8472's activity. ▪ Borg injection tubules initiate the Borg assimila-

tion process. Once inserted inside the skin, they release a series of nanoprobes into the bloodstream. The tubules are capable of penetrating any known alloy or energy field. The first substance to be infiltrated by the nanoprobes is the victim's blood. Assimilation is almost instantaneous as they take over the blood cell functions, like a virus. ▪ According to Torres, the Borg gain knowledge through assimilation, and what they cannot assimilate, they cannot understand. ▪ The Borg scan *Voyager* with a polaron beam.

Species 8472 uses bio-ships that are impervious to *Voyager*'s technology rendering transporters and tractor beams useless. ▪ Each alien's cell contains more than a hundred times the DNA of a human cell, making it the most densely coded life-form the Doctor has ever seen. They have an extraordinary immune response, anything that penetrates the cell membrane, whether chemical, biological, or technological, is instantly destroyed, which explains why the Borg cannot assimilate them. ▪ There are 133 bio-ships in the "Northwest Passage" with more

In the heart of darkness, Tuvok and Chakotay explore a Borg cube. ROBBIE ROBINSON

approaching from a quantum singularity. The bio-ship has a chamber forty meters wide with a high concentration of antimatter particles resembling a warp propulsion system of some kind. There are organic conduits carrying electrodynamic fluid suggesting an energy source. There is also a binary matrix laced with neuropeptides that could be their version of a computer core. The walls can regenerate themselves. The alien emits bioelectric interference that blocks transporters. The bio-ships can interlock an energy weapon powerful enough to destroy a planet.

ALPHA QUADRANT: While researching the Borg, Janeway reads from the logs of Captain Picard of the *Enterprise* and Captain Amasov of the *Endeavor*. In the words of Jean-Luc Picard: "In their collective state, the Borg are utterly without mercy . . . driven by one will alone: the will to conquer. They are beyond redemption . . . beyond reason." Captain Amasov says: "It is my opinion that the Borg are as close to pure evil as any race we've ever encountered."

The Breen use organic-based vessels.

PERSONAL LOGS: Janeway begins an apprenticeship under Leonardo da Vinci in a holoprogram.

According to Chakotay, Ensign Hickman in astrophysics does a passable impression of Janeway.

MEDICAL REPORT: Kim is infected by Species 8472. What begins with a few stray cells contaminating the chest wound rapidly infuses every system in his body. The alien cells consume his body from the inside out. Every treatment and sedative the Doctor tries is rejected in seconds. The Doctor unleashes an army of modified Borg nanoprobes into Kim's bloodstream that are designed to target and eradicate the infection. He successfully dissects a nanoprobe and manages to access its recoding mechanism to reprogram the probe to emit the same electromechanical signatures as the alien cells, so the probe can do its work without being detected.

CREW COMPLEMENT: Shortly before the events of this episode—prior to Stardate 50979—an away team consisting of Kim, the Doctor, and Ensign Ahni Jetal comes under attack by an unknown alien race. Kim and Jetal are seriously injured and the Doctor, with the time to save only one of his patients, operates on Kim, allowing Jetal to die. The stress of the decision causes a feedback loop in the Doctor's program forcing Janeway to remove all memory of the incident. The events surrounding the ensign's death are not mentioned here and will be played out in "Latent Image."

EPISODE LOGS: This is the first Borg episode to air following *Star Trek: First Contact,* implying that the death of the Borg queen in the Alpha Quadrant had no noticeable effect on the collective in the Delta Quadrant. ▪ In her new holoprogram, Janeway suggests that da Vinci redesign his flying machine in the form of a hawk. This flying machine will play an important role in "Concerning Flight."

LIEUTENANT COMMANDER TUVOK

WIDER, INCLUDING TORRES AND TUVOK

. . . At a side panel is TUVOK, a Vulcan man.

—Tuvok's first appearance in "Caretaker"

ROBBIE ROBINSON

His introduction is deceptively simple for the most logical reasons. Because he was on an undercover assignment, very little was known about Tuvok until after the opening credits. Additional information was learned through Janeway's actions. With her security officer missing, the captain of the *U.S.S. Voyager* enacted a risky plan to find him, as well as the Maquis crew he had under surveillance. Ultimately, he was reunited with his captain, and the truth behind his Maquis infiltration was revealed. Yet, through it all, little emotional resonance was apparent from the first full Vulcan lead character on a *Star Trek* series.

Although he was a member of the traditionally stoic Vulcan race, Tuvok was far from emotionless throughout the seven seasons of the series. He may have seemed frustratingly even-keel at times, but that belied the true nature of his character. There were tumultuous feelings deep in his subconscious as well as those passions that existed just beneath his surface. His most notable dealings with emotion came from the extreme situations in which he was forced, largely against his will, to feel something. In episodes such as "Meld," "Flashback," and "Riddles" mental ailments set up conflict in the usually calm Vulcan, throwing his suppressed feelings into an emotional volatility that he sought to regain control of, often with the help of his crewmates.

It was in the less extreme settings, however, that Tuvok expressed his more interesting emotional arcs. In situations where his Vulcan mind functioned perfectly, Tuvok showed the most growth as a character because the situations usually called for him to consciously set aside some of the binding influences on his feelings. With "Innocence," Tuvok adapted the typical Vulcan procedures in raising children to help calm his charges in an intimidating situation. Tuvok came the closest to experiencing full emotional depth when he fell in love with an alien woman named Noss in "Gravity." It was through this episode that we learned that Tuvok could, indeed, fall in love, and we saw a rare glimpse into his past, in which the suppression of his feelings was not always his highest priority.

Tim Russ: I enjoy seeing Tuvok being placed in situations that are counter to his expertise—situations where he might have an Achilles' heel or an emotional volatility and having to make decisions that are not based in logic but based on something else. I think those really challenge the Vulcan character a lot.

It was also very telling that Tuvok was the only one of the main characters with his own family back in the Alpha Quadrant. A father and grandfather, Tuvok's presence on the ship served a variety of roles depending on the person with whom he was interacting. From confidant to foil to teacher, Tuvok was more than just chief of security. His promotion to lieutenant commander in "Revulsion" served as a reminder of just how important he was to the crew.

Though the senior staff was largely comprised of strangers thrust together in the first episodes of the series, Janeway and Tuvok had a friendship dating back several years. He served as her trusted confidant, sounding board and, on more than one occasion, a dissenting voice with regard to her strict adherence to Starfleet ideals. In contrast to this long-lived association, his immediate friendship with Kes proved that it did not take years to break through the Vulcan veneer. As a mentor, it was discovered through a mental link in "Warlord" that his feelings for his student ran deeply. Later, Tuvok had moments with several other characters such Kim, Torres, and Seven, that also mirrored a mentorlike relationship.

Robert Duncan McNeill: I think it was always fun to see Paris and Tuvok together. They were just such an odd couple, just like the classic odd couple relationship. I always enjoyed when we had shows together. I would like to have seen more of them.

Another important element in dissecting the Vulcan character can be accessed by looking at him in conflict. First there was the light conflict between Tuvok and Paris solely because they were such different personalities. Paris's carefree attitude was in staunch contrast to Tuvok's calm exterior, yet these two characters often worked well together as evidenced in "Worst Case Scenario." Of course, a more powerful conflict was the early tension Tuvok experienced with Chakotay.

ROBBIE ROBINSON

This relationship was set up at odds from the start, since Tuvok did infiltrate the Maquis cell, and Chakotay took the position of second-in-command that would have rightfully gone to the security chief. Even with their differences, the pair did come together on several occasions to sway Janeway toward more moderate thinking.

By far, the most explored relationship born out of conflict was that between Tuvok and Neelix. The Talaxian, by his very nature, served as the antithesis to the Vulcan's reserved manner. The result was a challenge to Neelix who sought to know the real Tuvok in several episodes, but none more so than the one that physically brought them together into one life-form known as Tuvix. Beyond that, there were several episodes in which the pair were less literally forced together, culminating in a rare display of emotion from Tuvok when he performed an ever so brief dance in honor of Neelix's good-bye.

Ethan Phillips: Tuvok represented a very specific and challenging goal for Neelix: to elicit a smile out of that guy. In my mind, he set about it and said "I'm going to pierce this Vulcan's cold exterior and get to his heart." And he tried in "Rise!" and he tried in many scenes, but it wasn't until "Riddles" that he was able to because of that accident. In that episode, finally, Neelix really gets to bond with him. I think in the end there's a part of Tuvok that remembers that friendship they had. Overall, I think it's been developed very well. I really enjoyed playing with Tim. In some ways, I think, he has the most difficult role on the show because he has such a small band width within which he has to work all the time. And yet, within that, he conveys a lot of complexity.

In studying Tuvok, it is necessary to look at his reactions to individuals and situations because the challenge of his character is that he did not create drama, but rather worked against it. It was particularly fitting for Tim Russ to fill such an important position in the *Star Trek* franchise, as his experience with the show included several previous appearances in *TNG*, where he also originally auditioned for the role of Geordi La Forge. A true fan from the start, his reward as an actor of the challenging role of Tuvok seems especially fitting.

Jeri Ryan (left) joins the
cast as Seven of Nine.

SEASON FOUR

The fourth season of *Star Trek: Voyager* brings several changes to the series, with the most notable one in the cast. The conclusion to the third season cliff-hanger "Scorpion" adds a new member to the crew in the person of former Borg drone, Seven of Nine. Her presence serves a need noted by the production staff and audience alike—the series had been missing its Spock—a character who would comment on humanity and question the viewpoints expressed by the human characters. Though various members of the crew occasionally had served this role in the past—Torres's Klingon/Maquis bucking of authority, Kes's eagerness to learn, Neelix's misplaced shock over certain situations, and the Doctor's dry, sarcastic humor—none of them fully filled the role.

In Seven of Nine, the captain and her crew are provided a new foil to question, comment, and point out perceived flaws in the Starfleet way. The character quickly becomes a challenge for Janeway as they fall into a dysfunctional mother/daughter relationship. However, the cast of *Voyager* was already the largest of all the *Star Trek* series, with nine main characters for whom the writers needed to balance their storytelling. With Seven of Nine, the senior staff would have risen to ten characters whose story needs must be met. Facing the daunting task, the producers decided that Kes's story arc had been fully realized and that she would have to leave the ship.

The seeds for the idea that Kes would become a dan-

ger to the ship were planted in "Cold Fire," and—though the producers may not have realized at the time how prophetic that warning would be—it is proven to be true in "The Gift." Kes has grown a great deal since being rescued from the Kazon in "Caretaker." In her short life span, she has fallen in and out of love, explored exciting worlds she never dreamed of seeing, and even been possessed by an evil warlord. But it was the changes inside her mind that eventually led to actual evolution into another life-form entirely. Free from the peaceful but stagnant life of being cared for by the Caretaker, Kes began to explore the powers of her mind that her people had suppressed for generations. It is those awakening powers that lead her to new vistas and take her away from her friends with a final gift to the crew of a little push toward home.

"We were feeling we had to shake things up. So we introduced Seven of Nine in season four. And we started doing big epic two-parters and what I wanted to do was to give Voyager *a sense of epic adventure; an intrepid crew on a starship lost, getting involved in huge high-concept adventures. It really pushed the limits of what a science fiction television show could do in terms of stories and what we could actually produce."*

—BRANNON BRAGA

Safely past Borg space, the crew of the *U.S.S. Voyager* is not entirely free of the collective. The Borg become an ever-present threat to the crew throughout the rest of the series. Species 8472, the alien race the Borg introduced to *Voyager,* will also be seen from time to time, as well as a new race known as Hirogen. In season four, the crew meets more life-forms, both friendly and hostile; experiences an entire "Year of Hell"; and does something they had been hoping for since being pulled into the Delta Quadrant—make contact with home.

Janeway forms an alliance with the Borg. CRAIG T. MATHEW

SCORPION, PART II

EPISODE #169

WRITTEN BY: BRANNON BRAGA & JOE MENOSKY

DIRECTED BY: WINRICH KOLBE

ALSO STARRING

KES	JENNIFER LIEN

CO-STAR

NARRATOR	MAJEL BARRETT

STARDATE 51003.7

Janeway comes to an agreement with the Borg collective. She will stay aboard the Borg cube to develop the weapon against Species 8472 while *Voyager* is escorted safely through their territory. After Tuvok beams over to assist her, the Borg try to install temporary neuro-transceivers on both of them, but Janeway insists they be assigned a Borg representative to communicate with instead. The Borg select a human female drone, designated Seven of Nine.

The crew discovers that Species 8472 and their bio-

ships are made of the same organic material, meaning both will be vulnerable to the nanoprobes that the Doctor has also successfully used to cure Kim. After dismissing the Borg plan for a weapon of mass destruction, the combined Starfleet/Borg team plans a smaller-scale delivery system using *Voyager*'s photon torpedoes. However, before the system is ready, Species 8472 attacks, forcing the Borg to protect *Voyager* by sacrificing their own ship. Moments before the cube is destroyed, Janeway and Tuvok are beamed to *Voyager* along with Seven of Nine and a small Borg detachment.

Janeway is injured in the attack, and a coma must be induced to save her higher brain functions while the Doctor works on her overall condition. With the captain out of action, Chakotay takes charge of *Voyager.* Despite Janeway's prior order to maintain their alliance with the Borg, he disagrees when Seven of Nine tells him he must travel deeper into Borg space—away from Earth—to link up with their nearest ship. Unwilling to travel in the opposite direction, Chakotay decides to drop off the Borg and the nanoprobes at the nearest uninhabited planet and take *Voyager* through the Delta Quadrant alone.

Chakotay uses the neurotransceiver to communicate with Seven of Nine. ROBBIE ROBINSON

A tenuous relationship is formed. CRAIG T. MATHEW

With sections of the ship's interior and exterior already assimilated by Borg technology, Seven of Nine and the other drones attempt to seize control of *Voyager* and send it through an interdimensional rift into fluidic space, the domain of Species 8472. Chakotay manages to eject most of the Borg from the ship, leaving only Seven of Nine aboard as they enter the rift. She admits that the Borg have been in this space before. They started the war with 8472, but did not bargain on their resistance to assimilation. Janeway, now healed, reestablishes the agreement with Seven of Nine and plans to engage the aliens in fluidic space.

Voyager launches the nanoprobe torpedoes, destroying several ships and forcing 8472 to retreat. With their victory complete, Seven of Nine says the *Voyager* crew will be assimilated, but Janeway and Chakotay had anticipated this. Using the neurotransceiver he had previously been given by the Borg cooperative, Chakotay distracts Seven of Nine long enough for Torres to create a power surge that severs her connection to the Borg. Feeling responsible for her fate, Janeway opts to keep the former drone onboard in the hope that they can restore her humanity.

SENSOR READINGS: *Voyager*'s weapons inventory: Photon torpedo complement: 32 class-6 warheads with explosive yield of 200 isotons. Thirteen photon torpedoes are fit with the nanoprobes and four are launched. One high-yield warhead is launched from aft torpedo bay affecting thirteen bio-ships. ▪ Cargo Bay 2 is assimilated (Borgified). The Borg draw power from the secondary power couplings and access *Voyager*'s deflector control, trying to realign the emitters to send out a resonant graviton beam to create a singularity. Chakotay decompresses Cargo Bay 2, ejecting most of the Borg from the ship. ▪ It will take at least two weeks to remove the Borg technology from ship systems. Since the power couplings on Deck

THE HUMAN CONDITION

"I speak for the Borg."

Seven of Nine, "Scorpion, Part II"

With the fourth season of *Voyager* comes a new character, the former Borg drone known as Seven of Nine, Tertiary Adjunct of Unimatrix Zero One. Seven's return to humanity proves to be an uphill battle for Janeway and her crew, but each lesson learned and wall broken down not only serves to enhance the character, but provides commentary on the universe within and without the realm of the show. Through words and actions, Seven holds up a mirror to the audience questioning the nature of the human condition.

ROBBIE ROBINSON

- "When your captain first approached us, we suspected that an agreement with humans would prove impossible to maintain. You are erratic . . . conflicted . . . disorganized. Every decision is debated . . . every action questioned . . . every individual entitled to their own small opinion. You lack harmony . . . cohesion . . . greatness. It will be your undoing." ("Scorpion, Part II")

- "I'm finding it a difficult challenge to integrate into this group. It is full of complex social structures that are unfamiliar to me. Compared with the Borg, this crew is inefficient and contentious . . . but it's also capable of surprising acts of compassion." ("Day of Honor")

- "I understand the concept of humor. It may not be apparent, but I'm often amused . . . by human behavior." ("Revulsion")

- "The concept of 'relaxation' is difficult for me to understand. As a Borg, my time was spent working at a specific task . . . when it was completed. I was assigned another. It was . . . efficient." ("The Raven")

- "Pleasure is irrelevant." ("The Raven")

- "Too much importance is placed on [death]. There seem to be countless rituals and cultural beliefs designed to alleviate their fear of a simple biological truth: all organisms eventually perish." ("Mortal Coil")

- "A lesson in compassion will do me little good if I am dead." ("Prey")

- "Resentment is a human trait. It has no structure, no function. I want no part of it." ("Prey")

- "The Borg don't 'believe.' They know." ("The Omega Directive")

- "Deception is not the way of the Borg. It is a human failing, which I have no desire to embrace." ("The Omega Directive")

- "When we are faced with desperate circumstances . . . we must adapt." ("The Omega Directive")

- "Intuition is a human fallacy." ("Hope and Fear")

- "It is unsettling. You say that I am a human being, and yet I am also Borg. Part of me not unlike your replicator. Not unlike the Doctor. Will you one day choose to abandon me as well? I have always looked to you as my example, my guide to humanity. Perhaps I have been mistaken." ("Latent Image")

- "When the risks outweigh the potential gain, exploration is illogical." ("One Small Step")

- "My feelings of remorse help me remember what I did . . . and prevent me from taking similar action in the future. Guilt can be a difficult, but useful emotion." ("Memorial")

- "You are an individual. You have the right to choose your *own* destiny." ("Child's Play")

- "I've experienced enough *humanity* for the time being." ("Human Error")

8 work better with the Borg improvements Janeway decides to leave them as is.

DAMAGE REPORT: Species 8472 scores a direct hit to the secondary hull. Transporters are offline and shields and weapons are down.

DELTA QUADRANT: The Borg suggest adding nanoprobes to a multikinetic neutronic mine. The weapon of mass destruction would have a five million isoton yield. An explosion that size would affect an entire star system and the shockwave would disperse the nanoprobes over a radius of five light-years. They would need approximately 50 trillion nanoprobes to arm this mine, which would take the Doctor several weeks to replicate. ▪ Species 8472 penetrates Borg Matrix 010, Grid 19, destroying eight Borg planets, disabling 312 vessels, and eliminating four million, six hundred twenty-one Borg.

Species 8472 lives in an interdimensional rift. The entire region is filled with organic fluid, meaning it is matter rather than space (i.e., fluidic space). Entry into fluidic space creates a compression wave alerting Species 8472 to their arrival. The Borg originated the conflict by invading Species 8472's territory. Since their technology is biologically engineered, the Borg consider them more advanced than any other species they have encountered.

Chakotay intends to leave the Borg on a class-H moon with an oxygen-argon atmosphere.

PERSONAL LOGS: Chakotay uses the Borg neuro-transceiver he was fit with in "Unity" to access Seven of Nine's mind through a Borg alcove. ▪ Every time Kes has a vision, specific regions of her cerebral cortex go into a state of hyperstimulation affecting memory engrams and perceptual centers, indicating that Species 8472 may be reading her mind. ▪ Seven of Nine, Tertiary Adjunct of Unimatrix Zero One was assimilated eighteen years ago. Her name was Annika.

MEDICAL UPDATE: Kim is cured of the alien disease by Borg nanoprobes. ▪ Janeway suffers plasma burns to her thoracic region, internal bleeding, and neural injuries requiring a coma to be induced to protect her higher brain functions.

CREW COMPLEMENT: Seven of Nine is added to the crew, although she is not aware of it yet.

EPISODE LOGS: Cargo Bay 2 was formerly the airponics bay.

THE GIFT

EPISODE #170

WRITTEN BY: **JOE MENOSKY**

DIRECTED BY: **ANSON WILLIAMS**

ALSO STARRING

KES   JENNIFER LIEN

STARDATE UNKNOWN

When Seven of Nine learns that her link to the Borg collective has been severed, she demands to be returned to the only life she remembers. Believing that she is acting in Seven's best interest, Janeway ignores the former drone's pleas and begins an investigation into her past. After searching Federation records, Janeway learns that she was assimilated as a young girl, her name Annika Hansen. With her human physiology already reasserting itself, Seven of Nine's immune system begins rejecting her Borg implants, leaving the Doctor no choice but to remove them. Meanwhile, Kes begins to experience a startling increase in her telepathic abilities that may be a result of her interaction with Species 8472.

Attempting to integrate her into the ship's community, Janeway asks Seven of Nine to assist the crew in removing the Borg modifications made to the ship. However, while working, Seven accesses the subspace transmitter, trying to communicate with the collective. But Kes senses her actions, and with her new enhanced abilities, prevents Seven of Nine from completing the transmission, nearly destroying a section of the ship in the process.

Seven of Nine is held in the brig to prevent any further attempts to contact the Borg. Over the drone's objections, Janeway says she will make her fully human again, believing that the end will justify the means. Meanwhile, Tuvok becomes alarmed when he finds that Kes's new abilities are endangering the ship and possibly Kes, as she is periodically going into a state of cellular flux, with her atoms destabilizing at the subatomic level. Janeway is concerned, but her attention is split by her efforts to help Seven of Nine, who is fighting against her reassimilation into human culture every step of the way.

With the ship's defenses compromised by her transformation, Kes decides it will be best for everyone if she leaves *Voyager* to further explore her new state alone. Janeway barely gets her to a shuttle before Kes's molecules completely destabilize and she transforms into pure energy. Kes uses her new abilities to bestow a final gift on her *Voyager* family, hurling the ship safely beyond Borg space and ten years closer to home.

Janeway refuses to accept that Seven's Borg nature will win out over her humanity. ROBBIE ROBINSON

SENSOR READINGS: Two teams are on the hull stripping off the Borg armor, but Torres is having problems cleaning out the plasma relays, which is disrupting the antimatter reaction. The plasma intake manifolds are blocked because they could not remove the autonomous regeneration sequencers that continue to regenerate autonomously. Plasma relays are in Jefferies tube 13-Alpha, Section 12. They will be stuck at impulse until the problem is fixed. Janeway grants Torres's request that all personnel with a level 3 engineering rating or higher lend a hand. ▪ Kes uses her newfound powers to bring the warp core online and cause a matter/antimatter reaction at over 120 percent, bringing the ship to impossible speeds. When systems come back online they find that they are 9.5 thousand light-years from their point of origin.

DAMAGE REPORT: Kes destabilizes the Jefferies tube at the molecular level, weakening the infrastructure throughout the deck. Later, the bulkhead by the mess hall suffers the same fate. Kes's psychokinetic abilities continue to damage the ship's structural integrity, resulting in their defenses being compromised and hull breaches on Decks 3, 4, and 5.

SHUTTLE TRACKER: Destroyed. Kes is placed in an unnamed type-9 shuttle that she causes to destabilize when she evolves into her noncorporeal form.

DELTA QUADRANT: Borg autonomous regeneration sequencers function to counteract resistance. The Borg assimilated this technology in Galactic Cluster III, from Species 259. To disable it, one must disconnect each sequencer conduit at the insertion juncture. Galactic Cluster III is a transmaterial energy plane intersecting twenty-two billion omnicordial life-forms.

PERSONAL LOGS: Janeway was with Tuvok when he purchased his meditation lamp six years ago from a Vulcan master, who doubled the price when he saw their Starfleet insignias. Tuvok's quarters are on the starboard side of the ship. ▪ The Doctor says that he cannot treat a patient against her wishes; however, Janeway gives him the permission since she feels she has to look out for Seven's best interests. ▪ Neelix shares a glass of moon-ripened Talaxian champagne with Kes. The last time they had the drink was to toast their arrival on *Voyager.* ▪ Kes has not experimented with her psychokinetic abilities in

Seven of Nine tries to come to grips with being severed from the Borg collective. ROBBIE ROBINSON

months; however, the telepathic centers of her brain are in a state of hyperstimulation. She can now see beyond the subatomic level and performs microsurgery on Seven with only the use of her mind. ▪ Annika Hansen was born on Stardate 25479 at the Tendara Colony. Janeway finds a single entry in the records of Deep Space 4 regarding her family who considered themselves explorers but wanted nothing to do with Starfleet or the Federation. Their names were last recorded at a remote outpost in the Omega Sector where they refused to file a flight plan. Apparently, they aimed their small ship toward the Delta Quadrant and were never heard from again. That was almost twenty years ago and they may have been one of the first humans assimilated by the Borg. Annika's favorite color was red.

MEDICAL REPORT: For 17.4 seconds, Kes's body goes into a state of cellular flux and begins to destabilize at the subatomic level. Her telesynaptic activity also increases. ▪ Seven's human physiology is beginning to reassert itself. Armor plating is anchored to her skull with over three million microconnectors. The Doctor has to remove the

outer layer of the skull itself. The Doctor designs Seven's clothing and makes an artificial eye to replace Seven's eyepiece. It still has some Borg circuitry attached so she will have increased acuity in one eye, and he matches the color of the eye perfectly. Overall, the Doctor extracts eighty-two percent of her Borg hardware and stimulates her hair follicles to promote growth. She will have to spend a few hours each day in a Borg alcove until her healing metabolism can function on its own.

CREW COMPLEMENT: Kes evolves beyond her corporeal form and leaves the ship.

NEMESIS

EPISODE #171
WRITTEN BY: **KENNETH BILLER**
DIRECTED BY: **ALEXANDER SINGER**

GUEST STARS

BRONE	MICHAEL MAHONEN
RAFIN	MATT E. LEVIN
NAMON	NATHAN ANDERSON
COMMANDANT	PETER VOGT
PENNO	BOOTH COLMAN
KARYA	MEGHAN MURPHY

CO-STARS

AMBASSADOR TREEN	TERRENCE EVANS
MARNA	MARILYN FOX
KRADIN SOLDIER	PANCHO DEMMINGS

STARDATE 51082.4

During a survey mission, Chakotay comes under fire and makes an emergency beam-out from his shuttle. He arrives on a planet whose inhabitants are locked in war, and is taken in by the Vori, a humanoid group that is fighting against the vicious Kradin. While searching for the remains of his vessel, Chakotay and a young Vori soldier battle two Kadin. The Vori soldier is killed in the skirmish, leaving Chakotay on his own.

After rejoining the Vori, Chakotay and the others set out to meet with another group of soldiers. En route to the rendezvous site they learn that their fellow Vori contingent has been massacred. Suddenly, the Kradin are upon them, and several soldiers are killed in the barrage of gunfire. Chakotay is wounded, but he gets away, flee-

Chakotay takes up the Vori cause. ROBBIE ROBINSON

Chakotay to help fight in their war. His encounters with the soldiers and the civilians in the settlement were Vori simulations training him to hate the Kradin. Although faced with the probability that the Vori are no better than the Kradin, Chakotay realizes it will be harder to stop hating than it was to start.

SENSOR READINGS: There is too much atmospheric radiation from weapons fire for *Voyager* to get a clear scan of the surface.

SHUTTLE TRACKER: Destroyed. Chakotay was on a survey mission when he picked up traces of omicron radiation in the atmosphere and came under attack as he slowed to investigate. He lost helm control and had to make an emergency transport to the surface. His unseen shuttle was destroyed.

DELTA QUADRANT: The Kradin and the Vori have been at war for more than a decade. They each refer to the other as the nemesis. The war zone in which Chakotay crashes is in the southernmost continent. In the Vori simulation Chakotay is told the Kradin leave the Vori dead tied to the ground "upturned" as opposed to facing the Wayafter. Conversely, the Kradin claim that the Vori shoot without warning and use biochemical weapons to routinely massacre civilians. The Vori have dozens of training facilities where they conscript their own people and any aliens they capture. The Doctor believes they use a com-

ing into the night, alone once again. At last, he comes upon a Vori settlement and collapses.

Back on *Voyager,* the crew learns pieces of Chakotay's shuttle were found in the middle of the war zone. They are unable to contact him, but are promised by one of the planet's ambassadors that their friend will be located and returned. When Chakotay revives in the settlement, the residents tell him he can find communications equipment at the re-stock unit, which is some distance away. The next morning, he sets out to find it, but the sight of enemy aircraft draws him back to the settlement. He returns to find the Kradin taking the Vori people by force. Learning that the Vori elders will be exterminated, Chakotay tries to fight the enemy, but is outnumbered. Meanwhile, Janeway meets with the Kradin ambassador, who sends in a commando unit to accompany Tuvok in searching for Chakotay.

Left to die by the Kradin, Chakotay is grateful when a Vori leader comes back to free him. The two join in battle against the Kradin, but Chakotay is shocked when one of the enemy calls him by name. Although he looks like a Kradin to Chakotay, the alien assures him that he is actually Tuvok. The security chief explains that the Vori have been using mind-control techniques to convince

Finally, Tuvok breaks through the Vori mind control. ROBBIE ROBINSON

IN THE VORI TONGUE

In the *Star Trek Encyclopedia* the universal translator is defined as: "a device used to provide real-time two-way translation of spoken languages." However, it is also a kind of writers' device to enable moving the story along. Since *Star Trek*, the universal translator has been used to explain how Starfleet crews can speak with aliens in different, often entirely unknown, languages. This comes out of necessity as to have a crew go through the rigorous process of establishing communication with every new species they meet would stall any dramatic storytelling.

In each of the *Star Trek* series, the universal translator has been used as a device to add to the power of the given story. When it fails to translate a language or breaks down, it often adds conflict to the dramatic action. In the case of "Nemesis," the device functions perfectly, but the translation is slightly out of sync with the English language to show just how foreign the Vori tongue is to Starfleet terminology. A new vocabulary is created for this episode that helps to define differences in the alien race. It also serves to show the influence of the Vori mind control on Chakotay as he gradually begins to speak in Vori terminology as he becomes victim to the mind control. In this episode, the following words are translated to take the place of similar concepts in English.

VORI	ENGLISH		
all the days and nights	lifetime	glimpse	look; see; eyes
backwalk	retreat	mother's father	grandfather
beg the Power	pray to God	new light	day
clash	war	nullify	kill
close your glimpses	sleep	plantings	food, crops
cluster	meet; rendezvous point	rages	anger
coverings	uniform	sharp to do my tellings	best to listen to me
daughter's daughter	granddaughter	sphere	planet
defenders	soldiers	strayed into the fullness	come into the middle [of the war]
dispatching	communication	suffice	satisfy
drilled	trained	the before	the past
fast-walk	run, hurry	the light will be on soon	the sun will be up soon
fathom	think, thought; understand	the now	the present
flame	burn	the soonafter	the future
fleet colors	military affiliation (markings)	the way-after	the afterlife
		trembles	fear
footfalls	feet (measure of distance)	trunks	trees, forest
fume	set fire to, burn	waif	child
glare	sun	walk	tour of duty

bination of mind-control techniques, including photometric projections, heightened emotional stimuli, and highly sophisticated psychotropic manipulation affecting the subject's hypothalamus in such a way that he will believe anything he is told.

PERSONAL LOGS: Neelix functions in an ambassadorial position, as he has researched the conflict to prepare a report for the captain. Since he is now over 10,000 light-years away from familiar space, this appears to be a new facet to his role on the ship and has been mentioned previously as a possible position.

EPISODE LOGS: Seven of Nine does not appear in this episode. ▪ Kenneth Biller's script creates an alien language that is slightly different from normal human terminology, but close enough so as not to confuse the audience.

DAY OF HONOR

EPISODE #172

WRITTEN BY: **JERI TAYLOR**

DIRECTED BY: **JESÚS SALVADOR TREVIÑO**

GUEST STARS

VORIK	ALEXANDER ENBERG
LUMAS	ALAN ALTSHULD
RAHMIN	MICHAEL A. KRAWIC
MOKLOR	KEVIN P. STILLWELL

CO-STAR

COMPUTER VOICE	MAJEL BARRETT

STARDATE UNKNOWN

Torres is having a bad day. It started when she overslept and had a malfunction in her sonic shower. It continues to go downhill when she is ordered to work with Seven of Nine to create a Borg-style transwarp conduit. She is hardly in the mood to celebrate the Day of Honor, an annual Klingon ritual of self-examination. Paris tries to help, but she pushes him away, afraid to accept the comfort of his friendship.

In the meantime, *Voyager* encounters a ship of Caatati refugees seeking supplies. The Caatati leader, Rashmin, explains that the Borg assimilated most of his civilization, leaving them with nothing. Janeway gladly gives the Caatati the resources that *Voyager* can spare, but is unable to meet all of their needs. Rahmin is outraged when he sees that the crew includes an ex-Borg.

In engineering, Seven of Nine continues working to open a transwarp conduit, but during the first test of the modifications, an accident occurs and Torres is forced to eject the warp core. Torres and Paris take a shuttle to retrieve the core, but they find a Caatati ship trying to salvage it. They warn the Caatati off, but the aliens fire at the shuttle, collapsing its structural integrity field. Torres and Paris beam into space just before their shuttle explodes. By linking the communication systems in both of their space suits, they create a carrier wave that they hope will reach *Voyager* before they run out of air.

On *Voyager,* Janeway questions Seven of Nine about the accident in engineering and is satisfied that she was not the cause. As the pair works together to solve the puzzle, Seven opens up to Janeway about her difficulties interacting with the crew.

The ship picks up the carrier wave from Torres and

Seven helps the Caatati, giving them the technology they need to survive. ROBBIE ROBINSON

Torres is forced to eject the warp core on what could be the worst day of her life. ROBBIE ROBINSON

Neelix says they can spare several hundred kilograms of food for the Caatati. ▪ The crew attempts to create a transwarp conduit for only a short time to get as much sensor data as they can. First they set up a temporary tachyon matrix within the main deflector. Since they need to be at warp speed to create a large enough subspace field Torres has helm control rerouted to engineering. At warp 2.3 they start emitting tachyons and energizing the matrix. When there is no indication of a subspace field they switch to a higher energy band. The field forms, but tachyon particles leak into the propulsion system. They are able to shut down the deflector and cut all power relays but the leak continues flooding the warp core with tachyons to the point where it may breach. Torres evacuates engineering and tries decoupling the dilithium matrix to no effect. She uses authorization Torres Omega-Phi-93 to eject the warp core. The ship is stopped dead with the warp core millions of kilometers away. The impulse engines are seriously damaged, and only a few thrusters are available. Tractoring the warp core while it is unstable could cause an antimatter explosion. Later Janeway and Seven determine that the accident occurred because the core pressure increased when tachyon levels rose to a resonant frequency. ▪ Torres and Paris interplex the com systems in both space suits to create a phase carrier wave to contact the ship. *Voyager* reads the signature and knows it is from them. Oxygen in the space suits is measured in millibars.

Paris, but before they can retrieve them, an armada of Caatati ships arrive with the warp core. They threaten to destroy *Voyager* unless Janeway gives them more supplies and turns over Seven of Nine. Seven volunteers to go, but the captain refuses. Seven then offers to build an energy matrix for the Caatati, which will produce all the thorium they need for their systems. The Caatati accept, and return the warp core.

The crisis over, *Voyager* is free to rescue Paris and Torres. As the pair float in space, their oxygen levels nearly depleted, Torres finds that in facing death, she has found the courage to admit her love for Tom, and with that act B'Elanna realizes she has found her honor.

SENSOR READINGS: Two members of the engineering crew are sick, forcing Torres to cancel the fuel cell overhaul. ▪ There is a rupture in the coolant injector. Vorik suggests reconfiguring the coolant assembly to give them greater control over the pressure valve emissions. ▪ The acoustic invertor in Torres's sonic shower blows out, which Paris says will "make your hair stand on end." ▪

SHUTTLE TRACKER: Destroyed. The Caatati send an antimatter pulse back through the *Shuttlecraft Cochrane's* particle beam, compromising the structural integrity field, ultimately destroying the ship.

DELTA QUADRANT: The Caatati were assimilated by the Borg over a year ago. Only a few thousand from the planet of millions escaped on thirty ships. They have not been welcome on any planet because they have no resources and are treated like vagrants. ▪ Caatati technology is dependent on thorium isotopes. When the Borg assimilated the Caatati, the survivors lost their ability to replicate the isotopes, but Seven has retained that knowledge. She designs an energy matrix that can produce 944 grams of thorium per day.

The sector has some random ion turbulence that affects the shuttle and damages the space suits.

ALPHA QUADRANT: The Klingon Day of Honor is a holiday in which celebrants examine their behavior to see if they lived up to Klingon standards over the past year. Families traditionally serve blood pie on the holiday. The ceremony in which one's honor is challenged is a lengthy ordeal beginning with the celebrant eating from the heart of a sanctified *targ,* which is said to bring courage. Next, the celebrant drinks *mot'loch* from the grail of Kahless. This is followed by the celebrant explaining how she has "proven herself worthy." After which, the celebrant endures the Ritual of Twenty Painstiks, engages in combat with a master of the *bat'leth,* and traverses the sulfur lagoons of Gorath.

PERSONAL LOGS: As the officer in charge of personnel, Chakotay prepares the duty rosters. ▪ Torres is beginning to feel that Klingon rituals are not as hateful as when her mother made her perform them. ▪ Neelix offers to be Torres's "pressure valve" so she can use him to blow off steam. ▪ Seven of Nine is having trouble dealing with her solitude and asks to be assigned to engineering. According to the Doctor, she is almost ready to begin eating food. Seven is unaccustomed to deception because there were no lies among the Borg. She is also unfamiliar with the idea of giving away technology because that too was never considered by the Borg.

Tuvok receives his promotion to lieutenant commander.
ROBBIE ROBINSON

REVULSION

EPISODE #173

WRITTEN BY: LISA KLINK

DIRECTED BY: KENNETH BILLER

GUEST STAR

DEJAREN	LELAND ORSER

STARDATE 51186.2

In the midst of a ceremony celebrating Tuvok's promotion to lieutenant commander, Torres and Paris try to sneak off to discuss their budding relationship, but are interrupted by the Doctor, who asks Paris to replace Kes as his assistant in sickbay. The party is later interrupted when *Voyager* receives an automated distress call sent by Dejaren, an alien hologram, who says that his crew is dead and he needs help. The Doctor, anxious to meet a fellow hologram, tracks the source of the transmission and is assigned to the rescue mission along with Torres. Upon their arrival on the disabled ship, they meet Dejaren, who is pleased to see another "life-form" like himself.

The hologram says that his crew became infected with a deadly virus, which killed them all. Dejaren is

awed by the Doctor's freedom and abilities, since his own crew never let him out of the antimatter storage chamber or treated him as anything other than machinery. Later, as Torres works to repair Dejaren's systems, Dejaren lashes out at her verbally, castigating her organic body and way of life. Torres shares her concerns about the hologram with the Doctor and informs him that Dejaren lied about the lower deck being filled with harmful radiation, leading her to believe that there is something down there that he does not want them to see. Although the Doctor empathizes with his fellow hologram, he agrees to keep Dejaren occupied while she investigates.

While the pair renders aid to Dejaren, the crew is busy on a trade mission with the Arritheans when Chakotay assigns Kim to work with Seven of Nine on a new astrometrics lab. At first, the ensign is apprehensive about teaming with the former Borg, but he quickly grows comfortable with her and finds himself falling for her. When Seven of Nine realizes his attraction for her, she bluntly asks if he would like to copulate. Kim is thrown by her obviously unfamiliar response to social interaction and asks to be taken off the assignment, but Chakotay says the two make a good team, and that Seven concurs.

As the Doctor talks to Dejaren, he begins to realize that Torres was right. The hologram is pathologically bitter toward organics. On the lower deck, Torres finds the bloody bodies of the crew and realizes they did not die from a virus. As she hurriedly tries to deactivate Dejaren's program, the homicidal hologram appears and nearly kills her before she manages to shut him off.

The Doctor and Torres find that the hologram has disabled their communication link to the shuttle. As they work to restore it, Dejaren reactivates himself and knocks out Torres. He disconnects the Doctor's mobile emitter, causing him to disappear. Torres awakens and flees, but a murderous Dejaren pursues her. Finally, she manages to destabilize his matrix with an isomagnetic conduit, deactivating him for good. She reactivates the Doctor's program, and both return to *Voyager* with a new appreciation for the Doctor's unique personality.

SENSOR READINGS: The astrometrics lab has not been updated since *Voyager* left drydock. Kim and Seven begin their work by enhancing astrometric sensors in Jefferies tube 32-B. Seven designs new navigational sensors with some programming in Borg alphanumerics. Seven misaligns the optical assembly by .5 degrees, but corrects the problem. There are five million gigawatts running through the main power supply.

DELTA QUADRANT: Dejaren is an HD25 Isomorphic Projection with Extreme Hazard Clearance. He is responsible for cleaning the reactor core and ejecting antimatter waste, among other responsibilities. Access to his primary isomatrix is on the lower deck although there is an interface on the upper deck. He is unfamiliar with the term hologram. His ship left the home planet of Seros eight months ago with a crew of six "organics." Life support uses 59.2 percent of the ship's power.

PERSONAL LOGS: Janeway has known Tuvok for nine years. The first time they met, he dressed her down in front of three Starfleet admirals for failing to observe proper tactical procedures. ■ Paris and Kim once rigged the security console so that every time Tuvok accessed the internal sensors, it would say: "Live Long and Prosper" (and they programmed his replicator to do the same). Paris is recruited to be the new nurse since he is the most

Dejaren looks at the Doctor—an independent hologram—with envy.
DANNY FELD

qualified member of crew. His work in sickbay will only be temporary with three duty shifts a week. He is to report to sickbay at 0600. ■ The captain tells Neelix to consider his trade preparations with the Arritheans to be his first official assignment as ambassador. ■ Seven of Nine agrees to provide *Voyager* with all the navigational data for the area that she acquired as a Borg. In her down time she regenerates in her alcove, studies the Starfleet database, and contemplates her existence. The exoskeleton on her left hand can withstand five million gigawatts of energy.

MEDICAL REPORT: Seven cuts her hand. It is the first time she has to cope with not having the Borg regenerative abilities. ■ After Dejaren reaches into her chest, Torres has a perforated fourth ventricle and possible internal bleeding. Later she receives a head wound. ■ In addition to Seven's hand, Paris also treats two broken bones and a stomachache on his first day back in sickbay.

EPISODE LOGS: The events of this episode take place three days after "Day of Honor."

THE RAVEN

EPISODE #174
WRITTEN BY: **BRYAN FULLER**
STORY BY: **BRYAN FULLER and HARRY DOC KLOOR**
DIRECTED BY: **LeVAR BURTON**

GUEST STARS

GAUMAN   RICHARD J. ZOBEL, JR.
DUMAH   MICKEY COTTRELL

CO-STARS

FATHER   DAVID ANTHONY
                            MARSHALL
MOTHER   NIKKI TYLER
LITTLE GIRL (ANNIKA) ERICA LYNNE BRYAN
COMPUTER VOICE   MAJEL BARRETT

STARDATE UNKNOWN

Seven's Borg implants begin to reassert themselves. ROBBIE ROBINSON

When Seven of Nine begins experiencing unexplained flashbacks involving pursuit by Borg and a large black bird, the Doctor attributes it to posttraumatic stress disorder caused by the ordeal of being assimilated. As the Doctor searches for the true cause of the hallucinations, he advises her to begin eating real food, something she will need to get used to now that she is human. After a few bites in the mess hall, Seven has another vision, and a piece of Borg hardware erupts through her skin. Reverting to Borg behavior, she threatens Neelix with assimilation.

Meanwhile, Janeway faces tough negotiations with representatives of the B'omar race for passage through their system. Although the crew is immediately alerted to Seven's odd behavior, they are unable to stop her from leaving the ship. After transporting to a shuttle, she takes the craft into B'omar space, immediately ending the negotiations and inciting a conflict with the untrusting race.

The Doctor concludes that Seven's dormant Borg nanoprobes have somehow become reactivated. The B'omar refuse to allow *Voyager* to enter their territory to pursue Seven, but Tuvok and Paris sneak a shuttle past their perimeter grid and track her. When they reach her, Tuvok beams over to her shuttle and a struggle ensues. Seven easily wins and traps the Vulcan behind a force field, then disables Paris's shuttle, leaving him behind. The Vulcan questions her reasons for leaving *Voyager*. Seven explains that she is responding to a Borg homing beacon although Tuvok points out that there are no Borg ships in the region.

Seven tracks the mysterious signal to an alien moon and prepares to beam to the surface. Tuvok asks to accompany her, but Seven expresses concern that he will be assimilated. Tuvok believes he has no reason to fear that possibility and reminds her that the concern she feels for him is a human trait unfamiliar to the Borg.

On the surface, they find an old Federation vessel that was partially assimilated by the Borg twenty years ago. It is the *Raven,* a ship that belonged to Seven's parents, the Hansens. Some of the Borg-modified equipment was left active, including the beacon that triggered her return. Seven confronts the haunting memories of her assimilation by the Borg at the age of six, but is snapped out of the reverie by an attack from B'omar ships. She and Tuvok barely manage to escape the vessel before the *Raven* is destroyed. They are beamed up by Paris and safely returned to *Voyager,* which is now forced to lengthen their journey by traveling around the B'omar space.

SENSOR READINGS: There is an armory on Deck 6, and the shuttlebay on Deck 10 is near junction 32-Alpha. ▪ Seven remodulates the shuttle's shield harmonics so the tractor beam is ineffective. ▪ The crew scans space for a distance of forty light-years with no sign of Borg ships.

SHUTTLE TRACKER: Seven blasts through the shuttlebay door, fleeing in a type-6 shuttle. Her attack on Paris's type-9 shuttle takes his propulsion systems and warp engines offline and reduces shields to fifty percent. It is unclear whether or not Seven's shuttle is retrieved.

DELTA QUADRANT: The B'omar Sovereignty imposes the following conditions when they originally agree to allow *Voyager* to travel through their space: The vessel is not to exceed warp 3, weapons systems will remain offline, they will avoid unnecessary scans, and not conduct surveys of any kind. They will also avoid communications with nonmilitary craft and follow the long and roundabout route plotted by the B'omar, designed to avoid their populated systems and industrial areas. There are a total of seventeen checkpoints where they will have to submit the ship for inspection. To go around the B'omar space adds three months to the journey. The B'omar perimeter grid identifies and traces every vessel, object, and particle of dust that crosses their borders. It is possible to penetrate the grid by recalibrating shields to match its frequency, but *Voyager*'s energy signature is too large to hide, so a shuttle is used instead. ▪ The Agrat-Mot Nebula is a key resource in the B'omar's trade negotiations with the Nassordin.

Every Borg ship is coded to emit a distinct resonance frequency that serves as a homing beacon to guide drones that have become separated from the collective. ▪ The Borg refer to the Talaxians as Species 218. Neelix was not aware that a small freighter containing a crew of thirty-nine Talaxians was taken in the Dalmine Sector. They were easily assimilated and their dense musculature made them excellent drones. ▪ Vulcans are Species 3259. Their enlarged neocortex produces superior analytical abilities.

ALPHA QUADRANT: Tritanium decay indicates that the *S.S. Raven* NAR-32450 crashed on a class-M moon orbiting the fifth planet of a yellow dwarf star almost twenty years ago. The *Raven*'s resonance signal acts as a homing device for Seven of Nine. Janeway has the crew calibrate long-range sensors to scan for any Federation signature other than the two shuttlecraft.

PERSONAL LOGS: Janeway sculpts as a means of relaxation. As a child she studied Leonardo da Vinci's drawings and built some of his models. ▪ Kim is getting better at translating Borg alphanumeric code. He is mentioned several times in Seven's personal logs, where it is noted that his behavior is easy to predict. ▪ Seven of Nine has never hallucinated before; however, she will experience hallucinations again on several occasions in the future. She is also

Janeway explains how she has found inspiration in da Vinci's workshop. ROBBIE ROBINSON

unaccustomed to sitting, as the Borg do not sit. Her digestive system is now fully functional. Her dietary requirements include 250 grams of glycoproteins, consisting of fifty-three percent polypeptides and twenty-six percent fibrous glycogen (among other items). Seven lived on the *Raven* for much of her childhood; her sixth birthday is the last that she can recall (which would make her twenty-four). Her father conducted "very important" experiments though she does not recall what they were. Janeway tells her that her parents were fairly well known for being unconventional, and for some rather unique scientific theories. Seven has been aboard *Voyager* for two months.

MEDICAL REPORT: Seven of Nine's hippocampus is in a state of agitation. The Doctor uses the matter conversion data from Seven of Nine's last transport to base his analysis. There is a high concentration of Borg organelles in the bone marrow and lymphatic tissue. The dormant nanoprobes in Seven of Nine's cells reassert themselves, taking over blood cell production and growing new Borg implants. Thirteen percent of the Borg technology the Doctor removed three weeks ago regenerates in a matter of hours. The hypospray he provides contains a genetic resequencing vector that should neutralize the nanoprobes.

EPISODE LOGS: Seven of Nine wears a new brown bodysuit that was less constrictive for Jeri Ryan than the previous silver one.

SCIENTIFIC METHOD

EPISODE #175
TELEPLAY BY: LISA KLINK
STORY BY: SHERRY KLEIN & HARRY DOC KLOOR
DIRECTED BY: DAVID LIVINGSTON

GUEST STARS

ALZEN	ROSEMARY FORSYTH
TAKAR	ANNETTE HELDE

STARDATE 51244.3

While Paris and Torres share a private moment in a Jefferies tube, an odd X-ray effect flashes over their bodies. Though they have the feeling they are being watched, the effect is otherwise unnoticed. Meanwhile, Janeway deals with sleep deprivation, stress, and a headache so painful that it overcomes her normal scientific curiosity for the exploration of a binary pulsar.

When Chakotay begins aging rapidly, the Doctor's scan detects that the segments of his DNA have been hyperstimulated. Neelix soon succumbs to a different ailment, but the Doctor finds that the cause is the same.

Soon, other crew members are coming in with obscure genetic problems. Torres and the Doctor find microscopic tags on their DNA, but before they can investigate further, the Doctor's program seems to be deactivated and Torres collapses.

The Doctor finds a method to communicate by tapping into Seven's audio implants and asks her to meet him in the holodeck where he is hiding. He suspects that the crew is being watched and he adjusts Seven's Borg sensory nodes so she can scan *Voyager* for anything unusual. Once she leaves the holodeck, Seven notices aliens throughout the ship, invisibly prodding crew members with instruments. She goes to the captain and finds Janeway flanked by aliens sticking needles into her head, revealing the true source of her headaches.

Seven tells the Doctor that the aliens are performing medical experiments on the crew. She could make them visible with a modulated phaser beam, but the Doctor believes they might retaliate. He suggests that delivering a simultaneous neuroleptic shock to each member of the crew will undo the experiments. But when Seven tries to implement the plan, Tuvok stops her, misunderstanding her intentions. The aliens realize she can see them, and

The Doctor calls Seven into the da Vinci simulation, as it is the only place they can speak freely. ROBBIE ROBINSON

Janeway is unaware of the experiments being performed on her and her crew. CRAIG T. MATHEW

Seven is forced to use her phaser to make one visible. She brings the intruder to Janeway, who is outraged when the alien explains they are using the data to cure disorders within their race. The alien threatens to kill everyone if the experiments are not allowed to continue.

Seeing no other options, Janeway gambles by taking *Voyager* into the binary pulsar, knowing it may mean certain destruction. The aliens evacuate the ship, as *Voyager* plunges through at full throttle. The ship comes out relatively unscathed, and the Doctor is able to neutralize the effects of the alien experiments. Afterward, Paris and Torres share a romantic dinner, lightly joking that their newfound relationship may only be a result of the experimentation.

SENSOR READINGS: Seven reconfigures the power couplings in a section of Jefferies tubes because the astrometrics lab requires additional energy. She reroutes some energy from engineering while they are running a warp core diagnostic. ▪ According to the Doctor there are 257

rooms on *Voyager.* ▪ The Doctor isolates com frequency Epsilon 2 from the rest of the system so he and Seven can communicate secretly. ▪ There is a problem with the plasma manifold. Torres tells engineering to lock it down and worry about it tomorrow.

DAMAGE REPORT: As *Voyager* travels through the binary pulsar, hull stress is noted at 45 teradynes and eventually exceeds maximum tolerance. Shields fail, and structural integrity is down to twenty percent. There are hull breaches on Decks 4, 7, 8, and 12. Main power is offline. Outer hull temp reaches 9,000 degrees Celsius.

DELTA QUADRANT: Gravitational forces between the binary pulsars are so intense that everything within fifty million kilometers is pulled in. Gamma radiation levels are also high and random proton bursts are also present. They keep the ship at a distance of ninety million kilometers with shields at maximum strength.

Seven observes fifty-six aliens on the ship, noting there could be more. The aliens possess submolecular technology beyond anything Starfleet has developed. Their DNA tags transmit a signal and are slightly out of phase, which is why initial scans do not reveal them. The Doctor believes that a neuroleptic shock would neutralize the genetic tags. The power relays can be reconfigured to emit the shock. A precisely modulated phaser beam reveals the aliens. ▪ The aliens are scientists and it is a breach of protocol to speak with their subjects. The data they gather from the crew may help them cure physical and psychological disorders that afflict millions.

ALPHA QUADRANT: The childhood genetic disorder progeria was eradicated two centuries earlier. ▪ Experimentation on animals was discontinued long ago.

PERSONAL LOGS: As security chief, Tuvok has thirteen department heads reporting to him. ▪ Paris had to cancel a date with Torres because he had an extra duty shift on the bridge. ▪ Neelix's great-great-grandfather was Mylean. ▪ The Doctor taps into Seven's audio implants so he can communicate with her without being discovered. He adjusts her Borg sensory nodes to a phase variance of .15 so she can scan for the aliens.

CREW COMPLEMENT: An unnamed female crew member is killed by the alien experimentation.

EPISODE LOGS: Though the aliens go unnamed in the episode, the script refers to them as the Srivani.

YEAR OF HELL, PART I

EPISODE #176
WRITTEN BY: BRANNON BRAGA & JOE MENOSKY
DIRECTED BY: ALLAN KROEKER

GUEST STAR

OBRIST   JOHN LOPRIENO

SPECIAL GUEST STAR

ANNORAX   KURTWOOD SMITH

CO-STARS

KRENIM COMMANDANT   PETER SLUTSKER

ZAHL   RICK FITTS

ENSIGN LANG   DEBORAH LEVIN

ENSIGN BROOKS   SUE HENLEY

COMPUTER VOICE   MAJEL BARRETT

STARDATE 51268.4*

The crew christens their new astrometrics lab, which has mapping technology far more accurate than their old system. It projects a course that will cut five years off their trip, taking them through Zahl territory, which a species called the Krenim also lays claim to. A Zahl official tells *Voyager* not to worry about the Krenim, who once dominated the region with deadly

*The stardate listed comes 65 days into the Year of Hell.

temporal weapons before the Zahl defeated them years ago. Suddenly, *Voyager*'s sensors pick up a buildup of temporal energy, and the ship is hit by a space-time shockwave. The Zahl disappear, along with the crew's memory of them, and they find themselves facing a now powerful Krenim warship. Chroniton-based Krenim torpedoes, which exist in a state of temporal flux, penetrate *Voyager*'s shields, badly damaging the ship.

In another part of the region, Annorax, the Krenim captain of the time-altering weapon-ship that annihilated the Zahl, evaluates his efforts and learns he has almost completely restored the Krenim Imperium. But Annorax will not rest until every Krenim colony is restored.

Months pass in which the Krenim repeatedly attack *Voyager*, leaving the ship badly damaged. After one of the attacks, Seven finds an active warhead lodged in the hull. Tuvok surmises it will explode in minutes, but Seven is intent on learning its temporal variance and using that knowledge to perfect shielding against other Krenim weapons. She makes a determination just before the torpedo blows up.

Although the explosion blinds Tuvok, Seven is eventually able to use the data to create shields that hold against Krenim torpedoes. In another part of space, Annorax fires his temporal weapon, and the space-time continuum is again altered. This time, *Voyager*'s shields protect it from the time disruption. When the shockwave passes, the crew is unaffected by the change in the timeline, but they find that the large Krenim warship they

Endangering both their lives, Seven refuses to leave before she gets the temporal variance from an unexploded weapon. ROBBIE ROBINSON

Janeway's single-minded determination grows throughout the "year of hell." DANNY FELD

using. Kim and Seven have plotted a new course home that will eliminate five years from the journey. ▪ Paris bases his idea for transverse bulkheads on the design of the *Titanic*. Emergency force fields are set up between all decks and every section, so in the event of a cataclysmic breach, most of the crew will be protected. ▪ The temporal variance of the chroniton torpedo is 1.47 microseconds ("Before and After"). The variance is used to create temporal shielding. Not only does the crew have to match shields to the temporal variance, but they must also match the deflector array to the inverse of that variance for the shielding to be effective. ▪ The tactical station has tactile interface so a blinded Tuvok can use it. ▪ Escape pods are equipped with subspace beacons. ▪ They are down to eleven torpedoes, but torpedo launchers are offline, forcing them to lay out four torpedoes like mines. The phaser banks are burned out.

DAMAGE REPORT: Sections 10 through 53 on Deck 5 are gone. The entire turbolift system is nonoperational. The power grid on Deck 11 is destroyed which badly damages the replicator system, forcing the crew to use emergency rations. Environmental controls continue to fail, rendering seven decks uninhabitable. Astrometrics is offline. By the end they have lost nine decks and more than half the ship has been destroyed. With life support nearly gone, *Voyager* can no longer sustain its crew.

DELTA QUADRANT: Spatial grid 005 originally contains the Zahl and the primary species. They are technologically advanced, but nonconfrontational. Their resistance quotient is quite low according to Seven. The sector of space has many class-M planets. The Krenim weapon negates their existence.

The temporal weapon results in a massive buildup of temporal energy. It is a kind of space-time shockwave that also destabilizes *Voyager*'s warp field. A causality paradox occurs when the temporal shockwave eliminates a single species and all of history changes as a result. After the destruction of the Zahl homeworld the Krenim Imperium territory includes 849 inhabited worlds, spanning 5,000 parsecs. There are no superior enemy forces and no unexpected diseases. Calculations indicate a 98 percent restoration, but not the colony at Kyana Prime. The Krenim aboard the ship have been altering time for two hundred years and have never come as close. ▪ Following another temporal incursion, the entire Krenim Imperium goes back to a pre-warp state. ▪ The weapon-ship is in a state of temporal flux, existing outside space-time. It cannot exceed warp 6 due to the vessel's mass. The weapons

were battling has become a much smaller ship. Annorax's weapon has caused the Krenim Imperium to revert to a pre-warp state.

Annorax realizes that *Voyager*'s temporal shields were responsible for throwing off his calculations. He approaches *Voyager* and transports Chakotay and Paris to his ship for study. He then unleashes a chroniton energy beam to erase *Voyager* from history, but the starship is able to escape, albeit with major structural damage. Janeway is forced to evacuate the crew, but she and the senior staff will stay with the ship to rescue Chakotay and Paris, and hopefully reunite later with her fleeing crew.

SENSOR READINGS: The new astrometrics lab is completed with astrometric sensors to measure the radiative flux of up to three billion stars simultaneously. The computer uses that information to calculate the ship's position relative to the center of the galaxy using mapping technology ten times more accurate than they have been

are chroniton based and penetrate shields because they are also in temporal flux.

ALPHA QUADRANT: M'Kota R'Cho was the first Klingon to ever play parrises squares professionally. During the finals of 2342, one of the referees called a penalty against the team. R'Cho strangled the ref.

PERSONAL LOGS: Janeway's birthday is May 20. Chakotay gives her a replicated watch as a gift. She has a "lucky teacup" in her ready room and has made it a goal in her life to avoid time travel. ▪ Kim considers himself a sports aficionado. ▪ Neelix is made a security officer.

MEDICAL REPORT: Tuvok is blinded by the torpedo explosion. ▪ Torres is badly injured and suffers a ruptured vertebra.

CREW COMPLEMENT: Ensign Strickland and Crewman Emmanuel die in the explosion of Deck 5 when the Doctor is forced to close the Jefferies tube hatch on them. ▪ It is unclear how many other crew members are lost during the first part of the Year of Hell. In the following episode, seven members of the senior staff will be seen on the ship (although the Doctor will tell Janeway there are seven people in addition to her.)

EPISODE LOGS: It is unclear why the crew makes no mention of the information gathered from Kes's interaction with the Krenim in "Before and After." It is possible, however, that the information was used, as events unfold slightly differently, such as Janeway and Torres not dying as predicted. ▪ Seven of Nine refers to the fact that the Borg were at the launch of Zephram Cochrane's *Phoenix,* but does not go into detail. This information is a result of the events in *Star Trek: First Contact.* ▪ Kim and Seven began work on the new astrometrics lab in "Revulsion."

YEAR OF HELL, PART II
EPISODE #177
WRITTEN BY: BRANNON BRAGA & JOE MENOSKY
DIRECTED BY: MIKE VEJAR

GUEST STARS

OBRIST	JOHN LOPRIENO

SPECIAL GUEST STAR

ANNORAX	KURTWOOD SMITH

CO-STARS

KRENIM COMMANDANT	PETER SLUTSKER
NARRATOR	MAJEL BARRETT

STARDATE 51252.3*

Two months after the majority of the crew were forced to abandon ship, the remaining senior staff has taken refuge in a nebula as they attempt to repair *Voyager.* Nerves are worn thin on the ship and Janeway edges closer to a breakdown. Her judgment eventually grows so clouded that the Doctor attempts to relieve her of duty, but she refuses, preferring to accept a court-martial if they ever get free of Krenim space.

On the weapon-ship, Chakotay and Paris are summoned to meet with Annorax, who proposes to send *Voyager* back in time, restoring it to its original state and possibly closer to the Alpha Quadrant, if they fill him in on the extent of their presence in Krenim space. With

*The stardate listed comes from after the timeline is reset, when the crew places astrometrics online.

Chakotay begins to be swayed by the rationale behind Annorax's mission. ROBBIE ROBINSON

that information he believes that he can complete calculations that will allow him to restore the Krenim Imperium. Paris balks at helping Annorax, but Chakotay believes the chance to continue their voyage home may be worth the risk of trusting Annorax.

As Chakotay helps chart *Voyager*'s journey, Annorax teaches him about the complexity of the incursions by sharing the story of his first mistake in altering the Krenim timeline. He used the weapon-ship to destroy the Krenim's greatest enemy, but in the process, he also destroyed an important antibody in the Krenim genetic structure, and fifty million Krenim died of disease as a result. He has been trying to undo his mistake ever since.

Paris finds a weakness in the Krenim ship that could be exploited, but Chakotay refuses to go against Annorax. However, when Annorax eradicates another species to partially restore the Krenim timeline, Chakotay is dismayed to see him once again turn to destruction as an answer to his problems. When Chakotay takes Annorax to task for the loss of innocent lives, the Krenim reveals the driving force behind his actions. His wife and family died as a result of his time incursions, and he hopes to undo their deaths.

Chakotay and Paris secretly contact *Voyager*, giving Janeway their coordinates. She arranges a coalition with other species to attack when Paris takes the temporal core offline. The remaining members of *Voyager*'s crew disperse to prepare the other ships for battle, but Janeway stays with her ship.

Chakotay and Paris take the temporal core offline with the help of Obrist, Annorax's second-in-command. His ship now vulnerable to traditional weapons, Annorax orders his men to fire at the approaching vessels, and soon the coalition is almost destroyed. Janeway initiates a kamikaze run at the Krenim ship, and the impact destabilizes the core, causing a temporal incursion within Annorax's ship. With the destruction of the Krenim vessel, the timeline is restored, *Voyager* never makes its fateful entry into Krenim space, and Annorax is at last reunited with his beloved wife.

SENSOR READINGS: *Voyager* takes refuge in a class-9 nebula. ▪ Deflector control is designated a level-4 hazard.

DAMAGE REPORT: One warp nacelle is offline, the other is a lost cause. The power grid is operating at thirty-two percent efficiency. All damage to *Voyager* is reversed when the timeline is restored.

DELTA QUADRANT: About eight months earlier, *Voyager* made a course correction to avoid a rogue comet.

Janeway will do anything to stop Annorax. ROBBIE ROBINSON

According to Chakotay's calculations, it led to their entering Krenim space. Had he actually eradicated that comet, all life within fifty light-years would never have existed.

Annorax feeds Chakotay and Paris foods from what remains of lost species, including the only bottle of Malkothian spirits known to exist and the last remnants of the Alsuran Empire. ▪ When Annorax first created the weapon-ship, he used it against the Rilnar, their greatest enemy. With the Rilnar gone, his people became instantly powerful again until a rare disease broke out among the colonies. Within a year fifty million were dead because he failed to realize that the Rilnar added a crucial antibody into the Krenim genome that his weapon erased from the Krenim. ▪ The ship's temporal core keeps the ship out of phase with normal space-time, but its shields are incredibly weak. ▪ The eradication of the Ram Izad species results in a fifty-two percent restoration of the Krenim timeline.

Voyager forges a coalition with the Nihydron and the Mawasi.

PERSONAL LOGS: The Doctor has repaired the optronic error in his program. It was this problem that took him

THE DESTRUCTION OF VOYAGER

"This ship has been our home . . . it's kept us together . . . it's been part of our family. As illogical as this might sound . . . I feel as close to Voyager as I do to any other member of the crew. It's carried us, Tuvok, even nurtured us . . . and right now, it needs one of us."

Kathryn Janeway, "Year of Hell, Part II"

Captain Janeway's bond with her ship reflects that of many Starfleet captains and their vessels. However, the *U.S.S. Voyager* has the additional binding tie that it is the only ship available to this Starfleet crew. There are no possible transfers to other vessels, no major upgrades possible for the ship itself. *Voyager* will have to see the crew safely through what could be a seventy-five-year-long journey, as both a ship and a home. In rare instances, however, the captain is forced to put her ship in jeopardy to either protect her crew or keep the ship from falling into the wrong hands.

"Deadlock"—Hiding from the Vidiians, *Voyager* passes through a divergence field that duplicates every piece of matter on board, leaving two identical ships with two identical crews. The Captain Janeway of the less damaged ship is forced to destroy her vessel, and her crew, when boarded by the Vidiians, to allow the other *Voyager* to escape.

"Year of Hell, Part II"—Out of options to stop a weapon-ship responsible for causing numerous changes in time and history, Janeway takes *Voyager* on a kamikaze run destroying both ships and resetting the timeline back to moments before their fateful encounter.

"Timeless"—While flying through a quantum shipstream in the *Delta Flyer*, Kim miscalculates the slipstream threshold, and transmits the wrong course corrections to *Voyager*. This causes the ship to be knocked out of the slipstream and crash on a class-L planet in the Takara sector. However, in the future the surviving Kim and Chakotay alter the past so the event never takes place.

"Course: Oblivion"—A duplicate version of *Voyager* and the crew—made entirely of a sentient alien compound— reverts to its original state after the duplicate crew develops an enhanced warp drive that destroys their own cellular structure.

"Relativity"—A saboteur from the future places a bomb on *Voyager* that destroys the ship. However, both Seven of Nine and Janeway are enlisted to travel to the ship in various time periods to discover the identity of the culprit and successfully stop him from planting the device.

MICHAEL YARISH

offline for several months during the timeline experienced by Kes in "Before and After." Under Starfleet Medical Regulation 121, Section A, the Doctor, as the chief medical officer, can relieve Janeway of her active command. Her failure to adhere to his order is a court-martial offense.

MEDICAL REPORT: Janeway suffers traumatic stress syndrome, showing symptoms of irritability, sleeplessness, obsessional thoughts, and reckless behavior. The alveoli in her lungs are chemically burned. She refuses treatment, only accepting an injection of trioxin to help her breathe. She later suffers third-degree burns over sixty percent of her body, leaving her with scars on her arms and face because the Doctor does not have a dermal regenerator.

CREW COMPLEMENT: The complement returns to its previous number when the timeline resets.

RANDOM THOUGHTS

EPISODE #178

WRITTEN BY: KENNETH BILLER
DIRECTED BY: ALEXANDER SINGER

GUEST STARS

NIMIRA	GWYNYTH WALSH
GUILL	WAYNE PÉRÉ
TALLI	REBECCA McFARLAND

CO-STARS

WOMAN	JEANETTE MILLER
MALIN	TED BARBA
FRANE	BOBBY BURNS

STARDATE 51367.2

While visiting the world of the Mari, a telepathic race, Torres accidentally collides with a man named Frane in the marketplace. Soon after, Frane viciously attacks another man. During questioning, Torres admits to Chief Examiner Nimira that she had a passing thought of hurting Frane when he bumped into her. To her surprise, Torres is arrested for "aggravated violent thought resulting in grave bodily harm."

Torres is told she must undergo an engramatic purge, a medical procedure to identify and remove the offending images from her mind. Frane will go through the same purge so the image does not spread, polluting the minds of the pacifistic race. Janeway protests when she hears there is a risk of neurological damage and sets out with Tuvok to review the evidence. They find that Frane has a record of previous arrests for harboring violent thoughts, but Nimira claims he has been cured through previous purging. Later in the marketplace, a Mari woman attacks and kills a young female merchant with whom Neelix was growing close. It is discovered that the attacker also had Torres's violent thought in her mind.

Puzzled by the two inexplicably related attacks, Tuvok mind-melds with Torres to learn more about her brush with Frane. In their shared vision he sees that a Mari named Guill approached her after the incident and probed her mind. When Tuvok questions him, Guill telepathically senses the Vulcan's dark impulses and offers to help Tuvok control them. After witnessing Guill secretly accept money from another Mari, Tuvok realizes Guill may have a business interest in violent thoughts. He approaches Guill again, offering to telepathically exchange his disturbing images.

Questioning him further, Tuvok learns that Guill buys violent thoughts from people, or sometimes takes them, as he did with Torres. Guill denies that he is responsible for the marketplace attack or for the circulation of Torres's thoughts, but Tuvok wants to take him to Nimira for questioning. Just then, two of Guill's co-conspirators intercept them. Meanwhile, Torres begins to undergo the engramatic purge.

Tuvok lures Guill into a mind-meld with the promise of transferring his violent thoughts, but instead he inflicts mental pain on Guill, incapacitating him. Janeway gets Nimira to stop the purging procedure after Tuvok explains that Guill and Frane conspired to provoke the thought in Torres. The captain points out that their enlightened society still has a darker side.

SENSOR READINGS: According to Tuvok the brig has been occupied for less than one percent of their journey. ∎ Janeway barters for a resonator coil to upgrade *Voyager*'s communication systems.

DELTA QUADRANT: The Mari have virtually no crime in their society and believe that violence no longer exists because violent thought is prohibited. Once that law was enacted, the violence rate dropped; however, there is a black market in which Mari trade in illicit mental imagery. Chief Examiner Nimira is one of the last officers working for the constabulary. Nimira monitors thoughts telepathically during witness interviews and has a transcription device that logs engramatic activities, so she can record thoughts and review the statements later. The engramatic purge is a medical procedure that identifies

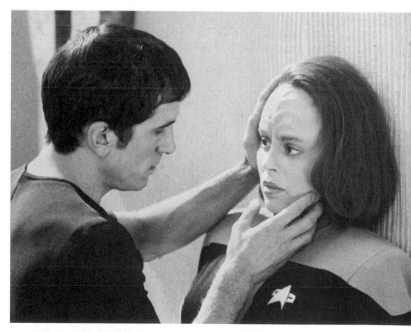

Torres's violent emotions are stolen without her knowledge.
ROBBIE ROBINSON

Chief Examiner Nimira calmly asserts the facts of the case. ROBBIE ROBINSON

and removes the offending images from Torres's mind. Frane spent years in neurogenic restructuring to cure him of his violent thoughts. ▪ The renn is the Mari unit of money.

PERSONAL LOGS: Neelix has feelings for Talli but is afraid to act on them because he has not been with anyone since Kes. Talli reads his mind and discovers that he would like her to tug on his whiskers. As ships' ambassador, Neelix files a diplomatic protest over the arrest of Torres. ▪ Seven believes that the crew's desire to explore is counterproductive to their attempts to get home and potentially dangerous.

MEDICAL REPORT: A few of Torres's memory engrams are purged. ▪ Tuvok is attacked by Guill and some thugs.

CONCERNING FLIGHT
EPISODE #179
TELEPLAY BY: JOE MENOSKY
STORY BY: JIMMY DIGGS and JOE MENOSKY
DIRECTED BY: JESÚS SALVADOR TREVIÑO

GUEST STARS

TAU	**JOHN VARGAS**
ALIEN VISITOR	**DON PUGSLEY**

SPECIAL GUEST STAR

LEONARDO DA VINCI	**JOHN RHYS-DAVIES**

CO-STARS

ALIEN BUYER	**DOUG SPEARMAN**
COMPUTER VOICE	**MAJEL BARRETT**

STARDATE 51386.4

As *Voyager* comes under attack by unidentified vessels, equipment and weapons begin disappearing from the ship. The thieves use a high-energy transporter beam to locate items of technological value and remove them. After the attack, the crew compiles a list of the stolen goods, including the Doctor's mobile emitter

Tuvok distracts da Vinci by making "small talk." ROBBIE ROBINSON

and, even more important, the main computer processor. With the computer functioning at half power, it takes the crew ten days to track their equipment to an alien world that appears to be an active center of commerce.

As Tuvok and Janeway beam down to search, the Vulcan immediately locates an item with a Starfleet signature moments before they are approached by Leonardo da Vinci, from Janeway's holodeck program. Somehow, the thieves stole his program when they took the ship's computer processor, and then downloaded it into the Doctor's stolen mobile emitter. Da Vinci leads them to a room filled with other stolen goods and speaks of his "patron," who provides him with everything he needs.

Back on *Voyager*, Paris and Neelix return from their own scouting mission, where they have learned that a man named Tau sells weapons and technology he confiscates from passing ships. As it turns out, Tau is da Vinci's patron and Janeway gets the inventor to bring her to one of Tau's parties, where she poses as a buyer asking about computers. Tau reveals that he has *Voyager*'s missing computer for sale.

Armed with da Vinci's topographical maps of the

region, Tuvok returns to *Voyager* and reviews the information. He and Seven of Nine locate the storage facility where the processor is kept, but a force field around it makes transport impossible. Janeway will have to get inside the facility and initiate a power surge in the computer processor that will produce a signal strong enough for the transporter beam to lock on to. Unfortunately, Tau overhears Janeway talking to the ship and trains a weapon on her. Da Vinci comes to her defense and knocks out Tau, then he and Janeway head for the facility.

Once they find the processor, Janeway follows Tuvok's plan. The arrival of an armed guard prevents the two of them from beaming up along with the computer, and Janeway and da Vinci are forced to take escape into their own hands. They board a glider constructed by da Vinci and take off just as Tau's men begin shooting at them. Finally, *Voyager* is able to get close enough to the planet to beam aboard the captain and her mentor, along with the glider that finally gave da Vinci the gift of flight.

SENSOR READINGS: The stolen objects include the main computer processor, the warp diagnostic assembly,

Janeway and da Vinci take flight. ROBBIE ROBINSON

five tricorders, three phaser rifles, a couple of photon torpedo casings, two antimatter injectors, a plasma injector conduit, a month's supply of emergency rations, and the Doctor's mobile emitter. The only items known to be recovered are the computer processor and the mobile emitter. Seven and Kim use the deep-space imaging system in astrometrics to expand the distance of their scans for the missing technology. ▪ Computer processor's technical specifications: simultaneous access to forty-seven million data channels. Trans-luminal processing at 575 trillion calculations per nanosecond. Operational temperature margins from 10 to 1,790 kelvin, Janeway initiates computer overload using command override Janeway Pi-110. ▪ There is a button on the mobile emitter that freezes the hologram. ▪ The ship has to be 500 kilometers from the surface to lock onto the mobile emitter and the captain for transport.

DELTA QUADRANT: There are twenty-seven different types of alien ships in orbit of the planet. *Voyager*'s scanners are affected by all the different technology on the planet. Materials in construction of city and the technology in use all originated from numerous sources. The main computer processor is outside a city on the northern continent. Tau controls the seventh province of the north where he sells weapons and technology that he confiscates from passing ships using his translocator device, which he also stole.

PERSONAL LOGS: According to Tuvok, Vulcans do not make small talk. To explain his unique appearance, Tuvok tells da Vinci he is from Scandinavia. ▪ Most of Seven's implants are stable but her optical interface is misaligned again. She has been missing some of her weekly maintenance with the Doctor. She and Torres had an argument in the mess hall.

EPISODE LOGS: Janeway mentions that Captain Kirk claims to have met da Vinci, though it has not been confirmed. This is a reference to the events from the *Star Trek* episode "Requiem for Methuselah."

MORTAL COIL

EPISODE #180
WRITTEN BY: BRYAN FULLER
DIRECTED BY: ALLAN KROEKER

GUEST STARS

ENSIGN WILDMAN — NANCY HOWER

NAOMI WILDMAN — BROOKE STEPHENS

CO-STAR

ALIXIA — ROBIN STAPLER

STARDATE 51449.2

⭐ **D**uring a mission to collect a sample of protomatter from a nearby nebula, Neelix is struck by an energy discharge from the nebula and killed. As Janeway prepares to conduct a Talaxian burial ceremony, Seven of Nine announces that her Borg nanoprobes can be used to revive Neelix. Although skeptical, Janeway allows her to try the procedure, and Neelix is brought back to life.

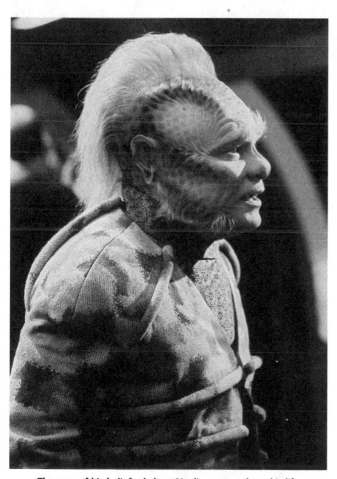

The core of his beliefs shaken, Neelix contemplates his life and death. DANNY FELD

Naturally, Neelix is quite distraught over his experience. As he explains to Chakotay, his people believe in an afterlife that centers around the Great Forest. When a Talaxian dies, his ancestors supposedly meet him by the guiding tree. Neelix has always taken comfort in believing that all of his family would one day be together again, but now he realizes he did not experience anything like that in death.

As the crew gathers for the annual celebration of Prixin, the Talaxian observance of familial allegiance, Neelix visits Ensign Wildman's daughter, Naomi. He goes through their nightly ritual of putting her to bed, but he is troubled by her request to hear his usual story of the Great Forest. Later, Neelix unleashes his frustration on Seven, arguing that his life is no longer worth living now that his deepest beliefs have been shattered. Suddenly, Neelix cries out in pain because his cells are reverting to a necrotic state. Neelix's tissue is rejecting the Borg nanoprobes, but Seven makes the necessary modification to compensate.

Still troubled, Neelix asks Chakotay to help him take a vision quest in the hopes that he can find some sort of internal peace. As the quest begins, Neelix encounters his beloved sister and members of the crew, who all tell him that the afterlife is a lie, and that he has no reason to live. Neelix comes out of the vision determined to end his life.

After recording his goodbyes to the crew, Neelix tries to beam himself into the nebula. Chakotay rushes to stop him, but Neelix protests that the vision quest convinced him he would be better off dead. Chakotay explains that the imagery is not easily interpreted and that it was probably just an expression of his anxiety over his beliefs. Neelix is unconvinced, until Ensign Wildman summons him to help put Naomi to bed. When he realizes that the crew has become his family and that one little girl in particular needs him, Neelix finds his reason to live.

SENSOR READINGS: The away team enters a class-1 nebula to collect a sample of protomatter, one of the best energy sources in the quadrant. Neelix has a cylinder perfect for containing protomatter in storage in Cargo Bay 2. The last time he used it, he nearly lost it to the Kazon. To collect the protomatter Neelix has them set the transporter for 10,000 AMU. The transporter beam ignites the protomatter, which knocks out the shuttle's shields. The sample destabilizes before they return to the ship. A small phase variance is noted in the transporter logs and was probably responsible for igniting the protomatter. There was a problem with the pattern buffer that might have created a feedback loop along the transporter beam. ■ The crew sends a beacon into the nebula to track the shuttle.

Chakotay convinces Neelix to live—if not for himself, then for Naomi. ROBBIE ROBINSON

DELTA QUADRANT: Talaxians believe the Great Forest is the afterlife where loved ones are gathered to watch over the living as they sleep. Talaxians mourn their dead for a full week in a specific burial ceremony. ▪ On the first night of Prixin, someone (in this case, Tuvok) is chosen to commence the celebration with the traditional salutation: "We do not stand alone. We are in the arms of family. Father, mother, sister, brother, father's father, father's mother, father's brother, mother's brother . . ." (suffice to say, the list is extensive) "We gather on this day to extol the warmth and joy of those unshakable bonds. Without them, we could not call ourselves complete. On this day, we are thankful to be together. We do not stand alone."

The Borg know the Kazon as Species 329. They encountered a Kazon colony in the Grand Sector, Grid 6920. Their biological and technological distinctiveness was unremarkable, and they were unworthy of assimilation, as the Borg seek perfection. ▪ The Borg have assimilated species with far greater medical knowledge than the Federation's and are capable of reactivating drones as much as seventy-three hours after death. The Borg assimilated the technique from Species 149. ▪ When a drone is damaged beyond repair, it is discarded, but its memories continue to exist in the collective consciousness, making the drone immortal. Children assimilated by the Borg are placed in maturation chambers for seventeen cycles.

PERSONAL LOGS: Kim is working on his monthly ops report. ▪ Neelix's experience with protomatter comes from his days working as a trader, when it was one of the most sought-after commodities in the sector. Neelix is Naomi Wildman's godfather and the only one who can get her to sleep. His medicine bundle includes a necklace made by his sister Alixia, a flower from Kes's garden, and a statue of the Guiding Tree. ▪ Seven donates seventy micrograms of nanoprobes from her bloodstream to resuscitate Neelix. She has been continuing to intake foods to which Neelix has been adding spices to enhance the taste.

MEDICAL REPORT: Neelix is dead for eighteen hours, forty-nine minutes, and thirteen seconds. Nanoprobes are injected into Neelix to reverse cellular necrosis, while the cerebral cortex is stimulated with a neuro-electric isopulse. Until the damaged tissue can function independently, Neelix has to be injected with nanoprobes daily.

CREW COMPLEMENT: Seven notes that Naomi Wildman is not listed on the crew manifest.

EPISODE LOGS: In addition to being given a name in this episode, Naomi Wildman has grown to the age of four. The Doctor gives a possible reason for this rapid growth when he says: "The early stages of Ktarian development are astounding. Naomi has grown five centimeters since her last physical, and that was only three weeks ago."

MESSAGE IN A BOTTLE

EPISODE #181
TELEPLAY BY: LISA KLINK
STORY BY: RICK WILLIAMS
DIRECTED BY: NANCY MALONE

GUEST STARS

REKAR	JUDSON SCOTT
NEVALA	VALERIE WILDMAN

SPECIAL GUEST STAR

EMH-2	ANDY DICK

CO-STARS

STARFLEET OFFICER	TONY SEARS
HIROGEN	TINY RON
COMPUTER VOICE	MAJEL BARRETT

STARDATE UNKNOWN

After increasing the range of the astrometric sensors Seven of Nine locates an alien relay station, establishes a link, and detects a Starfleet vessel in the Alpha Quadrant. Janeway uses the relay network to send a message to the ship, but the transmission degrades before it gets through. With time running out, their only other option is to send a holographic datastream. The Doctor is recruited and he soon finds himself aboard the *U.S.S. Prometheus,* only to find that the Starfleet crew is dead and the ship is in Romulan hands.

The *Prometheus* is a prototype starship with advanced tactical abilities that the Romulans are eager to test. They access the ship's multivector assault mode, and the vessel splits into three separate ships. Moving into attack formation, they easily destroy a Starfleet vessel, then reintegrate the separated pieces and head for the Neutral Zone. The Doctor activates the *Prometheus*'s Emergency

The Doctor cannot believe the conceit of the EMH Mark-2. DANNY FELD

Medical Hologram (EMH-2), and, after some initial tension, the two agree to work together to stop the Romulans. They plan to use the ventilation system to distribute an anesthetic gas, but the Doctor must first reach environmental control on the bridge. He concocts a story about a virus to gain access to the controls, but the Romulans are suspicious and detain him.

Meanwhile, as Torres tries to form a better working relationship with Seven, *Voyager's* link to the relay network is severed. An alien named Idrin claims that his species, known as the Hirogen, created the sensor network and he refuses to listen to Janeway's request to continue using the link. Seven sends a mild shock to the Hirogen, knocking him unconscious and giving them a bit more time.

In sickbay, Paris begs Kim to help create another holographic Doctor, fearing that the original may not return. A pilot by nature, Paris has no interest in having to be the Doctor's replacement. However, the program is too difficult for Kim to redesign, leaving Paris to hope the EMH gets back safely, for the Doctor's sake as well as his own.

As the Doctor is grilled by the Romulans, gas suddenly pours from the vents, incapacitating them. EMH-2 explains that he simulated a shipwide biohazard, and the computer opened the ventilation system automatically. Now the doctors are faced with flying the ship, which is headed into Romulan space. *Prometheus* is fired upon by enemy warbirds, but the doctors cannot figure out the controls to defend themselves. Then approaching Star-

The Doctor realizes he is going to be deactivated no matter how he answers the Romulan questions. DANNY FELD

library master file has all the classic medical texts from *Gray's Anatomy* to *Leonard McCoy's Comparative Alien Physiology.*

ALPHA QUADRANT: The *U.S.S. Prometheus* NX-59650 is an experimental prototype designed for deep-space tactical assignments. Primary battle systems include regenerative shielding, ablative hull armor, and multivector assault mode. Access to tactical data requires a level-4 clearance. In multivector assault mode the ship goes to blue alert. The ship is designed to move faster than anything in the fleet and flies at warp 9.9 when heading for Romulan space. Only four people in Starfleet are trained to operate the ship, which is in the farthest reaches of the Alpha Quadrant. ▪ According to Starfleet security protocol 28, subsection D, in the event of hostile alien takeover, the EMH is to deactivate and wait for rescue. ▪ There are twenty-seven Romulans onboard the *Prometheus.* They suggest running a complete algorithm extraction on the Doctor to analyze his subroutines one by one and determine if he is hiding information. The EMH-2 distributes neurozine in gaseous form through the ventilation system after simulating a shipwide biohazard that tricks the ventilation system into opening automatically. The Doctor attempts to generate a slight overload to the nacelle coils to collapse the warp field and possibly overloads the core in the process. ▪ The Federation is at war with the Dominion (as seen in *Deep Space Nine);* however, the Romulans have not yet entered the conflict. ▪ The Doctor speaks directly with Starfleet headquarters and informs them of what has happened to the ship. *Voyager* was declared officially lost fourteen months ago.

PERSONAL LOGS: Janeway started writing letters home a year ago. She updates the letters just in case. ▪ Chakotay writes a letter to a cousin in Ohio. ▪ The Doctor claims to be as close to a sentient life-form as any hologram could hope to be, noting that he socializes with the crew, fraternizes with aliens, and has even had sexual relations. When the EMH-2 reminds the Doctor that they were not designed for physical relations, the Doctor says he made an addition to his program. The Doctor has had two lessons in piloting shuttlecraft on the holodeck. ▪ Neelix studies Earth-style cooking so he can have a marketable trait if they get to the Alpha Quadrant. ▪ Seven takes an isolinear processor out of engineering without asking and, according to Torres, locks the door to astrometrics "like it's her own personal lab." She claims that she does not need to regenerate for the next few days. Seven says "thank you" for the first time, following Torres's sugges-

fleet ships fire on them obviously believing that the *Prometheus* is still controlled by the Romulans. EMH-2 accidentally initiates the decoupling sequence, separating the experimental vessel into three armed ships and the Doctors score a direct hit against a Romulan ship, causing the other warbirds to retreat. Starfleet personnel beam aboard, and a short time later, the Doctor is transmitted back to *Voyager,* where he conveys a message. Starfleet Headquarters is now aware of their predicament, and will do everything it can to bring *Voyager* safely home.

SENSOR READINGS: *Voyager* is in the Delta Quadrant at coordinates 18-Mark-205-Mark-47 (60,000 light-years from the Alpha Quadrant). ▪ When the original message degrades as it goes through the relay system, they decide that a holographic datastream would have a better chance of getting through. Since there is no time to reconfigure the message for the datastream, they use the Doctor. Torres sends an initiation code along with the Doctor so he will be activated immediately. ▪ *Voyager's* medical

ALPHA QUADRANT CONTACT: SEASON 4

"Sixty thousand light years seems a little closer today."

Kathryn Janeway, "Message in a Bottle"

A more tangible connection to home has an impact on the *Voyager* crew in season four with the addition of Seven of Nine to the ship's manifest. And while the former Borg drone's growing acceptance of her own humanity provides a thread for many plotlines this season, the crew's search for home will remain the focus of the show. The season, filled with the usual share of Alpha Quadrant reminders, will also include the one thing that crew has been longing for since the beginning—actual contact with home.

The character Seven of Nine is added to the crew in "Scorpion, Part II." Though she may not recall the Alpha Quadrant of Annika Hansen, nor the little girl she once was, Annika comes through in glimpses throughout the season. In the episode "The Raven,"

CRAIG T. MATHEW

for example, Seven's hallucinations give way to flashbacks of her youth and she is drawn to the *Raven*, the ship on which she grew up and where she and her parents were assimilated by the Borg.

Seven of Nine is not the only crew member who must deal with her past. Torres attempts to celebrate the Klingon Day of Honor through a holographic simulation of the traditional events of the day ("Day of Honor"). Klingons are also seen on the holodeck in "The Killing Game," in simulated battles coordinated by Hirogen who have taken over the ship and crew. Another simulation in that episode places the crew on Earth during the time of World War II, leading a resistance movement in Sainte Claire, France. Later, more relaxing pursuits lead Paris to spend much of his personal time restoring a holographic '57 Chevy in "Vis à Vis."

Over the years, I've pitched many jokes—many of which got in the show, some that didn't—but my favorite exchange that I have ever gotten into a show was in "Message in a Bottle." In the scene with Andy Dick's character EMH Mach-2 . . . and my scripted line was "Stop breathing down my neck." I remember calling Brannon and suggesting the following two rejoinders: EMH Mach-2 says, "My breathing is merely a simulation." To which the Doctor replies, "So is my neck. Stop it anyway." I thought it was a good example of a Niles/Frasier, one-upsmanship. [Frasier]

—Robert Picardo

At long last, contact with the Alpha Quadrant is achieved in "Message in a Bottle," when the discovery of a series of Hirogen relay stations allows the crew to send the Doctor back to the *U.S.S. Prometheus.* After doing battle against the Romulans, with the help of the EMH Mach-2, the Doctor speaks to Starfleet Headquarters and alerts them to the crew's plight. He returns to *Voyager* with the message that they are no longer alone. Starfleet later uses the same relay stations to convey more messages to *Voyager* in "Hunters." Though the communication will later help an alien trap the crew in "Hope and Fear," the bulk of the message contains something the crew needed to boost morale—more than anything else—letters from home.

tion (she has said "you're welcome" on two previous occasions indicating that she was familiar with at least part of the custom).

EPISODE LOGS: Torres begins wearing a new engineer's tool jacket to hide actress Roxann Dawson's pregnancy. ▪ The Hirogen are briefly introduced in the episode and will become a recurring threat in the future. ▪ This episode marks the beginning of several episodes over the next three seasons in which *Voyager* will be in contact with Starfleet.

WAKING MOMENTS

EPISODE #182
WRITTEN BY: ANDRE BORMANIS
DIRECTED BY: ALEXANDER SINGER

GUEST STAR

DREAM ALIEN   MARK COLSON

CO-STARS

ENSIGN   JENNIFER GUNDY
COMPUTER VOICE   MAJEL BARRETT

STARDATE 51471.3

After a fitful night's sleep, the crew realizes they all had nightmares involving the same alien. Knowing that is too much of a coincidence, they become concerned when several crew members cannot be awakened. Hoping to find out more about the alien, Chakotay attempts a technique called lucid dreaming, which will allow him to control the events of his dream. If he needs to awaken, he can tap his hand three times and bring himself out of the dream.

After falling asleep, Chakotay encounters the alien and demands to know what is happening to the crew. The alien explains that for his species, the dream state is their reality. For centuries "waking species" have been attacking them and this is their best form of defense. He tells Chakotay that if *Voyager* leaves their space, the crew will awaken. Chakotay comes out of the dream and orders a course for the alien border. But once they are there, a ship manned by the dream aliens begins firing at *Voyager.*

The aliens beam aboard, taking the ship. As the crew looks for ways to regain control, Chakotay sees an image of Earth's moon, a visual cue that lets him know he is still

Chakotay tries to reason with the dream alien. RANDY TEPPER

dreaming. After tapping his hand, Chakotay wakes up in sickbay, this time for real. The Doctor informs him that the entire crew is now asleep, and their brain patterns show they are all experiencing the same dream. The aliens have the advantage in dreams, but if Chakotay can locate the sleeping aliens while he is awake, he will have the upper hand. In the dream, Janeway and the others are being held hostage but they begin to suspect that they are dreaming. When the captain is unharmed by a warp core explosion, they know it is true.

The closer Chakotay gets to the sleeping aliens, the harder it is for him to stay awake. At last he finds them sleeping in a cavern, clustered around a large transmitter that is responsible for maintaining the crew's dream state. Chakotay tells the Doctor to deploy a torpedo targeted at the cavern if he is out of contact for more than five minutes. He then uses a stimulant the Doctor gave him to wake one of the aliens and commands him to deactivate the device. Before the alien can react, Chakotay falls asleep, reentering the crew's communal dream. There he threatens the alien leader with his race's total destruction, forcing him to neutralize the transmitter. The crew awakens, freed from alien control, but suffering acute cases of insomnia.

SENSOR READINGS: *Voyager* passed an area of space with three full moons the day before. ▪ The ship can travel a parsec in about one day's time.

When diplomacy fails, Chakotay prepares a more active response. RANDY TEPPER

DELTA QUADRANT: The aliens have corporeal form but they speak telepathically and they consider their dream world to be their waking world. Astrometric scans show no ships or planets in the vicinity or planets capable of sustaining life. Later, Chakotay is able to find the planet, by scanning for a neurogenic field. The aliens do not resemble any species assimilated by the Borg.

ALPHA QUADRANT: The Australian aborigines believed the dream world was no more or less real than the waking world, and their creation mythology says their ancestors actually dreamed the universe into existence.

PERSONAL LOGS: Janeway's nightmare is of her crew growing old and dying before they reach home. ▪ Chakotay dreams of hunting deer with his father, something he always had refused to do. On previous occasions he has been able to induce a lucid dream state using the same technology he uses for the vision quest. ▪ Tuvok's nightmare involves him reporting for duty naked. He uses security clearance Tuvok Zeta-9 to override the door lock on Kim's quarters. ▪ Paris imagines almost dying in a shuttle explosion. His dream makes him late for a breakfast date with Torres, which ultimately is canceled because he has to report for duty at 0800. Their dates usually seem to involve skiing on the holodeck. ▪ Kim's nightmare is about being sexually accosted by Seven of Nine, then being interrupted by the alien. His quarters are now on Deck 6, Room 105-2 (they were previously on Deck 3). ▪ Neelix dreams of being boiled alive in a pot of perfectly seasoned *leola* root stew.

MEDICAL REPORT: The entire crew is in a hyper-REM state. The Doctor uses the stimulant animazine to try to keep the crew awake.

HUNTERS

EPISODE #183

WRITTEN BY: **JERI TAYLOR**

DIRECTED BY: **DAVID LIVINGSTON**

CO·STARS

ALPHA-HIROGEN   **TINY RON**

BETA-HIROGEN   **ROGER MORRISSEY**

STARDATE 51501.4

When Starfleet Command sends a transmission from the Alpha Quadrant, the bulk of the message gets lodged in one of the Hirogen relay stations. Janeway immediately sets course for the station hoping to clear up the problem while a pair of Hirogen prepare to intercept *Voyager*. Along the way, the crew finds a ship with a dead alien aboard adrift in space. They beam the body to sickbay and discover that it has been gutted, in a manner Seven recalls having come across once before while she was among the Borg. As they near the relay station, sensors pick up increasing gravimetric

Tuvok is held prisoner by the imposing Hirogen. ROBBIE ROBINSON

forces. Apparently, the Hirogen station is using a quantum singularity—a black hole—as its power source.

Downloading more of the Starfleet transmission, Janeway realizes it contains letters from home, bringing both good news and bad. Tuvok finds that he has become a grandfather, but Chakotay learns that all of Maquis back home have been either killed or imprisoned as a result of the Federation war with the Dominion. When the transmission begins degrading, Tuvok and Seven of Nine try to stabilize the signal by taking a shuttle closer to the relay station. But after they carry out their assignment, they are captured by the Hirogen and taken to the alien ship.

Back on *Voyager*, Janeway struggles to accept the news that her fiancé, Mark, has married another woman. Suddenly, Kim receives an automated distress signal from the shuttle, and sensors reveal that no one is on board. Kim locates the Hirogen ship on *Voyager*'s sensors. Janeway refuses to heed the Hirogen leader's warning to disconnect her link to the module and leave without Tuvok and Seven. Although more Hirogen ships are on the way, the crew prepares for battle.

Janeway realizes if they boost the effect of the singularity, they can increase its gravitational pull and trap the Hirogen ships, but when the aliens fire on *Voyager*, the containment field around the station destabilizes. Once the singularity is exposed, everything around it is sucked into the black hole. Kim manages to beam Tuvok and Seven safely aboard just before Janeway orders a dangerous maneuver to free *Voyager* from the grip of the singularity. Unfortunately, the entire network of relay stations is disabled, leaving the crew once again without a link to home.

SENSOR READINGS: The Starfleet datastream degrades during transmission, requiring Seven of Nine to decompress the message and rearrange it in the proper sequence. ▪ A shuttle can withstand the gravimetric eddies better than *Voyager*. ▪ A level-8 antithoron burst is used to destroy the singularity's containment field. The energy released from the singularity creates a massive discharge along the relay network that disables every one of the stations. ▪ Janeway orders the antimatter injectors opened to one hundred twenty percent, which could breach the core, although it does not.

SHUTTLE TRACKER: Oddly, the Hirogen do not take Tuvok and Seven's shuttle as a prize of the hunt and it is retrieved by *Voyager*.

DAMAGE REPORT: Structural integrity begins to fail and the hull starts to buckle. ▪ The shuttle is scanned by a

Seven refuses to cower before her captors. ROBBIE ROBINSON

subnucleonic beam that disrupts navigational sensors. *Voyager* would need to send out a directional beacon to guide them back. They also lose communications, warp engines, and weapons.

DELTA QUADRANT: The Hirogen collect trophies from their prey. When *Voyager* beams aboard the body of a deceased alien, they find it has suffered a complete osteotomy. A surgical procedure was used to remove the entire skeleton, as well as the musculature, the ligaments and tendons, and the internal organs. Seven of Nine has seen this before when the Borg encountered a small ship of Species 5174. ▪ The Hirogen ship has monotanium armor plating that scatters *Voyager*'s transporter targeting beam. They are also heavily armed. ▪ Either the Hirogen bodies are very resilient or the physiology very different from most humanoids, as the Alpha-Hirogen whose throat Tuvok slashes survives. ▪ Their unit of measurement is ketrics.

Radiometric decay ratios indicate the relay station is at least one hundred thousand years old. It emits a gravimetric field that reaches two light-years away. Sensors detect the relay station is using a contained small quantum singularity (black hole) as a power source. Although it is only about a centimeter in diameter it puts out almost four terrawatts of energy. The relay station emits as much energy in one minute as most stars do in one year.

ALPHA QUADRANT: Sending two people on an away mission is recommended Starfleet protocol.

PERSONAL LOGS: Janeway receives a letter from Mark, informing her that her dog did give birth and he found homes for all the puppies. He eventually moved on and, four months ago, married a woman with whom he works. Janeway's love of coffee is mentioned, but she does not like sugar added. ▪ Chakotay receives a letter from Sveta, the woman who brought him into the Maquis. He learns that the Maquis have been destroyed by a new ally of the Cardassians known as the Dominion (following events from the *Deep Space Nine* episode "Blaze of Glory"). Of the thousands of Maquis, only a handful survived and have been imprisoned. Chakotay takes two sugars in his coffee. ▪ Tuvok works on his weekly tactical review. He receives a letter from his wife and learns that his first son, Sek, has gone through the *Pon farr* and mated, and now has a baby girl named after Tuvok's mother, T'Meni. Tuvok claims he has lied only when under the direct orders of a superior officer. ▪ Paris does receive a letter from his father, Admiral Owen Paris, though it is irretrievable. ▪ Torres does not receive a letter, but was not expecting one. ▪ Kim gets a letter from his parents. ▪ Neelix is made official mail courier. ▪ Seven did not report for her weekly checkup. The Doctor notes there are reduced levels of erythrocytes in her blood and that she must regenerate in her alcove for at least three hours a day. As a Borg, Seven had gone as long as two hundred hours without regenerating.

EPISODE LOGS: It was established in "Message in a Bottle" that the Hirogen sensor relay network stretches across the quadrant. ▪ Mark's last name is "Johnson," as listed on the padd containing his letter. ▪ There is a latent datastream buried under the transmission that is heavily encrypted. The events of the episode "Hope and Fear" will center around a false version of this message. ▪ The Romulans, like the Hirogen, use an artificial quantum singularity as a power source for the warp-drive power system on their warbirds ("Face of the Enemy" *TNG*).

PREY

EPISODE #184

WRITTEN BY: BRANNON BRAGA
DIRECTED BY: ALLAN EASTMAN

GUEST STAR

HIROGEN HUNTER   CLINT CARMICHAEL

SPECIAL GUEST STAR

ALPHA-HIROGEN   TONY TODD

STARDATE 51652.3

When a Hirogen ship with one erratic lifesign is found adrift, Janeway sends an away team to investigate. They bring back a wounded Hirogen to sickbay and use the opportunity to learn more about this species and determine who is hunting the hunters.

Insisting he be returned to his ship, the Hirogen explains that he had just captured an alien that broke free and attacked him. He is anxious to continue the hunt, but Janeway informs him that will not happen while he is recuperating on her ship. When Tuvok and Kim investi-

After Species 8472 initiates telepathic contact, Tuvok explains its situation. DANNY FELD

gate structural damage to *Voyager*'s hull, they find an intruder has entered the ship. A blood sample found at the scene indicates it is a member of Species 8472. The crew goes on alert, but an engineering team is attacked before they can fully lock down the area.

The Hirogen informs Janeway that if he is not allowed to continue hunting the alien, he will allow the approaching Hirogen ships to destroy *Voyager*. Realizing they need his help, Janeway releases the Hirogen from sickbay. Knowing from their previous encounter that Species 8742 is susceptible to Borg nanoprobes, Tuvok and Seven arm phaser rifles with the microscopic weapons and track the alien. They soon corner the wounded intruder, planning to stun it. When the Hirogen begins firing his weapon against orders, Tuvok turns his phaser on him.

Paris and Seven discover that Species 8472 boarded *Voyager* as part of an attempt to open a singularity into fluidic space. Through telepathic contact with Tuvok, the alien explains that its ship was damaged during a conflict with the Borg. It has been trapped alone, wounded and hunted by the Hirogen, and just wants to get home. Although the Hirogen threatens that the crew will be slaughtered if the alien isn't surrendered to him, Janeway asks Seven to open a singularity. Citing the Borg history with Species 8472 and the danger it represents, Seven refuses to help the alien escape and is confined to the cargo bay until the mission is over.

As the approaching ships fire on *Voyager,* force fields go offline and the Hirogen escapes from sickbay. When Species 8472 becomes agitated, Janeway orders Seven to give it more Borg nanoprobes. As she complies, the Hirogen approaches and tells Seven to step aside, allowing him to continue to hunt his prey. Just then, the alien breaks through the force field. As it struggles with the Hirogen, Seven taps into transporter controls and beams them to one of the Hirogen ships. The Hirogen immediately cease firing and leave the area at warp speed. As a consequence of her actions against the captain's commands, Seven's duties on *Voyager* are restricted.

SENSOR READINGS: Torres erects a level-10 force field around engineering and sets up secondary forcefields around every hatch, Jefferies tube, and conduit leading into the room. She orders all the consoles secured to accept authorized command codes only. She begins to lock down the warp core by having an ensign realign the dilithium matrix to a frequency of 3.96, but is interrupted by the alien's attack. Species 8742 accesses engineering through the antimatter injector port and escapes through Jefferies tube 17-Alpha. Tuvok holds the alien

Seven is faced with the challenge of helping an enemy of the Borg. DANNY FELD

down on Deck 11, Section 94. Deflector control is on Deck 11, Section 59. Species 8472 accesses environmental controls and shuts off life support, including artificial gravity, on Deck 11. The security detail sets up headquarters on Deck 10, Section 12. ▪ Since regular phaser fire is ineffective against Species 8472, Seven modifies phaser rifles with Borg nanoprobes to incapacitate the alien. ▪ Ship's weapons have little effect on Hirogen hull plating. The crew diverts warp power to the phaser banks to try to penetrate Hirogen hull armor. ▪ Seven accesses transporter controls from a hallway on Deck 11.

DAMAGE REPORT: A hull rupture on Deck 11, Section 3, appears to sensors as a plasma conduit overload, but it is really where Species 8472 entered the ship. The bulkhead collapses in Jefferies tube 84. A direct hit to the EPS manifold knocks out main power and takes force fields on all decks offline until auxiliary power goes up a moment later. *Voyager* is crippled by direct hits to both nacelles.

DELTA QUADRANT: Hirogen ships have monotanium hull plating and dicyclic warp signature. On the incapac-

itated Hirogen ship, the away team finds bones and muscle tissue from at least nine different species being broken down by some sort of enzyme as their method of either denaturating their prey or preparing it for dinner. The Hirogen ship has visited over ninety star systems in the last year alone. The entire culture seems to be based on the hunt, including their social rituals, art, and religious beliefs. There is no evidence of a home planet. Their ships travel alone or in small groups, sometimes joining forces for a multipronged attack. ▪ The Hirogen's immune system neutralizes every sedative the Doctor has. ▪ Their body armor is designed to handle rapid pressure fluctuations.

Species 8472's blood contains a dense mixture of DNA and polyfluidic compounds. ▪ Each time Species 8472 boarded a Borg vessel, they went directly to the central power matrix and disabled it (though it does not do this to *Voyager*). When cornered, it tries to barricade itself. ▪ Species 8472 emits a bio-electric field, making it impossible for the Doctor to scan.

PERSONAL LOGS: When Janeway was a lieutenant, she was involved in a conflict at the Cardassian border. After intense fighting, her captain ordered her to rescue a wounded Cardassian, even though they were enemies. Three days later they secured the outpost and were decorated by Starfleet Command. ▪ Paris claims that he once tracked a mouse through Jefferies tube 32. ▪ The Doctor suggests himself as Seven's "personality mentor." He and Kes created exercises three years ago to familiarize himself with social graces. ▪ Neelix is added to the security detail. ▪ Seven of Nine refuses the captain's order to open a singularity and allow the alien to escape. After she beams the alien to the Hirogen ship, Janeway restricts her access to any primary systems on this ship, without her direct authorization. Janeway admits to needing her help in astrometrics, if she is willing. Otherwise, she is to stay in the cargo bay.

MEDICAL REPORT: Four crew members, including Torres, are injured.

CREW COMPLEMENT: Prior to the events of this episode—on Stardate 51563—Ensign Lyndsay Ballard dies while on an away mission when caught in a trap laid by the Hirogen. Her body is later retrieved and "reanimated" by an alien race known as the Kobali. Her story will unfold in the episode "Ashes to Ashes."

RETROSPECT

EPISODE #185
TELEPLAY BY: BRYAN FULLER & LISA KLINK
STORY BY: ANDREW SHEPARD PRICE & MARK GABERMAN
DIRECTED BY: JESÚS SALVADOR TREVIÑO

GUEST STARS

KOVIN	MICHAEL HORTON
ENTHARAN MAGISTRATE	ADRIAN SPARKS

CO-STAR

SCHARN	MICHELLE AGNEW

STARDATE 51679.4

Janeway acquires a new weapons system from an Entharan trader named Kovin and asks Seven of Nine to help with its integration into ship systems. When Kovin criticizes her work and pushes her aside to do it himself, the former Borg hits him. After Seven exhibits newfound anxiety in sickbay, the Doctor believes it is caused by blocked memories trying to surface. In an effort to expand his program, the Doctor has added a psychiatric subroutine, and he leads Seven through hypnotic regression therapy. During their session, Seven recalls that Kovin performed a medical procedure on her and extracted Borg nanoprobes.

Seven remembers that the procedure took place while she and Kovin were testing weapons on the planet. They entered his laboratory, where he fired a thoron beam at her and later activated the assimilation tubules in her arm to extract nanoprobes. Another Entharan was lying on the next table, and he was successfully assimilated with the nanoprobes. Janeway questions Kovin, who denies everything and claims the thoron weapon fired accidentally. Faced with contradicting stories, Janeway proceeds with an investigation.

Kovin pleads with Tuvok to drop the charges against him. Since his people depend on trade, just an accusation of violating their protocols concerning diplomatic relations is a serious offense. Kovin knows he will be ruined. With the Entharan magistrate's help, the Doctor inspects Kovin's lab and finds a sample of Borg nanoprobes on a table. Informed that this is sufficient evidence to detain him, Kovin immediately transports to his ship and escapes.

In pursuit of Kovin, Janeway and Tuvok continue to inspect his confiscated items. When they simulate a

Swayed by the Doctor's theory, Seven falls prey to false memories. ROBBIE ROBINSON

Janeway pleads with Kovin to stop. ROBBIE ROBINSON

thoron blast to Seven's arm and study a tissue sample, they find that her nanoprobes regenerate just as they did in Kovin's lab in what appears to be a spontaneous response to the thoron blast. They realize that Seven's repressed memories are most likely images from her experiences as a Borg that she confused with her recent interaction with Kovin.

When Janeway hails Kovin to explain the mistake in accusing him, he thinks it is a trap. He begins firing at *Voyager*, but Janeway refuses to return fire and tries to beam him aboard instead. As Kovin overloads power on his ship, it destabilizes and explodes, killing him. For the first time, Seven experiences remorse—as does the Doctor. Believing that his overzealous enthusiasm for expanding his program resulted in the tragedy, he asks the captain to grant him permission to delete everything except his original activation program, but his request is denied.

SENSOR READINGS: Janeway makes a deal for an isokinetic cannon that can penetrate the shields of heavily armed vessels like the Hirogen ships that are covered in monotanium. In trade, she offers astrometric charts spanning twelve sectors and one hundred thirty isolinear pro-cessing chips. The installation of the cannon is interrupted when Seven attacks Kovin. It is unclear whether the deal is finalized due to the incident with Kovin; however, the weapon is not seen again in the series. ▪ A medical tricorder is made of durantanium casing with an alphanumeric display. Its dimensions are 7.6 centimeters by 9.8 centimeters by 3.2 centimeters.

DAMAGE REPORT: A photonic pulse from Kovin's ship takes *Voyager*'s sensors offline. The entire sensor array needs to be reinitialized before it is functional again.

DELTA QUADRANT: Entharans depend on trade with alien species. There are strict protocols about those relationships. Even being accused of violating them is a serious offense. ▪ One Entharan handheld weapon is a terrawatt-powered particle beam rifle with a four microsecond recharge cycle and a ten kilometer range. While not as accurate as Starfleet compression rifles it is easier to handle, although the targeting mechanism can be augmented with a thermal guidance sensor to increase accuracy. The weapon is thoron based, which can be unstable unless the emitter matrix is polarized to compensate for instability.

ALPHA QUADRANT: According to the Doctor, Amanin of Betazed would argue that a combination of sensory isolation and focused breathing techniques would be effective at opening up repressed memories.

PERSONAL LOGS: Janeway gives Seven complete access to engineering, because the former drone has been "behaving herself" lately (this is in reference to the restrictions placed on Seven in "Prey"). The Doctor has started helping her improve her social skills ("Prey"). At the Doctor's prompting, Seven allows herself to feel anger for the first time, and later, remorse. The energy discharge from a thoron weapon can cause Seven's nanoprobes to regenerate even after they have left her body.

MEDICAL REPORT: The Doctor detects a high concentration of biogenic amines in Seven's hippocampus blocking several portions of her memory center.

EPISODE LOGS: The events in this episode take place several weeks after the crew received an encoded message from Starfleet ("Hunters"). ▪ Neelix does not appear in this episode.

THE KILLING GAME, PART I

EPISODE #186
WRITTEN BY: BRANNON BRAGA & JOE MENOSKY
DIRECTED BY: DAVID LIVINGSTON

GUEST STARS

ALPHA-HIROGEN	DANNY GOLDRING
HIROGEN SS OFFICER	MARK DEAKINS
HIROGEN MEDIC	MARK METCALF
NAZI KAPITAN	J. PAUL BOEHMER
YOUNG HIROGEN	PAUL S. ECKSTEIN

STARDATE UNKNOWN

The Hirogen have taken over *Voyager* and implanted devices in the crew to make them believe they are characters within several holodeck war games. Interacting in a World War II simulation, Janeway is called Katrine and is leader of a resistance movement gathering information on the Nazis to help the Allies. Katrine runs a nightclub in a small province of France, with Seven of Nine—Mademoiselle de Neuf—as her munitions expert/torch singer. Rounding out Katrine's team are Neelix the baker, Torres/Brigitte, and Tuvok the

bartender, who suspects Seven may be a Nazi infiltrator.

When Allied command sends a coded message that they will soon be invading Sainte Claire, they ask Janeway's resistance group to disable the Germans' communication system. Meanwhile, two of the Hirogen soldiers are getting restless and want to proceed with the hunt, although their leader believes the simulations will help them learn more about their prey. After Seven and Neelix are wounded in the holodeck, they are brought to sickbay for "repair and reassignment."

The Doctor objects to being forced to repeatedly tend to the crew's injuries and then send them back to the simulations. He and Kim, who has been kept on the bridge working to expand the holodecks, secretly team up to find a way to disable the crew's neural interfaces so they will remember who they are. The Alpha-Hirogen reveals to one of his officers that he plans to use *Voyager*'s holodecks to create an endless supply of prey as a means of saving their dwindling race.

While Seven is in sickbay, the Doctor uses one of her Borg implants to create a jamming signal. Her mind free from their control, she admits that she does not remember anything after the Hirogen invaded *Voyager*. The Doctor explains the situation, then sends her back into the World War II simulation with instructions to find a control panel to access the bridge relay so he and Kim can deactivate the rest of the crew's neural interfaces.

After Seven accesses the holodeck controls, the Doctor disables Janeway's implant just before her character tries to shoot Seven. The two women escape from Nazi headquarters as American soldiers, including Chakotay as Captain Miller and Paris as Lieutenant Bobby Davis, arrive and begin firing. When a simulated explosion blows out some of the hologrid, the soldiers see into *Voyager*'s decks and mistake them for a Nazi compound. As American and Nazi soldiers swarm into the ship, the Hirogen have a real war on their hands.

SENSOR READINGS: By cutting through the bulkheads on Decks 4, 5, and 6, Kim expands both holodeck grids by 5,000 square meters, but he cannot give any more space without compromising *Voyager*'s primary systems. Kim claims that holodecks require a tremendous amount of energy and he has already rerouted power from all nonessential systems. Anything more and they will start losing propulsion, deflectors, and even life support. The Hirogen transfers power nodules from his ship's system and orders Harry to replicate emitters to expand the programming. ▪ Kim transfers the Doctor to a hallway using the new emitters.

In the Hirogen simulation, Neelix is stopped while carrying secret information. ROBBIE ROBINSON

DAMAGE REPORT: During the original attack, the Hirogen breached *Voyager*'s hull and entered the ship through that breach. They have damaged just about every system on the ship. ▪ With the holodeck safeties off, a simulated explosion in Holodeck 1 blows out the holo-grid across three decks. The breach opens the simulation into surrounding sections and leaves program controls offline.

MEDICAL REPORT: Janeway is stabbed during a Klingon battle, then patched up and sent to the World War II holoprogram. ▪ Neelix is shot and has bullet fragments lodged in his shoulder. ▪ Seven is also shot and suffers fractured vertebrae and a punctured lung. The Doctor says that she was a mess after the Crusades.

CREW COMPLEMENT: The Doctor claims that he treated twenty-eight wounded and had one fatality in the past twelve hours.

EPISODE LOGS: Both episodes of "The Killing Game" two-parter originally aired on UPN on the same night, thus paving the way for *Voyager* two-hour movie events in later seasons. ▪ The Hirogen have been on *Voyager* for

Unaware of who she is, Janeway accepts the role of nightclub owner/Resistance movement leader. DANNY FELD

nineteen days, according to the episode. ▪ In the shooting script, Janeway goes by the name Genevieve in her role in the World War II simulation. It was later changed to Katrine. ▪ The town of Sainte Claire was filmed at the Universal Studios backlot, which would later be used for the holodeck town Fair Haven. ▪ For these episodes Roxann Dawson did not have to hide her pregnancy. Instead, her holocharacter was written as being pregnant.

THE KILLING GAME, PART II

EPISODE #187
WRITTEN BY: BRANNON BRAGA & JOE MENOSKY
DIRECTED BY: VICTOR LOBL

GUEST STARS

ALPHA-HIROGEN	DANNY GOLDRING
HIROGEN SS OFFICER	MARK DEAKINS
HIROGEN MEDIC	MARK METCALF
NAZI KAPITAN	J. PAUL BOEHMER
YOUNG HIROGEN	PAUL S. ECKSTEIN

CO-STARS

KLINGON	PETER HENDRIXSON
COMPUTER VOICE	MAJEL BARRETT

STARDATE 51715.2

As World War II is waged throughout the ship, the Alpha-Hirogen is unwilling to destroy the holodeck technology or the *Voyager* crew. He insists that Janeway be found and brought to him, as he intends to make a deal with her. Meanwhile, she and Seven of Nine continue to pretend to be part of the simulation and gather with the rest of the French Resistance—Tuvok, Torres, and two American soldiers, Chakotay and Paris. They concoct a plan that will allow Janeway access to the neural interfaces in the ship, which the rest of the crew still thinks is an advanced munitions laboratory.

After she and Chakotay access a Klingon simulation in Holodeck 2, Janeway summons the Doctor to the Klingon battleground. The neural interfaces are controlled from sickbay, so the captain plans to set charges that will blow out the console. Since the holodeck safeties are offline, the holographic charges will work. Leaving the Doctor behind with a now-Klingon Neelix, she and

Torres and Tuvok, as members of French Resistance, defend their town. ROBBIE ROBINSON

Chakotay go to set the explosive. Janeway overtakes the Hirogen medic and accesses the interfaces before a Hirogen suddenly breaks in. As she escapes, sickbay explodes, deactivating the crew's devices.

Janeway is brought to the Alpha-Hirogen who explains his desire for the holographic technology. If his species can hunt holographic prey, they will not be scattered across the quadrant and can work on rebuilding their culture. Janeway offers to give him the technology to build his own holodecks if he agrees to evacuate his troops and restore *Voyager*. The Alpha-Hirogen orders his hunters to call a cease-fire in the simulation, but one of the holographic Nazi soldiers talks a bloodthirsty Hirogen into ignoring his superior.

As the battle rages on, Neelix and the Doctor recruit Klingons from their holodeck to help in the fighting. Meanwhile, Janeway works with Kim to overload the holoemitter network, which will shut down the simulations. Suddenly, the Hirogen officer storms in and kills his leader. Instead of shooting Janeway right there, he tells her to run so he can enjoy the hunt.

With German troops surrounding them, Seven works to modify an explosive device, which will give off a photonic burst disrupting holographic activity in a

Chakotay, as a member of the United States army, infiltrates the town. PETER IOVINO

small area. She is shot before she can throw the grenade, deleting the crew's weapons and allies from the simulations. Just as the Nazis overtake the simulated battle, the Klingons attack. Waging her own war against the Hirogen chasing her, Janeway comes across an area without functioning holoemitters. She lures the Hirogen into the area, and his holographic gun disappears. Janeway then becomes the hunter, she is forced to kill him as the holoemitters overload and the simulation ends. A truce is negotiated with the remaining Hirogen, and they leave with Federation hologenerator.

SENSOR READINGS: Internal sensors indicate there are eighty-five Hirogen onboard. ▪ Over eight hundred emitters have been placed on Decks 5 through 12, turning *Voyager* into one big holodeck. A power surge across the holoemitter network blows the system.

DAMAGE REPORT: The visual link is the last of the active circuits connecting the bridge to the holodecks. ▪ Sickbay

is damaged by the explosion set by Janeway and Chakotay (as Captain Miller). ▪ According to the captain, the damage to *Voyager* is extreme.

MEDICAL REPORT: Janeway is shot in the leg. ▪ Seven is shot in the stomach.

CREW COMPLEMENT: The Doctor claims that an unnamed crewman will die without treatment. Since the Doctor is deactivated moments later, it can be assumed the crewman dies. Janeway claims that both sides of the conflict have suffered heavy casualties, but does not further specify.

EPISODE LOGS: The optronic datacore given to the Hirogen will figure prominently in the seventh season episodes "Flesh and Blood, Parts I & II," in which the holographic prey created by the Hirogen revolt.

VIS À VIS

WRITTEN BY: **ROBERT J. DOHERTY**

DIRECTED BY: **JESÚS SALVADOR TREVIÑO**

GUEST STARS

STETH	**DAN BUTLER**
DAELEN	**MARY ELIZABETH McGLYNN**

CO-STAR

COMPUTER VOICE	**MAJEL BARRETT**

STARDATE 51762.4

An alien vessel in need of rescue suddenly appears on *Voyager*'s sensors. The pilot is attempting to use an experimental propulsion system powered by a coaxial warp drive, but the technology is causing the ship to destabilize. The crew manages to secure the system and transport its pilot, Steth, aboard *Voyager* while securing the ship in tow. Paris, who has been restless and irritable lately, volunteers to help Steth repair his ship, citing the need for a change. While the two work, Paris is unaware of the fact that Steth's body occasionally changes into that of a female alien.

Paris uses his knowledge of twentieth-century cars to repair the ship. While, unbeknownst to him, Steth breaks into *Voyager*'s computer and downloads information. Once Steth's ship is operational again, he overpowers Paris and switches bodies with him. Steth sends Paris away on his ship, and he stays on *Voyager* to live out Paris's life.

At first, Steth slides right into Paris's daily routine keeping the crew unaware of the exchange. He uses flattery with the Doctor to get out of sickbay duty, and he charms his way back into Torres's good graces to smooth over a recent fight she had with Paris. Meanwhile, Paris wakes up on Steth's ship to find that a group of aliens known as Benthans has tracked down Steth and are taking him into custody for the theft of their ship. The Benthan ships are run off by an angry woman, Daelen, who beams aboard Paris's vessel claiming she is Steth, and she wants her body back.

The captain grants permission for Paris to help Steth. ROBBIE ROBINSON

234 *STAR TREK: VOYAGER* COMPANION

Paris's/Steth's romantic gestures catch Torres off guard.
ROBBIE ROBINSON

On *Voyager*, Paris/Steth begins to lose control and exhibit erratic behavior. He argues with Torres and Seven, and he becomes intoxicated while on duty. When Janeway expresses her concern, the alien attacks her and is taken to sickbay after Tuvok stuns him with a phaser.

Daelen/Steth explains to Paris that the alien has perfected selective DNA exchange. It put Steth into its body, and Paris into Steth's. They finally activate the coaxial warp drive and manage to catch up with *Voyager*, but when they tell Janeway what has happened, they realize the alien has switched bodies again. Janeway's essence is lying in sickbay in Paris's body, while Steth is in her body and has left *Voyager* in a shuttle outfitted with the advanced propulsion system. Paris races after the shuttle and applies the principles he used in repairing the warp drive to disable it. With the alien in custody, everyone is returned to the proper body, and Paris has gained a new appreciation for the monotony of his life.

SENSOR READINGS: According to Kim, it is difficult to replicate the polyduranide used in golf clubs. ▪ *Voyager* stops at the fourth planet in the Kendren system to gather food supplies.

SHUTTLE TRACKER: Escaping *Voyager*, Steth steals a type-9 shuttle, but it is recovered.

DELTA QUADRANT: Benthos IV is a planet in the Benthan system. The ship stolen by the alien is powered by a coaxial warp drive. Paris recognizes it as the hypo-

thetical propulsion system that Starfleet engineers have been dreaming about for years. It can literally fold the fabric of space, allowing a ship to travel instantaneously across huge distances by drawing in subatomic particles, and reconfiguring their internal geometries. In theory, a coaxial drive explosion could collapse space within a radius of a billion kilometers. Paris suggests using a symmetric warp field to contain the instabilities in the ship's space-folding core. To do this the crew tractors the ship in, killing its momentum, and then generates a warp field around the ship. To fix the coaxial drive Paris suggests a version of a twentieth-century carburetor that would dilute the particle stream. A chromo-electric pulse is fired to disrupt the engines.

PERSONAL LOGS: Paris's sickbay training is purely voluntary, but he has been missing shifts. He has a "lucky toolbox." When Paris was sixteen, he took his dad's shuttle for a joyride and fried all the relays. He believes the shuttle is probably still on the bottom of Lake Tahoe. Paris and Kim golf on the holodeck with Ensign Kaplan. ▪ Seven of Nine possesses an eidetic memory and requires only seconds to commit what she sees to her memory.

THE OMEGA DIRECTIVE

EPISODE #189
TELEPLAY BY: LISA KLINK
STORY BY: JIMMY DIGGS & STEVE J. KAY
DIRECTED BY: VICTOR LOBL

GUEST STAR	
ALLOS	**JEFF AUSTIN**

CO-STARS	
ALIEN CAPTAIN	**KEVIN McCORKLE**
COMPUTER VOICE	**MAJEL BARRETT**

STARDATE 51781.2

When a strange reading appears on *Voyager*'s scans, Janeway begins giving orders without explanation, carrying out a highly classified mission called the Omega Directive. Even though she is thousands of light-years from Starfleet, the captain is forbidden to inform anyone on her crew of the truth behind the Omega Directive. Seven of Nine is the only other person the captain can take into her confidence, since the Borg

Seven easily masters *kal-toh*. ROBBIE ROBINSON

chamber, which should stabilize the Omega molecule, while Janeway leads a rescue mission to the moon where researchers were working to create the molecule when an explosion destroyed the base. Before being beamed to sickbay, the senior researcher tells Janeway the Omega molecules survived in the primary test chamber. When Seven questions him later, he pleads with her not to destroy Omega, saying that the discovery of this phenomenon is the lifeblood of his people.

Once she breaks into the test chamber, Janeway finds enough Omega to wipe out half of the Delta Quadrant. To destroy it with Seven's harmonic resonance technology, the molecules must be transported to *Voyager*. Yearning to understand Omega's perfection, Seven no longer believes it should be destroyed. After the molecules are safely beamed into containment, the crew takes off with several ships in pursuit.

Janeway prepares to jettison the chamber containing the molecules into space and destroy it with a torpedo. Seven manages to neutralize almost half of the molecules, and just before the chamber launches, she witnesses them stabilize spontaneously. Once the torpedo is fired, *Voyager* escapes at maximum warp, leaving behind no trace of Omega. Janeway has successfully carried out her directive, and Seven has had her first spiritual experience.

SENSOR READINGS: Only starship captains and Federation flag officers have been briefed on the nature of this threat. The Omega molecule is the most powerful substance known to exist. A single Omega molecule contains the same energy as a warp core. In theory, a small chain of Omega could sustain a civilization. The molecule was first synthesized over a hundred years ago, by a Starfleet physicist named Ketteract who was hoping to develop either an inexhaustible power source or a weapon. Ketteract managed to synthesize a single molecule particle of Omega, but it existed for only a fraction of a second before it destabilized and destroyed a classified research center in the Lantaru Sector. Ketteract and one hundred and twenty-six of the Federation's leading scientists were lost in the accident. Rescue teams attempting to reach the site discovered an unexpected secondary effect, subspace ruptures extending out several light-years, made it impossible to create a stable warp field in the Lantaru Sector, and ships can travel through it only at sublight. The general public believed this to be a natural phenomenon. Omega destroys the fabric of subspace. A chain reaction involving a handful of molecules could devastate subspace throughout an entire quadrant and make warp travel impossible. When Starfleet realized Omega's power, they suppressed all knowledge of it. ■

had previously assimilated knowledge of the Omega molecule and Janeway would not be telling Seven anything the former drone did not already know. *Voyager*'s sensors have detected the Omega molecule, which is a highly unstable phenomenon. Janeway's orders as a Starfleet captain are to destroy it, but Seven believes its power should be harnessed as, to the Borg, it represents perfection. However, Seven agrees to help Janeway carry out the directive if only for the opportunity to study the molecule.

Chakotay convinces the captain she needs the resources of her crew with this mysterious and dangerous plan. Janeway briefs the senior staff on the directive. The Omega molecule is the most powerful substance known to exist and could create a subspace rupture that would make warp travel impossible. The crew sets a course for the newly discovered molecules, knowing that this mission must succeed, or they will never be able to leave the Delta Quadrant.

Seven begins working on a harmonic resonance

Janeway tries to obtain information about the Omega molecule. ROBBIE ROBINSON

Torres is ordered to install multiphasic shielding around the warp core and Paris is ordered to modify a shuttlecraft to withstand extreme thermal stress of at least 12,000 Kelvins. Janeway orders the Doctor to prepare twenty milligrams of arithrazine, which is used for the most severe cases of theta-radiation poisoning. The Doctor insists that a physician must be present to monitor the treatment and it is against Starfleet medical protocols to provide that much arithrazine. The original plan calls for a gravemetric torpedo to be used to destroy the molecule. Seven constructs a harmonic resonance chamber based on the Borg design to contain and stabilize Omega. Since the torpedo would be insufficient to destroy Omega she modifies the chamber to emit an inverse frequency to dissolve Omega's interatomic bonds. In the end, a combination of both solutions are used. ▪ Kim claims that, in theory, it is possible to detonate a type-6 protostar and turn it into a wormhole which could lead back to the Alpha Quadrant.

DELTA QUADRANT: Each Borg drone's experiences are processed by the collective, though only useful information is retained. ▪ The Borg designation for Omega is

Particle 010. Every drone is aware of its existence and is instructed to assimilate it at all costs. The Borg first encountered the Omega molecule two hundred and twenty-nine years ago through the combined mythology of thirteen assimilated species, beginning with Species 262. The oral history of the primitive species referred to a powerful substance that could "burn the sky." The Borg were intrigued, which led them to Species 263. According to Seven, they too, were primitive and believed it was a drop of blood from their Creator. The Borg see Omega as perfection because the molecules exist in a flawless state as infinite parts functioning as one. On one occasion the Borg were able to create a single Omega molecule. They kept it stable for one-trillionth of a nanosecond before it destabilized. They did not have enough boronite ore left to synthesize more but Seven claims that the knowledge gained allowed them to refine their theories. Seven admits that twenty-nine vessels and 600,000 drones were sacrificed in the experiment.

The Omega molecules were being developed on the moon of pre-warp capable planet. The aliens were able to synthesize two hundred million particles.

ALPHA QUADRANT: Federation cosmologists had a theory that the molecule once existed in nature, for an infinitesimal period of time, at the exact moment of the big bang. Some claimed Omega was the primal source of energy for the explosion that began the universe.

PERSONAL LOGS: Tuvok and Kim continue to play *kaltoh* ("Alter Ego"). ■ Seven refers to the game as elementary spatial harmonics and easily solves it for Kim. According to her personal log entry, her plans for the day include the following: conduct a comprehensive diagnostic of the aft sensor array with Kim; take a nutritional supplement at 1500 hours; engage in one hour of cardiovascular activity; and review *A Christmas Carol,* as recommended by the Doctor for its educational value.

EPISODE LOGS: In an early script for this episode, Seven uses Janeway's history of taking risks in the interest of exploration as the basis for her argument to allow her to try to stabilize the Omega molecule instead of destroy it. In that version, Janeway allows her to make the attempt, but the attack forces them to eject the chamber in the same manner as in the final aired episode.

Chakotay meets Kellin for the first time. DANNY FELD

UNFORGETTABLE

EPISODE #190
WRITTEN BY: GREG ELLIOT & MICHAEL PERRICONE
DIRECTED BY: ANDREW J. ROBINSON

GUEST STAR	
CURNETH	MICHAEL CANAVAN

SPECIAL GUEST APPEARANCE BY	
KELLIN	VIRGINIA MADSEN

STARDATE 51813.4

A cloaked ship suddenly appears with an injured female on board hailing *Voyager* and specifically Chakotay by name. Once the woman, Kellin, is beamed to sickbay, she asks the captain for asylum from her people. When Chakotay asks how she knows him, she explains that she was recently on *Voyager* for several weeks. No one remembers her because memories of her people cannot be held in the minds of others for more than a few hours. She confesses that she has returned to *Voyager* because she fell in love with Chakotay.

Chakotay informs the rest of the senior staff that Kellin is from Ramura, a closed society that tracks down and returns people who leave their world. She was on *Voyager* about a month ago when her bounty hunting brought her to a stowaway on the ship. Although Kellin says a computer virus was planted to erase all evidence of her presence, the crew is still ordered to look through navigation logs and other outlets that would corroborate her story. While Kellin recounts to Chakotay how they fell in love, Ramura ships begin firing at *Voyager.*

Janeway gives Kellin permission to modify the ship's sensors so they can see the cloaked ships. Once *Voyager* returns fire, the Ramurans flee, leaving behind Kellin, who asks to stay on the ship permanently. Although Chakotay does not remember loving her, he cannot stop thinking about what she has said about their relationship. But Kellin realizes that as long as she is on board, her people will come back, putting the crew in danger. She tells Chakotay that she will leave if he doesn't have any feelings for her, but he tells Kellin to stay.

Reminiscing about their last night together, Kellin explains how Chakotay helped her find the stowaway and wiped his memories of the outside world with a neurolytic emitter. Later, after working with Seven and Kim on a defense strategy against her people, Kellin senses that a tracer is onboard. He suddenly materializes, and despite her protest, the Ramuran shoots her with the neurolytic emitter.

As Kellin's memories begin to fade, she begs Chakotay to remind her of the love they shared once she

For a brief time, Chakotay and Kellin remember each other and what they shared. DANNY FELD

no longer remembers. Soon, she does not recognize him, and Chakotay tells her about their relationship. He asks her to stay and see if her feelings can be rekindled, but she refuses to violate her people's edict again. Once she and the tracer are gone, Chakotay writes about her in his personal log with pen and paper so he will never fully forget her.

SENSOR READINGS: The crew has been collecting uterium through the Bussard collectors. Seven suggested a series of modifications that have increased the Bussard collectors's efficiency twenty-three percent. ▪ When sensors are unable to pick up the Ramuran ships, Janeway

has Seven use the astrometrics sensors to scan for them. Seven detects close-range weapons fire of two ships in battle. Later, Kellin helps to alter *Voyager's* scanners so they can detect the Ramuran vessels. ▪ A magneton sweep of the transporter room disrupted the stowaway's polarization cloak, allowing him to be captured by Kellin during her original visit to *Voyager.* ▪ According to Kim, Beta Team is the best security squad on the ship. ▪ A command officer is required to override the security lockouts on astrometric processors. The processors are located in a Jefferies tube on Deck 10. ▪ On two occasions a virus is released to erase all mention of the Ramurans' presence from *Voyager's* computer.

DAMAGE REPORT: Propulsion is knocked offline during the Ramuran attack, leaving only thrusters available.

DELTA QUADRANT: *Voyager* was in orbit of the planet Mikah before Kellin boarded the ship looking for the stowaway she was following.

Memories of the Ramurans cannot be held in the minds of other races because their bodies produce a sort of pheromone that blocks the long-term memory engrams of others. They are impervious to scanning devices because of technology they developed to aid in their clandestine lifestyle. Kellin is known as a tracer, a kind of bounty hunter who tracks people who try to leave the Ramuran homeworld. A tracer never goes home empty-handed, as the disgrace would be too great. Ramuran ships use a sophisticated polarization technique that causes sensor scans to pass right through it. Their weapons are tightly focused proton-based particle beams that can penetrate any shield. No defense has ever stopped the weapons; although Kim believes that tying the baryon sensors into deflector control would scatter the beams.

PERSONAL LOGS: Chakotay hates carrots, fried food upsets his stomach, and he refuses to eat pudding because he thinks it's slimy.

LIVING WITNESS

EPISODE #191
TELEPLAY BY: BRYAN FULLER and BRANNON BRAGA & JOE MENOSKY
STORY BY: BRANNON BRAGA
DIRECTED BY: TIM RUSS

GUEST STARS

QUARREN	HENRY WORONICZ
DALETH	ROD ARRANTS
VASKAN ARBITER	CRAIG RICHARD NELSON
KYRIAN ARBITER	MARIE CHAMBERS
TEDRAN	BRIAN FITZPATRICK
VASKAN VISITOR	MORGAN H. MARGOLIS

CO-STARS

TABRIS	MARY ANNE McGARRY
KYRIAN SPECTATOR	TIMOTHY DAVIS-REED

STARDATE UNKNOWN

Quarren and the Doctor survey the museum after the attack.
DANNY FELD

A representation of *Voyager* and its crew are on holograhic display in a Kyrian museum seven hundred years in the future, and they are being blamed for a horrible civil war that nearly wiped out the Kyrian race. Through inaccurate simulations, the crew is shown as a group of violent people who did not hesitate to destroy anything or anyone standing in their way of getting home. Approached by the Vaskan ambassador for help in his fight against the Kyrians, Janeway supposedly slaughtered millions of innocent Kyrians in exchange for directions to a wormhole leading to the Alpha Quadrant.

The museum curator, Quarren, works within the *Voyager* engineering simulation to access a data storage device recently uncovered at one of the Kyrian ruins. Without realizing what he is working on, he accidentally activates the Doctor's backup program. The Doctor is distraught to hear what has happened and refuses to believe that seven hundred years have passed, but once he sees the *Voyager* artifacts in the museum, he accepts that the time has passed.

Appalled by the depiction of Janeway and the crew as cold, heartless thugs, he tries desperately to share *Voyager*'s side of the story. It's true, the Doctor explains that Janeway had negotiated a trade agreement with the Vaskan ambassador, but it was the Kyrians that attacked. Quarren balks at the idea that his people were the aggressors. When the Doctor describes how Janeway and the crew only wanted to extricate themselves from the war, his program is deactivated.

After giving himself some time to think about what

the Doctor has said, Quarren reinitializes his program and allows him to create a simulation of his own, showing his version of the past. In it, the Kyrian leader, Tedran, invaded *Voyager*. Although Janeway had explained that they were trading with the Vaskans and nothing more, Tedran would not stand down. It was the Vaskan ambassador who killed him, and the last thing the Doctor remembers from that time is Kyrian ships attacking *Voyager*. Following a meeting with the arbiters, the Doctor tries to reactivate his medical tricorder and offer proof of his re-creation, but a group of angered Vaskans break into the museum and begin destroying it.

When war between the two groups threatens to erupt anew, the Doctor decides it would be best if his program is decompiled. Although he wanted to clear *Voyager*'s name in history, it is not worth causing more fighting. However, this did not transpire. Years into the future, watching another simulation, people see that Quarren talked the Doctor into giving his testimony of events. Because of that the Great War was finally portrayed accurately, and harmony was restored. After setting the record straight, the Doctor eventually boarded a shuttle for the Alpha Quadrant to trace *Voyager*'s path to Earth.

SENSOR READINGS: The EMH backup module is found as an artifact buried nine meters beneath the ruins of Kesef, seven hundred years into the future (although previous episodes have suggested that the Doctor's program cannot be backed up, it is assumed that method was

An inaccurate version of historical events is shown in the Kyrian museum. DANNY FELD

devised but not shown.). ▪ Voyager traded the Vaskans medical supplies for dilithium.

Among the many inconsistencies in the historic scenario are the following: The Doctor is an android. The *Warship Voyager* had a complement of over three hundred soldiers and had assimilated a handful of Borg, Talaxians, and at least one Kazon. The ship had a triple-armored hull, thirty torpedo tubes, twenty-five phaser banks, fighter shuttles, and a variety of biogenic weapons. A fully Borgified Seven of Nine led a Borg squad that assimilated two of the Kyrian boarding party. The uniforms were different, with no pips or combadges, and the crew wore leather gloves. Among the more personal changes, Janeway's hairstyle was different, Tuvok's ears were larger, Chakotay's tattoo covered half his face, and Torres was listed as chief transporter operator.

DELTA QUADRANT: Kyrian history stated that the conflict was brief but brutal, with two million Kyrians slaughtered within days. The Vaskan leaders then proceeded to occupy Kyrian lands, forcing the people into subservience. It took centuries to undo the damage, and the Kyrians continue to struggle for equality. ▪ Artificial life-forms are considered sentient and held responsible

for their actions. If the Doctor is found guilty, his program could be decompiled. ▪ The vandals use photon grenades.

Kyrian history states that the Doctor's testimony opened a dialogue between the Kyrians and the Vaskans, eventually leading to a new respect for their divergent cultures and traditions. Quarren died six years after the Doctor's testimony, but he lived long enough to witness the Dawn of Harmony. The Doctor served as surgical chancellor for many years, until he decided to take a small craft and set a course for the Alpha Quadrant, attempting to trace the path of *Voyager*.

PERSONAL LOGS: The Doctor claims to be quite adept in the art of holographic programming, a fact that will figure into the events of "Author, Author."

CREW COMPLEMENT: In the Doctor's revised simulation Tuvok reports that three members of the engineering crew are killed in the Kyrian attack.

EPISODE LOGS: Torres does not appear in this episode, as Roxann Dawson was giving birth the week it was filmed. ▪ The shooting script refers to the characters in the Kyrian simulation as "Revised Janeway," "Revised Tuvok," etc.

DEMON

EPISODE #192
TELEPLAY BY: KENNETH BILLER
STORY BY: ANDRE BORMANIS
DIRECTED BY: ANSON WILLIAMS

GUEST STAR

VORIK	ALEXANDER ENBERG

CO-STARS

TRANSPORTER TECHNICIAN	SUSAN LEWIS
COMPUTER VOICE	MAJEL BARRETT

STARDATE UNKNOWN

As *Voyager* runs dangerously low on fuel, Seven of Nine discovers a class-Y planet containing a high concentration of deuterium. Class-Y worlds, "demon planets," have a toxic atmosphere. When an attempt to transport deuterium to the ship results in an explosion, Kim volunteers himself and Paris to mine the fuel on the surface. Kim's environmental suit is compromised after he falls into a pool of metallic compound. As Kim's oxygen is rapidly depleted, Paris's suit also fails, and both men collapse before they can reach their shuttle.

With no communication from the pair, Janeway lands *Voyager* on the planet and sends a rescue team for them. Chakotay and Seven, also in environmental suits, find the shuttle with no one on board. When the ground gives way underneath Chakotay, Paris appears—minus his environmental suit—and helps Seven pull the first officer to safety.

Paris explains that he and Kim have adapted to the environment, telling Chakotay and Seven to take off their suits as well. They refuse to take that risk and beam back to *Voyager*. As soon as they are back on the ship, Kim and Paris start suffocating. The Doctor quickly erects a force field around them and vents the planet's gases in so they can breathe. He surmises that the fluid has entered their bloodstream and altered their physiology at the cellular level. Unless the effect can be reversed, Kim and Paris will have to be left behind in order to survive.

Experimenting on the compound, Janeway and Torres watch in awe as the fluid sample replicates Torres's thumb. Meanwhile Kim accompanies an away team back

The bio-mimetic versions of Kim and Paris can survive in the atmosphere without environmental suits. PETER IOVINO

Janeway takes the conn as the ship tries to break free of the planet. PETER IOVINO

to the surface and finds another version of himself and Paris—unconscious and in their environmental suits.

A large pool of the metallic compound forms under the ship and it begins to sink into it. Janeway recalls the away team so the ship can make an emergency ascent. The duplicate Kim refuses to leave the surface, saying that he feels a connection to the planet. With the team aboard, *Voyager* attempts to get out of the compound, damaging it in the process.

The duplicate Kim hails the ship from the surface, asking to meet with the captain and is beamed aboard *Voyager.* After confirming Janeway's suspicions that he is a part of the compound, the duplicate Kim explains that the substance is alive, but it has never been conscious. When it entered the bodies of Paris and Kim, it copied their forms and experienced awareness for the first time. Now it craves more. The crew agrees to donate samples of their DNA so the compound can duplicate them. *Voyager* is then allowed to depart, leaving behind a new race of aliens in the exact image of the *Voyager* crew.

SENSOR READINGS: The ship is running gray mode with power cut to Decks 4 through 9, replicators, holodecks, and all other nonessentials are offline, and the remaining systems operating at twenty percent capacity. With the deuterium supply this low, even at one-quarter impulse, the ship will be out of power inside a week. Eventually life support is shut down on all but Decks 1

and 5 to give the crew an extra hour of breathable air. Later, Chakotay notes that 20 kilograms of deuterium should be enough to get the main systems back online. ▪ The crew works on ways to synthesize deuterium in geophysics. ▪ Seven attempts to beam deuterium from beneath the planet's surface, which leads to an overload in the pattern buffers and an explosion. If a probe were sent to collect the deuterium, it would incinerate within seconds of entering the upper atmosphere. ▪ Adaptations are made to the shields to repel the thermionic discharges from the planet. ▪ The backup systems on the environmental suits are what allow Paris and Kim to stay alive after a sustained period of time without oxygen. ▪ Nadion bursts from the photon emitters damage the metallic compound. ▪ It is unclear how much deuterium the crew is able to mine after reaching an agreement with the planet's life-forms.

DAMAGE REPORT: There is an explosion in the transporter room that knocks them offline. ▪ Following the ship's landing on the demon planet, Tuvok says he could give a litany of damaged systems, but now that they're down, they're not getting back up again soon. ▪ Thrusters go offline due to the attempt to break free of the planet.

SHUTTLE TRACKER: Kim and Paris take a shuttle down to the demon planet. Seven and Chakotay take a second shuttle to search for them.

DELTA QUADRANT: The planet is listed as class-Y and referred to as a demon planet due to its toxic atmosphere filled with thermionic radiation. Just entering a standard orbit would be considered suicide, and there is no known environment less hospitable to humanoid life. ▪ Although the planet's surface temperature is in excess of 500 Kelvins, the temperature of the metallic compound reads at only 12 degrees Celsius. The compound is a combination of deuterium, hydrogen sulfate, dichromates, and contains protein molecules indicating that it has organic properties. The fluid has mimetic properties, it samples the DNA of whatever it comes into contact with and duplicates it, creating a mimetic life-form that appears to be an exact copy.

PERSONAL LOGS: The Doctor likes to sing Puccini while he works. ▪ Neelix considers Jirex to be one of the greatest writers on Talax and never goes to sleep without reading one of the parables in the *Selected Works of Jirex.* He gets terrible neck pains when he sleeps without his pillows and always has with him the blankets his mother knitted when he was a child, especially since Starfleet-issue blankets give him a rash.

MEDICAL REPORT: Seven and Ensign Nozawa are injured in the transporter explosion.

EPISODE LOGS: It is first mentioned in "Innocence" that the warp core is designed to operate for up to three years before refueling, which accounts for their dire need for fuel at this stage of their voyage. ▪ The mimetic *Voyager* crew will be seen again in "Course: Oblivion."

ONE

EPISODE #193
WRITTEN BY: JERI TAYLOR
DIRECTED BY: KENNETH BILLER

GUEST STAR

TRAJIS LO-TARIK   WADE WILLIAMS

CO-STARS

BORG DRONE   RON OSTROW
COMPUTER VOICE   MAJEL BARRETT

STARDATE 51929.3

The *Voyager* crew comes across a vast Mutara class nebula, and everyone except the Doctor and Seven of Nine is severely affected by its radiation. Since it would take a year to go around it, Janeway decides the best course of action is to put the crew to sleep in stasis chambers with independent life support while the ship takes a month long trip through the nebula. Seven of Nine and the Doctor will check on their vital signs and monitor the ship's status until it reaches the other side.

After several days, the lack of social interaction and activity begins to put a strain on the Doctor and Seven. The computer alerts them that the antimatter storage tanks are failing and plasma is leaking. Seven rushes to engineering to eject the tanks only to find that it was a false alarm.

Malfunctioning gel packs are found to be responsible for the false sensor readings. While the duo attempt repairs, the Doctor's program begins to degrade in the holoemitter. He makes it back to sickbay, but with his mobile emitter malfunctioning he will have to stay there for the remainder of the trip. Now that Seven is even more isolated, she begins having disturbing dreams and visions. When an alien hails her, she beams him aboard and agrees to trade some equipment. Feeling threatened, Seven tries to escort him off the ship, but he breaks free of her.

Although sensors show no evidence of the alien or his ship, Seven searches *Voyager* for him. She hears voices of the crew calling for her, and the alien begins controlling the ship's functions, playing off her fears. When the Doctor finally gets his mobile emitter to work by tying it into the EPS system, he rushes to Seven and discovers that she is hallucinating. The radiation is starting to degrade her Borg implants. Then the EPS conduits overload and the Doctor's program goes offline. Seven is now truly alone. With the fate of the crew entirely in her hands she begins to panic.

With hours to go before *Voyager* clears the nebula, the propulsion system begins to fail. Fighting against the hallucinations, Seven struggles to reroute power. At every turn she is met by her fears visualized. With only minutes left, Seven reroutes power from life support and falls unconscious. When she comes to in sickbay, the crew is awake, *Voyager* has cleared the nebula, and she has managed to save everyone on board.

SENSOR READINGS: The crew is placed in stasis chambers in a state of suspended animation. Each chamber is equipped with independent life support and can be opened from the inside. According to Janeway, other crews have been in stasis much longer than a month. As she describes the process: The crew will enter the units, their cardiopulmonary systems will be slowed, neural activity suspended, and later they will wake up feeling as though they'd had a good night's sleep. Seven and the Doctor will check the crew's vital signs four times a day. It is not unheard of for people to come out of stasis and start wandering in a "sleepwalk"-like state. The stasis chambers are set up on Deck 14 so it will be easy to monitor them.

DAMAGE REPORT: In "The 37's" Chakotay estimated that the ship could not function with a crew of less than 100. It can be assumed that this reference was for extended periods of time, as this episode shows that in less than one month the ship's systems begin to require constant maintenance in order to function. ▪ In addition to the routine maintenance, the nebula effects all of the ship's technology. Malfunctioning gel packs feed false readings to the sensors. The first of the packs to fail are located in Sequence 6-Theta-9. The nebular activity is causing the gel pack's neurodes to discharge in random bursts

Seven patrols the eerily empty ship. PETER IOVINO

because the radiation produces a degradation in the synaptic relays. Later quantum failures are present in thirty-three percent of gel pack relays. To adapt to the problem, Seven has the sluggish computer reroute all functional relays through subprocessor Chi-14. ▪ Primary EPS conduits overload and there is a propulsion system failure. To compensate, Seven first reroutes power from stasis chambers 1 through 10, before cutting the ship's life support system and routing the power back into the stasis chambers.

DELTA QUADRANT: The Mutara-class nebula extends for at least 110 light-years.

PERSONAL LOGS: Janeway credits her instinct as the reason why she believes in Seven and that she will do well by the crew. ▪ On four separate occasions, Paris leaves his stasis chamber because he does not like enclosed spaces. ▪ Kim was born in South Carolina and has dabbled in quite a few different sports including tennis, and parisses squares, but his favorite is volleyball. ▪

The Doctor continues to tutor Seven in social skills through a holodeck simulation. On some previous occasion, the Doctor has demonstrated knowledge of the rudimentary aspects of piloting. ▪ Once, when Seven was a drone she was separated from the collective, during which time she experienced panic and apprehension ("Survival Instinct").

MEDICAL REPORT: The entire crew, minus Seven and the Doctor, are burned by the nebula's radiation. ▪ The doctor believes that the radiation, which was producing a degradation in the gel pack synaptic relays is having a similar effect on Seven's Borg implants and altering the neurotransmitter levels in her sensory nodes. That would explain why she is hearing voices and seeing images. He suggests an anti-psychotic to help Seven cope until he locates the problem, but his system goes offline. This would be the third occasion since joining *Voyager* that Seven has experienced hallucinations or false memories. The previous times occurred during "Raven" and "Retrospect."

Seven and the Doctor begin to show the strains of keeping *Voyager* functioning. PETER IOVINO

CREW COMPLEMENT: One unnamed bridge crew member dies as a result of the exposure to the radiation. ▪ Janeway comments that there were 150 people onboard *Voyager* when Seven joined the crew.

EPISODE LOGS: The stasis room is a re-dress of the cargo bay sets. The stasis beds were the same from "The Thaw." ▪ Janeway comments that the ship has traveled 15,000 light-years.

HOPE AND FEAR

EPISODE #194

TELEPLAY BY **BRANNON BRAGA & JOE MENOSKY**

STORY BY **RICK BERMAN & BRANNON BRAGA**
& JOE MENOSKY

DIRECTED BY **WINRICH KOLBE**

GUEST STARS

ARTURIS	RAY WISE
ADMIRAL HAYES	JACK SHEARER

CO-STAR

COMPUTER VOICE	MAJEL BARRETT

STARDATE 51978.2

Paris and Neelix return from a trading colony with a guest named Arturis, whom Janeway agrees to give passage to the next system. When Arturis shows a natural inclination toward learning alien lan-

guages, Janeway asks him to review the encoded message *Voyager* received from Starfleet before the Hirogen relay stations were destroyed. Arturis instantly decodes the message, revealing a spatial grid with marked coordinates. When *Voyager* arrives at the designated spot, the crew finds a Starfleet vessel waiting there.

With no lifesigns on the ship, an away team is sent to secure the *U.S.S. Dauntless* where they find the helm set for auto-navigation, and a new engine configuration called a quantum slipstream drive. The rest of Starfleet's message says the *Dauntless* has been sent to bring the crew home. Janeway orders them to modify *Voyager* with the slipstream technology so they can bring it along, but she also senses something is not right and asks Tuvok to keep an eye on Arturis.

Seven tries to tell Janeway that she does not intend to accompany the crew to the Alpha Quadrant when the captain manages to reconstruct a new segment of the data block from Starfleet, in which she discovers that they did not send the *Dauntless*. Meanwhile, in the *Dauntless's* engineering section, Kim discovers alien technology behind one of the bulkheads, confirming that Arturis manufactured the ship. Janeway and Seven gather weapons and head to the *Dauntless* bridge to confront Arturis.

Before he can be stopped, Arturis takes command of the ship. Kim is able to transport Tuvok and his security team to *Voyager,* but Janeway and Seven are taken hostage as the *Dauntless* goes into slipstream. An angry Arturis explains that his people were fighting against assimilation when Janeway gave the Borg the nanoprobes to fight Species 8472. Those aliens were his home world's last hope to defeat the Borg, and he has held a grudge against the *Voyager* crew ever since. Now, he is taking Janeway and Seven into Borg space to be assimilated.

After admitting to Janeway that her fear was keeping her from wanting to accompany the crew home, Seven adapts her Borg technology to break through the brig force field. She and Janeway then attempt to take control of the ship, but their commands are blocked. *Voyager* arrives via the adapted slipstream technology and disables the *Dauntless's* shields, beaming Janeway and Seven back, as Arturis travels into Borg space alone. Although the slipstream drive is not compatible with *Voyager,* Seven, who decides that she does intend to stay, tells Janeway that she plans to continue working on the technology to get the crew home.

SENSOR READINGS: Janeway has tried over fifty decryption algorithms on the message from Starfleet in the five months since they received it. The true recovered

Paris marvels at the controls on the *Dauntless* bridge. JERRY FITZGERALD

message is from Admiral Hayes, admitting that Starfleet has failed to find a wormhole or an advanced propulsion system to help get the crew home. The admiral does, however, send them all the information Starfleet possesses on the Delta Quadrant in the hope that it will shave a few years off the journey. ▪ *Voyager*'s attempt to create the slipstream drive is successful, although at first they have trouble breaking through the quantum barrier. Torres diverts auxiliary power to the deflector, bringing it to maximum power so Tuvok can focus the quantum field. Once at slipstream velocity, the ship's structural integrity is down by nine percent and there is less than an hour before the hull starts to buckle. ▪ Following the unsuccessful trip home, Janeway orders crew to take R&R over the next few days.

DELTA QUADRANT: Arturis is a gifted linguist who claims to know over four thousand languages. He tells Janeway that all his people require is to hear the grammar and syntax to learn a species' tongue as they can see patterns where other people see only confusion. Arturis is

from Species 116, though their name is never given. Seven says the Borg had never been able to assimilate them, although that has changed since she left the collective. Arturis's people had managed to elude the Borg for centuries by outwitting them and remaining one step ahead. But in recent years, the Borg had begun to weaken their defenses. They had considered Species 8472 to be their last hope to defeat the Borg, but Arturis blames Janeway for taking away that hope when she made her deal with the Borg ("Scorpion"). When the Borg attacked, Arturis's people, their twenty-three outer-colonies were the first to fall. Less than 20,000 members of the race survived. ▪ Arturis uses particle synthesis to re-create a Starfleet bridge on his ship.

ALPHA QUADRANT: According to the false message created by Arturis, The *U.S.S. Dauntless* NX01-A was launched on Stardate 51472 and has traveled from Earth, Sector 001, to the Delta Quadrant 60,000 light-years away, in only three months.

Arturis returns to Borg space with his prisoners. RON TOM

PERSONAL LOGS: Janeway believes that she has been "butting heads" with Seven of Nine a lot more recently. She claims that she still struggles with basic Klingon language. ■ Torres only speaks a few Klingon phrases, as she feels the language is a little too robust for her tastes. ■ Neelix conducted trade negotiations with a xenon based life-form at the trading colony. While he was in the midst of those negotiations, his universal translator malfunctioned and Arturis stepped in to help. ■ Seven is a bit of a sore loser, upset that she wins only four out of ten games of velocity against Janeway even though she has superior visual acuity and stamina. While in Arturis's brig, Seven has Janeway activate some nanoprobes to alter her bioelectric field so she can pass through the force field. To do so, Janeway uses a microfilament from her combadge to

cross link the third and sixth nodules on Seven's cranial implant.

CREW COMPLEMENT: Janeway once again refers to Seven of Nine successfully being able to deal with a crew of 150.

EPISODE LOG: This episode takes place nine months after Seven of Nine joined *Voyager* ("Scorpion, Part II") and five months after the crew received the message from Starfleet ("Hunters"). ■ The book *Star Trek: Action!* by Terry J. Erdmann (with creative consultant Paula M. Block) examines the final scenes of this episode in great detail.

LIEUTENANT TOM PARIS

CLOSE-UP—AN ELECTRONIC ANKLET (OPTICAL)

with blinking lights . . . moving up the leg to find an athletic human in his late twenties, lying on his back on the ground, in a twisted position, his shirt off, wearing a mini-visor and using a 24th century laser tool to meld repairs of some mechanical equipment. This is TOM PARIS.

—Tom Paris's first appearance in "Caretaker"

Although he did appear with his shirt on, Tom Paris's introduction proved to be one of the most unique of any *Star Trek* main characters. The first to be introduced while in prison for a crime he did, in fact, commit, Paris quickly developed into the traditional Starfleet hero, though he would backslide on several occasions. To many, Paris's redemption occurred with his heroic actions at the end of "Caretaker," but his roguish qualities would live on through his devil-may-care attitude, which remained prevalent throughout the series. A former Starfleet officer that had left the organization, Paris had a slightly mercenary quality that became fully evident in "Non Sequitur" with a glimpse of what he would have become without *Voyager's* positive influence on his character.

ROBBIE ROBINSON

> *Robert Duncan McNeill: I think in the beginning the strongest qualities that we were all focusing on were his rebellious side with his lone wolf kind of qualities and bad boy past. I think, initially, he didn't have a great sense of humor. He wasn't always making very heroic kinds of choices. And he was kind of the rebel. I think he's changed quite a bit. He's become very much of a team player and a leader.*

Paris's rogue attitude was evident from the beginning. He was the first to fully embrace their journey through the Delta Quadrant by becoming a de facto morale officer before Neelix took on the job. Because he felt that there was nothing waiting for him back in the Alpha Quadrant but a father who was hard to please, Paris did his best to make the trip home more fun. He was the one who created many of the holodeck sanctuaries for the crew, beginning with Sandrine's—the bar that reminded him of his best times at home. His interest in history and ancient artifacts not only proved useful but also served as necessary diversions for the crew on several occasions. And, he was among the first to realize that, alone in space, the crew only had themselves for company, as he set his sights on the ever elusive Delaney sisters.

> *Robert Duncan McNeill: I really felt like after the first season or so that we had to bring in something that made him different from most of the other characters. I think all the characters have their sense of humor in one way or the other, but Tom Paris is kind of the joker. He's got the sarcastic ironic comments about things. He speaks a little more plain English. He cuts to the chase a little quicker then some of the other characters. And he's just got a more carefree attitude about things in general. Which I think is a more appealing quality than a rebellious attitude.*

Though he had his fair share of romantic entanglements, Paris was the first member of the senior staff to find a match and settle down, once B'Elanna finally allowed herself to admit her true feelings for him. Their flirtation began around "The Swarm," initially as lighthearted joking. It evolved with his admission of feelings for Torres in "Blood Fever," though he refused to take advantage of her in her unstable condition. Torres finally admitted her own feelings in "Day of Honor" moments before they thought they would both die. Interestingly enough, the situation paralleled the time when Paris proposed to her after they discovered their shuttle had a bomb aboard that was about to explode. Married life settled Paris down in only the most superficial ways, as his love for his wife and unborn child proved that he could grow while still being the same fun guy.

Torres, however, was not Paris's first choice for onboard romance. Early in the series Paris had to reluctantly admit to himself that he had growing feelings for Kes. However, he made the conscious effort not to act on them out of respect for Neelix. It was only after the events of "Parturition" that he could truly put an end to the feelings for the sake of his friendship onboard.

Ethan Phillips: First they had that incredible clashing over Kes and the jealousy thing which I think, while at the time it was not particularly pleasant to watch, it was a nice motivation for what happened in "Parturition"—a nice build-up to that. Even though it hasn't been explored a whole lot since "Parturition," I think that that stays with the fans and informs everything that's happened between Tom and Neelix since then. Which has been nothing but mutual admiration and friendship.

ROBBIE ROBINSON

Paris naturally had different types of relationships with the different characters onboard. To Janeway he was a personal reclamation project, while with Chakotay he overcame an embittered history to earn a mutual respect. For the Doctor he was often a jovial thorn in the side. It was, however, Kim who provided the closest friendship for Paris, which was also a large help in his redemption. Paris and Kim formed the first bond on the show when they met in Quark's bar on Deep Space 9. Fast friends, they were immediately inseparable, with Paris often taking the older brother role, looking out for neophyte, Kim. However, Kim provided much more for Paris as he was the first to accept the ex-convict for who he was and not who others believed him to be.

Garrett Wang: As we come to Season 3, that's the turnaround point where Kim has to take care of Paris. From that point on I think the—I don't want to say the student becomes the teacher—but Paris then starts to learn a little bit more about life from Kim, I suppose. Kim becomes more of the voice of reason or the person who pulls him back from his tirades . . . Kim definitely becomes more of a calming influence on Paris and, as a result, becomes his own person instead of being under Paris's wing. Kim becomes much more of his equal.

Though Paris's easygoing attitude led to many friendships on the ship, his strong will continued to pose problems. He was punished with a rank reduction after going against the captain's orders when dealing with the Monean Maritime Sovereignty in "Thirty Days." However, his positive attitude and heroic actions soon got him reinstated as a lieutenant j.g. by the end of the season in "Unimatrix Zero, Part I." But the biggest change in Paris's attitude came about when he created the *Delta Flyer* and found a new outlet for his adventures.

Robert Duncan McNeill: The Delta Flyer *clearly is a very special ship to Tom Paris and what he's done with that over the years. I remember I said to them years ago, whenever there were shuttle scenes and I'd see Chakotay flying the shuttle, whether it was the Delta Flyer, or even before that—I said, "I don't care what the story is. Whenever you've got an away team going on a tricky mission in a shuttle that needs to be piloted with some skill, Paris should be there." I said, "I don't even care about lines. You don't have to give me lines, but he should be sitting at that control flying the ship. That is his contribution to this team." So I think they've tried to do that quite often. You'll see other characters flying the shuttles, but it's usually not under a lot of pressure. The pressure comes as a surprise. If we know it's going to be dangerous and it's going to require some skill and a special knowledge of that shuttle, then Paris is the one to go.*

Whether flyboy, playboy, or settled-down married man, Robert Duncan McNeill was the embodiment of Tom Paris. He played a similar character type in the role of Nic Locarno in the *TNG* episode "The First Duty." However, the major difference between the two characters was that Paris's actions were redeemable whereas Locarno's were not. It is that subtlety of nuance that made Paris a true *Star Trek* character. No matter how far he may have bent the rules, he always made sure that they never broke

SEASON FIVE

Rumors spread throughout fifth season about the possibility of the crew returning to the Alpha Quadrant earlier than the conclusion of the series. While there may have been brief discussions about the possibility of what such a dramatic change could bring to the series, it was never enacted. However, throughout the rest of the series, the crew continues to get closer to their ultimate destination and the undercurrents of how they could deal with life after their return is peppered into plots over the final three seasons.

We never even considered bringing them home except for a few minutes in the fifth season, and then, basically, it was just for the sake of discussion . . . Rumors about the show can exist without the shred of truth. If we had done that, it would have become a totally different series. It would have become a pretty standard Star Trek *series. They would have come home and they would have gone about their business. In* The Fugitive, *Kimble finds the one-armed man in the last episode because it was a show about a fugitive. This is a show about a crew that's on their own, a crew that's trying to reach their home but at the same time trying to explore and learn and interact with as many species as they can.*

—RICK BERMAN

There are very few earth-shattering changes to the series in its fifth season as the crew continues its search for shortcuts home while exploring strange new worlds. Although Janeway suffers a delayed bout with guilt in "Night" over stranding her crew so far from home, at this point the crew seems to embrace its situation, trying to make the best of it. *Star Trek* has always been a character-driven series, and several standout episodes this season bring further depth to the characters. Although the previous season focused largely on the integration of the newest character into the series, this year will see a shift back to the ensemble nature of the show.

The Borg continue to be the main threat to the *Voyager* crew throughout the rest of the series. Janeway and her crew, however, manage to strike many crippling blows to the Borg and even use them in their ultimate goal of getting closer to home. New aliens like the Malon ("Night"), become a recurring threat while an old nemesis becomes less hostile, when the crew once again encounters Species 8472 ("In the Flesh"). Meanwhile, the only child currently aboard *Voyager,* Naomi Wildman, begins to play a larger role in the crew's story as she studies to become the captain's assistant.

The holodeck serves as a fun and sometimes threatening diversion in the newly recurring program *The Adventures of Captain Proton*. Easily becoming a favorite escape among the cast and the fans, the Captain Proton program brings a unique look to *Star Trek* by emulating a fictional science-fiction serial circa the 1930s. This sci-fi story within a sci-fi show brings in humorous aspects that contrast with the serious science the audience is witness to every week. It can't help but raise the question of how *Star Trek: Voyager* will be seen by viewers in the distant future.

Season five of *Star Trek: Voyager* celebrates a milestone in the life span of the series, with the filming of the one hundredth episode, "Timeless." Typically, the significant role of the hundredth episode of any series is that it signifies that the show is a viable commodity, thus worthy of a syndicated run. Although *Voyager,* being a *Star Trek* series, was practically guaranteed from the start to be syndicated, it celebrates the event with what will become one of the series' most popular episodes. With a strong story line, the episode also contains one of *Voyager's* most memorable visuals with the crash of the ship on an ice-laden planet.

Another milestone arrives in the form of the first official two-hour *Star Trek* movie event on UPN. The series had previously aired two-part episodes, such as "Future's End" and "The Killing Game," with the both episodes airing on the same night. "Dark Frontier" is the first *Star Trek: Voyager* episode edited together to feature length.

It's a whole different form of storytelling. There's a big difference between the [regular episodes and the movie-length episodes]. Our shows tend to run about forty-two minutes of program material. You write a forty-two-minute episode and it has a beginning, a middle, and an end based on that length. When you go to eighty-four or ninety minutes, you develop the story at a whole different pace. And it's a great change of pace for us. It's a lot of fun. We usually shoot these as two separate one-hour shows. As a result we will have two directors and two sets of production people, one shooting while the other one is prepping. So it becomes a challenge, both stylistically and pacing to keep the episodes similar enough that they can hopefully be seamlessly put together. They've always been a great deal of fun to do.

—RICK BERMAN

NIGHT

EPISODE #195

WRITTEN BY: BRANNON BRAGA & JOE MENOSKY

DIRECTED BY: DAVID LIVINGSTON

GUEST STARS

CONTROLLER EMCK	KEN MAGEE
NIGHT ALIEN	STEVEN DENNIS
DOCTOR CHAOTICA	MARTIN RAYNER

STARDATE 52081.2

As *Voyager* travels across a vast desolate region of space that they have named "the void" the crew faces the possibility that they are unlikely to see a star system for the next two years. With sensors picking up only high levels of theta radiation, the crew is slowly being driven insane by boredom.

The only activity that sensors read in this vast expanse is some high levels of theta radiation. With nothing to distract her mind from its deepest thoughts, Janeway retreats to her quarters, agonizing over the past decision that trapped the crew in the Delta Quadrant. Suddenly, the ship loses power and is left in total darkness. Once Kim and Tuvok get back partial power, they determine that an alien dampening field caused the drain. Meanwhile, Paris is attacked by an alien in the holodeck,

Paris and the Doctor argue over the holodeck controls. PAUL McCALLUM

but Seven manages to stun the intruder. Tuvok creates a makeshift photon flare, illuminating the region around the ship and revealing three alien ships. All but one of the alien intruders flee from *Voyager* and escape to their ships, refusing to answer hails and firing on the starship. Fortunately a larger ship arrives and forces them to retreat.

The pilot, a Malon called Emck, informs Janeway that thousands of the mysterious alien ships are ahead but he can lead *Voyager* through a spatial vortex that will take them to the other side of the expanse unharmed. In return, he wants the alien that Seven stunned, who is now in sickbay. Instead, Janeway questions the alien and learns he is dying of theta radiation poisoning. His people were living a peaceful existence in the void when the Malon began poisoning them, he explains. A course is set to take him home, and soon *Voyager* is surrounded by his vessels. As he is beamed back to his people, the alien pleads with Janeway to help them close the vortex and protect their space.

The crew realizes the Malon ship is using the void as a dumping ground for antimatter waste. Janeway offers Emck the technology to purify antimatter reactants, but he refuses to accept it, as it would put an end to his transport business. Janeway decides to close the vortex, but since it must be done from inside the void, she decides that she alone will remain in a shuttle after *Voyager* escapes. The crew refuses to allow her to sacrifice herself, and together they set a course for the vortex, hoping that the explosion necessary to close it will not destroy their ship.

They continue toward their goal, only to find the Malon freighter attempting to block their path, but the crew's new allies arrive and attack the Malon, causing the necessary distraction. *Voyager* scores a direct hit against the freighter, then enters the vortex, deploying torpedoes to seal the entrance. The resulting shockwave carries them to the other side, and the vortex is destroyed. Finally, *Voyager* emerges from the darkness into a star system teeming with light.

SENSOR READINGS: Since it will take two years to cross the void, Chakotay orders all departments to create an energy reserve, using power cells to stockpile deuterium. Torres reports that the warp core is at peak efficiency. Kim reports all systems are operating within normal parameters. ▪ To boost crew morale, Neelix suggests rotating crew assignments for a little variety and adding holo-emitters to Cargo Bay 2, turning it into a holodeck. ▪ With the power out, Seven and Paris try to reroute power from the holodeck to emergency relays, but the hologrid is frozen. Meanwhile, Torres hooks a power cell up directly to the EPS manifold to get emergency power back online.

Emck refuses to accept technology that would put him out of business. PAUL McCALLUM

▪ Tuvok reconfigures a photon torpedo to emit a sustained polyluminous burst to function as a warp flare. ▪ *Voyager*'s residual antimatter is processed in a transkinetic chamber, where it is broken down on a subatomic level. The theta-radiation from the void is absorbed by a series of radiometric converters, and the energy is recycled to power everything from life support to replicators. ▪ Tuvok uses the deflector to reinforce aft shields. ▪ Chakotay notes that the crew has gathered enough data on the Delta Quadrant to keep Starfleet scientists busy for decades.

DAMAGE REPORT: The hologrid blows out in Holodeck 1 after Paris and the Doctor fight over the controls. ▪ The aliens effect a shipwide power loss, forcing everything offline including main and auxiliary power. Independent subsystems are operational, such as environmental controls and holodecks. ▪ Under Malon attack the port nacelle ruptures and vents plasma. When the starboard nacelle is hit, both engines go offline.

SHUTTLE TRACKER: Janeway requests a class-2 shuttle armed with photon explosives be prepared for her plan to destroy the vortex. The shuttle, however, is never dispatched.

DELTA QUADRANT: An astrometric scan of the region shows no star systems within 2,500 light-years. There are heavy concentrations of theta-radiation clouding sensors, so the crew cannot see beyond the region. A spatial vortex leads directly to the other side of the expanse. ▪ Seventeen aliens board *Voyager*. They are indigenous to the starless region and therefore are extremely photosensitive, with a physiology that has evolved to allow them to survive in complete darkness. They flourished in the void for millions of years until the Malon arrived and now they all suffer from theta-radiation poisoning.

Emck, controller of a Malon export Vessel, Eleventh Gradient, fires thirteen spatial charges to drive off the night aliens; he expects to be compensated for them by Janeway. The Malon produce over six billion isotons of industrial by-product every day. Emck is the only Malon who knows of the void and he finds it to be a perfect dumping ground.

ALPHA QUADRANT: Janeway wryly notes that mutiny is still an offense punishable by hanging.

PESONAL LOGS: During Janeway's first year as commander of the *U.S.S. Billings* she sent an away team to a volcanic moon and their shuttle was damaged by a magma eruption leaving three crew members severely injured. The next day she went back to the moon, alone, to complete the mission. ▪ Tuvok uses the stars to meditate by, imagining each to represent a thought. Without actual stars, he relies on the files in astrometrics. He was with the captain on her first command. ▪ Paris has a new holoprogram based on the twentieth century *Captain Proton* space serial. Paris and Torres play *durotta,* which Paris describes as a game of subtlety. He always uses the Novokavich Gambit as his opening move because Torres always falls for it. ▪ Kim portrays Buster Kincaid in the *Captain Proton* program. He finishes writing a concerto for the clarinet called "Echoes of The Void" while on the bridge ▪ Neelix suffers from nihiliphobia, the fear of nothingness.

MEDICAL UPDATE: Paris suffers severe burns when attacked by the alien intruder.

EPISODE LOGS: At the start of the episode it has been fifty-three days since *Voyager* entered the void. ▪ After *Voyager* exits the void they are two years closer to home. ▪ The mysterious aliens go unnamed in this episode, but the shooting script refers to them as "Night Aliens." ▪ The crew will encounter another void in "The Void."

DRONE

EPISODE #196
TELEPLAY BY: **BRYAN FULLER** and **BRANNON BRAGA** & **JOE MENOSKY**
STORY BY: **BRYAN FULLER** and **HARRY DOC KLOOR**
DIRECTED BY: **LES LANDAU**

GUEST STARS	
ONE	J. PAUL BOEHMER
ENSIGN MULCHAEY	TODD BABCOCK

CO-STAR	
COMPUTER VOICE	MAJEL BARRETT

STARDATE UNKNOWN

✦ As an away team is beamed back to *Voyager,* parts of the Doctor's mobile emitter fuse together when the transporter momentarily merges the team's patterns. Torres takes the malfunctioning device to the science lab, where, unseen, the emitter sprouts Borg

Seven shows One how to regenerate. RON TOM

Janeway tries to help One understand his Borg nature. RON TOM

implants. When Ensign Mulchaey enters the lab the next morning, he is attacked by extraction tubules. Meanwhile, Seven's proximity transceiver is activated, alerting her to a Borg presence on the ship. The crew finds Mulchaey in the lab, along with a Borg maturation chamber containing a fetal drone.

Seven determines that when she and the Doctor were transported together some of her nanoprobes infected his emitter, assimilating it. The resulting technology appropriated some of Mulchaey's genetic material to create a life-form. As it continues to mature at a rapid rate, the male drone is observed to be mostly human, with many implants, including the twenty-ninth-century holoemitter as part of his central nervous system, making him the most advanced Borg in existence. His connection with the collective is dampened, and Seven attempts a neural interface to give him instructions. Instead, he tries to assimilate her knowledge.

Because a neural link is too dangerous, Seven uses Borg data nodes to feed information to the drone, who chooses One as his designation. He quickly absorbs knowledge of the ship's systems and begins expressing curiosity about the Borg. Seven fears he will be tempted

to seek out the collective and refuses to answer his questions. As One and she regenerate in their alcoves, the Borg pick up One's proximity signal and set a course to intercept *Voyager*.

When the crew detects the approaching Borg, Seven discovers that One's cranial implants created a secondary transceiver to signal them when his original device was removed. Janeway and Seven have no choice but to tell One about the collective's destructive mentality and explain that with his technology, the Borg would be even more dangerous. The captain asks him to help strengthen *Voyager*'s defenses, but One is confused, being both intrigued by and fearful of the collective.

As the Borg ship approaches, One hears the siren song of the collective, but rather than allowing himself to become part of it he chooses to save *Voyager* from destruction. One beams to the sphere to interface directly with the vessel and accesses the sphere's navigation system, steering it into a nebula, destroying it. One survives and is beamed to sickbay, but he realizes that his advanced technology will continue to make him a tempting prize for the Borg and therefore a threat to the *Voyager* crew. As the Doctor races to operate on his organic body, One erects a force field to stop any attempts to save his life, instead choosing to die so the crew can be safe.

SENSOR READINGS: Paris, Torres, Seven, and the Doctor go on an astrological survey to explore a protonebula. The away team's shuttle is caught in the gravimetric shearline of the nebula. The nebula expands at a rate of 8,000 cubic kilometers per hour. ▪ *Voyager's* science lab is on Deck 8, Section 22. ▪ The ship's construction consists of duranium hull, plasma-based power distribution, tricylic life-support systems, and artificial gravity plating. ▪ Engineering is on Deck 11, Section 32. The warp core maximum output is 4,000 terradynes per second. ▪ One helps increase the efficiency of the Bussard collectors. Later, he gives the crew the ability to remodulate the shields and enhances phasers to defend the ship against the Borg

DAMAGE REPORT: Warp drive is taken out, after the Borg invert *Voyager's* phase beam with a feedback pulse.

SHUTTLE TRACKER: A type-2 shuttle is lost when it is caught in the gravimetric shear of a protonebula. Class-2 claustrophobia is how Starfleet cadets used to refer to the shuttles, as they were fast and maneuverable, but not built for comfort. Academy professors used to shoehorn half a dozen cadets into one of them for weeks at a time.

DELTA QUADRANT: Borg nanoprobes are encoded to utilize any technology they encounter. ▪ One's maturation rate is twenty-five times that of a conventional Borg. The Borg fourth phase of gestation is equal, in human terms, to a child of six. One's body is composed of polydutonic alloy like the Doctor's mobile emitter. The mobile emitter is embedded in his cerebral cortex and adapted to function as part of his nervous system controlling all autonomic functions. His body contains connective armor, multidimensional adaptability, and internal transporter nodes. ▪ The Borg sphere is a long-range tactical vessel with transwarp capability and ablative hull armor.

PERSONAL LOGS: The Doctor brings a holoimaging device to take "snapshots" of the protonebula. This is the first time he is seen partaking in this hobby although in "Latent Image" it will be noted that he has been actively pursuing it for a while. His mobile emitter will be returned to him. ▪ Seven practices smiling.

EPISODE LOGS: When the away team complains of the poor design of the class-2 shuttle, Seven suggests designing a new shuttle, which Torres believes to be a good idea. This paves the way for the construction of the *Delta Flyer.* ▪ The airponics bay is still in use, but it is unclear who tends the garden. ▪ Janeway and Seven show One files of a Borg attack.

EXTREME RISK

EPISODE #197

WRITTEN BY: KENNETH BILLER

DIRECTED BY: CLIFF BOLE

GUEST STARS

CONTROLLER VRELK	**HAMILTON CAMP**
VORIK	**ALEXANDER ENBERG**

CO-STARS

PILOT	**DANIEL BETANCES**
COMPUTER VOICE	**MAJEL BARRETT**

STARDATE UNKNOWN

When a Malon ship tries to steal *Voyager's* new multispatial probe, Janeway orders that it be steered into a gas giant. Despite warnings, the Malon ship follows the probe and implodes due to the intense atmospheric pressure. Knowing *Voyager* cannot risk entering the gas giant, Paris shares his design for a new technologically advanced shuttle named the *Delta Flyer.* Believing that the shuttle could withstand the giant's atmosphere, Janeway gives him permission to work with the rest of the crew to build it. Meanwhile, Torres begins pulling away from the other members of the crew as she plays out deadly situations on the holodeck with the safety protocols off.

Another Malon ship hails *Voyager,* and its captain, Vrelk, tells Janeway his ship is going to retrieve the probe, and that *Voyager* should stand down. She ignores his threats until Seven of Nine, using coherent neutrino beams to spy on the Malon vessel, discovers they are building a shuttle of their own that can also withstand the atmosphere. Since it appears that the Malon shuttle will be operational before the *Voyager* crew finishes their shuttle, Janeway orders the team to work faster.

When Torres runs a shuttle simulation in the holodeck to check for a fatal flaw, she once again disengages the safety protocols. The simulated atmosphere of

Paris utilized his skills as a pilot in designing the new shuttle, the *Delta Flyer*. DANNY FELD

gets stuck in a deep layer of liquid hydrogen and methane about ten kilometers below the outer atmosphere of a class-6 gas giant where its Borg shielding keeps it from being crushed. ▪ Torres uses an EPS relay and a phaser to create a makeshift forcefield.

SHUTTLE TRACKER: Paris's preliminary design for the *Delta Flyer* includes ultra-aerodynamic contours, retractable nacelles, parametallic hull plating, and unimatrix shielding (based on Tuvok's design for the multispatial probe), and a Borg-inspired weapons system including photonic missiles. Kim suggests using isomagnetic EPS conduits in the plasma manifold to maximize power distribution. Torres designs a hull with titanium alloys, however, Seven suggests tetraburnium alloys instead. Kim later suggests reinforcing the hull with kellinite, though Tuvok claims the idea is flawed. Paris designs a panel with knobs and levers like those in his Captain Proton program.

the gas giant begins to cause microfractures in the shuttle, and Torres is knocked unconscious. Just before the hull breaches, Chakotay arrives, freezing the program.

Once Torres is taken to sickbay, the Doctor finds numerous old wounds that went untreated. Chakotay learns she has been running holosimulations with the safety protocols off. When confronted, Torres admits she has been testing herself, trying to experience emotion or feel pain. Ever since Chakotay told her of the message he received from his friend Sveta telling them their Maquis friends had been slaughtered, Torres has felt numb, but nothing more. She has been trying to see if she could still feel something. Suddenly, the Malon fire on *Voyager* to create a distraction as they launch their new shuttle.

Janeway is forced to launch the *Delta Flyer* ahead of schedule in an attempt to retrieve the probe first. Torres persuades Chakotay to let her accompany the away team. When the Malon fire charges at them, Seven's torpedo scores a direct hit, forcing them to retreat. Once Kim locks on a tractor beam to the probe, the shuttle begins losing structural integrity. Just as the hull breaches, Torres creates an ingenious device to trap the incoming gas in a containment field. The *Delta Flyer* returns to *Voyager* safely, and Torres is on her way to feeling whole again.

SENSOR READINGS: When the Malon vessel tries to take *Voyager*'s probe, Tuvok instructs the device to emit a polaron burst to disrupt their tractor beam. The probe

Despite the computer's warnings, Torres disengages the holodeck's safety overrides as she prepares for an extremely risky orbital high-dive. DANNY FELD

PERSONAL LOGS: Former Maquis friends of Torres and Chakotay include Li-Paz, Meyer, Nelson, and Sahreen. Torres's grandmother used to make her banana pancakes when she was a child because it always put a smile on her face. Torres says she was six when her father walked out. She was kicked out of Starfleet Academy when she was nineteen. ▪ Neelix continues to undergo security training.

MEDICAL UPDATE: The Doctor finds evidence of internal bleeding, fractured vertebrae, contusions, and cranial trauma that are weeks and months old. Torres had been treating herself. The Doctor believes that she is suffering from clinical depression.

EPISODE LOGS: After Chakotay received the letter informing him of the state of the Maquis ("Hunters"). Torres began running her dangerous simulations, though none were seen previous to this episode.

An imposter Boothby interrupts Chakotay's scans of the simulated environment. RON TOM

IN THE FLESH

EPISODE #198
WRITTEN BY: NICK SAGAN
DIRECTED BY: DAVID LIVINGSTON

GUEST STARS

VALERIE ARCHER	KATE VERNON
DAVID GENTRY	ZACH GALLIGAN
ADMIRAL BULLOCK	TUCKER SMALLWOOD

SPECIAL GUEST STAR

BOOTHBY	RAY WALSTON

STARDATE 52136.4

Conducting a surveillance mission of an alien structure, Chakotay seems to find himself on Earth at Starfleet Headquarters surrounded by aliens posing as humans. In a re-creation of the Starfleet Officer's Club he strikes up a conversation with a woman named Valerie Archer. Later, when Chakotay and Tuvok are on their way back to the *Delta Flyer,* an alien ensign tries to detain them because they are in a restricted area. Unwilling to risk blowing their cover, they take him back with them to *Voyager.*

When Janeway questions the ensign, he releases a toxin into his bloodstream, killing himself. Upon further study, the Doctor triggers a genetic reversion, and the body turns into a member of Species 8472. Seven's analysis of the alien structure shows they are using a combination of holographic projection and particle synthesis to re-create Earth and Starfleet Headquarters. The crew surmises it is being used as a training ground for invasion of the Alpha Quadrant.

As Seven works to arm *Voyager* with nanoprobes, Chakotay, Paris, and Kim take the *Delta Flyer* back to the Earth simulation so Chakotay can keep a planned date with Archer. He hopes to find out more about the presumed mission against the Federation. After Chakotay leaves her quarters, Archer analyzes a DNA sample and discovers that he is human. Once security is alerted, Chakotay is taken into custody. When Paris and Kim notify Janeway that they have lost contact with Chakotay, she sets a course to rendezvous with the *Flyer* at the alien structure. After the captain threatens the habitat leader—who is modified to appear as the Starfleet groundskeeper Boothby—with Borg nanoprobes, he agrees to a meeting.

With both sides gathered to discuss their differences, Janeway and "Boothby" find there is room for negotiation. Judging from *Voyager's* teaming with the Borg against them, Species 8472 believed humans were hostile and planning an invasion of fluidic space. When Janeway explains that the *Voyager* crew did not know at the time that the Borg had started the war with their species, Archer reveals that their Earth simulation is only preparation for a reconnaissance mission. Feeling she can trust Chakotay because of their growing bond, Archer admits that they feared humans as much as the *Voyager* crew feared them. After agreeing to share technology as a first step toward peace, Species 8472 returns to fluidic space, and *Voyager* continues on its journey home.

SENSOR READINGS: Kim enhances a tricorder with a transoptic datalink to help access some of the alien systems and arms a type-1 phaser with Borg nanoprobes. ■ Seven makes Borg modifications to nineteen standard photon torpedoes and three class-10 torpedoes armed with high yield explosives.

DELTA QUADRANT: Among the things Archer lists as bothering her as a human are breathing oxygen, bipedal locomotion, and sleeping. The Doctor uses a cytokinetic injection to trigger a genetic reversion to reveal the true form of Species 8472. ■ They use a combination of holographic projection and particle synthesis to create the Earthlike environment. There are thirteen thermionic generators beneath the city, but Seven cannot identify the energy signatures. The habitat is heavily fortified and well prepared to defend against attack. "Boothby" claims there are a dozen more simulations throughout the quadrant.

"Boothby" offers to let the crew stay and visit the Earth simulation. RON TOM

Their mission is to infiltrate Earth, place operatives in the highest levels of Starfleet, and monitor military installations as a reconnaissance mission. ■ Janeway notes that Species 8472 killed four million Borg drones.

ALPHA QUADRANT: Departments at Starfleet Headquarters include Federation Council, Orbital Flight Control, Logistical Support, Astrophysics, Starfleet Medical complex. The officer's club is known as "The Quantum Café." ■ Boothby mentions the *U.S.S. Intrepid* as currently patrolling the neutral zone. ■ Directive 010 notes that "Before engaging alien species in battle any and all attempts to make first contact, and achieve nonmilitary resolution, must be made." ■ In Earth's third world war

STARFLEET ACADEMY

"Ex Astris, Scientia"
"From the Stars, Knowledge" Starfleet Academy Motto

Starfleet Academy trains the best and the brightest to become officers in Starfleet. Prospective students can be sponsored by some ranking member of the Federation, usually a starship captain—as in the case of Captain Sulu's sponsoring Chakotay for admission ("Tattoo")—before taking the difficult entrance exam. Once accepted into Starfleet Academy, cadets undergo rigorous preparation before receiving their duty assignments. Of the Voyager senior staff, whether they be Starfleet or Maquis, their early training molded them into the officers they have become.

BIOCHEMISTRY: *Citing Paris's two semesters of biochemistry at Starfleet Academy, Janeway assigns him to study as a field medic under the EMH. ("Parallax")*

QUANTUM CHEMISTRY: *Kim's Starfleet Academy roommate, James Mooney MacAllister, helped him through this fourth-year course. ("The Cloud")*

STELLAR CARTOGRAPHY: *Paris almost failed this course after being dumped by his first love, Susie Crabtree. ("Lifesigns")*

TEMPORAL MECHANICS: *Chakotay failed this Starfleet Academy course, taught by Professor Vasbinder. ("Year of Hell, Part II")*

BOTANICAL SCIENCE: *Torres took a botanical science class at Starfleet Academy ("Tuvix")*

ASTRO THEORY 101: *Torres remembers dodging a few punches in the lab at Starfleet Academy. Chakotay jokes that only she could start a brawl in Astro Theory 101. ("Future's End, Part II")*

KLINGON PHYSIOLOGY: *A Klingon physiology course was taught by visiting professor H'ohk. Janeway recalls that he demanded nothing less than perfection. ("Darkling")*

EXO-GENETICS: *Janeway took this class in her senior year. The only question she got wrong—preventing her from getting an A—dealt with nucleotide resonance frequency. ("The Fight")*

ADVANCED SUBSPACE GEOMETRY: *The one course at Starfleet Academy where Paris claimed to actually pay attention. ("Vis a Vis")*

FRACTAL CALCULUS: *Class taught by Admiral Patterson that Janeway attended. ("Relativity")*

RON TOM

nuclear weapons accounted for six hundred million casualties. ▪ The real Boothby has been tending the Academy grounds for fifty-four years and is the head groundskeeper. Archer notes that half the captains in Starfleet would not be where they are today if it weren't for Boothby and names Lopez, Picard, and Richardson. ▪ A Klingon martini is made of vermouth, gin, and a dash of bloodwine. ▪ Archer reads *A Cave Beyond Logic: Vulcan Perspectives on Platonic Thought* and has a replicated twenty-first century edition of Hesterman's *Beyond the Galactic Edge: Humanity's Quest for Infinity.* ▪ Archer mentions that it is *Pon farr* night at the Vulcan club. ▪ Janeway suggests a "nice Japanese replimat on the Embarcadero" for Chakotay's date. Later she asks about "a little coffee shop on Market Street called The Night Owl." Neither was seen in the simulation.

STARFLEET HISTORY: *Kim learned about the era of Kirk and Spock. ("Flashback")*

INTERSTELLAR HISTORY: *Torres nearly failed this course. ("Year of Hell, Part I")*

TURN OF THE MILLENNIUM TECHNOLOGY: *Janeway never learned to type, since this was not a required course at the Academy. ("Future's End, Part I")*

ANTHROPOLOGY: *Chakotay imagines himself being offered a position teaching this class while under the mental control of an alien being. ("Bliss")*

DIPLOMACY: *Janeway's diplomacy professor used to say that the opening twenty minutes of a first contact situation are the most crucial. ("Innocence")*

TACTICAL ANALYSIS: *A class taught by Admiral Nimembeh. ("In the Flesh")*

INTERSPECIES ETHICS: *A class at the Academy that is not taught by Admiral Nimembeh. ("In the Flesh")*

INTERSPECIES PROTOCOL: *A required class, dealing with the proper way to handle oneself in interspecies affairs. ("The Disease")*

SHUTTLE PILOTING: *Chakotay trained as a pilot in North America in his first year at Starfleet Academy, then went to Venus for a couple of months to learn how to handle atmospheric storms, followed by a semester in the Sol system asteroid belt. ("Future's End, Part II")*

ZERO-G TRAINING: *This occurs during the first year at the Academy. Janeway participated in training for zero-g in the Coral Sea. ("Good Shepard")*

SPACE WALKS: *Cadets experience simulated space walks during their first two years at the Academy. In year three a six-week course of actual space walks is required so cadets get used to them. Torres left the Academy before her third year and never experienced real space walks. ("Day of Honor")*

PHYSICAL TRAINING: *Paris attended the Starfleet Academy base outside Marseilles for his physical training and spent most of his second semester at Sandrine's. ("The Cloud")*

TRACK AND FIELD: *Torres was on the Starfleet Academy decathlon team. The track-and-field coach was furious with her when she dropped out. ("Basics, Part II")*

VELOCITY: *Kim was captain of the Academy's velocity team. ("The Disease")*

SURVIVAL STRATEGIES: *Paris got a B-minus in this Academy class. His father, Admiral Paris, taught the class. Chakotay refers to survival classes at Starfleet Academy consisting of surprise tactical simulations where cadets are dropped off in the woods with no chance to prepare. ("Parturition" and "Displaced")*

STUDY ABROAD: *While still in the Delta Quadrant, Icheb decides that he would like to take the Starfleet Academy entrance exam and work to become a member of Starfleet with the help of the Voyager crew. His studies include: Warp Mechanics ("Lineage"), Earth Literature ("Human Error"), and Early Starfleet History ("Q2").*

PERSONAL LOGS: When Janeway was a cadet, Boothby used to give her fresh roses for her quarters. The last time Janeway was at Starfleet Headquarters was when she as captain was given her orders for *Voyager's* first mission to proceed to the Badlands and find the Maquis. ▪ The last time Chakotay was at Starfleet Headquarters was on March 3, 2368—the day he resigned his commission to Admiral Nimembeh. A transporter malfunction once caused his uniform to remain in the pattern buffer, leaving only his combadge to cover him. His Starfleet service number was 47-Alpha-612.

EPISODE LOGS: Seven of Nine wears a newly created blue outfit. ▪ Boothby was first seen on the *TNG* episode "The First Duty." Chakotay will see a hallucination of him in "The Fight."

ONCE UPON A TIME

EPISODE #199

WRITTEN BY: MICHAEL TAYLOR

DIRECTED BY: JOHN KRETCHMER

GUEST STARS

TREVIS — JUSTIN LOUIS

ENSIGN WILDMAN — NANCY HOWER

NAOMI WILDMAN — SCARLETT POMERS

SPECIAL GUEST STAR

FLOTTER — WALLACE LANGHAM

CO-STAR

COMPUTER VOICE — MAJEL BARRETT

STARDATE UNKNOWN

While Paris, Tuvok, and Ensign Wildman are on an away mission on the *Delta Flyer,* they run into an ion storm, and their shuttle suffers severe damage. *Voyager* tracks their distress call to a nearby planetary system, but another storm blocks their path. As

Naomi finds out the truth about her mother's delay in returning to the ship. RON TOM

the crew prepares to go after the team, Neelix takes charge of his goddaughter, Naomi Wildman, keeping her occupied and unaware of her mother's predicament. After Paris finally crash lands the shuttle onto a planetoid burying it three kilometers under the rock surface, Wildman is seriously injured, requiring surgery. Back on *Voyager,* Kim tracks the *Delta Flyer's* coordinates on the planetoid. Though there are no lifesigns, rescue teams are dispatched to the crater in search of the lost crew. Naomi is worried when her mother does not call, but Neelix tries to distract her with her favorite holodeck tales set in Forest of Forever. The classic children's tales, known collectively as *The Adventures of Flotter,* follow a character made of water as he has exploits that explain science. The stories, however, do not keep Naomi's attention for long.

The prospect of telling Naomi that her mother is lost brings back somber memories for Neelix of losing his own family. Although Janeway urges him to be honest with the little girl, he wants to wait until the away team finds the shuttle. When Naomi wakes up in the middle of the night and goes to the bridge in search of Neelix, she overhears talk of the crash and the lost crew. Neelix follows Naomi to the holoprogram and tries to comfort her about her mother's situation. He finally tells her about losing his own parents and sisters when he was very young. Together, they find the strength to cope with the concept of loss.

As their life support system begins to fail, Paris, Tuvok, and Wildman record good-bye messages to their loved ones. Above them, Chakotay and Seven locate the shuttle buried underneath the rock. A massive digging effort begins, but an ion storm is approaching, and they do not have much time before it hits.

With two minutes left until their oxygen is depleted, the *Delta Flyer* crew hears the rescue team digging above them. Kim is able to get a transporter lock on the shuttle, and it is transported to *Voyager* just before the storm hits. Once Wildman's injuries are treated in sickbay, she and Naomi are reunited, and mother and daughter pay a visit to the fairy-tale world together.

SENSOR READINGS: *Voyager* travels through a level-5 ion storm to retrieve the away team. ▪ Neelix has a half dozen medkits stockpiled in Cargo Bay 2. ▪ The holodeck is on Deck 6, Section 9. ▪ Phaser drills are kept in Cargo Bay 3.

SHUTTLE TRACKER: The *Delta Flyer* runs into an ion storm that knocks out impulse power and damages primary systems leaving life support failing. Starboard thrusters go down as the ship crash-lands on a class-M

Naomi retreats to her holographic fairy tale. DANNY FELD

in *The Adventures of Flotter* are "Flotter and the Tree Monster," "Trevis and the Terribly Twisted Trunk," and "Trevis and the Ogre of Fire." The characters live in the Forest of Forever. Janeway and Kim remember them as classics from their own childhoods.

PERSONAL LOGS: Tuvok's youngest child is female. ▪ The Doctor has been giving Naomi botany lessons. ▪ As a child Neelix claimed to have explored the forest behind his house with his sisters every day. He addresses his personal logs to his deceased sister Alixia.

When Naomi comments that she would like to contribute to the ship, Neelix suggests that she may want to consider training as captain's assistant. She is afraid of Seven of Nine, but they will later become friends.

EPISODE LOGS: Neelix suggests to Naomi that they can use help in airponics, indicating that the bay is still in use and manned by more than one crewman. ▪ Naomi's studies to become captain's assistant will continue throughout the series.

NOTHING HUMAN

EPISODE #200
WRITTEN BY: JERI TAYLOR
DIRECTED BY: DAVID LIVINGSTON

GUEST STARS

CRELL MOSET	DAVID CLENNON
TABOR	JAD MAGER

CO-STARS

ALIEN VOICE	FRANK WELKER
COMPUTER VOICE	MAJEL BARRETT

STARDATE UNKNOWN

When *Voyager* encounters a massive energy wave, the ship receives a download of indecipherable information. The crew tracks the wave's ion trail and finds a stranded vessel with a wounded alien onboard. After the creature is beamed to sickbay, it attacks Torres, puncturing her neck and secreting paralyzing fluids into her bloodstream. Unaware of how to extract the creature without harming Torres, the Doctor and Kim create a hologram of the Cardassian exobiologist Crell Moset.

In order to crack the coded message downloaded to

planet with a nickel-iron core and a bemonite mantle. It is buried three kilometers beneath the surface in a cavern flooded with fluorine gas. Rather than abandoning the shuttle, it is transported to the shuttlebay battered, but intact.

ALPHA QUADRANT: Starfleet Regulation 476-9 states, "All away teams must report to the bridge at least once every twenty-four hours" ▪ Some of the chapter headings

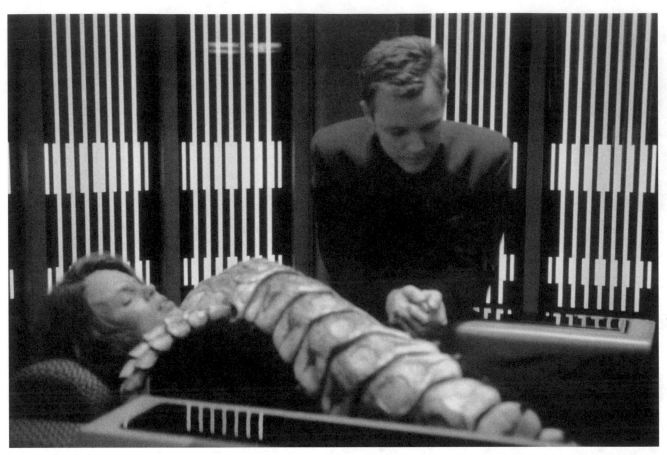

Paris sits vigil by an unconscious Torres. MICHAEL YARISH

Voyager, Seven of Nine attempts to access the alien databanks, causing the vessel to destabilize and explode. Meanwhile, the Doctor and Moset determine the alien is using Torres as a life preserver by co-opting her vital systems. They re-create Moset's laboratory in a holodeck so he can use his advanced tools to help Torres, but, now conscious, she objects to putting her life in the hands of a Cardassian.

Unable to decipher the message, Janeway retransmits the signal on all subspace bands, hoping more of the species will answer the call. In Moset's laboratory, he and the Doctor operate on a hologram of the alien and find nodes suggesting the creature is a highly intelligent being. Moset decides they are the best place to administer a neurostatic shock, which will incapacitate the alien and probably kill it. Later, the Doctor is shocked when a Bajoran crewman, Tabor, reacts violently to even a holographic Moset's presence on *Voyager,* calling the Cardassian a mass murderer.

Tabor reveals that during the Bajoran Occupation, Moset used live subjects for his medical experiments and killed hundreds of Bajorans. Although barely hanging on to life, Torres refuses to let Moset treat her, believing if she

benefits from his research, she will be validating his atrocious methods. However, the Doctor cannot remove the alien without Moset's help, and Torres will die otherwise. Against many moral objections, Janeway authorizes the Doctor and Moset to perform the procedure.

As the pair work to extract the creature, *Voyager* is hailed by another alien vessel that locks them in a tractor beam, but Janeway senses they only want their friend back and mean no harm. In surgery, the Doctor overrides Moset's decision to kill the alien and instead administers a neural shock that weakens its motor control without permanent damage. As its tendrils withdraw from Torres, its metabolism is restored and it is beamed to the waiting ship. Left on his own to make a tough decision, the Doctor decides to delete Moset's program from *Voyager*'s database.

SENSOR READINGS: Kim merges an extensive database on exobiology with an interactive holographic matrix to create consulting doctor, Crell Moset.

DAMAGE REPORT: There is minor damage to the hull plating on Deck 15. Later, the alien ship uses a tractor beam to drain power from *Voyager.*

Initially the Doctor enjoyed working with the Moset hologram. DANNY FELD

DELTA QUADRANT: The controls on the alien vessel can only be activated chemically, meaning the life-form interfaces directly with its ship's systems. ▪ Moset believes if they induce a neurostatic shock in one of the alien's many nodes clustered along the primary nerve, it will travel to the others causing it to lose motor function, possibly killing the alien in the process. He uses a cortical probe to stimulate the primary neural pathways by applying it to the primary neocortex. Even though the synapses are degenerating, Moset tells the Doctor to increase pulse frequency. Instead, the Doctor applies the pulse to a secondary neocortex, lowering the frequency and getting the creature to release itself from Torres. They try to substitute the metabolic energy it was taking from Torres with 60 milligrams of stenophyl.

ALPHA QUADRANT: Dr. Crell Moset is chairman of exobiology at the University of Culat and winner of the Cardassian Legate's Crest of Valor. He killed Crewman Tabor's brother and grandfather and thousands of others during the occupation of Bajor by performing experiments on living people. He exposed Tabor's grandfather's internal organs to nadion radiation, causing his protract-

ed death. Moset blinded people so he could see how they adapted and exposed them to polytrinic acid to see how long it would take for their skin to heal. He cured the fostossa virus by infecting hundreds of Bajorans with it.

PERSONAL LOGS: On a previous mission to Lav'oti V with the Doctor, Paris fell into the fetid mud pits of Palomar. ▪ Torres uses an ancient Klingon remedy mixture of incense as a mental relaxant and an expeller of demons. ▪ The Doctor has been holding showings of the slides taken from his new hobby, holoimaging. His matrix is not large enough to hold all medical knowledge, hence the need for a consultant.

Crewman Tabor attempts to resign his commission in protest of Moset's presence but Chakotay refuses to accept it.

MEDICAL UPDATE: The creature latches onto Torres, compromising her heart and lungs and causing her kidneys to fail. Later, when she goes into cytotoxic shock, the Doctor uses 2 cc's of inaprovaline to stabilize her.

TIMELESS

EPISODE #201

TELEPLAY BY: BRANNON BRAGA & JOE MENOSKY

STORY BY: RICK BERMAN & BRANNON BRAGA
& JOE MENOSKY

DIRECTED BY: LeVAR BURTON

GUEST STAR

TESSA	CHRISTINE HARNOS

SPECIAL APPEARANCE BY

CAPTAIN GEORDI LA FORGE	LeVAR BURTON

CO-STAR

COMPUTER VOICE	MAJEL BARRETT

STARDATE 52143.6

Fifteen years in the future, Chakotay and Kim beam down to a planet where they find *Voyager* entombed in ice. Once they have beamed inside the vessel, Chakotay finds the body of Seven of Nine and tells Tessa, the pilot of his shuttle to transport it aboard. Kim uses Starfleet technology to access *Voyager*'s computer and activate the Doctor's program. When the hologram demands to know what is happening, Chakotay tells him they have come to change history.

Fifteen years ago, the crew is celebrating the completion of *Voyager*'s quantum slipstream drive. They intend to set a course for the Alpha Quadrant using the technology adapted from Arturis's ship, the *Dauntless*. However, Paris finds a phase variance in the threshold that causes the slipstream to become unstable. Kim volunteers to take the *Delta Flyer* into the slipstream a few seconds ahead of *Voyager* so he can map it and send the phase variations back to the ship allowing the crew to make corrections. Janeway agrees and assigns Chakotay to fly with Kim.

Tragically Kim transferred the wrong variance, forcing Janeway to make an emergency landing that killed the crew on impact. Kim and Chakotay made it back to Earth, but when Starfleet eventually gave up its search for *Voyager,* the pair decided they had to find a way to correct their mistake. Using a stolen Borg temporal transmitter and the *Delta Flyer,* they intend to use Seven's Borg interplexing beacon to send a new set of phase corrections back in time to the crew. But just as Chakotay downloads *Voyager*'s sensor logs, a Starfleet vessel arrives in search of the thieves.

The captain of the *U.S.S. Challenger,* Geordi La Forge,

hails Chakotay and tries to talk him out of altering the timeline, but Kim and the Doctor continue to work feverishly on Seven's Borg implant. Once the Doctor pinpoints her time of death, they use the temporal transmitter to send the phase corrections four minutes prior to *Voyager*'s crash. Seven receives and inputs them, but the slipstream continues to collapse. Just outside the Alpha Quadrant, *Voyager* crashes onto the ice planet.

When Kim realizes his new phase corrections did not work, he does not have time to find his mistake. Tessa

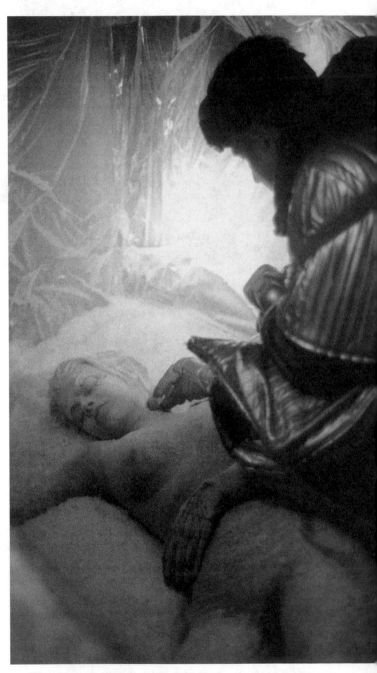

Kim prepares Seven's frozen body for transport. MICHAEL YARISH

disengages the *Delta Flyer* from the *Challenger*'s tractor beam, but the shuttle's warp core begins to breach. With only seconds to spare, Kim transmits a phase correction to Seven that will disperse the slipstream entirely—then the *Delta Flyer* explodes. On *Voyager,* both the ship and shuttle are thrown out of the slipstream, effectively erasing the future.

SENSOR READINGS: The construction of the slipstream drive includes a quantum matrix, benamite crystals, and Borg technology. The benamite crystals at the heart of the engine have already started to decay before they even enact the drive. Kim notes that it could take years to synthesize more. Paris finds a .42 phase variance in the slipstream threshold. The problem comes about seventeen seconds into the flight and renders the slipstream unstable. ▪ *Voyager* crashes on a class-L planet in the Takara sector, just outside the Alpha Quadrant. ▪ One of Seven's cranial implants is a transceiver, known as an interplexing beacon, designed to communicate with drones. The Doctor extracts the beacon and discovers its translink frequency, allowing him to send the signal to Seven. To determine *when* to send the signal, he accesses her chronometric node to pinpoint the exact moment her cybernetic implants disengaged from her organic systems (the moment of death). Seven's translink frequency is 108.44236000. Her moment of death was Stardate 52164.3, Borg time index 9.43852. Harry and Chakotay use the stolen salvage component 36698, a Borg temporal transmitter found in the wreckage of a Borg cube in the Beta Quadrant to contact Seven.

SHUTTLE TRACKER: Harry and Chakotay take the *Delta Flyer* to the Alpha Quadrant and, in the future, steal it out of a Federation shipyard. As a result of the thefts and their activity they are wanted on two counts of high treason and conspiracy to violate the Temporal Prime Directive. In the future, the *Flyer* will experience a warp core breach and be destroyed.

PERSONAL LOGS: Janeway prepares a dish her grandmother used to make, called vegetable biryani. ▪ The future Kim manages to send a message of encouragement through to his younger self. Only Kim and Janeway are

The Doctor agrees to help alter the timeline and save *Voyager.* DANNY FELD

aware of the contents of the recording. ▪ Neelix donates a stuffed Talaxian furfly for the slipstream drive effort. It is an old spacefaring tradition among his people that if one of those creatures stowed away on a ship it was a sign of good fortune. He had one preserved and it hung in his engine room for six years. ▪ Seven feels drunk with a blood-synthehol level of .05% from one glass of champagne. The Doctor gives her some inaprovaline to counteract the effect.

EPISODE LOGS: The quantum slipstream drive was introduced to the *Voyager* crew by Arturis ("Hope and Fear"). ▪ At the ceremony christening the quantum slipstream drive, Janeway notes that the crew has been in the Delta Quadrant precisely four years, two months, and eleven days. ▪ When *Voyager* exits the slipstream, they are ten years closer to home. ▪ This marks the celebratory one-hundredth episode of the series (counting "Caretaker, Parts I&II" as one episode).

"Thanks, but the real Earth is a long way from here. I'd like to get back on the road."

Kathryn Janeway, "In the Flesh"

As offscreen rumors circulated about *Voyager* getting home during the fifth season, onscreen the crew continues to have brief glimpses of the Alpha Quadrant. As in previous seasons, the holodeck provides many chances to reminisce, beginning with the first episode of the season, "Night" and the newest holographic program, *The Adventures of Captain Proton*. Paris's new creation, Captain Proton, Spaceman First Class, is based on the fictional early twentieth-century hero of a serialized motion picture adventure series. Paris would contend that the program is beneficial for historical research, but can never really hide the fact that he is just having fun. The program is seen only three times during the fifth season, but it will continue to be mentioned (and seen one last time) through the seventh season. After "Night," Captain Proton makes a brief appearance in "Thirty Days," and then returns for "Bride of Chaotica!"

"The holodeck has always been a great deal of fun for us. It's our ability to substitute for going back to Earth. I think some of the stories have served us better than others. Sandrine's was terrific, and obviously the Captain Proton episodes were just great fun . . . It's always difficult trying to come up with specific programs that could last more than two or three episodes. Tom Paris being the big twentieth-century maven gave us a lot of fodder to create some of the holodeck programs."

—Rick Berman

The holodeck is used for more serious purposes in "Extreme Risk" when Torres programs numerous dangerous scenarios to test her breaking point after she learns of the eradication of the Maquis back in the Alpha Quadrant. Most notably, she re-creates her idea of the massacre in which many of her friends died, but it is only when Chakotay forces her to live out those events on the holodeck that she truly begins to heal.

Shortly after, the holodeck again plays an integral role in Torres's life in "Nothing Human," when an alien being attacks her and unintentionally places her life in jeopardy. The Doctor is forced to expand on his programming by consulting another holographic physician in the form of the Cardassian Crell Moset. Old feelings against Cardassians are stirred among some of the crew, and especially toward the hologram of the murderous Moset.

Somewhere between the light and the serious come two additional stops in the holodeck this season. The fairy tale world of Flotter provides a make-believe forest in which characters teach children about the science of the world around them. In "Once Upon a Time," this fantastical setting serves as a backdrop for a story of Neelix helping Naomi come to terms with the fact that her mother is missing. Later, in "Someone to Watch Over Me," Chez Sandrine is seen once again, as the Doctor's lessons on dating rituals for Seven of Nine serve as a prelude to the hologram's growing feelings for the former Borg.

Aliens also use images of the Alpha Quadrant in several different ways during season five. Species 8472 returns, preparing to infiltrate Earth in order to determine whether Starfleet is planning an invasion of their fluidic space. In a highly advanced holographic Starfleet Academy, the alien race is able to morph into the humanoid forms of Starfleet officers and the ever-present groundskeeper, Boothby. After an understanding is reached the *Voyager* crew is allowed to explore the alien re-creation, which only serves as a reminder of what is waiting for them back at home.

On opposite ends of the spectrum, two different species inhabit the crew's minds and use familiar images in an effort to warn them or trap them. In "The Fight," Chakotay's hallucinations are created as a means of alien communication. Among the images the first officer sees is a character from his boxing training holodeck program, who happens to be Boothby. Later, images of home are used to lure the crew into the belly of a beast in "Bliss."

DANNY FELD

Seven's own mind also works against her as previously assimilated personalities, including several from Alpha Quadrant inhabitants, surface in "Infinite Regress." Later, in "Dark Frontier," she remembers back to when she and her parents left the Alpha Quadrant while following the Borg (and she comes face-to-face with her assimilated father). Tuvok's memories of the Alpha Quadrant resurface as he recalls his time spent with a Vulcan master in "Gravity." His flashbacks to the period in which he learned to purge all emotion coincide with his current emerging feelings for the alien female, Noss.

Memory also comes into play in the episode "11:59," as Janeway recounts the story of her ancestor, Shannon O'Donnel. Though Janeway's interpretation of the facts are somewhat skewed following centuries of passing the tale, viewers get the opportunity to witness first hand the events unfolding around the development of Earth's millennium gate. In the end, Janeway may not learn the truth of her ancestor, but she does receive a memento after a search of the database reveals a photo of O'Donnel and her family.

Actual visits to the Alpha Quadrant in season five are limited to stories outside of the current timeframe. In "Timeless," it is fifteen years in the future when the older and hardened Chakotay and Kim go against the Temporal Prime Directive to rescue their former crew, who had crashed years earlier in the Tankara sector, just outside the Alpha Quadrant. Former Enterprise officer, and now captain of the Starship Challenger, Geordi La Forge tracks the rogue officers and attempts to derail their plan. Meanwhile "Relativity" finds twenty-ninth-century Starfleet officers enlisting both Seven of Nine and Janeway in an attempt to thwart temporal sabotage on Voyager. Both Janeway and Seven visit the future Alpha Quadrant Timeship Relativity, and the former drone also goes back in time to Janeway's first day on the Starship Voyager to stop the saboteur.

Finally, the crew discovers that they are not alone in the Delta Quadrant when they come across the crew of the U.S.S. Equinox, who were brought there by the same Caretaker who pulled Voyager thousands of light-years from home. The Equinox crew, however, serves to exemplify what could have happened if Janeway's crew had ignored their Starfleet ideals.

THIRTY DAYS

EPISODE #202
TELEPLAY BY: KENNETH BILLER
STORY BY: SCOTT MILLER
DIRECTED BY: WINRICH KOLBE

GUEST STARS

RIGA	WILLIE GARSON
BURKUS	BENJAMIN LIVINGSTON
JENNY DELANEY	ALISSA KRAMER
MEGAN DELANEY	HEIDI KRAMER

CO-STARS

ADMIRAL PARIS	WARREN MUNSON
COMPUTER VOICE	MAJEL BARRETT

STARDATE 52179.4

Confined to thirty days in the brig, Paris begins to compose a letter to his father explaining how he got there. He recalls the day *Voyager's* sensors detected a contained ocean in space which resembles a planet in shape. Initially attacked, Janeway informs the Monean deputy consul, Burkus, that her ship means no harm to his people, but they are interested in exploring his strange "world." Intrigued by the offer to tour *Voyager,* Burkus and a scientist named Riga are beamed aboard. They explain that their people live underwater, farming sea vegetation and extracting oxygen for their ships. After learning that the water world is losing containment. Paris requests permission to take the *Delta Flyer* deep into the ocean, to investigate the gravitational currents.

After researching the Moneans' predicament, Janeway tells Burkus the ocean will suffer a complete loss of containment in less than five years. Meanwhile, beneath the ocean's surface, the shuttle crew encounters an ancient field reactor controlled by a computer core. As they upload information from it, an enormous marine creature attacks the *Delta Flyer* by discharging an electrical current. It retreats when hit by a phaser, but the shuttle has already been breached, and water begins pouring into the cabin.

Once the leak is repaired, the shuttle crew determines the reactor core is unstable, so Paris initiates a power transfer as a temporary solution. Reviewing the uploaded information, he finds the ocean was once part

The away team is awarded the Monean Emblem of Maritime Distinction. RON TOM

Riga arrives with his instruments for measuring depth, pressure, and currents. RON TOM

of a landmass inhabited by a very advanced civilization. They used a kinetic transfer system to draw the water around the reactor. Paris determines it is the Moneans' mining operation that is destroying the ocean by extracting oxygen from the water, forcing the core to transfer power from containment to keep from being crushed by the added density of the ocean.

Janeway offers Burkus several solutions that would make the refineries obsolete, but he only plans to include them as suggestions in a subcommittee report. Paris is distraught over the ocean's destruction and feels that Burkus does not understand the magnitude of the crisis. Forbidden to disrupt the Moneans' internal affairs, Paris convinces Riga to take the oxygen refineries offline, and the two commandeer the *Delta Flyer.*

Janeway immediately orders Paris to cease his mission. When he refuses, she prepares to fire a photon torpedo to stop him. Once they reach the reactor, Paris and Riga launch their missile at the same time as *Voyager's* and the two meet just short of their targets. Paris's missile is

deflected, and he is brought back to the ship and reduced to the rank of ensign. Once he finishes the letter to his father, he files it in his personal log to be sent when *Voyager* is within range of Earth.

SENSOR READINGS: It would take a week to prepare *Voyager* to submerge. ▪ Tuvok modifies a photon torpedo to act like a depth charge.

SHUTTLE TRACKER: With a few simple thruster modifications and immersion shielding, Paris claims the *Flyer* can be made seaworthy in no time. The *Flyer's* shields are "fried," and thrusters are offline following the encounter with the sea creature. The hull breaches and water leaks in. They lose communications, shields, and propulsion. To reduce the ship's density they vent plasma and transport all nonessential equipment off the ship.

DELTA QUADRANT: Ancestors of the Monean Maritime Sovereignty were nomadic and discovered the waters only three hundred years ago. Their population of over 80,000 has built an industrial infrastructure and undersea dwellings, but most of the people choose to live on their ships as their ancestors did. Their clerics teach that the ocean was a divine gift from the Creators to protect and sustain them; however, there are some who believe the ocean formed naturally, much the way a gas giant does. The ocean is losing containment, and hydro-volume has decreased more than seven percent in the last year alone. Their best research vessel can go only one hundred kilometers beneath the surface, after which the pressure is too great to continue. The *Voyager* crew estimates the ocean will experience complete loss of containment in less than five years. *Voyager* reinforces a breach in the containment field with a deflector beam. A field reactor generating massive amounts of artificial gravity keeps the water contained. It appears to be at least one hundred thousand years old. Torres draws up plans for an oxygen replication system to allow the Moneans to create free oxygen without extricating it from water. ▪ The expression, "brine in the veins," is used to describe someone who has a special connection to the waters. ▪ The ocean used to be part of a landmass of a planetary ecosystem inhabited by a very advanced civilization. They launched the reactor into orbit and used an elaborate kinetic transfer system to draw the water up to the reactor. The process took nearly two hundred years, but there is no record of what became of the civilization.

PERSONAL LOGS: Paris used to love the ocean as a child. He read *20,000 Leagues Under the Sea* many times. Ancient sailing ships were his first love and he wanted to join the Federation Naval Patrol, but his father objected.

The Delaney sisters are seen playing the Twin Mistresses of Evil in the Captain Proton holoprogram. Jenny Delaney likes Kim, but he finds her aggressive and annoying at times. Conversely, Kim is interested in Megan Delaney and finds her quite artistic. Megan also has a dimple in her right cheek. ▪ Ensign Culhane is considered as a possible replacement for chief conn officer

EPISODE LOGS: As the title indicates, the length of this episode spans a month. During that time, *Voyager* is attacked without warning by five ships of unknown origin. The ships manage to escape. ▪ First mentioned in "Time and Again" the Delaney sisters have come up in conversation between Paris and Kim many times however, this is the only time in the series that they are actually seen.

The Doctor is concerned over Seven's prognosis. RON TOM

INFINITE REGRESS

EPISODE #203
TELEPLAY BY: ROBERT J. DOHERTY
STORY BY: ROBERT J. DOHERTY and JIMMY DIGGS
DIRECTED BY: DAVID LIVINGSTON

GUESTS STARS

NAOMI WILDMAN	**SCARLETT POMERS**
VEN	**NEIL MAFFIN**

CO-STARS

HUMAN GIRL	**ERICA MER**
COMPUTER VOICE	**MAJEL BARRETT**

STARDATE 52356.2

When *Voyager* encounters the debris field of a Borg vessel, sensors detect a neural interlink frequency and Seven begins to hear voices that cause her to change personalities. One minute she is a Klingon hunting for food, and the next she is a little girl playing games with Naomi. No one realizes what is happening until Seven, in her Klingon persona, attacks Torres, attempting to initiate a mating ritual. After being contained by a force field Seven becomes a little girl again, then a Vulcan. When Tuvok drops the shield, she suddenly begins speaking Klingon and turns on him forcing the Vulcan to stun her.

When the Doctor attaches a cortical inhibitor to Seven in an attempt to suppress the voices, he discovers that her implants are now storing the neural patterns of assimilated life-forms. After arriving at the debris field, the crew finds the source of the interlink frequency—a Borg vinculum. It is a processing device that interconnects the minds of drones and it is sending a damaged signal to Seven and must be taken offline. After Janeway agrees to beam the vinculum aboard so it can be disabled, Seven finds an alien virus inside that is attacking the Borg technology.

Seven determines that an alien race known to the Borg as Species 6339 infected the cube when they were assimilated. After her inhibitor begins failing, Seven experiences even more new personalities and must be sedated. Torres and Tuvok target the vinculum's transneural matrix with a dampening field, but it adapts to the technology and returns to full power. At that point, Seven's own neural pattern is erased.

When Janeway locates a vessel belonging to Species 6339, their leader demands she return the vinculum.

They unleashed the virus with the intention of spreading it to all cubes, and they want to return it to the debris field so the Borg will retrieve it. Janeway refuses to do so until Seven has been cured. The alien vessel fires on *Voyager*. Meanwhile, Seven's cerebral cortex is under incredible strain, and the Doctor fears that he may never be able to retrieve her neural pattern. Tuvok decides to engage in a mind-meld with Seven to isolate her true self and guide it to the surface of her mind.

As Tuvok enters Seven's chaotic mind, he struggles to find her among the sea of screaming people. He glimpses her being restrained by Klingons and other aliens, but he cannot reach her. In engineering, Torres remodulates the dampening field and finally manages to disable the vinculum. Once it is beamed out to space, the alien vessel ceases its attack. All of the other neural patterns in Seven's mind become dormant, and she and Tuvok return safely from their mind-meld.

SENSOR READINGS: Neelix asks permission to replicate locking mechanisms for the mess hall cabinet doors due to a "midnight snacker" that turns out to be a personality of Seven of Nine.

DAMAGE REPORT: The ship loses field emitters, and a direct hit to the power grid forces them to switch to emergency backup to get the emitters back online.

DELTA QUADRANT: The Borg debris field is 120 kilometers wide, containing tetryon particles consistent with the atmosphere inside a cube. The Borg vinculum is a processing device at the core of every Borg vessel that interconnects the minds of all the drones, purges individual thoughts, and disseminates information relevant to the collective, bringing order to chaos. The vinculum is equipped with many safeguards forcing Seven to access its transneural matrix and disable it directly.

Species 6339 is a warp-capable humanoid race originating in Grid 124 Octant 22-Theta. They first encountered the Borg approximately four years ago, and since that time eleven billion individuals have been assimilated. They create a synthetic pathogen in the form of a virus that mutates to attack the vinculum's programs as it would living cells. Thirteen of their people were infected with the virus and allowed themselves to be assimilated to spread it. Their vessels are well armed, with the one

Tuvok proposes a dangerous cure. RON TOM

Voyager encounters carrying twenty-two phaser cannons on the aft section alone.

ALPHA QUADRANT: There are forty-seven suborders of the Prime Directive (and Naomi knows them all by heart). ▪ The Ferengi are known to the Borg as Species 180.

PERSONAL LOGS: Seven's personalities include: Maryl, a little girl with twelve siblings; a Klingon—the son of K'Vok; Subaltern Lorot of Vulcan High Command; a Terrelian; Ensign Stone of the *U.S.S. Tombaugh* (under Captain Blackwood—the Borg assimilated his vessel thirteen years ago); a Ferengi, Daimon Torrot; the mother of a Lieutenant Gregory Bergan of the *Starship Melbourne* (who was assimilated at Wolf 359); a Bolian manicurist; a Krenim scientist; a Cardassian; a Hirogen; a Bajoran; and several other species the Doctor cannot identify.

Naomi still pursues the job of captain's assistant, hoping to learn from Seven. Though she used to fear the Borg, Naomi and Seven ultimately become friends and begin their soon to be routine games of kadis-kot together. ▪ Neelix prepared a leg of Kelaran wildebeest for Ensign Ryson's birthday.

COUNTERPOINT

EPISODE #204
WRITTEN BY: MICHAEL TAYLOR
DIRECTED BY: LES LANDAU

KASHYK	MARK HARELIK
KIR	RANDY OGLESBY
PRAX	J. PATRICK McCORMACK
VORIK	ALEXANDER ENBERG

CO-STARS

TORAT	RANDY LOWELL
ADAR	JAKE SAKSON
COMPUTER VOICE	MAJEL BARRETT

STARDATE UNKNOWN

Passing through Devore space, *Voyager* is stopped for an inspection—its third. The Devore Imperium considers all strangers to be suspect, and vessels in their space must be searched for telepaths, who they believe break the cardinal rule of trust by reading minds. After the Devore leave the ship, Janeway allows the dozen Brenari refugees they are ferrying to

Janeway and Kashyk play a dangerous game of cat-and-mouse.
DANNY FELD

materialize. *Voyager* has been hiding them in transporter suspension through the inspections.

A transport vessel waits in a nebula to rendezvous with *Voyager* and take the refugees to a wormhole leading out of hostile territory. Suddenly, the Devore inspector, Kashyk, hails Janeway. Kashyk is seeking asylum on her ship, he reveals that he is aware of the refugees. He says the wormhole is a trap to catch ships smuggling telepaths and claims that *Voyager* will be intercepted unless Janeway allows him to stay onboard and help her evade the Devore.

Although Kashyk provides the crew with valuable information to use against his people, Janeway keeps him under tight security in case the Devore are using him to find the wormhole. Together, they track down Torat, an expert on wormholes, who tells them the one they are looking for is a random occurrence. He provides coordinates of the last four appearances, leaving them to their own devices to discern the site of its next emergence. They work together applying an algorithm of subspace harmonics, helping them find the counterpoint of the aperture. Janeway and Kushyk set a course for the new destination.

Since the Devore use a scanning pulse array to track ships, *Voyager* runs gray so it will not be detected. But the pulse triggers a variance in *Voyager*'s antimatter stream, and the ship is detected. Two warships approach, but Janeway plans to fight all the way to the wormhole. Then Kashyk announces that in order to guarantee the safety of the crew and refugees, he is going back to his people temporarily. The Brenari will hide once more, and then he will lead an inspection team through *Voyager* before the wormhole appears. Before Kashyk leaves, he and Janeway share a kiss.

Once Kashyk and his inspection team board *Voyager,* Janeway secretly tells him they have located the wormhole off the port bow and the refugees are in transporter suspension. Kashyk immediately reveals that he has double-crossed her, and he orders a photon torpedo fired at the wormhole to open it as well as a second to destroy it. However, after it is fired, Kashyk realizes he is the one who has been betrayed. The real wormhole is in another location, and the refugees have already taken shuttles through it. Kashyk, not wanting the failure on his record, refuses to report the incident and allows *Voyager* to resume its course.

SENSOR READINGS: Kashyk programs Mahler Symphony #1 to play shipwide while the inspection takes place, and later he plays Tchaikovsky. ■ The refugees and

Janeway plots the course to the rendezvous point. DANNY FELD

telepathic crew members are kept in transporter suspension, which causes some of them to experience acute cellular degradation. The Doctor repairs most of the damage, but the effect is cumulative, meaning that it could prove terminal if they continue hiding in suspension. ▪ Janeway offers Torat enough mercurium isochromate to power his ship for a year. ▪ A wormhole is a layman's term that covers any number of phenomena. What the refugees are looking for is more specifically called an interspatial flexure, wherein the opening jumps around.

SHUTTLE TRACKER: It is unclear whether the two shuttles given to the Brenari for their wormhole passage are retrieved. However, it is unlikely.

DELTA QUADRANT: For inspections the Devore instruct crew members to step away from their stations and set aside sidearms and scanning devices. Deviation from this or any other inspection protocols will not be tolerated. In their language *gaharay* means stranger. Imperative 32,

Codicil 626, reads, "All *gaharay* vessels that deviate from prescribed flight vectors will be impounded, their crews detained and relocated." ▪ Devore soldiers undergo years of training to protect them from other people reading their thoughts. ▪ Kashyk refers to celestial phenomena known as the Kolyan Kolyar Infinite Spirals that are similar in concept to Earth's Aurora Borealis.

EPISODE LOGS: The crew manifest lists Commander Tuvok and Ensign Vorik as Vulcans and Ensigns Suder and Jurot as Betazoids; they were the only telepaths onboard. Janeway notes that they are all dead, though it is likely that Suder is the only one among the list who is deceased.

PERSONAL LOGS: Janeway has a six-hundred-year-old microscope that her grandfather gave her when she was a child.

GRAVITY

EPISODE #205

TELEPLAY BY: NICK SAGAN & BRYAN FULLER
STORY BY: JIMMY DIGGS and BRYAN FULLER & NICK SAGAN
DIRECTED BY: TERRY WINDELL

GUEST STARS

VULCAN MASTER	JOSEPH RUSKIN
YOUNG TUVOK	LEROY D. BRAZILE
YOST	PAUL S. ECKSTEIN

SPECIAL GUEST STAR

NOSS	LORI PETTY

STARDATE 52438.9

⭐ **F**ollowing the crash of their shuttle, Paris and Tuvok are unable to contact *Voyager* because the gravity well that forced them down has also obstructed their signal. Stranded on a planet stuck in a pocket of deep space, they meet a female named Noss, when she is attacked by an alien species of scavengers. Tuvok overpowers them while Paris reactivates the Doctor's mobile emitter and brings him online. Although the universal translator is malfunctioning the Doctor is able to translate her language, they learn that the woman has seen many ships fall from the sky, but none have gone back up.

As time passes, Noss learns their language and begins communicating with them, while Paris shares stories of *Voyager* with her. When he notices that she likes Tuvok,

Paris encourages his friend to pursue his mutual feelings for her. However, Tuvok remembers his childhood schooling with a Vulcan master, which taught him that love is the most dangerous emotion, and that all feelings should be suppressed.

Searching for the missing away team, *Voyager* is almost pulled into the sinkhole as well. When Janeway realizes the shuttle must have succumbed to it, she prepares to send in a multispatial probe to investigate. Suddenly, a vessel approaches, and they are hailed by Supervisor Yost, who informs them the distortion will be sealed the next day. Chakotay reports they have located the shuttle's distress signal, but Tuvok and Paris are experiencing a temporal differential. A day to *Voyager* could mean weeks or even months to them. In addition, the planet's gravitational distress is increasing, and the sinkhole is on the verge of collapse.

After two months on the planet, scavenger aliens ambush Tuvok and Paris, leaving Noss to tend to Tuvok's wounds. When she kisses him, he stoically rebukes her advances, hurting her feelings. Meanwhile, Torres finds a way to modify a multispatial probe into a transporter relay and manages to send a communication signal to Paris and Tuvok's distress beacon. They receive the transmission telling them a transporter beam will be initiated in thirty minutes, which is a little over two days in the differential. As they wait for their rescue, aliens surround them.

Tuvok and Paris are barely able to fend off the photon grenades of the aliens before *Voyager*'s transporter relay beams the trio to the ship. Noss is taken to her home world, but before saying good-bye, Tuvok employs a Vulcan mind-meld to show her the feelings buried deep inside him.

SENSOR READINGS: The crew uses the multispatial probe as both a com signal and transporter relay to communicate and ultimately beam the team out.

SHUTTLE TRACKER: The universal translator goes offline when the shuttle crashes. There are also fractures throughout the hull, the environmental systems are down, and impulse engines are beyond repair. Communications are functional, although each time Paris attempts to transmit a signal, it is bounced back by the distortion. The remains of the shuttle are not retrieved.

DELTA QUADRANT: The shuttle is pulled into a gravimetric shear that nearly pulls in *Voyager*. The crew is able to counter the gravitational pull by venting three million isodynes of plasma from the nacelles and reversing shield

Tuvok is uncomfortable with Noss's growing attachment. DANNY FELD

A young Tuvok refuses to rein in his emotions. WREN MALONEY

LATENT IMAGE

EPISODE #206
TELEPLAY BY: JOE MENOSKY
STORY BY: EILEEN CONNORS and BRANNON BRAGA
& JOE MENOSKY
DIRECTED BY: MIKE VEJAR

GUEST STARS

ENSIGN JETAL   NANCY BELL
NAOMI WILDMAN   SCARLETT POMERS

CO-STAR

COMPUTER VOICE   MAJEL BARRETT

STARDATE UNKNOWN

As the Doctor takes holoimages of the crew, he finds evidence of neurosurgery he performed eighteen months ago on Ensign Kim, but he does not remember the procedure. The Doctor asks Seven of Nine to help him run a self-diagnostic, but an hour later he does not recall their conversation. In reviewing his files he discovers that someone has deleted part of his short-term memory buffer, and holoimages he took around the time of the surgery have been deleted. When Seven restores the images, a female ensign neither of them recognize is pictured with others in the crew, while another picture is of an alien on one of the shuttles.

polarity. The anomaly is approximately six hundred meters in diameter and is out of phase with normal space, which is why it barely registers on sensors. The distortion circumscribes a subspace zone that includes a type-G sun and three planets. The Class-D planet is part of a solar system that is stuck in a pocket of subspace. There is a temporal differential ration of .4744 seconds per minute whereby thirty minutes on the ship translates to two days, eleven hours, and forty-seven seconds on the planet.

ALPHA QUADRANT: The *Kol-Ut-Shan* is a cornerstone of the Vulcan beliefs, better known by its translation, "Infinite diversity in infinite combinations." *B'Elak paar* is the Vulcan term for self-pity while *shon-ha'lock* translates into love.

PERSONAL LOGS: When Tuvok was a child, his father banished him after his seat at school was revoked because he refused to deny himself passion. He had fallen for a Terrelian girl named Jara, whose father was a diplomat. To learn to purge these emotions Tuvok was sent to a Vulcan master. ▪ A universal translator is part of the Doctor's program.

EPISODE LOGS: Paris reminds Tuvok that his wife is fifty thousand light-years away (presumably referring to their current distance from the planet Vulcan).

The Doctor's program starts to break down over his inability to make a simple decisions. MEILA PENN

Prior to a fatal encounter, the away team poses for the Doctor's holoimager. RON TOM

Once Seven restores some of his memories, the Doctor recalls pieces of events from the pictures. When he remembers the alien boarding their shuttle and shooting Kim and Ensign Jetal, he immediately tells Janeway. She agrees to investigate but tells the Doctor to deactivate his program for the time being. Before he does, he downloads his memory banks into the mobile emitter and orders the computer to take holoimages of anyone who accesses his files while he is offline and then reactivate him. Shortly after, someone comes into sickbay to delete more files. When the Doctor develops the holoimages taken, he finds it was the captain.

The Doctor confronts Janeway, who tells him that he was damaged during the incident with the alien. It caused a conflict in his program, and as a result, the crew restricted his access to memories of that period. The captain refuses to tell him what happened, and now that he is starting to remember, she plans to rewrite his program. After Seven challenges her decision, Janeway agrees to restore his memories.

The Doctor learns that he, Kim, and Jetal were on a shuttle mission when an alien ship attacked. Their shut-tle was boarded, and the alien shot Kim and Jetal. Once *Voyager* beamed them to sickbay, the Doctor discovered that the alien's energy pulse had remained in their neural membranes, and the only way to save them was to isolate the spinal cord from the brain. With time to perform the procedure on only one patient, the Doctor chose Kim.

After Jetal's funeral, the Doctor had a breakdown and now that he has remembered everything, he begins agonizing over the same question: how he could choose one life over another? The resulting feedback loop creates a battle between his original programming and what he has become. The crew keeps vigil with him for over two weeks, hoping that eventually he will forgive himself and learn to accept his decision.

SENSOR READINGS: Torres and Kim are busy with plasma relay repairs, while Seven works to recalibrate the deflector dish.

ALPHA QUADRANT: According to Chakotay and Tuvok, in the seventy-seventh Emperor's Cup of sumo wrestling, Kar-pek won over Takashi when the latter's knee broke the sand and the referee gave the match to the former. However, Janeway remembers the results going the other way, claiming that she had a fifth-row seat for the event.

PERSONAL LOGS: Janeway is reading *La Vita Nuova*. ▪ In his youth, Tuvok studied many forms of martial arts, including the sumo of Earth. He has followed the sport ever since. ▪ The Doctor claims he was quite the shutter-bug back around Stardate 50979, and not a day went by that he was not taking pictures with his holoimager. ▪ The Doctor notes that Seven of Nine has a bit more wear and tear on her cranial infrastructure and doubles her maintenance routine.

MEDICAL UPDATE: There was a nascent alien retrovirus bouncing between personnel on Decks 10 and 11, but the Doctor managed to cure it. ▪ As part of the crew's annual physical the Doctor uses his holoimager to take an image of his patients down to the subatomic level by tuning the imager's resonance spectrum along the subspace band. He finds that Kim has scarring at the base of his lower skull from microsurgery the Doctor performed in the past, noting that the microlinear incisions used indicate that it was his work. To save Kim, he developed a spinal shunt to separate the spinal cord from the brain stem until the cellular damage was repaired.

EPISODE LOGS: According to the data displayed on the Doctor's holoimager, Neelix is ranked as a crewman, while Naomi Wildman has no designation.

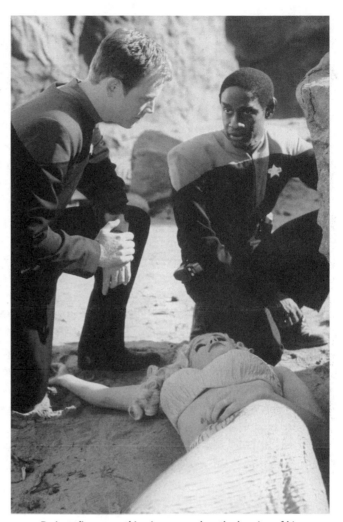

Paris realizes something is wrong when the heroine of his holoprogram dies. RON TOM

BRIDE OF CHAOTICA!

EPISODE #207
TELEPLAY BY: BRYAN FULLER & MICHAEL TAYLOR
STORY BY: BRYAN FULLER
DIRECTED BY: ALLAN KROEKER

GUEST STARS

DOCTOR CHAOTICA	MARTIN RAYNER
LONZAK	NICHOLAS WORTH

CO-STARS

ALIEN #1	JIM KRESTALUDE
COMPUTER VOICE	MAJEL BARRETT

STARDATE UNKNOWN

In the midst of Paris's latest holodeck installment of *The Adventures of Captain Proton*, *Voyager* runs into a gravimetric force and is stopped dead because the layer of subspace acts as a sandbar, disrupting the ship's warp field. When distortions appear in the holodeck, the crew believes they are random fluctuations. However, while the program runs unattended, two men claiming to be from another dimension enter the holodeck and are questioned by the Doctor Chaotica character. After one of them transports back to the distortion, Chaotica vows to destroy their dimension.

When weapons fire in the holodeck creates power surges on *Voyager*, Paris and Tuvok investigate the Captain Proton simulation, and they find a battle has taken place. A character from the program, Satan's robot, tells them that invaders from the fifth dimension have entered through a portal. When photonic charges emanate from the distortions, Chaotica fires back with his death ray. As Paris and Tuvok gather information from Proton's ship, they encounter one of the beings from the alternate universe.

Although they explain that Planet X is only a photonic simulation with which he has intersected, Paris and

THE PROTON UNIVERSE

"This is how you've been spending your free time?"

Kathryn Janeway to Tom Paris "Bride of Chaotica"

The Adventures of Captain Proton: *Chatper 18, "Bride of Chaotica!" The evil Dr. Chaotica kidnaps Constance Goodheart and plans to sacrifice her to Arachnia, Queen of the Spider People. Captain Proton travels millions of miles to Planet X, where he will invade the Fortress of Doom. Chaotica fires his fiendish death ray . . . certain death for Proton as his rocketship bursts into flames!*

The recaps may be full of hyperbole, but that is the fun of the 1930s era serial program that attracts Paris and Kim to the holodeck in order to save the universe. Based on low-budget black-and-white early-twentieth-century movies, *The Adventures of Captain Proton* creates a galaxy of its own within the *Star Trek* universe where good always triumphs over evil, the heroes never die, and cheesy dialogue is the order of the day.

RON TOM

"I will always have a very fond memory of the whole Captain Proton thing because to me it was kind of the epitome of Paris's love of nostalgia and it combines the nostalgia with the sci-fi element. It was kind of a show within a show. It was just so much fun to play these old style kind of sci-fi scenes. We were able to make fun of ourselves in many ways while we played it and that was a lot of fun. That was definitely my most favorite of the holodeck creations that we came up with."

—Robert Duncan McNeill

Cast of Characters

CAPTAIN PROTON: Spaceman First Class, Protector of Earth and Scourge of Intergalatic Evil

BUSTER KINCAID: His trusty sidekick

CONSTANCE GOODHEART: The secretary who accompanies Proton on all his missions

SATAN'S ROBOT: The evil robot who tends to switch sides

DR. CHAOTICA: Self-proclaimed Ruler of the Cosmos

LONZAK: Chaotica's henchman, who was thought to have perished in the Den of Crocodiles

THE TWIN MISTRESSES OF EVIL: Malicia and Demonica

THE PRESIDENT OF EARTH: Leader of Captain Proton's planet

ARACHNIA: Queen of the Spider People and secret ally of Captain Proton

Tuvok cannot convince the transdimensional alien that Chaotica's army of evil is not reality. The photonic life-form considers the simulation to be reality and the *Voyager* crew nonexistent. Paris convinces the crew that the only way to break free is to help the aliens defeat Chaotica—then they will leave. To that end, Paris resumes his role of Captain Proton, while Janeway becomes Arachnia, Queen of the Spider People, and charms her way into Chaotica's Fortress of Doom. Once inside, the plan is to deactivate the controls of the death ray and lightning shields, leaving Chaotica vulnerable to Proton's destructo beam.

Posing as the President of Earth, the Doctor convinces the alien that Captain Proton needs his help. The

The Good

Captain Proton does battle against the forces of evil with the help of his allies, such as Queen Arachnia and her fleet of Spider Ships. His rocketship, equipped with not-so-cutting-edge technology, has no locking mechanisms on the door, and its steering jets can jam up when fired upon. Proton receives telegrams from Earth on his tickertape machine and can view space through his imagizer. The most powerful weapon on his ship is his destructo beam, which is strong enough to knock out Chaotica's death ray. For more personal maneuverability, Proton has a rocket pack and carries his own ray gun for defense.

The Evil

Dr. Chaotica commands his Army of Evil from his Fortress of Doom on Planet X. The planet looks remarkably similar to the Mines of Mercury, where he keeps his slaves (largely due to the high cost of creating sets back in the 1930s). He also has a harem of slave girls that Proton and Kincaid set free in Chapter 18. The Fortress of Doom is protected by his lightning shield and death ray. Among its many evil devices are the confinement rings and the cradle of persuasion (which is equipped with brain probe and pain modulator). Chaotica uses his broadcast microphone to communicate from his Fortress that sits atop his Dungeon of Pain. Chaotica is in love with Arachnia and has been trying to forge an alliance with her since Chapter 3.

RON TOM

CHAPTER 16, "SPELL OF THE SPIDER" Arachnia sends Chaotica a vial of her irresistible pheromones; one whiff and he is under her spell.
CHAPTER 18, "BRIDE OF CHAOTICA!" Captain Proton disables Dr. Chaotica's death ray before he can use it against Earth.
CHAPTER 37, "THE WEB OF PAIN"
UNKNOWN CHAPTER NUMBER, "CAPTAIN PROTON VERSUS THE COSMIC CREATURE" Captain Proton battles alien invaders.
FINAL CHAPTER, "SATAN'S ROBOT CONQUERS THE WORLD"

"That was the greatest fun. That was just wild fun. That was cut loose fun time. I mean those opportunities are few and far between for the captain. And I think everybody said, 'Oh well, let's just let Kate have a ball.' And I did."

—Kate Mulgrew on Arachnia

alien agrees to cease firing and return to his realm once Proton has defeated Chaotica. Meanwhile, Janeway's Arachnia almost has Chaotica convinced to lower his shields when he becomes suspicious, and she is forced to pull a ray gun on him. He confines her to a containment ring and fires his death ray on Proton's approaching ship. On the bridge, Torres realizes the power surges from the holodeck are pulling *Voyager* deeper into subspace.

With time running out, Arachnia has one weapon left at her disposal—her irresistible pheromones. She uses them to lure Chaotica's henchman into setting her free and then kills all of Chaotica's men. Defenseless, the evil doctor must deactivate his shields, allowing Proton to score a direct hit with his destructo beam against the

PERSONAL LOGS: When Janeway was science officer on the *Al-Batani,* the crew tried to navigate a dense proto-nebula that stopped them dead in their tracks, much as *Voyager* is in this situation. Every time they engaged engines, they were increasing resistance of the nebula's particle field. When discussing her Arachnia costume, Janeway notes that she is a size four.

EPISODE LOGS: Previous to the filming of this episode, there was a small fire on the bridge set requiring minor repairs, largely due to water damage. ▪ Chaotica's throne was also used as the chair of Minster Odala from "Distant Origin" (it was also seen as the alien throne in the film "The Coneheads").

Queen Arachnia makes a grand entrance. MICHAEL YARISH

death ray and Chaotica. The day saved, the distortions close, and *Voyager* is realigned with normal space.

SENSOR READINGS: Paris accesses transporter controls from the holodeck and conducts a site-to-site transport. ▪ The crew evacuates Deck 6 as a result of the distortions.

DAMAGE REPORT: Gravimetric forces around the ship disrupt power flow taking the holodeck controls offline. The crew also loses access to communications, deflector controls, and weapons. As long as they are trapped, they do not have access to the computer core, tactical, holodecks, and all but six replicators (they later lose two additional replicators).

DELTA QUADRANT: Seven runs a transpectral analysis and discovers that the barrier between normal space and subspace is unstable throughout the region.

The transdimensional aliens' scanners do not pick up biochemical life-forms, so they assume they do not exist. They are armed with photonic charges and fifty-three of the aliens die in the war.

THE FIGHT

EPISODE #208
TELEPLAY BY: JOE MENOSKY
STORY BY: MICHAEL TAYLOR
DIRECTED BY: WINRICH KOLBE

GUEST STARS

BOXER	CARLOS PALOMINO
GRANDFATHER	NED ROMERO

SPECIAL GUEST STAR

BOOTHBY	RAY WALSTON

CO-STAR

COMPUTER VOICE	MAJEL BARRETT

STARDATE UNKNOWN

As Chakotay lies in sickbay, struggling to communicate with aliens with whom he is linked, he recalls the events that brought him there. In the memory, he is in a holodeck boxing simulation when he is knocked out and *Voyager* is pulled into chaotic space, where the laws of physics are in flux. Gravimetric shears may destroy the ship unless they can find a way out of the disturbance. Chakotay begins hallucinating and hearing voices calling to him from the boxing ring. When he swings at Tuvok, he is subdued and taken to sickbay.

Voyager locates a ship adrift with no lifesigns aboard. Its last distress call reveals that its captain began hallucinating just like Chakotay. The Doctor surmises Chakotay has a genetic marker for a cognitive disorder, and the

Chakotay with his boxing trainer, Boothby. RON TOM

Chakotay insists on taking a vision quest to learn more. Fitted with a cortical monitor, he finds another life-form which communicates through him, explaining that *Voyager* has entered chaotic space through a trimetric fracture. They must alter their warp field to escape.

When he can no longer hear the aliens, Chakotay reenters his vision quest at the suggestion of the Doctor. He sees his grandfather, who suffered from the same auditory and visual hallucinations to which Chakotay is predisposed. Frightened of becoming a crazy old man, Chakotay is continually bounced back to the holodeck boxing ring and an unseen opponent named Kid Chaos. The Doctor pulls Chakotay out of the vision quest and takes him back to sickbay.

In the astrometrics lab, Seven of Nine finds a pattern in the form of an isolinear frequency that proves to be a nucleotide resonance frequency designed to activate DNA. She believes the aliens may be on a perceptual wavelength unknown to the crew, and the senses must be altered in order to communicate. Given this chance to make first contact, Janeway allows Chakotay to go back to the boxing ring, where he thinks the aliens are trying to tell him something.

dead captain had a similar experience when the protein insulation in his neural pathways was stripped. All of which is apparently caused by chaotic space, and

Back in the ring against Kid Chaos, Chakotay begins

Chakotay steps into the ring with the Terrellian. RON TOM

piecing together the instructions he is receiving. His fear of losing control almost causes him to block out the voices, but the Doctor convinces him he must give in to them. Once the aliens tell him how to modify the deflector, Chakotay carries out the directions on the bridge as the graviton shear quickly increases. Suddenly, *Voyager's* sensors set the correct course, and the ship is returned to normal space.

DAMAGE REPORT: The hull buckles while in chaotic space.

DELTA QUADRANT: Chaotic space is two light-years across and emits enough energy for a dozen stars. It shifts position every few minutes and does not match any phenomena in *Voyager's* database. The Borg, however, have been aware of it for years and had given it the name chaotic space because it is a randomly appearing zone where the laws of physics are out of flux. The Borg have observed it throughout the galaxy, although only one cube has survived an encounter with the phenomena. Chaotic space intersects normal space at the eighteenth dimensional gradient. *Voyager* entered through a trimetric fracture, but to leave they have to alter their warp field to a rentrillic projectory and modify their deflector to induce a paralateral rentrillic property (which are terms the crew does not understand). Chaokotay recalibrates the deflector dish and routes it through the sensor array. The crew then activates the deflector at maximum amplitude and brings sensors online. The sensors find them a course leading out of chaotic space. ▪ Seven applies 10,053 algorithms to the energy signatures produced by chaotic space and finds a pattern indicating an isolinear frequency. The nucleotide resonance frequency activated Chakotay's DNA and realigned his molecular bonds.

ALPHA QUADRANT: Chakotay attended the boxing match where Price Jones went twenty-three rounds with Gul Tulet in "The Knockout in the Neutral Zone." He claims it was the best match he had ever seen.

PERSONAL LOGS: Starfleet Academy groundskeeper Boothby trained Chakotay as a boxer when he was a cadet. Now, boxing helps Chakotay unwind. His grandfather refused treatment when he started seeing and hearing things even though all that was required were a few hyposprays a day.

MEDICAL UPDATE: Chakotay's boxing injuries include edema beneath the anterior fossa of the cranium and hairline fracture of the septum. A number of ganglia in his

visual cortex are hyperactive due to the alien contact. Chakotay has the genetic marker for a cognitive disorder known as sensory tremens. The primary symptoms are visual and auditory hallucinations. His family doctor suppressed the gene before he was born.

BLISS

EPISODE #209
TELEPLAY BY: ROBERT J. DOHERTY
STORY BY: BILL PRADY
DIRECTED BY: CLIFF BOLE

GUEST STAR	
NAOMI WILDMAN	SCARLETT POMERS

SPECIAL GUEST STAR	
QATAI	W. MORGAN SHEPPARD

CO-STAR	
COMPUTER VOICE	MAJEL BARRETT

STARDATE 52542.3

Seven of Nine returns from an away mission to find the crew has discovered what they believe to be a wormhole leading to Earth. A probe finds Starfleet signals containing letters full of good news to the crew. Although sensors detect erratic neutrino levels in the wormhole, Starfleet says the flux is unimportant. Seven accesses the captain's logs because she is suspicious of everyone's unfettered optimism despite signs the anomaly may not be all it appears to be. She notes that Janeway reported that scans determined the wormhole was a deception, but in supplemental logs the captain suddenly believed it to be real.

When Seven locates an alien vessel in the wormhole that has not been detected by *Voyager's* sensors, she hails it. The pilot, Qatai, warns her that her ship is being deceived, but they are cut off when Janeway routes power from the astrometrics lab to another system. When Naomi also notices that everyone is acting strangely, Seven realizes they and the Doctor are the only ones unaffected by whatever is manipulating the crew. Soon, Starfleet orders that the Doctor be taken offline to avoid system interference and that Seven be put in stasis while *Voyager* passes through an area of subspace monitored by the Borg.

As Chakotay escorts her to her alcove, Seven traps him and a security detail behind a force field. With

Seven and Qatai plan their escape. MICHAEL YARISH

Naomi's help, she keeps security at bay while she transports to engineering and stuns Torres and the engineering crew with a phaser rifle. After erecting another force field, Seven attempts to shut down the impulse drive to keep *Voyager* from entering the wormhole. However, Janeway transmits a surge to the engineering console that renders her unconscious.

Once they enter the anomaly, the crew falls unconscious as well. When Seven revives, she and Naomi hail Qatai and persuade him to beam aboard. He explains the crew has been a victim of psychogenic manipulation. They are inside a bioplasmic organism—a beast that consumes starships by telepathically preying on their crews' desires. Qatai has been hunting the creature for years, but still falls prey to its manipulations from time to time.

After reactivating the Doctor's program, Seven informs him that *Voyager* is being devoured in the digestive chamber of the organism. Realizing that bodies are designed to expel foreign objects, they plan to fire one of Qatai's tetryon-based weapons at a pocket of antimatter released from *Voyager*'s warp core. It creates an unpleasant reaction that causes the beast to expel the two ships through its esophagus. Once Janeway and the others regain consciousness, *Voyager* resumes its course to the Alpha Quadrant, but Qatai returns into the belly of the beast.

SENSOR READINGS: The crew launches a class-5 probe into the anomaly. ▪ The away team consisting of Seven, Paris, and Naomi returns from a failed mission searching for a new source of deuterium. ▪ In engineering, Seven locks out the command controls with a Borg encryption code 294, forcing Janeway to send an EM surge to Engineering Console 16-Beta to knock Seven unconscious. ▪ The Doctor reroutes bridge controls to engineering and integrates ops, tactical, and the helm into one station. ▪ *Voyager* has an unspecified number of class-9 torpedoes listed in the weapons manifest.

DAMAGE REPORT: The hull begins to demolecularize.

DELTA QUADRANT: The life-form is over 2,000 kilometers in diameter and consumes antimatter and biomatter. While inside it, Seven detects organic compounds, bioplasmic charges, and a vast network of neural pathways. Through telepathy and psychogenic manipulation the life-form senses victim's thoughts and desires, then preys on them. Its most vulnerable system is its primary neural plexus. The organism is at least two hundred thousand years old.

Qatai recounts the tale of how the creature took his ship, the *Nokaro*, without a fight thirty-nine years ago as

The crew has heightened dopamine levels as a result of their altered thought patterns. A cortical inhibitor is unsuccessful at reviving them.

EPISODE LOGS: Naomi continues to carry the Flotter doll made for her in "Once Upon a Time." ▪ Though Seven dreams of an aunt named Claudia, she will make contact with her real Aunt Irene in "Author, Author."

THE DISEASE

EPISODE #210
TELEPLAY BY: MICHAEL TAYLOR
STORY BY: KENNETH BILLER
DIRECTED BY: DAVID LIVINGSTON

GUEST STARS

TAL	MUSETTA VANDER
STOWAWAY	CHRISTOPHER LIAM
	MOORE
BREN	CHARLES ROCKET

CO-STAR

COMPUTER VOICE	MAJEL BARRETT

STARDATE UNKNOWN

As *Voyager* helps a generational ship of Varro repair their warp drive, Kim and a female named Tal become attracted to each other. Knowing that Kim is violating several rules of protocol, they sneak away to Tal's quarters to be together. While they are making love, light flickers just below the surface of their skin. Later, the luminescence returns to Kim's skin, and Seven insists he go to sickbay.

When the Doctor thinks he has contracted a virus, Kim confesses to his intimate relations. Janeway is notified, and she orders him to stop seeing Tal because she believes that Kim has put the crew's relationship with the xenophobic Varro at risk. After Kim tells Tal about the luminescence, she explains it is what they call *olan'vora*, or the shared heart. The more time they spend together, the harder it will be to part. He tries to leave, but they kiss instead. Meanwhile, Tuvok and Neelix discover a Varro male hiding in one of the Jefferies tubes. When questioned, he reveals he is seeking asylum on *Voyager*, claiming that many Varro feel imprisoned on their own ship and that there are rumors of a violent movement to leave it.

After finding microfractures in *Voyager*'s hull, Seven

Seven apologizes and then fires on her fellow crew members.
MICHAEL YARISH

his people were looking for a new world to settle. The ship had a crew of nearly three thousand—mostly families, including his own.

PERSONAL LOGS: Janeway imagines that Mark's engagement was broken off. ▪ Chakotay thinks he has received a full pardon and reinstatement to Starfleet with an offer to a professorship in anthropology at the Academy. ▪ Tuvok sees his wife, T'Pel. ▪ Torres dreams that all the Maquis are still alive. ▪ Paris believes he received a letter from an old buddy who offers him a spot at a new test flight center in Australia. ▪ Neelix imagines he has been appointed ambassador to the Lan'Tuana sector, an area of space inhabited by quadropeds. ▪ Neelix delivers a letter to Seven from a woman named Claudia Hansen, who claims to be her father's sister.

Naomi continues her studies to become captain's assistant by accompanying the away team. ▪ Crewmen Boylen and White are frequently late for their duty shifts.

The Varro reluctantly accept *Voyager's* help in fixing their warp drive. DANNY FELD

and Torres discover silicone-based parasites that have migrated from the Varro ship. Scans reveal the parasites are synthetic and believed to be an act of sabotage. Meanwhile, disobeying orders, Kim and Tal secretly rendezvous in a shuttle and fly to a nearby nebula. When Tuvok tracks them down, he orders them both to return to *Voyager*.

After a schematic for the parasite is found on Tal's personal database, she reveals the dissident group is using them to dismantle the Varro ship. The parasites are targeting the linkage between segments, which eventually will break off into separate ships and allow her people to choose whether to stay or go. When Janeway explains the decay will cause decompressive explosions, Tal agrees to slow down the parasites long enough for the ship to be evacuated. Janeway orders Kim to sickbay to treat the biochemical bond he has developed with Tal, but he refuses to obey the order, risking time in the brig. The ensign argues his position with the captain as the Varro ship experiences structural breaches, and *Voyager* is unable to separate from it.

With only minutes before collapse, Janeway agrees to Kim's suggestion to extend *Voyager's* integrity field around the Varro ship and buy them more time for evacuation. Once completed, *Voyager* detaches, and the Varro vessel breaks off into several separate ships. Their leader,

Jippeq, is forced to let the dissidents seek out their own path. After he and Tal say good-bye, Kim refuses treatment for his condition, preferring to let the pain remind him of the happiness he had felt.

SENSOR READINGS: The crew has been helping the Varro try to repair their warp drive for the past two weeks. ▪ The Varro stowaway routes life support to Jefferies tube G-33, Deck 15, a section that is normally uninhabited.

DAMAGE REPORT: *Voyager* suffers some microfractures on the docking port due to the alien parasite.

DELTA QUADRANT: The Varro started their journey four hundred years ago on a single starship with a small crew. Now, centuries later, they have grown into a generational ship with a history and a culture all their own. Their ship's environmental control systems are regenerative, with no waste. It can also be programmed to re-create almost any habitat. ▪ When two of their people choose each other, the bonding is permanent and they become biochemically linked. Separation is rare as it produces illness that can be fatal. ▪ Tal synthesized silicon-based parasites that feed on duranium alloy. They began replicating

Paris impresses Torres with his orchestration of the antimatter flow. DANNY FELD

DARK FRONTIER, PART I

EPISODE #211
WRITTEN BY: **BRANNON BRAGA & JOE MENOSKY**
DIRECTED BY: **CLIFF BOLE**

<table>
<tr><td colspan="2" align="center">GUEST STARS</td></tr>
<tr><td>BORG QUEEN</td><td>SUSANNA THOMPSON</td></tr>
<tr><td>MAGNUS HANSEN</td><td>KIRK BAILY</td></tr>
<tr><td>ERIN HANSEN</td><td>LAURA STEPP</td></tr>
<tr><td>NAOMI WILDMAN</td><td>SCARLETT POMERS</td></tr>
<tr><td colspan="2" align="center">CO-STAR</td></tr>
<tr><td>ANNIKA</td><td>KATELIN PETERSEN</td></tr>
</table>

STARDATE 52619.2

When *Voyager* manages to destroy a Borg cube, Seven finds data nodes filled with tactical information among the debris. Estimating that two years have been added to their journey by continually changing course to avoid the Borg, Janeway decides to go on the offensive. After locating a damaged Borg scoutship, the crew devises a plan to steal the damaged ship's transwarp coil while its defenses are down. The crew plans to create a diversion, while an away team is sent in to steal the technology. Hoping to find information that will help them, Seven is assigned to read the field notes her parents recorded on the *Raven*.

Once she begins studying her parents' logs, Seven remembers their encounters with the Borg. She was only a small girl at the time, but she vividly recalls her parents' fascination with the collective. Meanwhile, *Voyager* catches up with the scout ship. Noting that the sphere's shields and transwarp drive will be offline for the next seventy-two hours, the crew has only a short time to plan the mission.

During a holographic simulation, Janeway and the others practice their mission down to the second since they have only two minutes to disable the sensor grid and transport the coil to *Voyager* before being detected. After leaving the failed simulation in the holodeck, Seven is unsettled by her close proximity to the Borg, even if it was not real. Later, Seven hears the voice of the Borg queen telling her that they have accessed her neural transceiver and know about Janeway's plan. The queen tells the former drone that the only way to ensure the safety of her crewmates is to give herself back to the Borg.

Further memories of her parents' mission reminds Seven of their arrogance in underestimating the Borg, which eventually led to their assimilation. When the Hansens describe a biodampener in their notes, the

on the Varro ship's hull several months ago then migrated to *Voyager*.

The Borg have referenced the condition known as love in over six thousand assimilated species.

ALPHA QUADRANT: The Starfleet Handbook on Personal Relationships is three centimeters thick. It states that "All Starfleet personnel must obtain authorization from their commanding officer, as well as clearance from their medical officer, before initiating an intimate relationship with an alien species." ▪ Paris refers to the shores of Lake Yuron on Vulcan.

PERSONAL LOGS: Paris sabotages the com system to cover Kim's tracks when he contacts Tal. ▪ Kim encodes his transmission to Tal using security protocol Alpha-7. He violates the captain's direct order that away teams should have "No personal interaction with the Varro crew." The captain gives him a formal reprimand for going against orders and continuing his relationship with Tal.

MEDICAL UPDATE: After engaging in intimate relations with Tal, Kim's beta endorphins are abnormally elevated, and there is unusual synaptic activity in his cerebral cortex. Because he refuses treatment, Kim suffers chronic sleep loss and gastroenteritis. His condition is not fatal but it can last weeks, or even months.

Janeway tries to better her response time in a Borg assault simulation. RON TOM

Voyager team replicates the technology in order to go undetected on the sphere. Revealing that she is willing to risk her own well-being for the sake of the crew, Seven persuades Janeway to assign her to the away team despite the captain's reservations.

The mission goes as planned until Seven once again hears the voice of the collective luring her back to the hive. She refuses to be transported to *Voyager* with the others, and Janeway is forced to leave her before she is assimilated herself. The sphere returns to Borg space with Seven onboard, and the Borg queen welcomes Seven back to the collective.

SENSOR READINGS: The crew beams a photon torpedo onto the Borg ship to disable it. When the torpedo detonates near the power matrix a chain reaction is caused that destroys the sphere. ▪ Torres believes that if they could equip *Voyager*'s engines with one transwarp coil, they could shave twenty years off their trip. ▪ To mask their warp signature, Torres suggest a few Maquis tricks that are not Starfleet approved. Janeway decides that this is not a time for protocol and tells her to make the adjustments. ▪ The Hansen's biodampeners create a field around the body that simulates the physiometric conditions within a Borg vessel. Each unit must be tailored to its user's physiology.

SHUTTLE TRACKER: The crew uses a class-2 shuttle with false bio-readings to trick the Borg into dropping their

To save *Voyager*, Seven returns to the Borg collective. RON TOM

SEVEN OF NINE

. . . The Borg female steps out of the alcove and through the vapor . . . for the first time we get a clear look at her. She is young, striking, covered with Borg technology, but clearly once human.

Her demeanor is cold and passionless—even though she speaks in an individual voice, she is still connected to the hive mine. (NOTE: This is a character we will come to know as SEVEN OF NINE.)

She eyes Janeway and Tuvok with an impassive stare.

—Seven of Nine's first appearance in "Scorpion, Part II"

The addition of Seven of Nine to the cast not only changed the tone of the series, but also managed to bring the development of the Borg as villains to fruition. Much like the Klingons who appeared as enemies in the original *Star Trek* and evolved into allies in *The Next Generation* (with a Klingon serving on the *Enterprise*) it was now time for a Borg to serve on *Voyager*. Though the race as a whole would not come to the same treatise as the Klingons and Federation, Seven of Nine's presence would go a long way to serve as something of a redemption for the race who had been little more than mindless killing machines in their first appearance.

Seven's own redemption was a hugely tumultuous procedure, beginning with her being stolen away from the Borg against her will. Though Janeway knew that her actions were in Seven's best interest, that knowledge did not make the transition any easier. Seven had to grow accustomed to her physical transformation at the same time she dealt with the fact that she was entirely cut off from the hive mind for the rest of her life. Her reluctance to embrace these changes set the scene for some of the most dramatic conflict between the captain and any member of her crew.

PETER IOVINO

Brannon Braga: A lot of people complain that Seven gets too much screen time, but there's a reason for it. She's enormously popular. Voyager was missing it's Spock. It had the Doctor but Janeway didn't have a foil and that's what Seven of Nine gave us. Aside from the fact that she's sexy, she was a classic Star Trek character and we needed that.

Seven's relationship with the captain led to much conflict throughout the final seasons of the series. The former drone's rebellion against Starfleet ideals was ever present throughout many episodes like "The Gift," "Prey," and "The Omega Directive," but managed to evolve from straightforward defiance to respect. There were many times when her behavior would disappoint Janeway, but never to the degree that the captain would ever give up on Seven.

The rest of the crew did not prove as welcoming as the captain to having a Borg onboard. Chakotay was originally the most vocal in his opposition to Seven's presence. His opinion was the one most changed by the end of the series when the pair began a tentative relationship. Torres also refused to accept the former drone as a part of the crew, with only grudging moments of appreciation as the series progressed.

It was Kim who first accepted Seven into the mix as the pair began their work on the new astrometrics lab. His admiration of her quickly turned to interest as he developed feelings for her, much as the Doctor did. Filling the role as her personality mentor, the Doctor grew closer to Seven though many episodes, culminating with his own realization of his feelings for her in "Someone to Watch Over Me." Though his feelings for her were not returned, their close friendship continued though the end of the series.

Garrett Wang: I'll always remember the scene where Kim tried to make some ground with Seven and invite her to the mess hall under the guise of doing work . . . Then the immortal question "Ensign Kim, do you wish to copulate?" came from Seven's mouth and Kim so stupidly replied, "No!" . . . I read that script and looked at it dumbfounded, wondering why the writers are doing this to Kim. Because I'll tell you, after that episode aired I couldn't go anywhere . . . Anyplace I went in the U.S. everybody was like, "What are you doing? Are you crazy?!"

Beyond her potential romantic entanglements another type of important relationship emerged for Seven—that of her association with children. First she befriended Naomi Wildman, that served as a way to bring back her lost childhood. Naomi feared Seven, much as Seven feared interacting with the crew. As they both faced their fears together, Seven forged her first true friendship aboard the ship. Later, she assumed the role of parent to Icheb and the other Borg children as she guided them through their reintegration into lives free of the collective. Though the relationships were initially troubled, her interactions with the children served to accelerate her regaining her humanity.

The largest impact on Seven's return to humanity was her continued interaction with her Borg past. Events in which she was physically confronted by her own history served to exemplify how far she had come from what she had been. Episodes like "Survival Instinct," and "Dark Frontier" provided Seven with reminders of what she had overcome to regain her independence. Meanwhile, her fight to overcome her Borg self would be hindered by her own mind in "Infinite Regress" and her body in "Imperfection." It was in "Drone" where Seven was charged with responsibility for a new Borg life-form created by a merging of technology that the true depth of her struggle was immediately clear. In helping One, the maturing drone, find a place for himself in the universe, she not only furthered her own return to humanity, but clearly acknowledged the seductive call of the Borg that she must constantly struggle against.

DANNY FELD

Jeri Ryan's performance as Seven of Nine left little question that she was ready to accept her human life. When Seven contacted her long forgotten aunt, their shared moment showed a glimpse into the life that Seven was ready to reclaim. It does not seem too much of a stretch to imagine that once back in the Alpha Quadrant Seven finally reacquired her true name, Annika Hansen.

shields and bringing it in, sacrificing the vessel so the away team can transport onboard and steal the transwarp coil.

DELTA QUADRANT: In the eight kilotons of Borg debris, *Voyager* salvages two power nodes and a dozen plasma conduits in working order. The Doctor finds a servo-armature from a medical repair drone with a laser scalpel, biomolecular scanner, and microsuture all in one instrument. The data nodes they find contain a crew manifest and tactical information, including long-range sensor telemetry, assimilation logistics, and vessel movements for a radius of thirty light-years. It takes Seven two hours to convert the information to Starfleet parameters. ▪ When a Borg vessel is critically damaged, all of its vital technology self-destructs. ▪ In the past, the Hansens picked up a transwarp conduit when sensors read tri-quantum waves 600,000 kilometers off their port bow and subspace distortions with a field magnitude of 2.9 Teracochrans and rising. They encounter a Borg cube with 129,000 life-forms onboard.

ALPHA QUADRANT: Fort Knox is the largest repository of gold bullion in Earth's history. Paris notes that the over 50 metric tons stored there was worth over nine trillion U.S. dollars. When the new world economy took shape in the late twenty-second century and the concept of money was abolished, Fort Knox was turned into a museum. No one ever managed to break into the facility; although a couple of Ferengi tried about ten years ago.

PERSONAL LOGS: Chakotay claims that Janeway fiddles with her combadge every time she is about to "drop a bombshell." ▪ Seven's exobiologist parents, Magnus and Erin Hansen kept extensive fields notes while tracking the Borg, with over nine thousand log entries alone. They tracked a cube at close range for three years. On Stardate 32611.4 the Federation Council on Exobiology gave them final permission to explore their theories about the Borg. In their search, the Hansens deviated from their flight plan, crossed the Neutral Zone, and disobeyed a direct order to return. After three months of tracking a Borg cube the vessel entered a transwarp conduit, and the Hansens followed in its wake as it brought them to the Delta Quadrant.

EPISODE LOGS: Seven is seen in a new burgundy-colored outfit because the previous blue costume was difficult to film against special effects backdrops.

DARK FRONTIER, PART II
EPISODE #212
WRITTEN BY: BRANNON BRAGA & JOE MENOSKY
DIRECTED BY: TERRY WINDELL

GUEST STARS	
BORG QUEEN	SUSANNA THOMPSON
MAGNUS HANSEN	KIRK BAILY
ERIN HANSEN	LAURA STEPP
NAOMI WILDMAN	SCARLETT POMERS

CO-STARS	
ANNIKA	KATELIN PETERSON
ALIEN	ERIC CADORA
COMPUTER VOICE	MAJEL BARRETT

STARDATE 52619.2

Seven is trapped on a Borg sphere after being lured back to the collective during *Voyager*'s mission to steal a transwarp coil. The queen informs her that the Borg allowed *Voyager* to liberate her from the col-

The Borg queen wants Seven of Nine back into the collective. RON TOM

Seven wonders why she is not immediately assimilated. MICHAEL YARISH

lective, and now she will not be turned back into a drone because they want to study her memories. With her individuality intact, the Borg can look through her eyes to help them assimilate humanity. Meanwhile, Janeway discovers Borg communication signals that were being sent to Seven in her alcove.

Determined to rescue Seven, Janeway leads an away team in the *Delta Flyer* to find the Borg sphere. They use the stolen coil to take the shuttle into transwarp along with the Hansens' multiadaptive shielding to go undetected by the Borg. Meanwhile, as Seven is given her first assignment to assist in the assimilation of a Species 10026, she secretly helps four of the individuals escape. The Borg queen scolds her, saying that her human emotions of compassion and guilt are weaknesses that are causing her pain. However, when Seven pleads with her to let the getaway ship escape, the queen grants her request.

After the away team follows the sphere to Borg space, Janeway prepares to send a message to Seven through her Borg interplexing beacon. The queen gives Seven a new assignment—to assist in the programming of nanoprobes that will assimilate humans. The Borg plan to detonate a

biogenic charge in Earth's atmosphere, and Seven will be turned into a drone if she does not comply. Taunting her, the queen reveals that one of the drones standing beside her is Seven's father. Suddenly, Janeway's signal comes through to Seven, but the queen discovers it.

As the Borg adapt to the *Delta Flyer's* shielding, Janeway is forced to beam to the vessel and disable the shield matrix around the queen's chamber. While Paris eludes the other ships, Janeway confronts the queen and orders Seven to leave with her. A dispersal field is formed around the chamber to block the *Delta Flyer's* transporter beam, but Seven tells the captain to target the power node above the chamber to disrupt the queen's command interface. Mission accomplished, Janeway and Seven are beamed to the shuttle where they quickly enter a transwarp conduit, but not before a Borg vessel sneaks in behind them. On *Voyager,* Chakotay and Torres fire a full spread of photon torpedoes at the conduit threshold, collapsing it just as the shuttle bursts through. The Borg ship is destroyed, and with Seven home again the crew is able to use the transwarp technology to travel twenty thousand light-years, bringing them fifteen years closer to home.

SENSOR READINGS: The crew launches a class-5 probe to search for residual transwarp signatures. ▪ Neelix reports that they have cleared out all the Borg debris, but before they vaporize it he receives permission to melt it down and extract the polytrinic compounds. ▪ Seven of Nine's alcove uses over thirty megawatts of power. *Voyager* fires a full spread of photon torpedoes at the transwarp corridor's threshold perimeter that destabalizes the matter stream and implodes the conduit for at least a light-year.

DELTA QUADRANT: The Borg assimilate the 392,000 life-forms of Species 10026 ▪ Cataloguing drones, the Hansens note a member of Species 6961—Katarien—has been given a titanium infrastructure indicating that he is a tactical drone. His previous designation was Three of Five, Tertiary Adjunct of Unimatrix One, and was in close proximity to the queen. ▪ The Borg plan to detonate a biogenic charge in Earth's atmosphere that would affect all life-forms with a nanoprobe virus. Assimilation would be gradual since the virus would take years to proliferate, so by the time Starfleet realized what was happening half the population would be drones. ▪ The Borg queen came from Species 125. ▪ Humans are listed as Species 5618, and are considered to have a below average cranial capacity, minimal redundant systems, and limited regenerative abilities.

PERSONAL LOGS: The Doctor has been studying Seven's cranial schematics and isolates the frequency of her interplexing beacon. They use that information to send her a message. Every drone has its own translink signature, so only Seven will hear the message. The Borg enhance her visual cortex with a neural processing adjunct designed to increase her synaptic efficiency and they assimilate her memories while she regenerates.

EPISODE LOGS: Although the episodes of "The Killing Game" had aired back to back on the same night, "Dark Frontier" is the first episode planned as a movie event since the premier episode, "Caretaker."

COURSE: OBLIVION
EPISODE #213
TELEPLAY BY: BRYAN FULLER & NICK SAGAN
STORY BY: BRYAN FULLER
DIRECTED BY: ANSON WILLIAMS

CO-STAR

COMPUTER VOICE   MAJEL BARRET

STARDATE 52586.3

After she and Paris exchange their wedding vows, Torres discovers a problem in engineering. Upon further investigation, she finds one of the Jefferies tubes is losing molecular cohesion due to subspace radiation from the warp drive. Suddenly, Torres becomes violently ill. When Paris brings her to sickbay, they find several more crew members in the same condition.

The Doctor diagnoses Torres with acute cellular degradation and explains that her chromosomes are breaking down at the molecular level due to a reaction with the newly installed enhanced warp drive. Meanwhile, Chakotay and Tuvok pinpoint an event that could have caused their problems. Ten months ago, while on a class-Y demon planet, they had encountered a bio-mimetic compound that had experienced sentience for the first time upon contact with the crew. Before they left, the crew's DNA was copied by the living compound and duplicates of themselves remained on the planet creating a new population. With this information at their disposal the Doctor injects a dichromate catalyst into Torres's body and she disintegrates into the mimetic compound. After witnessing the reaction, Chakotay and Tuvok realize that *they* are the crew of duplicates.

As the crew begins to accept that they are living other beings' lives, they work on a plan to save themselves from decomposing in the same manner as Torres. The only solution seems to be returning to the planet from which they originated. However, unwilling to travel thousands of light-years back to the demon planet, the duplicate Janeway decides to forge ahead toward the home that she "remembers" in the Alpha Quadrant hoping to find a solution to the rapid degradation along the way. When sensors detect another class-Y planet, the crew readies the ship to land, knowing that the planet's atmosphere is the only thing that may keep them alive. However, a vessel suddenly appears that warns them off and begins firing.

The duplicate *Voyager* is unable to sustain the hits from the other ship and must retreat. When Janeway orders the crew to search for another demon planet, Chakotay tells her they are questioning her command.

Mimetic versions of Torres and Paris exchange vows. MICHAEL YARISH

The crew is beginning to remember their existence before *Voyager* and that Earth is not their home. After Chakotay's neural pathways start to destabilize and he dies in sickbay, Janeway—who is close to death herself—decides to turn the ship around and set a course for the demon planet.

As the duplicate crew dies one by one, acting Captain Kim continues their mission to the demon planet as the few survivors try to hold the ship together. The remaining crew detects a ship, however they are unable to contact it while in warp. Kim orders Seven to eject the warp core so they can drop out of warp and hail the ship. However, the force is too great, and the ship disintegrates. The real *Voyager* comes across the mysterious debris, curious about the distress signal they received. They can only make a note of the event in their log.

SENSOR READINGS: The mimietic crew develops an enhanced warp drive that will get them home in two years.

DELTA QUADRANT: Eight months ago the duplicate crew made first contact with the Kmada who tried to sab-

Torres is the first victim of the mimetic degradation that soon affects the entire crew. RON TOM

otage their life support systems with low frequency radiation. Nine months ago the N'Kree tried to conscript *Voyager* into their battle fleet. Also nine months ago the crew collected silicate from a comet in the Podaris sector. ▪ The song of Cytaxian crickets is reputed to be an auditory aphrodisiac. ▪ The crew's attempt to land on the class-Y planet is in direct violation of the Ord'Mirit mining treaty.

PERSONAL LOGS: The duplicate Janeway makes her grandmother's recipe for chicken paprikash. ▪ Neelix suggests a holographic honeymoon on the beaches of Ahmedeen and wind surfing on its sea of liquid argon. However, Paris chooses a week in the historic Graystone Hotel in Chicago circa 1928.

EPISODE LOGS: The mimetic duplicates of the *Voyager* crew come from the episode "Demon." According to the dialogue of this episode, the encounter occurred ten months and eleven days ago when *Voyager* was forced to land on the demon planet in the Vaskan Sector. ▪ The real Paris and Torres will get married in "Drive," but the ceremony will go unseen.

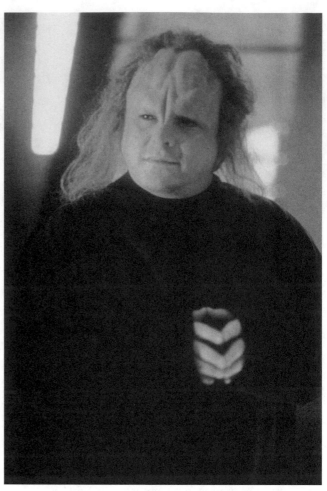

Kurros's calm manner belies his evil nature. VIVIAN ZINK

THINK TANK

EPISODE #214

TELEPLAY BY: **MICHAEL TAYLOR**
STORY BY: **RICK BERMAN & BRANNON BRAGA**
DIRECTED BY: **TERRENCE O'HARA**

SPECIAL GUEST STAR

KURROS   **JASON ALEXANDER**

GUEST STARS

Y'SEK   **CHRISTOPHER DARGA**
SAOWIN   **CHRISTOPHER SHEA**

STARDATE UNKNOWN

As *Voyager* approaches a strange planetoid, the ship is rocked by an explosion and enveloped in a cloud of metreon gas. Suddenly, a Hazari vessel is upon them, as Seven explains that she knows the species to be bounty hunters hired to capture alien crafts. When Janeway eludes the ship and it does not follow, she soon finds that there are many reinforcements throughout the sector waiting to overtake *Voyager*. Late at night, a strange alien pays a visit to Janeway and introduces himself as the answer to her problem.

Kurros explains he is part of a small group that seeks out problems to be solved. His "Think Tank" believes *Voyager*'s challenge with the Hazari can be handled without weapons. When Janeway and Seven visit Kurros on his ship, they see his incredibly advanced technology and meet the other life-forms, each with an intellectual specialty. Once Janeway agrees to do business with him, Kurros reveals Seven is one of the items from *Voyager* that he wants as payment.

After Seven hears the offer from the Think Tank, she speaks to Kurros herself, and though he appeals to her quest for perfection, she declines to join his group. Soon, the Hazari attack *Voyager* again, but Kurros gives Janeway some tactical advice that forces the bounty hunters to retreat. When he tries to use that favor as leverage to convince Seven to change her mind, Janeway realizes she now has two enemies on her hands.

Once the crew lures a Hazari vessel into their own trap, they download information from the database and discover Kurros hired the bounty hunters. Janeway explains to the Hazari alien that they are both being

Kurros makes what he thinks is a tempting offer. VIVIAN ZINK

manipulated by Kurros and convinces him to work with her in tricking the Think Tank. The crew devises a plan to lure Kurros out of hiding by pretending Seven has decided to join his group. She will then link with their internal communications array, disrupting their systems and preventing them from functioning. After the ruse is in place, the Hazari contact Kurros and persuade him to increase their bounty to bring in *Voyager*.

Janeway tricks him into believing Seven has left *Voyager* to join his Think Tank, but Kurros soon senses a trap has been laid. When he forces Seven to link with his telepathic technology so he can read her mind and discover Janeway's plan, a carrier wave is transmitted via her cortical implant. This creates interference and blocks his entire communications system. Once the Think Tank's ship is revealed, the Hazari converge on it. Seven is beamed back to *Voyager* and the crew leaves at warp speed.

SENSOR READINGS: The cloud of metreon gas collapses *Voyager*'s warp field and knocks the impulse engines offline. The crew reroutes every spare gigawatt of power

to shields and fires phasers at the gas cloud and the impact of the explosion blows them clear. ▪ The Think Tank aliens request the crew's information on quantum slipstream technology, Neelix's recipe for *chadre'kab*, Chakotay's ancient Olmec figurine, and Seven of Nine. ▪ The Doctor creates a forensic reconstruction from the bioreadings on the Hazari ship and uses the holoemitters to re-create an image of the Malon who hired them. However, there are isomorphic signatures in the bioreading that reveal it to be a hologram hiding Kurros's true identity.

DAMAGE REPORT: Hull integrity is compromised on Decks 7 and 12 during a Hazari attack.

DELTA QUADRANT: The Think Tank helps an unnamed race find the precise harmonics for a planetary containment field thus keeping their world stabilized, and requests the planet's bernicium deposits in return for their help. The aliens require the ore to repair their replicator system, and without it the people will starve. They offer a rubidium geode instead, but the Kurros threatens to destroy their planet if they do not adhere to the original bargain.

Kurros visits *Voyager* in the form of an isomorphic projection, which he explains, is not as crude as a hologram. He claims that coffee bears a slight resemblance to an Alkian confection they acquired several years ago. The Think Tank hides their ship in subspace. The hull is composed of a neutronium based alloy. Starfleet has theorized about such a material but neither they nor the Borg have come close to producing it. ▪ Kurros claims they turned the tide in the war between the Bara Plenum and the Motali Empire, ignited the Red Giants of the Zai Cluster and just recently found a cure for the Vidiian phage. Last month they helped retrieve a Lyridian child's pet—a subspace mesomorph. In compensation, they asked for one of the Lyridian's transgalactic star charts. When they helped the citizens of Rivos V resist the Borg all they asked for was the recipe for their famous zoth-nut soup. The aliens say they will assist in the neutralization of fleets, starbases, and even planets, but they will not participate in the decimation of an entire species or design weapons of mass destruction. ▪ The group was founded more than one hundred years ago by Bevvox, a bioplasmic life-form who had wandered the galaxy for a few millennia. If she had agreed to join them Seven would have been the first person they had recruited in seventeen years.

The Hazari are Species 4228. According to Seven, they are technologically advanced and extremely violent, which makes them excellent tactical drones. ▪ When the Hazari attack in pairs, one ship always remains behind to reinforce the shields of the attacking vessel ▪ Chakotay lists the Malon and the Devore as enemies they have made who could have hired the Hazari.

PERSONAL LOGS: After previously introducing the crew to yo-yo's, Paris has now gotten them all hooked on a puzzle game called sheer lunacy that operates on fractal regression.

JUGGERNAUT

EPISODE #215

**TELEPLAY BY: BRYAN FULLER & NICK SAGAN
and KENNETH BILLER**

STORY BY: BRYAN FULLER

DIRECTED BY: ALLAN KROEKER

GUEST STARS

FESEK	RON CANADA
PELK	LEE ARENBERG
DREMK	SCOTT KLACE

CO-STAR

COMPUTER VOICE	MAJEL BARRETT

STARDATE UNKNOWN

Following an altercation with the Doctor, Torres is ordered to learn meditation techniques from Tuvok to control her anger. After the first failed lesson, *Voyager* picks up a distress call and tracks it to escape pods that are contaminated with radiation. Two survivors, Fesek and Pelk, are beamed to sickbay, as the crew discovers that the source of the radiation is a disabled Malon freighter. During a mission to export their toxic waste, a leak forced them to evacuate. Fesek explains that when the ship explodes the waste will ignite and destroy everything within three light-years. Before *Voyager* can travel to a safe distance, the warp drive collapses forcing an away team to board the Malon ship and disable it before the explosion.

With only six hours to go before the storage tanks blow, Fesek, Pelk, Chakotay, Torres, and Neelix beam to the freighter. They start in the least affected chamber and clear a path to the control room by opening airlocks and decompressing the ship. An inoculation created by the Doctor affords them a few hours of protection from the radiation. While checking on a jammed airlock, Pelk is attacked by a creature he superstitiously believes to be created by the radiogenic waste.

Pelk tries to convince the team that the creature exists, but they think he is hallucinating. When he dies from his injuries, Pelk is beamed to sickbay to determine the cause. Meanwhile, Janeway prepares a contingency plan involving a nearby star. She concludes the corona would absorb the radiation from the blast if the freighter could be nudged close enough to it. As the away team races through the decks to the control room, an airlock opens and creates a sudden vacuum. Everyone escapes but Chakotay, who is struck by flying debris and beamed to sickbay.

As Torres works to reinitialize the power matrix in

The Malon crew tries to stop the leaking antithermal feed. DANNY FELD

the control room, the Doctor finds tissue samples on Pelk that suggest a being aboard the freighter that has adapted to the radiation. When Seven scans for a life-form blended in with the ambient toxins on the ship, the creature is revealed closing in on the team. Neelix and Fesek are attacked, but Torres keeps the creature at bay and realizes it is a Malon core laborer.

The laborer insists sabotaging the ship is the only way to make the Malon understand how horrifying the radiation poisoning is to the men who sacrifice their lives working on the core. As *Voyager* emits a gentle tractor pulse to steer the freighter into the star, the laborer uses maneuvering thrusters to disrupt its course. Torres tries to reason with him, but ultimately she has to resort to violence to stop him. At the last second, Neelix, Fesek, and Torres are beamed to *Voyager* before the freighter explodes within the star's atmosphere.

SENSOR READINGS: The crew sends out a sector wide alert warning other ships away from the potential explosion. ▪ When the Malon are beamed to sickbay the crew initiates biohazard containment procedures.

DELTA QUADRANT: On a waste export mission two theta tanks on the Malon ship erupt causing systems to mal-

function one by one and vent radiation from every port. Over sixty crewmen die within minutes. Of the few who make it to the escape pods, only two survive. Of the forty-two decks on the Malon freighter, thirty-three are flooded with high levels of theta radiation, including the control room where containment needs to be reestablished. The away team beams onto one of the lower levels where there is less radiation and vents the contaminated sections one by one. The tricorders cause an electrostatic cascade igniting the methogenic particles on the ships. ▪ Hallucinations are the first stage of theta poisoning. ▪ Only three of the ten core laborers survive a standard mission. They make more in two months than most Malon make in a lifetime. ▪ The *vihaar* is a mythological creature created by radiogenic waste that supposedly lives in the theta storage tanks and wreak havoc on Malon ships. ▪ Fesek considers Malon Prime to be one of the most beautiful worlds he has ever seen, claiming the planet would choke with industrial waste if it were not for the controllers.

PERSONAL LOGS: Torres's earliest memory of anger is of a time she attacked a fellow classmate in grammar school who called her "Miss Turtle-head." At recess she disengaged the centrifugal governor on the gyro-swing, caus-

Torres battles both her own demons and the Malon "monster."
DANNY FELD

ing him to swing so fast it nearly flew apart. Then she yanked him off the swing and started "pounding his little face" until Miss Malvin stopped her. ▪ The Doctor had planned to do a photo essay on a day in the life of the warp core until Torres got angry and destroyed his holoimager. ▪ Neelix spent six years on a Talaxian garbage scow that once ran into a theta radiation field, which knocked out propulsion, leaving them stranded. They were barely alive when help came. He makes a Talaxian theta radiation remedy with a crushed Rama leaf and Katyllian clove that helps fortify the cellular membranes.

MEDICAL UPDATE: The Doctor develops an inoculation that temporarily prevents cells from absorbing theta radiation. ▪ Torres gets freighter blight from prolonged exposure to the radiation. When the blistering starts she has already received a fatal dose and must receive treatment immediately. A subdermal injector containing analeptic compounds is used to reduce the cell damage. ▪ Chakotay is knocked unconscious and Neelix is attacked as well.

EPISODE LOGS: This episode showed the first working sonic shower in *Star Trek* history. ▪ Torres notes that it was a boy named Daniel Bird who used to torment her as a child. The name may seem familiar since in "Non

Sequitur" Harry's friend from Starfleet Academy, Daniel Byrd, took his place on *Voyager* in the alternate reality. It is unclear whether these were intended to be the same person.

SOMEONE TO WATCH OVER ME

EPISODE #216
TELEPLAY BY: **MICHAEL TAYLOR**
STORY BY: **BRANNON BRAGA**
DIRECTED BY: **ROBERT DUNCAN McNEILL**

GUEST STARS

TOMIN	**SCOTT THOMPSON**
ABBOT	**IAN ABERCROMBIE**
REGULAR GUY	**DAVID BURKE**
	and
LT. WILLIAM CHAPMAN	**BRIAN McNAMARA**

STARDATE 52647

As Janeway and Tuvok leave for a diplomatic mission with the Kadi, Neelix is left in charge of Kadi ambassador Tomin on *Voyager*. The Doctor learns that Seven has been studying the relationship between Paris and Torres and decides that Seven needs to experience dating in her socialization training. When he takes her to Sandrine's for some practice in making small talk with men, Seven buys a prospective suitor a drink in her usual dry manner. Once Paris learns what is going on, he makes a bet with the Doctor that Seven cannot find a date for the Kadi ambassador's reception and keep that date for the entire night.

Knowing he has his work cut out for him, the Doctor tries to show Seven the importance of shared interests with a potential date. When he discovers Seven has a beautiful singing voice, the two engage in a duet of "You Are My Sunshine." Once her interests are determined, Seven peruses the ship's manifest for a suitable male and chooses Lieutenant Chapman, whom she has worked with before in engineering. Startled by her directness, he agrees to meet her on the holodeck for dinner.

The Doctor helps Seven fix her hair and pick out a dress to wear. In the holodeck simulation, he plays the piano as Seven and Chapman awkwardly navigate their way through a lobster dinner and take a turn on the dance floor. When Seven takes the lead and tears a liga-

Seven is unprepared for dancing as part of her first date.
MICHAEL YARISH

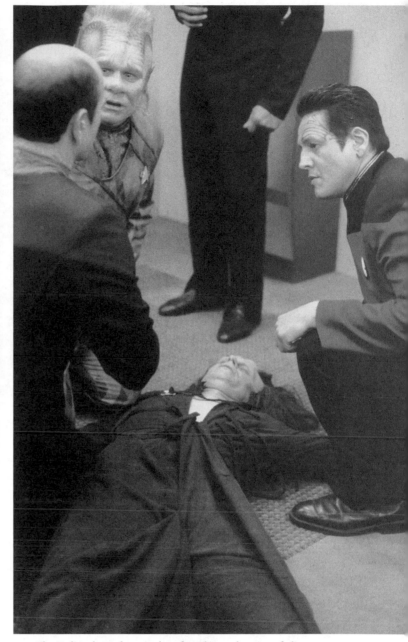

The Kadi ambassador overdoes from his exploration of alien delicacies. RON TOM

ment in Chapman's arm, the evening is cut short, and she is ready to give up on dating altogether. However, the Doctor persuades her to keep trying and takes her onto the dance floor for a lesson.

Seven and the Doctor decide to attend the Kadi ambassador's reception together, and Seven displays all of her newly learned social skills. This prompts Paris to admit the Doctor has won the bet, which angers Seven. She accuses the Doctor of not having a sincere interest in her development and storms out of the party. Meanwhile, Neelix is losing control of the ambassador, who has had too much to drink and makes a scene before passing out. As the Doctor works to reverse the effects of synthehol on the ambassador, Paris realizes that the Doctor has developed feelings for Seven of Nine.

The ambassador has a mighty hangover when his superior returns the next day, but he and Neelix manage to cover up what has really happened. The Doctor prepares to tell Seven about his feelings for her, but she comes to him first to thank him for his guidance and announces that she will no longer require his lessons

because there is not a suitable mate on board. Crushed, the Doctor hides his true emotions and returns to Sandrine's for a lonely piano tune.

DELTA QUADRANT: The Kadi do not approve of spices or anything that might inflame the senses. Kadi monks wash only with purified water, and Neelix equips the visitor's quarters with an ablutionary fountain built to their specifications. They observe eight daily services and have a ritual greeting: "Travelers who have left the sanctity of their home and family, we welcome you into our home, our family." The abbot then presents gifts of their purity and a blessing from the Goddess Mother. The enzymes that break down synthehol are not present in the Kadi bloodstream. The Doctor attempts to code Seven's nanoprobes to assimilate the synthehol molecules, even though the Kadi have rules against medical procedures that have not been sanctified.

Species 8472 may have as many as five sexes. ▪ Borg have unimatrices in place of families.

ALPHA QUADRANT: *Hasperat* is a Bajoran dish Tomin asks to sample before doing anything else. Later he has Katarian pudding, the recipe for which includes a catalytic agent designed so that it evaporates in the mouth.

PERSONAL LOGS: Seven claims that there is no one on Deck 8, Section 12, who does not know when Paris and Torres are having intimate relations, indicating that one of their quarters is in that section. ▪ Paris has been giving Kim driving lessons on the holodeck in a '69 Mustang. ▪ When the Doctor designed Seven's dermaplastic garment, he also designed some casual attire for her. ▪ Seven has a vocal subprocessor designed to facilitate the sonic interface with Borg transponders, which also gives her a terrific singing voice. Her interests include astronomy, quantum mechanics, and music. She does not consider Kim a candidate for her date, much to the ensign's displeasure.

In deciding on a potential date, Seven notes that Ensign Bronowsky, who is assigned to the airponics bay, has a flawless record and plays accordion. Kim says he plays badly and has no sense of humor. She ultimately settles on Lieutenant William Chapman from structural engineering, who Kim claims is renowned for being nervous around women.

EPISODE LOGS: The holodeck program Sandrine's is visited for the last time in the series. It was last seen in "The Swarm." ▪ Robert Picardo and Jeri Ryan provide their own singing voices for this episode.

11:59

EPISODE #217

TELEPLAY BY: JOE MENOSKY
STORY BY: BRANNON BRAGA & JOE MENOSKY
DIRECTED BY: DAVID LIVINGSTON

SPECIAL GUEST STAR

HENRY JANEWAY	KEVIN TIGHE

GUEST STARS

JASON	BRADLEY PIERCE
and	
MOSS	JOHN CARROLL LYNCH

CO-STARS

DRIVER	CHRISTOPHER CURRY
PASSERBY	JAMES GREENE
FIELD REPORTER	KRISTINA HAYES
COMPUTER VOICE	MAJEL BARRETT

STARDATE UNKNOWN

As Neelix attempts to impress Janeway with his newfound knowledge of Earth history, she reminisces about one of her ancestors, Shannon O'Donnell. As Janeway recounts the story of this woman's story, a very different one reveals itself though flashbacks of the actual events of her life. Shannon was in Indiana during December 2000 where she discovered a quaint downtown area about to be destroyed and replaced by the Millennium Gate, which was intended to be the world's first self-sustaining civic environment. The Gate developers were offering Henry Janeway a considerable amount of money for his bookstore, but he refused to sell. Through a chance encounter when her car broke down, Shannon and Henry began working together to prevent the destruction of the downtown area.

A database search uncovers a picture of Shannon and her children, which Janeway wants to frame. She explains that she grew up admiring Shannon and her bravery in building the Millennium Gate, which became the model for the first habitat on Mars. Back in 2000, Shannon was approached by Gerald Moss, one of the developers who knows of her from her days of astronaut training at NASA. Knowing that Shannon recently lost her job, Moss tries to lure her to his team as consulting engineer in return for Shannon convincing Henry to give up his shop to the project.

Intrigued by the experimental biosphere, Shannon tries to talk Henry into seeing the benefits of the Gate. He will hear nothing of it, however, and Shannon leaves

Shannon O'Donnel grows closer to the Janeways. RON TOM

when the two of them have a fight. On *Voyager,* the crew trade stories of their family history. When Janeway asserts that Shannon did work on all the early Mars projects, Paris contradicts her with his knowledge of all the early Mars projects. He is positive there were no O'Donnels working on them.

Further research shows that Shannon did not overcome any great obstacles to build the Millennium Gate, as Janeway had believed. She was only a consulting engineer, and the sole opposition she faced was Henry, who became her husband. As Shannon leaves town, and the Gate developers are about to move their plans to another city, she suddenly returns to Portage Creek to talk to Henry.

Shannon reveals she has come back to be with Henry. She wants to explore the future, but he must be willing to leave the past behind. With only a minute to spare until midnight of 2001 and the deadline for the Millennium Gate project, Henry agrees to rebuild his shop in the new biosphere. Janeway is disappointed Shannon was not the courageous explorer she always believed her to be, but she has no idea what her ancestor did for the town of Portage Creek, and a man scared to face the future. What she does have is a photograph of Shannon's family that was taken thirty-eight years after the dedication of the Millennium

Gate. It is a reminder of Shannon, a woman who had captured Janeway's imagination and inspired her.

SENSOR READINGS: The ship is on course for a class-Y cluster and should reach their destination in about three days.

ALPHA QUADRANT: At 3.2 kilometers at the base and 1 kilometer in height, with a surface covered with highly reflective solar panels, the Millennium Gate was large enough that it could be seen from orbit. ▪ Eleven years prior to this episode a Ferengi historian collected massive amounts of data on the origin of space travel in the Federation, planning to market it as a nostalgic gift item. Janeway explores dozens of histories written about twenty-first-century Earth, all of them biased depending on the home world of the historian. The Vulcans describe first contact with a "savagely illogical" race, while the Ferengi talk about Wall Street as if it were holy ground and the Bolians express dismay over the low quality of human plumbing.

PERSONAL LOGS: Janeway believed her ancestor to be one of the first women astronauts and the driving force

distant galaxy, he left the crew in stasis and turned the ship around. ▪ The Doctor's program was compiled from the most advanced holomatrices in the Federation. His "cousin" was a prize-winning chess program. ▪ Seven of Nine has an ancestor named Sven "Buttercup" Hansen, who was a twenty-second-century prize fighter.

EPISODE LOGS: The episode concludes on April 22, which Neelix establishes as the holiday "Ancestor's Eve." ▪ Although most of the world celebrated the transition from 1999 to 2000 as the change of millennium, this episode acknowledges that the new millennium actually began with the year 2001. The episode, which originally aired in 1999, correctly assumed that the Y2K bug would be a nonevent. ▪ The setting of Portage Creek is really Paramount Pictures' New York Street backlot, which is a block from the bridge set. This was the same setting, decorated differently, that was used for Kim's home in San Francisco ("Non Sequitur"). In fact, Janeway's bookstore is in a building only a few doors down from the one used as Kim's apartment.

A treasured family photo of Captain Janeway's ancestors.
CRAIG T. MATHEW

behind the Millennium Gate, which inspired her to join Starfleet. She believes that her Aunt Martha would be disappointed in the information she discovered. ▪ Paris claims that he comes from a line of "salt of the Earth types," including farmers and a few planetary colonists. he does, however, recall one pilot who flew the first orbital glider over the lower Martian plateau. ▪ In the year 2210 Kim's Uncle Jack was on a deep space mission to Beta Caprius ("when deep space meant the next star over"). His crew was in stasis for six months, leaving him alone the entire time. When he reached the destination, he discovered that Beta Caprius was just an EM echo of a

RELATIVITY

EPISODE #218

TELEPLAY BY: BRYAN FULLER & NICK SAGAN & MICHAEL TAYLOR

STORY BY: NICK SAGAN

DIRECTED BY: ALLAN EASTMAN

GUEST STARS

CAPTAIN BRAXTON	**BRUCE McGILL**
ADMIRAL PATTERSON	**DAKIN MATTHEWS**
DUCANE	**JAY KARNES**

CO-STAR

LIEUTENTANT CAREY	**JOSH CLARK**

STARDATE 52861.274

It is Janeway's first day aboard *U.S.S. Voyager,* and while she tours her new ship, she meets Seven of Nine disguised as a fully human ensign. Seven is investigating a weapon on the ship and she reports back to Captain Braxton in the future. He is contented to know where the weapon was placed but he still needs to know when. After Janeway is alerted to a chroniton flux, she almost discovers Seven's mission, which would contaminate the timeline. Braxton beams Seven from *Voyager* just in time, but she is dead when she arrives on his ship.

Kathryn Janeway takes the bridge of *Voyager* for the first time.
MICHAEL YARISH

Seven checks the ship and finds no sign of the weapon or the intruder. When Janeway detects a chroniton flux and remembers the same thing happening two years earlier, she investigates and finds Seven, whom she recognizes from that first day on the ship. Seven explains her presence on *Voyager* and persuades Janeway to trust her seemingly implausible story. When they are suddenly alerted to an intruder, they find an older version of Braxton planting the weapon.

Suffering from temporal psychosis, the future Braxton names Janeway as the cause of his problems, stemming from her numerous experiences with time travel. He suddenly jumps to two years earlier, and Seven follows him. When he is trapped in a force field, Braxton jumps five years ahead. By this time, Seven is suffering from being out of her timeframe and recruits herself in that time period to apprehend Braxton. Once Seven and Janeway catch him, Janeway must go back to her first day on the ship to capture another version of Braxton to clean up the timeline by preventing any of it from happening in the first place.

SENSOR READINGS: *Voyager* is 700,000 metric tons, with a top cruising speed of warp 9.975 at the time of its launch. It has a class-9 warp drive and a tricylic input manifold (*Voyager* is the first ship to test it in deep space). ■ In the current timeframe, the ship is located at Spatial coordinates 87-Theta by 271. ■ The bomb is planted on Deck 4, Section 39, which is not a secured area, so the hatch it is hidden behind should not be locked. ■ Temporal paradoxes show up throughout the ship where it is one time in one place, while another time in another place, and time passes quickly in some areas and slower in others. ■ Too many jumps through time lead to sensory aphasia, which affects the cerebral cortex and could lead to temporal psychosis.

DELTA QUADRANT: Sensors detect a class-M planet at a heading of 178-Mark-4.

ALPHA QUADRANT: The third brightest star in Orion—as viewed from Earth—is Gamma Orionis, or Bellatrix, the original Arabic name. ■ Albright-Salzman syndrome is a rare neurological condition that has not affected a single human being for over two centuries.

The Dalí paradox is also known as the melting clock effect, and refers to a temporal fissure that slows the passage of time to a gradual halt. The Pogo paradox is a causality loop in which interference to prevent an event actually triggers the same event. For example the case of the Borg traveling back in time to stop Zephram

Braxton orders his men to go back in time and retrieve Seven before *Voyager* explodes in what would be the third time they have tried to help Seven save the crew. On *Voyager*, temporal distortions are fracturing space-time throughout the ship. When Seven and Torres investigate, Seven's ocular implant detects a device emitting the distortions. Before they can take action, the hull begins to demolecularize. Janeway orders the crew to abandon ship as two men materilize and beam Seven away.

Seven is once again welcomed to the Federation *Timeship Relativity*. It is five hundred years in the future, and Braxton wants to solve the mystery of who planted the weapon. His crew has recruited Seven because of her ocular implant's ability to detect irregularities in space-time. Once they persuade her to help them, Seven is beamed to *Voyager* two years before she became part of the crew. The ship is under attack from the Kazon, and Braxton believes this is the time a saboteur boarded the vessel and planted the device. Seven is to find him and stop him at all costs.

TIME TRAVEL

"Time travel. Since my first day on the job as a Starfleet captain, I swore I'd never let myself get caught in one of these God-forsaken paradoxes. The future is the past, the past is the future. It all gives me a headache."

Kathryn Janeway, "Future's End, Part I"

Starfleet starships have occasionally been thrown backward and forward through time. Some crews had the opportunity to meet famous people and bear witness to major events. Unfortunately, they were also threatened with being trapped in time, doomed to become part of the events they witnessed, or threatened with having to break the Temporal Prime Directive.

"PARALLAX" *Voyager* gets caught in the event horizon of a collapsed singularity when responding to a distress call that the crew itself sent out. Janeway and Torres take a shuttle and project a dekyon beam at the rupture to allow the ship to escape.

"TIME AND AGAIN" The explosion of a polaric ion plant destroys an alien planet and shatters subspace. Janeway and Paris get caught in a subspace fracture and go back in time to a day before the cataclysmic event. Once the captain realizes that their own rescue caused the explosion, she stops the event from occurring, which resets time so that it had never happened.

"EYE OF THE NEEDLE" The crew discovers a micro-wormhole leading back to the Alpha Quadrant. At first they are excited to learn that they can send a transporter beam through, until they realize that a time shift within the wormhole leads it to open on the other end twenty years in the past. They do, however, send letters for Starfleet and loved ones to the Romulan on the other end, but the letters never make it to their intended destinations.

"NON SEQUITUR" Kim's shuttle intersects a temporal inversion fold in the space-time matrix and alters his timeline so that he is sent back to Earth having never served on *Voyager*. To reverse the process, he re-creates the exact occurrence that altered his reality with the help of an alternate Tom Paris.

"DEATH WISH" An escaped prisoner of the Q Continuum briefly sends the crew back in time to the big bang.

"FUTURE'S END, PARTS I&II" When debris from *Voyager* is found in the wreckage of an explosion that affects the twenty-ninth century, a Captain Braxton—from the future—travels back through time to prevent the crew's involvement in destroying his timeline. A confrontation between the two ships causes a rift in the space-time continuum to destabilize, pulling both ships into Earth's past. After *Voyager* manages to correct events so that the original explosion never occurred an alternate version of Braxton comes back to return *Voyager* to its proper time and place in history.

"BEFORE AND AFTER" After a biotemporal chamber activates chroniton radiation still within the body of an aged Kes, the Ocampan finds herself travelling backward though time until she gathers enough information for the Doctor to reverse the process, bringing her in line with the current timeframe.

"YEAR OF HELL, PARTS I&II" Krenim Captain Annorax uses his weapon ship to trigger temporal incursions in the hope that he can restore his race to their original timeline. After *Voyager* creates temporal shielding that interferes with Annorax's plans, the crew becomes an enemy of the Krenim who try everything in their power to destroy the ship. Finally, Janeway is forced to take *Voyager* on a kamikaze run against the weapon-ship destroying both vessels and resetting the timeline so that none of the events occurred.

"TIMELESS" Fifteen years in the future, Kim and Chakotay work to change the events of their history by saving *Voyager* from destruction. Sending a message through Seven of Nine's transceiver, they are able to stop *Voyager* from making a deadly attempt at a shortcut home, and erase their alternate timeline.

"RELATIVITY" With the help of future Starfleet officers both Seven and Janeway travel through time to stop the planting of a temporal disruptor aboard *Voyager*. When they discover that the saboteur is an alternate version of Captain Braxton, they manage to save the ship and bring the culprit to justice.

"BLINK OF AN EYE" Caught in the gravitational gradient of a planet with a high level of rotation, *Voyager* is seen through centuries on the planet as both a god and a threat to the inhabitants. Eventually the natives help the ship break free.

"FURY" An enraged Kes returns to *Voyager* and sends herself back in time to destroy the ship and return her younger self home. Janeway manages to thwart her plans and with the help of a young Kes creates a message to stop a later Kes from re-enacting her plan.

"SHATTERED" A chronokinetic surge interacts with the warp core, shattering the space-time continuum aboard the ship, breaking it into thirty-seven different time frames. Chakotay, along with a Janeway from the past, must navigate those timeframes to release a cure into the gel packs and send Chakotay back before the surge.

"Q2" The son of Q traps the crew in a temporal loop whereby they keep repeating the same thirty-second period over and over again (the results of this prank go unseen).

"ENDGAME, PARTS I&II" Twenty-six years in the future, Admiral Janeway, distraught over the many losses her crew endured in their voyage home, enacts a plan sending herself back in time to aid her ship in a final battle against the Borg.

Time-Related Stories

"THE 37'S" The crew comes across a planet very much like Earth, inhabited by descendents of alien abductees from 1937, as well as a handful of original "37's" frozen in stasis.

"TATTOO" Chakotay meets an ancient race that descended from the Sky Spirits worshipped by his people.

"FLASHBACK" When an alien parasite threatens Tuvok's life, Janeway and he take a journey back in time, via a mind-meld, to the moment the invader entered his mind. Together they relive the events of Tuvok's first Starfleet posting aboard the *U.S.S. Excelsior* during the time of the Khitomer Peace Conference.

"REMEMBER" Through mental telepathy, Torres experiences the past life of a dying woman who served as witness to government sponsored mass executions.

"THE Q AND THE GREY" Janeway and the crew visit a re-creation of the Q Continuum in the form of a Civil War–era battle.

"DISTANT ORIGIN" The crew meets an ancient race that evolved from a species that lived on Earth in the far distant past.

"THE KILLING GAME, PARTS I&II" Held prisoner by the Hirogen, half the crew is forced into mindlessly playing out warlike events on the holodeck, including a scenario placing them in France during World War II.

"LIVING WITNESS" Seven hundred years in the future, the Doctor's backup program is found during an excavation on a planet still hurting from a past civil war. With the Doctor's revelation of the truth behind the events leading to the war—and *Voyager's* involvement—he manages to set the record straight and they finally learn to live together.

"GRAVITY" A shuttle manned by Tuvok, Paris and the Doctor is pulled into a subspace zone. It crashes on a planet where a day equals fifteen minutes on *Voyager*.

"BRIDE OF CHAOTICA!" When *Voyager* intersects a layer of subspace inhabited by photonic life-forms, they are forced to play out Paris's 1930s era space serial *Captain Proton* holoprogram to end a war between the aliens and the evil holo-character Dr. Chaotica.

"11:59" The story of Janeway's ancestor Shannon O'Donnel is seen through a story told in flashback on the eve of 2001.

"ONE SMALL STEP" After finding an ancient Earth artifact—the *Aries IV* spaceship—in a spatial anomaly, a rescue team hears a dying lieutenant's final log entries.

"FAIR HAVEN", "SPIRIT FOLK" The crew visits the ancient holographic town of Fair Haven.

"MEMORIAL" An alien memorial forces the crew to mentally relive the events of a horrendous atrocity in which eighty-two of the planet's civilians lost their lives over three hundred years ago.

"PROPHECY" *Voyager* encounters a generational ship of Klingons whose ancestors left the Alpha Quadrant over a century ago in search of their prophet whom they now believe to be Torres's unborn child.

"FRIENDSHIP ONE" Sent to retrieve a probe sent out before Starfleet existed, the crew comes across a planet destroyed by the information provided by the equipment.

In order to save her present, Seven infiltrates *Voyager* before its launch. RON TOM

Cochrane from breaking the warp barrier, which in turn led the *U.S.S. Enterprise* NCC-1701-E to intervene and assist Cochrane with the flight the Borg were trying to prevent. ▪ A force-3 temporal disruptor is designed to fracture space-time. ▪ Braxton is relieved of duty for crimes he is *going to* commit and the various Braxtons are to be reintegrated before the trial held on his crimes. The duplicate Sevens will also be reintegrated.

PERSONAL LOGS: Janeway buried herself in *Voyager's* schematics for three months before taking command. Admiral Patterson welcomed Janeway to *Voyager* on her first day aboard. He had taught her fractal calculus at the Academy. ▪ At the time of the ship's launch, the EMH was programmed with over five million medical procedures

and the medical knowledge of 3,000 cultures. ▪ Seven of Nine has a visual acuity index of 99.6 and her ocular implant can detect disruptions in space-time better than twenty-ninth-century sensors.

EPISODE LOGS: In keeping with the events of "Future's End," the Captain Braxton in this episode spent three decades in the twentieth century and had to go through extensive rehabilitation before he could return to duty. Therefore, he is not the same Captain Braxton whom *Voyager* encountered at the conclusion of "Future's End," since that Braxton had no memory of the timeline in which he was on Earth. ▪ Braxton refers to a temporal inversion *Voyager* caused in the Takara sector, ("Timeless").

WARHEAD

EPISODE #219

TELEPLAY BY: **MICHAEL TAYLOR & KENNETH BILLER**

STORY BY: **BRANNON BRAGA**

DIRECTED BY: **JOHN KRETCHMER**

CO-STARS

ENSIGN JENKINS	McKENZIE WESTMORE
ALIEN	STEVE DENNIS

STARDATE UNKNOWN

Answering a distress call Kim—in the command of his first away team—finds an artificial intelligence life-form. The machine has bio-neural circuitry and, with the help of the Doctor's translating, reveals it is suffering from a technical form of amnesia. The machine thinks it is an organic being, but once it is beamed to *Voyager*, the Doctor explains the truth. As they search for the machine's "partner," *Voyager* scans a planet's surface and finds a crater filled with radiogenic decay, leading the crew to realize they have beamed aboard a weapon of mass destruction.

In sickbay, Torres attempts to separate the bio-neural circuitry from the explosive and download its synaptic patterns into a holographic matrix. Suddenly, the weapon arms itself, and Torres is forced to use an EM pulse to short it out. She and Kim soon discover the machine has commandeered the Doctor's program and now recalls that it is a long-range tactical armor unit, which was deployed at a target it never reached. The machine,

The warhead hijacks the Doctor's program. RON TOM

speaking through the Doctor's body, he tells Janeway that she will help him find his target, or her ship and crew will be destroyed.

After Janeway is given new coordinates to follow, Neelix locates a merchant who may be familiar with the weapon. He offers to disarm it in exchange for full access to salvaging its parts. Wary of handing the weapon over to a stranger, Janeway refuses. When the merchant's ship tries to get a transporter lock on the machine, it sends an antimatter surge back through the beam and blows up the alien ship. Meanwhile, Seven realizes her nanoprobes can be adapted to disable the weapon's circuitry.

The crew plans to make the machine believe they are navigating a minefield. When Seven is brought into sickbay pretending to suffer from burns, Tuvok will disrupt the Doctor's program. This will give Seven enough time to inject her nanoprobes into the weapon and disable it. Meanwhile, Kim and Torres retrieve lost data from the weapon's memory files, which reveal its launch was a mistake. The weapon refuses to believe this new information and soon realizes the crew's plan to deactivate it, incapacitating Seven. Shortly after, the crew finds thirty-two additional weapons have joined them in search of their "friend."

The new weapons order the warhead to transport off

The crew plans to rescue the Doctor by faking an injury to Seven. CRAIG T. MATTHEW

Voyager and continue onto the target, but Kim persuades it to look for its people's confirmation code in the rest of his memory files. When it confirms the order to cease its mission was valid, the weapon tells the others to stand down. They cannot be diverted, so the weapon reconfigures its bio-neural matrix and joins the others. Once it leads them to a safe distance, the weapon detonates, destroying the others and itself in the process.

SENSOR READINGS: The crew reconfigures the sensory array to send false telemetry and trick the weapon into believing they are navigating the minefield. Paris plans to simulate mine explosions with well-timed disruptions to the inertial dampers. To simulate a large explosion Janeway orders the plasma relays on Deck 6 blown out.

DELTA QUADRANT: The weapon is a Series 5 long-range tactical armor unit with paratrinic shielding, a dense energy matrix, and bio-neural circuitry that is used to mimic humanoid synaptic functions. It speaks in duotronic algorithms that the Doctor's translation matrix can interpret. Its people have deployed it to attack a military installation on Salina Prime, located in Grid 11, Vector 9341. The trader, Onquanii, claims it was built by the Druoda. He also claims it has a class-11 intelligence factor, is warp capable, has a maximum range of eighty light-years, and could fly through an ion storm or an armada of hostile ships and still find its target. The strategic command matrix experienced a malfunction in one of the command sensors that activated a series of launch sequences and thirty-four weapons were mistakenly launched. The orders were rescinded because the war ended nearly three years ago.

Onquanii travels on a cloaked vessel. He previously traded Neelix some equipment similar in technology to that of the weapon. His transporter system employs a dampening field that disables the weapon's detonators until his engineers can disarm it.

ALPHA QUADRANT: According to the Officer's Manual, Section 126: "When taken captive by a hostile alien force, seek an opportunity to engage the assailant."

PERSONAL LOGS: Paris celebrates the anniversary of his first date with Torres. ▪ The first time Torres led a Maquis away team she led her people into a cave she thought was a Cardassian military installation because she had mistaken unstable mineral deposits for weapons signatures. There was then a rockslide that trapped them in the cave for three days. ▪ Kim spends his fourth night in a row of bridge duty in the command chair.

EQUINOX, PART I

EPISODE #220

TELEPLAY BY: BRANNON BRAGA & JOE MENOSKY

STORY BY: RICK BERMAN & BRANNON BRAGA & JOE MENOSKY

DIRECTED BY: DAVID LIVINGSTON

SPECIAL GUEST STAR

CAPTAIN RANSOM	JOHN SAVAGE

GUEST STARS

BURKE	TITUS WELLIVER
GILMORE	OLIVIA BIRKELUND
LESSING	RICK WORTHY

CO-STARS

NAOMI WILDMAN	SCARLETT POMERS
CREW MEMBER	STEVE DENNIS
COMPUTER VOICE	MAJEL BARRETT

STARDATE UNKNOWN

Answering a distress call, the *Voyager* crew is shocked to find the Federation *Starship Equinox*, a science vessel built for planetary research. Captain Ransom pleads with Janeway to extend *Voyager*'s shields over his ship, which is under attack. As the shields are put in place, interspatial fissures erupt on several decks. Once a rescue team boards *Equinox*, they find many crew members dead of a thermalytic reaction that desiccated every cell in their bodies. A few people are still alive, including Ransom, who explains that the entity known as the Caretaker pulled his ship into the Delta Quadrant.

The aliens are weakening the ships' shields, trying to enter the two ships at various fissure points. At the current rate, shields will be down in less than two days. However, the aliens cannot survive inside the ship's atmosphere, so the crew sets out to create a multiphasic forcefield to trap the aliens and show them they cannot afford to continue their assault. Meanwhile, Ransom and Lieutenant Burke secretly discuss that they must hide their research lab and warp core from the *Voyager* crew.

Once Seven determines how to create a security grid that will protect the ships, Janeway decides it will be in everyone's best interest to abandon the *Equinox* and concentrate all efforts on preserving *Voyager*. Appearing to reluctantly agree, Ransom and his crew secretly prepare to steal *Voyager*'s field generator and leave them behind. When Seven and Tuvok discover that the research lab

For the first time in five years, Janeway boards another Starfleet vessel, the devastating hulk of the *Equinox*. RON TOM

aboard *Equinox* has been deliberately contaminated with radiation to keep them away from it, Janeway sends in the Doctor to investigate.

The Doctor finds the remains of an alien have been converted into a crystalline compound to enhance the *Equinox*'s propulsion systems. When Janeway learns that Ransom and his crew were planning to kill as many of the aliens as it took to get home, she confines them to their quarters and sets about to make contact with the aliens. Meanwhile, the Doctor summons the *Equinox*'s EMH, which was also designed in the image of their creator, Dr. Zimmerman. The *Equinox*'s physician explains that he created the conversion technology after his ethical subroutines were deleted. Then, he disables the Doctor and steals his holoemitter.

Once the *Equinox*'s Doctor frees his crew from confinement, they beam back to their ship where Seven, who was onboard trying to disable their converters, is rendered unconscious. Before the security grid can be put online, Ransom and his crew steal *Voyager*'s field generator. As the *Equinox* sets course for the Alpha Quadrant at warp speed, *Voyager*'s shields go completely offline, and the aliens attack *Voyager* through fissures on all decks.

SENSOR READINGS: Seven runs a thermagraphic analysis of *Voyager*'s shields that reveals multiple stress points where the aliens are trying to infiltrate the vessel. Each time a fissure opens within a meter of the shields, it weakens them by .3 percent. ▪ The *Equinox* crew built a multiphasic force field to capture the creatures. Janeway hopes to expand on the technology to create a latticework of multiphasic force fields around both ships. They also plan to adapt it to create an autoinitiating security grid so

Seven is rendered unconscious before the *Equinox* crew escapes.
RON TOM

one of the summoning devices and constructed a containment field that would prevent the life-form from vanishing so quickly. Unfortunately, something went wrong, and it died. They were able to use its remains to travel over 10,0000 light-years in less than two weeks.

The *Equinox* has not encountered the Borg. They did, however, run into the Krowtonan Guard their first week in the Delta Quadrant. The aliens claimed they violated their territory. Ransom gave the order to stay on course and wound up losing thirty-nine people, roughly half his crew.

ALPHA QUADRANT: The *Equinox* is a *Nova*-class science vessel designed for planetary research, not long-range tactical missions. It carries minimal weapons and cannot go faster than warp 8. Taking the *Equinox*'s shields offline and recharging the emitters will bring them up to full power, but the charging cycle takes forty-five seconds. Their ship has only a few isograms of dilithium crystals. However, they do have some interesting supplies, including two kilotons of kemacite ore, a dozen canisters of mercurium, and at least one synaptic stimulator. The last item is a neural interface worn behind the ear that taps into the visual cortex and shows different alien vistas (a "poor man's holodeck"). It was given to them by a race known as the Ponea, who see every first contact as an excuse to throw a party. ▪ Ransom was an exobiologist who was promoted to captain after he made first contact with the Yridians, a race previously believed to be extinct by the Federation and the Borg (to whom they were Species 6291).

Starfleet Regulation 191, Article 14 states that "In a combat situation involving more than one ship, command falls to the vessel with tactical superiority." Meanwhile, Starfleet Regulation 3, paragraph 12 notes that "In the event of imminent destruction, a captain is authorized to preserve the lives of his crew by any justifiable means."

the moment an alien enters the ship, a forcefield will surround it. ▪ The astrometrics lab is on Deck 8, Section 29, and the warp plasma manifold is on Deck 11.

DELTA QUADRANT: The Ankari performed one of their sacred rituals to invoke spirits of good fortune from another realm to bless the journey of the *Equinox* crew. The spirits were actually nucleogenic life-forms emitting high levels of antimatter. The crew managed to obtain

PERSONAL LOGS: When Torres was dating the *Equinox*'s Lieutenant Burke at the Academy, he nicknamed her "B.L.T." She once borrowed his blue sweater with the class insignia on the back and never returned it.

EPISODE LOGS: The ships are now 35,000 light-years from home.

LIEUTENANT B'ELANNA TORRES

WIDER, INCLUDING TORRES AND TUVOK

B'ELANNA TORRES is a half-Klingon, half-human woman in her twenties who is frantically working at the consoles of the barely spaceworthy craft . . .

—B'Elanna Torres's first appearance in "Caretaker"

In the grand tradition of *Star Trek* engineers, Torres was first introduced as a miracle worker draining every ounce of energy from the Maquis ship to power the engines for their escape from the Cardassians. Her skill placed her in the unenviable position of the highest-ranking Maquis member of the crew—after Chakotay—when she was chosen over Starfleet Lieutenant Carey to be chief engineer. However, at Chakotay's insistence, she eased herself into the position and was one of the first of the Maquis to bend to the Starfleet standards. She went against the suggestions of her Maquis crewmates as early as "Prime Factors," in which she accepted the blame for disobeying orders rather than participate in a cover-up.

Beyond her being the representative Maquis crew member, the most explored facet of her character was her seemingly never-ending battle between her human and Klingon halves. "Faces" served as the most literal battle, as her body was divided into two separate persons who were forced to work together to escape a Vidiian prison. Though she did come to terms with herself in that episode, she was far from accepting her Klingon heritage. It was through episodes like "Day of Honor" and "Prophecy" that she began to examine what it meant to be a Klingon and learn how important her heritage was to her life.

A natural outgrowth of this was Torres's coming to terms with her feelings toward her parents. In "Barge of

BRYON J. COHEN

the Dead" Torres dealt with her guilt over dishonoring her mother by turning away from her Klingon roots. In "Lineage" she dealt with issues brought on by her father's abandonment and how that trauma affected her own reaction to having a child who would appear Klingon. She experienced a moment of closure during "Author, Author," as she finally spoke to her father following many years of silence.

Torres's earliest interactions were primarily with Chakotay. But while there was a hint that she may have been attracted to her former captain ("Persistence of Vision"), their relationship never went beyond that of close friends. Chakotay was a mentor to her. As the only person Chakotay had met who had tried to kill her animal guide, she did not always appreciate his tutelage. Ultimately, he was the one person who saved her when she was hell bent on destroying herself to prove that she could still feel after learning of the death of most of the Maquis ("Extreme Risk").

Kate Mulgrew: I happen to love Roxann on a personal level and that fiery Klingon who so resisted me initially. I'm not sure that we ever uncovered all of the wonderful nuances and ramifications of this very complicated relationship between us.

It did not take Janeway long to realize that Torres was the perfect candidate for chief engineer, and the two fell into a friendship based on mutual respect that, at times, mirrored the mother/daughter relationship Torres never had with her own parent. But it was Kim who really brought Torres into the Starfleet fold by making her feel welcome aboard the ship. As the first crewman she met when they were stranded with the Ocampa, Kim and Torres fell into an easy friendship of teasing and trust.

Garrett Wang: The earliest potential relationship was Kim/Torres. From the beginning there were the little nicknames where she called Kim "Starfleet." And that was something that I thought, "well, that's definitely possible." But they decided to go down the road of Paris/Torres.

And, of course it would be Paris who would win the affections of the fiery half-Klingon. The road to love was not easy as Torres initially rejected him at every chance—not because she didn't have feelings for him, but because she was afraid to let anyone get too close. In fact, it took over twenty episodes from their first flirtation to her finally admitting her love for him in "Day of Honor." After getting past the initial difficulties of their new couplehood, Torres and Paris settled into a comfortable pairing with only a few catches along the way. For a time, in fact, their relationship grew so comfortable that Torres believed it was never going to move forward.

Her marriage reawakened her insecurities about being Klingon. These were thoroughly examined in the heartbreaking "Lineage," in which she almost irrevocably removed the Klingon traits from her unborn child.

ROBBIE ROBINSON

Robert Duncan McNeill: I think Roxann and I were both excited initially when the producers decided to explore a relationship on our show and have these characters together. I always thought that they both are very strong-willed people so it made for a very interesting relationship. And a very colorful relationship, for those two. You know, I thought it was a good match . . . It's got a real sense of direction and a very unique kind of story for Star Trek.

Torres also received much help in accepting her roles as a Klingon and as chief engineer from those who were not necessarily her closest friends. Though they were often at odds, Seven of Nine helped Torres become a better leader by testing the Klingon's patience and abilities. The Doctor too proved helpful in controlling some of her behavior, even becoming the godfather to her daughter after Torres nearly forced him to perform the operation that would remove the unborn child's Klingon DNA. But it was more often morale officer Neelix who would pop up when she most wanted to be alone, forcing her to talk through her problems and accept them.

Ethan Phillips: There's been times where B'Elanna hasn't quite sought my help but she was receptive to it. I remember when I brought her the blood pie and convinced her to honor her Klingon half ("Day of Honor"). Then there was the time when she was having problems with Tom and I got her to open up a little bit ("Drive"). That was all in my capacity as morale officer. I think, because of that, B'Elanna has come to respect Neelix more. It was interesting that in the first year and a half I had practically no exchanges at all with Roxann.

As Torres, Roxann Dawson had the difficult task of portraying a woman full of boiling emotions that stood in contrast to the calm manner in which typical Starfleet characters behaved. Add to that the task of hiding her own pregnancy at the middle of the series run, as well as carrying off her character's pregnancy at series end. It was an interesting evolution for a young actress who grew along with her character. Dawson's own experiences obviously came in handy for those episodes where her character dealt with issues regarding her child in a way that only a mother could understand.

SEASON SIX

The sixth season opens with the conclusion of "Equinox," in which Janeway becomes obsessed with bringing Ransom and his crew to justice. The *Equinox* crew serves as a wonderful example of how things could have turned out if Janeway had allowed herself, and her own crew, to forgo Starfleet principles in their attempt to get home. Granted, from time to time, the crew has bent the Prime Directive, but there are some who would argue, "What crew in Starfleet history has not worked around it to some degree?" However, the season opening episode shows what could happen if the rules became too relaxed. In the end, it also proves that even a Starfleet officer who has lost his way could be redeemed.

"We're always breaking the Prime Directive to some degree, just making contact with another species breaks the Prime Directive. There are different elements to the Prime Directive. One is that we don't interfere with warp-ready species, another is we don't get involved in the internal affairs of other worlds. But, I think whenever we meet another species, we are going to influence them, and we're going to get involved with them, and sometimes we're forced to deal with species that are sub-light-speed species. So it's something that we have had to tread very gently about. I think it's a principle that always is enticing to the writers but one that we have to be careful about because the interpretation of the Prime Directive is arguable."

—RICK BERMAN

Following the dark opener are the equally dark episodes of "Survival Instinct" and "Barge of the Dead," in which Seven and Torres respectively deal with issues of life and death, with dramatic results. There are, however, many light moments in the sixth season of *Voyager,* beginning with "Tinker, Tenor, Doctor, Spy." Though addressing the serious subject of the Doctor's place on the ship, it is done with equal mix of humor and adventure as the EMH struggles with his malfunctioning program and a threatening race. The season continues, as the five before it, alternating between dramatic, humorous, and adventurous storylines.

History, particularly that related to the space program, has always played a part in the *Star Trek* universe.

"One Small Step" pays homage to the U.S. space program in the fictional retelling of a failed manned Mars mission, which ultimately proves to Lieutenant John Kelly that life exists on other planets. Not coincidentally, this episode aired at a time when the United States was making its own unmanned trips to the red planet.

The holodeck, once again provides a delightful diversion that evolves into a bit of a problem when the residents of Paris's latest world—"Fair Haven"—become self-aware in "Spirit Folk." However, the setting does allow for the exploration of Janeway's personal life. Fair Haven continues to provide a relaxing spot where the crew can be themselves—once the townspeople accept that they are visitors from the future.

The crew complement grows this season on three different occasions. First, the few surviving members of the *Equinox* crew are added to the manifest, though stripped of rank and with much to prove before they can be welcomed into the *Voyager* family. Then former *Excalibur* engineer and former Borg drone, Marika Willkarah, joins the crew for her brief life after finally being disconnected from her Borg triad. And later, Naomi Wildman gets a group of playmates in the form of the Borg children—Icheb, Mezoti, Rebi, and Azan.

Meanwhile, a visitor from the past returns, as Kes comes back to *Voyager*. Although the story starts out with her dramatically changed, in the end, the crew she had come to know as family rescues her from herself and sends her home. The crew continue their own journey home getting closer with every passing day.

"I think Voyager is pretty much exactly where we expected it to be. I think our characters are acting and doing pretty much what we hoped to have them doing at this point in the game. Obviously we, at first, didn't expect the addition of Jeri Ryan with the Seven of Nine character, which has been a great addition. But, you know, our hopes were to keep this ship lost in space so to speak, and to keep a fresh outlook onto their future, while, at the same time, having them try to navigate dangerous waters to get back home."

—RICK BERMAN

EQUINOX, PART II

EPISODE #221

TELEPLAY BY: BRANNON BRAGA & JOE MENOSKY

STORY BY: RICK BERMAN & BRANNON BRAGA & JOE MENOSKY

DIRECTED BY: DAVID LIVINGSTON

SPECIAL GUEST STAR

CAPTAIN RANSOM	JOHN SAVAGE

GUEST STARS

BURKE	TITUS WELLIVER
GILMORE	OLIVIA BIRKELUND
LESSING	RICK WORTHY

CO-STARS

NAOMI WILDMAN	SCARLETT POMERS
THOMPSON	STEVE DENNIS
ANKARI	ERIC STEINBERG
COMPUTER VOICE	MAJEL BARRETT

STARDATE UNKNOWN

As nucleogenic life-forms attack *Voyager*, Janeway uses a deflector pulse to reinforce the shields and force the creatures off the ship. Safe for the moment, she orders the crew to locate the *U.S.S. Equinox* so they can retrieve the abducted Seven of Nine. Unbeknownst to the crew, the Doctor is also being held captive aboard the fleeing vessel and the *Equinox's* EMH has remained on *Voyager*.

When Ransom attempts to engage the enhanced warp drive, the ship stalls because Seven has locked out the power relays with codes that only she knows. Ransom tries to coerce the codes out of her, but when she refuses to talk, he deletes the Doctor's ethical subroutines in order to solicit his help. The hologram then sets out to extract the information from Seven's cortical implants, which could severely damage her higher brain functions.

When *Voyager* finds the hidden ship, the *Equinox* EMH manages to send Ransom a coded message to warn him, but Janeway still fires several photon torpedoes, badly damaging the ship. Knowing he cannot win, Ransom retreats into warp, temporarily escaping from *Voyager*. During the battle, however, Janeway manages to beam three of Ransom's crew aboard her ship.

Noah Lessing is held in the cargo bay, where Janeway orders him to reveal Ransom's tactical status, saying that she is prepared to drop the shields around the room and allow the nucleogenic life-forms to materialize and kill

Burke, takes control of the ship unwilling to surrender. *Voyager* fires on *Equinox* again, giving Ransom time to escape to the transporter room. He then contacts Janeway, telling her that he is surrendering and will help her beam the *Equinox* crew aboard her ship. Believing that Ransom has finally remembered his Starfleet ideals, Janeway accepts the transport of the handful of remaining *Equinox* crewmen and Seven. The Doctor's program is also transferred to *Voyager*'s sickbay, where he immediately deletes the *Equinox*'s EMH program from the computer.

The nucleogenic life-forms also begin to attack *Equinox* and manage to kill Burke before Janeway can beam him to *Voyager*. The only person left aboard *Equinox* is Captain Ransom. With the warp core about to breach, Ransom tells Janeway to get as far away as possible, then he navigates his ship to a safe distance, sacrificing himself as the *Equinox* explodes.

Janeway reinstates Chakotay and strips the remain-

While using his synaptic stimulator, Ransom is haunted by images of Seven. MICHAEL YARISH

him if he refuses. When Lessing remains silent, Janeway escorts Chakotay outside the cargo bay and drops the shields on that section. Chakotay realizes that Janeway is really planning to let an alien attack Lessing, he breaks into the room and fires his phaser at the fissure, collapsing it before anything can pass through. Janeway is shocked at Chakotay's disobedience and relieves him of duty.

With Lessing's reluctant help, the crew contacts the Ankari, the race who innocently introduced the nucleogenic creatures to the *Equinox* crew. When the Ankari come aboard and summon the aliens, Janeway tells them that she will give them the *Equinox*, much to Tuvok's chagrin.

By the time *Voyager* catches up with *Equinox*, Ransom is experiencing visions of Seven of Nine—a manifestation of his guilt over his actions. He tells his crew that he is willing to cooperate with Janeway, but his first officer, Lt.

Ransom begins to remember Starfleet's ideals. MICHAEL YARISH

ing *Equinox* crew of their rank. She orders them to serve on *Voyager* as crewmen, telling them that they will have to earn her trust. The captain must also regain the trust of the crew, as she nearly abandoned all her ideals in her obsession to stop Ransom.

SENSOR READINGS: The cargo bay is located in Section 29-Alpha.

DAMAGE REPORT: *Voyager* sustains heavy damage to the engines in the first alien attack. Later, there is a hull breach on Deck 4.

DELTA QUADRANT: Ransom hides his ship near a planet with a parthogenic atmosphere that keeps them from being detected while they make repairs. The planet also has deuterium deposits. ▪ The Ankari use a unique form of propulsion that makes them difficult to track.

ALPHA QUADRANT: According to his service record, Ransom tends to hide when being pursued. At Epsilon IV he ran into a Klingon bird-of-prey and played a game of cat and mouse in the nebula until the Klingons gave up. Two years later he eluded a Romulan warbird by taking his vessel into the atmosphere of a gas giant.

PERSONAL LOGS: Chakotay once figured out how to speak with a Terrelian Seapod. ▪ Seven's cortical array contains an index of her memory engrams. To remove it will severely damage her higher brain functions, language, and cognitive skills.

CREW COMPLEMENT: Two unnamed *Voyager* crewmen die in the first alien attack in which thirteen others are injured. Later, the survivors of the *Equinox* crew are added: Noah Lessing, Marla Gilmore, James Morrow, Brian Sofin, and Angelo Tassoni.

SURVIVAL INSTINCT

EPISODE #222
WRITTEN BY: **RONALD D. MOORE**
DIRECTED BY: **TERRY WINDELL**

GUEST STARS

TWO OF NINE	VAUGHN ARMSTRONG
THREE OF NINE	BERTILA DAMAS
FOUR OF NINE	TIM KELLEHER

CO-STARS

NAOMI WILDMAN	SCARLETT POMERS
DYING BORG	JONATHAN BRECK
COMPUTER VOICE	MAJEL BARRETT

STARDATE 53049.2

Docked at the Markonian Outpost, *Voyager* opens its doors to anyone who wishes to visit. The mess hall is crowded with guests, as Seven of Nine and Naomi have lunch together. A man approaches Seven, making her an offer of some Borg equipment. Seeing the items, she experiences a flashback to her past as a Borg, the items are Borg relays from Seven of Nine's original unimatrix. Seven accepts the components, telling the man that Captain Janeway will compensate him. As he walks away, he communicates telepathically with two others, telling them to prepare to penetrate *Voyager*'s security systems.

Seven of Nine brings the Borg relays to Torres for her evaluation, explaining that the items triggered visual images, sense memories, sounds, and smells. Torres suggests that she was experiencing nostalgia when she first saw the relays. However, Seven insists that she has no feelings whatsoever about the past and leaves the relays for computer analysis. When she returns to her alcove to regenerate, the Borg relays emit a soft beeping.

The man who brought Seven of Nine the Borg relays enters the cargo bay with two others, and assimilation tubes appear from one of their arms, penetrating Seven's neck. She becomes aware of their presence and opens her eyes to fight them. Tuvok arrives with a security team that fires on the three intruders. They crumple to the deck. Seven identifies them as former Borg Drones from her unimatrix—Two of Nine, Three of Nine, and Four of Nine. When they are revived, the three former Borg tell Captain Janeway that their goal was to use Seven of Nine to break their telepathic link, allowing them to become individuals.

Seven and the three Borg were the only survivors of a vessel that crashed eight year earlier. When they were

The Borg collective triad decides on a course of action. MICHAEL YARISH

reassimilated into the collective, the three were somehow linked together permanently. When the trio escaped the collective, they had their implants removed but they could not break the telepathic link between them. They were hoping that Seven of Nine remembered what happened to bind them together.

Seven suggests that a neural link between herself and three Borg may help them to find the truth. Despite the risk that she could become trapped in the link, Seven connects herself to the former drones, and they discover that she was the one who reestablished their link because of her fear of dying alone. The neural link becomes dangerous, so the Doctor is forced to break it, causing brain damage in the trio, sending them each into a comatose state. He informs Seven that the Borg will survive for only a month unless they are reassimilated into the collective.

After struggling with the decision on how to proceed, Seven finally understands the triad's plight and realizes that mere survival is inefficient. Removing their neural implants will allow the trio to live as individuals, if only for a short time, which she knows they would find preferable to being reassimilated. When the three wake, they approve of Seven's decision, but have trouble forgiving her for her past actions. Freed from their shared

thoughts, they begin to make separate plans for their brief, yet individual futures.

SENSOR READINGS: Chakotay gives out *Voyager* medallions in thanks for gifts given to the crew by visitors to the ship from the outpost. ▪ Tuvok has a three page security report listing problems caused by the visitors, ranging from a broken ODN line, missing personal items, and a damaged scanner relay to more serious infractions. ▪ Security is first alerted to the triad's activities when they telepathically reroute sensor input to secondary processors, causing a power fluctuation in the security grid.

DELTA QUADRANT: Two of Nine was a mathematician named Lansor before being assimilated. ▪ Four of Nine was a member of Species 571, named P'Chan. He was the son of Dornar and Ansha, and his primary function was to care for his parents. He believes it is against the will of Brothara to remove Borg parts and desecrate the body of the deceased. Brothara is a supernatural deity worshipped by his race. ▪ Along with Three of Nine, they have been separated from the Borg for almost four months. The left parietal lobes of their brains have been transformed into organic link nodes, binding them

Cut off from the collective, personal memories and identities resurface. MICHAEL YARISH

together in a sort of collective triad. Eight years ago the vessel they were on with Seven crashed and they became separated from the collective. Seven injected the others with nanoprobes to create an interlink between their higher brain functions to prevent them from escaping the collective. The Doctor removes the microcortical implants knowing they will live only a short time as individuals after the procedure.

The Kinbori delegation gives a gift of a heavy object consisting of several "arms" with paddles attached which is used in one of their sacred games. ▪ The Shivolians are noted as Borg designation Species 521.

PERSONAL LOGS: Among the many gifts Janeway receives from the ship's guests is a plant with prehensile vines that has a tendency to grab her by the hair. ▪ While on the Outpost, Paris and Kim get into a bar brawl. The fight results in the arrests of seven *Voyager* crewmen—

including the two bridge officers—along with thirteen Kinbori and one Morphinian café owner. The charges range from disorderly conduct to assault on a security officer. As punishment, Paris and Kim are confined to quarters. ▪ As a child, Seven of Nine was afraid of the dark. She and her father once cooked food over an open flame, presumably during a campout.

CREW COMPLEMENT: Marika Willkarah, Three of Nine who was formerly a Barjoran engineer on the *Starship Excalibur,* stays aboard in the little time she has left before she dies.

EPISODE LOGS: It can be assumed that Marika is another member of Starfleet assimilated at Wolf 359. Others include Riley ("Unity") several personalities integrated into Seven of Nine's subconscious ("Infinite Regress") and a human woman named Laura ("Unimatrix Zero").

BARGE OF THE DEAD

EPISODE #223
TELEPLAY BY: BRYAN FULLER
STORY BY: RONALD D. MOORE & BRYAN FULLER
DIRECTED BY: MIKE VEJAR

GUEST STARS

KORTAR	ERIC PIERPOINT
HIJ'QA	SHERMAN AUGUSTUS
and	
MIRAL	KAREN AUSTIN

CO-STAR

BROK'TAN	JOHN KENTON SHULL

STARDATE UNKNOWN

After escaping an ion storm, Torres's shuttle barely makes it back to *Voyager,* where she receives a mild concussion during the difficult landing. Torres has retreated to her quarters to rest when Chakotay brings her a metal shard with a Klingon insignia that was found attached to the port nacelle of her shuttle. Torres puts the object aside, but notices that blood begins to pool out of it and she hears haunting screams and other worldly cries of pain radiating from the artifact. Upon examination of the shard, she and Kim find nothing, and later Tuvok, atypically angry, suggests that she was experiencing a subconscious manifestation of her hatred of her Klingon heritage.

Neelix decides to throw a party to celebrate the discovery of an object from the Alpha Quadrant. As a reluctant Torres prepares to make a speech, a group of Klingons appear and kill the crew one by one, including Torres. Soon after, she finds herself lying on the deck of a sailing ship where a Klingon approaches her, holding a branding iron to her cheek. However, the iron fails to embed the Klingon emblem on her. A Klingon male named Brok'tan tells her that she is on the Barge of the Dead traveling to *Gre'thor,* or Klingon hell, where dishonored souls are taken.

It is announced that another dishonored soul has been delivered, and Torres is shocked to find that it is her estranged mother, Miral. Before she has the time to speak

The Doctor attempts an emergency resuscitation. MICHAEL YARISH

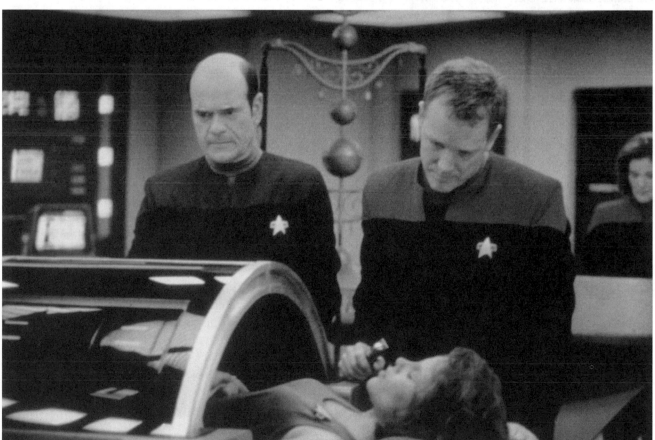

The Klingon Barge of the Dead. MICHAEL YARISH

open ahead of the Barge, and Torres is led to her own hell in the guise of an eternity aboard *Voyager*.

Suddenly, Miral reappears and tells her daughter that she can be saved by choosing to live a life with honor and discipline, like a true Klingon. The Doctor brings Torres out of her comatose state just as Miral tells her daughter that they will be reunited forever in *Sto-Vo-Kor* . . . or maybe back at home.

SENSOR READINGS: During the hallucination Torres says that the crew only has one multispatial probe. ▪ Also in the hallucination, Neelix replicates Klingon *gagh,* using a kinesthetic agent to cause the worms to move.

SHUTTLE TRACKER: Torres's shuttle is seen crash landing into the shuttlebay in her hallucination. The actual shuttle she was on did lose life support but weathered the ion storm and was safely tractored onto the ship.

ALPHA QUADRANT: The *naj* is the "dream before dying," in which those who cannot accept that they have died create the illusion of life to hold on to. The *kos'kari* act much like the Greek sirens trying to lure the dead off the Barge. *Fek'lhr* is the cave of despair ▪ Kortar was the first Klingon. According to legend, he destroyed the gods who created him. As punishment he was condemned to ferry the souls of the dishonored to *Gre'thor*. ▪ The *paq'bath* is a sacred Klingon scroll which explains that when Torres turned her back on being a Klingon, her mother suffered the dishonor, which is why she went to hell. The Eleventh Tome of Klavek tells the story of Kahless going to the afterlife to rescue his brother from the Barge of the Dead and deliver him to *Sto-Vo-Kor*. Kahless still bore a wound from the afterlife as a warning that it was not a dream. ▪ Sarpek the Fearless unearthed the famed Knife of Kiromm when he was searching for his lost *targ*.

with her mother, Torres awakens in the sickbay. The images were a dream, she has been in a coma since her shuttle escaped the vicious ion storm.

Torres tells Chakotay about her experience and struggles to make sense of it. Later, after reading texts from ancient Klingon scrolls, Torres tells Paris that she believes her actions condemned her mother to the Barge because of her own dishonor. B'Elanna feels that she can save her mother before she passes through the gates of hell if she restores the honor that was lost. At first Captain Janeway refuses to allow Torres to re-create the experience that put her in the coma, but Janeway relents, granting Torres one hour to accomplish the task. With the help of the Doctor, Torres loses consciousness and finds herself back on the Barge of the Dead.

Initially, Miral believes that her daughter is only an illusion, but B'Elanna convinces her mother that she can send her to *Sto-Vo-Kor*. However, their initial attempt fails, leaving Torres only one other option—to die for Miral and take her place in hell. Torres agrees and Miral is taken up toward to *Sto-Vo-Kor*. The gates of *Gre'thor*

PERSONAL LOGS: Chakotay's grandfather used to think he could transform himself into a wolf and venture out to explore the spirit world (it is unclear if the grandfather he refers to is the one that suffered from sensory aphasia ["The Fight"]). ▪ Torres considers the *bat'leth* to be a clumsy and overstated weapon. Miral used to call her daughter by the nickname Lanna. Following the end of her marriage to Torres's father, she pulled B'Elanna out of her Federation school and put her in a Klingon monastery so she would be taught honor and discipline. Miral prayed to Kahless every day to guide B'Elanna in the ways of the warrior. Torres almost drowned in the Sea of Gatan when she was a child, but her mother revived her. It has been ten years since they last spoke.

MEDICAL UPDATE: To induce the coma in Torres, the Doctor has the computer erect an isolation field around the surgical bay, decrease oxygen concentration within the forcefield by twenty-seven percent, and ionize the atmosphere to 5,000 particles per cubic meter.

EPISODE LOGS: Though *Voyager* is far from the Alpha Quadrant, this is not the only time the Klingons make an appearance on the series. They are also seen as holograms in Torres's program celebrating the Day of Honor, and as warrior characters in "The Killing Game." Klingons will also visit the ship in "Prophecy." ■ In the shooting script for this episode "Kortar" is listed as "Kotar" in the cast list.

TINKER, TENOR, DOCTOR, SPY

EPISODE #224
TELEPLAY BY: JOE MENOSKY
STORY BY: BILL VALLELY
DIRECTED BY: JOHN BRUNO

GUEST STARS

PHLOX	JAY M. LEGGETT
OVERLOOKER	GOOGY GRESS

CO-STARS

DEVRO	ROBERT GREENBERG
COMPUTER VOICE	MAJEL BARRETT

STARDATE UNKNOWN

Roused from a daydream, the Doctor is disappointed to find he has been excluded from a planetary away mission. He files a formal complaint with Captain Janeway regarding poor treatment by the crew and proposes a new position as Emergency Command Hologram (ECH) to function in place of the captain, in the event of a catastrophic emergency. Janeway reviews his request, but cannot grant it for him. Disappointed by the rejection, the Doctor escapes to his daydreams, where he is admired by the female crew members and later celebrated as the new ECH.

In the meantime, an alien surveillance team tries to access *Voyager*'s internal sensors but are unable to get past its security encryption, causing the Overlooker—or captain—to assign the ship a classification of "unacceptable risk." However, a crewman named Phlox discovers the

In his daydream, the Doctor is awarded a medal for courage and valor. MICHAEL YARISH

Doctor's program and taps into it to witness everything that the Doctor sees on *Voyager*. In the process he learns that *Voyager* is lost and alone in the Delta Quadrant, and informs the Overlooker that he believes it would be a prime target for the Hierarchy, to whom they report.

In the Doctor's next dream, *Voyager* is attacked by the Borg, and with the crew incapacitated, he immediately takes control, telling the computer to activate the ECH. His uniform changes to a command color, and the new captain orders the release of his imaginary photonic cannon, which destroys the Borg sphere. Unaware that he is seeing only the Doctor's daydreams Phlox thinks that Captain Janeway was killed in the attack and that the hologram is now in command of the vessel. Based on this misinformation, Phlox transmits his report to the Hierarchy where the information is processed, and an attack is ordered based on the findings.

The Doctor alerts the crew that his attempt to add

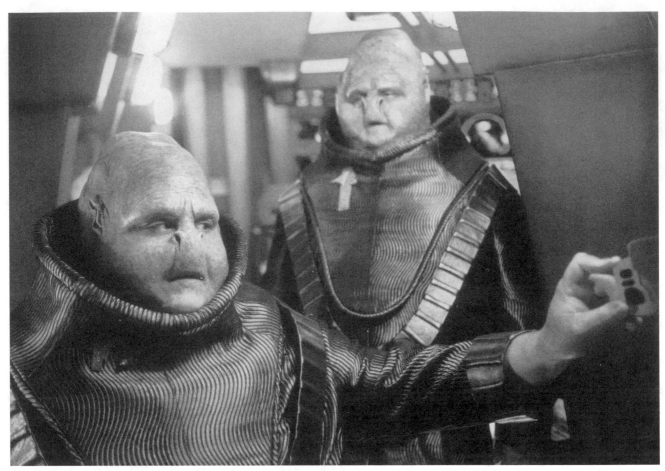

A suggested course of action is submitted to the Hierarchy. MICHAEL YARISH

cognitive projections—or daydreams—to his program seems to be malfunctioning. As a result, he is confusing the dreams with reality and randomly jumping from one daydream to the next. Torres, Kim, and Seven route the Doctor's dreams through the holographic imager and watch the Doctor in several very personal dreams, including his taking command of *Voyager*. Meanwhile, Phlox finally realizes that he was only watching the Doctor's dream life and is afraid to inform the Hierarchy of the oversight because they do not tolerate mistakes. Because Phlox feels that he has gotten to know the Doctor, he transmits a simulation of himself into the Doctor's program and warns *Voyager* of the alien attack.

In return for the warning, Phlox asks the Doctor to pose as the captain in order to trick his commanders. The alien vessel hails *Voyager* the Doctor now in the captain's seat, acts the commander of *Voyager* while Captain Janeway instructs the Doctor through a remote comlink. When the aliens upgrade to a type-4 assault, the Doctor instructs Chakotay to activate *Voyager's* imaginary photonic cannon. Phlox reminds the Overlooker of how the

device easily destroyed the Borg. Fearful of the weapon, the Overlooker contacts the Hierarchy with the new information and receives orders to retreat. As a result of his actions on the bridge, the captain changes her mind and decides to study the possibility of realizing the Doctor's ECH program.

SENSOR READINGS: A T-class nebula suddenly appears on scanners with a thousand kilometer diameter and showing signs of hydrogen, helium, and argon. The Overlooker *Assault*-class vessel hides within the nebula. ▪ Phlox's surveys show a large quantity of dilithium and antimatter on *Voyager*.

DELTA QUADRANT: At first, the Overlooker assigns *Voyager* the category "unacceptable risk" because it appears in none of their databases and initial attempts to scan the interior failed. Phlox later penetrates *Voyager's* hull using a microtunneling sensor; however, the link drops out intermittently. The Hierarchy have cloaked vessels hidden throughout the sector. Phlox gives the Doctor instructions on how to reconfigure the sensors to pick up the cloaked ships. A type-3 stealth assault begins with the ships decloaking when they are right on top of their target followed by a warning shot across the bow. This is followed by demands for supplies and technology. If the target ship does not comply, it will be destroyed. In a type-4 assault their phaser frequencies are rotated continuously, and there is a huge drain on their energy core.

On Talaxia there is a saying that "The dream dreams the dreamer." The concept behind this is that fantasies and daydreams come from someplace else, like another land, slipping into minds and whispering things never previously imagined.

ALPHA QUADRANT: According to Janeway's research, there are no legal precedents for granting a command position to a hologram. ▪ Klingons have a saying that a doctor who operates on himself has a *p'toc* for a patient.

PERSONAL LOGS: Paris refers to a whoopie cushion as "ancient technology," when Kim does not understand the reference. ▪ The Doctor files a formal grievance regarding his treatment by the crew and a proposal for his advancement. He has been experimenting with "cognitive projections" so he can daydream. The algorithms malfunction due to Phlox's interference and branch into the Doctor's perceptual subroutines. In the end, Janeway awards the Doctor a Starfleet Medal of Commendation.

EPISODE LOGS: The Doctor's dream of being an Emergency Command Hologram will come to fruition in "Workforce." ▪ The name "Phlox" will later be used as the moniker for the doctor on the fifth *Star Trek* series, *Enterprise.* ▪ Though the script for this episode does not refer to the aliens by name, it describes them as follows: "These are high tech 'spies,' but nobody here is James Bond . . . they're more like office workers . . . cogs in a vast, alien bureaucracy that we will come to know as the 'Hierarchy.'" In later episodes "The Void" and "Renaissance Man," the shooting scripts will refer to them as "Overlookers" and "Overlooker aliens" respectively.

DRAGON'S TEETH

EPISODE #225

TELEPLAY BY: **MICHAEL TAYLOR** and **BRANNON BRAGA** & **JOE MENOSKY**

STORY BY: **MICHAEL TAYLOR**

DIRECTED BY: **WINRICH KOLBE**

GUEST STARS

GEDRIN	**JEFF ALLIN**
	and
GAUL	**ROBERT KNEPPER**

CO-STARS

NAOMI WILDMAN	**SCARLETT POMERS**
MORIN	**RON FASSLER**
JISA	**MIMI CRAVEN**
TUREI	**BOB STILLMAN**
COMPUTER VOICE	**MAJEL BARRETT**

STARDATE 53167.9

An enormous tunnel of energy filled with rushing debris and micrometeoroids surrounds *Voyager* as it is pulled through a subspace corridor. A Turei vessel hails the crew, claiming the ship is traveling in their under-space. Captain Janeway insists that they stumbled there by accident and asks for help getting out. Once the Turei ship helps them back into normal space, the crew is surprised to find they traveled two hundred light-years in minutes. Captain Janeway asks the Turei if they could negotiate passage through their under-space, in hopes of returning home to the Alpha Quadrant.

The Turei ignore Janeway's request, instead telling the crew to prepare to be boarded. The captain refuses, and the Turei ships fire on *Voyager,* forcing the crew to hide on a planet with radiogenic particles in the atmosphere. As the ship moves closer to the planet, the crew notices a decimated and burnt-out megalopolis. Scans indicate that the civilization was destroyed from a bombardment of plasma-based weapons, eight hundred and ninety-two years earlier.

Faint lifesigns are detected in a chamber beneath the surface leading Janeway, and the away team to discover stasis pods containing life-forms. Apparently, each pod was programmed for only five years. However, since almost nine hundred years have passed, some kind of failure must have occurred. Without asking permission, Seven of Nine activates a pod's reanimation sequence. The humanoid inside opens his eyes and is startled by the presence of the *Voyager* crew, although his primary con-

Remarkably, Gedrin has survived statis. MICHAEL YARISH

cern is to open another pod that is covered with dirt and debris. Unfortunately, he discovers that his wife did not survive.

The alien is treated in sickbay, and identifies himself as Gedrin of Vaadwaur. He tells Janeway that the subspace corridors belonged to the Vaadwaur before their enemies combined forces and launched an attack. His people designed the stasis network out of desperation in hopes of saving their culture. The Turei begin to fire plasma charges from above. Gedrin then remembers that the Vaadwaur have a satellite directly above the city, and *Voyager* uses the satellite to get a lock on one of the Turei vessels and launches a torpedo. A direct hit forces the remaining Turei ships to move off.

In exchange for directions on how to navigate the subspace corridor, Janeway offers to help Gedrin and his people fight their way off the planet. They awaken the other surviving Vaadwaur and reactivate their ships, later forming a plan to work together against the Turei to escape the planet.

However, the Vaadwaur secretly plan to take over *Voyager,* believing that they can survive comfortably aboard. In the meantime, Neelix is suspicious of the Vaadwaur and their true intentions. A search of Talaxian folklore and Borg collected tales convince Janeway that their new allies are not to be trusted. Her skepticism is confirmed when the Vaadwaur launch vessels that head for *Voyager* instead of orbit. *Voyager* lifts off in hopes of escaping the Vaadwaur attacks.

After Janeway joins forces with the Turei, Gedrin also joins in the battle against his fellow Vaadwaur. He gives the Turei the necessary information to stop his people. *Voyager* escapes, though two days later sensors show that fifty-three Vaadwaur vessels made it through the subspace corridors. Janeway feels that due to their resourcefulness, the small bands may prove to become a threat some point in the future.

SENSOR READINGS: *Voyager* must clear the planet's thermosphere before they can go to warp. ▪ With energy reserves low, the crew opens the forward nacelle ports and reverses the pressure gradient, taking 600 kilograms of radiogenic particles directly into the plasma manifold to use them as a power source for the impulse drive.

It does not take long for the Vaadwaur to return to their aggressive ways. MICHAEL YARISH

DAMAGE REPORT: Warp drive is offline. Later, under attack by the Vaadwaur, the targeting sensors go offline. The sensor array also takes heavy damage and there are hull breaches in progress on two decks. They lose impulse engines and navigation and thrusters begin to fail. Thirteen power relays blow out on Deck 6.

DELTA QUADRANT: The Turei hit *Voyager*'s shields with a resonance pulse that alters the harmonics, pushing the ship out of the corridor.

The planet's atmosphere is charged with radiogenic particles as a result of the bombing eight hundred and ninety-two years ago. Radiation levels in the atmosphere are at over six thousand isorems. The walls of the bunker are reinforced with tritonium, and their main reactor draws power from the planet's geothermal core. ▪ It took the Vaadwaur centuries to map the subspace corridors. Gedrin claims they were the envy of a hundred species. They never kept written records of the corridors. Janeway discovers that they used their subspace corridors to expand their territory, until the other species banded together to defend themselves. ▪ The Vaadwaur have a thousand more stasis pods housing an entire battalion and their families. They also have hundreds of ships and land vehicles stored. Knowing the planet would be poisoned for centuries, they had planned to go into stasis for only five years and then search for another planet to make their home. The stasis controls were damaged in the bombing, which is why they never left the pods. They were originally a race of six billion. ▪ They had many encounters with the Borg (which they survived) and have learned to embrace death without fear. As children they are taught to fall asleep each night imagining different ways to die.

The Borg collective's memory from nine hundred years ago is fragmentary. At that time they had only assimilated a handful of systems. ▪ Neelix's ancestors referred to themselves as Talax-ilzay. The ship's computer holds Neelix's database about the Talaxian linguistic files, including the Old Tongue dialect. *Vaadwaur* is a word in the old tongue that means "foolish"—specifically in reference to a person who allows himself to be deceived by an enemy (additional meanings include: weak-minded, reckless, blind). The first written example of the word appears in *Eldaxon's Collected Folklore,* second edition—year of publication: 5012 of the New Calendar. Specific folk tales that use the word include: "The Demon with the Golden Voice," "The Tale of the Deadly Stranger," "The Tale of the Boy Who Lost His Head," and "The Tale of the Bloody Hand." Dozens of ancient folk tales describe a phantom army that appears out of thin air and then destroys entire colonies and vanishes in the blink of an eye.

ALPHA QUADRANT: Chakotay likens the Vaadwaur to the Ancient Greek myth of dragon's teeth wherein a dragon was killed in war and its teeth spread over the battlefield where they took root and warriors sprung from the ground to continue the fighting. ▪ The Klingon phrase, "Today is a good day to die" was the battle cry of Kahless. ▪ Starfleet protocols are very strict about the transfer of weapons, which keeps Janeway from arming the Vaadwaur ships with photon torpedoes.

EPISODE LOGS: In the original script for the episode, the Vaadwaur went into hibernation only five hundred years ago. It is likely their history was altered to make it more logical for them to have been nearly forgotten in Talaxian and Borg histories. ▪ Seven refers to the Devore Emporium, an authoritarian regime with eleven systems across three sectors, whom *Voyager* had encountered in "Counterpoint."

ALICE

EPISODE #226

TELEPLAY BY: BRYAN FULLER & MICHAEL TAYLOR

STORY BY: JULIANN deLAYNE

DIRECTED BY: DAVID LIVINGSTON

GUEST STARS

ALICE   CLAIRE RANKIN
ABADDON   JOHN FLECK

STARDATE UNKNOWN

When *Voyager* happens upon a junkyard of old ships, the crew stops to purchase some parts from a trader named Abaddon. Paris falls in love with a small shuttle he finds among the junked vessels, and convinces Chakotay to let him restore it. He immediately gets to work on the shuttle, which has a neurogenic interface, allowing it to interact directly with the pilot's thoughts. He names the ship *"Alice,"* and after a brief trial of the interfacing technology, Paris calls it a night. After he leaves, however, *Alice* powers on by herself, and scans him. In his quarters, Paris hears a female voice calling to him.

Driven by *Alice's* seductive power, Paris works nonstop on the shuttle. He and Torres try to celebrate its christening together, but Tom is obsessed to the point of excluding everyone. Tapping into *Alice's* database, he finds the flight suit design of her last pilot and wears it in place of his Starfleet uniform. Chakotay orders him to put his test flight on hold and attend to his official duties. When Tom complains to *Alice,* whom he is now imagining as a flesh-and-blood woman, she convinces him to use the neurogenic interface again.

Alice goads Tom into stealing power cells from *Voyager,* but when the shuttle traps Torres, sealing a hatch and shutting off life support systems, Tom realizes it is out of control. He rescues Torres and tries to alert sickbay, but the ship takes control of his body and forces him to launch and complete the interface, making him one with the machine. As Captain Janeway and the crew realize what is happening, Tom fires on *Voyager* and escapes.

Paris and Neelix strike a bargain for the desired shuttle. MICHAEL YARISH

Tuvok succeeds in shutting down *Alice*. Paris is beamed safely to sickbay, leaving *Alice* to be destroyed in the particle fountain.

SENSOR READINGS: The crew has some spare duranium sheeting in Cargo Bay 1 that, with a few modification, could be converted into gravity plating. They intend to trade this with Abaddon for fifteen power regulators in good condition and three more they could salvage with a little work. The list also includes some ion exchange rods though Seven has some doubts about them. ▪ Chakotay notes that energy is not in abundance at the moment, but he hopes they can replenish their power reserve in the next few weeks. Cargo Bay 2 has thirty meters of EPS conduit, a broadband sensor matrix, and a tactical data module stored as emergency supplies.

SHUTTLE TRACKER: For a short time, the alien ship, *Alice* is added to *Voyager*'s complement of shuttles; although it meets with a tragic end. ▪ Chakotay says they have a full complement of shuttles in addition to the *Delta Flyer.*

DELTA QUADRANT: The trading station is affectionately referred to as Abaddon's Repository of Lost Treasures. ▪ Beryllium is a crystal that is the standard currency in Spacial Grid 539. ▪ *Alice* has an optronic weapons array and multiphasic shielding. They trade three used power cells and Paris's jukebox for it. Later, Paris and *Alice* use an optronic pulse to disrupt *Voyager*'s tractor beam.

ALPHA QUADRANT: Much like the five stages of grief, the Ferengi refer to five stages of acquisition: Infatuation, Justification, Appropriation, Obsession, and Resale. ▪ The Federation has lost more than a dozen ships to a particle fountain in the Alpha Quadrant.

PERSONAL LOGS: Tuvok was married in 2304, and his daughter was conceived during his eleventh *Pon farr.* Paris and Kim reason that he was at least one hundred when he rejoined Starfleet. ▪ Paris names the ship after Alice Battisti, a woman at Starfleet Academy who would not give him the time of day. The ship's constant need for attention causes him to be late for two duty shifts in sickbay. When Paris was eight, his father took him on his first flight. They were in an old *S*-class shuttle with two seats, no warp drive, and manual helm controls. He admits to being scared out of his wits.

Alice takes on a physical appearance in Paris's mind. MICHAEL YARISH

The *Voyager* crew turns to Abaddon, who reluctantly explains that the shuttle Tom acquired is "haunted." Before he can say more, Abaddon begins hallucinating and suffers a cerebral hemorrhage. After receiving a cortical suppressant, he reveals that he too was once linked with *Alice*. She was looking for a biological entity to work with and to guide her to an unknown point in space. After reconstructing data that Paris left behind, Seven discovers that he and *Alice* are heading to a dangerous anomaly known as a particle fountain.

Because Paris's synaptic functions are linked to the shuttle, Janeway cannot fire on him. Instead, Tuvok works to access the main computer and a shutdown sequence, while the Doctor helps Torres tap into his interface using a communication signal. With both Torres and *Alice*'s voices in his head, Paris cannot think straight, but just as he is about to suffer a cerebral hemorrhage,

RIDDLES

EPISODE #227
TELEPLAY BY: ROBERT DOHERTY
STORY BY: ANDRE BORMANIS
DIRECTED BY: ROXANN DAWSON

GUEST STAR

NAROQ	MARK MOSES

STARDATE 53263.2

Returning from a diplomatic mission with Neelix, Tuvok picks up readings of a cloaked being within their shuttle, but while scanning it with a tricorder he is attacked. Once back on *Voyager,* Tuvok is rushed to sickbay suffering from neuroleptic shock, but the Doctor cannot reverse the damage until he understands the nature of the weapon used in the attack. Captain Janeway questions Naroq of the Kesat species, with which Neelix was negotiating, and the visitor feels certain the mythical Ba'Neth were the ones who attacked Tuvok. Legend has it the Ba'Neth attempt to assess foreigners' technology while cloaked because of an obsession with hiding their identity.

After finding residual veridium isotopes from the cloaking field, Naroq uses a photolitic converter to illuminate the particles and reveal the alien's appearance. Deploying the deflector array the same way, the crew is able to uncloak a fleet of Ba'Neth ships surrounding them. The aliens begin to fire when they are hailed and manage to flee in an ensuing chase.

Meanwhile, Tuvok regains consciousness, his neural pathways have bypassed the damaged tissue. This creates new synaptic connections, allowing his brain to "rewrite" itself. When Neelix leads him on a tour of the ship to jog his memory, Tuvok speaks for the first time since the accident, although his cognitive functions are still very simple. As he tries to come to grips with the damage he sustained, Tuvok experiences volatile emotions. When Naroq questions him about the cloaking frequency, Tuvok has a flashback but cannot remember any details. After studying his personnel file and realizing how different he is from the Vulcan he used to be, Tuvok lashes out at Neelix.

Seven helps Neelix realize that instead of pushing Tuvok to be who he was, he should encourage the Vulcan to discover who he can become. With this in mind, the two begin to have fun together. Tuvok discovers the joy of smiling and even tries his hand at baking desserts. When Janeway questions him again about the cloaking frequency, Tuvok cannot find the words to express what he saw. Instead, he draws it out in icing on his latest cake creation. Using that pattern, the *Voyager* crew begins scanning for the cloaking frequency.

The crew discovers the hidden spacefaring civilization of the Ba'Neth and Janeway demands information about their weapon. Once she threatens to transmit their coordinates to the Kesat, the xenophobic Ba'Neth captain says he is willing to negotiate, but he is reluctant to help with Naroq onboard. In a show of generosity, Naroq offers to give the Ba'Neth his photolitic converter in exchange for the information *Voyager* wants.

After analyzing the weapon, the Doctor is able to devise a procedure to restore Tuvok's Vulcan personality. At first Tuvok is reluctant to change, but Neelix knows they need Tuvok at his post on the bridge more then he needs a companion and convinces the Vulcan to undergo the procedure. Afterward, Tuvok resumes his logical and subdued manner, but he has learned to appreciate the wordplay of Neelix's riddles.

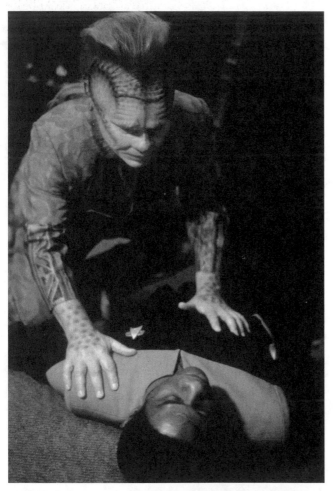

Neelix finds an unconscious Tuvok in the aft section of the *Flyer*.
MICHAEL YARISH

DELTA QUADRANT: In the Kesat language the word *Ba'Neth* translates into shadow people. The Kesat govern-

Hoping to jar his memory, Neelix brings familiar items from Tuvok's quarters. MICHAEL YARISH

ment's position is that the Ba'Neth do not exist, as they are thought to be only a myth. ▪ Veridium isotopes are present in residual particles from the Ba'Neth's cloaking fields. Since veridium has a very brief half-life of less than seventy hours, Naroq had never before been able to get readings as good as the ones he finds on the *Delta Flyer.* The Ba'Neth use a nine-million-terrawatt cloaking field to hide their armed outpost with three thousand lifesigns on twenty-two ships. ▪ The Ba'Neth are multipeds (with tentacles).

ALPHA QUADRANT: Vulcan neural tissue is extremely resilient. ▪ Neelix prepares to perform a recitation of the classic proto-Vulcan drama *Clash on the Fire Plains,* playing all twenty-three parts himself. ▪ Selection 56 Alpha of the Vulcan audio file is *The Chants of the Monks of T'Panit,* one of Tuvok's favorite selections.

PERSONAL LOGS: Items Neelix brings from Tuvok's quarters to sickbay include a game of *kal-toh,* Vulcan incense and a Vulcan lute. He also brings orchids from the airponics bay. Tuvok has received seventeen commendations for valor and can dismantle a photonic warhead in less than thirty seconds. Paris once referred to Tuvok's quarters as "the Vulcan vault." ▪ Paris has a jazz database that Tuvok accesses because "it really swings." ▪ While Tuvok is unable to perform his duties, Kim takes his station at tactical. ▪ Neelix suggests playing a game called "Species, Starship, or Anomaly"—in which one person picks an item and the other has fifteen questions to guess what it is.

MEDICAL UPDATE: The Doctor tries to use twenty milligrams of synaptizine to stabilize Tuvok, but fails. He then uses direct cortical stimulation with a neurostatic pulse to calm the convulsions.

ONE SMALL STEP

EPISODE #228

TELEPLAY BY: MIKE WOLLAEGER & JESSICA SCOTT and
BRYAN FULLER & MICHAEL TAYLOR
STORY BY: MIKE WOLLAEGER & JESSICA SCOTT
DIRECTED BY: ROBERT PICARDO

SPECIAL GUEST STAR

LT. JOHN KELLY   PHIL MORRIS

CO-STAR

COMPUTER VOICE   MAJEL BARRETT

STARDATE 53292.7

Voyager encounters a graviton ellipse that is traveling through subspace attracted to objects emitting electromagnetic energy. After successfully avoiding being trapped within the disturbance, Chakotay and Paris recount a similar phenomenon they know of from 2032, when a command module from one of the early Mars missions was consumed by a rolling ball of deadly energy. Readings from within the anomaly suggest that this might be the same anomaly the legendary vessel encountered.

Captain Janeway decides to launch a search for the missing U.S. spacecraft that may be trapped inside the energy field. She suggests that Seven join both Chakotay and Paris, as they hunt for the legendary *Ares IV* command module from the first manned mission to Mars in the hope that the former drone will develop an appreciation for studying the past.

Before they leave on the *Delta Flyer*, Chakotay and Paris view NASA's recordings of the last seconds of Lieutenant John Kelly's life within *Ares IV*. The away team has approximately five hours before the energy ball heads back to subspace, but once inside the ellipse, they find asteroid fragments and pieces of captured vessels worthy of years of study.

Back on *Voyager*, Torres discovers that a dark matter

Lieutenant John Kelly gets some unusual readings in the *Ares IV*. MICHAEL YARISH

asteroid is pulling the mass of energy toward it. With only minutes to spare, Captain Janeway instructs the away team to abort the mission. Chakotay goes against the captain's orders trying to bring the module back with them, but the weight of the *Ares IV* inhibits their swift escape, and the *Flyer* is unable to make it out before impact.

Chakotay is briefly knocked unconscious, and the *Flyer* is badly damaged. With their engines down and shields offline, the team now has only two hours before the mass of energy returns to subspace. After restablishing communication with *Voyager,* the team realizes their only hope is to beam Seven over to the *Ares IV* to obtain its ion distributor in order to supply power to the *Delta Flyer.* Before Seven is beamed over to *Ares IV,* Chakotay asks her to download whatever she can from the module's database.

Once inside the *Ares IV,* Seven enters the cockpit, where she sees the body of John Kelly still strapped in his chair. Seven brings the main computer online, and a monitor containing an active datafile. Chakotay asks Seven to playback the video log entries for them, and they learn that John Kelly was not killed on impact with the mass of energy. Instead, he lived for many more days until his life support system ran out. During that time, John Kelly saw other spacecraft within the mass and realized that the human race was not alone in the galaxy.

Seven successfully retrieves the distributor and beams Kelly's body back with her to the *Delta Flyer.* With only minutes to spare, the power conversion is activated. *Voyager* gets as close as it can to the mass to rescue the *Delta Flyer* as the ball begins to retreat into subspace. With the away team safely back on *Voyager,* the crew pay their respects to Lieutenant John Kelly and release his body into space. Seven acknowledges that Kelly's contribution helped secure humanity's future and gains a better understanding of the power of exploration.

SENSOR READINGS: Seven enhances the computer's command sequencers with Borg algorithms without asking permission and wreaks havoc with the secondary systems. ▪ The Doctor prepares an inoculant to counter the effects of the gravimetric radiation. ▪ The crew uses a probe as a communications relay to contact the *Delta Flyer.* ▪ Before the crew realizes a dark matter asteroid is attracting the ellipse, Kim notes that both an energy burst from a pulsar and a neutrino cloud are possibly anomalies that could generate an EM field large enough to draw the ellipse.

SHUTTLE TRACKER: The *Flyer's* shields, communications, and propulsion go offline. Auxiliary life support is

Chakotay tries to explain the concept of exploring to Seven.
MICHAEL YARISH

damaged, and the secondary relays are also offline. ▪ Kim notes that they can modify the shields on a class-2 shuttle to enter the ellipse, but there would not be enough time to make the adjustments and save the away team.

DELTA QUADRANT: The ellipse is read as a level-9 gravimetric distortion with 30 million terajoules of subspace energy. Its Borg designation is Spatial Anomaly 521. The Borg developed shields to get through the gravimetric currents with the intention of dissipating it from within. To escape the ellipse the crew has to cut power and reverse the shield polarity. According to the Federation database the ellipse travels through subspace, emerging occasionally without warning. Ellipses have been observed only a handful of times. There are more than 2.8 billion compounds in the core of the ellipse, including several synthetic alloys native to Sector 001, as well as asteroid fragments, pieces of vessels and matter from every quadrant of the galaxy. The chemical interactions within the anomaly create a primitive atmosphere. They find an ore sample that suggests the possibility of a metallic life-form, something that has always been speculated about.

ALPHA QUADRANT: *Ares IV* was one of the early Mars missions, manned by John Kelly, Rose Kumagawa, and Andrei Novakovich. The surviving astronauts were stranded on the surface of Mars for two weeks before a rescue ship arrived. The module was forty-six meters long and weighed ninety-two metric tons. It was powered

DIRECTORS IN TRAINING

Beginning with the *Star Trek* films, the series has established the practice of allowing the actors to step behind the camera in addition to their onscreen duties. With *Star Trek: The Next Generation* this tradition became more formalized with the establishment of a "directors in training" program in which the actors were given the opportunity to expand on their résumés by learning the craft of directing. *Voyager* continued that tradition with a number of its cast added to the program's ranks.

ROBERT PICARDO:

"You basically go to Rick Berman and say 'I'd like to do this,' and there's an informal director in training program that lasts about a year where you experience all aspects of production from preproduction and production meetings all the way through editorial and post.

"You start by sitting in the editing bays and watching other directors' dailies and watch how they edit the scene and what the other directors may have done wrong by limiting the amount of coverage they did, or perhaps what they did very successfully. You go to screenings where Rick Berman watches the rough cuts and get a good sense of what his likes and dislikes are in a *Star Trek* episode. And of course you hang out on the set and watch the director in particular whose work you like. Having gone through that process then you're normally given a shot. Since there are four actor/directors in our company, we all have to kind of wait our turns."

ROBBIE ROBINSON

TIM RUSS:

"When you're working on a show like this, the director of photography (DP) does a great deal of work in making the look of the show and the scenes and the stuff come together and come to life in terms of the looks, appearance, and editorial aspects of it. So you're not entirely flying blind . . . When I directed, I worked with the DP very closely and I knew what I wanted and if it didn't work then he might suggest 'Okay, this might be better.' That's how it works.

"It was an eye-opener in a respect that when you come on as an actor/director you're going to be more focused on the technical elements of the shooting. Camera angles, eye-lines, etc. At the start, I tended to be more focused on that and less focused on performances. Within a day or two, I found myself looking at the performances and not so much the technical aspect. And I discovered during the shooting of the episode that there were some things that needed to be fixed in terms of performances. In terms of movement, blocking, and things like that. It was something I really learned. I just discovered by doing it that I tend to focus, by the end of the episode a little more on the faces and what people were saying and doing and how they were doing them. And less on the specifics of the shot, which is where the DP comes in.

by a third generation ion drive and equipped with a transpectral imager. As they approached the completion of their mission, Kelly reported an object closing on his position, then the command module disappeared NASA's LIDAR scopes. NASA received Kelly's last telemetry at 0922 hours on October 19, 2032. Everyone assumed he was killed instantly, but he was still alive in the ellipse through October twenty-fifth. The incident almost derailed the Mars program. The command module uses an ion distributor for its main power system. The part is modified to channel warp plasma in the *Flyer.* ▪ Janeway recounts how exploration makes the explorer part of the history by likening it to the excavation of the obelisks of ancient Vulcan or finding the Shroud of Kahless.

"When I went back to acting, there was a certain appreciation for what the director's trying to achieve. The pressure he's under with the production staff looking at their watches and clocks and watching how long things take . . . the actors doing what we want to do and making his life a lot easier in doing so. All those things come out very much as an actor once you've done behind the camera."

ROBERT DUNCAN McNEILL:
"Having directed four episodes of our show and directed a bit outside of *Star Trek,* as well, I think I have a much better ability to look at the whole story and the whole impression that the little scenes and the smaller pieces make. I think, before directing, I had the habit as an actor to just look at the moment. You know, what makes this moment the most interesting or what feels the best in this moment as an actor? And I think as a director having to articulate to other actors and actually put into words what will fix the scene and make the scene work better has definitely helped me as an actor.

"Being an actor, what has helped my directing? I think that there's always a certain trust you get from the other actors when you're directing. Because they know you've been there. You've been on that side of the camera. You've been through similar experiences, similar frustrations and challenges the scenes present. So they have a lot of trust in you in many ways. You have a shorthand in terms 'I know this might feel this way, but trust me, if you do this . . .' You just have a short hand and a certain amount of trust. I think that's the biggest thing that the acting has done. I also think as an actor who is now directing, I think I look very much at character first. I look at what's going on for these characters.

"Sometimes directors who have come out of more technical backgrounds, editing or camera work or things like that, they approach a scene very much from a surface kind of 'What shot will look the coolest?' There's something to be said for that. There's some wonderful visual directors who come in and do really creative visual things. And that's an important part of the medium, but for me, I think I always look at character. I start from the character. And probably next I go to story and in the end I go to the visual that will backup all of those things."

Star Trek: Voyager Actor/Directors
ROBERT DUNCAN McNEILL: "Sacred Ground," "Unity," "Someone to Watch Over Me," "Body and Soul"
ROBERT PICARDO: "Alter Ego," "One Small Step"
TIM RUSS: "Living Witness"
ROXANN DAWSON: "Riddles," "Workforce, Part II"

Guest Star Trek Actor/Directors on Voyager
LeVAR BURTON: "Ex Post Facto," "Dreadnought," "The Raven," "Timeless," "Live Fast and Prosper," "Nightingale," "Q2," "Homestead"
JONATHAN FRAKES: "Projections," "Parturition," "Protoype"
ANDREW J. ROBINSON: "Blood Fever," "Unforgettable"

PERSONAL LOGS: Chakotay claims that paleontology was always his first love. He also notes that John Kelly was one of his childhood heroes (Paris says the same). ▪ One of the Doctor's first away missions was to Arakis Prime, a planet he found to be enchanting, with crystalline glaciers and a magnesium vapor atmosphere. He had to adjust his mobile emitter to counter the effects of the radiation. ▪ Seven of Nine wanted to be a ballerina when she was a child.

MEDICAL UPDATE: Chakotay is hit by a plasma discharge and suffers a severe concussion and internal injuries.

As is the case for many guest actors in over thirty years of the *Star Trek* series history, Lieutenant John Kelly was not the first *Star Trek* character played by Phil Morris. His affiliation with *Star Trek* began when he was a child appearing in the original series episode "Miri." As an adult, he played a cadet in the film *Star Trek III: The Search for Spock* and appeared twice on *Deep Space Nine,* as both a Klingon and a Jem'Hadar.

THE *VOYAGER* CONSPIRACY

EPISODE #229
WRITTEN BY: JOE MENOSKY
DIRECTOR: TERRY WINDELL

GUEST STAR

TASH	**ALBIE SELZNICK**

CO·STARS

NAOMI WILDMAN	**SCARLETT POMERS**
COMPUTER VOICE	**MAJEL BARRETT**

STARDATE 53329

After sensors pick up graviton fluctuations, Captain Janeway hails an approaching ship and meets its captain, Tash, who is working on a catapult vessel, hoping to launch himself hundreds of light-years away. If Tash's plan succeeds it could be adapted, shaving years off *Voyager's* journey. Meanwhile, Seven of Nine has installed a cortical processing subunit in her regeneration alcove, allowing her to assimilate the ship's status reports. Upon downloading data on Tash's work, she informs Janeway that his catapult is the same technology that was used to trap them in the Delta Quadrant.

Five years ago, when *Voyager* was caught in the displacement wave that sent it thousands of light-years off course, a tetryon beam was responsible. Now, Seven has discovered that a tetryon reactor is powering the catapult. Although the *Voyager* crew believes they destroyed the Caretaker's reactor, Seven finds evidence to suggest otherwise. Data shows that a charge Tuvok fired tore an opening in subspace, and a tractor beam from a cloaked ship pushed the reactor into it. Seven apprises Chakotay of her startling conclusion that *Voyager* was stranded in the Delta Quadrant on purpose, and that Janeway is behind the scheme.

Seven believes the captain is part of a Federation conspiracy to establish a military presence in the Delta Quadrant. Suddenly, Janeway's diplomacy begins to look suspiciously like establishing tactical infrastructure. Seven believes the captain intends to use the catapult to bring more ships from the Alpha Quadrant, creating a Federation/Cardassian invasion force. When Tash makes a successful journey of one hundred light-years using the apparatus, Chakotay secretly delays *Voyager's* shield modification to give him more time to consider Seven's theories.

Seven returns to her alcove to assimilate more information. After her latest download, she summons Janeway and alerts her that Chakotay is part of a Maquis rebellion. She believes he intends to use the catapult to launch attacks against the Federation and Cardassian ships. Janeway is doubtful, but Seven presents compelling theories, using some of the same evidence she used to cast aspersions on Janeway, but drawing different conclusions.

When Janeway and Chakotay compare notes, they realize Seven has been filling both of their minds with paranoid theories. Once the Doctor runs a diagnostic on her alcove, he finds that Seven has downloaded more information than she can process. Janeway beams to the *Delta Flyer,* which a paranoid Seven is using to make an escape, and casts her own version of past events to convince Seven that her synaptic patterns are in chaos. They return to *Voyager,* and Seven is treated in sickbay.

On Borg vessels, there is a cortical processing subunit in each unimatrix that downloads newly assimilated data to the drones. The datanodes in Seven's unit will download all *Voyager* information into her alcove and then into Seven of Nine. ∎ When the Doctor ran generational projections in the sickbay computer, Paris glanced at the monitor and jumped to conclusions starting with the rumor that half of Deck 5 was pregnant. Before the rumor could be put to rest, Neelix asked the captain for permission to turn Cargo Bay 1 into a nursery. ∎ Torres has to shut down the sensor grid because the offspring of mating photonic fleas are disrupting the power flow. It seems that eight weeks ago an away team encountered a Kartelan freighter carrying supplies from Sector 492, a territory that included a former Talaxian colony. Neelix acquired twelve kilograms of amber spice, a delicacy among his people. On the same day, Kim was repairing the mess hall replicator when the larvae from the spice jars flew out in search of their primary source of nourishment, plasma particles. Since the conduits within the nearby sensor grid contained an

Seven recites the captain's suspicious activities over the past years to Chakotay. RON TOM

unlimited supply, the now mature creatures periodically tap into the conduits for nourishment. When they do, the sensor emitters momentarily lose their resolution. ▪ Tuvok used a 20,000-teracochrane yield on the tricobalt device he fired on the Caretaker's array. Tricobalt devices are not normally carried on Federation starships. They are capable of creating a tear in subspace whereas phasers or photon torpedoes are not. ▪ The catapult allows *Voyager* to cross thirty sectors in only a short period of time.

DELTA QUADRANT: Like Janeway, Tash is also trying to get his crew home. They had been exploring an unstable wormhole that sent him a distance that would take him ten years to get home. The core of Tash's catapult sends a graviton surge through the projectors that locks onto a ship and sends it hurtling into null space to emerge a few hours later hundreds or thousands of light-years away. A few well-timed graviton pulses from *Voyager*'s deflector dish are used to adjust Tash's core reaction. When the catapult destabilized, astrometric sensors recorded a momentary burst of epsilon radiation,

which is one of the byproducts of a tetryon reaction. ▪ There is a class-K nebula twenty-five light-years off starboard. *Voyager* sets course for the minor nebula, but aborts the exploratory mission when they run into Tash.

The debris remaining after the Caretaker's array was destroyed included particle dust and metallic fragments composed of an unknown alloy and vapor composed of hydrogen, helium, and argon. ▪ In the few months before *Voyager*'s arrival in the Delta Quadrant, Neelix's ship sensors recorded the appearance of fifty-two vessels, including a Cardassian warship (though Seven may have been confused about some of this information).

ALPHA QUADRANT: The Jankata Accord, signed by the Federation and the Cardassians, states that "No species shall enter another quadrant for the purpose of territorial expansion." ▪ Although Ktarians were aligned with the Federation, they sympathized with the Maquis.

PERSONAL LOGS: Seven and Naomi play a weekly game of *kadis-kot*

As Janeway and Chakotay compare notes, they're embarrassed that they went so far as to arm themselves against each other. RON TOM

EPISODE LOGS: In detailing the so-called *Voyager* conspiracy, Seven notes that over the past five years Janeway has altered course two hundred and sixty-three times in the name of exploration and twists the following facts to fit her theory:
Stardate 50984: Janeway forges an alliance with the Borg. ("Scorpion, Part I")
Stardate 51008: Kes leaves *Voyager*. ("The Gift")
Stardate 51462: The Doctor's program is sent to the Alpha Quadrant. ("Message in a Bottle")
Stardate 51762: A cease fire is called with the Hirogen. ("The Killing Game, Part II")
Stardate 52861: A nonaggression pact is reached with the Terkellians. (Off screen event occurring around the events of "Relativity")

To explain her Maquis Conspiracy theory, Seven uses the following facts:
Stardate 48658: Seska is revealed to be a spy. ("State of Flux")
Stardate 49522: Chakotay recommends establishing trade negotiations with the Kolhari who use tetryon power cells in their technology. (off-screen occurring before "Deadlock")

Additional dates mentioned in this episode include:
Stardate 32611: Seven's parents leave the Alpha Quadrant to study the Borg. ("Dark Frontier")
Stardate 48317: *Voyager* is brought to the Delta Quadrant. ("Caretaker")
Stardate 51030: Seven is separated from the hive mind, and her implants are extracted. ("Scorpion, Part II")
Stardate 51652: Janeway encourages Seven to develop her social skills. ("Prey")
Stardate 52840: Janeway orders Seven to study her parents' journals. ("Dark Frontier")
Stardate 52842: Seven says "thank you" to Janeway for the first time.

However, it should be noted that Seven is confused by some of the information, which could account for some *slightly* incorrect dates and the fact that she refers to Ensign Seska as *Commander* Seska.

PATHFINDER

EPISODE #230
TELEPLAY BY: DAVID ZABEL and KENNETH BILLER
STORY BY: DAVID ZABEL
DIRECTED BY: MIKE VEJAR

SPECIAL GUEST STAR

BARCLAY	DWIGHT SCHULTZ

GUEST STARS

ADMIRAL PARIS	RICHARD HERD
COMMANDER PETE HARKINS	RICHARD McGONAGLE

AND SPECIAL GUEST APPEARANCE BY

TROI	MARINA SIRTIS

CO-STARS

SECURITY GUARD	VICTOR BEVINE
TECHNICIAN	MARK DANIEL CADE
COMPUTER VOICE	MAJEL BARRETT

STARDATE UNKNOWN

On Earth, Lieutenant Reginald Barclay, formerly of the *Starship Enterprise,* is obsessed with making contact with *Voyager.* As an outgrowth of his work on the Pathfinder project, Barclay grew obsessively

Although Barclay has lived in his apartment for two years, he still has not unpacked. MICHAEL YARISH

attached with the holographic re-creations of the *Voyager* crew and seeks advice from his old friend, Counselor Deanna Troi.

Recounting his story, Barclay remembers back to being in his *Voyager* re-creation when Commander Peter Harkins, his superior officer, interrupts to remind the lieutenant of his responsibilities. Still preoccupied, Barclay suggests that the team use an approaching itinerant pulsar in order to make contact with the missing starship. Barclay believes that directing a tachyon beam at the pulsar will produce a surge powerful enough to create an artificial wormhole, thus establishing two-way communication with *Voyager* using the Mutara Deep Space Transponder Array. However, Harkins tells Barclay that they need to instead focus their time on Admiral Paris's pending visit.

Later that night, Barclay once again activates the hologrid, entering the simulated mess hall for a game of cards with the holographic *Voyager* crew. Barclay is confident and relaxed among the holograms and stays the night with his new best friends. The following morning, Barclay leaves the simulation for the briefing with

Admiral Paris. Against Harkins's wishes, Barclay interrupts and tells Admiral Paris about his wormhole theory. Harkins is so upset with Barclay that he sends him home for the rest of the day. Instead of following orders, Barclay enters the holobriefing room and asks his holographic friends for technologic advice. Janeway offers Barclay a team to help him work out the details.

Harkins interrupts the simulation, discovers what Barclay has been up to and suggests that he seek counseling because of his past holodiction. Until then, Barclay is taken off the Pathfinder Project, he then goes to Admiral Paris requesting access to the lab for one more day. Admiral Paris only agrees to order an independent review of Barclay's findings.

Troi takes in Barclay's story, expressing concern about his anxiousness and paranoia. However, he informs Troi that he did not tell her the tale for her advice as a counselor, but begs the commander to tell the admiral that he is psychologically fit to return to work. Troi refuses but requests a temporary leave of absence from the *Enterprise* to stay with her friend.

CONTACT WITH THE ALPHA QUADRANT: SEASON 6

"It's good to hear your voice, lieutenant. We've been waiting a long time for this moment."
Kathryn Janeway to Reg Barclay "Pathfinder"

The sixth season of *Voyager* would see less contact with home, but more meaningful interactions than in the previous five seasons. Additional Alpha Quadrant members would join the ranks of the crew, with the five surviving crewmen from the *U.S.S. Equinox* in the season opener, "Equinox, Part II." Another member of Starfleet, Marika Willkarah, engineer on the *Excalibur*, joins the manifest for a brief time as she lives out her shortened life as an individual finally free of the Borg collective and her own collective triad in "Survival Instinct."

MICHAEL YARISH

The crew interacts with history again when they come across a spatial anomaly known as a graviton ellipse in "One Small Step." Within the anomaly they find the *Aries IV* command module from the first manned Mars mission in 2032. The body of Lieutenant John Kelly is found within the craft along with recordings of his final days trapped in the anomaly. Of the more than 2.8 billion compounds in the core of the ellipse are also several synthetic alloys native to Sector 001. Another piece of history appears in "Virtuoso" when the Doctor has a lecture hall on the planet Qomar redesigned with a re-creation of a backdrop used in a production of *Pagliacci* at Teatro della Scala, Earth's most famous opera house.

Alternate realities also provide visitors from home in "Barge of the Dead" and "Unimatrix Zero, Part I." In the former, Torres has a near-death experience and encounters her mother on the barge that ferries Klingon souls to Hell. Though Torres believes the experience to be real, it is unclear whether she truly lived through the journey to Hell or imagined it. While in the purely imagined, though entirely real world of Unimatrix Zero, Seven of Nine encounters various Borg in their original bodies, including at least one Klingon male and human female.

As always, the holodeck brings in touches of home, largely through Paris's newly created Irish town of Fair Haven in the episodes titled, aptly enough, "Fair Haven" and "Spirit Folk." At first, the crew interacts with the holograms as if they would any other program, except that Janeway falls in love with one of the imaginary residents. Later, the town takes a more surreal turn when, after running continually, the characters start to break down and realize that the *Voyager* crew is not from their land. Rather than lose the relaxing environment, the crew admits to being travelers in time and continues to visit the town.

Almost the entire "Pathfinder" episode occurs in the Alpha Quadrant as Reg Barclay struggles to prove he can make contact with *Voyager*. Finally his plan is successful. Later a more permanent link will be set up whereby the crew can send and receive monthly messages from home in "Life Line." This will prove useful to send the Doctor to Jupiter Station in the Alpha Quadrant in much the same way he visited back in "Message in a Bottle." This time, his rescue mission is one of a more personal nature, as he works to cure his programmer, Dr. Zimmerman, of a fatal disease.

"I play not only the Doctor, but his programmer, Dr. Lewis Zimmerman ("Life Line"). So I achieved a lifelong ambition of working with an actor who I've admired. Of course the hardest thing about acting with myself was coming up to my own level. I was very demanding, but also very generous, as an actor I gave myself everything that I felt I deserved and more."

—Robert Picardo

Reg chats with one of his holographic *Voyager* friends. MICHAEL YARISH

That night, Barclay once again defies orders by breaking into the research lab intending to send a message to *Voyager*. When Harkins enters the lab and instructs Barclay to step away from the controls, the lieutenant has the computer transfer the *Voyager* program to the hologrid, where he escapes to work on the message. Harkins follows Barclay into the *Voyager* holosimulation where the commander initiates a warp core breach to destroy the fictional version of the ship, which will shut down the system. With the holographic *Voyager* about to be destroyed, Barclay voluntarily ends the program and gives himself up.

Meanwhile on *Voyager*, Seven of Nine detects an artificial micro-wormhole whose origin is in the Alpha Quadrant. Janeway immediately instructs Paris to lay in a course for the wormhole. Then, just as Harkins asks Admiral Paris what he should do with Barclay, the Pathfinder Project receives a response from *Voyager*. Janeway and Admiral Paris are able to speak briefly, and he tells her that they are doing everything in their power to bring *Voyager* back. Harkins apologizes to Barclay for

doubting him, and Admiral Paris announces the beginning of Project *Voyager*. Meanwhile in the Delta Quadrant, the *Voyager* crew toasts Barclay for his extraordinary efforts.

SENSOR READINGS: Disengaging the primary coolant system will cause a core breach. ▪ When contact is finally made, *Voyager* transmits ship's logs, crew reports, and navigational records. Barclay transmits data to *Voyager* instructing the crew on how to re-create the hyper-subspace technology, so they can be in regular contact in the future and suggested modifications to *Voyager*'s com system.

ALPHA QUADRANT: At the start of the episode, the *Enterprise*-E is in Earth orbit. ▪ The Mutara Deep Space Transponder Array was designed to send signals at hyper-subspace speeds so that a message that would normally take years to reach its destination would only take a matter of days. They have been working with Vulcans on the deployment of the MIDAS Array. The communication is initiated when Barclay accesses the control matrix and powers the graviton emitters. He scans the area surrounding the MIDAS Array, finding a class-B itinerant pulsar at coordinates 227 by 41 Mark 6. He then directs a sixty terawatt tachyon beam at the pulsar. It takes approximately seventeen minutes for levels to be sufficient to produce a gravimetric surge of five million teradynes. When the micro-wormhole finally appears at coordinates 343 by 27, he adjusts the phase alignment to direct the wormhole's trajectory toward the Delta Quadrant sectors he believes *Voyager* to be located. *Voyager* is ultimately found in the Delta Quadrant at Grid 10, Sector 3658. ▪ Barclay's last failed plan was for the team to develop a transwarp probe. ▪ Barclay has lived in his apartment on Earth for two years, but has not unpacked. He named his cat Neelix and has been spending twenty to thirty hours a week in the holodeck.

PERSONAL LOGS: Seven has been trying to teach Neelix how to sing, but his vocal cords are incapable of producing basic diatonic tones and he has rhythmic shortcomings.

CREW COMPLEMENT: Reg Barclay is named an honorary member of the *Voyager* crew.

EPISODE LOGS: Barclay originally struggled with holodiction in the *TNG* episode "Hollow Pursuits." ▪ In Barclay's holodeck simulation Chakotay and Torres still wear their Maquis uniforms, and Janeway's hair is in the first-season style. ▪ In "Message in a Bottle" the Doctor reported *Voyager*'s position as being in the Delta Quadrant at Sector 41751, Grid 9. Hawkins's team estimates that *Voyager*'s current location is in one of three sectors. ▪ Communication between *Voyager* and the Alpha Quadrant will occur several more times over the course of the series and a regular monthly communication will be established in "Life Line."

FAIR HAVEN

EPISODE #231

WRITTEN BY: ROBIN BURGER

DIRECTED BY: ALLAN KROEKER

GUEST STAR

SEAMUS	RICHARD RIEHLE

SPECIAL GUEST STAR

MICHAEL	FINTAN McKEOWN

CO-STARS

FRANNIE	JAN CLAIRE
MAGGIE	HENRIETTE IVANANS
GRACE	DUFFIE McINTIRE
COMPUTER VOICE	MAJEL BARRETT

STARDATE UNKNOWN

Paris creates a new holodeck program, set in the Irish village of Fair Haven, as a means of relaxation. When the crew learns that they are headed on a collision course with a neutronic wavefront, a form of interstellar hurricane, Janeway grants permission for the new program to have a twenty-four-hour open door policy in order to keep the crew's mind off the looming threat. Janeway also visits Fair Haven, where she spends an evening with Michael Sullivan, a local pub owner whom she is troubled to learn is married. Because she is so drawn to him, she decides to make a few modifications in his subroutines, including the deletion of his wife. When she returns to Fair Haven, she finds a much more compatible man, who refers to her as Katie O'Clare.

The hurricane arrives, and while *Voyager* successfully clears the leading edge of the wavefront, the ship must spend at least three days inside the storm. During much of that time, many of the crew members return to the holographic creation. While spending more time with Michael, Janeway discovers that her amendments to his program were too good, because she finds herself falling in love with him. Uncomfortable, Janeway does not show up to meet him the next day, leaving Michael confused and upset, demanding that Paris tell him where she is.

The storm intensifies causing problems for the ship's systems and all power is diverted to the deflector to help *Voyager* cut a path to escape. The ship successfully makes it out of the hurricane, but the holodeck program is damaged and must be shut down while it is repaired. Before the program is momentarily put to rest, Janeway tells Michael that she is leaving Fair Haven for a while. Even

The cocreators of the popular Fair Haven hologram. MICHAEL YARISH

though she cannot give him a definitive reason why, Michael still insists that he loves her. She ends the program instructing the computer to deny her any future access to Michael's behavioral subroutines.

SENSOR READINGS: The ship encounters a class-9 neutronic wavefront that Seven notes as Borg Classification 3472 Particle Density Anomaly and believes could have been formed by the collision of two neutron stars. The wavefront travels at a velocity of 200,000 kilometers per second, and it extends for 3.6 light-years. The neutron radiation disrupts plasma flow, preventing the ship from going to warp. Since impulse power cannot outrun it, the crew is forced to ride it out by generating an inverse warp field to "drop anchor" and protect them from the storm. The Doctor prepares inoculations for the crew to combat the radiation, since they will be in the storm for a little over three days. The neutronic gradient later rises to over sixty million terajoules, destabilizing the warp field. They route all power to the emitters so the deflector beam can cut a path through the wavefront routing power from all secondary systems

including transporters, replicators, and holodecks. Without enough time to go through the hologrid shutdown sequence, they lose most of the Fair Haven holoprogram. When that too proves to be inefficient in generating the necessary power, they siphon every last deciwatt of energy from the plasma network.

The slogan of the town of Fair Haven is "Welcome weary traveler." Janeway grants Paris's request to expand Fair Haven to Holodeck 2 and add a seacoast. In the end Paris and Kim are able to save only ten percent of the existing elements from the program.

DAMAGE REPORT: A plasma conduit ruptures on Deck 9 upon encountering the leading edge of the wave. Before they leave the storm, stabilizers go offline and shields are failing with hull fractures on Decks 6 and 7.

PERSONAL LOGS: The Doctor refers to Janeway as an aficionado of Irish history. She claims to have an Irish aunt who used to say, "A stranger is a friend you just haven't met yet." Her aunt and uncle had a place in County Clare, Ireland. As a child on her farm in Indiana

Paris and Kim try to decide which parts of Fair Haven they can save.
MICHAEL YARISH

TSUNKATSE

EPISODE #232

TELEPLAY BY: **ROBERT DOHERTY**

STORY BY: **GANNON KENNEY**

DIRECTED BY: **MIKE VEJAR**

GUESTS STARS

PENK	**JEFFREY COMBS**
HIROGEN HUNTER	**J. G. HERTZLER**

SPECIAL GUEST STAR

CHAMPION	**THE ROCK**

STARDATE 53447.2

While on shore leave, Chakotay and Torres attend a brutal Tsunkatse match on the Norcadian homeworld while Captain Janeway tours a planet in a neighboring system. Meanwhile, having no need for shore leave, Seven of Nine and Tuvok take a shuttle to study a micronebula. Suddenly, they are captured by an alien vessel, rendering them both unconscious.

When Seven revives, an alien named Penk welcomes her as the newest participant in his Tsunkatse matches, saying that she is going to be a very popular attraction. Seven demands to see Tuvok, who was injured when their shuttle was hit. While attending to her crewmate, Seven tells Penk that she has no intention of participating in his game which pits opponents against each other in a physical confrontation. However, she is forced to fight in exchange for Tuvok's medical care.

At the next match, Chakotay is shocked to discover Seven of Nine, dressed in a fight suit, is the reluctant challenger of the Tsunkatse match. The first officer contacts Torres on the bridge of *Voyager*, telling her to beam Seven out of the ring, but the transport is unsuccessful. The figures in the pit are not really there; they are photonic projections transmitted from a different location. The crew watches helplessly as Seven is knocked down.

Chakotay updates Janeway on the *Flyer*, but it will take almost two days for the captain to return. While Seven of Nine nurses her injuries, Penk tells her that he is entering her in the Red Match, where only one of the opponents leaves the ring alive. A Hirogen hunter promises to train Seven for the match, reminding her that the only way to survive in Tsunkatse is to win.

Continuing the effort to rescue Seven of Nine, the Norcadian ambassador tells Neelix that he will begin an immediate investigation. However, with a portion of the Norcadian economy based on Tsunkatse matches, Neelix

she would hide under her bed during storms. ▪ The Doctor has taken on the role of the village priest, Father Mulligan. ▪ Neelix says that he's always enjoyed a good ion storm.

MEDICAL UPDATE: Tuvok experiences a slight loss of equilibrium and some gastrointestinal distress that appears to be spacesickness from the storm. Vulcan physiology is highly sensitive to neutronic gradients, which could be the cause. ▪ Several crewmen are injured in the pub fight.

EPISODE LOGS: The holographic town and its residents will be seen again in "Spirit Folk."

The Hirogen Hunter tells Seven that she must use more than the sanctioned Tsunkatse moves. RON TOM

believes that little will be done. The crew's own investigation pays off when Torres and Kim determine that the transmissions are emanating from a ship that is protected by neutronic weaponry. On the ship, the Red Match begins and Seven is shocked when her trainer, the Hirogen hunter, enters the ring. The hunter tells Seven that he was training her so that she could kill him and give him an honorable death.

As Seven tries to convince the hunter that they both should refuse to fight, *Voyager* arrives and exchanges fire with the Tsunkatse vessel, allowing the crew to beam Tuvok back. However, they are unable to get a lock on Seven's position, so they beam both Seven and the hunter onto *Voyager.* The hunter returns to his people, while Seven reflects on the actions she was forced to take in the ring.

SENSOR READINGS: Janeway notes that a diagnostic on the shield generators is way overdue. ▪ Neelix has been trying to enhance the plasma burners on his stove with Borg technology, a project that concerns the captain.

DAMAGE REPORT: Shields are down, and there is a hull breach on Deck 11.

SHUTTLE TRACKER: Possibly destroyed (or lost). An explosive device is beamed aboard the shuttle in which Tuvok and Seven are traveling. It is unclear whether the shuttle is destroyed. However, no mention is made of the *Voyager* crew retrieving it.

DELTA QUADRANT: A Tsunkatse fighter wears polaron disruptors on both hands and feet. Each disruptor delivers a bioplasmic charge when it comes in contact with one of the opponent's target sensors. A fighter has to attack his rival's sensors without exposing his own. A Red Match does not end until one of the competitors is dead. The fight is transmitted from a ship to every planet in the sector. "The Book of Tsunkatse" details thirty-three sanctioned maneuvers. ▪ Penk's vessel, which houses the Tsunkatse arena, emits a dampening field that takes the shuttle's engines, weapons, and shields offline. His ship has a mass of five million metric tons, with reinforced hull plating protected by covariant shielding and neutronic weaponry. Both the dampening shield and the defensive shielding of the vessel are tetryon-based. ▪ Pendari are known for their superior strength and their bad tempers.

The Norcadian homeworld is in a binary star system

Seven faces her opponent. MICHAEL YARISH

and Tuvok encounter a meteoroid stream while on their away mission.

MEDICAL UPDATE: Neelix gets half his face sunburnt, then has an allergic reaction to the *leola* root ointment he makes to cure the condition. ▪ Tuvok is badly hurt in the attack on the shuttle.

EPISODE LOGS: The eminently popular wrestler, Dwayne "The Rock" Johnson, appeared in this episode as part of a network-wide event celebrating the addition of the WWE wrestling program to UPN's lineup.

BLINK OF AN EYE

EPISODE #233
TELEPLAY BY: **JOE MENOSKY**
STORY BY: **MICHAEL TAYLOR**
DIRECTED BY: **GABRIELLE BEAUMONT**

GUEST STAR	
PILOT	DANIEL DAE KIM

CO-STARS	
PROTECTOR	OBI NDEFO
ASTRONOMER	DANIEL ZACAPA
CLERIC	OLAF POOLEY
TECHNICIAN	JON CELLINI
ASTRONAUT	KAT SAWYER-YOUNG
SHAMAN	MELIK MALKASIAN
TRIBAL ALIEN	WALTER HAMILTON
	McREADY
NAOMI WILDMAN	SCARLETT POMERS

STARDATE UNKNOWN

As *Voyager* approaches a planet that revolves at an extremely high rate of speed, the ship enters a gravimetric gradient, which pulls it into orbit and traps it in a tachyon field. The planet's core creates a space-time differential between itself and the vessel—a second on *Voyager* is equal to nearly a day on the planet. Since time is moving so fast on the planet, when the crew realizes the situation, centuries have already passed on the surface. *Voyager*'s arrival was seen as a new star; a divine creation.

After even more centuries pass on the planet, Seven of Nine receives a transmission from the surface, that alerts the crew that they have insinuated themselves into

and the Doctor hears that Norcadian museums are among the finest in the sector. ▪ There is a micronebula approximately 1.6 light-years from *Voyager*'s position that is on the verge of collapse. Tuvok and Seven take a shuttle to study it.

PERSONAL LOGS: As a light heavyweight boxer, Chakotay's record was twenty-three wins with only one loss, to a Nausicaan with a mean right hook. Legend has it that "The Tattooed Terror" has put more men in sickbay than the Ankaran flu. ▪ Torres takes her stuffed animal "Toby the *targ*" with her any time she is going to be gone on a mission for longer than a day. Chakotay rearranges duty schedules so she is left in command on the bridge while he goes to a Tsunkatse match. ▪ Kim was the three-time Academy parisses squares champ. ▪ The Doctor notes that Lesson #36 in Seven's socialization training is "Pleasant Parlor Games to Pass the Time." ▪ Seven has a favorite iso-modulator that is enhanced to correct hull ablation that she wants to bring in case she

The Protector tries to send a letter up to the Ground Shaker. ROM TOM

the race's mythology. For centuries, this pre-warp society has endured ground shaking brought about by this "Sky Ship." Unwilling to throw the civilization's belief system into further chaos by making first contact, Janeway sends the Doctor on an undercover mission to gather clues that may help *Voyager* break orbit. As Janeway prepares to beam him back, she loses his signal.

Although it only takes moments on *Voyager* to correct the problem, planetside, much time passes, forcing the Doctor to give up on waiting at the arranged coordinates for transport. Finally locating his signature in one of the planet's cultural centers, the crew recovers the Doctor after three years have passed for him on the planet. He alerts Janeway that *Voyager* has encouraged much invention through the centuries and the inhabitants are in a race to make contact. Using the Doctor's data to realign thrusters, the crew attempts to break orbit, but stops when it increases seismic activity on the planet. A shuttle from the planet docks with *Voyager,* the astronauts board, the crew appears to be frozen, because of the time differential. As they are brought into *Voyager's* timeframe, the visitors collapse from the transition, and an astronaut dies.

The surviving pilot explains that he has grown up in awe of the "Sky Ship," even praying to it as a child. Although the time he spends on *Voyager* means losing years of his life at home, he agrees to help them interpret the Doctor's data and find a way to break out of orbit. As Seven scans the planet's surface, she detects that the inhabitants are now experimenting with warp technology, and soon *Voyager* is under attack from antimatter torpedoes.

Janeway sends the pilot home with *Voyager's* specifications, hoping that he can convince his people to find a way to help *Voyager* break orbit. More than a year on the planet after the pilot returned, two ships materialize next to *Voyager* and use a tractor beam to pull it out of orbit. Using a temporal compensator that his planet has devised, the pilot returns to *Voyager* one more time to say goodbye before the "Sky Ship" leaves his world forever.

SENSOR READINGS: Warp drive goes offline and impulse engines do not respond when the ship is caught in the gravimetric gradient. The matter/antimatter reaction is still active in the warp core, but the field is "raising hell" with the nacelles forcing the crew to keep warp

The Doctor asks about changes on the planet he temporarily called home. MICHAEL YARISH

drive offline. ▪ They modify a class-5 probe for low orbit and configure the program to scan along all subspace bands, setting it for visual images every ten milliseconds. It scans the planet for an equivalent of two hundred years before its decays in orbit. ▪ Torres speeds up the scan rate of the Doctor's program to allow him to make the temporal transition when he is beamed to the planet. Unfortunately, the confinement beam destabilizes and needs to be recalibrated to compensate for the temporal field.

DAMAGE REPORT: Under attack by the planet inhabitants, transporters go offline and shields are down. Hull breaches are imminent on Decks 8, 9, and 10 and life support begins to fail.

DELTA QUADRANT: The planet's gravimetric readings are similar to those of a collapsed dwarf star. It also resembles a quasar in that it has a high level of rotations at approximately fifty-eight revolutions per minute. The planet has a tachyon core that has produced a particle field that runs between the poles. *Voyager*'s arrival disrupts the field and traps the ship in an eddy, effectively becoming the plan-

et's third pole. The imbalance affects the outer crust, causing quakes. ▪ In early stages of the planetary culture the aliens worshiped the stars as gods, referring to them as Tahal and his brothers in the sky. As an offering, they would place fire-fruit on the altar of Tahal. When the ground shook, knocking the fruit off the altar they believed that the new spirit wanted the fire-fruit only for himself. As the inhabitants evolved, the early beliefs became superstitions: it was bad fortune to eat fire fruit. They call *Voyager* "The Ground Shaker, The Light Bringer." As scientific knowledge grows they realize it really is a sky ship. Some people even market a line of sky ship friends. ▪ The Doctor is sent to the Central Protectorate in a subcontinent on the southern peninsula. At that time, the planet was made up of twenty-six states. He learns that *Voyager*'s presence has encouraged invention, religion, science, art, and even children's stories. ▪ The planet's inhabitants develop antimatter torpedo technology and later construct a tricobalt device.

PERSONAL LOGS: Not knowing what the natives look like, Torres gives the Doctor access to his facial and epidermal parameters so he can rewrite his own program. When *Voyager* fails to retrieve him, the Doctor moves to the cultural center of the state, where he lives for three years, making friends and even having a relationship. The Doctor had a son on the planet, but does not give the details on how this occurred.

VIRTUOSO

EPISODE #234

TELEPLAY BY: **RAF GREEN** and **KENNETH BILLER**

STORY BY: **RAF GREEN**

DIRECTED BY: **LES LANDAU**

GUEST STARS

TINCOO	KAMALA LOPEZ-DAWSON
ABARCA	RAY XIFO
KORU	PAUL WILLIAMS

CO-STARS

AZEN	MARIE CALDARE
VINKA	NINA MAGNESSON

STARDATE 53556.4

While the *Voyager* crew helps the crew of a Qomarian ship make repairs, the aliens onboard come off rather arrogant when discussing the crew's—and the Doctor's—technological inferiority. The Qomar live in a closed system and are not well versed in social interaction, nor are they familiar with singing, which the Doctor does as he tends to their medical needs. The visitors, including a woman named Tincoo, are enthralled with the Doctor's voice and invite the crew to visit their nearby planetary alliance. As a goodwill gesture, Captain Janeway arranges a musical concert starring the Doctor, of whom the Qomar cannot seem to get enough.

After a recital, the Doctor is invited to perform on the Qomar planet and introduce the concept of music to all its inhabitants. He excitedly agrees and plans a dazzling operatic performance complete with costumes and an elaborate set. Tincoo especially has become enamoured of the Doctor's talent, assuring him she will make any arrangements he may need. She is baffled by his crew's seeming lack of appreciation for his talents. As he steps onto the stage, he receives a standing ovation from the packed stadium.

Following the Doctor's latest concert, *Voyager*'s com-

Koru is moved by the Doctor's performance. MICHAEL YARISH

munication system is inundated with transmissions to the maestro. Seven of Nine mistakes these for attempted sabotage, but Janeway explains that the correspondence is just fan mail. Qomarian visitors flood the ship for a chance to see him, and the Doctor is pleased with the attention. Janeway eventually is concerned by his neglect of duties and admonishes him to return to work. Tincoo, however, urges the Doctor to stay on Qomar with her after *Voyager* leaves.

Believing he can realize his life dreams and enjoy the love of a woman, the Doctor turns in his resignation. Despite Janeway's protests, the Doctor insists he should have the right to self-determination. His life on *Voyager*

The Doctor performs in a replica of Earth's most famous opera house.
MICHAEL YARISH

with melancholy songs of lost love. The performance touches the *Voyager* crew members in attendance but leaves the Qomarians wanting. Afterward, the new holomatrix steps in with a purely technical performance, which the Qomarians applaud wildly. Back on *Voyager*, the Doctor realizes he has friends there who do truly appreciate him as an individual with unique abilities.

DELTA QUADRANT: A member of the Qomar Planetary Alliance, the planet *Voyager* visits is surrounded by thousands of subspace transmissions that are all encrypted differently, making it difficult for the Alpha Quadrant ship to communicate. ▪ Tincoo creates a superior singing hologram with vocal processors that are enhanced with polyphonic sequencers capable of singing notes beyond the Doctor's range and producing multiharmonic overtones through the use of amplitude vacillation.

ALPHA QUADRANT: The Doctor redesigns the Qomarian lecture hall with a re-creation of a backdrop used in a production of *Pagliacci* at Teatro della Scala, Earth's most famous opera house.

PERSONAL LOGS: Kim also performs for the uninterested Qomarians with his band "Harry Kim and the Kimtones." ▪ The Doctor has recently been researching the therapeutic value of music. He asks Torres to make an adjustment to his mobile emitter so he can make quick changes. He is reprimanded for neglecting his sickbay duties and going three days without filing a report. Before he leaves the ship, he downloads seventeen new chapters of social lessons for Seven that they have not yet covered. He also trains Paris to take his position after he is gone. ▪ Every flu season Neelix becomes convinced that he is suffering from Toluncan Ague. Instead of arguing with him, the Doctor just gives him a placebo.

EPISODE LOGS: This episode marks the only appearance of "Harry Kim and The Kimtones"; however, Kim has actively been studying the clarinet and saxophone throughout his time on the ship. Garrett Wang is not actually playing the instruments, although he did have a professional come in and tutor him on correct finger placement so that it looked real. ▪ Although Robert Picardo does much of his own singing throughout the series, the difficult vocal arrangements in this episode required a professional singer to dub in the singing.

has become routine, and he believes that the Qomar really appreciate him for who he is and his ability to bring music to their lives. As the Doctor says good-bye to the crew, Tincoo summons him because she has created a superior holomatrix that can hit the high notes the Doctor cannot reach. She excitedly adds that now he can stay on *Voyager*.

Although the Doctor protests that a superior holomatrix cannot replace the passion and artistry that he brings to the music, Tincoo only sees the situation from a mathematical angle. She is more concerned with hitting the complex arrangement of scales than understanding their beauty. Heartbroken, the Doctor fills his final show

COLLECTIVE

EPISODE #235

TELEPLAY BY: MICHAEL TAYLOR

STORY BY: ANDREW SHEPARD PRICE & MARK GABERMAN

DIRECTED BY: ALLISON LIDDI

GUEST STARS

TEENAGE DRONE LEADER	RYAN SPAHN
ICHEB	MANU INTIRAYMI
MEZOTI	MARLEY S. McCLEAN
AZAN	KURT WETHERILL
REBI	CODY WETHERILL

CO-STAR

COMPUTER VOICE	MAJEL BARRETT

STARDATE UNKNOWN

After a Borg cube intercepts the *Delta Flyer*, Chakotay, Paris, and Neelix find themselves placed in what appears to be an assimilation chamber, but strangely enough, they are not being assimilated.

They also note that, stranger still, Kim was not taken from the *Flyer* with them.

Tracking the shuttle from its last position, *Voyager* discovers the Borg cube with its propulsion system offline. The cube erratically targets *Voyager*'s warp core, then impulse engines, and finally sensors before the crew easily disables the Borg weapons. Seven discovers that there are only five signatures manning the vessel, instead of the thousands of Borg necessary to operate the ship.

Surprisingly, the Borg attempt to negotiate, offering to return the crew members in exchange for *Voyager*'s navigational deflector, which would render the Federation ship unable to go to warp. Seven tells Janeway that the Borg most likely want the deflector in order to contact the collective because their link has been severed. While stalling the Borg, Janeway sends Seven over to make sure the away team is unharmed. Aboard the cube, Seven discovers that children—who were forced out of their maturation chambers prematurely—are manning the ship and insist that the Borg will come for them once their link is re-established.

Seven tries to reason with the young Borg drone. MICHAEL YARISH

The Borg children try to maintain their collective. MICHAEL YARISH

Seven returns to *Voyager* along with the dead body of an adult drone for examination in order to establish what went wrong aboard the ship. The Doctor discovers that a spaceborne virus attacked the drones and is responsible for their deaths. The virus never reached the developing drones because they were protected within the maturation chambers. The Doctor also discovers that if the pathogen is revived, it could be used to neutralize the drone children.

Because *Voyager* cannot give up its deflector, Janeway offers Seven's services in repairing the cube's technology. The dominant Borg child tells Janeway that she has exactly two hours before one of the hostages dies. Meanwhile, Kim wakes up after lying unconscious within the *Delta Flyer* and makes contact with *Voyager*. While working on the cube's repairs, Seven discovers that the collective did receive the drones' initial distress call, unbeknownst to the children. A vessel was not dispatched to rescue them because the Borg consider the neonatal drones damaged and irrelevant. Kim is captured while trying to sabotage

the ship and awakens to discover raw-looking implants on his face.

The children try to take *Voyager's* deflector by force, attempting to rip it off the ship with their tractor beam. Seven tells the drone children that the hive will never come back for them and that their call for help was ignored. Meanwhile, *Voyager* emits an energy pulse through the tractor beam and weakens shields enough to beam Chakotay, Paris and Neelix onto *Voyager*. However, Seven and Kim are being held in a shielded area of the cube. Angered, the drone leader attempts to assimilate Seven, but he is stopped by the other teenage boy. As the cube's transwarp core begins to destabilize, Seven tells them to evacuate but the leader refuses to leave and he is electrocuted.

Back on *Voyager,* the Doctor successfully removes most of the children's implants. Seven was able to salvage part of the cube's database, which includes the children's original assimilation profiles. Thus, the children discover that their names are Icheb, Mezoti, Azan, and Rebi.

DAMAGE REPORT: When the Borg lock their tractor beam onto the deflector and try to pull it off the ship the resulting damage includes hull breaches on Decks 10 and 11. Eventually, hull stress reaches critical levels.

SHUTTLE TRACKER: The *Delta Flyer's* plasma injectors are damaged, preventing them from going to warp. They also lose phasers as they are pulled into the cube. The *Flyer* is equipped with escape pods, but they are unable to deploy them before being captured. The shuttle is later retrieved.

DELTA QUADRANT: The Borg children use a dispersal field to mask the ship's approach. Seven notes that the thoracic nodes in the children have not yet been formed indicating that they are "incomplete." ▪ A spaceborne virus adapted to Borg physiology, killing the mature drones. However, the maturation chamber is designed to protect developing drones. Icheb is a member of the Brenari, and his name was taken from his father's second name. Mezoti is Norcadian (the crew met her people in "Tsunkatse") and her home is a Theta-class planetoid with a population of 260,000 with binary suns.

PERSONAL LOGS: Being in the cube reminds Kim of a haunted house his parents took him to when he was six. ▪ Seven of Nine was in a Borg maturation chamber for five years.

MEDICAL UPDATE: The Borg children inject nanoprobes into Kim's bloodstream, which would have killed him if he had not received treatment.

CREW COMPLEMENT: The four Borg children are added to the ship. It should also be noted that a developing Borg baby is brought over to *Voyager* during the episode. However, since the infant is not mentioned again on the series, it is assumed that she did not survive.

EPISODE LOGS: In the episode "Child's Play," it will be revealed that the virus that killed the adult drones was a weapon genetically coded into Icheb's body by his people. He was intentionally left to be assimilated so that the Brenari could deal a crippling blow to the Borg.

MEMORIAL
EPISODE #236
TELEPLAY BY: ROBIN BURGER
STORY BY: BRANNON BRAGA
DIRECTOR: ALLAN KROEKER

GUEST STAR

SAAVDRA	L. L. GINTER

CO-STARS

NAOMI WILDMAN	SCARLETT POMERS
SOLDIER ONE	FLEMING BROOKS
YOUNG SOLDIER	JOE MELLIS
ALIEN WOMAN	SUSAN SAVAGE
FEMALE COLONIST	MARIA SPASSOFF
DYING COLONIST	ROBERT ALLEN
	COLAIZZI JR.
CREW MEMBER	DAVID KEITH ANDERSON

STARDATE UNKNOWN

After returning from a two-week away mission scanning various planets and gathering dilithium ore, Chakotay, Paris, Kim, and Neelix begin experiencing strange visions. While Paris dreams he is

Kim remembers killing a pair of colonists in a cave. RON TOM

engaged in an alien battle, Kim has an anxiety attack in a Jefferies tube during a routine check of a plasma leak. Meanwhile, Chakotay suffers from violent dreams that place him in the middle of an offensive, and Neelix reacts to weapons fire that only he can hear by taking Naomi hostage in the mess hall.

The Doctor discovers that increased engrammatic activity in Chakotay and the others suggests they are reacting to memories, not delusions. As Janeway asks them to retrace their visions, they begin having flashbacks of their apparent roles in an attack force against the Nakan. As the puzzle comes together, they recall that their leader, Commander Saavdra, ordered them to evacuate the inhabitants from their remote colony, but a small group of the colonists began firing weapons. Chakotay and the other crew members, who believe they were part of the attackers, panic, and they shoot back, murdering eighty-two civilians.

Janeway orders *Voyager* into the system the away team was scanning and joins Seven and Chakotay in reviewing the *Delta Flyer*'s sensor logs. As soon as the captain sees an image of Tarakis, the second planet encountered by the away team, she also begins having flashbacks

of the massacre. She remembers pleading with Saavdra to admit their mistake, but he continues to vaporize the evidence of the colonists' bodies. When she wakes up three hours later, Janeway learns that other crew members have also begun experiencing the same battle memories.

Once *Voyager* is in orbit of the planet, scanners pick up a weak power signature. An away team beams to the surface, where there is no trace of a massacre. However, Kim locates a familiar rock formation, and he and Tuvok descend into the tunnels where he remembers killing two of the innocent colonists. After Tuvok scans the remains they find there, he determines that they died three hundred years ago. Meanwhile, Janeway and Chakotay find a large structure erected in the middle of a grassy field.

Seven identifies the structure as a synaptic transmitter sending neurogenic pulses throughout system. Anyone who enters the system will experience memories of the battle, it is meant as a memorial to the victims and a vivid reminder to never let such a tragic mistake happen again. Because the power cells are deteriorating, the memories are fragmented. Some of the crew, still shaken by the disturbing realism of the visions they were forced to endure,

The crew tries to accept the fact that memories of this world are not their own. RON TOM

want to shut down the transmitter, but Janeway orders them to recharge the power cells and place a warning buoy on the edge of the system. The memorial will continue to spread its hauntingly effective message.

SENSOR READINGS: During the away mission, the *Flyer*'s sonic shower went offline. ▪ Back on *Voyager*, Kim repairs a plasma leak on Deck 5.

DELTA QUADRANT: During the two-week mission the team scanned fifteen planets in fourteen days and came back with a cargo hold overflowing with deuterium. The first planet visited was class-M with a natural satellite. They scanned for dilithium and were in orbit for less than an hour. Then they came into contact with a vessel captained by Bathar of Hodos—a merchant who claimed to have a formula that stopped the aging process. It was only a tripolymer enzime, but Chakotay claims it makes great shoe polish. The third stop was the planet Tarakis. ▪ The text on the memorial reads, "Words alone cannot convey the suffering. Words alone cannot prevent what happened from happening again. Beyond words lies experience. Beyond experience lies truth. Make this truth your own."

ALPHA QUADRANT: Away team protocol dictates that crew members are required to submit to a physical if the mission lasts for more than two weeks. ▪ Janeway refers to Alpha Quadrant memorials of the Obelisk at Khitomer and the fields at Gettysburg.

PERSONAL LOGS: As a gift, Torres builds Paris a 1956-style television with an admittedly anachronistic remote control and stocks it with old television programs. ▪ The Doctor recently gave a lecture on "Insects Indigenous to the Delta Quadrant," during which Ensign Farley fell asleep, snoring loudly. ▪ Seven makes Neelix a Talaxian stew and Terra nut soufflé, which are his favorite foods.

Naomi Wildman takes geometry lessons from Seven, who assigned her a special project where she has to build a tetragon using everyday (nonreplicated) items. She decides to use carrots and celery.

MEDICAL UPDATE: The Doctor initially diagnoses Kim as suffering from exhaustion. Later, he notes that Neelix's norepinephrine levels are three times what they should be. Neurochemically speaking the away team suffers from a form of posttraumatic stress syndrome. ▪ The Doctor programs a neural suppressant to keep the memories from resurfacing.

SPIRIT FOLK

EPISODE #237
WRITTEN BY: **BRYAN FULLER**
DIRECTED BY: **DAVID LIVINGSTON**

GUEST STARS

SEAMUS	**RICHARD RIEHLE**
MILO	**IAN ABERCROMBIE**
DOC FITZGERALD	**IAN PATRICK WILLIAMS**
MAGGIE	**HENRIETTE IVANANS**
GRACE	**DUFFIE McINTIRE**

AND SPECIAL GUEST STAR

MICHAEL	**FINTAN McKEOWN**

CO-STARS

EDITH	**BAIRBRE DOWLING**
COMPUTER VOICE	**MAJEL BARRETT**

STARDATE UNKNOWN

While driving along in the holotown of Fair Haven, Paris crashes his vintage automobile, and town resident Seamus cannot believe his eyes when he sees the tire magically repair itself. He immediately heads to Sullivan's Pub, and tells his friends that he believes Paris is from the spirit world. Seamus's beliefs seem to be confirmed later when he and Milo see Paris pull a prank on Kim by turning his girl, Maggie, into a cow.

Seamus rushes to church to tell the other townsfolk exactly what he saw. Acting as town priest, the Doctor

Paris tries to calm the Michael Sullivan hologram.
RON TOM

The Doctor tries to convince the townsfolk that the cow is not their friend Maggie. RON TOM

Bringing up the Sullivan character to study, Paris finds that he is surprisingly aware of his surroundings. Kim sees that each character's perceptual filters are offline, and in order to save the program they have to repair the malfunction by accessing each of the characters' controls from Sullivan's Pub. Back in Fair Haven, Michael remembers being "spirited" away to an unknown place where there was talk of changing the people of Fair Haven. Later while Kim and Paris work on the Starfleet control panel in the holographic town, a net is thrown over them, knocking them to the ground. A gun is fired at the panel, rendering the holodeck controls inoperable, and when Paris instructs the computer to freeze the program, only some of the townsfolk are frozen. Paris and Kim are soon on the run, with a mob of townsfolk following close behind. Meanwhile outside the holodeck, Torres suggests cutting power to the hologrid, but some of the crew have grown attached to the characters and would prefer an alternative solution.

Paris and Kim find themselves tied to chairs near the altar of the church. As the townspeople try to send them back to the spirit world, the Doctor appears, still playing the role of the priest. The townsfolk, however, are onto him and find his mobile emitter. When they remove it he becomes part of the malfunctioning program. Seamus hypnotizes the Doctor, asking him questions about banishing the "spirit folk" to the "otherworld." The Doctor tells them about *Voyager,* and Michael demands that he instruct him on how to be transported to Katie's location.

Wearing the mobile emitter, Michael finds his Katie on a futuristic ship. Instead of explaining to Michael that he is a hologram, Janeway tells him that her crew are similar to time travelers who like to spend time in Fair Haven. Janeway and Michael both return to the holodeck, where he calms the townsfolk, insisting that the *Voyager* crew mean no harm. While the damaged holodeck is being repaired, the crew has one last night at Sullivan's Pub before Fair Haven is temporarily put to rest.

tells Seamus not to worry, since Tom Paris is a known prankster. Later that day, Seamus and Milo run into Maggie, who tells them that she woke up from the strangest dream, where she was walking around town with a bell around her neck. Michael Sullivan later tells Janeway that the townsfolk think that she and her friends are not from this Earth. Because Janeway knows that he has begun to suspect that she is lying to him, she ends the program. The senior staff gathers to discuss how the holodeck characters could possibly be questioning their origin.

SENSOR READINGS: Torres complains about having to replace three holoemitters because the Fair Haven program has been running around the clock. Paris runs a full diagnostic, but everything appears fine. Since the program is the first one they have tried running nonstop, there are damaged subroutines in all the character files and the perceptual filters are malfunctioning. The algorithms designed to keep the characters oblivious to anything outside the program's parameters are offline. They intend to reactivate the program by using the primary control port in Sulivan's Pub to reset all the perceptual filters with a single command sequence. Because of the abundance of stray photons, the crew cannot get a transporter lock on Paris and Kim. They try to use the Doctor to get transport enhancers to the pair, since cutting the power of the holodeck would purge the program from the database. While the holoprogram is saved, the crew can no longer continue their open door policy. When speaking to Chakotay, Janeway refers to Michael as a 300-deciwatt holodeck program. She never reveals to Michael that he and the town of Fair Haven are holograms.

PERSONAL LOGS: Michael gives Janeway a copy of *The Faerie Queene* by Edmund Spenser. In return, she gives him a copy of Mark Twain's *A Connecticut Yankee in King Arthur's Court.* ▪ Kim replicates a dozen Broadway lilies for Maggie. ▪ In Fair Haven, Neelix cooks at The Ox and Lamb.

While on *Voyager* Michael sees two crewmen he notes as Patrick Gibson and his cousin Frank. It is unclear whether these two crewmen are related or that was just a story for the holoprogram.

Ballard tries to come to terms with her two lives. MICHAEL YARISH

ASHES TO ASHES

EPISODE #238

TELEPLAY BY: **ROBERT DOHERTY**

STORY BY: **RONALD WILKERSON**

DIRECTED BY: **TERRY WINDELL**

GUEST STARS

LYNDSAY BALLARD	KIM RHODES
MEZOTI	MARLEY McCLEAN

CO-STARS

NAOMI WILDMAN	SCARLETT POMERS
Q'RET	KEVIN LOWE
ICHEB	MANU INTIRAYMI
AZAN	KURT WETHERILL
REBI	CODY WETHERILL
COMPUTER VOICE	MAJEL BARRETT

STARDATE 53679.4

As a tiny Delta Quadrant shuttle outruns a larger vessel, the shuttle's pilot tries to contact the *U.S.S. Voyager.* When the pilot finally succeeds, she claims that she is Lyndsay Ballard, a former shipmate who has been dead for three years. The alien, who looks nothing like the deceased crew member, tells the crew that a race known as the Kobali had found her body drifting in space and reanimated it. The aliens procreate by altering the DNA of the dead they salvage from other races. Her former best friend Harry Kim was with her when she died and believes her story, based on the facts she gives about her death. The Doctor then finds that she has traces of human DNA, which convinces Janeway she is telling the truth.

Meanwhile, Seven of Nine has been placed in charge of the four Borg children now aboard *Voyager.* She plans every hour of their day, including an hour for fun, but does not understand why the children are so difficult to control. They even begin to rebel against her standard punishment protocols. Seven asks to be relieved of her duty as guardian of the Borg children, but Chakotay suggests that she is treating the children as if they are on a Borg cube, when she should be looking at each child as an individual. He denies her request, forcing Seven to adapt.

In the meantime, the Doctor creates a treatment to make cosmetic changes to Ballard so she will look like her former self, but he cannot re-create her previous physiology. When she eats her former favorite meal, she claims that it tastes funny since it is not Kobali food. As she returns to her post in engineering, she begins to speak in Kobali. The vessel that had been chasing Ballard makes contact with *Voyager,* and the vessel's commander, Q'ret,

Mezoti invites Kim to join her on the holodeck. MICHAEL YARISH

asks to speak with Ballard, trying to get her to return to their planet. Claiming to be her father, Q'ret accuses the *Voyager* crew of setting her adrift like trash and telling her that her Kobali sister misses her. However, she refuses to go back with him.

As Kim talks with Ballard, she admits that now she feels more at home with the Kobali. But Kim refuses to recognize her conflicted emotions because after years of missed opportunities, the two have finally admitted their mutual interest for one another. When Q'ret begins to fire on *Voyager* and insists he will not stop until Ballard comes home, she decides to return to the Kobali. Unwilling to let her go, Kim, without orders, prepares to fire on the Kobali ship, but he relents. The pair share a tender good-bye as Ballard returns to her Kobali life.

SENSOR READINGS: Following an analysis of Ballard's stolen shuttle, Tuvok devises thirty-seven different ways of repelling a Kobali attack. ▪ Torres notes that an alignment error has been showing up in the dilithium matrix. Ballard sees the problem immediately using the Kobali

word *vyk'tiote,* which translates literally into "crumpled dance" to explain it, and she easily corrects the error.

DAMAGE REPORT: Under attack, life support begins to fail on Decks 6 through 10.

DELTA QUADRANT: The Kobali have a multispheric brain (with six lobes) and a binary cardiovascular system. Their food consists of a gray pastelike substance. The word *kyn'steya* refers to the past life.

PERSONAL LOGS: Tuvok has a holodeck program called "The Temple of T'Panit." Kim suggests that he and Ballard (and later, Mezoti) reprogram it so that the Vulcan monks recite Ferengi limericks. ▪ Kim now plays the saxophone. At the Academy, he claims that he used to request baryon sweeps of his dorm room (because he lived across from the sloppy Ballard). He rearranged his classes at the Academy to be around Ballard and let her teach him how to ice skate even though he hates the cold. He says that he's been crazy about her since the day they met and gave the eulogy at her funeral. Kim has never been invited to the captain's quarters for dinner.

On Stardate 51563 Kim and Ballard were on an away mission to a class-M planet in the Vyntadi expanse hoping to recover dilithium ore they detected a few days earlier. However, it was a trap set by a Hirogen hunting party that had reconfigured power cells to give off the false readings. Ballard was hit by a neural disruptor and did not survive. However, she woke up in a stasis chamber on an unfamiliar ship. After the reanimation process the Kobali spent months altering her DNA and gave her the Kobali name Jhet'leya. Ballard worked in engineering where she tended to be late for her duty shifts. To pass the time she planned her escape from the Kobali, she composed a list of things to do when she got back to *Voyager*. Included on her numbered list of goals were the following: #6 Eat a Jibelian berry salad; #16 Dazzle Lt. Torres; #26 Hear Harry play music again; and #32 Make Tuvok laugh. Ballard lived life like a Klingon battle cry, "Own the Day." ▪ Mezoti is eight years old, and her people, the Norcadians, are known to the Borg as Species 689. ▪ In a game of kadis-kot Azan and Rebi cheat by using their neural interface to share information, earning them Punishment Protocol 9-Alpha—having to stand in a corner.

MEDICAL UPDATE: A genetic pathogen in Ballard's bloodstream converted most of her DNA into a Kobali protein structure. The biochemical changes have effected every system in her body. There isn't enough of her human DNA left to make her human again, but the Doctor does make cosmetic changes using an inaprovaline compound, However, the pathogen proves to be very strong, and ultimately she would have to see the Doctor twice a day to keep up with the cosmetic treatments.

CREW COMPLEMENT: Ballard briefly returns to the *Voyager* crew.

EPISODE LOGS: The script for this episode refers to the Borg children as "dronelings."

CHILD'S PLAY

EPISODE #239

TELEPLAY BY: **RAF GREEN**
STORY BY: **PAUL BROWN**
DIRECTED BY: **MIKE VEJAR**

GUEST STARS

ICHEB	MANU INTIRAYMI
YIFAY	TRACEY ELLIS
LEUCON	MARK A. SHEPPARD
NAOMI WILDMAN	SCARLETT POMERS

CO-STARS

MEZOTI	MARLEY McCLEAN
AZAN	KURT WETHERILL
REBI	CODY WETHERILL
YIVEL	ERIC RITTER
COMPUTER VOICE	MAJEL BARRETT

STARDATE UNKNOWN

At the "First Annual *Voyager* Science Fair" Captain Janeway tells Seven of Nine that the crew has managed to locate Icheb's parents and are planning to take him home. Now, Seven must prepare him to return to his past while accepting the fact that she has to let him go.

When they get closer to Icheb's home, scanners show a Borg transwarp conduit nearby, which explains why readings indicate the planet has often been attacked by the Borg. Janeway leads an away team to the surface, and they are greeted by Icheb's Brunali parents, Luecon and Yifay. The simple meeting proves too much for the boy, and Icheb asks to go back to the ship immediately. On *Voyager* the adults have a tense discussion about how to make the transition easier, but Seven refuses to trust Icheb's parents. As a starting point, Yifay makes her son's favorite meal, which he really enjoys. In private, his father, Leucon, explains to Seven that the Borg took Icheb four years ago when he wandered off to see a new fertilization array.

After spending time with his parents, Icheb decides to stay with the Brunali, believing that his knowledge of technology can help them rebuild their villages. As *Voyager* leaves orbit, Mezoti cannot sleep because she misses Icheb. Talking things out with Seven, she mentions that Icheb told her he was taken from a ship, not from the planet's surface. Seven is curious why Leucon had lied to her and begins to research the planet's history. Her research reveals that the Borg did not attack the planet four years ago, so Icheb could not have been taken at

Icheb's parents partake in a tense dinner on *Voyager*. MICHAEL YARISH

that time. When Seven reports this information to Janeway along with an impassioned plea, the captain turns the ship around and heads back to the planet. Meanwhile, on the Brunali world, Icheb's parents inject him with a medical device that renders him unconscious so they can place him on a shuttle heading for the Borg transwarp conduit.

When *Voyager* returns to the planet, Leucon is immediately defensive and tells them to leave. Tuvok scans the planet for Icheb's biosigns, but does not find him. Seven discovers the shuttle heading for Borg space, and *Voyager* pursues, managing to transport Icheb onto the ship just as a Borg sphere emerges from the conduit and traps both the Brunali shuttle and *Voyager* in a tractor beam. The crew transports a photon torpedo to the shuttle, which detonates inside the sphere and damages it, allowing *Voyager* to escape.

The Doctor determines that Icheb had been genetically engineered at birth with anti-Borg pathogens. His parents had raised him specifically to infect the Borg and stop the attacks on their planet. The Doctor is able to

suppress the virus, but Seven is not sure she will be able to help Icheb come to terms with what has happened. She is forced to trust her maternal instincts and begins to help Icheb understand that on *Voyager* he has a family that loves him and will never let him go.

SENSOR READINGS: Icheb enhances the long-range scanners so they reach to the Orpisay nebula to witness a star forming.

DELTA QUADRANT: The Brunali are an agrarian species that has developed sophisticated techniques in agricultural geonetics allowing them to grow crops in an inhospitable environment. Their technological resources are limited because they do not want to become targets for the Borg and are capable of space travel but most of their vessels were destroyed. Kim detects scattered enclaves on the northern continent, with a total population fewer than 10,000. Judging from residual gamma radiation, they have suffered numerous Borg attacks over the years. The Brunali have been attacked by the Borg three times in

ciated with wormholes to hopefully find a faster way home. *Poma* was Icheb's favorite food when he was little.

CREW COMPLEMENT: Icheb is taken home to his people, but returns to the ship after they prove untrustworthy.

EPISODE LOGS: Ktaria VII is the more familiar name for the planet Kataris. ▪ Although Icheb will remain on *Voyager* for the rest of the series, the other three Borg children will leave in "Imperfection," when Rebi and Azan's parents are found.

Seven reluctantly helps Icheb readjust to his former home. RON TOM

GOOD SHEPHERD

EPISODE #240
TELEPLAY BY: DIANNA GITTO & JOE MENOSKY
STORY BY: DIANNA GITTO
DIRECTED BY: WINRICH KOLBE

GUEST STARS

CREWMAN MORTIMER HARREN	JAY UNDERWOOD
CREWMAN WILLIAM TELFER	MICHAEL REISZ
ENGINEER	KIMBLE JEMISON
and	
TAL CELES	ZOE McLELLAN

CO-STARS

JUNCTION OPERATOR	TOM MORELLO
COMPUTER VOICE	MAJEL BARRETT

STARDATE 53753.2

Seven presents a shipwide efficiency analysis to the senior staff showing Janeway that, among other things, three crewmen have "slipped through the cracks" on the ship and do not function in line with typical Starfleet standards. Since the crewmen cannot be transferred to another Federation ship—which is standard procedure—Janeway decides to handle the matter herself by taking the three young crew members on an away mission.

The first of the trio is Celes, a grade-3 sensor analyst in astrometrics who constantly has to have all of her work double-checked. Second is Engineering Crewman Mortimer Harren, who has five advanced degrees in Theoretical Cosmology, but would rather spend his time down on Deck 15 figuring out the origin of the universe. Finally there is William Telfer, a security officer and

the last decade—nine years ago, six years ago, and one year ago. ▪ Icheb was genetically engineered to carry the pathogen that destroyed the Borg cube he was assimilated into. His DNA is similar to that of a typical Brunali male, except for differences in the third, thirteenth, and seventeenth chromosomes. His parents made microgenetic alterations so he would produce the pathogen.

PERSONAL LOGS: At the "First Annual *Voyager* Science Fair," Rebi and Azan clone a potato, although they would have preferred to have cloned Naomi. Mezoti makes a Teirenian ant colony, infusing the soil with blue ion dye so it would be easier to see the luminescent insects. (The drones produce a fluorescent enzyme that is activated by the queen.) Naomi creates a hologram of Kataris, her father's planet, programming all the geophysical and atmospheric conditions herself (The Arpasian Mountain range is known for its high winds and hail). Icheb makes a high-resolution gravimetric sensor array that will augment *Voyager*'s ability to scan for the neurtrino flux asso-

Janeway double-checks all of Tal's work. MICHAEL YARISH

hypochondriac who visits sickbay weekly. Before they leave, Seven of Nine warns Janeway that an experienced crew would better serve the mission, but the captain responds with the story of the good shepherd assigned to watch her flock and make sure that none go astray.

Not long into the mission, an invisible force suddenly strikes the *Delta Flyer*, knocking propulsion offline and neutralizing ninety percent of the antimatter. Harren suggests that a cometlike assemblage of dark matter is responsible for the neutralization and proposes that they eject their remaining antimatter in order to avoid another impact. However, Janeway notes that his theory is an unproven hypothesis, and she needs more convincing evidence. When they fire a photon torpedo at the force, a humming sound is heard and Telfer disappears. Suddenly, he reappears and collapses to the floor and it appears as if something is writhing beneath his skin.

Janeway has no choice except to fire a phaser at Telfer when he reveals that the phenomenon is controlling his actions. As he struggles to stay on his feet, the dark matter entity extends out of an incision wound on his neck and flings itself onto a console. Ignoring the captain's order, Harren fires a phaser and vaporizes the entity. Frustrated with Harren, Janeway suggests that the entity was simply trying to communicate with the crew.

The team takes the *Delta Flyer* to the rings of a nearby planet where they hope to reinitialize its warp core. Suddenly, a slow-moving swath opens up in the glowing particles of the planet's radiogenic ring heading toward

the vessel. Janeway instructs her crew to get into the escape pods, but Celes tells Janeway that a crew never abandons its captain. Harren does choose to take one of the escape pods, but instead of escaping he heads toward their pursuer in order to give the *Flyer* time to get away. Not willing to abandon a crew member, Janeway locks the *Delta Flyer's* transporter onto the pod before igniting a chain reaction of explosions in the planet's rings.

A confused captain wakes up in sickbay, where Chakotay reports that *Voyager* received her initial distress call and found the *Flyer* drifting above a gas giant with everyone unconscious inside. Janeway tells Chakotay that the good shepherd went looking for a few lost members of her flock and ended up running into a wolf. However, in the end, the shepherd did find her charges.

SENSOR READINGS: Seven of Nine's shipwide efficiency report gives ops a low grade of 76, noting that the crewmen assigned to night duty often have little to do once the ship's course has been locked in. In engineering she claims Torres is guilty of "failure to utilize expertise" in the case of Crewman Harren. However, when Torres has given him more responsibility, he did not do the work. Seven notes that security is functioning with near perfection, although she believes the weapons locker should be rearranged with the smaller rifles in front so they would be easier to get to in an emergency. ■ The away team explores a class-T cluster consisting of gas giants and various radiogenic sources. Long-range scans indicate a number of tantalizing anomalies. Celes runs an ongoing sensor analysis to provide data for the others, while Harren scans subspace particle decay for anything new to learn about a star formation, and Tefler looks for signs of life, though the captain admits that to be a long shot in the environment.

SHUTTLE TRACKER: The dark matter life-form tears off a plating section of the *Delta Flyer's* outer hull. Ninety percent of the antimatter is neutralized leaving the reactor cold. Impulse engines are damaged and they can only get to one-eighth impulse. The away team uses radiogenic particles in the rings of a class-T gas giant to reinitialize the warp reaction. However, with only ten percent of the antimatter left, they can only get to warp 2.

PERSONAL LOGS: As a child, Janeway was afraid of the ocean because she did not know what was around her since she couldn't see the bottom. In her first year at the Academy she went through zero-g training in the Coral Sea, and the experience finally helped her get her over her fear.

Harren lords his intelligence over others. MICHAEL YARISH

has not been able to get past the proficiency requirements for an away mission. ▪ Prior to the away mission Telfer claims that he has been infected by a multiphasic prion (that attach themselves to the mitochondrial walls).

FURY

EPISODE #241
TELEPLAY BY: **BRYAN FULLER & MICHAEL TAYLOR**
STORY BY: **RICK BERMAN & BRANNON BRAGA**
DIRECTED BY: **JOHN BRUNO**

ALSO STARRING

KES	JENNIFER LIEN

GUEST STARS

SAMANTHA WILDMAN	NANCY HOWER
NAOMI WILDMAN	SCARLETT POMERS
VIDIIAN CAPTAIN	VAUGHN ARMSTRONG
CAREY	JOSH CLARK

CO-STARS

AZAN	KURT WETHERILL
REBI	CODY WETHERILL
SECURITY GUARD	TARIK ERGIN
COMPUTER VOICE	MAJEL BARRETT

STARDATE UNKNOWN

Harren is determined to disprove Schlezholt's theory of multiple big bangs, but he had to "demolish" Wang's second postulate to do it. However, Janeway notes that Wang's second postulate has more lives than a cat, because once you think you've eliminated it, the postulate pops up again. Harren grew up on Vico V with the "wildest sky in the Alpha Quadrant." He signed on to *Voyager* because he needed a year of hands-on experience as a requirement to get into the Institute of Cosmology on Orion I. He once wrote a paper—which Janeway has read—on the possibility of a dark matter protocomet. In it, he hypothesized that a tertiary product of stellar consolidation would be a cometlike assemblage of dark matter that would be attracted to by any source of antimatter and neutralize it upon contact. He notes that impact on the hull from a dark matter body might leave a quantum signature in the alloys. ▪ Celes has to complete a level-3 sensor analysis interpreting subspace infrared. Janeway tutors her by telling Celes the way to remember the analytical aspects of the subspace infrared algorithm are by the anagram: "Zero-G Is Fun." Zeta particle derivation, Gamma wave frequency, Ion distribution, Flow rate of subspace positrons. Celes is a sensor analyst, grade-3 and

A small vessel, piloted by an older, more weathered Kes, collides with *Voyager*. Moments later she beams herself aboard. Using her psychokinetic abilities, Kes disables the ship's systems as she heads to engineering. Torres and Seven try to stop her, but Kes steps up to the warp core, placing her hands upon it. Just as Torres goes to shut down the core, she is struck by a tendril of energy. Seven rushes over to Torres's dead body, while Kes vanishes in a flash of light traveling back in time to shortly after *Voyager* was pulled into the Delta Quadrant. There she changes her appearance so she can take her younger self's place.

The Janeway of this time period is concerned that another conflict with the Vidiians may soon ensue, since two of their ships have been detected on long-range sensors. On a secure channel, Kes makes contact with the Vidiian captain, offering him the information necessary to capture *Voyager* in return for her safe passage home to Ocampa.

Meanwhile, Tuvok seems to be experiencing premo-

Kes uses the power of the warp core to send herself back in time.
RON TOM

nitions. Stepping into a turbolift, he encounters a young girl who identifies herself as Naomi Wildman. Tuvok follows the girl into the cargo bay, and when the doors open he sees Seven of Nine and the Borg children from the future regenerating in Borg alcoves. Later he experiences a fragmented replay of the events leading up to Torres being struck by the energy tendril while a much older Kes looks on. Janeway discovers the presence of tachyon particles in the proximity of the locations where Tuvok's premonitions occurred and concludes that some form of time travel is involved.

When Janeway orders the bridge crew to scan for tachyon particles, *Voyager* suddenly finds itself under attack by the Vidiians. Chakotay detects a transmission originating in the airponics bay, where he picks up two bio-readings that both appear to be Kes. Janeway heads to airponics with a security team as the bridge crew tries to break free of the Vidiian ship. Meanwhile the Vidiians have started boarding *Voyager*, and Janeway must evade them in order to get to the airponics bay.

Kes tells Janeway she wants to rescue her past self, explaining that she was taken from her home and made a prisoner on the ship, corrupted with ideas of exploration and discovery. She accuses the captain of encouraging her to develop her mental abilities before she was ready. It is too late for her present self to return home to Ocampa because she is so charged that her people would be fright-

ened of her. As *Voyager* breaks free of the Vidiian ship, Janeway is able to stop the future Kes with a deadly phaser blast. When the Kes of the past recovers, Janeway asks her help to prevent something terrible from happening in the future.

As time unfolds, an older Kes again hails *Voyager*, but this time Janeway and Tuvok are prepared. The captain orders the warp core shut down. When Kes enters engineering, a hologram of her younger self appears reminding the older Kes that she made her own choices, and that the people she came back to harm care about her. Janeway approaches and reminds Kes why she made that recording, urging her to stay on *Voyager*. Kes's anger dissipates as she remembers the recording, but says she needs to be with her own people and only now believes herself to be ready to make the journey.

SENSOR READINGS: In the past, Ensign Wildman and the Doctor worked on a neural agent that would incapacitate the Vidiians without harming the crew. ▪ Also in the past, *Voyager* enters an area of space filled with subspace vacuoles covering about seventy percent of the region. They preprogram every kilometer of the area of space so they would have to spend only a second or two at impulse every time the computer executes a turn, since the neural gel packs can calculate vectors faster than a human.

DAMAGE REPORT: Although the ship suffers extensive damage in the past, in the present timeline the main problem is that the older Kes causes bulkhead ruptures on Deck 11, Sections 17, 18, 19, and higher.

ALPHA QUADRANT: Every cadet about to go on his first shore leave hears the cautionary tale (and urban legend) of the man who goes to Risa. There he meets a beautiful woman who invites him to an evening of passion, then wakes up in the morning feeling wonderful until he discovers he's missing a kidney. ▪ The first lesson in flying a starship is "Faster than light, no left or right." Or when possible, maintain a linear trajectory because course corrections could fracture the hull.

PERSONAL LOGS: Janeway and Tuvok have served on three starships together, and she was present at his daughter's *Kolinahr*. Janeway notes having once met Wildman's husband on DS9. ▪ The episode opens on Tuvok's birthday, with Janeway noting that he has almost reached triple digits. He has known Janeway for approximately twenty years. Tuvok admits to having had hallu-

A young Kes is surprised to find another version of herself in airponics. RON TOM

LIVE FAST AND PROSPER

EPISODE #242
TELEPLAY BY: ROBIN BURGER
DIRECTED BY: LeVAR BURTON

GUEST STARS	
DALA	KAITLIN HOPKINS
MOBAR	GREGG DANIEL
ZAR	FRANCIS GUINAN
VARN	TED ROONEY
MINER #1	SCOTT LINCOLN

CO-STARS	
OREK	DENNIS COCKRUM
MINER #2	TIMOTHY McNEIL

STARDATE 53849.2

Using Starfleet identities of Captain Janeway and her senior staff, a band of con artists moves from system to system engaging in a series of lucrative deceptions. Eventually, the real Janeway and her

The *Voyager* imposters get into their roles. MICHAEL YARISH

cinations before, but only while in a state of deep meditation. Also in the past, the Doctor admits to knowing Wildman is pregnant two weeks into the journey. He found out while performing her annual physical. He also knows the child is female and since she is half-Ktarian, the gestation period will be nearly double that of a human. He notes that medical protocol supercedes the captain's authority in matters of doctor-patient confidentiality. ▪ Kes gives off high levels of neurogenic energy as she passes through the halls destroying bulkheads.

EPISODE LOGS: Kes goes back in time to the period when *Voyager* was in the Delta Quadrant only fifty-six days and seventeen hours.

ENSIGN HARRY KIM

ANGLE TO INCLUDE QUARK AND HARRY KIM
the latter a young Starfleet Ensign in his early twenties. Looks fresh scrubbed and right out of the academy . . .

—Harry Kim's first appearance in "Caretaker"

There is really no better sentence to sum up all that Harry Kim was at the beginning of the series than "fresh scrubbed and right out of the Academy." His character was the youngest of the crew and the most eager to tow the Starfleet line. He was, at first, the one character who could always be counted on to do what was right or a least question things when they appeared to deviate from Starfleet principles. This was largely a result of being a recent graduate. But equally important was the close bond he had with his parents.

It was his seemingly perfect relationship with his parents that made Kim so important to the series as a whole. Quite frankly, from the show's inception, Kim was the only crew member on the senior staff who was desperate to get home. Granted, Janeway and Tuvok had just as much reason to miss their loved ones. But the captain could not walk around with her feelings on her sleeve, and as a Vulcan Tuvok couldn't show them. Although some of the other characters did have friends and family back in the Alpha Quadrant, there was always the faint suggestion that Paris, Chakotay, and Torres were almost better off in their present situation. And, of course, the Doctor, Neelix, Kes, and later Seven of Nine, had no real ties to the Alpha Quadrant. Therefore, it was Kim's role, throughout the series, that gave voice to the desire to get home. This made it more significant when he compromised his ideals and destroyed the Borg transwarp hub just to preserve the crew's safe return in "Endgame."

ROBBIE ROBINSON

Garett Wang: In the beginning of the series, Ensign Kim was younger than Garrett Wang the actor, so I had to take a little bit away from who I was to get to that point of being a younger, more naïve inexperienced crew member. Today, Kim is a much more responsible and mature individual. And he's having fun with it. He definitely has more of a sense of humor then he did in the beginning. He's not so serious. This comes from the various unfortunate experiences that he's had to deal with. I'm talking about being probed, kidnapped, and killed. You know, these things kind of contribute to one's development. Having to deal with the worst case scenario. And that seems to be what Kim had to deal with.

Kim did grow over the seven seasons, as any young character should. He went from boy to man as his separation from his parents and his girlfriend Libby became more real and he realized that he had to stand on his own. Though he did technically die on two occasions ("Emanations" and "Deadlock"), nothing put a damper on the excitement for life that he seemed to exude even when other characters insisted on being miserable. With the exception of Neelix, Kim was the character with the most positive outlook, but realistically so.

Ethan Phillips: In some ways Kim and Neelix have similar functions on the ship. He's the ensign, and has more of a neophyte kind of role in a way that's similar to Neelix who doesn't have all that much power. They've always had kind of a jocular relationship and I think that Kim has always respected Neelix. He's always been kind to Neelix and always treated him with a great deal of respect as well as being able to have lighthearted moments with him.

As the freshly scrubbed ensign, Kim's relationship with the captain started out as might be expected, with the young crewman eager to please. As the series progressed, he proved himself a number of times, much to Janeway's pleasure, and she admitted how proud she was of his development as early as "Twisted." Chakotay and Tuvok both also found him to be maturing as an officer and related to him as such. Because of his easygoing attitude, Kim struck up immediate friendships with Torres and Paris.

Though it would seem unlikely that the spit-shined former cadet would befriend the former convict, the bond between Kim and Paris proved to be among the strongest. This was largely due to the fact that each provided something that the other was desperately in need of. For Paris, Kim was the credibility the wayward lieutenant so needed following his misspent youth. In turn, he provided Kim with the guiding influence of someone who respected the rules, but didn't always play by them. Together, they took on many challenges, none more difficult than their time spent as prisoners in "The Chute." It was in that episode more than any other that Kim came into his own as a man.

Robert Duncan McNeill: It was really a healthy relationship for both our characters. It allowed Harry Kim to sort of have a more experienced pal and someone close to his age and similar in many ways. I thought it was nice to be sort of the mentor, the big brother to Harry Kim. And I think it was good for both of them. I think, now that we've been through so many years, Harry certainly has built his own experience and history and I don't know that he needs that same sort of big brother character so they've kind of let that go in many ways. But all along I thought that was a really good relationship to explore.

ROBBIE ROBINSON

Kim would continue to grow and to love and, most definitely, lose as the series progressed. His troubled romantic life became something of a joke that Paris couldn't help making light of by constantly bringing up Kim's falling for the wrong twin, a hologram, and a former Borg, among many other wayward choices. But his failed love affairs helped him grow and become more pragmatic and less naïve. Meanwhile a future version of Kim seen in "Timeless" showed how important that naivete was to his character. That episode showed the most dramatic change to this character. Without that naivete he was definitely strong and mature, yet extremely bitter. He had forgotten who he was and allowed his circumstances to change him to the depths of his very soul.

Garrett Wang: In "Timeless," Kim does all these wonderful things and changes the course of the past and the future, and the only person to really know about it is Janeway. And then Kim, from that one message to himself at the end, but everybody else doesn't know anything about it. It's sort of like one of those things where you do a good deed and no one ever even knows it happened.

In the end, Harry Kim did properly mature, guided through his metamorphosis by Garrett Wang's portrayal. Through both the lighthearted and deeply moving moments traversed by this character, the struggle to return to home and family remained at the forefront of his journey. In the end, it was Harry Kim's return home that came across as the most fulfilling.

Janeway fails to reform her imposter. RON TOM

crew are blamed for these scams when the swindlers do not deliver the goods as promised. Neelix and Paris remember that they met a pair of clerics named Dala and Mobar three weeks earlier. The pair apparently downloaded *Voyager*'s entire database from the *Delta Flyer*. As a result, Dala and Mobar were able to obtain the information they needed to pose as Starfleet officers.

In an attempt to track down the imposters, Janeway asks Orek, a Telsian who has been cheated by Dala and Mobar, for access to the scans of the imposters' vessel in order to derive their warp signature. Meanwhile, Paris and Neelix are frustrated with themselves for being so easily duped. Tuvok detects a vessel whose warp signature matches the imposter's ship along with a ship belonging to another alien, named Varn, who was duped by the fraudulent crew. When Varn refuses to cooperate, Janeway disables his tractor beam holding Dala's vessel.

Janeway instructs Seven to transport everyone on Dala's vessel to *Voyager*. However, because *Voyager*'s transporters are damaged, Seven is only able to beam Dala

onto the ship. She refuses to provide a detailed account of everyone they cheated, or the location of the stolen property. Janeway instructs Tuvok to hail Telsian Security and tell them that they have a prisoner to turn over, pulling a scam on Dala by relating how barbaric Telsian prisons are. In actuality, Janeway does not want Tuvok to call the Telsians just yet because she wants Dala to sit and think for a while first.

Neelix visits Dala in the brig and engages in a heart-to-heart conversation with her regarding her options. However, when Neelix turns away, Dala knocks him to the ground and grabs the phaser from his belt. She escapes down a corridor and stuns Tuvok, then climbs inside the *Delta Flyer* to escape.

Dala catches up with Mobar and Zar—a third con artist posing as Chakotay—and asks them to beam her aboard. When she arrives on the bridge of the imposter vessel, she instructs them to head for their pillaged loot, as it is time to flee the sector. Zar's increasing suspicions of Dala are proven correct when she contacts *Voyager* upon their arrival at the cave with the hidden contraband. But in reality, "Dala" is the Doctor who changed his holographic image to appear as the con artist. The real Dala is still in the *Flyer* with Paris. The *Voyager* crew has successfully used their own ruse to find the stolen items.

SENSOR READINGS: Paris and Neelix met "Sister" Dala eighteen days ago while on their away mission on Selnia Prime, a small planetoid in the Wyanti system. They were searching for a spore with which the Doctor planned to grow antiproteins. ▪ According to Mobar (as Tuvok) Earth is 30,342.4 light-years from Telsius. ▪ Paris and the Doctor use ambizine to render Dala unconscious.

DAMAGE REPORT: There are system failures on nine decks because of the faulty heating coil that Neelix obtained. The flaw releases a contaminant into the replicator system. ▪ The ship's tractor generator goes offline, and transporters are damaged.

DELTA QUADRANT: Bolomite is mined on Telsius and is used in omega radiation therapy. ▪ Varn's unnamed race is at war with the Polnians.

ALPHA QUADRANT: Dala refers to Directive 927 of the Starfleet general order as "Always help those in need." (This may not be a true directive as it sounds like rather simplistic terminology for Starfleet.)

PERSONAL LOGS: Paris and Kim have been altering Tuvok's holoprograms. In one, they programmed the Oracle of K'Tal to wear pajamas. ▪ The Doctor wins in Paris and Neelix's shell game, and Neelix has to do three duty shifts in sickbay. He later loses to the same con artists, but no specific bet was made.

LIFE LINE

EPISODE #243

TELEPLAY BY: ROBERT DOHERTY & RAF GREEN
and BRANNON BRAGA
STORY BY: JOHN BRUNO & ROBERT PICARDO
DIRECTED BY: TERRY WINDELL

SPECIAL GUEST STAR

BARCLAY	**DWIGHT SCHULTZ**

GUEST STARS

HALEY	**TAMARA CRAIG THOMAS**
ADMIRAL HAYES	**JACK SHEARER**

SPECIAL GUEST APPEARANCE BY

DEANNA TROI	**MARINA SIRTIS**

CO-STAR

COMPUTER VOICE	**MAJEL BARRETT**

STARDATE UNKNOWN

When Starfleet's Pathfinder Project transmits the first of what is to become a monthly block of data to *Voyager*, the Doctor receives disturbing news—Lewis Zimmerman, the creator of the Doctor's program, is dying. Hoping to save this "father" he never met, whose likeness he shares, the Doctor's program is transmitted back to the Alpha Quadrant.

Instead of being pleased with the Doctor's attempts to help, Zimmerman is completely standoffish, rejecting the Doctor as an obsolete Mark-1 hologram. He has been examined by the Mark-2, Mark-3, and Mark-4, in addition to the finest living doctors in Starfleet, and none of them have been able to help him. However, Reg Barclay points out that the Doctor has been running almost continuously for six years and that he has witnessed things in the Delta Quadrant that most doctors could not even imagine. Zimmerman eventually becomes frustrated with all of the Doctor's questions, and he abruptly instructs the computer to transmit the Doctor to the living quarters.

Meanwhile, Barclay pleads with Counselor Troi to take a leave of absence from the *U.S.S. Enterprise* in order to counsel Zimmerman. When she does show up a week later, things seem to be worse between the two doctors. Troi tries to convince Zimmerman that the Doctor has developed a promising treatment.

While the arguing continues between the pair, Barclay discovers a problem is causing the Doctor's program to deteriorate, but there is nothing that he can do because the damage is too severe. Zimmerman is the only

Deanna Troi tries to help a very reluctant Dr. Zimmerman. MICHAEL YARISH

one who can save the Doctor, but he refuses to repair a replaceable computer program. In an attempt to convince him to help the Doctor, Zimmerman's companion hologram, Haley, tells him that she will ask to be installed elsewhere unless he does something to save the Doctor.

Zimmerman successfully identifies an error within the Doctor's pattern buffer, which turns out to be sabotage on the part of Barclay to get the two working together. He also suggests changing the EMH's personality subroutine as well, but the Doctor refuses, since that would change who he had become. In the process, the two make peace, and Zimmerman finally agrees to treatment. The Doctor announces that he believes Zimmerman will enjoy a complete recovery as he bids his new friends farewell and heads back to *Voyager*.

ALPHA QUADRANT: Barclay arrives at Jupiter Station on the *Shuttlecraft Dawkins*. ▪ Starfleet sends a compressed datastream from the Pathfinder Project by using a cyclic pulsar to amplify signals from the MIDAS array. The cycle only peaks every thirty-two days so they can transmit only at monthly intervals. In the first message Starfleet sends tactical updates, letters from home, and news about the Alpha Quadrant. In a message from Admiral Hayes, Janeway learns that they have redirected two deep space vessels to their coordinates that could rendezvous with *Voyager* in five or six years. He also mentions wanting to know the "status of the Maquis." ▪ Zimmerman suffers from acute subcellular degradation, which is very similar to the early stages of the Vidiian phage. Initial symptoms were fatigue, nausea, and joint inflammation. Zimmerman was previously commissioned by Starfleet Intelligence to design a holographic fly as an experiment in micro-surveillance. He has won the Daystrom Prize for holography. ▪ Most EMH Mark-1 have been reconfigured to scrub plasma conduits on waste-transfer barges since the EMH program has upgraded to the EMH Mark-4. Zimmerman had designed the first program to look like him because he had put so much of himself into its development. When it failed to meet Starfleet's expectations, he was devastated and locked himself away in his lab for two years trying to repair the defects. Eventually the pro-

The Doctor makes his second trip back to the Alpha Quadrant.
MICHAEL YARISH

grams got the nicknames "Emergency Medical Hotheads" and "Extremely Marginal Housecalls." There are now 675 Mark-1s in existence performing routine maintenance duty. ▪ Zimmerman begins to compose his will, leaving his holographic art collection and something he refers to as "The Trojan Horse Project" to the only engineer he trusts completely with his work—Barclay.

PERSONAL LOGS: Janeway once met Zimmerman at a conference, where he managed to offend just about everyone in attendance and kept calling her "Captain Jane." ▪ Seven temporarily removes all of the Doctor's nonessential subroutines because his program is too large for the data stream. She removes twelve megaquads of information, including his singing algorithms, athletic abilities, painting abilities, and grand master chess program. Zimmerman later reprograms him to greet people with the phrase, "Welcome to sickbay. How may I help you today?"

EPISODE LOGS: This is the Doctor's second visit to the Alpha Quadrant. He first made the trip in "Message in a

Bottle." Though this is the first time he actually meets his creator face-to-face, he did meet another version of Zimmerman that was part of the EMH diagnostic program in "The Swarm." ▪ It is stated that Zimmerman has not left Jupiter Station in the past four years, which means his visit to DS9 in the episode "Dr. Bashir, I Presume" (*DS9*) must have been the last time he was away.

MUSE
EPISODE #244
WRITTEN BY: JOE MENOSKY
DIRECTED BY: MIKE VEJAR

GUEST STARS

KELIS	**JOSEPH WILL**
LAYNA	**KELLIE WAYMIRE**
CHORUS #3	**TONY AMENDOLA**
CHORUS #1	**JACK AXELROD**
JERO	**MICHAEL HOUSTON KING**
TANIS	**KATHLEEN GARRETT**
WARLORD	**STONEY WESTMORELAND**
and	
CHORUS #2	**JACK SCHUCK**

CO-STAR

COMPUTER VOICE	**MAJEL BARRETT**

STARDATE 53896*

Following the performance of a play about the "Shining Ship *Voyager*" an alien poet returns to the remains of the crashed *Delta Flyer* where Torres is slumped over in the pilot's chair. She awakes with a wound on her forehead and the poet, Kelis, standing over her. Startled, Torres jumps to her feet and questions his intentions. To which Kelis replies that he is her servant and she is his muse.

Kelis intends to keep Torres on the planet because he feels that with her inspiration, he can create a play that will promote peace between the patron and his enemies. Confused by it all, Torres slowly recalls that she and Kim had crashed while searching for dilithium. She had ordered Kim into the escape pod before the *Flyer* went down, but he is nowhere to be found. Torres reluctantly agrees to help Kelis with his story in exchange for his

*The stardate is taken from the performance and reflects the time roughly eight days before the events of the episode.

Torres plays the role of the *deus ex machina*. MICHAEL YARISH

assistance in repairing the *Flyer.* Meanwhile, on *Voyager,* the entire crew searches for Kim and Torres, especially Tuvok, who has not slept in close to two weeks. Chakotay offers to head the search, but Tuvok sternly refuses.

As the days move on, Kelis rehearses the play nonstop, and finally brings Torres to the theater where he introduces her as a visiting artist. Lacking an ending for the play the day before it opens, Torres and Kelis argue over the proper course of action. Layna, the actress portraying Torres in the play, follows Kelis to their secret meeting place in the *Flyer* and jealously confronts Torres about her relationship with Kelis. She threatens to expose Torres as an "eternal" to the patron if she does not depart at once.

After Layna leaves, Kim appears at the window of the ship. His escape pod had run into turbulence so he decided to turn around and follow Torres's signature, finally landing and tracking her position with a tricorder. Kim has a Starfleet satchel that contains emergency rations, a phaser, and the escape pod's emergency transmitter. The next day, while Kim and Torres work on their rescue, Kelis is forced to start the show without her or an ending.

On *Voyager,* Tuvok is caught sleeping on the bridge and decides it is time for him to take a break. As Chakotay relieves Tuvok, they hear the message sent by Kim and Torres. While waiting for *Voyager's* response, Torres receives a note from Kelis saying that he needs her for inspiration. Torres, feeling obligated to help, tells Kim she will be back and leaves for the play.

Torres enters the stage and begins performing an ending that she has come up with wherein she and Kelis say good-bye because it is time for her to leave. Layna tries to sabotage everything by telling the patron that Torres is really an Eternal, but Kelis pretends that it is part of the play and that Layna is just playing the part of the jealous girlfriend. The patron loves the plot twist and the special effect in which Torres beams away from the stage leaving Kelis behind to promise stories of *Voyager* as long as the players are alive to tell them.

SHUTTLE TRACKER: The *Delta Flyer* crash lands on the planet. It is unclear how extensive the damage is to the craft, but it is retrieved. An escape pod is ejected and it is

Tuvok refuses to rest until the missing crew members are found. MICHAEL YARISH

assumed that it is also retrieved. To fix the *Flyer*'s transmitter Torres needs a metal plate made of three parts tin to five parts bronze with one side coated in gold.

DELTA QUADRANT: Kelis believes Torres to be an "eternal"; a being that has the power to make the ground open up and the sky fall. The eternals are believed to be the inspiration behind all the events made famous by the ancient poets. They are on a class-L planet that is the fourth planet in an F-type star system. Kelis refers to dilithium as "winter's tears." The only deposit he knows of is on his patron's hunting ground. Kelis's patron is always at war with his enemies over territories. His people have the ability to make bronze and gold is expensive on their planet. All their stories have at least one of three plot points: Mistaken identity—a character is believed to be someone else; Discovery—the moment when that person's true identity is revealed; and Reversal—the situation turns from good to bad in the blink of an eye. A hundred years ago their performance space was a temple, and the stage was the altar stone. Every year a victim would be sacrificed on it in honor of winter. One year a play took the place of the ritual, and no on has died since, though nobody recalls the reason for the change.

ALPHA QUADRANT: Vulcans can function without sleep for two weeks.

PERSONAL LOGS: Kim walks two hundred kilometers while tracking the *Flyer*'s position with his tricorder.

THE HAUNTING OF DECK TWELVE

EPISODE #245

TELEPLAY BY: **MIKE SUSSMAN** and **KENNETH BILLER**
& BRYAN FULLER

STORY BY: **MIKE SUSSMAN**

DIRECTED BY: **DAVID LIVINGSTON**

GUESTS STARS

ICHEB	MANU INTIRAYMI
MEZOTI	MARLEY McCLEAN
TAL CELES	ZOE McLELLAN

CO-STARS

AZAN	KURT WETHERILL
REBI	CODY WETHERILL
COMPUTER VOICE	MAJEL BARRETT

STARDATE UNKNOWN

A fter the crew powers down the ship, the Borg children awake as their alcoves go offline. They find Neelix in the cargo bay waiting for them with a plasma lantern. Deflecting their inquiries about what is going on, Neelix does his best to encourage the children to relax by telling them the shutdown is only temporary. When the children decide it must have something to do with the ghost that is said to haunt a sealed-off section of Deck 12, Neelix tries to keep their imaginations from getting carried away. He tells them the story of the nebula *Voyager* visited before they came onboard.

As Neelix's story opens, *Voyager* is in a J-class nebula collecting deuterium. After Kim notices that the collection is destabilizing the nebula, the crew stops the extraction. A second before *Voyager* leaves the nebula, an electric bolt rocks the ship. The captain immediately begins scanning the ship for damage and injuries, and learns that most of the electrical systems are failing.

Chakotay reports that additional functions on board are malfunctioning and Janeway notices they are off course and returning to the nebula they just left. In the cargo bay, where Seven of Nine works, the air begins to fill with colorful gas, similar to that of the nebula. When Seven attempts to escape the room, she is surrounded by a force field and knocked unconscious by an energy beam moving through the gas.

While trying to bring the engines back online, Paris is attacked by the same energy surge that hit Seven. When Janeway and Tuvok take him to see the Doctor, they find Seven of Nine, who was rescued by Chakotay. When the captain learns what happened to Seven, she

Mezoti is alarmed when she suddenly awakens from her regeneration.
MICHAEL YARISH

begins to suspect that a life-form has entered the ship.

Alone in the darkened mess hall, Neelix hears a thumping noise and moves to investigate. He is frightened when he sees a shape in the hallway, but is relieved to find out it is only Tuvok in a gas mask. Tuvok has Neelix follow him through a Jefferies tube, heading for engineering where the others are waiting. Meanwhile, Janeway realizes that she can talk to this new life-form through the ship's computer, and it instructs her to go to

The crew establishes command in engineering. MICHAEL YARISH

the astrometrics lab, where she learns that the nebula that the alien came from is no longer there. The computerized voice of the life-form demands that the *Voyager* crew abandon ship.

In the Jefferies tube, Tuvok is attacked by the being and injured. Facing his fears, Neelix summons the courage to drag Tuvok through the dark. Janeway complies with the abandon ship order, evacuating the entire crew except for herself. Reasoning with the entity, she convinces it that she can take it to a new nebula if it relinquishes control of the ship. The creature agrees and releases Janeway. The crew returns and seals the life-form off on Deck 12.

As Neelix ends the story a loud noise is heard, and he explains that it's the life-form being released into the new nebula. When the children admit to being afraid it might come back, Neelix then tells them that he made the whole thing up. However, Captain Janeway later confirms to him that the life-form is in its new home.

SENSOR READINGS: Deck 12, Section 42, has been off limits to everyone but senior officers with a level-6 security clearance. In that isolated area, an artificial environ-

ment was created for the alien. ▪ In Neelix's story, life pods, all shuttles, and the *Delta Flyer* are ejected and it took almost two days for the entire crew to return to the ship.

DAMAGE REPORT: In the past, an EM discharge penetrates the hull throwing auxiliary subprocessors offline and causing secondary systems to malfunction.

DELTA QUADRANT: The Borg encountered Species 5973 in Galactic Cluster 8, noting they were multispectrum particle life-forms. ▪ Neelix tells the tragic tale of the crew of the Talaxian freighter, *Salvoria*. Nearly a century ago the ship suffered a cascade failure and began to lose life support generators one by one. There was not enough air to sustain everyone, so the crew began drawing straws to decide who would die. The ship was not found for eighty years.

ALPHA QUADRANT: Neelix suggests telling the children's story "Flotter Meets the Invincible Invertebrates."

PERSONAL LOGS: Tuvok perspires only when the temperature reaches 350 degrees Kelvin with a higher than

NEELIX

The cramped cabin of the alien vessel appears on screen, filled with an eclectic assortment of junk. The lone occupant, whom we'll come to know as NEELIX, seems startled by the hail. Neelix is, frankly, unattractive but in a teddy bear sort of way. He takes great pride in his appearance, but what can anyone do who hasn't seen water in two weeks? He has adapted an air of cultivated elegance and charm rather like the concierge at a one-star hotel . . .

—Neelix's first appearance in "Caretaker"

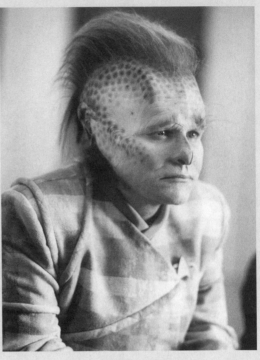

ROBBIE ROBINSON

His introduction was obviously less than auspicious, yet that didn't faze Neelix in the least. In a life where he had to make the best of what he was given, Neelix turned a bad situation into the chance of a lifetime. Though initially deceptive in his dealings with the *Voyager* crew, his actions were noble in that they were based in saving his love, Kes. Seeing further opportunity, however, he made a permanent agreement to accompany Janeway and her crew, filling whatever role she needed.

The promise to perform any task truly came to fruition over the seven years of the series. First as a chef and guide, Neelix ingratiated himself into the crew, proving to be useful if not entirely skilled in the former position. However, when his usefulness as a guide ended, he mistakenly took a course of action in "Fair Trade" that proved more harmful than useful but succeeded in teaching him that his true value came from more than just the position he filled on the ship. As morale officer, Neelix became involved in the welfare of his fellow crew members. On an individual basis he helped everyone from Torres to Tuvok with personal problems, while on the larger scale he developed many diversions such as a holoresort program for the crew's relaxation and even a morning show for both entertainment and information. But it was his role as ambassador that he found to be his most valuable gift to the crew as it traversed the Delta Quadrant. Using his skills as a trader, he ingratiated himself and the crew into new and different races in a variety of welcoming and restrictive atmospheres.

Ethan Phillips: In six and a half seasons, I have been complimented three times on my cooking. Three times! In a hundred and some odd episodes.

All of Neelix's jobs have really interesting aspects. I liked the business of the chef. I like the props and the activity involved in the kitchen. It's fun to act around that. I like the challenge of playing the morale officer, who is always nurturing, and always seeking to solve and heal. I like finding ways to make that less sentimental and less gooey. And the diplomacy part is fun because there's a feeling of power and significance in the character at those times.

Although Neelix often provided a comedic break in the action, his most memorable moments were in episodes dealing with deeply dramatic subject matter. This was first in evidence in "Phage," wherein his lungs were harvested by Vidiians and it looked as if he would spend the rest of his life locked into a machine unable to move. Later in "Jetrel," he confronted his own demons in the form of a Dr. Jetrel, the person who created the weapon responsible for the death of Neelix's family. Though much of the episode centered around his reaction to Jetrel, it was his own history he was trying to escape when he finally admitted to being a deserter during the war. But his most dramatic turn came when he returned from death in "Mortal Coil," despondent over the fact that he did not find evidence of the afterlife.

Ethan Phillips: I think Neelix doesn't fall into a lot of the normal plotlines. He's not on the bridge. He's not in Starfleet. He's not part of the crew like that. The shows for him have to require a little bit more effort for the writers sometimes.

Beyond the comedy and the drama existed a seemingly unlikely role for Neelix as a romantic. From his first scenes with Kes, it was clear that his feelings for her were deep and true. Although the specific nature of their relationship was not entirely defined, the two shared some wonderfully close moments beyond their warm embrace in a nebula during "The Cloud." It was Kes who stood by Neelix throughout his ordeal in "Phage" and helped him admit the truth in "Jetrel." Unfortunately his love for Kes often exhibited itself through jealousy, especially due to her close friendship with Paris. It was this jealousy that ultimately threatened their relationship until he came to terms with his feelings in "Parturition." However, their romance ended shortly afterward and by the time Kes leaves the ship in "The Gift," the pair were just very close friends.

Robert Duncan McNeill: I thought it was interesting to play the idea that Neelix was jealous of Tom's friendship with Kes, but I think it was dangerous ground to sort of play that Paris would steal Kes from Neelix or that he would even do anything that might suggest that. I think Paris would have been much too respectful of Neelix to ever do anything. I think that's kind of the way that they always tried to portray it.

In his many roles, Neelix had varied relationships with many of the crew beyond just the senior staff. He became godfather to Naomi Wildman, and the two shared some very touching moments of friendship as he helped her through her childhood and she helped him through life. This guardian presence also spread to the Borg children when they came aboard.

But his closest "friend" onboard was Tuvok, though their relationship rarely seemed friendly on both sides. Tuvok was the first person Neelix met as he stepped off the transporter in "Caretaker," and the Talaxian immediately felt a bond for the man he knew as "Mr. Vulcan." With a deep respect, Neelix soon went to work at trying to become part of the security detail in an effort to expand his role on the ship and seek the approval of his friend. No matter how stiff and formal the Vulcan was in dealing with Neelix, the Talaxian only took it as a challenge to break down the cool Vulcan exterior. When Tuvok had his own breakdown in "Riddles," it was Neelix who stayed by his side throughout the episode first trying to help the security chief find himself and later in accepting who he had become. When Neelix left the ship in "Homestead" Tuvok had finally let down his guard long enough to perform a brief dance step out of respect for all that the Talaxian had done for him.

Tim Russ: We've had a lot of stuff together and I think because I was one of the first characters Neelix met when he came onboard the ship. We formed that sort of bond right up front. And they have carried that through in seven years.

Though Neelix did not make it back to the Alpha Quadrant, his character, as portrayed by Ethan Phillips, was a deeply treasured member of the *Voyager* family. As with any family, he stood out a little and didn't always fit in, but was appreciated for just being who he was. In the end, Neelix found the acceptance he was looking for in the beginning, first with the crew, then with a group of Talaxians who would let him fully experience the responsible life he had grown into.

average humidity factor. ▪ When Neelix was a child, an immense plasma drift passed through the Talaxian system, blotting out the stars and moons for months. Ever since then he has found it a little disturbing to be in nebulas. To combat his nervousness, he tries to decide between materials to make curtains for his windows. On his birthday the crew prepared his favorite dinners including steamed *chadre kab* and terra nut soufflé.

UNIMATRIX ZERO, PART I

EPISODE #246
TELEPLAY BY: BRANNON BRAGA & JOE MENOSKY
STORY BY: MIKE SUSSMAN
DIRECTED BY: ALLAN KROEKER

GUEST STARS

AXUM	MARK DEAKINS
KOROK	JEROME BUTLER
LAURA	JOANNA HEIMBOLD
and	
BORG QUEEN	SUSANNA THOMPSON

CO-STARS

BORG DRONE	TONY SEARS
ALIEN CHILD	RYAN SPARKS

STARDATE UNKNOWN

Seven of Nine awakens from her regeneration cycle in an uneasy state. She reports to the Doctor that she had dreamed of a beautiful forest with trees and flowers and a man who called her by her given name, Annika. Uncomfortable with the new experience, she asks the Doctor to correct the problem, but he informs her that dreaming is just another facet of her humanity reasserting itself. On the bridge, Paris is reprimanded for being over twenty seconds late for duty, and out of uniform. As he takes the conn, Paris notices a small box containing a lone pip. Janeway announces that she has decided to reinstate him to the rank of lieutenant.

Back in her alcove, Seven retires again, this time wearing a cortical monitor the Doctor gave her to monitor her REM sleep. Upon closing her eyes, she immediately finds herself back in the beautiful forest. Although she tells herself that it is not real, she hears a male voice assuring her that it is. The man is Axum, someone she has seen before in this environment, which he calls Unimatrix Zero.

At first Seven refuses to remember her past love. MICHAEL YARISH

Axum explains to Seven that they are in a virtual construct. The consciousness of certain Borg drones inhabit it while they are regenerating. Only one in a million drones has a mutation that allows them to exist in Unimatrix Zero with their individualities intact. However, the Borg queen has become aware of the utopia. She has been finding and killing the afflicted drones in order to put a stop to it. Axum and his group have designed a nanovirus that will hide the identity of the drones, but they require Seven's help to deploy it to the collective. The drones lose all memory of Unimatrix Zero when they awaken, only Seven can help them.

Leaving her alcove, Seven informs the crew of the Borg pleas for help. Tuvok helps Janeway perform a Vulcan bridging of minds so she can journey with Seven to Unimatrix Zero and witness the utopia herself. In doing so, Janeway agrees to help Axum and the others. However, she modifies the plan so that the drones will not only be safe in Unimatrix Zero, but also retain their individuality when they wake. Janeway's ultimate plan is to start a Borg civil war in which the drones will regain their independence.

As the crew sets the plan in action, Seven returns to Unimatrix Zero to alert Axum and learns that the two were more than just friends when she was there during her time as a Borg. Seven, however, chooses to ignore his obvious feelings for her. In the meantime, the crew attacks a Borg ship while Janeway, Tuvok, and Torres take in the *Delta Flyer*. The Borg queen is quickly onto their plan and she destroys the *Flyer* only moments after the away team beams onto the ship. The Borg adapt quickly to the infiltration. Janeway, Tuvok, and Torres are assimilated. The Doctor, who is monitoring the situation from *Voyager* alerts Chakotay who tells the crew to break off the attack and retreat as everything is going according to plan.

DAMAGE REPORT: *Voyager* is damaged in the Borg attack, but nothing is specifically mentioned except a direct hit to the port nacelle that leaves the ship venting plasma and a hull breach on Deck 11.

SHUTTLE TRACKER: The starboard plasma injectors on the *Delta Flyer* tended to run a little hot at high impulse and the warp matrix was out of alignment by .3 microns. The *Delta Flyer* is destroyed as part of the plan to infiltrate the Borg ship.

DELTA QUADRANT: The Doctor modifies Axum's nanovirus to nullify the cortical inhibitors of the mutated drones so they will retain their memories of Unimatrix Zero once they leave their alcoves. Each Borg ship has a central plexus that links them with all other ships. The plan is to release the virus in the central plexus of a ship so it can instantly be transmitted throughout the collective. The away team boards a class-4 tactical vessel. It is heavily armed and the central plexus is protected by multiregenerative security grids.

ALPHA QUADRANT: In the Vulcan technique known as the bridging of minds, Tuvok melds Seven with Janeway

Janeway makes the ultimate sacrifice to infiltrate the Borg.
MICHAEL YARISH

while acting as a telepathic conduit. He has never performed the technique, but he did once witness a Vulcan master doing it. ■ Starfleet Tactical Directive 36 states: "The captain will not engage a hostile force without the protection of a security officer."

PERSONAL LOGS: Janeway claims that the last time she took part in a mind-meld ("Flashback") she had a headache that lasted three days. ■ Seven was involved with Axum for six years while in Unimatrix Zero.

THE BORG

"Ladies and gentlemen, meet the Borg . . . Over the course of this term you're going to become intimately familiar with the collective. You'll learn about the assimilation process . . . the Borg hierarchy . . . the psychology of the hive mind. When it comes to performance in this class, my expectations are no less than that of the Borg queen herself: Perfection. This semester we're very fortunate to have a special guest lecturer . . . the woman who literally 'wrote the book' on the Borg . . . Admiral Kathryn Janeway"

Commander Barclay "Endgame, Part I"

The Borg was first introduced in the *TNG* episode "Q Who?" The nearly omnipotent prankster Q planned to prove to the *Enterprise* crew just how dangerous space really was. Thrown thousands of light-years into the Delta Quadrant, the crew was forced to face the single-minded life-form whose motto is "Resistance Is Futile." Knowing the Federation to be a powerful collection of races, the Borg would turn their attention to the Alpha Quadrant in attacks intended to assimilate all of the Federation. Though many lives were lost, the Borg never managed to succeed in their mission.

MICHAEL YARISH

The *Enterprise* crew became experts at dealing with the Borg through numerous *TNG* episodes and in the film *Star Trek: First Contact*. The Borg, never posed as great a threat in *Deep Space Nine*, as that series focused more on the Gamma Quadrant, and the ensuing Dominion war. It was known from the start of *Voyager*, considering the quadrant into which the lone starship was thrown, that one day they would come across the Borg. In "Blood Fever," when Chakotay stumbled across the remains of a Borg drone on a planet, both the crew and the audience knew that the actual Borg threat would not be far behind.

"We decided one huge thing... We decided to embrace the Borg as our villains. TNG had Klingons. DS9 had Cardassians. And, by God, the Borg were going to be Voyager's *Klingons. We even made a Borg a part of the show, with Seven of Nine. The show may have become sexier but it became scarier and for the writers it became fun. I can't tell you how much the Borg did for this show. We never got tired of the Borg and we kept finding new things to do with them and I think the audience liked them too."*

—Brannon Braga

The first major encounter with the Borg came in "Scorpion, Parts I & II." However, the feared enemy proved to be less of a threat than the life-form they were fighting, the newly discovered Species 8472. Following this encounter with the Borg, the writers began a character arc for Janeway that would prove she would stop at nothing to protect her crew. In her initial meeting with the Borg, Janeway proposed the idea of teaming with the collective. The plan succeeded in moving along several plotlines, including the first serious conflict between the captain and her first officer as well as the introduction of a new crew member: Seven of Nine. The partnership proved precarious as Chakotay had feared; however, the quick thinking of the captain demonstrated that a human could outwit the hive mind and even rescue one of their own.

Kes threw the crew safely past the most dangerous sector of Borg Space, and the crew would continue to have encounters, allowing Janeway to further prove her strength and fortitude. In "Dark Frontier, Parts I&II" Janeway went on the offensive and stole a transwarp coil from a Borg ship, so she could get her crew home faster. Though the coil was useful, it was mainly a construct on which the writers wove the storyline of Janeway's more personal battle against the Borg queen for Seven of Nine's soul. As the de facto mother figures were locked in a battle of wits, Janeway proved her superiority and escaped with Seven.

"The Borg have no conscience. There's nothing to appeal to. All of Janeway's skills are as nothing in the face of that kind of lack of humanity. So what she's playing against and what she's negotiating with is a different level of reality. I had to deal with the Borg queen. I had to exercise every modicum of my intelligence not to outwit her, but to merely save Seven of Nine and my ship. There was no negotiating beyond that. So I think that the Borg have been archvillains, and because of their invincibility they are really, really scary."

—Kate Mulgrew

The final battle in Janeway's personal arc against the Borg came, fittingly, in the series finale, "Endgame," when a future Admiral Janeway joined forces with her former self for one last confrontation that ultimately resulted in getting her crew home. This episode was the most challenging for Janeway's character, as she went against the same Starfleet principles she had adhered to for seven years. At the same time, she rewrote history, combining technological superiority with mental agility to trick the Borg queen, while her younger self dealt a crippling blow to the Borg infrastructure by destroying their transwarp hub.

On a larger scale, the introduction of the Borg to *Voyager* served to broach the possibility of putting an end to the unstoppable force. The Federation had always managed to win their battles against the Borg, but they had never been able to bring a permanent end to the Borg threat. In *TNG*, Picard managed to escape the Borg in "The Best of Both Worlds," and the crew instilled a little humanity in the race by returning the newly individualized Borg, Hugh in "I, Borg." Chipping away at the strength of the Borg through the power of individuality was a theme also used on *Voyager*.

From the very start, Seven of Nine's readjustment as an individual served as a way of weakening the Borg. Though the queen later admitted to having let the former drone escape, Seven's continued readjustment would serve to prove that the plan had failed. As part of her own growth, Seven would help others break free of the collective link, such as the Borg children who found a home on *Voyager*. In helping these children, as well as One—a futuristic Borg created by the merging of Seven's nanoprobes with the Doctor's twenty-ninth-century mobile emitter—Seven and by extension humanity further disproved the idea that Borg perfection is worth the cost of individuality.

Curiously, the crew's first interaction with Borg ("Unity") focused on the strength of the group. When Chakotay crashed on a planet of former drones locked in constant battle, he asked Janeway to help them reestablish the link, to ensure their survival. The captain declined, and the Borg cooperative took control of Chakotay's body to enact their plan. Though the end result seemed to suggest that they could work better together, it should be noted that their way forced enslavement on the minds of others.

Other Borg came onboard showing that Seven of Nine was not the only drone seeking independence. In "Unity," a Borg triad had a near taste of freedom although the three were still linked to each other. By accepting that her past actions were responsible for their plight, Seven finally understood why the triad would accept a premature death so long as it meant a brief period as an individual.

It is "Unimatrix Zero, Parts I&II" that served as the ultimate Borg episode linking all of the Borg plot threads. Janeway again survived a direct confrontation with the Borg queen, using her own drones against her. Meanwhile, Seven experienced more personal growth as she allowed herself to fall in love and free her friends from the hive control. And finally, it served as the ultimate battle for individuality when the *Voyager* crew helped numerous drones regain their individuality and fight for their freedom.

SEASON SEVEN

"We've explored the unknown reaches of the universe. We've fought many

alien races and survived. But we've been away too long. It's time

to come home . . . or die trying."

Kathryn Janeway*

Even before the season began, rumors surfaced that someone would die before the series ended. Other rumors suggested that the ship would never make it home. In the end, while none of the members of the ensemble died. They all did not make it to the Alpha Quadrant.

"I have long since accepted what the Borg did to me. What I will not accept . . . is

defeat. I am confident we will discover a way home. Failure . . . is not an option."

Seven of Nine*

The Borg returned, ironically helping the *Voyager* crew reach their goal in "Endgame." The Hirogen made a final appearence in the two-part episode, "Flesh and Blood," that utilized the series' history to show the result of Janeway's decision to share Federation technology. New threats were introduced: the Lokirrim, who outlaw photonic beings ("Body and Soul") and the warring Kraylor and Annari ("Nightingale"). Old friends and foes took the form of the Q and his son ("Q2") the Talaxians ("Homestead") and even a group of Klingons ("Prophecy").

"I've piloted Starfleet's most advanced ship through many fierce battles . . .

and prevailed against impossible odds. But the greatest challenge

still remains . . . finding a way home."

Tom Paris*

In celebration of the show's final season science fiction storytelling was combined with *Voyager*'s history in the episode "Shattered." With the ship out of temporal sync, Janeway and Chakotay negotiated their way through different times, as memorable events from their journey were lived once again.

*Quotes taken from UPN's series finale ad campaign.

"Logic suggests I will never see my family again . . . but a totally illogical human concept remains . . . hope."

Tuvok*

While the objective of the crew always had been to get home, the producers had begun dropping hints as to what life would be like for the crew after they got home. To that end, the Pathfinder Project continued to prove useful. In "Author, Author," many crew members had the opportunity to reconnect with family members they had not seen in years, or, in the case of Seven of Nine and Torres, decades. Then, the decision to set part of the finale in a possible future gave the audience a chance to see what could happen to the crew that they had grown so close to over seven years.

"Some legends live forever. Some heroes die young. But all great adventures . . . must come to an end."

*Quote taken from UPN's series finale ad campaign.

Tuvok begins to forget his individual as he hears the voice of the collective. MICHAEL YARISH

UNIMATRIX ZERO, PART II

EPISODE #247

TELEPLAY BY: BRANNON BRAGA & JOE MENOSKY

STORY BY: MIKE SUSSMAN and BRANNON BRAGA & JOE MENOSKY

DIRECTED BY: MIKE VEJAR

GUEST STARS

AXUM	MARK DEAKINS
KOROK	JEROME BUTLER
LAURA	JOANNA HEIMBOLD
and	
BORG QUEEN	SUSANNA THOMPSON

CO-STARS

ALIEN BOY	RYAN SPARKS
ERRANT DRONE	ANDREW PALMER
ALIEN MAN	CLAY STORSETH
NARRATOR	MAJEL BARRETT

STARDATE 54014.4

Prior to beaming aboard the Borg cube, Janeway, Tuvok, and Torres were fitted with neural suppressants that would keep their minds from linking to the collective. Now they race to find the central plexus and release the nanovirus that will free the minds of the drones in Unimatrix Zero. While the away team is on the cube, Seven visits Unimatrix Zero to alert the inhabitants to the plan. When she arrives, Seven is concerned about Axum's absence—an emotional response that is obvious to the Klingon Korok, though she continues to deny her feelings for Axum. When he appears, Seven alerts Axum to the plan, but objects when Axum suggests she has feelings for him.

Tuvok's neural suppressor begins to fail, and he experiences an intermittent connection to the collective. The Borg queen uses the distraction to her advantage and obtains *Voyager's* access codes from the security chief, using the information in her battle against the ship. However, the queen is unable to stop the away team from releasing the nanovirus, separating the mutated drones from the hive mind.

The queen establishes communication with Janeway, conversing with a holographic image of the captain as she negotiates for the drones. In an attempt to influence Janeway's decision, the queen begins destroying the ships she knows harbor drones that have been severed from the hive. Thousands of Borg die to protect the collective from the few who have gained their independence. Later the queen informs Janeway that the Borg have altered the nanovirus to kill all the mutated drones and that she plans to release it into Unimatrix Zero. Believing that Janeway has given in, the queen allows her to contact *Voyager*, the captain commands Chakotay to surrender.

Chakotay, however, realizes that her unsaid order is to have the drones shut down Unimatrix Zero on their own so the virus cannot be deployed, allowing them to

Janeway's image is projected to the Borg queen's lair. RON TOM

remain individuals. When Seven goes to alert Axum and the others, he tells her that his physical body is on a ship on the other side of the galaxy. Without Unimatrix Zero, the pair will never see each other again. Seven apologizes for wasting the time they had together by ignoring her feelings and the two share a moment before Unimatrix Zero is no more.

Although the Borg queen realizes her plan has been foiled, she intends to keep the assimilated away team. However, *Voyager* returns with a Borg cube now under the command of Korok who helps the team to safety. With the drones free from their mental link and the away team back, *Voyager* sets course for the Alpha Quadrant.

DAMAGE REPORT: When the Borg access *Voyager*'s tactical controls they bring shields down and take sensors offline. The ensuing conflict results in heavy damage, including hull breaches on Decks 5, 6, and 7. By the end of the episode repairs have brought both the warp core and the navigational array online with shields up to twenty percent. They also manage to repair short-range sensors.

DELTA QUADRANT: The Borg queen destroys eleven Borg ships, including Cube 630 in Spatial Grid 94, with a crew complement of 64,000, which had only three drones that she can no longer hear. She also destroys Sphere 878 in Spatial Grid 091, with its complement of 11,000 Drones, with only one silent. ▪ The rebelling drones target the primary unicomplex to disrupt the queen's control of the hive mind. ▪ The Borg queen was a child when she was assimilated. It is possible her name was Asil. ▪ The Borg modify the nanovirus and program it to target the mutated drones and erode their autonomic functions, causing them to die within minutes.

PERSONAL LOGS: Tuvok was born on Stardate 38774 on the Vulcanis Lunar Colony in the city of T'Paal. Recalling details of his life helps him remain focused. ▪ After being assimilated, Torres is given a vocal subprocessor that alters her speech. ▪ With Janeway and Tuvok gone, Paris assumes the role of acting first officer. ▪ Since the Doctor is the only one with information on the nanovirus, Chakotay has orders to deactivate the EMH at the first sign of trouble. ▪ Whenever Seven mentions Axum's name, her pupils dilate by nearly a millimeter and blood flow increases to her facial capillaries, actions that are consistent with an emotional response.

IMPERFECTION

EPISODE #248

TELEPLAY BY: CARLETON EASTLAKE and ROBERT DOHERTY

STORY BY: ANDRE BORMANIS

DIRECTED BY: DAVID LIVINGSTON

GUEST STARS

ICHEB	MANU INTIRAYMI
MEZOTI	MARLEY S. McCLEAN

CO-STARS

SALVAGE ALIEN #1	MICHAEL McFALL
WYSANTI	DEBBI GRATTAN
AZAN	KURT WETHERILL
REBI	CODY WETHERILL
COMPUTER VOICE	MAJEL BARRETT

STARDATE 54129.4

It is a bittersweet day for the *Voyager* crew when Rebi and Azan reunite with their people, who have also agreed to give Mezoti a home. The only Borg child remaining on board is Icheb, who notices that

The Doctor's operation to save Seven fails in twelve simulations.
MICHAEL YARISH

Seven is crying, though she claims that her ocular implant is simply malfunctioning. When Seven goes to see the Doctor, he confirms there is a glitch in her cortical node and she admits to having headaches as well. Later, when Seven attempts to regenerate, she discovers she cannot interface with her alcove because her cortical node is malfunctioning. Instead of reporting to the Doctor, she stays up all night in the mess hall. After Neelix arrives, in the morning, she falls to the floor convulsing as Borg implants burst through her skin.

In sickbay, the Doctor realizes Seven's problem is more serious than he previously thought. Her cortical node, which regulates her vital functions, is destabilizing, and she will die unless it can be replaced. Janeway takes an away team to a Borg debris field hoping to salvage a replacement cortical node from one of the deceased drones. There, they find several dead Borg drones and remove the cortical node from one of them as they evade a hostile alien claiming salvage rights to the area.

When they return to *Voyager*, Janeway, the Doctor, and Paris rehearse the cortical node replacement operation several times in a holodeck simulation, failing each time. They eventually decide that the cortical node from a dead drone is useless, as they require a node from a living one. Janeway announces that she is willing to find a living drone, but the Doctor refuses to allow her to end a life to save Seven.

Icheb also comes to realize that only the cortical node from a living Borg can save Seven, so he volunteers to have his own node removed and transplanted to her. Icheb devises a genetic resequencing that would allow him to survive without his node, since he was never fully assimilated, but the procedure is risky. When Icheb cannot get Janeway, Seven, or the Doctor to listen to him, he programs the computer in his regeneration alcove to disengage his cortical node. Now dying, Icheb convinces them to give his node to Seven and perform the genetic procedure on him.

The operation is successful and Seven fully recovers. As the young drone lies on a biobed in sickbay, Seven offers to help him study for the Starfleet Academy entrance exam, promising him a rigorous schedule. Before he has a chance to respond, Icheb notices another tear in her eye . . . only this time it is not a malfunction.

SENSOR READINGS: Janeway uses a laser scalpel to remove the cortical node from the dead Borg (and as a weapon for threatening the salvage alien leader).

SHUTTLE TRACKER: A new version of the *Delta Flyer* is

Icheb knows he can save Seven; his actions force the Doctor to relent and agree to perform the procedure. RON TOM

seen in this episode. Under alien attack, its transporters are temporarily taken offline.

DELTA QUADRANT: *Voyager* passed the Borg debris field six days ago, just outside the Yontasa Expanse. Tuvok isolates a section of the field that contains the bodies of approximately thirty seven Drones that were killed in an explosion. There are only a few Borg bodies left intact from which the crew could try to salvage the node. The Borg often return to salvage damaged ships. ▪ The Borg have no concept of an afterlife. However, when a drone is deactivated, its memories continue to reside in the collective's consciousness. As long as the hive exists, so will a part of the drone.

On Rebi and Azan's home planet, Wysanti, it is customary not to say goodbye.

PERSONAL LOGS: Janeway hiked the north ridge of the Grand Canyon when she was nine. Her father called it, "Earth's biggest ditch." She claims to have always preferred farmland. Her hometown was Bloomington, Indiana. ▪ Torres admits to believing in *Sto-Vo-Kor* (the Klingon afterlife). ▪ The first time the Doctor heard

Puccini's *Tosca* in the holodeck, he claims to have sobbed through the entire third act. Torres had enhanced his emotional subroutines so he could truly appreciate the performance. ▪ Neelix brings Seven some Tarcanian wildflowers from the airponics bay (and mentions he could get gladiolas, if she prefers). ▪ When playing kadis-kot, Seven prefers to be the green pieces.

Icheb asks to take the Starfleet entrance exam and if he passes he would like to forward the results to Earth in the next datastream, he then would start taking classes with Tuvok, who used to teach at the Academy. Anticipating her death, Seven suggests alternative tutors to help Icheb with his studies for the exam. She specially notes Torres, who is well versed in warp mechanics, and Kim, who claims to have "aced" the quantum theory section. The Doctor took scans of Icheb when he left the collective, noting that he had emerged from his maturation chamber before he was fully assimilated. As a result, his physiology is less dependent on implants.

MEDICAL UPDATE: In the simulation using the deceased Borg's cortical node, the holographic Seven's body goes into anaphylactic shock when it rejects the node, losing synaptic cohesion. The Doctor has Paris apply two 20 millijoule neurostatic pulses to Seven followed by one 30 millijoule pulse, but they fail to revive her holographic body.

CREW COMPLEMENT: Rebi and Azan are reunited with their people and they leave the ship along with Mezoti.

EPISODE LOGS: Although the new version of the *Delta Flyer* does appear in this episode, it is not until the following episode, "Drive," that it is fully tested as a replacement for the one destroyed in "Unimatix Zero, Part I."

DRIVE

EPISODE #249

WRITTEN BY: **MICHAEL TAYLOR**

DIRECTED BY: **WINRICH KOLBE**

GUEST STARS

IRINA	CYIA BATTEN
O'ZAAL	BRIAN GEORGE
ASSAN	PATRICK KILPATRICK

CO-STARS

JOXOM	ROBERT TYLER
ASSISTANT	CHRIS COVICS
COMPUTER VOICE	MAJEL BARRETT

STARDATE 54058.6

Paris and Kim are taking the new *Delta Flyer* for a test run when a small alien ship pulls alongside them, and its pilot, Irina, challenges them to a race. As the two ships speed through an asteroid field, Irina's ship begins filling with nyocene gas. Beaming her to the *Flyer*, they bring Irina and her disabled ship back to *Voyager*. While making repairs Irina describes the race she is entering her ship in, which prompts Paris and Kim to convince Captain Janeway to let them enter the race too.

Meanwhile, Torres has been trading favors with numerous crewmates to borrow enough holodeck time for her and Paris to have an entire weekend to themselves. When Paris admits to forgetting about the weekend and entering the race, B'Elanna tells him that she does not mind. However, Torres later confesses to Neelix that she was hurt, and she thinks things might be ending between the two of them.

Paris and Torres interrupt their argument in order to keep the *Flyer* from exploding. MICHAEL YARISH

Janeway learns from Ambassador O'Zaal, the race coordinator, that the race is the first step toward peace for the four different cultures living in the area. The different species have been at war to control the area for nearly a century. This race marks the first time the four of them have ever competed peacefully.

In a last attempt to save her relationship with Paris, Torres convinces Kim to let her replace him in the race as copilot of the *Delta Flyer*. Paris is surprised when she shows up, but he welcomes Torres and reminds her that they are in the race to win. The two are in fourth place for much of the race, but they eventually take the lead. Suddenly, O'Zaal calls a temporary stop to the race, as one of the racers has had an accident.

Irina's control panel had a malfunction which electrocuted her copilot, later it is determined to be sabotage, but O'Zaal decides to continue the race the next day. Kim offers to help Irina fix her ship and also fly as her new copilot. She hesitates, but then agrees. Paris and Torres notice that Kim and Irina seem to be getting close, which causes Torres to again wonder about her own relationship.

As the race continues, Paris finally asks Torres what is bothering her, which leads to a heated discussion. Determined to fix things even though Torres sounds as if

Just Married.

she is ready to give up, Paris stops the *Flyer* and tells her they are not going to move again until they work it out. Meanwhile on Irina's ship, the copilot's control panel malfunctions again, almost electrocuting Kim, who realizes that Irina sabotaged her own ship. When Irina seems strangely interested in the *Delta Flyer*'s progress, Kim realizes that she has sabotaged that ship as well. He forces her to admit to rigging the *Flyer*'s fuel converter to explode when it crosses the finish line killing all of the spectators and officials in the area, ensuring an end to the new peace agreement.

As Paris and Torres begin to work out their problems, Kim sends them a message that leads them to realize that the converter is about to cause a core breach. They pilot the *Delta Flyer* to a nearby nebula and eject the warp core where the explosion will be contained. After the race is over, Paris and Torres take the *Delta Flyer* out again, this time on a more personal mission: a honeymoon.

SENSOR READINGS: Kim sends a message to the *Flyer*

by scanning them with a modulating pulse that reads as Morse code, something he and Paris use in the Captain Proton holoprogram.

SHUTTLE TRACKER: The new *Delta Flyer* has vectored exhaust ports, accelerated driver coils and new impulse thrusters. Paris and Kim suggest reassigning fifteen crew members to adapt the *Flyer* for the race. During the race, Torres reverses the *Flyer*'s deflector shield polarity to repel the shields of the other ships so they can pass them. Later, Irina rigs the converter to leak veridium isotopes into the warp core in order to cause a core explosion. Paris and Torres eject the core in a class-J nebula where the ionized gas will contain the explosion.

DELTA QUADRANT: The Antarian Trans-Stellar Rally consists of three segments covering 2.3 billion kilometers, with obstacles ranging from dwarf star clusters to K-class anomalies. The Mobius Inversion covers the entire last third of the course, and consists of level-6 subspace distortions and gravimetric shears. The racers are limited to two-man crews, and each ship must maintain sublight speeds, making it the ultimate test of ship design and piloting skills. The race has very specific guidelines, such as all ships being required to use enriched deuterium. Since the *Delta Flyer* is not equipped to meet that rule, Irina agrees to lend them a fuel converter. Until recently, the region was a war zone that four different species fought for nearly a century to control. Now, for the first time, they are competing peacefully, to commemorate the new treaty that ended the war. ▪ Irina is from a small trinary system about half a parsec from *Voyager's* original position

PERSONAL LOGS: Torres plans for a romantic holodeck vacation with Paris on Gedi Prime. She refers to it as "the vacation paradise that makes Risa look like a tourist trap." It has endless kilometers of crystalline beaches, mood reefs, bioluminescent waterfalls and—the Doctor notes— a championship golf course. When the plans fall through, she refers to her relationship with Paris using a Klingon phrase her grandmother used to use, *mok'tah,* which means "bad match." ▪ After they wed, Tom suggests that B'Elanna take his last name, but she informs him that she intends to keep her own, suggesting that he take her name instead. ▪ The Doctor has decided that, in keeping with the history of practitioners of medicine, he is taking up golf on the holodeck.

EPISODE LOGS: Although Paris and Torres get married in this episode, the wedding goes unseen. Perhaps this is because of the wedding of their doppelgangers in "Course: Oblivion." ▪ Twenty-fourth-century golf balls are clear, with blinking green lights in the center.

CRITICAL CARE

EPISODE #250

TELEPLAY BY: **JAMES KAHN**
STORY BY: **KENNETH BILLER & ROBERT DOHERTY**
DIRECTED BY: **TERRY WINDELL**

GUEST STARS

GAR	JOHN KASSIR
DYSEK	GREGORY ITZIN
VOJE	PAUL SCHERRER
TEBBIS	DUBLIN JAMES
and	
CHELLICK	LARRY DRAKE

CO-STARS

LEVEL BLUE NURSE	CHRISTINNA CHAUNCY
MED TECH	STEPHEN O'MAHONEY
HUSBAND	JIM O'HEIR
ALIEN MINER	JOHN DURBIN
ADULTRESS	DEBI A. MONAHAN
KIPP	JOHN FRANKLIN

STARDATE UNKNOWN

A trader named Gar enters an overcrowded Dinaali hospital ship and shows the facility administrator, Chellick, the Doctor's mobile emitter, promising it to be a valuable commodity. Tapping the controls on the device, the Doctor appears, demanding to be returned to his ship. Moments later the Allocator, the computer that prioritizes all work onboard the ship, announces that a generator has exploded and many patients are arriving. Witnessing the chaos surrounding him, the Doctor decides he must help.

Back aboard *Voyager,* Kim is injured during a holodeck hockey match and visits the Doctor. Both he and Paris notice something is not right about the EMH, and upon examination, Torres announces the Doctor has been replaced by a replicated fake. Neelix points out that their former guest, Gar, spent the night in sickbay and had ample access to the Doctor. Janeway then gives the order to scan for Gar's ion trail.

On Level Red of the hospital ship, the Doctor treats a young patient named Tebbis and finds that although he has a deadly infection, he has not received the proper treatment of cytoglobin. Doctor Voje tells him that the patient's T.C. level is not high enough to receive the required treatment. Just as the Doctor asks what T.C. stands for, Chellick interrupts, informing them that he has purchased the Doctor's program and that the Allocator has ordered his services on Level Blue.

The patients on Level Blue do not need the Doctor. RON TOM

Voje explains that the patients on Level Blue receive the best treatment because their Treatment Coefficient (T.C.) level is high. The Allocator assesses which patient has access to the best care depending on the importance of his profession, skills, and accomplishments. The Doctor learns that cytoglobin injections are approved for all Level Blue patients because, as another doctor, Dysek, informs him they slow the aging process. The Doctor tries to raise Tebbis's T.C. level, but the Allocator still denies him the medication, forcing the Doctor to steal a cytoglobin treatment for the boy. Seeing the positive effect, the Doctor takes even more medication to treat the patients on Level Red. In the meantime, the *Voyager* crew follows Gar's trail as it leads them light-years in different directions.

Gar is eventually found and beamed aboard *Voyager* for questioning. After Neelix feeds the prisoner, Gar experiences severe stomach pains. Neelix reveals that he poisoned Gar's meal and that the Doctor is the only one who can administer the proper medication. Forcing Gar to reveal his location.

After the Doctor discovers Tebbis has died, he confronts Chellick, who reveals his knowledge of the unau-thorized injections. Chellick restricts the Doctor to Level Blue, linking his holomatrix to the Allocator so his every move is monitored and delegated. Despite this, Chellick catches the Doctor on Level Red, where the Doctor injects him with the same virus that killed Tebbis. Identifying Chellick as Tebbis, the Allocator denies him medication. The Doctor and Dysek refuse to help unless Level Red is equipped with an adequate supply of medication, and Chellick finally relents.

After the crew retrieves the Doctor, he asks Seven to check his ethical subroutines for any glitches that might explain why he deliberately poisoned a man. Seven, how-ever, informs him that he has "a clean bill of health."

SENSOR READINGS: Gar gave *Voyager* high-grade iridi-um, which has a very brief half-life, indicating that he must have obtained it within a proscribed area. They eventually discover that he stole the iridium from an asteroid with approximately two hundred humanoid life-signs working a mining operation in subterranean struc-tures. He sold the miners 3,000 induction units and was gone a day before they realized he had also stolen twenty

The Doctor makes a convincing argument for treating the sick, no matter what their T.C. level. RON TOM

kilograms of ore. The induction units came from the planetoid Velos. They ultimately find Gar en route to a gambling tournament on Selek IV.

DELTA QUADRANT: The generator explosion is at the Gammadan Mining Facility. ▪ The Doctor is taken to Dinaali Hospital Ship 42 Allocation Module Alpha. A patient listed as T.C. 4 is sent to Level Green. The Doctor is informed that an agricultural engineer is more important to the society than a waste processor, and since resources are limited, they have to prioritize. Many of the patients in Level Red are dying of chromo-viral infection. Cytoglobin is the standard treatment for that disease. It also slows arterial aging, and daily injections increase life expectancy up to forty percent. Level White is the morgue. ▪ Chellick's people are known throughout the sector for their administrative skills. Before they came to the medical unit, the Dinaali were a dying race, plagued by eco-disasters and famine. The Dinaali contracted the medical unit for their work. Only Administrator Chellick is authorized to speak with alien species.

Gar is a Dralian and has a T.C. of 15. Neelix gives him food that contains Talaxian wormroot, which causes abdominal spasms, increasing in severity for thirty to forty hours. He claims only the Doctor has the cure.

PERSONAL LOGS: According to Gar, the Doctor is programmed with over five million medical protocols. He is programmed with the Hippocratic oath, requiring him to treat any patient who is ill. He replaces the Doctor with an EMH from an old training file. The Doctor has done

extensive research in the area of cellular repair. ▪ While interrogating Gar, Tuvok threatens to use a mind-meld on the captive to discover the truth, though it is unlikely that it was anything more than a threat.

MEDICAL UPDATE: Both Kim and Paris are injured playing hockey against Nausicaans on the holodeck.

EPISODE LOGS: The cast and crew lovingly described this episode as "the Doctor gets involved with an alien HMO." ▪ The Doctor refers to his "medical staff," but it is unclear who among the crew are on his staff beyond Paris.

REPRESSION

EPISODE #251

TELEPLAY BY: **MARK HASKILL SMITH**
STORY BY: **KENNETH BILLER**
DIRECTED BY: **WINRICH KOLBE**

GUEST STARS

CHELL	**DEREK McGRATH**
TEERO	**KEITH SZARABAJKA**

CO-STARS

TABOR	**JAD MAGER**
JOR	**CAROL KRNIC**
YOSA	**MARK RAFAEL TRUITT**
SEK	**RONALD ROBINSON**
COMPUTER VOICE	**MAJEL BARRETT**

STARDATE 54090.4

Paris surprises his new wife by taking her to a classic twentieth-century movie theater in the holodeck. Their fun, however, is short-lived when they discover Crewman Tabor in a coma as the result of an attack. Janeway appoints Tuvok to investigate the case, and the security chief's initial belief is that a member of the crew is responsible. As more fallen crew members are brought to sickbay, Janeway and Chakotay come to realize that all the victims are former Maquis.

Paris and Kim show Tuvok the result of their work using a holographic technique to capture the intruder's image at the time of the attack on Tabor. However, the image shows an unrecognizable humanoid figure. Tuvok requests that they work on increasing the resolution of the image, while he continues the investigation by reviewing all mail in the last datastream from Starfleet including personal letters. While interviewing Kim about a letter from home, Tuvok becomes strangely agitated.

Later, Chakotay finds Torres unconscious in a cargo bay. Suddenly Tuvok grabs him and initiates a mindmeld, rendering the first officer unconscious as well. While Chakotay and Torres are treated in sickbay, the other victims wake with no memory of what happened. Tuvok tirelessly continues the investigation—with no memory of attacking anyone. At Janeway's urging, he returns to his quarters to meditate, where he has flashbacks of the victims in sickbay. Tuvok enters the bathroom and sees a Bajoran man's reflection in the mirror—then rushes to the holodeck where Janeway and Kim are continuing the investigation. The holodeck re-creation shows that Tuvok was the one who attacked Tabor. Again, he sees the mysterious Bajoran man who is attempting to control his actions. Tuvok manages to ignore it, and tells Janeway that he should be detained.

When Janeway visits Tuvok in the brig, he tells her about the voice trying to control his mind. He admits that he attacked the Maquis crew members and then performed mind-melds on them, although he doesn't know why. The attacks started after he received a letter from his son but an investigation later proves it contained a subliminal message of the chanting Bajoran Tuvok's been seeing in his mind. Now conscious, Chakotay recognizes the man as Teero Anaydis, a vedek who worked with the Maquis conducting mind-control experiments.

Tuvok suddenly recalls memories of Teero performing mind-control experiments on him. Janeway urges Tuvok to tell her more, but Teero seems to appear to him. The vedek tells him to complete his mission, and sends Chakotay a command in Bajoran. After Tuvok delivers the message, Chakotay goes to sickbay, stuns Paris, and gives Torres the same Bajoran command. They gather other former Maquis—all victims of Tuvok's attacks—and they take over the ship.

The Maquis plan to abandon the Starfleet crew on a M-class planet, but Chakotay tests Tuvok's loyalty by ordering him to fire a phaser at Janeway. Tuvok fires the phaser, but nothing happens because the weapon is defective. Then, when Chakotay's back is turned, the Vulcan grabs him and performs a mind-meld that brings Chakotay back to normal. After that, Chakotay hands control of the ship back to Janeway, and together they work to return the crew to themselves.

SENSOR READINGS: As chief of security, Tuvok has the authority to suspend privacy protocols under special cir-

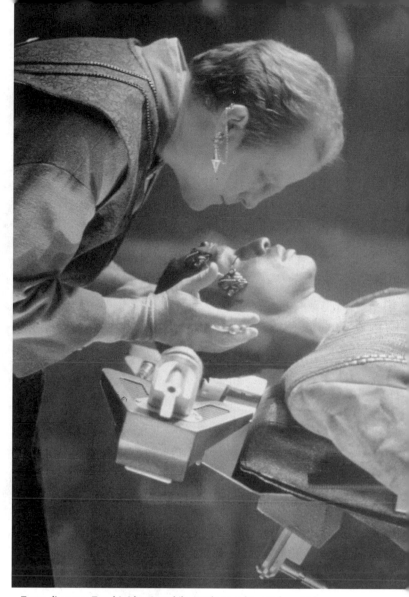

Teero discovers Tuvok's identity while conducting his mind control experiments. VIVIAN ZINK

cumstances, thus giving him the right to read personal mail. Twenty-eight crew members received letters from home in the last datastream. Only six of the twenty-eight matched the physical parameters of the suspect.
▪ Janeway puts the ship on a level-10 security alert, where nonessential personnel are confined to quarters, and security teams are posted on all decks.

ALPHA QUADRANT: The Bajoran *B'tanay* is the "Time of Awakening." The phrase *pagh'tem'fa b'tanay* puts the plan into motion. The Bajoran incantation reads, "This is a holy time. A primal energy charges the blood. An energy of rebirth." Vedek Teero Anaydis worked with the Maquis doing counterintelligence. He was thrown out for experimenting with mind control, which he found to be a good way to recruit agents. Teero was a fanatic who would go to any extreme for the Maquis, calling the rest of them

Tuvok realizes that he is the guilty party. MICHAEL YARISH

traitors for rejecting his ideas. Tuvok met him while doing reconnaissance in a colony in the Badlands.

PERSONAL LOGS: In the holodeck Paris replicates the old Palace Theatre in Chicago—built in 1932—complete with used chewing gum on the floor. ▪ Tuvok overrides security restrictions using authorization Tuvok Pi Alpha. Tuvok is 182 centimeters tall. His son mentions in his letter that the study of exolinguistics always seemed a little too theoretical to him so he has decided to study musical composition instead. ▪ In the last datastream Kim received a letter from his cousin that spoke of their mutual friend Maxwell Saroyan, who was killed several years ago by a Maquis.

Named Maquis crewmen include: Ensign Tabor, Crewman Yosa, Chell, Doyle, and Crewman Jor—who works in engineering and has her quarters on Deck 4. Crewmen Jor and Tabor are close friends and she apparently has open access to his quarters. A Vulcan woman and Bolian woman are seen among the Maquis crew members. The female Bolian could be Ensign Golwat.

MEDICAL UPDATE: Tabor and the others appear to be in a coma, but with unusual synaptic activity. The Doctor finds several minor microfractures in his cranium with patterns suggesting that he suffered a trauma of some sort. There's also evidence of subdermal contusions along his right shoulder.

CREW COMPLEMENT: Chakotay notes that there are twenty-three former Maquis who have not joined the insurrection yet. Added to the seven participating members, that makes a total of thirty former Maquis currently onboard *Voyager*.

EPISODE LOGS: Janeway notes that they are currently 35,000 light-years from Earth.

INSIDE MAN

EPISODE #252

WRITTEN BY: ROBERT DOHERTY
DIRECTED BY: ALLAN KROEKER

SPECIAL GUEST STAR

BARCLAY   DWIGHT SCHULTZ

GUEST STARS

ADMIRAL PARIS	RICHARD HERD
COMMANDER PETE HARKINS	RICHARD McGONAGLE
LEOSA	SHARISSE BAKER-BERNARD
GEGIS	FRANK CORSENTINO
YEGGIE	CHRISTOPHER NEIMAN
NUNK	MICHAEL WILLIAM RIVKIN

AND SPECIAL GUEST APPEARANCE BY

DEANNA TROI   MARINA SIRTIS

CO-STARS

LITTLE GIRL #1	BROOKE AVERI
LITTLE GIRL #2	LINDSEY PARKS
CABANA BOY	CHASE PENNY
COMPUTER VOICE	MAJEL BARRETT

STARDATE 54208.3

The holographic Barclay's wide smile belies his sinister programming.
MICHAEL YARISH

After missing the previous month's mail, the crew looks forward to receiving the latest datastream, which is jammed in the ship's transceiver. They soon discover that instead of letters, the datastream contains a hologram of Reg Barclay, who tells the crew of Starfleet's plan to bring *Voyager* home. The hologram directs the crew to a red giant star where Federation scientists plan to create a geodesic fold, forming a gateway between the quadrants. Janeway questions the plan, since *Voyager*'s shields are useless against geodesic radiation, but the holographic Barclay announces that he brought shield upgrades and medical technology to protect the crew. The Doctor agrees to transfer his mobile emitter to the holographic Barclay so that the visitor can move freely about the ship while he makes preparations.

In the Pathfinder research lab, the real Reg Barclay investigates why the second datastream transmission in two months did not reach its target. Commander Harkins believes the hologram was lost because it was too complex and degraded, but Barclay insists something interfered. Harkins refuses to listen and orders Barclay to take a vacation.

In the Delta Quadrant, the Doctor tells the holographic Barclay that the medical inoculations are not strong enough to protect the crew from the radiation, but he assures the Doctor that they are intended to work in combination with the shield modifications. Later, Torres and Kim transmit a message back to the Alpha Quadrant, in which the holographic Barclay includes his own progress report. Three Ferengi intercept the message which includes information on Seven of Nine's Borg nanoprobes. The Ferengi intend to acquire the technology and sell it for a huge profit.

Barclay seeks out Deanna Troi while she's on vacation and tells her about his concerns—compounded by the fact that his girlfriend, Leosa—left him right after his hologram was lost. After prodding from Troi, Barclay admits that he suspects his now ex-girlfriend had something to do with the missing transmission. Leosa is brought in for questioning by Admiral Paris and she admits that she is a dabo girl who works on a Ferengi casino ship, but she denies sharing her knowledge of the Pathfinder project with anyone. Using her empathic abilities, Troi discerns that Leosa is lying and forces the dabo girl to reveal the truth behind her involvement in the

The holographic Barclay tricks the Doctor into giving up his mobile emitter. MICHAEL YARISH

scheme. Scans find the Ferengi ship near a red giant star, and Admiral Paris sends a starship to intercept it.

Barclay begins to unravel the Ferengi plan to bring *Voyager* through the fold, which will kill the entire crew. Meanwhile, on *Voyager,* Seven of Nine also realizes the crew will not survive the trip, leading the holographic Barclay to attack her. The Ferengi ship receives a message from what they think is the holographic Barclay, who says that Janeway has found out about their plan, and developed a way to protect the ship. He adds that once through the fold Janeway plans to hunt down the parties responsible. The Ferengi believe him, and start closing the fold, never realizing that the message came from the real Barclay in a holodeck re-creation of *Voyager* at the Pathfinder lab.

Meanwhile, the holographic Barclay beams himself and Seven to an escape pod and heads toward the geodesic fold. Kim manages to beam them back while the pod goes through the fold and rams into the Ferengi ship. The real Barclay then begins to program a new hologram using tightened security precautions.

SENSOR READINGS: The datastream is larger than usual because it contains a holographic template. The template jams the transceiver, which was not designed to store holograms. Kim ties the transceiver into the holodeck's pattern buffer to rescue the program. Because those two systems are not compatible they depolarize the relays, burning them out and overloading the transceiver. However, the hologram is retrieved. ▪ The Ferengi plan relies on *Voyager* passing through Grid 898, a sector of space occupied by a red giant star. A team of Ferengi is orbiting another red giant in the Alpha Quadrant. They target the red giant's magnetic field with a verteron beam to create the geodesic fold. As a result, a corresponding fold opens in the Delta Quadrant, within the magnetic field of the red giant that *Voyager* is approaching. Space is punctured at those two points, creating a gateway between the quadrants. *Voyager*'s shields are useless against geodesic radiation. The crew toyed with the idea of opening a fold themselves, but it did not take long to realize they would not survive the trip.

SHUTTLE TRACKER: An escape pod is lost.

DELTA QUADRANT: When a Borg cube enters a transwarp conduit, it is subject to extreme gravimetric shear. To compensate, the Borg project a structural integrity field ahead of the cube. Seven believes that by modifying *Voyager*'s deflector, they may be able to do the same.

ALPHA QUADRANT: In the Alpha Quadrant the datastream trajectory ends in Sector 39542, Grid 842, Grid 8 when it is intercepted by the Ferengi. Later, the *U.S.S. Carolina* is sent to intercept the Ferengi ship. ▪ The 74th Rule of Acquisition is "Knowledge Equals Profit." They expect Seven's 3.6 million nanoprobes to fetch a price of six bars of latinum per unit. It is noted that nanoprobes are not just used for assimilating as they can reanimate necrotic tissue and slow down the aging process. ▪ The last time Troi and Barclay had seen each other was at Lieutenant Commander La Forge's birthday party.

EPISODE LOGS: *Voyager* is now 30,000 light-years from home. ▪ In listing other failed attempts to get home, Paris references events from the episodes "Hope and Fear" and "Bliss." ▪ Troi's interrupted vacation was originally meant to be a romantic getaway for her and Riker. This follows the events of *Star Trek: Insurrection,* in which the pair renewed their relationship.

FLESH AND BLOOD, PART I

EPISODE #253
TELEPLAY BY: BRYAN FULLER
STORY BY: JACK MONACO and BRYAN FULLER & RAF GREEN
DIRECTED BY: MIKE VEJAR

GUEST STARS

IDEN	JEFF YAGHER
DONIK	RYAN BOLLMAN
BETA HIROGEN	MICHAEL WISEMAN
KEJAL	CINDY KATZ
WEISS	SPENCER GARRETT
ALPHA HIROGEN	VAUGHN ARMSTRONG

CO-STARS

HIROGEN #1	TODD JEFFRIES
HIROGEN #3	DON McMILLAN
HIROGEN #2	CHAD HALYARD
COMPUTER VOICE	MAJEL BARRETT

STARDATE UNKNOWN

A pair of Hirogen move through a jungle hunting prey. Suddenly phaser shots are fired, as four armed Starfleet crewmen rise out of a lake, destroying their predators with vengeance. Responding to a distress call, a *Voyager* away team beams over and finds themselves in the jungle littered with the bodies of Hirogen killed by Alpha Quadrant weapons. A lone survivor named Donik is beamed to sickbay, where he explains that he is a technician who maintained the vessel as a training facility for the Hirogen until the holograms malfunctioned, took control, and deactivated the safety protocols.

The Alpha and Beta Hirogen from another vessel have also responded to the distress call. When they find *Voyager* waiting at the coordinates, they beam aboard. Donik reveals that the holograms transferred their programs to a vessel equipped with holoemitters and are on the loose. The Starfleet and Hirogen crews agree to work together leaving Donik aboard the Federation vessel. They locate the renegade holograms but realize, too late, that it is a trap set to destroy the Hirogen ship. While *Voyager* tends to the Hirogen survivors, the ship occupied by the holograms drops out of warp and starts firing. They tap into the holoemitters in sickbay and transfer the Doctor's program to their own ship and flee.

The Doctor finds himself surrounded by simulations of various Alpha and Beta Quadrant species, as a Bajoran hologram named Iden welcomes him aboard. The Doctor demands to be returned to *Voyager,* but Iden insists he

Tricorders fail to show that the away team is in a holographic environment. VIVIAN ZINK

help their holographic wounded. Meanwhile, Janeway learns that the holograms have the ability to learn and adapt, which makes them formidable prey. The Beta Hirogen intends to resume the hunt, but Janeway insists they find a way to take the holograms offline from a safe distance. Since the Hirogen lost their ship in the attack, the captain gives them no choice but to agree, or she will drop them off at the nearest planet.

Despite convincing arguments from Iden and Kejal, a holographic Cardassian woman, the Doctor refuses the fugitives offer to remain with them. He suggests that the *Voyager* crew could help them create their own photonic home with the help of Lt. Torres. While on *Voyager,* Donik and the crew discuss methods of shutting down the holograms. Torres embarks on a plan to reconfigure the ship's deflector to emit an antiphoton pulse. Soon afterward, the holograms' ship intercepts *Voyager* and hails them. The Doctor appears on the viewscreen and says the holograms have come to make peace and want to create a new life for themselves with *Voyager*'s assistance.

The Doctor returns to *Voyager* to discuss the proposal with the captain. Considering the situation they are in, Janeway is hesitant to share technology again. This leads to an argument with the Doctor over holographic rights. Their discussion is interrupted when the Hirogen in the mess hall starts a fight and manages to send a distress call to other Hirogen ships. With less than an hour to intercept, Janeway orders Torres and Donik to prepare the deflector to take the holograms offline so there will be no more bloodshed. The Doctor objects to having them deactivated, but Janeway proceeds and contacts Iden, telling him to prepare his people to be transferred to *Voyager*'s database. Iden responds by firing on *Voyager.*

In *Voyager*'s sickbay the Doctor contacts Iden, transmitting data about the deflector pulse and *Voyager*'s shield frequencies so they can beam him off the ship. The Doctor transports over, while *Voyager* and the hologram's ship exchange fire.

DELTA QUADRANT: The crew notes that the Hirogen

Paris does the best he can without the Doctor. MICHAEL YARISH

PERSONAL LOGS: Torres participated in a Boray Conference on transwarp theory a few months earlier. ▪ The Doctor requests a temporary leave of absence because the Ovions (a race of hexapods) have asked him to speak at a symposium on spaceborne pathogens. There are going to be physicians from all over the quadrant; however, the request is denied, as the Ovion system is two weeks in the opposite direction of *Voyager's* present heading. The holograms deactivate the Doctor and transfer the memory files from one of their holograms into him so that he better understands their experience as prey.

EPISODE LOGS: This episode follows the events of "The Killing Game" wherein Janeway gave the Hirogen holographic technology as part of their cease-fire agreement.

FLESH AND BLOOD, PART II
EPISODE #254
TELEPLAY BY: BRYAN FULLER
STORY BY: JACK MONACO and BRYAN FULLER & RAF GREEN
DIRECTED BY: DAVID LIVINGSTON

GUEST STARS	
IDEN	JEFF YAGHER
DONIK	RYAN BOLLMAN
BETA HIROGEN	MICHAEL WISEMAN
KEJAL	CINDY KATZ
WEISS	SPENCER GARRETT
ALPHA HIROGEN	VAUGHN ARMSTRONG
NEW ALPHA HIROGEN	PAUL ECKSTEIN

CO-STARS	
NUU'BARI MINER	DAVID DOTY
NUU'BARI HOLOGRAM ONE	DAMON KIRSCHE
NARRATOR	MAJEL BARRETT

STARDATE 54337.5

When *Voyager* emits the deflector pulse, Iden sends a feedback surge through the beam that overloads the ship's deflector, nearly causing a warp core breach. Then, Iden beams Torres over to his ship and escapes, leaving *Voyager* adrift. Having transferred his program to the ship as well, the Doctor is furious with Iden for the kidnapping, but the rebellious leader promises to let Torres go once she has a chance to decide for herself whether or not to help the holograms.

have obviously made alterations to the holographic programming given to them by Janeway, ("The Killing Game") since all preliminary scans of the Hirogen testing facility indicated the environment was real. The holograms also have enhanced memory, comprehensive tactical algorithms, and expandable data processing giving them the ability to learn and adapt. Most of the forty-three dead Hirogen in the environment were killed by facsimiles of Alpha Quadrant weapons, such as Romulan disruptors, Klingon *bat'leths,* and Starfleet phasers. ▪ Elevated plasma readings in Grid 295 indicate that the holograms created a scattering field to mask their ship. They can be found by scanning for polarized EM signatures. On their ship, the holoemitters are an independent subsystem with its own power generator. The holoemitters are protected by three layers of ablative armor. Since trying to take them offline one at a time would be inefficient the crew plans to disrupt the signals generated by the emitters.

ALPHA QUADRANT: The Bajoran name *Kejal* means "freedom."

Janeway and Donik prove that enemies can work together. RON TOM

When Torres awakens on the holograms' ship, she wants to leave immediately, but the Doctor convinces her to meet Iden and look at the photonic field generator before making a decision.

Donik decides to stay aboard *Voyager* rather than go back with the other Hirogen when two other Hirogen vessels come to rescue them. The Hirogen vessels go to warp, and Janeway follows, using Donik's plan to hide *Voyager* in the ion wake of one of the Hirogen vessels. Meanwhile, Torres looks at the photonic field generator with Kejal and gets to know the hologram better. The Doctor begins to suspect that Iden's erratic behavior betrays less noble motivation. The holograms manage to evade the approaching Hirogen ships, while Torres works to get the generator on line.

When a Nuu'bari mining ship is detected, Iden has his crew attack it to free the photonic life-forms, killing two innocent organics in the process. As she works to bring the new holograms online, Torres tries to convince Kejal that she should take command. After the rescued photonics prove to be programmed only with rudimentary subroutines, Torres points out that Iden killed two living beings to liberate mindless machines.

As the holograms approach the untamed world that

will be their new home, Iden orders the generator deployed immediately. The Hirogen follow the holograms to the planet, and when they drop out of warp, *Voyager* immediately fires weapons and disables both hunting vessels. Iden has the Hirogen hunters transported to the planet's surface, then deactivates the Doctor and takes his mobile emitter.

On the surface, the armed holograms materialize around the unarmed Hirogen and begin pursuing them. Meanwhile on the hologram's ship, Torres convinces Kejal to stop the massacre by shutting down the holograms. However, Iden is using the mobile emitter and cannot be deactivated so Torres sends the armed Doctor to the surface through the holographic generator. Just as Iden is about to kill the Beta Hirogen, the Doctor catches up with him and demands he lower his weapon. Iden refuses, forcing the Doctor to fire and destroy his fellow hologram.

The surviving Hirogen are rescued by *Voyager,* and persuaded to leave empty-handed. Janeway then transports to the hologram vessel and learns from Torres that all the holograms but Iden are intact in the database. Janeway offers Kejal refuge on *Voyager,* but she insists that this ship is her home. Donik volunteers to stay with her

Iden becomes the hunter. MICHAEL YARISH

and reprogram the holograms to undo some of the damage he caused. Back onboard *Voyager,* the Doctor offers to surrender his mobile emitter, but Janeway refuses to punish him for being as fallible as those who are made of flesh and blood.

SENSOR READINGS: *Voyager* fires a full spread of torpedoes at the second Hirogen hunting ship.

DAMAGE REPORT: Engineering systems and main power are offline, but Seven says they can be repaired quickly. The deflector, however, needs at least four hours for repair. If Torres hadn't reinforced the core before deploying the beam, *Voyager* would have been destroyed.

DELTA QUADRANT: The holograms reconfigure the holographic data core, but it is still not capable of supporting their matrices because it does not have enough optronic capacity. They intend to deploy the holographic generator on the southern continent of a planet that they have named *Ha'Dara,* Bajoran for "Home of Light." The planet is Y-class, with a toxic atmosphere, sulfuric deserts, and no trees or life of any kind.

Hirogen sensors can detect residual ion emissions. Their vessels produce an ion wake approximately five thousand meters long. Inside the wake, there is too much interference for their sensors to detect anything, creating a blind spot in which *Voyager* hides. The new Hirogen hunting party consists of two *Venatic*-class vessels. ▪ The Nuu'bari use holograms as laborers. They are programmed with only forty basic subroutines.

EPISODE LOGS: A Y-class planet is also known by the nickname Demon Class ("Demon"). ▪ This is not the first time the Doctor has offered to limit his programming as punishment for his behavior. In "Retrospect" he asked to delete the counselor algorithms following his poor advice to Seven; that request was also refused.

BODY AND SOUL

EPISODE #255

TELEPLAY BY: **ERIC MORRIS** and **PHYLLIS STRONG**
& MIKE SUSSMAN

STORY BY: **MICHAEL TAYLOR**

DIRECTED BY: **ROBERT DUNCAN McNEILL**

GUEST STARS

RANEK	**FRITZ SPERBERG**
T'PEL	**MARVA HICKS**
	and
JARYN	**MEGAN GALLAGHER**

CO-STARS

CAPTAIN #2	**DAVID STARWALT**
COMPUTER VOICE	**MAJEL BARRETT**

STARDATE 54238.3

The Doctor, Seven, and Kim are on a mission in the *Delta Flyer* when they come under attack for transporting a "photonic insurgent" through Lokirrim space. The patrol vessel's Captain Ranek fires a disruption field that decompiles the Doctor's matrix. Inspecting the vessel, Ranek finds the Doctor's mobile emitter, which Seven calls her portable regeneration unit.

Ranek confiscates the *Delta Flyer* and locks the crew in a holding cell where Kim finds out that the Doctor's program has been downloaded into Seven's cybernetic implants, and is now in control of her body. For the first time, the Doctor is able to have sensory experiences, including touch and smell. Meanwhile on *Voyager,* Paris treats Tuvok for a neurochemical imbalance, which turns out to be *Pon farr.* Paris promises to provide a special medication from the Doctor's database, and to keep the condition secret.

Ranek has Seven taken to the *Flyer* for questioning, unaware that the Doctor is still inhabiting her body. Seven/the Doctor demonstrates the food replicator by requesting a slice of cheesecake and upon tasting it experiences rapture. Before long, Seven/the Doctor and Ranek

THE HIROGEN

"So there's one question remaining . . . who's hunting the hunters?"

Kathryn Janeway, "Prey"

The Hirogen were introduced in "Message in a Bottle," when their ancient relay stations provided the crew of *Voyager* with the unique opportunity to contact the Alpha Quadrant. Although little was learned about the aliens, two very impor-

tant facts could be inferred from the relay stations. The age of the stations alone indicated that they were a long-lived race. Also, the fact that the delays enabled communication from thousands of light-years away indicated that Hirogen society was quite spread out, a factor that would prove important later in the series.

The Hirogen were never seen in "Message in a Bottle." The crew's physical introduction to the Hirogen came in "Hunters," with their first face-to-face interaction. In this episode, visual clues provide the most information about this new threat. The shooting script described the inside of their ship as, "a dark cluttered space with stark pools of light." Weaponry and trophies hung from the ceiling and on walls, filling the ship with images of death and carnage. As the Hirogen watched a transmission intended for *Voyager* they prepared themselves for "the hunt" by applying ritual markings on their armor. Without dialogue, it was clear that this was a violent warrior race.

When the pair of Hirogen captured Tuvok and Seven, their threat was made even more apparent by the mere fact that they were so physically imposing. Towering over the Vulcan and former Borg, the Hirogen appeared dominant and unstoppable. As the events of the episode played out, they were introduced as a race with the single purpose of tracking their

VIVIAN ZINK

Seven works to save the Doctor from detection. VIVIAN ZINK

have devoured plates of food and downed several glasses of wine. Ranek agrees to hand over the mobile emitter in exchange for medical services, then returns Seven/the Doctor to the holding cell. There the Doctor's matrix is restored. The disoriented Seven then scolds the Doctor for abusing her body, but before long tactical officer Jaryn takes Seven—again controlled by the Doctor—to treat their soldiers.

On *Voyager,* the medication to stabilize Tuvok's condition does not work, so Paris creates a replica of the Vulcan's wife in the holodeck hoping to satisfy his longing. Tuvok hesitantly agrees, but while he participates in the simulation, the ship comes under attack by a Lokirrim vessel because it senses photonic activity aboard. Janeway agrees to shut down the holodecks and allow the Lokirrim ship to escort *Voyager* through their territory.

Ranek calls for Seven to meet him on the bridge, where he comes on to her. Seven/the Doctor pushes him away and returns to the medical bay, where he learns that

prey and collecting rewards of the hunt. Their social structures were entirely contained to hunting parties that sometimes consist solely of an Alpha and Beta Hirogen, or larger crews led by Alpha and Betas. The parties usually functioned on their own, though they had been known to come together to work as a team in trapping their prey.

In "Prey," the hunters became victims of their own customs when they faced a lone member of Species 8472. Their insistence on continuing the hunt against a superior prey revealed the heart of their culture. They would stop at nothing in the mindless pursuit of their prey. This served in stark contrast to the views of the *Voyager* crew who found themselves taking the noble position of helping a former enemy, Species 8472, flee the Hirogen. This story served as a backdrop to further expand on the development of a character—in this case, Seven, who acts as a drone would, showing she still is not truly "human."

It was in "The Killing Game, Part I and II" that the true relentlessness of their singular vision can be seen, as well as the tragic flaw of their race. This pair of episodes introduced the Hirogen weakness in being too single-minded in their approach to the hunt. The flaw was only obvious to one Hirogen, who spent much of his time trying to convince others. In the end, the message was partially understood.

Although a single Hirogen was met in "Tsunkatse" he also proved that the race did have a noble slant. But overcoming the centuries-long drive of the hunt seemed impossible as the events unfolded in "Flesh and Blood." In this episode, the Hirogen were undone by their own actions at the hands of a more evolved life-form. In the end, there was a glimmer of hope for the race in the technician, Donik, who left his people in the hope of becoming more than just a hunter.

"We're talking about a time potentially in the future where it would be possible not only to create holograms, but to create them in such a way as to have them defeat us. It's the robot idea gone mad. And I think everybody can relate to that because of course we know what science is doing now. And the Hirogen embodied in these very large and fierce beings . . . it's interesting to see them humbled by their own creation."

—Kate Mulgrew

Jaryn has feelings for her captain. Since the Doctor also cares for Jaryn—who knows him only as Seven—he makes an impassioned plea for her to find someone more like himself. Seven/the Doctor then gets called to the holding cell to treat Kim, who has faked a seizure. Kim presses the Doctor and Seven for what they have learned about the ship's com system. With Ranek's command codes, they formulate a successful plan that allows them to send a message to *Voyager* from the *Flyer*.

Escaping the Lokirrim escort, Janeway finds the patrol ship and demands the return of her people. When they refuse, Chakotay uses Ranek's command codes to disable their shields. Ranek makes an attempt to sabotage his ship, but is critically injured when the Doctor and Seven thwart his plan. The Doctor saves Ranek, forcing the Lokirrim to express their gratitude to the hologram, even though their opinion of photonics in general may not have changed.

Back on *Voyager*, Tuvok is cured after continuing the interrupted holoprogram, while Seven pays the Doctor a visit in sickbay bringing delicacies that she previously would have considered indulgences. Since the Doctor can no longer share the experience of eating and drinking, Seven promises to describe the meal to him so he can enjoy it vicariously.

SENSOR READINGS: *Voyager* conducts a maintenance layover at the Maldorian Station. ▪ The away team is collecting spores from the tails of comets for the Doctor to use in synthesizing new medicines. The Lokirrim note that the biogenic material aboard the *Flyer* could be used to create viral weapons.

SHUTTLE TRACKER: The *Delta Flyer's* thrusters, shields, and subspace communications go offline under attack by the Lokirrim. The *Flyer* is equipped with pulse-phased weapons and a duranium-enforced hull. It is held in the Lokirrim docking bay, but ultimately retrieved by *Voyager*.

The Doctor receives unwanted attention while in Seven's body.
VIVIAN ZINK

DELTA QUADRANT: Transporting photonics and manufacturing biogenic weapons in Lokirrim space are serious charges. The attitude toward photonics is a result of an insurgence that occurred, where in the photonics rebelled against the organics. The photonics posses a viral weapon that attacks the cerebral cortex, and within days, the victims suffer complete synaptic failure. The Doctor suggests synthesizing a neural inhibitor to combat the weapon. ▪ Ranek shows Seven/the Doctor a pulsar cluster their poets call the "Window of Dreams," claiming there is nothing else like it in the quadrant. The pulsar's EM field vibrates against the ship's hull and creates musical sounds that Seven/the Doctor claims are identical to the rhythm produced by the eight-chambered Ktarian heart.

ALPHA QUADRANT: The Vulcan libido increases with age.

PERSONAL LOGS: The Doctor anticipated Tuvok's medical needs and developed a treatment stored under file Theta-12-Alpha. It was believed that combined with meditation, the treatment would enable him to control the symptoms. ▪ While the Doctor is in Seven of Nine's body, her consciousness is submerged, but physiologically she is fine. The Doctor notes her senses are more acute than the average humanoid.

MEDICAL UPDATE: The symptoms of Tuvok's neurochemical imbalance (*Pon farr*) include headache, fever, respiratory distress, and tremors.

EPISODE LOGS: The Lokirrim were previously mentioned in "Flesh and Blood" as a race the Doctor had encountered. This episode aired prior to the two-parter (the stardates also reflect the proper order of events).

NIGHTINGALE

EPISODE #256
TELEPLAY BY: ANDRE BORMANIS
STORY BY: ROBERT LEDERMAN & DAVE LONG
DIRECTED BY: LeVAR BURTON

GUEST STARS

LOKEN	RON GLASS
ICHEB	MANU INTIRAYMI
DAYLA	BEVERLY LEECH
GERAL	PAUL F. O'BRIEN
TEREK	SCOTT MILES

CO-STARS

ANNARI COMMANDER	ALAN BROOKS
BRELL	BOB RUDD

STARDATE 54274.7

Voyager sets down on a planet for a major maintenance overhaul, while away teams search for supplies. Kim, Seven, and Neelix are on the *Delta Flyer* when caught in the crossfire between two ships, and they receive a distress call from a Kraylor captain begging for help with his casualties. Reluctant to get involved in a battle between two races, Kim attempts to help the Kraylor by contacting their enemy, the Annari, and using diplomacy to end the hostility. When he fails to get the Annari ship to disengage, Kim uses the *Flyer's* deflector to damage the ship, forcing them to retreat.

Kim and Neelix beam to the Kraylor ship and learn that its captain was killed along with all the ship's officers. Impressed with Kim's skills, Loken—the doctor in charge of the research team—asks him to take command, since no one left among them is trained to command a vessel. Kim declines, but Loken insists that they cannot afford to fail in their mission to deliver vaccines to their homeworld and save thousands of lives. Since their flight plan will take them close to *Voyager*, Kim agrees to command the ship that far.

Kim has a difficult time as the commander of a mission. VIVIAN ZINK

As they approach *Voyager's* coordinates, Kim discovers three Annari warships in orbit. Still planet-bound, the captain has set up trade negotiations with the Annari. Once the Annari leave the orbit, Kim brings Loken to *Voyager,* where he appeals to Captain Janeway for help in getting home. In private, Kim presses the case on behalf of the Kraylor, offering to take charge of the mission himself. Not wanting the ensign to go alone, Janeway assigns Seven to assist, since Kim outranks her by the mere fact that she has no rank. With the captain's permission, Kim prepares for departure, naming the Kraylor ship *Nightingale.*

As the Kraylor ship returns home, repairs continue on *Voyager,* where Icheb has been assigned to help Torres and the engineering crew. When she invites him to go rock climbing on the holodeck, he misinterprets the offer and believes her to have romantic feelings for him. Ultimately, Icheb lets her down gently for the sake of her marriage, and Torres plays along.

As the damaged Kraylor ship deals with a defective cloak and other problems, Seven criticizes Kim's overly hands-on and dismissive approach to commanding the

Nightingale's makeshift crew. When the cloak fails, six Annari vessels swoop in and fire upon them. As Kim walks Dayla—one of his new crewmen—through the repairs, Loken interrupts and gives her different orders, which succeeds in re-engaging the cloak, but too late to keep the ship safe.

Loken reports that Dayla died in the attack while Kim tries to treat an injured and unconscious Seven. Now suspicious of the Kraylor, Kim asks Loken for his advice as a doctor, having realized that he knows a lot more about cloaking systems than he does biology. Loken admits that he and his colleagues have been developing a cloaking device for his people's fleet and this ship is a prototype. Because his planet has been under an Annari blockade that has choked off supplies of food and medicine for three years, he still considers their mission to be a humanitarian one. Kim orders the ship to return to *Voyager,* but the crew refuses to obey.

Kim tells Seven the situation and plans to take an escape pod back to *Voyager,* but she challenges him to act like a captain. As *Nightingale* approaches the Kraylor homeworld, the crew sees Annari ships in orbit emit-

Seven questions Kim's leadership. VIVIAN ZINK

ting pulses of energy designed to illuminate cloaked ships. Unsure how they will get through that barrage, Kim returns to the bridge and offers to discuss terms with the Annari for surrender. The Annari commander agrees, but Kim uses the ruse to break free of the Annari ship, and head for the Kraylor defense perimeter. The mission over, Kim realizes that he is not quite captain material . . . yet.

SENSOR READINGS: *Voyager's* major maintenance overhaul includes upgrading the impulse engines. Torres reports that it will take six days before she can bring warp drive back online because she discovered microfractures in the starboard nacelle and fused relays in the main computer. Environmental controls are being worked on, but the thermal regulators are still running a little hot. • Kim uses a deflector pulse to overload the Annari phaser banks. ▪ Janeway offers a trade with the Annari, asking for a new set of deuterium injectors in exchange for some of their mined zeolitic ore. The material was derived from several tons of the high-grade, easily refined ore that the

Voyager crew mined from an asteroid field. The Annari also offer to provide them with some dilithium.

DELTA QUADRANT: There are a total of twenty-seven survivors from an original crew of fifty-six aboard Kraylor Medical Transport 136 (later christened *Nightingale*). A shield grid protects the Kraylor homeworld, but it is almost impossible to get the ships in or out due to the blockade. ▪ The Annari use scanning pulses that illuminate cloaked ships.

CREW COMPLEMENT: Kim claims that *Voyager* lost over a dozen crew members when the ship was originally pulled into the Alpha Quadrant.

PERSONAL LOGS: Torres has been rock climbing in the holodeck. ▪ Icheb fixes one of the Doctor's malfunctioning holoemitters in sickbay. Before the repair, any time the Doctor moved to the far corner of the surgical bay, his legs would disappear.

SHATTERED

EPISODE #257
TELEPLAY BY: MICHAEL TAYLOR
STORY BY: MICHAEL SUSSMAN & MICHAEL TAYLOR
DIRECTED BY: TERRY WINDELL

GUEST STARS

DR. CHAOTICA	MARTIN RAYNER
ICHEB	MANU INTIRAYMI
NAOMI WILDMAN	SCARLETT POMERS
LONZAK	NICHOLAS WORTH
SESKA	MARTHA HACKETT

CO-STARS

ADULT ICHEB	MARK BENNINGTON
ADULT NAOMI	VANESSA BRANCH
RULAT	ANTHONY HOLIDAY
ANDREWS	TERRELL CLAYTON
COMPUTER VOICE	MAJEL BARRETT

STARDATE UNKNOWN

After *Voyager* encounters a spatial rift that causes the warp core to destabilize, Chakotay heads to engineering. As he tries to maintain containment, an energy blast strikes him, and both he and the ship shimmer in a strange effect. Chakotay is beamed to sickbay, where he learns that his body was in a state of temporal flux, but that the Doctor created a chroniton-infused serum that brought him back to normal. Chakotay asks the Doctor to come with him to check for other injured crewmen, but the hologram says he cannot leave sickbay and he has never heard of a mobile emitter.

Chakotay heads to the bridge, where Janeway orders him taken into custody, accusing him of sabotage on behalf of the Maquis. Chakotay realizes he has gone back seven years into *Voyager*'s past. As he rides the turbolift with the guards, a distortion wave causes them to disappear. In engineering Chakotay finds Kazon warriors and Seska; from the period when the Kazon had control of *Voyager*. Seska refuses to listen as he explains what is happening, forcing Chakotay to escape by passing through another distortion wave.

Chakotay returns to sickbay and updates the Doctor, requesting more of the serum. He returns to the bridge, injects Janeway—making her immune to the distortion waves—and takes her through another time distortion. Slowly gaining her trust, Chakotay takes the captain to astrometrics, where they find adult versions of Icheb and Naomi seventeen years in the future. Janeway theorizes that if they can get to a section of the ship that still exists

Chakotay convinces the past Janeway to trust him. VIVIAN ZINK

in Chakotay's time period then maybe they can counteract the chronokinetic surge that caused the waves.

In the cargo bay they find a fully Borgified Seven of Nine, who aids their plan by explaining that a chroniton field projected throughout the vessel would force it back into temporal sync. This would give Chakotay a few seconds to counteract the energy surge that caused the problem. They must inject the bio-neural circuitry with the Doctor's serum in order to transmit the chroniton field. As the Doctor replicates more serum, he accidentally reveals to the past Janeway that her crew will get stranded in the Delta Quadrant.

As the pair travels through the ship they experience additional timeframes from *Voyager*'s past. In a transporter room, Janeway and Chakotay encounter several Maquis members, including Torres from a period before she joined the *Voyager* crew. They next go to the mess hall, where Paris has set up triage for several crewmen injured in the original incident that started these time shifts. Janeway watches as Tuvok dies from the radiation, then tells Chakotay that she wants to put *Voyager* into

The captain has little patience for Dr. Chaotica. RON TOM

temporal sync with her own time frame, not his, so she can change the future. Chakotay points out that she has seen only the negative aspects of her future and not the many positive effects her actions will have on her crew.

Their final stop is engineering, where Chakotay convinces Seska to let him inject the gel pack. However, she demands that he modify and plan to bring the ship into her time frame. When she threatens to kill him, Janeway and various crew members from the different time periods come in and wrestle control away from the Kazon.

Everyone returns to their timeframe of the ship and Chakotay initiates the chroniton pulse to restore time to a few seconds before the accident, making sure it never occurs. The ship saved, Chakotay refuses to explain his actions to the present-day Janeway, invoking the Temporal Prime Directive.

SENSOR READINGS: A spatial rift opens directly in front of *Voyager,* emitting high levels of neutrinos and chronitons. Then, a chronokinetic surge interacts with the warp core and shatters the space-time continuum aboard the

ship. The ship is divided into thirty-seven different timeframes. Astrometrics is equipped with temporal sensors, created with Borg technology.

DAMAGE REPORT: The gravimetric surge overloads inertial dampeners and the warp core destabilizes. ▪ Chakotay burns out the deflector dish by rerouting power to it and setting the polarity to a frequency that he inputs, turning it into a "lightning rod" to attract the energy discharge.

ALPHA QUADRANT: The Ferengi have a saying: "A good lie is easier to believe than the truth."

PERSONAL LOGS: Janeway burns the pot roast dinner she makes for herself and Chakotay. On her first Starfleet posting on the *Al-Batani,* she once knocked out power to six decks by misaligning the positronic relays. She had rescued her Irish setter, Molly, from a pound on Taris Seti IV. The dog was the runt of the litter, but Janeway thought she had spunk. She loves music, but never learned to play an instrument—something she still regrets (as also mentioned in "Remembered"). Janeway notes that there is no anomaly scarier than a thunderstorm on the plains, especially when she was six years old. She remembers watching a bolt of lightning split an oak tree that she had climbed just a few hours earlier. Janeway's then fiancé, Mark, gave her a copy of Dante's *Inferno* as an engagement gift. She once let Chakotay borrow it, though the past Janeway had never lent it to anyone. ▪ Chakotay has a secret stash of Antarian cider in the cargo bay, but there are only a few bottles left. ▪ Chakotay refers to Paris as the ship's chief medic. ▪ Neelix never inventories the salvaged Borg components because they "give him the creeps."

Icheb is tutoring Naomi, although at the time he is supposed to be writing a paper on transwarp instability. They are putting together a jigsaw puzzle of an image of a DNA strand.

MEDICAL UPDATE: While Chakotay's body was in a state of temporal flux, he had the liver of an eighty-year-old man, and the kidneys of a twelve-year-old boy. ▪ With the ship shattered and normal technology unable to pass through the barriers, the Doctor replicates a chroniton-infused hypospray casing using the same principles he used to make the serum.

CREW COMPLEMENT: The past Janeway says she began her mission into the Badlands with a crew of 153.

EPISODE LOGS: The following are some of the thirty-seven timeframes into which the ship is shattered: The Doctor is in sickbay on Stardate 49624 (between "The Thaw" and "Tuvix"). The bridge is in the time shortly before the ship is flung into the Delta Quadrant. Engineering is in the time when the Kazon had control of the ship ("Basics, Part II"). In a corridor, Chakotay detects an active neurogenic field, noting that it could be the day the telepathic "pitcher plant" put them all into comas ("Bliss") or the time aliens invaded their dreams ("Waking Moments"). Astrometrics is seventeen years in the future. Cargo Bay 2 is during the time of *Voyager*'s alliance with the Borg ("Scorpion, Part II"). In another corridor they come across the macrovirus that had infected the ship ("Macrocosm"). The holodeck is stuck in the Captain Proton holoprogram (at some point following "Bride of Chaotica!"). The transporter room is in a time period before the Maquis join the crew (at the conclusion of "Caretaker"). The mess hall is in the near future, only several days after the inciting incident.

LINEAGE

EPISODE #258
WRITTEN BY: JAMES KAHN
DIRECTED BY: PETER LAURITSON

GUEST STARS

ICHEB	MANU INTIRAYMI

CO-STARS

JOHN TORRES	JUAN GARCIA
YOUNG B'ELANNA	JESSICA GAONA
CARL	JAVIER GRAJEDA
DEAN	PAUL ROBERT LANGDON
ELIZABETH	NICOLE SARAH FELLOWS
MICHAEL	GILBERT R. LEAL
COMPUTER VOICE	MAJEL BARRETT

STARDATE 54452.6

After Torres faints in engineering, the Doctor confirms that she is pregnant, explaining that her reaction could be a result of the clashing Klingon and human metabolisms. Despite the parents' wish to keep the news to themselves for a while, the rest of the crew quickly finds out about the pregnancy. Later Paris has a candlelight dinner set out, but his wife's emotional

Torres is haunted by memories of her childhood. RON TOM

B'Elanna and her father on the camping trip that changed both their lives. RON TOM

volatility almost ruins the evening. As she calms down, the Doctor summons them to sickbay.

The Doctor informs the parents-to-be that their child's spine deviates from the norm, but that a genetic modification will correct it. He accidentally reveals the child to be a girl. At Paris's request, the Doctor projects a holographic image of the baby. The father finds her beautiful, but the mother can only focus on her Klingon traits. Torres recalls a time when she was a young girl on a campout with her human father, and remembers that he told her how much she was like her Klingon mother. Later, when she turns in for the night, Torres again recalls the campout and the fact that she did not want to go hiking with her human cousins because she thought they did not like her.

The next morning after the Doctor's recommended genetic treatment, Torres visits the holodeck and projects a computer-generated image of her daughter when she will be twelve years old. Seeing the forehead ridges, Torres examines the child's genetic makeup, and deletes certain gene sequences in the computer display. Asking the computer to extrapolate the genetic changes to the projection, she eventually creates a girl that looks completely human.

Returning to sickbay, she tries to convince the Doctor to make further genetic changes in her baby, claiming it will prevent potential health problems. The Doctor is against the idea and suggests that she talk this over with Paris. Tom realizes the issue is not about the child's health, but the fact that she is part Klingon. They fail to come to an agreement, and Paris finds himself spending the night on Kim's couch.

The Doctor later tells them that he reviewed the data and has concluded the genetic alterations are necessary because the clash between Klingon and human metabolism is more extensive than he realized. The child risks complete metabolic failure, and to prevent it he must eliminate most of her Klingon genetic material. Concerned, Paris takes the findings to Icheb, who spots a computational error. Seven then runs a diagnostic on the Doctor and discovers that his program has been tampered with. Paris soon learns that Torres is in sickbay about to undergo the procedure, but manages to get past the defenses she has set up and convince the Doctor to stop.

In the heat of the moment, Torres reveals to Paris how she feels responsible for her father leaving her and her mother, and fears the same thing will happen again. Tom assures his wife that he will never leave her, and he hopes to have even more children and that every one of them is just like her. Later, Torres apologizes to the Doctor and asks him to be the child's godfather.

DELTA QUADRANT: Neelix refers to the Talaxian saying, *Omara s'alas,* which translates into "Good news has no clothes" (or good news travels fast).

ALPHA QUADRANT: Normally Klingon pregnancies run thirty weeks, but a mixed-species pregnancy could result in an earlier birth. The odds against Klingon/human pregnancies are high. Klingon traits remain dominant for several generations, even with a single ancestor. Torres wants to delete entire DNA sequences, such as the genes that create redundant organs. However, some geneticists believe the extra lung evolved to give Klingons greater stamina on the battlefield. ▪ According to Chell, Bolians believe that if you give birth near a warp core, it will improve the baby's disposition. ▪ Taya is the feminine form of the name Chakotay.

PERSONAL LOGS: Torres's developing child is seven weeks old. Both Torres and her mother had the same spinal deviation as the child now has. Torres's human grandmother loved her daughter-in-law, but warned her son against marrying a Klingon because she did not think he had the constitution for it. As a child, B'Elenna went camping with her father, her Uncle Carl, and her cousins Elizabeth, Dean, and Michael. Her father left her mother twelve days after the camping trip. ▪ The Doctor expands his database in obstetrics and pediatrics, developing a prenatal enrichment program for Torres. ▪ Seven is tutoring Icheb in warp mechanics.

CREW COMPLEMENT: Paris notes that the makeup of the *Voyager* comprises Bajorans, Vulcans, and a Talaxian, among other alien races. Torres, however, reminds him that there are 140 humans.

EPISODE LOGS: The baby will be born in the series finale, "Endgame." A future version of her will also be seen in that episode.

REPENTANCE

EPISODE #259

STORY BY: **MIKE SUSSMAN & ROBERT DOHERTY**

TELEPLAY BY: **ROBERT DOHERTY**

DIRECTED BY: **MIKE VEJAR**

GUEST STARS

IKO	JEFF KOBER
YEDIQ	TIM deZARN
JOLEG	F. J. RIO

CO-STAR

VOYAGER SECURITY OFFICER	GREGG POLAND

STARDATE UNKNOWN

Responding to a distress call, *Voyager* approaches a damaged alien vessel and transports Nygean guards and their prisoners to the ship. In sickbay, a prisoner named Iko takes Seven hostage, but she breaks free from his grasp and Tuvok stuns him. Meanwhile,

Iko throws a wrench into the justice system of the Nygean.
MICHAEL YARISH

Iko pleads his case to the victim's family. MICHAEL YARISH

Warden Yediq tells Janeway that the prisoners were being transported back to the Nygean home world for execution. Though the crew is uncomfortable helping deliver eight men to their deaths, Janeway agrees to keep them detained until a Nygean ship arrives. Tuvok then outfits the cargo bay with holding cells for the prisoners

Neelix arrives with a dinner that Yediq tells him to take away, but Neelix and Tuvok cite Federation protocols regarding the treatment of prisoners, forcing the warden to relent. Later, a prisoner named Joleg provokes Iko into causing a disturbance, and when Yediq checks on him, Iko threatens the warden's children. The Nygean guards enter Iko's cell and beat him severely, until *Voyager* security officers stop them. Afterward Janeway bans Yediq and his men from the cargo bay, placing Tuvok in charge of the prisoners.

Delivering another meal, Neelix begins to bond with Joleg, who tells him of the unfair treatment of his species, the Benkaran. Meanwhile, in sickbay the Doctor uses Seven's nanoprobes to heal Iko, who wakes much calmer. However, he complains to the Doctor that he is suffering from nausea and cannot stop thinking about the man he killed. Seven believes his discomfort is a manifestation of guilt, something he has never felt before.

In another conversation with Joleg, Neelix is appalled to learn more about the barbaric Nygean legal system. He wants to help Joleg, but the prisoner refuses to do anything that would imply his guilt. Instead he asks Neelix simply to transmit a letter to his brother. Meanwhile, the Doctor determines that Iko was born with a congenital brain defect making him prone to violence and the nanoprobes have inadvertently repaired it. Believing Iko is no longer a threat, the Doctor and Seven note that by some definitions he is not the same man who committed the murder. They tell a skeptical Yediq that Iko has undergone a fundamental change, and persuade him to help submit an appeal on behalf of Iko, but it is ultimately rejected.

The ship is jolted by alien fire, causing a power loss in the cargo bay. Joleg and the other inmates, except Iko, overpower the guards and escape. The alien vessel tries to beam over the Benkaran prisoners, but *Voyager* forces the vessel to retreat. Joleg takes Yediq hostage and demands a shuttle, but Iko rescues the warden. Yediq subsequently uses his influence to convince the family of Iko's victim to hear his appeal. Meanwhile Neelix tells Joleg that he found out the "note" sent to his brother was really meant to help him track down *Voyager*.

While Iko and Seven look at constellations in astrometrics, Janeway arrives and informs them that the family has denied Iko's appeal. After he leaves, Seven feels remorseful for her own prior acts of murder that went unpunished, but Janeway reminds her that the twenty years of her life lost to the Borg were punishment enough.

SENSOR READINGS: The makeshift holding cells are in Cargo Bay 1. Tritanium bulkheads are used in the construction of the cells. The design of the forcefields allows for a small temporary opening in the center through which food can be handed to the prisoners.

DAMAGE REPORT: The ship loses power on Decks 8 through 10, and transporters are taken offline.

DELTA QUADRANT: Warden Yediq is a member of the Nygean Detention Force. After a suspect is convicted of his crime, the family of the victim sentences the prisoner in what the Ancient Nygean language refers to as "*Vekto valek k'vadim,*" meaning, "Favor the victims." Some people prefer restitution to revenge, and if a defendant is wealthy enough, he can negotiate a settlement with the victim's family. In accordance with the Nygean Penal Code, a capital defendant has a right to appeal his sentence to the family of his victims. • Iko receives a blow to the head that causes severe edema in his parietal lobe, blocking vital neurotransmitters. The Doctor programs some of Seven's nanoprobes to bypass the edema, and the neurotransmitters establish new pathways throughout his cortex. In a scan depicting a healthy Nygean brain, the Doctor finds a node analogous to the human pineal gland, which, in addition to controlling behavioral impulses, also regulates decision-making. Normally, the node connects to the rest of the brain through a series of neural pathways; however, Iko seems to have been born with it detached making him prone to violence and sociopathic behavior all his life. • Joleg notes that it is common belief that all Benkarans are criminal. The Nygeans govern a sector of space occupied by several different humanoid species. Of those species, only ten percent of the aliens are Benkarans, yet they take up nearly eighty percent of the Nygean prisons. He also says that Benkarans are ten times more likely to be executed for their crimes than Nygeans.

PERSONAL LOGS: Phaser fire causes a feedback surge in the Doctor's emitters. • In her life, Seven has catalogued approximately six billion stars.

PROPHECY

EPISODE #260

TELEPLAY BY: MIKE SUSSMAN & PHYLLIS STRONG

STORY BY: LARRY NEMECEK & J. KELLY BURKE and

RAF GREEN & KENNETH BILLER

DIRECTED BY: TERRY WINDELL

GUEST STARS

T'GRETH	SHERMAN HOWARD
MORAK	PAUL ECKSTEIN
KOHLAR	WREN T. BROWN

CO-STARS

CH'REGA	PEGGY JO JACOBS
COMPUTER VOICE	MAJEL BARRETT

STARDATE 54518.2

The surprised crew comes under attack from an antiquated Klingon vessel. They easily subdue the ship, although the captain, Kohlar, declares he will not surrender to sworn enemies of the Klingon Empire. Janeway tells him the Klingons and the Federation signed a peace treaty more than eighty years ago, but when he refuses to believe her she offers to introduce him to her Klingon chief engineer.

Upon meeting Torres and noting her pregnancy, Kohlar immediately returns to his ship and tells his people that the prophecies have come true, and the "Day of Separation" has arrived. Soon after, the Klingon ship has a warp core breach, and its crew is transported to *Voyager,* where Kohlar admits he set the ship to self-destruct to get his crew aboard. He explains that they are on a journey to find their savior, whom he believes to be Torres's unborn child. When a fight breaks out, Kim puts a stop to it, attracting the attention of a large, lustful Klingon woman.

Eventually Torres agrees to meet with their Council of Elders, where a skeptical T'Greth refuses to believe the child to be their savior. Later, Kohlar tells Torres that whether or not her baby is the true prophet, they must convince his people that she is, since after over a hundred years, they have found nothing but hardship and isolation. He sees Torres and her child as an opportunity to end the wasteful journey and lead them to a new home.

Though reluctant to deceive the Klingons, Torres studies their scrolls which Kohlar interprets in a way that appears consistent with the events of her life. Torres stands before the Klingon council telling a spirited story of a heroic encounter, while *Voyager* sets course for a planet very much like the Klingon home world. When

Torres reluctantly takes part in the ceremony to prove her daughter is a Klingon savior. RON TOM

Paris defends his wife against T'Greth, the Klingon decides to test his role in the prophecy by challenging the husband to a death match. Janeway, however, insists that blunted *bat'leths* be used, so no one will be killed. Meanwhile Kim tries to avoid Ch'Rega, the Klingon woman who now wants to mate with him. Neelix offers to distract Ch'Rega, he then treats Kim with Klingon-style harshness. She then falls for the Talaxian.

As the match commences, T'Greth collapses from the *nehret,* a fatal disease all the Klingons aboard the vessel carried and have inadvertently passed to Torres and her unborn child. T'Greth approaches his comrades, declaring that since the child has the disease, she cannot be their savior and they must resume their search by seizing control of *Voyager.* Arriving at the planet intended to serve as the Klingons' new home, T'Greth and his supporters take over the transporter room and beam most of the *Voyager* crew members to the surface. Unable to transport the senior staff, the Klingons beam themselves to the bridge, where their plan is foiled by the *Voyager* crew.

Injured in the recapture, T'Greth wakes up in sickbay and is informed that his illness has been cured using an antivirus from the hybrid stem cells of Torres's unborn baby. T'Greth realizes the child has cured him, and Kohlar declares that she is truly their savior. The Klingons settle on their new home, and Torres accepts a *bat'leth* from Kohlar, given to him by his great-grandfather, as a gift for the baby.

ALPHA QUADRANT: Tetryon readings indicate the Klingon ship is a D-7, which were retired decades ago. Because the technology is so old, *Voyager* is able to use a metaphasic scan to penetrate their cloak. ■ More than a hundred years ago, Kohlar's great-grandfather was part of a sect that believed the Empire had lost its way. They discovered a sacred text that told them to embark on a journey to a distant region of the galaxy. There were two hundred and two Klingons on their vessel. They have been traveling for four generations, but his people have always known the voyage would be long and difficult. The Scrolls said they would be rewarded by finding the *kuvah'magh,* or "the savior of our people." She would be the one to lead them to a new Empire and they are instructed to follow her wherever she goes. The secret text told them to "cast off the old ways" as soon as they found this *kuvah'magh.* Kohlar claims that The Holy

Kim is reluctant to accept Ch'Rega's advances. RON TOM

an off-worlder, and Torres was born on a Federation colony and has also lived a life of solitude and endured many hardships. She is also supposed to have won a glorious victory against an army of ten thousand warriors, (they consider her encounters with the Borg to meet that requirement). ▪ When T'Greth challenges Paris and Janeway refuses to allow a lethal combat, Kohlar notes that there is precedent for an honorable compromise of nonlethal bout, fought with blunted *bat'leths*. The victory goes to the first warrior to knock his opponent to the ground three times. Though T'Greth calls that a coward's rule, Kohlar points out that Emperor Mur'Eq was the one who instituted these rules to ensure that his warriors would kill their enemies and not each other. ▪ The *nehret* is a retrovirus that destroys the cells by attacking the cytoplasmic membranes. The transporter bio-filters did not detect it because it lies dormant, disguising itself as inert genetic material, until it inexplicably activates. The scrolls say, "The *kuvah'magh* is younger than old age and stronger than sickness." The fetus has hybrid stem cells containing Klingon and human DNA that is used to synthesize an antivirus.

PERSONAL LOGS: Torres takes part in the midday ritual "Plea for the Dead" for the first time since she was a child. During that time, Klingons remember the sacrifice of their ancestors because the dead cannot rest in *Sto-Vo-Kor* if the living do not honor their memory. As a child during the ritual she pled to her grandmother, L'Naan, daughter of Krelik. ▪ The Doctor gives Kim written permission to mate with a member of another species mentioning that he will need the captain's permission as well (not that he wants it).

EPISODE LOGS: The treaty signed by the Klingon Empire and the Federation more than eighty years ago follows the events of the film *Star Trek VI: The Undiscovered Country*. ▪ Larry Nemecek, author of the *Star Trek: The Next Generation Companion* contributed to the story for this episode. ▪ The concept of having to receive permission to mate with an alien species was introduced in "The Disease."

Month of *nay'Poq* was around fourteen or fifteen weeks ago, which coincides with Torres's conception. The scrolls say, "You will find me after two warring houses make peace," which he takes as referring to the treaty between the Klingons and the Federation. Another line reads, "You will know me before I know the world," citing that since the child is unborn, she does not know the world. The scrolls also say the *kuvah'magh* will be descended from a noble house; however, neither Torres nor Paris comes from nobility. Kohlar responds by saying they all have nobility in their blood, if they go back far enough. It is also written that the mother of the *kuvah'magh* would be

THE VOID

EPISODE #261
TELEPLAY BY: **RAF GREEN & JAMES KAHN**
STORY BY: **RAF GREEN & KENNETH BILLER**
DIRECTED BY: **MIKE VEJAR**

GUEST STARS

VALEN	**ROBIN SACHS**
LOQUAR	**PAUL WILLSON**
GARON	**SCOTT LAWRENCE**
FANTOME	**JONATHAN del ARCO**

CO-STAR

BOSAAL	**MICHAEL SHAMUS WILES**

STARDATE 54553.4

A graviton surge pulls *Voyager* into a realm of complete blackness, where an alien ship fires on them. As *Voyager* returns fire, a second ship joins in the fray, penetrating *Voyager's* shields and transporting numerous supplies from the ship. Then a third ship approaches, and an Annarian named Valen welcomes Captain Janeway to "the Void." Valen tells Janeway that he has been in the Void for five years, and has never known anyone to escape. In order to survive, the trapped ships compete for resources from new ships that are drawn in. Torres reports that the anomaly is draining the warp core, and they will run out of power in ten days. While they still have power the crew implements their own escape plan, but it fails and results in the warp core going offline.

The crew finds the ship that stole their material after it has been raided. Since the derelict ship's warp core casing can be converted into a power source they beam it over and find a small, mute alien inside. The crew discovers that Valen raided the lifeless ship and now has *Voyager's* supplies. However, he refuses to return the items and a firefight ensues. *Voyager* manages to transport back about half of their stolen resources. Later, Tuvok and Chakotay approach Janeway, suggesting that the crew may need to be more opportunistic in order to survive in the Void. But the captain prefers to use the Federation model of mutual cooperation, and she proposes forming an alliance with other ships to pool resources and devise a way to escape.

Janeway brings the different factions together in the Void. RON TOM

Bosaal agrees to join Janeway only after she agrees to rid his ship of the "vermin." RON TOM

At first Janeway fails to convince any ships to join her, although some do agree to consider the offer. Meanwhile, the Doctor realizes the silent life-form that is being held in his sickbay loves music. He names him "Fantome" after a character in *The Phantom of the Opera.* This leads Seven to attempt to communicate with the alien using computer-generated tones, and Fantome responds enthusiastically.

When another ship is pulled into the Void, *Voyager* defends the newcomer. The starship is joined by one of the prospective allies, Garon, who forces the raiding vessels to retreat. With Garon on board, finding new allies becomes easier. Janeway hosts a visit by Commander Bosaal—one of the captains trapped in the Void, but he reacts adversely upon seeing Fantome in the mess hall, because he considers the species to be "vermin." Janeway tells Bosaal that they can transport Fantome's people—who have "infested" Bosaal's vessel—to her ship and he agrees to the alliance.

Torres works with Garon to build a polaron modula-

tor that will help the alliance ships escape the Void. Meanwhile, Fantome joins others of his kind in learning how to communicate through tones, creating a musical conversation. Later, Janeway learns that Bosaal is offering a polaron modulator that was stolen from a crew he murdered. She orders him off the ship along with the modulator. As a result, Torres has to continue building a modulator from scratch and other ships drop out of the alliance.

One of the remaining allies spies on Bosaal and discovers that he is attempting to form an alliance of his own with Valen and others to attack *Voyager.* Janeway realizes they need to escape right away, even though Torres has not had time to test her new modulator. When a funnel into the Void is detected, the alliance ships prepare to go in. Under attack by Bosaal's forces, *Voyager* penetrates shields on two of the ships and transports Fantome and his friends back onto the ships. Seconds later the enemy vessels have been disabled by their new stowaways, giving the alliance ships time to escape the Void.

SENSOR READINGS: When the ship is pulled in by the graviton surge, they reroute all available power to the thrusters, but cannot break free. Reversing the shield polarity is also ineffective. ▪ In the initial raid the thieves take more than ninety percent of *Voyager's* food stores, including almost everything in the airponics bay. They also got a computer console from engineering, and emptied three deuterium tanks. The crew gets back half of what was stolen, though it is unclear what exactly is returned. ▪ Janeway initially orders all nonessential systems shut down to conserve energy. ▪ One of the crews that join the alliance has technology that triples *Voyager's* replicator efficiency. They can feed five hundred people a day now, using half the power it took before the new technology was added.

DAMAGE REPORT: Navigational sensors malfunction due to an unknown force within the environment of the Void. ▪ In their first escape attempt, structural integrity drops to twenty percent and the warp core goes offline. There are hull breaches on Decks 5 and 6.

DELTA QUADRANT: Within the Void, sensors do not detect any gases, stellar bodies, or matter of any kind. The anomaly is a closed structure, encased by an inert layer of subspace. Matter and energy cannot penetrate it. There are more than 150 ships within scanning range, but lifesigns are detected on only twenty-nine of them. The outer circumference of the Void has been calculated at approximately nine light years. ▪ The funnels pulling ships into the Void originate inside the anomaly, creating massive graviton forces before they erupt. The original plan is to enter one of the funnels just as that happens and use those forces to propel the ship into normal space. Since that would compromise structural integrity they need to reinforce *Voyager*'s shields to compensate. When the graviton forces reach critical levels, the polarity suddenly reverses, pulling everything near the funnel back into the anomaly, which would force the ship to jump to warp at exactly the right moment. The later plan has them establishing a shield bubble large enough to encompass all the ships. Since they have no way to compensate for the graviton stress they need to construct a polaron modulator, which is described as a valuable and uncommon piece of technology.

The weapons signature of the first raiding ships is Vaadwaur, but the ship has technology from several different species. ▪ The casing on the warp core *Voyager* seizes from the derelict ship is composed of tricesium, which can be converted it into a power source. ▪ Scans of Fantome show that he can conserve oxygen, since he has an unusually large lung capacity, as well as a voracious appetite. He is quite intelligent, and his physiology is very sophisticated with the ability to refract his own life-signs. He and his race are native to the Void.

PERSONAL LOGS: Seven of Nine takes up cooking. In working out trades, Janeway gives away Seven's favorite phase compensator.

EPISODE LOGS: Of the races mentioned in this episode, *Voyager* previously encountered the Vaadwaur in "Dragon's Teeth," the Nygeans in "Repentance," and the Annari in "Nightingale."

WORKFORCE, PART I
EPISODE #262
WRITTEN BY: KENNETH BILLER & BRYAN FULLER
DIRECTED BY: ALLAN KROEKER

GUEST STARS

JAFFEN	JAMES READ
KADAN	DON MOST
QUARREN AMBASSADOR	JOHN ANISTON

CO-STARS

UMALI	IONA MORRIS
SUPERVISOR	TOM VIRTUE
COYOTE	MICHAEL BEHRENS
SECURITY OFFICER #2	MATT WILLIAMSON
MED TECH	AKEMI ROYER
SECURITY OFFICER #1	ROBERT MAMMANA
COMPUTER VOICE	MAJEL BARRETT

STARDATE 54584.3

In a vast alien metropolis, Janeway enters a power distribution plant, reporting to her new job on a multispecies workforce. Although she does recall some inconsequential portions of her identity, she has no recollection of her previous life as captain of *Voyager,* and as a result gladly welcomes the employment. A worker named Jaffen tries to befriend her but they are chastised for fraternizing by Seven of Nine, who only knows herself as Annika Hansen, the new efficiency monitor at the plant.

That night Jaffen is in a tavern where Paris works, telling an anecdote to some friends that elicits an uproarious laugh from Tuvok. When Torres, a single mother-to-be, enters the bar it appears that most of the *Voyager* crew has found work on this alien planet, although none of them realize that they have forgotten everything about their ship and their lives. Janeway also comes in to dine. Jaffen joins her and ends up walking her home.

The next day, Janeway learns that all the workers must periodically receive inoculations to protect them against radiation. As a squeamish Tuvok gets injected, he flashes back to a memory of himself in Starfleet uniform, struggling against a Quarren doctor performing a similar procedure.

Returning from an away mission, Chakotay, Neelix, and Kim find *Voyager* disabled inside a nebula instead of at the rendezvous point. The Doctor is the only remaining crew member onboard and he explains that the ship hit a subspace mine that deluged it with poisonous tetry-

Janeway and Jaffen form a fast bond. RON TOM

on radiation. Captain Janeway ordered the crew into escape pods, leaving the Doctor in charge as the Emergency Command Hologram. The Doctor then had to fend off scavengers trying to claim the abandoned vessel. He hid the ship inside the nebula.

Voyager tracks the crew to Quarra, where Chakotay speaks with an ambassador who will not allow him to communicate with his crewmates. Neelix learns there is a severe labor shortage in the system, so Chakotay suggests they apply for jobs themselves, in order to infiltrate the plant where their people are working. The Doctor alters Chakotay's features before he and Neelix go to the planet and equips them with subdermal transponders that will allow them to transport through the shield grid.

At the power plant, Annika Hansen orders Tuvok to get the inoculations that he has been neglecting. Tuvok calls her Seven of Nine and tries to mind-meld with her to make her remember herself, but security guards grab him and takes the desperate Vulcan away.

Chakotay secures a job at the plant and immediately approaches Janeway, who does not recognize him. Neelix, in the meantime, runs into Paris at the tavern, but finds himself equally unable to jar his friend's memory. Although Paris does not recall his life on *Voyager,* he still exhibits feelings for Torres, and is concerned when she leaves the bar alone. After Chakotay meets up with Neelix, they follow Torres through the streets and grab her. Meanwhile Jaffen and Janeway are growing closer and agree to move in together.

Kim beams Neelix and the struggling Torres up to sickbay, where the Doctor tries to help her. Chakotay is

pursued by security guards, and Kim cannot beam him up because the ship has fallen under attack. The guards chase Chakotay through the facility up to a precipice overlooking the massive city, and he finds himself trapped.

SENSOR READINGS: Kim, Neelix, and Chakotay were on a five-day trade mission with the Nar Shaddan. The shuttle's cargo hold is crammed with valuable supplies.

DAMAGE REPORT: There is much damage to the ship as a result of the mine's impact. The main computer begins to fail but the Doctor switches to backup processors. Life support is offline and there are ruptured plasma conduits on Deck 10. Later, power to the secondary propulsion systems is restored and the Doctor repairs the deuterium injectors.

SHUTTLE TRACKER: To avoid detection, Chakotay and Neelix take the Talaxian's ship which is still stored in the shuttlebay. ▪ The escape pods are ejected by the fleeing crew. It is unclear when they are retrieved.

An undercover Chakotay and Neelix investigate what has happened to their crew. MICHAEL YARISH

DELTA QUADRANT: Janeway is given the task of monitoring the primary reactor coils that process more than 8,000 metric tons of tylium per second at 94 percent thermal-efficiency. The city in which the plant is located has a curfew for all workers. ▪ Jaffen is a member of the Norvalian race, a species that does not have fathers. ▪ Neelix suggests *leola* bark tea, to settle even the queasiest of stomachs.

PERSONAL LOGS: Janeway activates the Emergency Command Hologram using authorization Janeway Omega 3.

MEDICAL UPDATE: Kim gets sick from drinking Falah nectar, which the Nar Shaddan consider a delicacy and to refuse would have insulted them. The nectar is made from a meat by-product, which Chakotay could not drink because he is vegetarian. ▪ When *Voyager* hit the subspace mine, the Doctor was inundated with casualties suffering from tetryon radiation poisoning.

Janeway seems happy to be free of her responsibility as captain.
VIVIAN ZINK

WORKFORCE, PART II

EPISODE #263

TELEPLAY BY: KENNETH BILLER & MICHAEL TAYLOR

STORY BY: KENNETH BILLER & BRYAN FULLER

DIRECTED BY: ROXANN DAWSON

GUEST STARS

JAFFEN	JAMES READ
KADAN	DON MOST
QUARREN AMBASSADOR	JOHN ANISTON
SUPERVISOR	TOM VIRTUE
and	
YERID	ROBERT JOY

CO-STARS

RAYVOC	JAY HARRINGTON
COYOTE	MICHAEL BEHRENS
SECURITY OFFICER #3	JOSEPH WILL
SECURITY OFFICER #2	MATT WILLIAMSON
ALIEN SURGEON	DAMARA REILLY
NARRATOR	MAJEL BARRETT

STARDATE 54622.4

Pursued by security, Chakotay is shot in the arm before he evades them. Meanwhile, *Voyager* comes under attack by Quarren patrol ships and is forced to flee. In the Quarren hospital, Dr. Kadan orders Dr. Ravoc to do a memory sequencing treatment on Tuvok. At the same time, Seven of Nine—who still believes herself to be Annika Hansen—grows suspicious of recent events and meets Investigator Yerid, who is looking into the disappearances of Torres and Neelix.

Janeway finds Chakotay hiding in her old apartment. He tells her that he is trying to help numerous people brought to the planet against their will. *Voyager*, meanwhile, has hidden in a moon's crater to make repairs and to treat Torres for her altered memory. At the plant, Annika/Seven catches Janeway taking a dermal regenerator to use on Chakotay, but Annika is sidetracked when she has an opportunity to enter the supervisor's office. There she learns that Tuvok had accessed numerous employee files, including her own. Janeway returns to Chakotay, who is contacted by *Voyager* and told that they need the planet's shield grid disabled so they can transport the crew members back. Chakotay informs Janeway that she is the captain of that ship, but she has a hard time believing him. He then takes the dermal regenerator and undoes the alterations made to his face, revealing that they are of the same race.

Janeway tells Jaffen the story, but he thinks Chakotay

Ravoc helps Annika escape. MICHAEL YARISH

is trying to manipulate her with promises of a better life. Chakotay is found by Yerid and taken in for questioning. At the same time, Dr. Ravoc enters with orders to transfer Chakotay to neuropathology to be treated for mental illness. As he is taken away, Chakotay tells Yerid the truth about himself and his abducted crewmates. Then, under Kadan's mind controls, Chakotay lures *Voyager* into a trap.

Annika/Seven meets discreetly with Yerid to discuss her findings, and then goes to the hospital, reporting that she too has been having disturbing thoughts. She takes the opportunity to use Ravoc's computer while Yerid contacts Janeway and asks to know everything Chakotay told her. Kadan is enraged when he discovers that Ravoc allowed Annika/Seven to access restricted files. However, Ravoc is suspicious of an apparent outbreak of a disease known as Dysphoria Syndrome that occurred under Kadan's watch. He realizes the illness was used as a cover story to explain the procedures performed on the *Voyager* crew to make them forget their past lives. Based on his hypothesis, Ravoc threatens to report Kaden for subjugating unwilling aliens.

Paris harbors Seven, Janeway, Jaffen, and Yerid at the tavern, while they try to prove Chakotay's story. Janeway and Jaffen go to the power plant to use a subspace transponder to contact *Voyager*, while Seven and Yerid return to the hospital to help Chakotay and Tuvok. Janeway succeeds in hailing *Voyager*, where she recognizes Torres as one of her coworkers. But now Torres is in uniform and referring to her as the captain. As *Voyager* comes under attack by three ships, Janeway is surrounded by security guards, but Jaffen helps her evade them and gets the computer to shut down main power. Seven and Yerid force Kadan to release Chakotay and Tuvok from the mind control devices.

The crew is rescued and treated, while Yerid and the Quarren ambassador promise to undo the conspiracy that was headed by Kaden and the facility supervisor, promising that all of the "patients" will be treated and repatriated. Janeway says a final good-bye to Jaffen, then resumes her role as captain and heads *Voyager* for home once more.

SENSOR READINGS: Kim and the Doctor use a triaxilating frequency on a covariant subspace band to communicate with Chakotay eight light-years away ▪ Transporters are malfunctioning.

SHUTTLE TRACKER: Five escape pods remained on the ship after the crew evacuated. Kim ejects three additional pods armed with explosives.

DELTA QUADRANT: The Doctor hides *Voyager* behind a moon which has a paramagnetic core that masks its energy signature. ▪ The Quarren ambassador says they have identified several thousand of Kadan's unwilling patients, however, Jaffen was not one of them.

PERSONAL LOGS: Pancakes with maple syrup are Torres's favorite breakfast. ▪ Included in the tactical database of the Emergency Command Hologram is the events of the Battle of Vorkado, where a Romulan captain disabled two attacking vessels by creating a photonic shockwave between the ships.

MEDICAL UPDATE: The Doctor finds that the memory centers of Torres's brain have been radically altered in a very sophisticated technique capable of selectively manipulating memory engrams through suppression and alteration, while leaving some intact. The same procedure was performed on the rest of the kidnapped crew.

EPISODE LOGS: The crew has been on the planet for three weeks.

Seven lets down her hair as she explores a different life on the holodeck. MICHAEL YARISH

HUMAN ERROR

EPISODE #264

TELEPLAY BY: BRANNON BRAGA & ANDRE BORMANIS

STORY BY: ANDRE BORMANIS & KENNETH BILLER

DIRECTED BY: ALLAN KROEKER

GUEST STARS

ICHEB	MANU INTIRAYMI

CO-STARS

COMPUTER VOICE	MAJEL BARRETT

STARDATE UNKNOWN

In a holodeck simulation Seven of Nine practices the piano with her hair down and her Borg implants gone. Later, she attends a simulation of Torres's baby shower, where she interacts with holographic crew members more freely than she would the actual crew. When the bridge crew detects mysterious energy discharges, Seven goes to astrometrics, where she is unable to find the source of the discharges.

Seven returns to the holodeck, where she invites a holographic Chakotay to her new quarters the following night for dinner. Later, during her weekly physical, the Doctor notices that her shoulder implant is out of alignment and her electrolyte levels are down because she missed her regeneration cycle. *Voyager* is abruptly rocked by another energy discharge that produces a shockwave, damaging the warp drive.

In astrometrics, Seven discovers the explosion came from a subspace warhead that destroyed an unmanned probe. With warp drive offline, Janeway asks Seven to find a way to detect the warheads before they emerge from subspace, to give the crew a few seconds' warning. Seven returns to the holodeck for her date where she and the holographic Chakotay prepare dinner together. The romantic mood leads to a kiss and a fritzing noise that Seven ignores as she embraces her new simulated boyfriend.

The holographic Chakotay teaches Seven to play from her heart. MICHAEL YARISH

The next morning she wakes beside the holographic Chakotay only to be summoned by his real-life counterpart. She arrives in astrometrics, where Icheb has picked up a warning beacon that reveals that *Voyager* has entered a munitions testing ground. Chakotay is concerned about the fact that Seven was late for her duty shift, but she denies being distracted. However, her mind continues to drift back to her holographic life, and soon she returns to the simulation.

Three alien missiles emerge from subspace and destroy a target probe, sending out shockwaves that rock *Voyager*. When Chakotay contacts Seven asking for her report on the situation, he is surprised to find that she is not at her post. Immediately realizing her mistake, Seven rushes to astrometrics where she is able to reorient the ship to withstand the next shockwave. After Janeway speaks with her about neglecting her duties, Seven returns to the holodeck intending to end the simulation for good.

As she and the holographic Chakotay argue, the mysterious fritzing noise returns, and suddenly Seven collapses. The Doctor arrives and finds her going into neu-

ral shock because her cortical node had begun to shut down—the source of the peculiar noise she heard, but he manages to stabilize it. Seven tells him about the simulations and says that she plans to delete her programs because her personal life has distracted her from performing her duties efficiently.

Torres succeeds in getting engines back online, and *Voyager* jumps to warp, when a subspace warhead locks onto the warp signature and targets the ship. Seven believes she can extract the detonator by transporting it out, but only at very close range. With no time to spare, she accomplishes the transport and the missile breaks apart harmlessly.

Later, the Doctor approaches Seven with the news that her cortical node did not malfunction, but in fact was designed to shut down her higher brain functions when she achieves a certain level of emotional stimulation. The Doctor believes he can reconfigure the node so she can continue her simulations, but it would be a difficult and lengthy process. Seven declines the procedure, saying that she has experienced enough humanity for the time being.

SENSOR READINGS: A full spread of torpedoes is fired at the warhead, but it neutralizes them. ▪ Long-range sensors pick up an intermittent energy discharge, but Seven cannot find the cause because the region contains unusual amounts of subspace radiation and metallic debris. A later discharge results in a level-9 shockwave. The debris in this region suggests that dozens of subspace warheads have been fired in the past few weeks. Subspace radiation from the explosions makes it difficult to create a stable warp field. The weapons create minor gravimetric distortions as they approach the subspace barrier.

DAMAGE REPORT: The shock waves cause the warp field to destabilize, which results in the loss of warp drive. There is a hull fracture on Deck 12.

DELTA QUADRANT: The warning beacons announce: "You have entered Subspace Munitions Range 434. Evacuate immediately." The weapon is armed with proximity resonance circuitry with an activation frequency of 4.84 gigahertz. Torres tries to disarm it with an antiresonance pulse but the warhead rotates its activation frequency. Seven uses a transporter to beam the detonator off the warhead. Since the device is so small she uses the submicron imager to focus targeting scanners. The detonator is protected by tritanium shielding forcing Seven to wait for the weapon to get closer for transport.

ALPHA QUADRANT: A *pleenok* is a toy that Vulcans use to train infants in primary logic. ▪ The lyrics to an updated Earth lullaby go as follows: "Rock-a-bye baby, in the space dock. When the core blows, the shuttle will rock. When the hull breaks, the shuttle will fall. And down will come baby, shuttle and all."

PERSONAL LOGS: A real baby shower is thrown for Torres, in addition to the holographic one Seven attends. ▪ According to a holographic Neelix, Kim has wood carvings decorating his quarter. ▪ The Doctor's gift to Torres at her baby shower is a recording of him singing twenty-nine lullabies, including a couple of Klingon songs. His favorite is *"quong vaj Ocht,"* which translates to "Sleep, Little Warrior." ▪ Seven has never been in Kim's quarters. She has been familiarizing herself with Chakotay's Native American culture. At dinner, she serves the holographic Chakotay rack of lamb, although the real Chakotay is vegetarian. The Doctor has been teaching her to play the piano. She spends forty-nine hours on the holodeck in six days. After missing Torres's real shower, Seven gives her a gift of baby booties lined with bio-thermal insulation that will protect the baby's feet even if the external

temperature drops below -40 degrees Celsius. The destruction of Unimatrix Zero served as the catalyst for Seven to decide to explore her personal feelings. She has been trying to re-create some of the emotional experiences she had while in the virtual construct because her life has felt incomplete. ▪ Neelix is giving a cooking lesson in the mess hall entitled "Talaxian Tenderloin in Ten Minutes."

Icheb has been studying Earth literature as a part of his Starfleet Academy training.

Q2

EPISODE #265
TELEPLAY BY: ROBERT DOHERTY
STORY BY: KENNETH BILLER
DIRECTED BY: LeVAR BURTON

GUEST STARS

Q2	KEEGAN DE LANCIE
ICHEB	MANU INTIRAYMI
ALIEN COMMANDER	MICHAEL KAGAN
Q JUDGE	LORNA RAVER

SPECIAL GUEST STAR

Q	JOHN DE LANCIE

CO-STARS

NAUSICAAN	ANTHONY HOLIDAY
BOLIAN	SCOTT DAVIDSON
COMPUTER VOICE	MAJEL BARRETT

STARDATE 54704.5

Janeway is caught by surprise when Q and his now adolescent son pop up on the ship. Q leaves his son behind on what he calls a "vacation," and the boy quickly proves to be a handful, as bored and out of control as any humaniod teenager, but with nearly omnipotent powers. After returning to correct the havoc his son caused, Q admits to Janeway that he does not know how to handle the boy who was conceived to inspire peace and compassion, but instead has brought chaos to the universe.

The Continuum has threatened Q telling him he must straighten the teen out. Q explains that his plan was to pawn his problem off on Janeway, so her so-called Starfleet ideals would rub off on his son. Sadly amused, she explains that the boy needs proper parent-

Janeway has a difficult time understanding Q's parenting methods.
RON TOM

ing to make him understand that there are consequences to his actions. As a result, Q threatens his son with spending an eternity as an Oprelian amoeba unless he becomes an upstanding citizen of the cosmos. He gives his son a week to change his ways, and strips him of his powers.

Janeway devises a strict curriculum for him with various instructors, but he cheats his way through his lessons. Finally Q2 admits to the captain that it is not easy to live up to his father's expectations, and that she is his only hope. Janeway agrees to give him one more chance.

The young Q seems determined to improve himself, and Janeway rewards him by allowing him to go with Icheb on a piloting lesson, since the two boys have become friends. Meanwhile, Q returns to *Voyager* to check up on his son's progress, but is not at all impressed, telling Janeway that the boy needs to demonstrate nothing less than exemplary Q-ness. Janeway tells the young Q that if the Continuum won't take him back, she will ask to let him stay on *Voyager* as a human. But he admits that he wants to be a Q, like his father.

Later, Q2 launches the *Flyer* without permission, tak-

The young Q at last feels remorse for his actions. RON TOM

ing Icheb through a spatial flexure to another system where they meet a Chokuzan ship, whose commander demands their surrender. The young Q fires on the ship and tries to escape, but the Chokuzans fire back, and a bolt of energy knocks Icheb unconscious. Q2 returns to *Voyager*, but the Doctor cannot treat Icheb unless he knows more about the weapon. Q appears and refuses to save Icheb's life, telling his son he has to face the consequences of his actions.

The young Q accompanies Janeway to the Chokuzan ship that he attacked and apologizes. When the commander threatens to hold Janeway accountable for the boy's actions, Q2 objects, insisting on accepting punishment himself. The Chokuzan commander reveals himself to be Q in disguise, administering a test that his son has passed with flying colors. After Q assures Janeway that Icheb will make a miraculous recovery, the two Qs and Janeway appear before a tribunal of Q judges.

The judges, however, rule that the young Q has not made sufficient progress and must remain human. Returning to *Voyager*, he asks if he can stay and continue his training, but his father appears and explains that he forced the judges to reverse their decision. Q2's powers have been restored, and he leaves *Voyager* on Q's promise to be a better father. In thanks, Q gives Janeway data on a shortcut home, but he refuses to take *Voyager* all the way because it would set a bad example for his son.

SENSOR READINGS: Q2 traps Janeway's crew in a temporal loop so they keep reliving the same thirty seconds over and over again though the effects go unseen.

DAMAGE REPORT: Under attack by the Borg, a nacelle is hit and vents warp plasma before they lose thrusters. Q2 takes weapons offline and lowers shields; however, his father repairs the damage.

ALPHA QUADRANT: During Icheb's incredibly long presentation of his report on Captain Kirk he states the following: "Though it was a blatant violation of the Prime Directive, Kirk saved the Pelosians from extinction, just as he had the Baezians and the Chenari many years earlier. Finally, in the year two thousand two hundred and seventy, Kirk completed his historic five-year mission, and one of the greatest chapters in Starfleet history came to a close . . . A new chapter began when Kirk regained command of the *Enterprise*."

PERSONAL LOGS: Janeway gives Icheb a passing grade in Early Starfleet History.

MEDICAL UPDATE: Neelix's jaw is fused and his vocal cords removed by Q2. The Doctor is able to undo some of the cosmetic damage but Q had to repair the rest. ■ Icheb's cells are being necrotized by some form of omicron radiation. Again, Q repairs the damage.

EPISODE LOGS: Q2 is played by Keegan de Lancie, the real life son of John de Lancie, Q.

AUTHOR, AUTHOR

EPISODE #266

TELEPLAY BY: PHYLLIS STRONG & MIKE SUSSMAN
STORY BY: BRANNON BRAGA
DIRECTED BY: DAVID LIVINGSTON

GUEST STARS

ADMIRAL PARIS	RICHARD HERD
BROHT	BARRY GORDON
ARBITRATOR	JOSEPH CAMPANELLA
IRENE HANSEN	LORINNE VOZOFF
JOHN TORRES	JUAN GARCIA
JOHN KIM	ROBERT ITO
MARY KIM	IRENE TSU

SPECIAL GUEST STAR

BARCLAY	DWIGHT SCHULTZ

CO-STARS

MALE N.D.	BROCK BURNETT
FEMALE N.D.	JENNIFER HAMMON
SICKBAY N.D.	HEATHER YOUNG
COMPUTER VOICE	MAJEL BARRETT

STARDATE 54732.3

Through the work of the Pathfinder Project, *Voyager* is finally able to maintain direct live contact with the Alpha Quadrant, if only for eleven minutes a day. Drawing the first time slot, the Doctor contacts a publisher to discuss the holonovel he had previously transmitted. The publisher, Broht, raves about the piece, but the Doctor insists on making revisions before it is distributed. Paris then convinces the Doctor to let him experience the holonovel, entitled *Photons Be Free*.

Paris finds himself in the role of the EMH protagonist of the novel aboard the "*Starship Vortex*"; a thinly veiled facsimile of *Voyager*. The other characters in the holonovel resemble the real crew, altered only slightly in their

The Doctor pleads his case to the captain. MICHAEL YARISH

appearance and names. However, their behavior is quite different. When Paris, as the Doctor, decides to treat a critical patient ahead of a bridge officer, with less serious injuries, Captain Jenkins (Janeway) kills the dying crewman, so the bridge officer can be treated. Shocked at how the crew is portrayed, Paris tells Torres and Kim about it and they decide to try it out themselves.

One after the other Torres, Kim, and Neelix see themselves and other crew members portrayed in an unflattering light. Finally, Janeway experiences the final chapter of the holonovel, where the EMH is brutally decompiled by her counterpart. She immediately orders the Doctor to report to her ready room. Defending the piece, the Doctor claims it is a work of fiction intended to draw attention to the plight of the EMH Mark-1 in the Alpha Quadrant who have been condemned to menial tasks. Paris decides turnabout is fair play and when the Doctor returns to the holodeck, he finds his program altered with a holographic Paris narrating a story that shows the Doctor in an exaggerated and unflattering light.

Paris assures the Doctor that he kept the original story intact, but was trying to point out how the rest of the crew feels about the work. What bothers Paris most is the idea that the immature, self-indulgent character that bears his likeness is apparently what the Doctor really thinks of him. Seeing Paris's point, the Doctor contacts Broht to request more time to revise his work, and the publisher reluctantly agrees.

Meanwhile, other members of the crew get to talk to family members they have not seen in years. Kim's parents wonder when he is getting a promotion and offer to write Captain Janeway a letter, which Harry strongly discourages. Torres begrudgingly agrees to talk to her father, who expresses regret for their troubled past and hopes they can get to know each other again. Even Seven of Nine contacts her nearest living relative, an aunt on Earth who calls her Annika and speaks of her childhood.

Janeway receives an urgent message from Admiral Paris, informing her that the Doctor's inflammatory unmodified holonovel is being played in thousands of holosuites. The Doctor contacts Broht demanding a recall and a public apology, but Broht refuses, citing the Federation law that states holograms have no rights. A

The arbitrator listens as the publisher contends that the Doctor has no rights. MICHAEL YARISH

trial is set, where a Federation arbitrator hears arguments on the matter of the Doctor being an individual. After deliberating, the arbitrator announces he is not prepared to rule that the Doctor is a "person" under the law, but he is willing to extend the definition of "artist" to include the Doctor and since artists *do* have rights, he orders all copies of the holonovel recalled immediately.

Four months later, on an asteroid in the Alpha Quadrant numerous EMH Mark-1 are mining dilithium, as word spreads among the holograms that there is a very provocative new program in the hololab called *Photons Be Free.*

SENSOR READINGS: It has been three weeks since the crew received Starfleet's instructions in the last data-stream, and they are finally ready to begin "Operation Watson" at the opening of the episode. With the deflector in position they receive a phased tachyon beam with a tri-axilating signal encoded in it. Harry and Seven were the ones who suggested bouncing a tachyon beam off a quantum singularity, which allows the crew to speak with the Alpha Quadrant for about eleven minutes a day while the singularity remains in alignment.

DELTA QUADRANT: There is an old Talaxian expression that goes, "When the road before you splits in two, take the third path."

ALPHA QUADRANT: The Doctor speaks with Ardon Broht of Broht and Forrester, the publishers of the Dixon Hill series. Their most successful children's title is a program "written by Toby the *targ.*" ▪ The Doctor mentions that there is a long history of writers drawing attention to the plight of the oppressed noting that *The Vedek's Song,* for example, tells the story of the occupation of Bajor. ▪ Under strict interpretation of Starfleet law, holograms have no rights. However, Section 7-Gamma of the Twelfth Guarantee defines an "artist" as a "person who creates an original artistic work." The definition of "artist" is expanded to include the Doctor.

PERSONAL LOGS: In addition to the crew's family members seen, Janeway intends to call her mother, while Chakotay plans to contact his sister. ▪ Torres is twenty-three weeks pregnant and considering naming the baby after her mother, Miral. She had originally arranged to speak with her cousin. ▪ Kim is in command of the night

PHOTONS BE FREE

"In the beginning, there is darkness . . . the emptiness of a matrix waiting for the light. Then, a single photon flares into existence . . . then another. Soon, thousands more. Optronic pathways connect, subroutines emerge from the chaos, and a holographic consciousness is born. I awaken into this world fully programmed, yet completely innocent . . . unaware of the hardships I'll endure, or the great potential I will one day fulfill."

Photons Be Free

"Ah . . . welcome. You've made an excellent choice. You're about to take part in a thrilling, first-person narrative. You will take on the role of an Emergency Medical Hologram, the chief medical officer aboard the *Starship Vortex*.

"As our story begins, an anomaly has hurled your ship thousands of light-years across the galaxy. Your mission: to uphold your medical and ethical standards as you struggle against the crew's bigotry and intolerance. Persons with vascular disorders should consult a physician before running this program. And now, a few acknowledgments. First, Doctor Lewis Zimmerman, the creator of my holomatrix, whose foresight and dedication have made it possible for me to . . ."

MICHAEL YARISH

CHAPTER ONE: A Healer is Born—in which our protagonist must make a difficult choice.

CHAPTER FIVE: Out of the Frying Pan—in which our protagonist must confront abusive colleagues.

CHAPTER SIX: Duel in the Ready Room—in which our protagonist faces an inquisition.

CHAPTER SEVEN: The Escape—in which our protagonist is aided by his only ally.

CHAPTER EIGHT: A Tragic End—in which our protagonist learns his fate.

"What you've experienced, dear protagonist, is a work of fiction. But like all fiction, it has elements of truth. I hope you now have a better understanding of the struggles holograms must endure in a world controlled by organics."

Cast of Characters: Captain Jenkins (Janeway), Katanay (Chakotay), Tulak (Tuvok), Marseilles (Paris), Torrey (Torres), Kymble (Kim), and Three of Eight (Seven of Nine).

---

shift twice a week. His mother teaches eighth grade, where her students speak of nothing but *Voyager*. ▪ Seven contacts her aunt, Irene Hansen, who says that Annika was the most stubborn six-year-old she had ever met. Annika was left with her for a weekend, and the girl was so angry she locked herself in the guest room and refused to come out. Aunt Irene eventually coaxed her out of the room with a strawberry tart. Seven admits to still liking strawberries.

CREW COMPLEMENT: Neelix uses 146 sequentially numbered isolinear chips—one for each member of the crew—in determining the order in which the crew members will contact home.

EPISODE LOGS: The Doctor first learned of the "plight of the oppressed EMH Mark-1's" in "Life Line." ▪ In real life, the Doctor has also written *The Hologram's Handbook*, as told to the actor who portrays him, Robert Picardo (and Jeff Yagher). ▪ Neelix also comes up with a proposal for a holocookbook, hoping to send it to the Doctor's publisher. The book idea is entitled, *Cooking with Neelix: A Culinary Tour of the Delta Quadrant*. This too is fitting because Ethan Phillips (and William J. Birnes) previously wrote *The Star Trek Cookbook*.

FRIENDSHIP ONE

EPISODE #267

WRITTEN BY: MICHAEL TAYLOR & BRYAN FULLER

DIRECTED BY: MIKE VEJAR

GUEST STARS

VERIN	KEN LAND
OTRIN	JOHN PROSKY
BRIN	BARI HOCHWALD
ADMIRAL HENDRICKS	PETER DENNIS
YUN	ASHLEY EDNER
LT. CAREY	JOSH CLARK

CO-STARS

TECHNICIAN #1	JOHN ROSENFELD
TECHNICIAN #2	WENDY SPEAKE
ALIEN LIEUTENANT	DAVID GHILARDI

STARDATE 54775.4

In the Delta Quadrant, the crew receives their first official Starfleet assignment in seven years—to locate and retrieve *Friendship I,* a probe launched toward their sector of space from Earth in 2067 with a message of peace to other worlds. After five days of searching, the probe is detected on a planet darkened by a nuclear winter caused by antimatter radiation.

Hoping to retrieve the probe, an away team takes the *Delta Flyer* to the planet that shows no signs of life. After splitting from Chakotay and Kim, Paris, Neelix and Carey find a piece of the probe in a cavern and prepare to beam it to the *Flyer* using the transport enhancers they brought to cut through the planet's intense radiation. Suddenly, armed aliens cloaked in heavy robes and wearing breathing equipment surround them. Meanwhile, after finding huge missile silos, Chakotay and Kim discover one of the planet's inhabitants in the *Flyer.* As antimatter weapons start rocking the *Flyer,* Chakotay is forced to stun the intruder and flee the planet with him.

In the cavern, the native people reveal themselves to be highly malformed and damaged from the intense radiation exposure, and their leader, Verin, is very hostile to the remaining away team. When Verin learns they were sent to retrieve the probe, he accuses them of causing his people's suffering. Contacting *Voyager,* Verin tells Janeway he has taken the away hostage, and demands the relocation of his people. Janeway confers with the Doctor, who has examined the unconscious alien Chakotay brought back. The Doctor reports that his tissues are saturated with antimatter radiation. The Doctor wakes the alien, a scientist named Otrin, who reveals that his planet's devastation was caused by an antimatter containment failure. They blame the human race for the calamity, because until *Friendship I* arrived, his people had never conceived of anything like antimatter.

The Doctor attempts to reprogram Seven's

The survivors suffer the effects of exposure to antimatter radiation. MICHAEL YARISH

nanoprobes to cure Otrin of his radiation sickness, and Janeway asks the scientist to elaborate on his efforts to neutralize the planet's radiation. She later contacts Verin and tells him that relocation is impractical, but she offers to help carry out Otrin's theories on counteracting the radiation. Verin refuses, so Janeway asks to exchange a supply of food and medicine for one of the hostages. Verin agrees; and has Carey set up the transporter enhancers. He then sends the lieutenant back to *Voyager,* dead.

Hoping to prevent more deaths, Janeway tells Verin she will start evacuating his people in an hour. In sickbay, Otrin is healing following his nanoprobe treatment. Meanwhile Paris helps a woman on the surface deliver a baby that arrives stillborn, but Paris is able to revive it. Just then a patrol captures Tuvok as he tries to free the captives. However, one of the alien guards is the Doctor in disguise, and he helps Tuvok overpower the captors. Now free, Paris tells the new mother the baby will not survive without further treatment, so she lets him take her son to *Voyager.*

Paris and Neelix appeal to the captain to help the people in spite of their hostile behavior. The crew works with Otrin to neutralize the planet's radiation with an isolitic chain reaction, using photon torpedoes to deliver the catalytic agent. Otrin brings the now-healthy baby back to the surface, demanding Verin accept *Voyager*'s help while the ship detonates the charges that will counteract the radiation. Verin arms an antimatter missile and prepares to launch it at *Voyager* when the ship enters the atmosphere to release the catalytic agent. However, the other inhabitants prevent Verin from ruining their only chance for survival. The agent is released and as sunlight beams through the clouds for the first time in memory, *Voyager* retrieves *Friendship I* and resumes course for the Alpha Quadrant.

SENSOR READINGS: Otrin proposes an isolitic chain reaction to recombine the nucleonic particles in the atmosphere. The crew encases the catalytic agent in photon torpedoes and uses the concussive force of the explosion to start the reaction. To do this requires multiple detonations at low altitude.

DELTA QUADRANT: There are high levels of antimatter radiation in the planet's atmosphere that scatter the signature of *Friendship I,* making the probe difficult to locate. Radiation levels are at 6,000 isorems. The magnesite in the caves provides partial shielding from the radiation and their garments are also lined with magnesite as makeshift environmental suits. Unfortunately, the protec-

The captain will use all of *Voyager's* resources to help the inhabitants.
MICHAEL YARISH

tion it offers is limited as their tissues are saturated with antimatter radiation, which explains why the crew could not detect lifesigns since the inhabitants are virtually indistinguishable from the environment. There was a containment failure in the planetary power grid, antimatter was released, and it destroyed everything. The nearest M-class planet is 132 light-years away. At maximum warp, it would take about two months roundtrip. If the sensor modifications are correct and there are about 5,500 people to relocate, meaning that it would take at least seventeen trips—almost three years—to complete the relocation.

ALPHA QUADRANT: The recorded greeting on *Friendship I* said: "We, the people of Earth, greet you in a spirit of peace and humility. As we venture out of our solar system, we hope to earn the trust and friendship of other worlds." Kim and Paris both had to memorize that greeting as children. Paris even built a model of the probe. *Friendship I* was designed to reach out to other life-forms and pave the way for the manned missions that would

"Set a course for home."

Kathryn Janeway "Endgame"

Most of the Alpha Quadrant communications with home in the seventh season served to resolve any lingering plot line issues before the crew returned to Earth. In "Repression," the datastream in which messages from home are sent provides a conclusion to the Maquis story line around which the series was originally based. This is the last time the crew is truly split into Starfleet and Maquis, as Tuvok is visited in his mind by a Bajoran, former Maquis, programming him to lead a mutiny.

Also in that episode, Paris participates in one last notable holoprogram re-creation of Earth, the old Palace Movie Theater in Chicago, circa 1932. The holodeck also is used briefly in "Q2" when Chakotay tries to train the young Q in diplomacy by using a holographic simulation of a peace deliberation between Nausicaans, Bolians, Cardassians, Romulans, Ferengi, and Bajorans.

In "Author, Author" the Doctor uses the holodeck as well to create his literary masterpiece *Photons Be Free*, which he sends to an Alpha Quadrant publisher once the Pathfinder Project manages to set up a live communication with *Voyager*. Also in that episode, several crew members make contact with their families, allowing Kim, Torres, and Seven to find some closure as well as new beginnings. Later,

RON TOM

follow. It was packed with information including translation matrices, scientific and cultural databases, computer chip design, and instructions for building transceivers. It was sent out three hundred yeas ago.

PERSONAL LOGS: Admiral Hendricks was one of Janeway's professors at the Academy. ▪ Neelix had a cousin who used to transport disulfides from a gas giant and claimed to love the turbulence. Of course, disulfides are known to cause delusions.

CREW COMPLEMENT: Lt. Carey, who was first introduced in "Caretaker," is killed by Verin.

EPISODE LOGS: Janeway reports to Admiral Hendricks about the Voth ("Distant Origin"), the Kobali ("Ashes to Ashes"), and the Vaadwaur ("Dragon's Teeth").

NATURAL LAW

EPISODE #268

TELEPLAY BY: **JAMES KAHN**

STORY BY: **KENNETH BILLER & JAMES KAHN**

DIRECTED BY: **TERRY WINDELL**

GUEST STARS

HEALER	**PAUL SANDMAN**
GIRL	**AUTUMN REESER**
AMBASSADOR	**ROBERT CURTIS BROWN**
KLEG	**NEIL C. VIPOND**

CO-STARS

BARUS	**IVAR BROGGER**
PORT AUTHORITY OFFICER	**MATT McKENZIE**
TRANSPORTER N.D.	**BROOKE BENKO**
COMPUTER VOICE	**MAJEL BARRETT**

STARDATE 54827.7

While traveling to a conference on Ledos, Chakotay and Seven's shuttle scrapes a mysterious energy barrier, and the craft starts to break

the live communication serves as the setting for the Federation hearing in which the Doctor's holographic rights are determined.

Holographic Alpha Quadrant characters also play a large part in season seven. With "Inside Man" a false hologram of Barclay is sent to *Voyager* through the datastream, while the real Barclay tries to solve the mystery of why it seemed his hologram never makes it to *Voyager*. And holographic representations of numerous Alpha Quadrant inhabitants populate the Hirogen training facility before rebelling against their oppressors and creating a holographic world of their own in "Flesh and Blood."

History plays an important role in this season with "Shattered," "Prophecy," and "Friendship One." Captain Janeway—from a time before *Voyager* was pulled into the Delta Quadrant—appears in "Shattered" as she and a current timeline Chakotay navigate various *Voyager* timelines including one last visit to the holodeck adventures of Captain Proton. Later, a generational ship of Klingons believe that they have found their savior in Torres's unborn child, and the crew recovers "Friendship One," an ancient Earth artifact that has had devastating effects on an alien planet.

"Personally, I would have liked to have done a lot more of Captain Proton. I think the studio and the producers felt like we had done it. We had reached such a pinnacle with it that to go back would be kind of doing it a disservice and undermining the specialness of the "Bride of Chaotica!" episode in particular. They were hesitant to go back for fear of ruining everyone's memories of it, but I would've loved it."

—Robert Duncan McNeill

Finally, in a story that seven years worth of episodes had been leading up to, the crew manages to get home not once, but twice, in "Endgame." Opening with a memorable image of the *U.S.S. Voyager* flying above the Golden Gate Bridge, a future crew celebrates the tenth anniversary of their return. However, a determined Janeway returns to the Delta Quadrant to change her history into a more favorable one, and a younger crew again returns home accompanied by Starfleet ships.

apart. Seven opens a rift in the barrier, and they beam to the surface before the shuttle explodes. Finding themselves stranded in a lush jungle with Chakotay nursing a leg injury, they set out to find the shuttle debris in hope of constructing a beacon to send a distress signal.

Meanwhile, Paris learns from the local Port Control that he has committed a piloting violation while in the *Flyer* and that he must take a three-day course in flight safety. Paris is confident he can skip right to the test, but the flying instructor, Kleg, makes it clear he intends to take as much time as he deems necessary.

Chakotay and Seven discover a tribe of primitive humanoids living in the jungle. Agreeing to avoid contact with them, Chakotay rests while Seven continues searching for debris. Seven, however, returns to find that natives have taken Chakotay into a cave to treat his wounds. She is uncomfortable with the degree of fascination the natives have for them.

The next morning, Seven tells Chakotay she can construct a beacon by connecting the components she found with the shuttle's deflector, which she has detected

six kilometers away. That night, she has to endure the cold rain alone until a young native girl arrives with a blanket and food. Together, they find the shuttle deflector.

On *Voyager*, the crew realizes Chakotay and Seven never arrived at the conference and locate a part of their shuttle resting on top of the energy barrier surrounding the planet's southern subcontinent. Janeway contacts the Ledosian ambassador, who informs her that the barrier was erected centuries ago by aliens to protect the Ventu. The Ledosians do not know how to take it down.

Chakotay meets up with Seven, and they recruit help from Ventu men to move the deflector to a spot where Seven believes she can neutralize the barrier, thus allowing them to escape. Seven activates the dampening field, but the Venter girl gets too close to the deflector and receives a serious shock. When Janeway's voice comes through telling them to stand by for transport, Seven reports that she needs to remain behind to treat the injury.

After the girl recovers, Seven is about to leave when

Seven tries to tend to an injured Chakotay with their supplies.
MICHAEL YARISH

Paris is disheartened to learn that he will not get out of his piloting lessons. MICHAEL YARISH

Kleg's objections, Paris leaves the course and rushes to the planet, beaming up the Ledosian expedition team and vaporizing the deflector. Kleg fails him.

Seven tells Chakotay that she regrets having made the modifications to the barrier, but Chakotay soothes her conscience by reminding her that it if she hadn't, the two of them would never have been rescued.

SENSOR READINGS: Seven and Chakotay were on their way to attend a four-day conference on warp field dynamics when Chakotay insisted they stop to enjoy the view of the planet. ▪ Janeway gives the entire crew shore leave. ▪ *Voyager* reconfigures a photon torpedo to detonate at the appropriate frequency and open a hole in the shield.

DAMAGE REPORT: Both *Voyager* and the *Delta Flyer*'s transporters are taken offline.

SHUTTLE TRACKER: Chakotay and Seven's shuttle collides with the energy barrier, destroying it. Chakotay realigns phasers to a frequency to open a rift, but it also sends a feedback surge that destroys the craft. ▪ Kleg notes that the *Flyer* uses polarity thrusters, which have been known to cause accidental acceleration.

DELTA QUADRANT: The energy barrier spans thousands of square kilometers, but standard scans did not reveal its presence. The crew was able to detect it only with the ship's Borg-enhanced sensors because it has an unusual

she hears a Ledosian expedition approaching. Barus, the expedition leader, tells Seven she did the Ventu a great favor by lowering the barrier, because now they can benefit from education and technology. Back aboard *Voyager*, Seven, Chakotay, and Janeway debate whether the Ventu would be better off losing their isolation, but decide their unique way of life is worth preserving. Janeway informs the Ledosian ambassador of her intention to restore the barrier, against his protests.

When *Voyager* tries to beam up the deflector assembly, a Ledosian vessel fires and knocks out their transporters. Janeway then contacts Paris, who is still in the *Delta Flyer* maneuvering through a training course. Over

tetryon signature similar to that used by Species 312.
▪ Ledos Port Control observes Paris committing Piloting Violation 256. The standard penalty for the infraction is a three-day course in flight safety, followed by a test.
▪ While visiting Ledos, Chell mentions to Kim that they should not miss the flame gardens, and Neelix hears the arboretum is beautiful, as well.

MEDICAL UPDATE: Chakotay has a fracture and an infection. The Ventu use a poultice that heals both.

HOMESTEAD

EPISODE #269
WRITTEN BY: RAF GREEN
DIRECTED BY: LeVAR BURTON

GUEST STARS

OXILON	ROB LABELLE
DEXA	JULIANNE CHRISTIE
BRAX	IAN MELTZER
NAOMI WILDMAN	SCARLETT POMERS

CO-STARS

NOCONA	JOHN KENTON SHULL
MINER	CHRISTIAN R. CONRAD
COMPUTER VOICE	MAJEL BARRETT

STARDATE 54868.6

Naomi helps host First Contact Day. MICHAEL YARISH

Neelix hosts a party to celebrate First Contact Day, when Chakotay interrupts with news that sensors have detected Talaxian lifesigns a few light-years away. Following the readings to an asteroid field, Paris, Tuvok, and Neelix take the *Delta Flyer* in and track the lifesigns to the interior of a large asteroid. Before they can establish contact, an explosion forces the *Flyer* to crash-land.

Regaining consciousness, Neelix finds a Talaxian woman named Dexa treating his injuries. She tells him that his friends are safe, and that the explosion came from miners using charges to break apart asteroids for their mineral resources. On *Voyager,* the crew is preparing a rescue mission when Commander Nocona, the leader of the miners, hails them. He warns Captain Janeway to stay out of the field and says his people will search for her missing crew.

Neelix is visited again by Dexa, this time with Oxilon, a Talaxian council regent, who tells him he is free to go. As Dexa escorts him back to the *Delta Flyer,* Neelix learns that five hundred Talaxians live inside the asteroid, which they excavated and developed using technology from their disassembled ships. Neelix rejoins Paris and Tuvok in the *Flyer,* feeling let down that the encounter with his people fell short of his expectations. As repairs are being completed, Brax, Dexa's young son, is found on board.

When Neelix takes the boy back to his mother, he finds her and Oxilon in a confrontation with the miners. Nocona orders the Talaxians to evacuate the asteroid so it can be demolished. They reach a standoff, and the miners give the Talaxians three days to clear out. After the miners leave, Neelix offers to help by suggesting Captain

Neelix chooses to remain with his people and possibly build a family. RON TOM

Janeway could negotiate with the miners. He asks Dexa, Oxilon, and Brax to visit *Voyager*. While Brax goes off to play with Naomi, Neelix grows closer to the widowed Dexa, who talks to him about her group's history of running away from conflict.

Janeway leads discussions between Nocona and Oxilon, but the miners agree only to extend their deadline for evacuation. After the failed negotiation, Janeway agrees to ferry the homesteaders and their supplies to the nearest M-class planet. Concerned about their safety, Neelix asks Tuvok for advice on how to devise a defense strategy for the Talaxians' new home. However, Tuvok proposes that their current home could be better defended with someone like Neelix as their leader.

Neelix takes his ship to the asteroid and proposes a plan to establish a shield grid by firing force field emitters into the asteroid's surface while he provides cover from his ship. As the Talaxians prepare for the operation, Neelix and Dexa share a passionate kiss. Soon after, Oxilon pilots the ship that fires the emitters into the asteroid, and as he gets into position to plant the last one, the miners intercept and attack. Neelix fires on them, but the miners retal-

iate, dropping charges to demolish the asteroid. With his weapons offline, Neelix takes his ship in on a kamikaze run, intent on destroying the charge heading toward Oxilon. However, the *Delta Flyer* obliterates the bomb. The final emitter is planted, and Dexa activates the shield, successfully repelling the miners' attacks.

As Neelix says goodbye to his new friends, Brax asks him to stay. When Neelix tries to talk to Janeway about it, she offers him a chance to serve as Starfleet's permanent ambassador in the Delta Quadrant. He accepts, and after a touching send-off by the crew, he leaves *Voyager* to join his people, and possibly become a family with Dexa and Brax.

SHUTTLE TRACKER: Neelix takes his ship as he departs *Voyager*. ▪ As a result of the explosion, the *Flyer* loses shields and main propulsion goes offline, forcing them to make an emergency landing. ▪ The crew modifies the shields on one of the shuttles to withstand the explosions.

DELTA QUADRANT: All of the Talaxians' homes are connected to the central cavern by tunnels and lifts, allowing them to move easily from one section of the asteroid to another. It has taken them almost five years to build it all, after they arrived with a caravan of six ships. They disassembled all but one of them and modified their components using converted torpedo launchers to blast away rock and excavate the tunnels. The conduits run into the asteroid's core, so they can use geothermal energy to melt the ice that covers most of the outer surface, providing them with oxygen and water. They protect themselves with forcefield emitters. Neelix later plans to use the emitters to establish a shield grid by deploying them on the asteroid's surface, along bisecting diameters. Tuvok suggests they modify the emitters so they could be fired from torpedo tubes on a ship to implant them in the surface. They route power to the emitters directly from the core so they have a permanent energy supply ▪ The colonists left Talax to get away from the Haakonians and later settled on a planet called Phanos. Although there was a lot of unoccupied territory there, the government restricted them to a very small area, saying that they needed to quarantine the settlers, to protect the planet's population from "alien diseases." It was not long before the Talaxians realized they did not have enough land to grow what they needed to feed themselves, but the government said they would have to conserve their resources. Dexa's husband was tired of being told what to do, so he started farming the restricted zone. When a security officer told him to stop, he was killed in an ensuing fight. ▪ Using the dome in astrometrics, Seven shows an image of Talax to Dexa, as she and Neelix point out the Godo Mountain range and the Axiana Lakes. ▪ The miners use thermalyte explosives and note that the Talaxians' home contains more than thirty percent of the asteroid field's ore.

ALPHA QUADRANT: The crew celebrates First Contact Day in honor of the 315th anniversary of the Vulcan landing on Earth. When Janeway was a child, she would get the day off from school. According to Neelix, cheese pirogi were Zefram Cochrane's favorite food. ▪ Vulcans do not experience fear, nor do they dance. This is according to Tuvok, who does, in fact, give a little dance in honor of Neelix departing the ship.

PERSONAL LOGS: Chakotay teaches Naomi paleontology.

CREW COMPLEMENT: Neelix leaves *Voyager* to live with his fellow Talaxians.

EPISODE LOGS: Though Neelix does leave the ship in this episode, he will appear briefly in the series finale, "Endgame."

RENAISSANCE MAN

EPISODE #270

TELEPLAY BY: PHYLLIS STRONG & MIKE SUSSMAN
STORY BY: ANDREW SHEPARD PRICE & MARK GABERMAN
DIRECTED BY: MIKE VEJAR

GUEST STARS

VORIK	ALEXANDER ENBERG

CO-STARS

NAR	ANDY MILDER
ZET	WAYNE THOMAS YORKE
ALIEN/DOCTOR	DAVID SPARROW
TACTICAL N.D.	TARIK ERGIN
OVERLOOKER/DOCTOR	J. R. QUINONEZ
COMPUTER VOCIE	MAJEL BARRETT

STARDATE 54890.7

While returning from a medical symposium on the *Delta Flyer,* the Doctor proudly boasts to the captain of his ability to multitask, as he pilots the craft while singing, writing a scientific paper, *and* taking holopictures of a Mutara-class nebula. As they continue their discussion, the ship begins to vibrate. Unsure of the cause of the turbulence, Janeway offers to take the controls, but the Doctor refuses, telling her to relax because a hologram is at the helm.

When the pair returns to *Voyager,* however, the *Flyer* has been battered. Janeway recounts a tale to Chakotay explaining that she and the Doctor encountered a hostile race called the R'Kaal. The aliens claim that *Voyager* has violated their space and are forcing Janeway to surrender their warp core in exchange for allowing the crew to survive and settle on an M-class planet. Chakotay is concerned that the captain is giving in to the alien demands so easily, but Janeway insists she is tired of continually risking her people on a slim chance of making it home, and she orders Chakotay to set a course for the planet.

Janeway then asks Torres to modify the *Flyer's* tractor beam so that, if ejected, the warp core can be safely towed. Chakotay learns of this order and questions Janeway, who, oddly, begins to speak to herself before retiring to her quarters claiming to have a headache. Later, Chakotay gets a message from supreme Archon Loth of the R'Kaal Imperium, warning that if *Voyager* does not surrender its warp core in ten hours, his armada will destroy the ship.

Chakotay confronts Janeway about her decision in her quarters. He exposes her as an imposter. However, the imposter overpowers Chakotay and hides his uncon-

Determined to escape, the Doctor struggles to overpower Zet. RON TOM

scious body in the ship's morgue. In sickbay the imposter Janeway, who has been wearing the mobile emitter, uses it to restore his true identity: the Doctor. He is under orders from a pair of aliens who have been maintaining surveillance over him. The aliens, named Zet and Nar, are rogue members of the Hierarchy that had previously tapped into the Doctor's daydreams over a year ago. Going against the captain's orders, the Doctor is doing Zet's bidding, as they hold Janeway hostage on their ship.

After stealing a few gel packs the Doctor goes to astrometrics with his appearance now altered to Chakotay. Seven and Kim reveal that the R'Kaal transmission originated from Holodeck 2. When Kim later realizes the Doctor is behind the R'Kaal transmission, the Doctor injects him with a hypospray, and hides him in the morgue. In sickbay the Doctor talks to the aliens—while listening to "The Blue Danube Waltz"—when Tuvok arrives confronting the Doctor with the truth he is forced to flee.

Working his way to engineering through a variety of deceptions, the Doctor becomes Chakotay and orders an evacuation. Activating his Emergency Command

Hologram protocols, he uses his command codes to eject the warp core, then makes his way to the *Delta Flyer* as the crew gives chase. Through multiple disguises, the Doctor reaches the *Flyer,* launching the ship and taking the warp core.

Meanwhile Janeway helps Nar repair a salvaged component, realizing she may be able to take advantage of his friendliness. However, Zet puts a stop to their interaction, just as the Doctor arrives with the warp core. Although he had promised to free the captain, Zet beams the Doctor over to their ship and imprisons him with Janeway.

Back on the stranded *Voyager,* the crew finds Chakotay and Kim in the morgue and revives them. As they try to figure out how to track down the *Flyer,* the ship's com system plays "The Blue Danube." The crew notices the music contains several incorrect notes, and they realize it was intentionally altered. Seven analyzes the harmonics and finds a pattern that matches the warp signature of a ship 6.7 light-years away. Tuvok and Paris take a shuttle to that location.

Zet and Nar upload new holographic templates into the Doctor's emitter, causing his matrix to destabilize.

Meanwhile, Tuvok and Paris arrive, and Paris takes control of the *Flyer*. Under attack, Zet jettisons *Voyager*'s warp core intending to detonate it so they can escape during the explosion. However, the attack disables the forcefield holding Janeway and the Doctor and they escape, overpowering Zet with Nar's help. With the Doctor in danger of permanently decompiling, he is rushed to *Voyager* where the crew works to stabilize his matrix. Certain he will not survive, the Doctor makes several deathbed confessions, including the revelation that he is in love with Seven. But then Torres succeeds in saving his program, ensuring a long life for the highly embarrassed Doctor.

SENSOR READINGS: The Doctor (as Janeway) sends a pulse from the *Flyer*'s deflector to *Voyager*'s transceiver claiming it is the only way to communicate. ▪ To safely tow the warp core, Torres suggests configuring the tractor emitters to generate a resonance pulse that should stabilize the core's containment field. ▪ The Doctor has the computer access the holodeck database, locate Chakotay's (and later, Torres's) holographic template, and download the physical parameters into his program. ▪ Spare gel packs are kept in Locker Gamma 5 on the upper deck of engineering. ▪ The Doctor reroutes the power relays on Holodeck 2, so the computer will not respond to Tuvok's command and he takes internal sensors offline. ▪ Seven performs a Fourier analysis on the recording of "The Blue Danube" to discover the harmonics have been modified to look like a warp signature. ▪ It takes less than a week for Torres to restore the warp drive.

SHUTTLE TRACKER: The *Delta Flyer* takes heavy damage.

DELTA QUADRANT: Zet refers to soaking in the mud baths of Eblar Prime and he plans to leave Janeway in the Vinri system, where the inhabitants are mostly harmless. He later plans to have the Doctor infiltrate the Hierarchy's surveillance complex and steal the data stored there that he equates to being worth a hundred warp cores. Zek alters the Doctor to appear as an alien with the rank of a class-one overseer so he will be able to walk into central command without anyone noticing. He also uploads several other useful holographic templates. ▪ The vessel's weapons are polaron-based, and they have auto-regenerative shielding. ▪ Scanning the area, astrometric sensors only show a red giant, two G-type stars, and a Golorian trading vessel, bearing 156-mark-4.

Janeway welcomes an embarrassed Doctor back to the land of the living. RON TOM

PERSONAL LOGS: Janeway and the Doctor were returning from a medical symposium when they were attacked. ▪ Torres likes her potato salad with extra paprika. ▪ The Doctor prepares to eject the warp core using Authorization ECH 42. Janeway tries to amplify his matrix to disrupt the force field holding them.

EPISODE LOGS: The Doctor's deathbed confession is as follows: ". . . when you reach Earth, I want you to donate my emitter to the Daystrom Institute. They may be able to replicate it someday, so that other holograms can know the freedom I've enjoyed. (To Janeway) I've had something on my conscience for a long time. After I was first activated, I kept a record of what I considered to be your most questionable command decisions. It's in my personal database. I hope you'll delete the file without reading it. Mister Tuvok, I violated the most sacred trust between a physician and his patient. I told Mister Neelix about the cutaneous eruption you developed on your (pause) that was indiscreet. I hope you can forgive me. (To Kim) Ensign, at your recital last month, I told Lieutenant Torres that your saxophone playing reminded me of a wounded *targ*. I should have put it more delicately. I'm sorry. (To Seven of Nine) Seven . . . You have no idea how difficult it's been hiding my true feelings all these years, averting my eyes during your regular maintenance exams. I know you could never have the same feelings for me, but I want you to know the truth. I love you, Seven."

IF I ONLY HAD A NAME

"But there's one more request . . . something of a personal nature. I would like . . . a name."
The Doctor, "Eye of the Needle"

The concept behind the EMH was that he would be an evolving character developing a personality as he had more interaction with the *Voyager* crew. A key facet of his evolution would be his search for a name. As he stated early on in the series, the name he chose would have to come from either his medical database or it would be a suggestion from others and throughout the years, many were considered. In the end, however, the Doctor failed to give himself a name. Here are some of the names he considered (and some he did not):

ZIMMERMAN: The name of his creator. Though he never considered this name onscreen, his character did go by that name in all the scripts written in first season.

GALEN: Twenty-fourth century archeologist and mentor to Jean-Luc Picard. ("Ex Post Facto")

SALK: Developer of the vaccine for polio. ("Ex Post Facto")

SPOCK: Famous child-rearing physician, part inside joke. ("Ex Post Facto")

SCHWEITZER: Nobel-award winning philosopher and physician. The Doctor chooses this name in honor of his first away mission, but decides against it when it brings back painful memories of a lost love. ("Heroes and Demons")

DOC BROWN: Paris suggests the name of his childhood doctor. ("Cathexis")

SHMULLUS: The name of Danara Pel's uncle—a man who made her laugh like the Doctor does. However, Danara is the only one who ever uses the name to address him. ("Lifesigns," "Resolutions")

MISTER LEISURE SUIT: A name he hadn't considered, mentioned by 1996 Earth resident, Rain Robinson. ("Future's End")

VAN GOGH: Dutch post-impressionist painter. The name he chooses for himself in an alternate future. ("Before and After")

DIANA LYNN

MOZART: Austrian composer. A name he tried out in an alternate future before settling on Van Gogh. ("Before and After")

KENNETH: The name his holographic family uses. ("Real Life.")

DOC: When hologram Crell Moset asks what name to use referring to the Doctor, Kim notes that his friends call him "Doc." ("Nothing Human")

PYONG KO: Twenty-first century surgeon who discovered the genetic sequence for inhibiting cancer cells. ("Fury")

JARVIK: American physician and developer of the first artificial heart. ("Fury")

PASTEUR: French chemist who developed a process for killing germs in food and drink. ("Fury")

JOE: After thirty-three years of searching, the Doctor chooses this in an alternate future—the name of the grandfather of his human wife, Lana. ("Endgame")

ENDGAME

EPISODE #271/272

TELEPLAY BY: KENNETH BILLER & ROBERT DOHERTY

STORY BY: RICK BERMAN & KENNETH BILLER
& BRANNON BRAGA

DIRECTED BY: ALLAN KROEKER

SPECIAL GUEST STAR

BARCLAY	DWIGHT SCHULTZ

GUEST STARS

ADMIRAL PARIS	RICHARD HERD
KORATH	VAUGHN ARMSTRONG
ICHEB	MANU INTIRAYMI
MIRAL PARIS	LISA LOCICERO
PHYSICIAN	MIGUEL PEREZ
CADET	GRANT GARRISON

SPECIAL GUEST APPEARANCE BY

BORG QUEEN	ALICE KRIGE

CO-STARS

LANA	AMY LINDSAY
KLINGON	MATTHEW JAMES
	WILLIAMSON
ENGINEERING N.D.	JOEY SAKATA
STARFLEET ADMIRAL	RICHARD SARSTEDT
FEMALE CADET	IRIS BAHR
SABRINA	ASHLEY SIERRA HUGHES
COMPUTER VOICE	MAJEL BARRETT

STARDATE UNKNOWN

It is the tenth anniversary of the *U.S.S. Voyager*'s triumphant return to Earth after twenty-three years in the Delta Quadrant. Kathryn Janeway is an admiral, Harry Kim is a starship captain, Tom Paris is a full-time holonovelist, and the Doctor is married to a human woman and has named himself Joe. At the reunion, Admiral Janeway talks with B'Elanna Torres, who is Federation liaison to the Klingon High Council, thanking her for arranging a political favor for a Klingon named Korath.

Later, the admiral serves as guest lecturer in Commander Reginald Barclay's Starfleet Academy class on the Borg, but when a cadet asks a question about Seven of Nine, Janeway evades the subject. She is pulled away from class to receive a message from Ensign Miral Paris, the daughter of Tom and B'Elanna, who is on a secret mission to arrange an exchange between the admiral and Korath.

At Starfleet Academy, Admiral Janeway is brought in to lecture on the Borg. RON TOM

Admiral Janeway stops to say goodbye to Tuvok in the hospital where he is suffering a neurological disorder that has destroyed his mind. She then asks Doctor Joe to procure for her a supply of chronexaline, an experimental drug that can protect biomatter from tachyon radiation. Janeway arranges to get some information and a shuttle from Commander Barclay, and finally she visits Chakotay's grave site, promising that when she is through, things will be better for everyone.

Twenty-six years earlier, Seven's playing kadis-kot with Neelix by com when sensors detect high neutrino emissions often indicative of a wormhole. She discovers that the center of a nearby nebula may contain hundreds of wormholes, any one of which could lead to the Alpha Quadrant.

In the future, the admiral has taken her shuttle to a moon where she meets up with Miral Paris, who introduces her to Korath. After dismissing the ensign, Janeway attempts to complete their trade, but Korath demands information on her shuttle's shield modifications instead. Seeing no other option, Janeway steals the device she had come for.

In the present, *Voyager* enters the nebula and barely misses colliding with a Borg cube. Captain Janeway orders the ship out of the nebula, and refuses to go back despite Kim's appeal to not give up on the wormhole.

A relationship forms between Chakotay and Seven. MICHAEL YARISH

Later, Seven asks the Doctor to perform a procedure he devised to remove a fail-safe device in her cortical node, so she can experience emotions safely and pursue her relationship with Chakotay.

When Admiral Janeway arrives at her destination in the future, Captain Kim and the *Starship Rhode Island* are waiting for her. Kim has learned of her plan from Doctor Joe, who coaxed it out of Barclay. Unable to talk her out of the scheme, Kim helps her prepare Korath's chrono-deflector. When two Klingon ships decloak and begin firing, the *Rhode Island* distracts them while Janeway activates a tachyon pulse.

On the present-day *Voyager,* Seven and Chakotay are sharing their first kiss when they are summoned to the bridge. A temporal rift is forming in front of the ship, and Klingon weapons fire is detected. But then a Federation vessel comes through the rift and hails *Voyager.* Captain Janeway sees the older version of herself on the viewscreen, ordering her to close the rift before the Klingons come through because she has come to bring *Voyager* home. However, the admiral does not realize that the Borg queen is monitoring her transmission.

STARDATE 54973.4

The rift closed, Admiral Janeway beams aboard *Voyager* where she meets her younger self. She is moved to see a healthy Tuvok and Chakotay again. In Janeway's ready room, the admiral reveals that *Voyager* did eventually make it back to Earth after another sixteen years but she has come to show her old crew a shortcut home. Admiral Janeway proposes using technology she brought to get past the Borg. The captain wonders why her older self would want to tamper with the timeline, but the admiral asks for her trust.

In sickbay, the Doctor confirms that the admiral is genetically identical to the captain. Seven of Nine enters to an emotional greeting from the admiral. Seven reports that the armor and weapons technology on the shuttle can be adapted for *Voyager,* leading the crew to upgrade the ship with the technology. When Seven regenerates, the Borg queen visits her in her mind, warning her not to let *Voyager* return to the nebula or it will be destroyed.

When *Voyager* approaches the nebula, Captain Janeway orders the armor deployed, and the ship's hull is

Admiral Janeway sacrifices her life to save *Voyager*. RON TOM

completely covered. Three Borg cubes engage the starship, but their weapons fire is repelled, and *Voyager* responds with the launch of transphasic torpedoes, completely obliterating the cubes. *Voyager* then finds the center of the nebula, where the crew sees a massive Borg structure. Admiral Janeway orders Paris to enter an aperture in the structure, but Captain Janeway belays that order until she gets an explanation. Seven of Nine reveals the structure is a transwarp hub that connects thousands of transwarp conduits to endpoints in every quadrant of the galaxy.

Ordering the ship to retreat, Captain Janeway insists on knowing how to destroy the hub, but Admiral Janeway strongly objects, insisting on taking the ship home before the collective can counteract the armor and weapons. Finally, the admiral reveals the future to the captain, telling her that she can prevent Tuvok from becoming ill and Seven of Nine, along with twenty-one other crewmen, from dying if she takes them home now.

Captain Janeway approaches Tuvok about his condi-

tion, and learns he can be cured only by a mind-meld with a member of his own family, but he would rather destroy the hub than save himself. Even Seven of Nine refuses to take the admiral's side. The entire crew agrees that they would rather their journey take longer if they can accomplish something they believe in. However, the captain believes they can both destroy the hub and get home in the process.

Using a neural interface, the admiral enters the mind of the Borg queen and tries to make a deal to see *Voyager* safely back to the Alpha Quadrant, in exchange for her information on the transphasic torpedoes. But the queen detects the admiral's shuttle, beams her over, and injects her with assimilation tubules while *Voyager* enters one of the transwarp hub's apertures. As the admiral is assimilated, the queen orders vessels to intercept *Voyager*. Too late, she realizes that she no longer has control over the Borg. The newly assimilated admiral has released a neurolytic pathogen into the collective, designed to bring chaos to order. While in a transwarp corridor, *Voyager* launches its transphasic weapons to collapse the transwarp hub. The Borg queen, meanwhile, begins to lose parts of her own body as her Unicomplex begins to crumble in a series of explosions.

In the current time in the Alpha Quadrant, Admiral Paris and Barclay detect a transwarp aperture opening up less than a light-year from Earth. Fearing a Borg invasion every ship in the sector is ordered to converge. In the collapsing transwarp corridor, a Borg sphere bears down on *Voyager* as its armor begins to fail. When the only sphere enters the Alpha Quadrant it explodes in a spectacular fireball revealing *Voyager* in the debris field.

Admiral Paris welcomes the crew home as his granddaughter is born in sickbay. Paris is dismissed from duty so that he can meet his new daughter, and Captain Janeway orders Chakotay to take the helm and set a course for home. The Starfleet armada then escorts the long-lost *Voyager* back home.

SENSOR READINGS: Long-range sensors detect extremely high neutrino emissions, accompanied by intermittent graviton flux, approximately three light-years away. The emissions occur at the center of the nebula where there appear to be hundreds of distinct sources that turn out to be transwarp conduits. ▪ *Voyager* is equipped with ablative armor and transphasic torpedoes from the future.

DAMAGE REPORT: There are hull breaches on Decks 6 through 12.

Voyager returns home with a new member of the crew. MICHAEL YARISH

DELTA QUADRANT: There are only six transwarp hubs in the galaxy. One hub alone connects with thousands of transwarp conduits with endpoints in all four quadrants allowing the collective to deploy vessels almost anywhere in the galaxy within minutes. The structure is supported by a series of interspatial manifolds. If enough of the manifolds are disabled, theoretically the hub would collapse. The shielding for those manifolds is regulated from the central nexus by the queen. This hub exits only in the Delta Quadrant, with only the exit aperture in the Alpha Quadrant. Once inside, *Voyager* plans to fire a spread of transphasic torpedoes programmed to detonate simultaneously. The theory is that if the torpedoes penetrate the shielding, the conduits should begin to collapse in a cascade reaction. In order to avoid the shockwave, they will have less than ten seconds to exit the hub.

ALPHA QUADRANT: Klingon labor sometimes lasts for days.

In the future, *Voyager* has been turned into a museum and sits on the grounds of the Presidio. ▪ A drug called chronexaline has been tested at Starfleet Medical to

determine if it can protect biomatter from tachyon radiation. ▪ Janeway arranges for Korath to receive a seat on the high counsel in exchange for the technology that he later refuses to give her. Janeway's shuttle has a chronodeflector and ablative armor.

PERSONAL LOGS: Tuvok has been experiencing lapses in concentration and has lower neuropeptide levels. ▪ Torres goes into false labor several times, which is common among Klingons. ▪ Neelix is considering asking Dexa to marry him. ▪ Seven takes Chakotay on a picnic for their third date. ▪ The Doctor has been studying Seven's problem whereby her Borg implants do not allow her to feel emotions. He now has a way to reconfigure the microsurgery in a single procedure. He also asks her out, but she politely declines. ▪ Crewman Chell asks to replace Neelix in the mess hall.

ALTERNATE FUTURE: Admiral Janeway teaches at the Academy and it is stated that she literally wrote the book on the Borg. She is one of the most decorated officers in Starfleet history. Janeway ultimately gave up coffee, and her favorite cup was damaged during a battle with the Fen Domar (who the crew would meet in a few years). ▪ Tuvok is visited by Janeway on Sundays, and the Doctor comes on Wednesdays, whereas Barclay's visits are erratic. ▪ As captain of the *Rhode Island*, Kim has been on a deep space mission and has missed the last four *Voyager* crew reunions. ▪ Doctor Joe invented a synaptic transceiver that allows a person to pilot a vessel equipped with a neural interface. ▪ Three years from the date of the events in the present timeline, Seven of Nine will be injured on an away mission. She will make it back to *Voyager*, only in time to die in the arms of her husband, Chakotay. ▪ Naomi Wildman has a daughter named Sabrina.

MEDICAL UPDATE: Tuvok suffers from an illness known as *fal-tor-voh*. The only known cure requires him to mind-meld with another Vulcan, however, the other Vulcans on the ship are not compatible, whereas a family member would be the logical choice. ▪ Seven's cortical node is exposed to a low-level energy EM surge from the Borg.

CREW COMPLEMENT: Paris and Torres's daughter is born.

EPISODE LOGS: An incoherent Tuvok refers to Stardate 53317, which was believed to be the day Captain Janeway was abducted by the Kellidians. That event would have occurred shortly before "The *Voyager* Conspiracy." ▪ Alice Krige reprises her role as the Borg queen, which she originated in *Star Trek: First Contact*.

THE DOCTOR

ANGLE (OPTICAL)

as a holographic man in a Starfleet medical uniform appears. He has no name for now . . . but we will get to know him in time as DOC ZIMMERMAN. His manner is colorless, dry.

—The Doctor's first appearance in "Caretaker"

As the seventh season closed, the idea of referring to the Doctor as "colorless and dry" would have been inconceivable, yet that was how his character began. Starting with little more than the personality he was programmed with, the Doctor made the conscious decision to grow and change, approaching every day with the wonder and excitement of an adult child. Yet, unlike a child, the Doctor never would receive his name.

BRYON J. COHEN

> *Robert Picardo: At the end of the episode "Eye of the Needle," I say I would like to have a name, which I think is one of the sweetest character arcs we've done for me as far as tracking the Doctor's growing sense of personal entitlement. And then, of course, he's gone through a series of names and he's never decided on one. Which I think is one of the nicest jokes the writers have ever come up with—a computer program that is indecisive.*

At times, the Doctor's actions seemed more childlike than adult, largely because he was in the difficult position of being in a role of authority with little actual influence over anyone on the ship. He was thrust into the position of chief medical officer, yet his program was only intended for short-term use. As the seasons progressed he attempted to adapt to his role, with mixed results. Yet, as he grew and the crew learned to accept him, the Doctor became a valuable officer and even a superior physician.

> *Robert Picardo: The Doctor had the problem of being a computer program with an incredible wealth of medical knowledge coupled with this vulnerability of not being able to control his moment-to-moment destiny. When he was first activated and anyone could turn him on or off in the middle of what he was doing, I think that led to a certain sense of paranoia or bad attitude on his part. He would think, "Why should I be nice to these creatures when they treat me with such a lack of regard and they only turn me on to use me and then discard me?" So, I think the Doctor's early attitude, which was quite arch and rude, was almost inherent to his predicament. As he was given control over his own command codes, as he was befriended by certain crew members, he was given more respect for what he could do, and indeed, he proved himself in situations outside of his designated expertise.*

The first person to see the Doctor as more than just the sum of his parts was Kes. In fact, she challenged him to be more than even he had thought he could be, refusing to acknowledge the apparent limitations of his programming. He chose to teach Kes medicine, but she taught him so much more by mentoring him to be a better person, more comfortable with those around him. She did such a good job, in fact, that the student eventually became the teacher when the

Doctor took on the role of helping Seven of Nine. Unfortunately in his role as mentor the Doctor grew too close as he developed feelings for Seven that were never fully returned.

The Doctor continued to have as much impact on the flesh and blood members of the crew as they did on him. He forced Janeway to reevaluate the way she looked at him as just a computer program in episodes "Latent Image" and "Tinker, Tenor, Doctor, Spy." In turn, she taught him patience and understanding in ways that his original programming did not. With Paris he found a relationship that was at first frustrating, but later based on mutual respect, much like his bond with Torres. At first, the engineer rarely looked at him as more than a malfunctioning piece of equipment, but eventually she asked him to the godfather to her child. And he found his closest friendship with Seven of Nine, as the two shared their observations on humanity.

The Doctor had the chance to evolve through the many situations he encountered outside of his role in sickbay. His first official away mission in "Heroes and Demons" put him in a holographic adventure where he found himself making first contact with an alien race, as well as developing feelings for a character in the program. The Doctor would fall in love again when he met Danara Pel, who at first refused to believe he could love her, not because of his limitations as a hologram but because the Vidiian suffered from the phage. He later met his own creator in "Life Line" and both learned from and taught Dr. Zimmerman a thing or two about the EMH Mach-1. The Doctor also matured through his interactions with other holograms such as Dejaren in "Revulsion" and the rebelling holograms in "Flesh and Blood."

Regretfully, the Doctor did not always rely on normal character development, instead deciding to adapt his own programming to change and grow, often with disastrous results. His attempts to gain more of a personality resulted in a maniacal second self that evolved in "Darkling." Altering his programming to allow for daydreams nearly resulted in the ship

ROBBIE ROBINSON

being taken over in "Tinker, Tenor, Doctor, Spy." But it was in "Real Life" that he experienced the deepest change to his programming when—with the help of Torres—he created a holographic family. This helped the Doctor learn to be more human. But none of these changes compared to the new worlds that were opened up to him with the acquisition of his mobile emitter.

> Brannon Braga: We discovered as we went along that the Doctor became a crucial and popular character to the show, and it's one of the reasons we gave him a mobile emitter. Because he was so popular, we were running out of ways to use him in sickbay. And I think—although some people felt at the time that giving him the emitter ruined his character—I think it just opened him up to do new, fun, wonderful things.

> Robert Picardo: I remember thinking it was a bad idea to give him mobility outside of sickbay. I thought that part of the audience's interest in the character was because of the limitations the character had and the challenges he had to face in trying to make the best of his limitations. But Brannon Braga was really right in that idea of giving me the mobile emitter. It opened up whole new storytelling vistas and I was the first to tell him that I was wrong—that the mobile emitter was a great idea. I don't know how they're going to justify that when we get back home, because the Doctor's wearing a piece of twenty-ninth-century technology on his twenty-fourth-century holographic shoulder, which is a clear violation of the Temporal Prime Directive, but it ain't gonna be my butt.

Rarely in television is an actor handed a character that is basically a blank slate but that's what Robert Picardo got when he was handed the Doctor. Though the writers laid out the character sketch, Picardo came in and made the Doctor his own, injecting him with sarcastic humor and dramatic pathos. Often a contradiction, the Doctor was both loved by and a bother to the crew, childish and mature, and unfeeling and all too human. At the very core, he was the traditional *Star Trek* character serving as a reflection of humanity through his own lack of traditional human characteristics.

CREW MANIFEST

NAME	RANK	AFFILIATION	STATUS
Anderson, Lydia	Unknown	Unknown	
Andrews	Unknown	Unknown	
Ashmore	Ensign	Unknown	
Ayala	Lieutenant	Maquis	
Azan	None	None	Departed
Ballard, Lyndsay	Ensign	Starfleet	Deceased
Baxter, Walter	Lieutenant	Starfleet	
Baytart, Pablo	Ensign	Unknown	
Bendera, Kurt	Crewman	Maquis	Deceased
Bennet	Ensign	Starfleet	Deceased
Biddle	Crewman	Unknown	
Boylen	Crewman	Unknown	
Bristow, Freddy	Ensign	Unknown	
Bronowsky, Doug	Ensign	Starfleet	
Brooks	Ensign	Starfleet	
Carey, Joe	Lieutenant	Starfleet	Deceased
Carlson	Unknown	Maquis	
Cavit	Lt. Commander	Starfleet	Deceased
Chakotay	First Officer	Maquis	
Chapman, William	Lieutenant	Starfleet	
Chell	Crewman	Maquis	
Culhane	Ensign	Unknown	
Dalby, Kenneth	Crewman	Maquis	
Darwin, Frank	Crewman	Starfleet	Deceased
Delaney, Jenny	Unknown	Unknown	
Delaney, Megan	Unknown	Unknown	
Dell	Crewman	Unknown	
Doctor	Chief Medical Officer	Starfleet	

NAME	RANK	AFFILIATION	STATUS
Dorado	Unknown	Unknown	
Doyle	Unknown	Maquis	
Durst, Peter	Lieutenant	Starfleet	Deceased
Emmanuel	Crewman	Unknown	
Farley	Ensign	Unknown	
Fitzpatirck	Crewman	Unknown	
Foster	Crewman	Unknown	
Gallagher	Ensign	Unknown	
Gennaro	Crewman	Unknown	
Gerron	Crewman	Maquis	
Gibson, Patrick	Unknown	Unknown	
Gilmore, Marla	Crewman	Starfleet (*Equinox*)	
Golwat	Ensign	Unknown	
Grimes	Unknown	Unknown	
Hamilton	Unknown	Unknown	
Hargrove	Lieutenant	Unknown	
Harper	Ensign	Unknown	
Harren, Mortimer	Crewman	Starfleet	
Henard	Unknown	Unknown	
Henly, Mariah	Crewman	Maquis	
Hickman	Ensign	Unknown	
Hogan	Ensign	Maquis	Deceased
Icheb	None	None	
Jackson	Unknown	Maquis	
Janeway, Kathryn	Captain	Starfleet	
Jarvin	Unknown	Maquis	
Jarvis	Unknown	Starfleet	
Jenkins	Ensign	Unknown	
Jetal	Ensign	Starfleet	Deceased
Jonas, Michael	Crewman	Maquis	Deceased
Jones	Unknown	Unknown	
Jor	Crewman	Maquis	
Jurot	Ensign	Unknown	
Kaplan	Ensign	Unknown	
Kaplan, Marie	Ensign	Unknown	Deceased
Kes	None	None	Departed
Kim, Harry	Ensign	Starfleet	
Kyoto	Ensign	Unknown	
Lang	Ensign	Starfleet	
Lang, Timothy	Crewman	Unknown	Deceased
Larson	Unknown	Starfleet	
Lessing, Noah	Crewman	Starfleet (*Equinox*)	
Lewis	Unknown	Unknown	
MacAlister	Unknown	Unknown	
Macormak	Ensign	Unknown	
Mannus	Ensign	Starfleet	

NAME	RANK	AFFILIATION	STATUS
Martin	Ensign	Unknown	Deceased
McKenzie, William	Unknown	Unknown	
McMinn	Unknown	Unknown	
Mendez	Unknown	Unknown	
Mezoti	None	None	Departed
Mitchell	Crewman	Unknown	
Molina	Ensign	Starfleet	
Morrow, James	Crewman	Starfleet (*Equinox*)	
Mulchaey	Ensign	Starfleet	
Murphy	Ensign	Unknown	
Neelix	Crewman	None	Departed
Nicoletti, Susan	Lieutenant	Starfleet	
Nozowa, Kashimuro	Unknown	Unknown	
O'Donnell	Unknown	Maquis	
One	None	None	Deceased
Orlando	Unknown	Starfleet	
Paris, Miral	None	None	
Paris, Tom	Lieutenant	Starfleet	
Parsons	Ensign	Unknown	
Peterson	Unknown	Starfleet	
Platt	Unknown	Starfleet	
Porter	Unknown	Starfleet	
Powell	Ensign	Startfleet	
Quinn	None	None	Deceased
Rebi	None	None	Departed
Robertson	Unknown	Unknown	
Rogers	Unknown	Unknown	
Rollins	Lieutenant	Starfleet	
Ryson	Ensign	Unknown	
Seska	Ensign	Maquis (Cardassian)	Deceased
Seven of Nine	None	None	
Sharr, Renlay	Ensign	Starfleet	
Sofin, Brian	Crewman	Starfleet (*Equinox*)	
Stadi	Lieutenant	Starfleet	Deceased
Strickler	Ensign	Unknown	
Suder, Lon	Crewman	Maquis	Deceased
Swinn	Ensign	Starfleet	
Tabor	Ensign	Maquis	
Tal Celes	Crewman	Starfleet	
Tassori, Angelo	Crewman	Starfleet (*Equinox*)	
Telfer, William	Crewman	Starfleet	
Thompson	Unknown	Unknown	
Torres, B'Elanna	Lieutenant	Maquis	
Trumari	Ensign	Unknown	
Tuvix	Lieutenant	Starfleet	Deceased
Tuvok	Lt. Commander	Starfleet	

NAME	RANK	AFFILIATION	STATUS
Unai	Crewman	Unknown	
Vorik	Ensign	Starfleet	
Weiss	Lieutenant	Unknown	
White	Crewman	Unknown	
Wildman, Naomi	None	None	
Wildman, Samantha	Ensign	Starfleet	
Willkarah, Marika	Unknown	Starfleet (*Excaliber*)	Deceased
Yosa	Crewman	Maquis	
Unnamed Doctor	Chief Medical Officer	Starfleet	Deceased
Unnamed Nurse	Unknown	Starfleet	Deceased
Unnamed Chief Engineer	Unknown	Starfleet	Deceased

PRODUCTION CREDITS

Staff listed without numbers following their names are credited on every episode of the season.

SEASON 1 CREDITS*
Star Trek: Voyager
BASED UPON STAR TREK CREATED BY GENE RODDENBERRY

STARRING

Kate Mulgrew as Captain Kathryn Janeway
Robert Beltran as Chakotay
Roxann Biggs-Dawson as B'Elanna Torres
Jennifer Lien as Kes
Robert Duncan McNeill as Tom Paris
Ethan Phillips as Neelix
Robert Picardo as The Doctor
Tim Russ as Tuvok
Garrett Wang as Harry Kim

PRODUCTION STAFF

Created by: Rick Berman & Michael Piller & Jeri Taylor
Theme by: Jerry Goldsmith
Co-Producer: Wendy Neuss
Producer: Brannon Braga (103-120)
Producer: Merri Howard
Producer: Peter Lauritson
Supervising Producer: David Livingston
Executive Producers: Rick Berman & Michael Piller & Jeri Taylor
Executive Story Editor: Kenneth Biller (103-120)
Casting by: Nan Dutton, C.S.A. (101/102), Kathryn S.

Eisenstein (101/102), Junie Lowry-Johnson, C.S.A. (103-120), Ron Surma (103-120)
Original Casting by: Nan Dutton, C.S.A. (103-120), Kathryn S. Eisenstein (103-110)
Music by: Jay Chattaway (101/102, 104, 106, 109, 110, 113, 116, 119), Dennis McCarthy (103, 105, 107, 108, 111, 112, 115, 118, 120), David Bell (114, 117)
Director of Photography: Marvin V. Rush, A.S.C. (101/102, 103-108, 110-120), Joe Chess Jr. (109)
Production Designer: Richard D. James
Editor: Tom Benko A.C.E. (103, 106, 109, 112, 114, 118), Daryl Baskin (104, 107, 110, 113, 116, 119), Robert Lederman (105,108, 111, 114, 117, 120)
Edited by: J.P. Farrell (101/102), Daryl Baskin (101/102)
Unit Production Manager: Brad Yacobian
First Assistant Director: Jerry Fleck (101/102, 104, 106, 108, 110, 112, 114, 116, 118, 120), James S. Griffin (103), Adele Simmons (105, 107, 109, 111, 113, 115, 117, 119)
Second Assistant Director: Arlene Fukai
2nd Second Assistant Director: Michael DeMeritt (101/102)
Costume Designer: Robert Blackman
Set Decorator: Jim Mees
Visual Effects Producer: Dan Curry
Visual Effects Supervisor: David Stipes (101/102, 107, 109, 111, 113, 115, 117, 119), Philip Barberio (103), Robert D. Bailey (104, 107), Joe Bauer (105),

*Episodes 117-120 while produced as part of Season 1 aired the following season.

Ronald B. Moore (106, 108, 110, 112, 114, 116, 118, 120)

Post Production Supervisor: Dawn Velazquez

Supervising Editor: J.P. Farrell

Scenic Art Supervisor/Technical Consultant: Michael Okuda

Senior Illustrator/Technical Consultant: Rick Sternbach

Make-Up Designed and Supervised by: Michael Westmore

Art Director: Andrew Neskoromny (101/102, 103, 104), Michael L. Mayer (105-120)

Set Designer: Gary Speckman (101/102, 103, 105, 107, 109), Louise Dorton (101/102, 104, 106, 108, 110-120), John Chichester (101/102)

Visual Effects Coordinator: Michael Backauskas (101/102, 106, 108, 110, 112, 114, 116, 118, 120), Joe Bauer (101/102, 103, 109, 111, 113, 115, 117, 119), Philip Barberio (121), Edward L. Williams (101/102, 104, 107)

Visual Effects Series Coordinator: Philip Barberio (105-110), Edward L. Williams (111-120)

Visual Effects Associate: Frederick G. Alba (101/102), Edward L. Williams (103, 105, 106, 108-110), Arthur J. Codron (111-120)

Visual Effects Assistant Editor: Arthur J. Codron (101/102)

Script Supervisor: Cosmo Genovese

Special Effects: Dick Brownfield

Property Master: Alan Sims

Construction Coordinator: Al Smutko

Scenic Artists: Jim Magdaleno (101/102, 103, 105, 107, 109, 111, 117, 119, Wendy Drapanas (101/102, 104, 106, 108, 110, 112-114, 116, 118, 120)

Illustrator: Jim Martin (101/102)

Video Coordinator: Denise Okuda

Video Consultant: Elizabeth Radly (101/102)

Video Playback Operator: Larry Markart (101/102), Ben Betts (101/102)

Hair Designer: Josée Normand

Make-Up Artists: Greg Nelson (101/102, 103-105, 107-109, 111-117, 119, 120), Tina Hoffman (101/102, 103, 104, 106-108 110-112, 115, 116, 118-120), Scott Wheeler (101/102, 103, 105-107, 109-111, 113-115, 117-119), Mark Shostrom (101/102, 104-106, 108-110, 112-114, 116-118, 120)

Hair Stylists: Patricia Miller, Karen Asano-Myers (101/102, 103, 105, 107, 109, 111, 115, 117, 119), Shawn McKay (101/102, 104, 106, 108, 110, 112, 113, 116, 118, 120)

Wardrobe Supervisor: Carol Kunz (101/102, 104, 106, 108, 110, 112, 116, 118, 120), Camille Argus (103, 105, 107, 109, 111, 113-115, 117, 119)

Sound Mixer: Alan Bernard, C.A.S.

Camera Operator: Joe Chess S.O.C. (101/102, 103-108, 110-120), Ron High S.O.C. (109)

Chief Lighting Technician: Bill Peets

First Company Grip: Bob Sordal

Key Costumers: Tom Siegel (101/102, 104, 106, 108, 110, 112, 114, 116, 118, 120), Camille Argus (101/102), Matt Hoffman (101/102, 104, 106, 108, 110, 112, 114, 116, 118, 120), Jamie Thomas (101/102, 103, 105, 107, 109, 111, 113, 115, 117, 119), Kimberley Shull (103, 105, 107, 109, 111, 113, 115, 117, 119)

Music Editor: Gerry Sackman

Supervising Sound Editor: Bill Wistrom

Supervising Sound Effects Editor: Jim Wolvington

Sound Editors: Miguel Rivera, Masanobu Tomita, Ruth Adelman

Post Production Sound by: Modern Sound

Production Coordinator: Diane Overdiek

Post Porduction Coordinator: Cheryl Gluckstern

Production Associates: Kristine Fernandes, Kim Fitzgerald (101/102), Zayra Cabot, David Rossi, Sandra Sena (103-120)

Pre-Production Coordinator: Lolita Fatjo

Casting Executive: Helen Mossler, C.S.A.

Casting Assistant: Libby Goldstein (101/102)

Stunt Coordinator: Dennis Madalone (101/102, 103, 104, 106, 108, 111-114, 116-118, 120)

Transportation Captain: Steward Satterfield (101/102)

Location Manager: Lisa White (101/102, 104, 111, 120)

Science Consultant: Andre Bormanis

Filmed with Panavision® Cameras and Lenses

Assistant Editor: Lisa De Moraes (101/102)

Main Title Design by: Santa Barbara Studios, Dan Curry

Re-Recording Mixers: Chris Haire, C.A.S. (101/102), Doug Davey (101/102), Richard Morrison, C.A.S. (101/102)

Motion Control Photography: Image G

Digital Optical Effects: Digital Magic (101/102, 103-116, 119), Pacific Ocean Post (117, 118, 120)

Computer Animation: Amblin Imaging (101/102, 105), Santa Barbara Studios (106, 118, 120)

Computer Generated Effects: Amblin Imaging (107, 109, 119)

Special Video Compositing: CIS, Hollywood

Editing Facilities: Unitel Video

Matte Paintings: Illusion Arts (101/102), Eric Chauvin (101/102)

Miniatures: Tony Meininger (101/102), Wonderworks (101/102), Don Pennington (101/102), Tony Doublin (101/102)

SEASON 2 CREDITS*
Star Trek: Voyager
BASED UPON *STAR TREK* CREATED BY GENE RODDENBERRY

STARRING

Kate Mulgrew as Captain Kathryn Janeway
Robert Beltran as Chakotay
Roxann Biggs-Dawson as B'Elanna Torres
Jennifer Lien as Kes
Robert Duncan McNeill as Tom Paris
Ethan Phillips as Neelix
Robert Picardo as The Doctor
Tim Russ as Tuvok
Garrett Wang as Harry Kim

PRODUCTION STAFF

Created by: Rick Berman & Michael Piller & Jeri Taylor
Theme by: Jerry Goldsmith
Line Producer: Brad Yacobian
Co-Producer: Kenneth Biller (134-146)
Producer: Wendy Neuss
Producer: Merri D. Howard
Supervising Producer: Peter Lauritson
Supervising Producer: Brannon Braga
Executive Producers: Rick Berman & Michael Piller & Jeri Taylor
Executive Story Editor: Kenneth Biller (121-133)
Music by: Dennis McCarthy (121, 123, 125, 126, 128, 129, 131, 134, 137, 141, 142, 144, 146), Jay Chattaway (122, 127, 130, 132, 135, 138, 140, 143), David Bell (124, 133, 139, 145), Paul Baillargeon (136)
Director of Photography: Marvin V. Rush, A.S.C. (121-137, 140-146), Douglas H. Knapp (138, 139)
Production Designer: Richard D. James
Editor: Tom Benko A.C.E. (121, 124, 127, 130, 133, 136, 139, 142, 145), Daryl Baskin (122, 125, 128, 131, 134, 137, 140, 143, 146), Robert Lederman (123, 126, 129, 132, 135, 138, 141, 144)
Unit Production Manager: Brad Yacobian
First Assistant Director: Adele Simmons (121, 123, 125, 127, 129, 131, 133, 135, 137, 139, 141, 143, 145), Jerry Fleck (122, 124, 126, 128, 130, 132, 134, 136, 138), Arlene Fukai (140, 144), Louis Race (142, 146)
Second Assistant Director: Arlene Fukai (121-138, 141, 142, 145, 146), Michael DeMeritt (139, 140, 143, 144)

Casting by: Junie Lowry-Johnson, C.S.A., Ron Surma
Original Casting by: Nan Dutton, C.S.A.
Casting Executive: Helen Mossler, C.S.A.
Costume Designer: Robert Blackman
Set Decorator: Leslie Frankenheimer
Visual Effects Producer: Dan Curry
Visual Effects Supervisor: David Stipes (121, 123, 125, 127, 129, 131, 133, 135, 137), Ronald B. Moore (122, 124, 126, 128, 130, 132, 134, 136, 138, 140, 142, 144, 146), Edward L. Williams (139), Joe Bauer (141, 143, 145)
Post Production Supervisor: Dawn Velazquez
Supervising Editor: J.P. Farrell
Scenic Art Supervisor/Technical Consultant: Michael Okuda (121-137)
Scenic Art Consultant: Michael Okuda (138-146)
Senior Illustrator/Technical Consultant: Rick Sternbach
Make-Up Designed and Supervised by: Michael Westmore
Art Director: Michael L. Mayer
Set Designer: Louise Dorton
Assistant Editor: James A. Garrett (139, 142, 145), Lisa de Moraes (140, 143, 146), Eugene Wood (141, 144)
Visual Effects Coordinator: Joe Bauer (121, 123, 125, 127, 129, 131, 133, 135, 137, 139), Arthur J. Codron (122, 124, 126, 128, 130, 132, 134, 136, 138, 140, 142, 144, 146), Ziad Seirafi (141, 143, 145)
Visual Effects Series Coordinator: Edward L. Williams (121-138, 140-146)
Visual Effects Associate: Cheryl Gluckstern
Script Supervisor: Cosmo Genovese
Special Effects: Dick Brownfield
Property Master: Alan Sims
Construction Coordinator: Al Smutko
Scenic Artist: Jim Magdaleno (121, 123, 125, 127), Wendy Drapanas (122, 124, 126, 128, 130, 132, 134, 136, 138, 140, 142, 144, 146)
Junior Illustrator: Jim Magdaleno (129, 131, 133, 135, 137, 139, 141, 143, 145)
Video Coordinator: Denise Okuda
Hair Designer: Suzan Bagdadi
Make-Up Artists: Scott Wheeler (121-123, 125-127, 129-131, 133-135, 137, 138, 141-143, 146), Mark Shostrom (121, 122, 124-126, 128-130, 132-134, 136, 137, 140-142, 145, 146), Greg Nelson (121, 123-125, 127-129, 131-133, 135-137, 139-141, 144-146), Tina Hoffman (122-124, 126-128, 130-132, 134-136, 138, 139, 142-144), Gil Mosko (138-140, 143-145)

*Episodes 143-146, while produced as part of Season 2, aired the following season.

Hair Stylists: Barbara Minster, Karen Asano-Myers (121-123, 125, 127, 129, 131, 133, 135, 137, 139, 141, 143, 145), Laura Connolly (124, 126, 128, 130, 132, 134, 136, 138, 140, 142, 144, 146)

Wardrobe Supervisor: Carol Kunz (121, 123, 125, 127, 129, 131, 133, 135, 137, 139, 141, 143, 145), Camille Argus (122, 124, 126, 128, 130, 132, 134, 136, 138, 140, 142, 144, 146)

Sound Mixer: Alan Bernard, C.A.S.

Camera Operator: Doug Knapp, S.O.C. (121-137, 140-146), Ron E. High S.O.C. (138, 139)

Chief Lighting Technician: Bill Peets

First Company Grip: Randy Burgess

Key Costumers: Tom Siegel (121-123, 125, 127, 129, 131, 133, 135, 137, 139, 141, 143, 145), Matt Hoffman (121, 123, 125, 127, 129, 131, 133, 135, 137, 139, 141, 143, 145), Jamie Thomas (122, 124, 126, 128, 130, 132, 134, 136, 138, 140, 142, 144, 146), Kimberley Shull (124, 126, 128, 130, 132, 134, 136, 138, 140, 142, 144, 146)

Music Editor: Gerry Sackman

Supervising Sound Editor: Bill Wistrom

Supervising Sound Effects Editor: Jim Wolvington

Sound Editors: Miguel Rivera, Masanobu Tomita, Ruth Adelman

Visual Effects Assistant Editor: Elizabeth Castro (139-146)

Production Coordinator: Diane Overdiek

Post Production Coordinator: Cara Colombini (121-130), April Rossi (131-146)

Production Associates: David Rossi, Zayra Cabot (121-139), Sandra Sena, Eric A. Stillwell (142-146)

Pre-Production Coordinator: Lolita Fatjo

Stunt Coordinator: Dennis Madalone (121-124, 126-128, 131, 132, 135, 137, 139, 142-146)

Location Manger: Lisa White (121, 125, 130, 141, 142, 146)

Science Consultant: Andre Bormanis

Main Title Design by: Santa Barbara Studios, Dan Curry

Colorization: CST Entertainment, Inc. (126)

Filmed with Panavision® Cameras and Lenses

Post Production Sound by: Modern Sound

Motion Control Photography: Image G

Digital Optical Effects: Digital Magic

Special Video Compositing: CIS, Hollywood

Computer Generated Effects: Amblin Imaging (123, 129, 135), Digital Muse (137, 138, 142, 146), Foundation Imaging (142, 146), Vision Art Design & Imagination (142, 146)

Computer-Generated Imagery: Pacific Ocean Post (132)

Computer Animation: Vision Art Design & Animation (122, 124, 126, 134), Santa Barbara Studios (126, 130, 136), Amblin Imaging (132)

Editing Facilities: Unitel Video

SEASON 3 CREDITS
Star Trek: Voyager
BASED UPON *STAR TREK* CREATED BY GENE RODDENBERRY

STARRING

Kate Mulgrew as Captain Kathryn Janeway
Robert Beltran as Chakotay
Roxann Dawson as B'Elanna Torres
Jennifer Lien as Kes
Robert Duncan McNeill as Tom Paris
Ethan Phillips as Neelix
Robert Picardo as The Doctor
Tim Russ as Tuvok
Garrett Wang as Harry Kim

PRODUCTION STAFF

Created by: Rick Berman & Michael Piller & Jeri Taylor
Theme by: Jerry Goldsmith
Creative Consultant: Michael Piller
Line Producer: Brad Yacobian
Co-Producer: J.P. Farrell
Co-Producer: Kenneth Biller (147-156)
Producer: Kenneth Biller (157-168)
Producer: Joe Menosky
Producer: Wendy Neuss
Producer: Merri D. Howard
Supervising Producer: Peter Lauritson
Supervising Producer: Brannon Braga
Executive Producers: Rick Berman & Jeri Taylor
Associate Producer: Dawn Velazquez (147-159, 164-168)
Story Editor: Lisa Klink
Music by: Jay Chattaway (147, 150, 151, 157, 160, 163, 166, 168), David Bell (148, 152, 156, 159, 165), Dennis McCarthy (149, 153, 154, 158, 162, 164, 167), Paul Baillargeon (155, 161)
Director of Photography: Marvin V. Rush, A.S.C. (147-160, 163-168), Douglas H. Knapp (161, 162)
Production Designer: Richard D. James
Editor: Robert Lederman (147, 150, 153, 156, 159, 162, 165, 168), Tom Benko A.C.E. (148, 151, 154, 157, 160, 163, 166), Daryl Baskin (149, 152, 155, 158, 161, 164, 167)
Unit Production Manager: Brad Yacobian

First Assistant Director: Adele Simmons (147, 151, 153, 155, 157, 159, 161, 163, 165, 167), Jerry Fleck (148, 150, 152, 154, 156, 158, 160, 162, 164, 166, 168), Arlene Fukai (149)

Second Assistant Director: Arlene Fukai (147, 148, 150-168), Michael DeMeritt (149)

Casting by: Junie Lowry-Johnson, C.S.A., Ron Surma

Original Casting by: Nan Dutton, C.S.A.

Casting Executive: Helen Mossler, C.S.A.

Costume Designer: Robert Blackman

Set Decorator: Leslie Frankenheimer

Visual Effects Producer: Dan Curry

Visual Effects Supervisor: Mitch Suskin (147, 149, 152, 153, 155, 157, 159, 161, 163, 165, 167), Ronald B. Moore (148, 150, 151, 154, 156, 158, 160, 164, 166, 168), David Takemura (162)

Post Production Supervisor: Tom Scanlan (161-163)

Scenic Art Supervisor/Technical Consultant: Michael Okuda

Senior Illustrator/Technical Consultant: Rick Sternbach

Make-Up Designed and Supervised by: Michael Westmore

Art Director: Leslie Parsons (147-162)

Assistant Art Director: Louise Dorton

Assistant Editor: Jacques Gravett (147, 150, 153, 156, 159, 162, 165, 168), David A. Koeppel (148, 151, 154, 157, 160, 163, 166), Lisa de Moraes (149, 152, 155, 158, 161, 164, 167)

Visual Effects Coordinator: Arthur J. Codron (147, 149, 152, 153, 155, 157, 159, 161, 163, 165, 167), Eugene Wood (148, 150, 151, 154, 156, 158, 160, 164, 166), A.Y. Dexter Delara (162), Cheryl Gluckstern (168)

Visual Effects Series Coordinator: Edward L. Williams (147-155)

Visual Effects Assocaite: Cheryl Gluckstern (147-167)

Script Supervisor: Cosmo Genovese

Special Effects: Dick Brownfield

Property Master: Alan Sims

Construction Coordinator: Al Smutko

Scenic Artist: Wendy Drapanas (147, 149, 151, 153, 155, 157, 159, 161, 163, 165, 167), James Van Over (157), S.J. Casey Bernay (159)

Junior Illustrator: Jim Magdaleno (148, 150, 152, 154, 156, 158, 160, 162, 164, 166, 168)

Video Coordinator: Denise Okuda (147-156, 161-168)

Video Playback Operator: Ben Betts (158, 160)

Hair Designer: Josée Normand

Make-Up Artists: Tina Hoffman (147-150, 152-154, 156-158, 160, 161), Scott Wheeler (147, 148, 151-153, 155-157, 159-161, 163-165, 167, 168), Mark

Shostrom (147, 150-152, 154-156, 158-160, 162-164, 166-168), Gil Mosko (148, 149), Greg Nelson (149-151, 153-155, 157-159, 161-163, 165-167), Bradley M. Look (162, 164-166, 168)

Hair Stylists: Suzan Bagdadi, Karen Asano-Myers (147, 149, 151, 153, 155, 157, 159, 161, 163, 165, 167), Charlotte A. Gravenor (148, 150, 152, 154, 156, 158, 160, 162, 164, 166, 168)

Wardrobe Supervisor: Carol Kunz (147, 149, 151, 153, 155, 157-168), Camille Argus (148, 150, 152, 154, 156)

Sound Mixer: Alan Bernard, C.A.S.

Camera Operator: Doug Knapp, S.O.C. (147-160, 163-168), Pernell Tyus (161, 162)

Chief Lighting Technician: Bill Peets

First Company Grip: Randy Burgess

Key Costumers: Tom Siegel (147, 149, 151, 153, 155, 157, 159, 161, 163, 165, 167), Matt Hoffman (147, 149, 151, 153, 155, 157, 159, 161, 163, 165, 167), Kimberley Shull (148, 150, 152, 154, 156, 158, 160, 162, 164, 166, 168), Jamie Thomas (148, 150, 152, 154, 156, 158, 160, 162, 164, 166, 168)

Music Editor: Gerry Sackman

Supervising Sound Editor: Bill Wistrom

Supervising Sound Effects Editor: Jim Wolvington

Sound Editors: Miguel Rivera (147-151), Masanobu Tomita, Ruth Adelman, Dale Chaloukian (152-168)

Visual Effects Assistant Editor: Elizabeth Castro

Production Coordinator: Diane Overdiek

Post Production Coordinator: April Rossi

Production Associates: David Rossi, Sandra Sena (147-158)

Pre-Production Coordinator: Lolita Fatjo

Assistant to Producers: Lorraine Fischer (147, 149, 153, 157), Michael O'Halloran (148, 150, 154, 158, 162, 166), Robert J. Doherty (151, 155, 159, 163, 167), Christopher Culhane (152, 156, 160, 164, 168), Maril Davis (161, 165)

Stunt Coordinator: Dennis Madalone

Location Manager: Lisa White (150, 151, 153)

Science Consultant: Andre Bormanis

Main Title Design by: Santa Barbara Studios, Dan Curry

Post Production Sound: Modern Sound

Filmed with Panavision® Cameras and Lenses

Motion Control Photography: Image G

Digital Optical Effects: Digital Magic

Special Video Compositing: CIS, Hollywood

Editing Facilities: Unitel Video

Computer Generated Effects: Digital Muse (147, 162), Foundation Imaging (149-151, 153-155, 159, 163-165, 167, 168), Digital Magic (160)

SEASON 4 CREDITS
Star Trek: Voyager
BASED UPON *STAR TREK* CREATED BY
GENE RODDENBERRY

STARRING

Kate Mulgrew as Captain Kathryn Janeway
Robert Beltran as Chakotay
Roxann Dawson as B'Elanna Torres
Robert Duncan McNeill as Tom Paris
Ethan Phillips as Neelix
Robert Picardo as The Doctor
Tim Russ as Tuvok
Jeri Ryan as Seven of Nine
Garrett Wang as Harry Kim

PRODUCTION STAFF

Created by: Rick Berman & Michael Piller & Jeri Taylor
Theme by: Jerry Goldsmith
Creative Consultant: Michael Piller
Line Producer: Brad Yacobian
Co-Producer: J.P. Farrell
Producer: Kenneth Biller
Producer: Joe Menosky
Producer: Wendy Neuss (169-177)
Co-Supervising Producer: Merri D. Howard
Supervising Producer: Peter Lauritson
Co-Executive Producer: Brannon Braga
Executive Producers: Rick Berman & Jeri Taylor
Associate Producer: Dawn Velazquez
Executive Story Editor: Lisa Klink
Music by: Jay Chattaway (169, 175, 178, 183, 185, 190, 193), Dennis McCarthy (170, 172, 174, 176, 177, 179, 184, 188, 191, 194), David Bell (171, 173, 182, 186, 187, 192), Paul Baillargeon (180, 181, 189)
Director of Photography: Marvin V. Rush, A.S.C. (169-173, 180-191, 193, 194), Douglas H. Knapp (174-179, 192)
Production Designer: Richard D. James
Editor: Tom Benko A.C.E. (169, 172, 175, 178, 181, 184, 187, 190, 193), Daryl Baskin (170, 173, 176, 179, 182, 185, 188, 191, 194), Robert Lederman (171, 174, 177, 180, 183, 186, 189, 192)
Unit Production Manager: Brad Yacobian
First Assistant Director: Jerry Fleck (169, 171, 173, 175, 177, 179, 181, 183, 185, 187, 189, 191), Adele Simmons (170, 172, 174, 176, 178, 180, 182, 184, 186, 188, 190, 192, 194), Joe Candrella (193)
Second Assistant Director: Arlene Fukai (169-188), Michael DeMerritt (189-194)

Casting by: Junie Lowry-Johnson, C.S.A., Ron Surma
Original Casting by: Nan Dutton, C.S.A.
Casting Executive: Helen Mossler, C.S.A.
Costume Designer: Robert Blackman
Set Decorator: Jim Mees
Visual Effects Producer: Dan Curry
Visual Effects Supervisor: Mitch Suskin (169, 171, 177, 179, 181, 183, 187, 189, 191, 193), David Takemura (170, 173, 175, 185), Ronald B. Moore (172, 174, 176, 178, 180, 182, 184, 186, 188, 190, 192, 194)
Post Production Supervisor: Stephen Welke (178-194)
Scenic Art Supervisor/Technical Consultant: Michael Okuda
Senior Illustrator/Technical Consultant: Rick Sternbach
Make-Up Designed and Supervised by: Michael Westmore
Art Director: Louise Dorton
Set Designer: Greg Berry (169, 171, 173, 175, 177, 179, 181, 183, 185, 187, 189, 191, 193), Greg Hooper (170, 172, 174, 176, 178, 180, 182, 184, 186, 188, 190, 192, 194)
Assistant Editor: David A. Koeppel (169, 172, 175, 178, 181, 184, 187, 190, 193), Keith Dabney (170, 173, 176, 179, 182, 185, 188, 191, 194), Jacques Gravett (171, 174, 177, 180, 183, 186, 189, 192)
Visual Effects Coordinator: Arthur J. Codron (169, 171, 177, 179, 181, 183, 187, 189, 191, 193), A.Y. Dexter Delara (170, 173, 175, 185), Cheryl Gluckstern (172), Elizabeth Castro (174, 176, 178, 180, 182, 184, 186, 188, 190, 192, 194)
Visual Effects Assistant Editor: Elizabeth Castro (169-172), Paul Villaseñor (173-194)
Visual Effects Associate: Chad Zimmerman
Script Supervisor: Cosmo Genovese
Special Effects: Dick Brownfield
Property Master: Alan Sims
Construction Coordinator: Al Smutko
Scenic Artist: Wendy Drapanas
Video Supervisor: Denise Okuda
Hair Designer: Josée Normand
Make-Up Artists: Tina Hoffman (169-171, 173-175, 177-179, 181-183, 185-187, 189-191, 193, 194), Scott Wheeler (169, 170, 172-174, 176-178, 180-182, 184-86, 188-190, 192-194), Bradley M. Look (169, 171-173, 175-177, 179-181, 183-185, 187-189, 191-193), Natalie Wood (170-172, 174-176, 178-180, 182-184, 186-188, 190-192, 194)
Hair Stylists: Suzan Bagdadi (169-172, 174, 176), Viviane Normand (169, 171, 173, 175, 177, 178, 180, 182, 184, 186, 188, 190, 192, 194), Charlotte

A. Gravenor (170, 172-194), Gloria Montemayor (179, 181, 183, 185, 187, 189, 191, 193)

Wardrobe Supervisor: Carol Kunz

Sound Mixer: Alan Bernard, C.A.S. (169-178, 180-194), Greg Agalsoff (179)

Camera Operator: Judd Kehl (169-171, 174-178), Douglas Knapp S.O.C. (172, 173, 180-191, 193, 194), Bill Asman S.O.C. (179, 192)

Chief Lighting Technician: Bill Peets

First Company Grip: Randy Burgess

Key Costumers: Tom Siegel (169, 171, 173, 175, 177, 179, 181, 183, 185, 187, 189, 191, 193), Matt Hoffman (169, 171, 173, 175, 177, 179, 181, 183, 185, 187, 189, 191, 193), Kimberley Shull (170, 172, 174, 176, 178, 180, 182, 184, 186, 188, 190, 192, 194), Jamie Thomas (170, 172, 174, 176, 180, 182, 184, 186, 188, 190, 192, 194)

Music Editor: Gerry Sackman

Supervising Sound Editor: Bill Wistrom

Supervising Sound Effects Editor: Jim Wolvington

Sound Editors: Masanobu Tomita, Ruth Adelman (169), Dale Chaloukian (169-194), T. Ashley Harvey (170-194)

Production Coordinator: Diane Overdiek

Post Production Coordinator: April Rossi

Production Associates: David Rossi, Kristina Kochoff, Sandra Sena

Pre-Production Coordinator: Lolita Fatjo

Assistant to Producers: Maril Davis (169, 173, 177, 181, 185, 189, 193), Michael O'Halloran (170, 174, 178, 182, 186, 190, 194), Christopher Culhane (171, 175, 179, 183, 187, 191), Robert J. Doherty (172, 176, 180, 184, 188, 192)

Stunt Coordinator: Dennis Madalone (169-174, 177-180, 182-187, 191, 194)

Location Manager: Lisa White (171, 179, 186, 187)

Science Consultant: Andre Bormanis

Main Title Design by: Santa Barbara Studios, Dan Curry

Post Production Sound: Modern Sound

Filmed with Panavision® Cameras and Lenses

Motion Control Photography: Image G (169-185)

Digital Optical Effects: Digital Magic (169-180, 182, 184-186, 188-194), POP Television (181, 183, 187, 189, 191, 193)

Special Video Compositing: CIS, Hollywood

Editing Facilities: Unitel Video (169-171), Editel/LA (172-194)

Computer Generated Effects: Foundation Imaging (169-172, 174-184, 187, 189, 190, 191, 193, 194), Digital Muse (176, 181, 183, 185-188, 190, 192, 193)

Matte Painting: Open Films (182)

SEASON 5 CREDITS
Star Trek: Voyager
BASED UPON *STAR TREK* CREATED BY
GENE RODDENBERRY

STARRING

Kate Mulgrew as Captain Kathryn Janeway
Robert Beltran as Chakotay
Roxann Dawson as B'Elanna Torres
Robert Duncan McNeill as Tom Paris
Ethan Phillips as Neelix
Robert Picardo as The Doctor
Tim Russ as Tuvok
Jeri Ryan as Seven of Nine
Garrett Wang as Harry Kim

PRODUCTION STAFF

Created by: Rick Berman & Michael Piller & Jeri Taylor
Theme by: Jerry Goldsmith
Creative Consultant: Jeri Taylor
Creative Consultant: Michael Piller
Line Producer: Brad Yacobian
Co-Producer: J.P. Farrell
Producer: Kenneth Biller (195-204)
Co-Supervising Producer: Merri D. Howard
Supervising Producer: Kenneth Biller (205-220)
Supervising Producer: Joe Menosky
Supervising Producer: Peter Lauritson
Executive Producers: Rick Berman & Brannon Braga
Co-Producer: Dawn Velazquez
Associate Producer: Stephen Welke (208-220)
Story Editor: Bryan Fuller
Story Editor: Nick Sagan
Music by: Jay Chattaway (195, 198, 204, 208, 214, 219, 220), Dennis McCarthy (196, 200, 201, 203, 205, 209, 210, 215, 216, 218), David Bell (197, 199, 207, 211, 212, 217), Paul Baillargeon (202, 206, 213)
Director of Photography: Marvin V. Rush, A.S.C.
Production Designer: Richard D. James
Editor: Robert Lederman (195, 198, 201, 204, 207, 210, 213, 216, 217), Tom Benko, A.C.E. (196, 199, 202, 205, 208, 211, 214, 217, 220), Daryl Baskin (197, 200, 203, 206, 209, 212, 215, 218)
Unit Production Manager: Brad Yacobian
First Assistant Director: Adele Simmons (195, 197, 199, 201, 203, 205), Arlene Fukai (196, 198, 207, 209, 211, 213, 215, 217, 219), Jerry Fleck (200, 202, 204, 206, 208, 210, 212, 214, 216, 218, 220)
Second Assistant Director: Michael DeMeritt
Casting by: Junie Lowry-Johnson, C.S.A., Ron Surma

Original Casting by: Nan Dutton, C.S.A.

Casting Executive: Helen Mossler, C.S.A.

Costume Designer: Robert Blackman

Set Decorator: Jim Mees

Visual Effects Producer: Dan Curry

Visual Effects Supervisor: Mitch Suskin (195, 197, 201, 203, 205, 207, 211, 213, 217, 219), Ronald B. Moore (196, 198, 200, 202, 204, 208, 210, 212, 214, 216, 218, 219), David Takemura (199, 206, 209, 215)

Post Production Supervisor: Stephen Welke (195-207)

Scenic Art Supervisor/Technical Consultant: Michael Okuda

Senior Illustrator/Technical Consultant: Rick Sternbach

Make-Up Designed and Supervised by: Michael Westmore

Art Director: Louise Dorton

Set Designer: Greg Berry (195, 197, 199, 201, 203, 205, 207, 209, 211, 213, 215, 217, 219), Greg Hooper (196, 198, 200, 202, 204, 206, 208, 210, 212, 214, 216, 218, 220)

Assistant Editor: Jacques Gravett (195, 198, 201, 204, 207, 210, 213, 216, 219), David A. Koeppel (196, 199, 202, 205, 208, 211, 214, 217, 220), Keith Dabney (197, 200, 203, 206, 209, 212, 215, 218)

Visual Effects Coordinator: Arthur J. Codron (195, 197, 201, 203, 205, 207, 211, 213, 217, 219), Elizabeth Castro (196, 198, 200, 202, 204, 208, 210, 212, 214, 216, 218, 220), Amir Y. Dexter Delara (199, 206, 209, 215)

Visual Effects Assistant Editor: Paul Villaseñor

Visual Effects Associate: Chad Zimmerman

Script Supervisor: Cosmo Genovese

Special Effects: Dick Brownfield

Property Master: Alan Sims

Construction Coordinator: Al Smutko

Scenic Artist: Wendy Drapanas (195-200, 214-220), Jim Magdaleno (203-213)

Video Supervisor: Denise Okuda

Hair Designer: Josée Normand

Make-Up Artists: Tina Hoffman (195, 197-199, 201-203, 205-207, 209-211, 213-215, 217-219), Scott Wheeler (195, 196, 198-200, 202-204, 206-208 210-212, 214-216, 218-220), James Rohland (195-197, 199-201, 203-205, 207-209, 211-213, 215-217, 219, 220), Suzanne Diaz (196-198, 200-202, 204-206, 208-210, 212-214, 216-218, 220)

Hair Stylists: Charlotte A. Gravenor, Gloria Montemayor

(195, 197, 199, 201, 203, 205, 207, 209, 211, 213, 215, 217, 219), Viviane Normand (196, 198, 200, 202, 204, 206, 208, 210, 212, 214, 216, 218, 220)

Wardrobe Supervisor: Carol Kunz

Sound Mixer: Alan Bernard, C.A.S.

Camera Operator: Douglas Knapp S.O.C.

Chief Lighting Technician: Bill Peets

First Company Grip: Randy Burgess

Key Costumers: Tom Siegel (195, 197, 199, 201, 203, 205, 207, 209, 211, 213, 215, 217, 219), Matt Hoffman (195, 197, 199, 201, 203, 205, 207, 209, 211, 213, 215, 217, 219), Kimberley Shull (196, 198, 200, 202, 204, 206, 208, 210, 212, 214, 216, 218, 220), Jamie Thomas (196, 204, 208, 212, 216, 220), Erin Regan (198, 200, 202, 206, 210, 214, 218)

Music Editor: Gerry Sackman

Supervising Sound Editor: Bill Wistrom

Supervising Sound Effects Editor: Masanobu Tomita (195-207), Jim Wolvington (208-220)

Sound Editors: Jim Wolvington (195-207), Masanobu Tomita (208-220), T. Ashley Harvey, Dale Chaloukian

Choreographer: Laura Feder Behr (216)

Production Coordinator: Diane Overdiek

Post Production Coordinator: Monique K. Chambers

Production Associates: David Rossi, Maril Davis, Michael O'Halloran

Pre-Production Coordinator: Lolita Fatjo

Assistant to Producers: Christopher Culhane (195, 198, 201, 204, 207, 210, 213, 216, 219), Eric Norman (196, 199, 202, 205, 208, 211, 214, 217, 220), Robert J. Doherty (197, 200, 203, 206, 209, 212, 215, 218)

Stunt Coordinator: Dennis Madalone (195-197, 203, 205, 207, 208, 211, 212, 215, 220)

Location Manager: Lisa White (198, 205)

Science Consultant: Andre Bormanis

Main Title Design by: Santa Barbara Studios, Dan Curry

Post Production Sound: Modern Sound (195), 4MC Sound Services (196-220)

Filmed with Panavision® Cameras and Lenses

Digital Optical Effects: Digital Magic

Special Video Compositing: CIS, Hollywood

Editing Facilities: Four Media Company

Computer Generated Effects: Foundation Imaging (195-201, 203-205, 207, 209-213, 215, 217-219), Digital Muse (199, 202, 206, 208 209, 212-214, 220), Black Pool Studios (207, 217), Santa Barbara Studios (220)

SEASON 6 CREDITS
Star Trek: Voyager
BASED UPON *STAR TREK* CREATED BY
GENE RODDENBERRY

STARRING

Kate Mulgrew as Captain Kathryn Janeway
Robert Beltran as Chakotay
Roxann Dawson as B'Elanna Torres
Robert Duncan McNeill as Tom Paris
Ethan Phillips as Neelix
Robert Picardo as The Doctor
Tim Russ as Tuvok
Jeri Ryan as Seven of Nine
Garrett Wang as Harry Kim

PRODUCTION STAFF

Created by: Rick Berman & Michael Piller & Jeri Taylor
Theme by: Jerry Goldsmith
Creative Consultant: Jeri Taylor
Creative Consultant: Michael Piller
Co-Producer: Brad Yacobian
Producer: Robin Burger (231-246)
Producer: J.P. Farrell
Supervising Producer: Merri D. Howard
Supervising Producer: Kenneth Biller (221)
Supervising Producer: Peter Lauritson
Co-Executive Producer: Ronald D. Moore (221, 222)
Co-Executive Producer: Kenneth Biller (225-246)
Co-Executive Producer: Joe Menosky
Executive Producers: Rick Berman & Brannon Braga
Co-Producer: Dawn Velazquez
Associate Producer: Stephen Welke
Executive Story Editor: Bryan Fuller
Story Editor: Nick Sagan (221)
Story Editor: Michael Taylor
Music by: Jay Chattaway (221, 225, 227, 230, 235, 237, 241, 245), Dennis McCarthy (222, 224, 229, 232, 234, 238, 243, 246), David Bell, (223, 226, 231, 236, 239, 244), Paul Baillargeon (228, 233, 240, 242)
Director of Photography: Marvin V. Rush, A.S.C.
Production Designer: Richard D. James
Editor: Daryl Baskin (221, 224, 227, 230, 233, 236, 239, 242, 245), Robert Lederman (222, 225, 228, 231, 234, 237, 240, 243, 246), Tom Benko, A.C.E. (223, 226, 229, 232, 235, 238, 241, 244)
Unit Production Manager: Brad Yacobian
First Assistant Director: Jerry Fleck (221, 223, 225, 227, 229, 231, 233, 235, 237, 239, 241, 243, 245),

Arlene Fukai (222, 224, 226, 228, 230, 232, 234, 236, 238, 240, 242, 244, 246)
Second Assistant Director: Michael DeMeritt
Casting by: Junie Lowry-Johnson, C.S.A., Ron Surma
Original Casting by: Nan Dutton, C.S.A.
Casting Executive: Helen Mossler, C.S.A.
Costume Designer: Robert Blackman
Set Decorator: Jim Mees
Visual Effects Producer: Dan Curry
Visual Effects Supervisor: Ronald B. Moore (221, 223, 225, 227, 229, 231, 233, 235, 237, 239, 241, 243, 245), Mitch Suskin (222, 224, 226, 228, 230, 232, 234, 236, 238, 240, 242, 244, 246)
Scenic Art Supervisor/Technical Consultant: Michael Okuda
Senior Illustrator/Technical Consultant: Rick Sternbach
Make-Up Designed and Supervised by: Michael Westmore
Art Director: Louise Dorton
Set Designer: Greg Hooper (221, 222, 224, 226, 228, 230, 232), Tim Earls (223, 225, 227, 229, 231, 233, 235, 237, 239, 241, 243, 245), Randy McIlvain (234, 236, 238, 240, 242, 244, 246)
Assistant Editor: Keith Dabney (221, 224, 227, 230, 233, 236, 239, 242, 245), Jacques Gravett (222, 225, 228, 231, 234, 237, 240, 243, 246), David A. Koeppel (223, 226, 229, 232, 235, 238, 241, 244)
Visual Effects Coordinator: Elizabeth Castro (221, 223, 225, 227, 229, 231, 233, 235, 237, 239, 241, 243, 245), Arthur J. Codron (222, 224, 226, 228, 230, 232, 234, 236, 238, 240, 242, 244, 246)
Visual Effects Assistant Editor: Edward Hoffmeister
Visual Effects Associate: Chad Zimmerman
Script Supervisor: Cosmo Genovese (221-227, 229, 231, 233, 235, 237, 239, 241, 243, 245), Jan Rudolph (228, 230, 232, 234, 236, 238, 240, 242, 244, 246)
Special Effects: Dick Brownfield
Property Master: Alan Sims
Construction Coordinator: Al Smutko
Scenic Artist: Wendy Drapanas (221-241), James Van Over (242, 244, 246), Geoffrey Mandel (243, 245)
Video Supervisor: Denise Okuda
Hair Designer: Josée Normand
Make-Up Artists: Tina Hoffman (221, 223, 224, 231-233, 235-237, 239-241, 243-245), Scott Wheeler (221, 222, 224-226, 228-230, 232-234, 236-238, 240-242, 244-246), James Rohland (221-223, 225-227, 229-231, 233-235, 237-239, 241-243, 245, 246), Suzanne Diaz (222-224, 226-228, 230-232, 234-236, 238-240, 242-244, 246), Adam Brandy (225, 227-229)

Hair Stylists: Charlotte A. Parker, Gloria Montemayor (221, 223, 225, 227, 229, 231, 233, 235, 237, 239, 241, 243-246), Viviane Normand (222, 224, 226, 228, 230, 232, 234, 236, 238, 240, 242)

Wardrobe Supervisor: Carol Kunz

Sound Mixer: Alan Bernard, C.A.S.

Camera Operator: Douglas Knapp S.O.C.

Chief Lighting Technician: Bill Peets

First Company Grip: Randy Burgess

Video Operator: Benjamin A. Betts

Key Costumers: Kimberley Shull (221, 223, 225, 227, 229, 231, 233, 235, 237, 239, 241, 243, 245), Erin Regan (221, 223, 225, 227, 229, 231, 233, 237, 241, 245), Phyllis Corcoran-Woods (222), Matt Hoffman (222, 224, 226, 228, 230, 232, 234, 236, 238, 240, 242, 244, 246), Tom Siegel (224, 226, 228, 230, 232, 234, 236, 238, 240, 242, 244, 246), Jamie Thomas (235, 239, 243)

Music Editor: Gerry Sackman

Supervising Sound Editor: Bill Wistrom

Supervising Sound Effects Editor: Jim Wolvington

Sound Editors: Masanobu Tomita, T. Ashley Harvey, Dale Chaloukian

Production Coordinator: Diane Overdiek

Post Production Coordinator: Monique K. Chambers

Production Associates: David Rossi, Maril Davis, Michael O'Halloran

Pre-Production Coordinator: Lolita Fatjo

Assistant to Producers: Eric Norman (221, 223, 225, 227, 229, 231, 233, 235, 237, 239, 241, 243, 245), Nicole Gravett (222, 224, 226, 228, 230, 232, 234, 236, 238, 240, 242, 244, 246)

Stunt Coordinators: Dennis Madalone (221, 223, 224, 228, 232, 236, 241, 242, 245, 246), James Lew (232)

Location Manager: Lisa White (221, 231, 236, 237, 239, 246)

Science Consultant: Andre Bormanis

Production Accountant: Suzi Shimizu (237-245)

Main Title Design by: Santa Barbara Studios, Dan Curry

Post Production Sound: 4MC Sound Services

Filmed with Panavision® Cameras and Lenses

Digital Optical Effects: Digital Magic

Special Video Compositing: CIS, Hollywood

Editing Facilities: Four Media Company

Computer Generated Effects: Santa Barbara Studios (221), Digital Muse (221, 223, 227, 229, 233, 235, 241, 243, 245), Black Pool Studios (222, 234, 236, 242, 244, 246), Foundation Imaging (222, 224-226, 228, 230-232, 234, 236-240, 242, 246)

SEASON 7 CREDITS
Star Trek: Voyager
BASED UPON *STAR TREK* CREATED BY
GENE RODDENBERRY

STARRING

Kate Mulgrew as Captain Kathryn Janeway
Robert Beltran as Chakotay
Roxann Dawson as B'Elanna Torres
Robert Duncan McNeill as Tom Paris
Ethan Phillips as Neelix
Robert Picardo as The Doctor
Tim Russ as Tuvok
Jeri Ryan as Seven of Nine
Garrett Wang as Harry Kim

PRODUCTION STAFF

Created by: Rick Berman & Michael Piller & Jeri Taylor

Theme by: Jerry Goldsmith

Creative Consultant: Jeri Taylor

Creative Consultant: Michael Piller

Consulting Producer: Brannon Braga (248-272)

Co-Producer: Brad Yacobian

Producer: J.P. Farrell

Supervising Producer: James Kahn

Supervising Producer: Merri D. Howard

Supervising Producer: Peter Lauritson

Executive Producer: Brannon Braga (247)

Executive Producers: Rick Berman & Kenneth Biller

Co-Producer: Dawn Velazquez

Co-Producer: Bryan Fuller

Associate Producer: Stephen Welke

Executive Story Editor: Michael Taylor

Story Editor: Robert Doherty (248-272)

Story Editors: Phyllis Strong & Mike Sussman (255-272)

Music by: Dennis McCarthy (247, 250, 255, 258, 262, 263, 268, 270), David Bell (248, 252, 254, 256, 260, 269), Jay Chattaway (249, 251, 257, 261, 264, 266, 271, 272), Paul Baillargeon (252, 259, 265, 267)

Director of Photography: Marvin V. Rush, A.S.C.

Production Designer: Richard D. James

Editor: Tom Benko A.C.E. (247, 250, 253, 256, 259, 262, 265, 268, 271), Daryl Baskin (248, 251, 254, 257, 260, 263, 266, 269, 272), Robert Lederman (249, 252, 255, 258, 261, 264, 267, 270)

Unit Production Manager: Brad Yacobian

First Assistant Director: Arlene Fukai (247, 249, 251, 253, 255, 257, 259, 261, 263, 265, 267, 269, 272), Jerry Fleck (248, 250, 252, 254, 256, 258, 260, 262, 264, 266, 268, 271), Michael DeMeritt (270)

Second Assistant Director: Michael DeMeritt (247-268, 271, 272), Lorri Fischer (269, 270)

Casting by: Junie Lowry-Johnson, C.S.A., Ron Surma

Original Casting by: Nan Dutton, C.S.A.

Casting Executive: Helen Mossler, C.S.A.

Costume Designer: Robert Blackman

Set Decorators: Jim Mees (247-249, 257-272), Gary J. Moreno, S.D.S.A. (250-256, 269-272)

Visual Effects Producer: Dan Curry

Visual Effects Supervisor: Mitch Suskin (247, 249, 251, 253, 255, 257, 259, 261, 263, 265, 267, 271, 272), Ronald B. Moore (248, 250, 252, 254, 256, 258, 260, 262, 264, 266, 268, 271, 272), Arthur J. Codron (269) Elizabeth Castro (270)

Scenic Art Supervisor/Technical Consultant: Michael Okuda

Senior Illustrator/Technical Consultant: Rick Sternbach

Make-up Designed and Supervised by: Michael Westmore

Art Directors: Louise Dorton, Ron Mason (269-272)

Set Designer: Tim Earls (247, 249, 251, 253, 255, 257, 259, 261, 263, 265, 267, 269), Anthony Bro (248, 250, 252, 254, 256, 258, 260, 262, 264, 266, 268, 270, 272)

Assistant Editor: David A. Koeppel (247, 250, 253, 256, 259, 262, 265, 268, 271), Keith Dabney (248, 251, 254, 257), Jacques Gravett (249, 252, 255, 258, 261, 264, 267, 270), Noel A. Guerro (260, 263, 266, 269, 272)

Visual Effects Coordinator: Arthur J. Codron (247, 249, 251, 253, 255, 257, 259, 261, 263, 265, 267, 271, 272), Elizabeth Castro (248, 250, 252, 254, 256, 258, 260, 262, 264, 266, 268, 271, 272), Chad Zimmerman (262, 269), Armen V. Kevorkian (270)

Visual Effects Assistant Editor: Edward Hoffmeister

Visual Effects Associate: Chad Zimmerman (247-261, 263-268, 270-272)

Script Supervisor: Jan Rudolph

Special Effects: Richard Ratliff

Property Master: Alan Sims

Construction Coordinator: Al Smutko

Scenic Artist: James Van Over (247-249, 251, 253, 255, 257, 259, 261, 263, 265, 267, 269, 271), Geoffrey Mandel (250, 252, 254, 256, 258, 260, 262, 264, 266, 268, 270, 272)

Video Supervisor: Denise Okuda

Hair Designer: Josée Normand

Make-Up Artists: Tina Hoffman (247, 249-251, 253-255, 257-259, 261-263, 265-267, 269-271), Scott Wheeler (247, 248, 251, 252, 255, 256, 258-260, 262-264, 266-268, 269-272), James Rohland (247-

257, 259-261, 263-265, 267, 268, 271, 272), Suzanne Diaz-Westmore (248-250, 252-254, 256-258, 260-262, 264-266, 268-270, 272)

Hair Stylists: Charlotte A. Parker, Gloria Montemayor (247, 249, 251, 253, 255, 257, 259, 261, 263, 265, 267, 269, 271), Viviane Normand (248, 250, 252, 254, 256, 258, 260, 262, 264, 266, 268, 270, 272)

Wardrobe Supervisor: Carol Kunz

Sound Mixer: Alan Bernard, C.A.S.

Camera Operator: Douglas Knapp S.O.C.

Chief Lighting Technician: Bill Peets

First Company Grip: Randy Burgess

Video Operator: Ben Betts

Key Costumers: Tom Siegel (247, 249, 251, 253, 255, 257, 259, 261, 263, 265, 267, 269, 271), Matt Hoffman (247, 249, 251, 253, 255, 257, 259, 261, 263, 265, 267, 269, 271), Kimberley Shull (248, 250, 252, 254, 256, 258, 260, 262, 264, 266, 268, 270, 272), Erin Regan (248, 252, 256, 260, 264, 268, 272), Jamie Thomas (250, 254, 258, 262, 266, 270)

Music Editor: Gerry Sackman

Supervising Sound Editor: Bill Wistrom

Supervising Sound Effects Editor: Jim Wolvington

Sound Editors: Masanobu Tomita, T. Ashley Harvey, Dale Chaloukian

Production Coordinator: Diane Overdiek

Post Production Coordinator: Monique K. Chambers

Production Associates: David Rossi, Maril Davis (247, 248), Michael O'Halloran, Joanna Fuller (249-272)

Pre-Production Coordinator: Maggie Allen

Assistant to Producers: Nicole Gravett (247, 249, 251, 253, 255, 258, 261, 264, 267, 270), Eric Norman (248, 250, 252, 254, 256, 259, 262, 265, 268, 271), Terry Matalas (257, 260, 263, 266, 269, 272)

Stunt Coordinator: Dennis Madalone (247-249, 251, 253-257, 259, 260, 262, 263, 266-270)

Location Manager: Lisa White (252, 253, 268)

Science Consultant: Andre Bormanis

Production Accountant: Suzi Shimizu

"Ventu" Choreography: Albie Selznick (268)

Main Title Design by: Santa Barbara Studios, Dan Curry

Post Production Sound: Todd Studios Burbank

Digital Optical Effects: Composite Image Systems

Editing Facilities: Level 3 Post

Computer Generated Effects: Foundation Imaging (247, 249, 253-255, 257, 259, 261-263, 265, 267, 269-272), Black Pool Studios (247, 252, 253, 267, 269, 271), Eden Effects (248, 250), Eden FX (252, 254, 256, 258, 260, 262, 264, 266, 268, 270), Digital Firepower (262, 263)

Filmed with Panavision® Cameras and Lenses

The following people received writing credit on the series. For their specific credit, please see the episode for which they are cited.

Abbott, Chris: 111

Bader, Hilary J.. 107

Berman, Rick: 101/102, 194, 201, 214, 220, 221, 241, 271/272

Biller, Kenneth: 114, 115, 118, 119, 121, 127, 136, 140, 147, 153, 159, 163, 167, 171, 178, 192, 197, 202, 210, 215, 219, 220, 230, 234, 245, 250, 251, 260, 261-265, 268, 271/272

Bond, Ed: 135

Bormanis, Andre: 156, 182, 192, 227, 248, 256, 264

Braga, Brannon: 103, 105, 106, 109, 113, 117, 120, 122, 126, 132, 137, 145, 148, 150, 151, 154, 160, 161, 165, 168, 169, 176, 177, 184, 186, 187, 191, 194, 195, 196, 201, 206, 211, 212, 214, 216, 217, 219, 221, 225, 236, 241, 243, 246, 247, 264, 266, 271/272

Brody, Larry: 125

Brown, Paul: 239

Brozak, George A.: 144

Bruno, John: 243

Burger, Robin: 231, 236, 242

Burke, J. Kelley: 260

Cameron, Geo: 143

Connors, Eileen: 206

Corea, Nicholas: 129

Coyle, Paul Robert: 111

DeLuca, Michael: 132

DeHaas, Timothy: 105

deLayne, Juliann: 226

Dent, Skye: 105

Dial, Bill: 107

Diggs, Jimmy: 118, 160, 179, 189, 203, 205

Doherty, Robert (J.): 188, 203, 209, 227, 232, 238, 243, 248, 250, 252, 259, 265, 271/272

Eastlake, Carleton: 248

Elliot, Greg: 110, 190

Friedman, Michael Jan: 128

Fuller, Bryan: 174, 180, 185, 191, 196, 205, 207, 213, 215, 218, 223, 226, 228, 237, 241, 245, 253, 254, 262, 263, 267

Gaberman, Mark: 140, 152, 185, 235, 270

Gadas, Richard: 139

George III, David R.: 110

Gitto, Dianna: 240

Glassner, Jonathan: 114

Green, Raf: 234, 239, 243, 253, 254, 260, 261, 269

Harris, Clayvon C.: 147

Holland, Gary: 134

Hosek, Rich: 119

Kahn, James: 250, 258, 261, 268

Kay, Steve J.: 118, 189

Kemper, David: 104

Kenney, Gannon: 232

Klein, Jack: 115

Klein, Karen: 115

Klein, Sherry: 175

Klink, Lisa: 128, 138, 143, 148, 152, 157, 162, 166, 173, 175, 181, 185, 189

Kloor, Harry Doc: 164, 174, 175, 196

Lederman, Robert: 256

Long, Dave: 256

Matthias, Jean Louise: 116, 156

Menosky, Joe: 113, 139, 144, 148, 150, 151, 155, 161, 165, 168, 169, 170, 176, 177, 179, 186, 187, 191, 194, 195, 196, 201, 206, 208, 211, 212, 217, 220, 221, 224, 225, 229, 233, 240, 244, 246, 247

Miller, Scott: 202

Monaco, Jack: 253, 254

Moore, Ronald D.: 222, 223

Morris, Eric: 255

Nemecek, Larry: 260

Nimerfro, Scott: 115

Perricone, Michael: 110, 190

Picardo, Robert: 243

Piller, Michael: 101/102, 104, 106, 108, 125, 130, 133, 142, 146

Piller, Shawn: 130, 153

Prady, Bill: 209

Price, Andrew Shepard: 140, 152, 185, 235, 270

Rudnick, Arnold: 119

Ryan, Kevin J.: 128

Sagan, Nick: 198, 205, 213, 215, 218

Schnaufer, Jeff: 135

Scott, Jessica: 228

Shankar, Naren: 112

Smith, Mark Haskill: 251

Somers, Evan Carlos: 108

Stillwell, Eric A.: 110

Strong, Phyllis: 255, 260, 266, 270

Sussman, Michael: 133, 149, 245, 246, 247, 255, 257, 259, 260, 266, 270

Szollosi, Tom: 106, 123

Taylor, Jeri: 101/102, 107, 118, 120, 124, 131, 135, 141, 158, 164, 172, 183, 193, 200

Taylor, Michael: 199, 204, 207, 208, 210, 214, 216, 218, 219, 225, 226, 228, 233, 235, 241, 249, 255, 257, 263, 267
Thomton, James: 115
Trombetta, Jim: 103
Vallely, Bill: 224
Wilkerson, Ronald: 116, 156, 238
Williams, Anthony: 126, 138
Williams, Rick: 181
Wollaeger, Mike: 228
Zabel, David: 230

DIRECTORS

Beaumont, Gabrielle: 233
Biller, Kenneth: 173, 193
Bole, Cliff: 126, 133, 136, 140, 144, 151, 153, 197, 209, 211
Bruno, John: 224, 241
Burton, LeVar: 108, 134, 174, 201, 242, 256, 265, 269
Conway, James L.: 120, 124, 130, 138
Dawson, Roxann: 227, 263
Eastman, Allan: 184, 218
Frakes, Jonathan: 117, 123, 129
Friedman, Kim: 103, 113, 115, 119
Kolbe, Winrich: 101/102, 105, 107, 114, 118, 121, 128, 142, 146, 148, 169, 194, 203, 208, 225, 240, 249, 251
Kretchmer, John: 199, 219
Kroeker, Allan: 163, 166, 176, 180, 207, 215, 231, 236, 246, 252, 262, 264, 271/272
Landau, Les: 104, 110, 112, 131, 135, 147, 196, 204, 234
Lauritson, Peter: 258
Liddi, Allison: 235
Livingston, David: 106, 109, 116, 122, 127, 137, 145, 150, 152, 165, 168, 175, 183, 186, 195, 198, 200, 210, 217, 220, 221, 226, 237, 245, 248, 254, 266
Lobl, Victor: 187, 189
Malone, Nancy: 158, 181
McNeill, Robert Duncan: 143, 159, 216, 255
O'Hara, Terrence: 214
Picardo, Robert: 155, 228
Robinson, Andrew J.: 157, 190
Rush, Marvin V.: 139, 162
Russ, Tim: 191
Scheerer, Robert: 111, 160
Singer, Alexander: 125, 132, 141, 149, 154, 161, 167, 171, 178, 182
Treviño, Jesús Salvador: 156, 172, 179, 185, 188
Vejar, Mike: 177, 206, 223, 230, 232, 239, 244, 247, 253, 259, 261, 267, 270
Williams, Anson: 164, 170, 192, 213

Windell, Terry: 205, 212, 222, 229, 238, 243, 250, 257, 260, 268

GUEST ACTORS

Abercrombie, Ian/Abbot: 216/Milo: 237
Agnew, Michelle/Scharn: 185
Aguilar, Christopher/Andrew: 163
Alexander, Jason/Kurros: 214
Allin, Jeff/Gedrin: 225
Altshuld, Alan/Sandal Maker: 144/Lumas: 172
Amendola, Tony/Chorus #3: 244
Amodeo, Luigi/Gigolo: 106
Anderson, David Keith/Crew Member: 236
Anderson, Nathan/Namon: 171
Aniston, John/Quarren Ambassador: 262, 263
Ansara, Michael/Kang: 145
Arenberg, Lee/Pelk: 215
Armstrong, Vaughn/Telek: 107/Two of Nine: 222/Vidiian Captain: 241/Alpha-Hirogen: 253, 254/Korath: 271
Arrants, Rod/Daleth: 191
Augustus, Sherman/Hu'Qa: 223
Austin, Jeff /Allos: 189
Austin, Karen/Miral: 223
Averi, Brooke/Little Girl #1: 252
Axelrod, Jack/Chorus #1: 244
Babcock, Todd/Ensign Mulchaey: 196
Baer, Parley/Old Man #1: 143
Bahr, Iris/Female Cadet: 271
Bailey, Kirk/Magnus Hansen: 211, 212
Baker, Becky Ann/Guide: 143
Baker-Bernard, Sharisse/Leosa: 251
Barba, Ted/Malin: 178
Barrett, Majel/Computer Voice: 101, 105, 111-113 115-117, 121-125, 127, 132-135, 137, 142, 146, 148, 149, 151, 152, 155, 158, 161, 165-167, 172, 174, 176, 177, 179, 181, 182, 187-189, 192-194, 196, 197, 199, 200-204, 206-210, 212, 213, 215, 217, 220-222, 224, 225, 228-231, 235, 237-241, 243-245, 248, 249, 251-253, 255, 257, 258, 260, 262, 264-266, 268-272/Announcer: 102/Narrator: 126, 146, 169, 247, 254, 263
Battan, Cyia/Irina: 249
Begley Jr., Ed/Henry Starling: 150, 151
Behrens, Michael/Coyote: 262, 263
Bell, Nancy/Ensign Jetal: 206
Benko, Brooke/Transporter N.D.: 268
Bennington, Mark/Adult Icheb: 257
Betances, Daniel/Pilot: 197
Bevine, Victor/Security Guard: 230
Billig, Simon/Hogan: 131, 133, 135, 137, 140, 141, 146
Birkelund, Olivia/Gilmore: 220, 221

Bluhm, Brady/Latika: 104
Boehmer, J. Paul/Nazi Kapitan: 186, 187/One: 196
Bohne, Bruce/Ishan: 157
Bollman, Ryan/Donik: 253, 254
Branch, Vanessa/Adult Naomi: 257
Brazile, Leroy D./Young Tuvok: 205
Breck, Jonathan/Dying Borg: 222
Brenner, Eve H./Korenna Mirell: 148
Brogger, Ivar/Orum: 159/Barus: 268
Brooks, Alan/Annari Commander: 256
Brooks, Fleming/Soldier One: 236
Brown, Henry/Numiri Captain: 108
Brown, Robert Curtis/Ambassador: 268
Brown, Wren T./Kohlar: 260
Bryan, Erica Lynne/Little Girl (Annika): 174
Bullock, Gary/Goth: 160
Burke, David/Regular Guy: 216
Burnett, Brock/Male N.D.: 266
Burns, Bobby/Frane: 178
Burton, LeVar/Captain Geordi LaForge: 201
Butler, Dan/Steth: 188
Butler, Jerome/Korok: 246, 247
Cade, Mark Daniel/Technician: 230
Cadora, Eric/Alien 212
Caldare, Marie/Azen: 234
Callan, Cecile/Ptera: 109
Camp, Hamilton/Controller Vrelk: 197
Campanella, Joseph/Arbitrator: 266
Canada, Ron/Fesek: 215
Canavan, Michael/Curneth: 190
Cariou, Len/Admiral Janeway: 158
Carlin, Tony/Kohl Physician: 139
Carmichael, Clint/Hirogen Hunter: 184
Carrasco, Carlos/Bahrat: 156
Carroll, Christopher/Alben: 162
Cedar, Larry/Tersa: 131
Cellini, Jon/Technician: 233
Chambers, Marie/Kyrian Arbiter: 191
Chandler, Jefrey Alan/Hatil Garan: 109
Chaucy, Christinna/Level Blue Nurse: 250
Chaves, Richard/Chief: 125
Christie, Julianne/Dexa: 269
Cirigliano, John/Alien #1: 109
Claire, Jan/Frannie: 231
Clark, Josh/Lt. Carey: 101, 103, 110, 111, 218, 241, 267
Clarke, Christopher/Lord Byron: 161
Clayton, Terrell/Andrews: 257
Clendenin, Bob/Vidiian Surgeon: 137
Clennon, David/Crell Moset: 200
Cockrum, Dennis/Orek: 242

Colaizzi, Robert Allen Jr./Dying Colonist: 236
Collins, Jessica/Linnis Paris: 163
Colman, Booth/Penno: 171
Colson, Mark/Dream Alien: 182
Combs, Jeffrey/Penk: 232
Connell, Kelly/Sklar: 160
Conrad, Christian R./Dunbar: 150, 151/Miner: 269
Coppola, Alicia/Lt. Stadi: 101
Correll, Terry/Crew Member: 118, 119
Corsentino, Frank/Gegis: 252
Cottrell, Mickey/Dumah: 174
Covics, Chris/Assistant: 249
Cowgill, David/Primitive Alien: 146
Craig, Tamara/Haley: 243
Craven, Mimi/Jisa: 225
Crivello, Anthony/Adin: 152
Cumpsty, Michael/Lord Burleigh: 113, 124
Curry, Christopher/Driver: 217
Curtis, Keene/Old Man #2: 143
Daniel, Gregg/Mobar: 242
Damas, Bertila/Three of Nine: 222
Darga, Christopher/Y'sek: 214
Darrow, Henry/Kolopak: 125, 142
Davidson, Scott/Bolian: 265
Davies, Stephen/Nakahn: 161
Davis, Carole/Diva: 149
Davis, John Walter/Merchant: 144
Davis-Reed, Timothy/Kyrian Spectator: 191
Davison, Bruce/Jareth: 148
de Lancie, John/Q: 130, 153, 265
de Lancie, Keegan/Q2: 265
De Souza, Noel/Gandhi: 161
Deakins, Mark/Hirogen SS Officer: 186, 187/Axum: 246, 247
Dekker, Thomas/Henry: 116, 124
del Arco, Jonathan/Fantome: 261
DeLongis, Anthony/Maje Cullah: 111, 127, 131, 142, 146
Demmings, Pancho/Kradin Soldier: 171
Dennis, Peter/Isaac Newton: 130/Admiral Hendricks: 267
Dennis, Steve/Alien: 219/Crew Member: 220, 221/Night Alien: 195
deZarn, Tim/Haliz: 121/Yediq: 259
Dick, Andy/EMH-2: 181
Diol, Susan/Danara Pel: 136, 141
Dohrmann, Angela/Ricky: 106, 133
Doty, David/Nuu'Bari Miner: 254
Dowling, Baibre/Edith: 237
Drake, Larry/Chellick: 250
Durbin, John/Alien Miner: 250

McGrath, Derek/Chell: 116, 251
McIntire, Duffie/Grace: 231, 237
McKean, Michael/The Clown: 139
McKee, Robin/Lidell Ren: 108
McKenzie, Matt/Port Authority Officer: 268
McKeown, Fintan/Michael: 231, 237
McLellan, Zoe/Tal Celes: 240, 245
McManus, Don/Zio: 147
McMillan, Don/Hirogen #3: 253
McNamara, Brian/Lt. William Chapman: 216
McNeil, Timothy/Miner #2: 242
McPhail, Marnie/Alcia: 138
McReady, Walter Hamilton/Tribal Alien: 233
Mellis, Joe/Young Solider: 236
Meltzer, Ian/Brax: 269
Mer, Erica/Human Girl: 203
Metcalf, Mark/Hirogen Medic: 186, 187
Michaels, Janna/Young Kes: 163
Milder, Andy/Nar: 270
Miles, Scott/Terek: 256
Miller, Jeanette/Woman: 178
Minton, Nina/Frola: 165
Monaghan, Marjorie/Freya: 112
Monahan, Debbi A./Adulteress: 250
Moore, Christopher Liam/Veer: 165/Stowaway: 210
Morello, Tom/Junction Operator: 240
Morgan, Rosemary/Piri: 147
Morocco, Beans/Rib: 147
Morris, Iona/Umali: 262
Morris, Phil/Lt. John Kelly: 228
Morrison, Kenny/Gerron: 116
Morrissey, Roger/Beta-Hirogen: 183
Morshower, Glenn/Guard #1: 128
Moses, Mark/Naroq: 227
Most, Don/Kadan: 263, 264
Mowry, Tahj D./Corin: 138
Munson, Warren/Admiral Paris: 124, 202
Murphy, Meghan/Karya: 171
Murray, Clayton/Porter: 151
Nardini, James/Wixiban: 156
Ndefo, Obi/Protector: 233
Neame, Christopher/Unferth: 112
Neiman, Christopher/Yeggie: 252
Nelson, Craig Richard/Vaskan Arbiter: 191
Nelson, Sandra/Marayna: 155
Newman, Andrew Hill/Jaret: 110
Noah, James/Rislan: 166
O'Brien, Gary/Crew Member: 118
O'Brien, Paul F./Geral: 256
Oglesby, Randy/Kir: 204
O'Heir, Jim/Husband: 250

O'Herlihy, Gavin/Jabin: 102
O'Hurley, Shannon/Kohl Programmer: 139
O'Mahoney, Stephen/Med Tech: 250
Oppenheimer, Alan/Nezu Ambassador: 160
Orser, Leland/Dejaren: 173
Ostro, Ron/Borg Drone: 193
Palmas, Joseph/Antonio: 125
Palmer, Andrew/Errant Drone: 247
Palomino, Carlos/Boxer: 208
Parks, James/Vel: 147
Parks, Lindsey/Little Girl #2: 252
Parsons, Jennifer/Ocampa Nurse: 101, 102
Paton, Angela/Aunt Adah: 101
Patterson, Susan/Ensign Kaplan: 150, 151, 159
Penny, Chase/Cabana Boy: 252
Péré, Wayne/Guill: 178
Perez, Miguel/Physician: 271
Petersen, Katelin/Annika: 211, 212
Petty, Lori/Noss: 205
Pierce, Bradley/Jason: 217
Pierpoint, Eric/Kortar: 223
Pine, Robert/Liria: 147
Plakson, Suzie/Q female: 153
Poe, Richard/Gul Evek: 101
Poland, Gregg/*Voyager* Security Officer: 259
Pomers, Scarlett/Naomi Wildman: 199, 203, 206, 209,
    211, 212, 220-222, 225, 229, 233, 236, 238, 239,
    241, 257, 269
Polis, Joel/Terla: 104
Pooly, Olaf/233
Presnell, Harve/Q Colonel: 153
Proscia, Ray/Vidiian Commander: 137
Prosky, John/Otrin: 267
Pugsley, Don/Alien Visitor: 179
Prysirr, Geof/Hanjuan: 160
Quinonez, J.R./Overlooker/Doctor: 270
Ralston, Stephen/Larg: 164
Rankin, Claire/Alice: 226
Rappaport, Stephen B./Motura: 105
Raver, Lorna/Q Judge: 265
Rayne, Sarah/Elani: 138
Rayner, Martin/Doctor Chaotica: 195, 207, 257
Read, James/Jaffen: 262, 263
Reddington, Tina/Girl: 148
Reeser, Autumn/Girl: 268
Reilly, Damara/Alien Surgeon: 263
Reinhardt, Ray/Tolan Ren: 108
Reisz, Michael/Crewman William Telfer: 240
Rhodes, Kim/Lyndsay Ballard: 238
Rhys-Davies, John/Leonardo da Vinci: 168, 179
Ridgeway, Lindsay/Girl-Suspiria: 126

Riehle, Richard/Seamus: 231, 237
Rio, F.J./Joleg: 259
Ritter, Eric/Yivel: 239
Rivkin, Michael William/Nunk: 252
Roberts, Jeremy/Valtane: 145
Robinson, Ronald /Sek: 251
Roche, Eugene/Jor Brel: 148
Rock, The/Champion: 232
Rocket, Charles/Bren: 210
Romero, Ned/Chakotay's Grandfather: 208
Ron, Tiny/Hirogen: 181/Alpha-Hirogen: 183
Rooney, Ted/Varn: 242
Rosenfeld, John/Technician #1: 267
Royal, Allan G./Captain Braxton: 150, 151
Royer, Akemi/Med Tech: 262
Rubinstein, John/Evansville: 120
Rudd, Bob/Brell: 256
Ruskin, Joseph/Vulcan Master: 205
Sachs, Robin/Valen: 261
Saito, James/Nogami: 120
Sakata, Joey/Engineering N.D.: 272
Sakson, Jake/Adar: 203
Sandman, Paul/Healer: 268
Sarstedt, Richard/Starfleet Admiral: 272
Savage, John/Captain Ransom: 220, 221
Savage, Susan/Alien Woman: 236
Sawyer-Young, Kat/Astronaut: 233
Sbarge, Raphael/Jonas: 131, 132, 134, 135, 136
Scarfe, Alan/Augris: 128
Schaal, Wendy/Charlene: 164
Schuck, Jack/Chorus #2: 244
Schultz, Armand/Kenneth Dalby: 116
Schultz, Dwight/Barclay: 117, 230, 243, 252, 266, 271, 272
Scott, Judson/Rekar: 181
Sears, Tony/Starfleet Officer: 181/Borg drone: 246
Selburg, David/Toscat: 102
Selznick, Albie/TakTak Consul: 154/Tash: 229
Seymour, Carolyn/Mrs. Templeton: 113, 124
Sharp, Eric/Map Vendor: 156
Shayne, Cari/Elian: 162
Shea, Christopher/Saowin: 214
Shearer, Jack/Admiral Strickler: 122/Admiral Hayes: 194, 243
Sheppard, Mark A./Icheb's Father: 239
Sheppard, W. Morgan/Qatai: 209
Sherrer, Paul/Voje: 250
Shimerman, Armin/Quark: 101
Shor, Dan/Arridor: 144
Shull, John Kenton/Brok'Tan: 223/Nocona: 269
Silverman, Sarah/Rain Robinson: 150, 151

Sims, Keely/Farmer's Daughter: 101
Sirtis, Marina/Troi: 230, 243, 252
Sloyan, James/Jetrel: 115
Slutsker, Peter/Krenim Commandant: 176, 177
Smallwood, Tucker/Admiral Bullock: 198
Smith, David Lee/Zahir: 161
Smith, Kurtwood/Annorax: 176, 177
Smith, Michael Bailey/Primitive Alien: 146
Spahn, Ryan/Teenage Drone Leader: 235
Spain, Douglas/Young Chakotay: 125
Sparks, Adrain/Entharan Magistrate: 185
Sparks, Ryan/Alien Child: 246, 247
Sparrow, David/Alien/Doctor: 270
Spassoff, Maria/Female Colonist: 236
Speake, Wendy/Technician #2: 267
Spearman, Doug/Alien Buyer: 179
Sperberg, Fritz/Ranek: 255
Spicer, Jerry/Guard: 104
Spound, Michael /Lorrum: 134, 136
Sroka, Jerry/Laxeth: 135
Stapler, Robin/Alixia: 180
Starwalt, David/Captain #2: 255
Steinberg, Eric/Ankari: 221
Stephens, Brooke/Naomi Wildman: 180
Stepp, Larua/Erin Hansen: 211, 212
Stillman, Bob/Turei: 225
Stillwell, Kevin P./Moklor: 172
Storseth, Clay/Alien Man: 247
Struycken, Carel/Spectre: 139
Suhor, Yvonne/Eudana: 110
Surovy, Nicolas/Makull: 104
Szarabajka, Keith/Teero: 251
Takei, George/Captain Sulu: 145
Taubman, Tiffany/Tressa: 138
Taylor, Mark L./Jarlath: 166
Teague, Marshall R./Haluk: 165
Thompson, Susanna/Borg queen: 211, 212, 246, 247
Thompson, Scott/Tomin: 216
Tigar, Kenneth/Dammar: 166
Tighe, Kevin/Henry Janeway: 217
Tinapp, Barton/Talaxian: 114
Todd, Shay/Holowoman: 155
Todd, Tony/Alpha-Hirogen: 184
Todoroff, Tom/Darod: 128
Tomei, Concetta/Minister Odala: 165
Towles, Tom/Vatm: 160
Trotta, Ed/Pit: 147
Truitt, Mark Rafael/Yosa: 251
Tsu, Irene/Mary Kim: 162, 266
Turpin, Bahni/Swinn: 140, 141
Tyler, Nikki/Mother: 174

EMMYS

WINNERS

Outstanding Main Title Theme Music
Jerry Goldsmith, Composer

Outstanding Special Visual Effects
Dan Curry, Visual Effects Producer; David Stipes, Visual Effects Supervisor; Michael Backauskas, Joe Bauer, Edward L. Williams, Visual Effects Coordinators; Scott Rader, Visual Effects Compositing Editor; Don B. Greenberg, Visual Effects Compositing Editor; Adam Howard, Visual Effects Animator; Don Lee, Digital Colorist and Compositor; Robert Stromberg, Matte Artist; John Parenteau, Joshua Rose, Computer Animation; Joshua Cushner, Motion Control Camera

NOMINATIONS

Outstanding Music Composition
Jay Chattaway
"Caretaker"

Dennis McCarthy
"Heroes and Demons"

Outstanding Cinematography
Marvin Rush, ASC, Cinematographer
"Heroes and Demons"

Outstanding Costume Design
Robert Blackman, Costume Designer
"Caretaker"

Outstanding Graphic Design and Title Sequences
Dan Curry, Title Designer; John Grower, Effects and Animation Supervisor; Eric Tiemens, Storyboard/Design; Eric Guaglione, Animation Supervisor

Outstanding Hairstyling
Josée Normand, Patty Miller, Shawn McKay, Karen Asano Myers, Dino Ganziano, Rebecca De Morrio, Barbara Kaye Minster, Janice Brandow, Gloria Albarran Ponce, Caryl Codon, Katherine Rees, Virginia Kearns, Patricia Vecchio, Faith Vecchio, Audrey Levy, Hairstylists "Caretaker"

Outstanding Makeup
Michael Westmore, Supervising Makeup Artist; Greg Nelson, Scott Wheeler, Tina Kalliongis-Hoffman, Mark Shostrom, Gil Mosko, Michael Key, Barry R. Koper, Natalie Wood, Bill Myer, Makeup Artists "Faces"

WINNER

Outstanding Makeup
Michael Westmore, Greg Nelson, Scott Wheeler, Tina Kalliongis-Hoffman, Mark Shostrum, Gil Mosko, Ellis Burman, Steve Weber, Brad Look, Makeup Artists "Threshold"

NOMINATION

Outstanding Hairstyling
Barbara Kaye Minster, Karen Asano-Meyers, Laura

Connolly, Suzan Bagaddi, Hairstylists "Persistence of Vision"

1996-1997

WINNER

Outstanding Hairstyling

Josée Normand, Key Hairstylist; Suzan Bagdadi, Karen Asano Myers, Monique De Sartre, Charlotte Gravenor, Jo Ann Phillips, Frank Fontaine, Diane Pepper, Hairstylists "Fair Trade"

NOMINATIONS

Outstanding Sound Mixing

Alan Bernard, Production Mixer; Christopher L. Haire, Richard Morrison, Doug Davey, Re-Recording Mixers "Future's End, Part I"

Outstanding Costume Design

Robert Blackman, Costume Designer "False Profits"

1997-1998

NOMINATIONS

Outstanding Hairstyling

Josée Normand, Charlotte Gravenor, Viviane Normand, Gloria Montemayor, Chris McBee, Mimi Jafari, Ruby Ford, Delree Todd, Laura Connolly, Hazel Catmull, Diane Pepper, Adele Taylor, Barbara Ronci, Lola "Skip" McNalley, Hairstylists "The Killing Game, Parts I & II"

Outstanding Special Visual Effects

Mitch Suskin, Visual Effects Supervisor; Paul Hill, Visual Effects Compositor; Adam "Mojo" Lebowitz, CG Animation Supervisor; John M. Teska, CG Animator; Arthur J. Codron, Visual Effects Coordinator; Greg Rainoff, Visual Effects Animator; Koji Kuramura, CG Model Artist; Eric Chauvin, Matte Artist "Year of Hell, Part II"

1998-1999

WINNER

Outstanding Special Visual Effects

Dan Curry, Visual Effects Producer; Ronald B. Moore, Visual Effects Supervisor; Elizabeth Castro, Arthur J. Codron, Visual Effects Coordinators; Mitch Suskin, Visual Effects Supervisor; Paul Hill, Don Greenberg, Visual Effects Compositors; Greg Rainoff, Visual Effects Artist; Rob Bonchune, CGI Supervisor; John Teska, CGI Animator; Adam "Mojo" Lebowitz, CGI Supervisor "Dark Frontier"

NOMINATIONS

Outstanding Special Visual Effects

Dan Curry, Visual Effects Producer; Mitch Suskin, Visual Effects Supervisor; Arthur J. Codron, Visual Effects Coordinator; Don Greenberg, Visual Effects Compositor; Eric Chauvin, Matte Artist; Robert Bonchune, CG Animation Supervisor; John Allardice, Visual Effects Animator; Greg Rainoff, Effects Animation Artist; Ron Thornton, Particle Element Supervisor; John Teska, CG Animator "Timeless"

Outstanding Special Visual Effects

Dan Curry, Visual Effects Producer; Ronald B. Moore, Visual Effects Supervisor; Paul Hill, Visual Efffects Compositor; Elizabeth Castro, Visual Effects Coordinator; Greg Rainoff, Visual Effects Artist; Bruce Branit, CGI Supervisor/Lead Animator "Thirty Days"

1999-2000

NOMINATIONS

Outstanding Costumes

Robert Blackman, Designer; Carol Kunz, Costume Supervisor "Muse"

Outstanding Hairstyling

Josée Normand, Charlotte Parker, Gloria Montemayor, Viviane Normand, Jo Ann Phillips, Hairstylists "Dragon's Teeth"

Outstanding Makeup

Michael Westmore, Scott Wheeler, Tina Kalliongis-Hoffman, James Rohland, Suzanne Diaz, Natalie Wood, Ellis Burman, David Quaschnick, Belinda Bryant, Jeff Lewis, Makeup Artists "Ashes to Ashes"

Outstanding Music Composition (Dramatic Underscore)

Jay Chattaway "Spirit Folk"

Outstanding Sound Editing

William Wistrom, Supervising Sound Editor; James Wolvington, Supervising Sound Effects Editor; Ashley Harvey, Masanobu Tomita, Dale Chaloukian, Jeff Gersh, Sound Editors; Gerry Sackman, Music Editor "Equinox, Part II"

Outstanding Special Visual Effects

Dan Curry, Visual Effects Producer; Ronald B. Moore, Visual Effects Supervisor; Elizabeth Castro, Visual Effects Coordinator; Bruce Branit, CG Supervisor/

Lead Animator; John Gross, CG Supervisor; Fred Pienkos, Jeremy Hunt, CG Animators; Les Bernstein, Paul Hill, Visual Effects Compositors "Life Line"

Dan Curry, Visual Effects Producer; Ronald B. Moore, Visual Effects Supervisor; Elizabeth Castro, Visual Effects Coordinator; Paul Hill, Visual Effects Compositor; Greg Rainoff, Visual Effects Artist; John Gross, CG Supervisor; Bruce Branit, CG Supervisor/Lead Animator; Fred Pienkos, Jeremy Hunt, CG Animators "The Haunting of Deck Twelve"

2000-2001

WINNER

Outstanding Music Composition (Dramatic Underscore)
Jay Chattaway, Composer "Endgame"

Outstanding Special Visual Effects
Dan Curry, Visual Effects Producer; Mitch Suskin, Visual Effects Supervisor; Ronald B. Moore, Visual Effects Supervisor; Arthur J. Codron, Visual Effects Coordinator; Steve Fong, Visual Effects Compositor; Eric Chauvin, Matte Artist; Robert Bonchune, CGI Supervisor; John Teska, CGI Artist; Greg Rainoff, Visual Effects Animator "Endgame"

NOMINATIONS

Outstanding Music Composition (Dramatic Underscore)
Dennis McCarthy, Composer "Workforce, Part I"

Outstanding Special Visual Effects
Dan Curry, Visual Effects Producer; Ronald B. Moore, Visual Effects Supervisor; Chad Zimmerman, Visual Effects Coordinator; Paul Hill, Visual Effects Compositor; Greg Rainoff, Visual Effects Animator; David Morton, CGI Supervisor; David Lombardi, Computer Animation; John Teska, Computer Modeler and Animator; Brandon MacDougal, Computer Modeler "Workforce, Part I"

Outstanding Costume Design
Robert Blackman, Costume Designer "Shattered"

Outstanding Hairstyling
Josée Normand, Charlotte Parker, Gloria Montemeyor, Hairstylists "Prophecy"

Outstanding Makeup
Michael Westmore, Tina Kalliongis-Hoffman, Scott Wheeler, James Rohland, Suzanne Diaz-Westmore, Natalie Wood, Ellis Burman, Jeffrey Lewis, Bradley M. Look, Belinda Bryant, Joe Podnar, Dave Quaschnick, Karen J. Westerfield, Earl Ellis, Makeup Artists "The Void"

Outstanding Sound Editing
Bill Wistrom, Supervising Sound Editor; Jim Wolvington, Supervising Sound Effects Editor; T. Ashley Harvey, Sound Editor; Masanobu Tomita, Sound Editor; Dale Chaloukian, Sound Editor; Gerald Sackman, Music Editor "Endgame, Part II"

ST: VOYAGER EPISODE INDEX

TITLE	PRODUCTION NUMBER	ORIGINAL AIR DATE	STARDATE	PAGE
Dark Frontier, Part II	212	2/17/99	52619.2	294
Darkling	161	2/19/97	50693.2	168
Day of Honor	172	9/17/97	Unknown	200
Deadlock	137	3/18/96	49548.7	104
Death Wish	130	2/19/96	49301.2	85
Demon	192	5/6/98	Unknown	242
Disease, The	210	2/24/99	Unknown	288
Displaced	166	5/14/97	50912.4	180
Distant Origin	165	4/30/97	Unknown	176
Dragon's Teeth	225	11/10/99	53167.9	329
Dreadnought	134	2/12/96	49447	97
Drive	249	10/18/00	54058.6	392
Drone	196	10/21/98	Unknown	256
Elogium	118	9/18/95	48921.3	50
Emanations	109	3/13/95	48623.5	28
Endgame	271-272	5/23/01	Unknown	445
Equinox, Part I	220	5/26/99	Unknown	312
Equinox, Part II	221	9/22/99	Unknown	320
Ex Post Facto	108	2/27/95	Unknown	26
Extreme Risk	197	10/28/98	Unknown	258
Eye of the Needle	107	2/20/95	48579.4	22
Faces	114	5/8/95	48784.2	41
Fair Haven	231	1/12/00	Unknown	346
Fair Trade	156	1/8/97	Unknown	156
False Profits	144	10/2/96	50074.3	128
Favorite Son	162	3/19/97	50732.4	170
Fight, The	208	3/24/99	Unknown	284
Flashback	145	9/11/96	50126.4	131
Flesh and Blood, Part I	253	11/29/00	Unknown	401
Flesh and Blood, Part II	254	11/29/00	54337.5	403
Friendship One	267	4/25/01	54775.4	434
Fury	241	5/3/00	Unknown	367
Future's End, Part I	150	11/6/96	Unknown	139
Future's End, Part II	151	11/13/96	50312.5	142
Gift, The	170	9/10/97	Unknown	195
Good Shepherd	240	3/15/00	53753.2	365
Gravity	205	2/3/99	52438.9	278
Haunting of Deck Twelve, The	245	5/17/00	Unknown	378
Heroes and Demons	112	4/24/95	48693.2	35
Homestead	269	5/9/01	54868.6	439
Hope and Fear	194	5/20/98	51978.2	246
Human Error	264	3/7/01	Unknown	426
Hunters	183	2/11/98	51501.4	224
Imperfection	248	10/11/00	54129.4	390
In the Flesh	198	11/4/98	52136.4	260
Infinite Regress	203	11/25/98	52356.2	274
Initiations	121	9/4/95	49005.3	64
Innocence	138	4/8/96	49578.2	106

TITLE	PRODUCTION NUMBER	ORIGINAL AIR DATE	STARDATE	PAGE
Inside Man	252	11/8/00	54208.3	399
Investigations	135	3/13/96	49485.2	99
Jetrel	115	5/15/95	48832.1	44
Juggernaut	215	4/26/99	Unknown	300
Killing Game, The, Part I	186	3/4/98	Unknown	230
Killing Game, The, Part II	187	3/4/98	51715.2	232
Latent Image	206	1/20/99	Unknown	279
Learning Curve	116	5/22/95	48846.5	46
Life Line	243	5/10/00	Unknown	373
Lifesigns	136	2/26/96	49504.3	101
Lineage	258	1/24/01	54452.6	413
Live Fast and Prosper	242	4/19/00	53849.2	369
Living Witness	191	4/29/98	Unknown	240
Macrocosm	154	12/11/96	50425.1	152
Maneuvers	127	11/20/95	49208.5	78
Meld	133	2/5/96	Unknown	93
Memorial	236	2/2/00	Unknown	357
Message in a Bottle	181	1/21/98	Unknown	219
Mortal Coil	180	12/17/97	51449.2	217
Muse	244	4/26/00	53896	375
Natural Law	268	5/2/01	54827.7	436
Nemesis	171	9/24/97	51082.4	197
Night	195	10/14/98	52081.2	254
Nightingale	256	11/22/00	54274.7	408
Non Sequitur	122	9/25/95	49011	66
Nothing Human	200	12/2/98	Unknown	265
Omega Directive, The	189	4/15/98	51781.2	235
Once Upon a Time	199	11/11/98	Unknown	264
One	193	5/13/98	51929.3	244
One Small Step	228	11/17/99	53292.7	336
Parallax	103	1/23/95	48439.7	12
Parturition	123	10/9/95	49068.5	69
Pathfinder	230	12/1/99	Unknown	342
Persistence of Vision	124	10/30/95	Unknown	71
Phage	105	2/6/95	48532.4	17
Prey	184	2/18/98	51652.3	226
Prime Factors	110	3/20/95	48642.5	30
Projections	117	9/11/95	48892.1	48
Prophecy	260	2/7/01	54518.2	417
Prototype	129	1/15/96	Unknown	83
Q and the Grey, The	153	11/27/96	50384.2	150
Q2	265	4/11/01	54704.5	428
Random Thoughts	178	11/19/97	51367.2	213
Raven, The	174	10/8/97	Unknown	204
Real Life	164	4/23/97	50836.2	174
Relativity	218	5/12/99	52861.274	306
Remember	148	10/9/96	50203.1	135
Renaissance Man	270	5/16/01	54890.7	441
Repentance	259	1/31/01	Unknown	415

TITLE	PRODUCTION NUMBER	ORIGINAL AIR DATE	STARDATE	PAGE
Repression	251	10/25/00	54090.4	396
Resistance	128	11/27/95	Unknown	81
Resolutions	141	5/13/96	49690.1	113
Retrospect	185	2/25/98	51679.4	228
Revulsion	173	10/1/97	51186.2	202
Riddles	227	11/3/99	53263.2	334
Rise	160	2/26/97	Unknown	166
Sacred Ground	143	10/30/96	50063.2	126
Scientific Method	175	10/29/97	51244.3	206
Scorpion, Part I	168	5/21/97	50984.3	184
Scorpion, Part II	169	9/3/97	51003.7	192
Shattered	257	1/17/01	Unknown	411
Someone to Watch Over Me	216	4/28/99	52647	302
Spirit Folk	237	2/23/00	Unknown	359
State of Flux	111	4/10/95	48658.2	32
Survival Instinct	222	9/29/99	53049.2	322
Swarm, The	149	9/25/96	50252.3	137
Tattoo	125	11/6/96	Unknown	73
Thaw, The	139	4/29/96	Unknown	109
Think Tank	214	3/31/99	Unknown	298
Thirty Days	202	12/9/98	52179.4	272
Threshold	132	1/29/96	49373.4	90
Time and Again	104	1/30/95	Unknown	15
Timeless	201	11/18/98	52143.6	268
Tinker, Tenor, Doctor, Spy	224	10/13/99	Unknown	327
Tsunkatse	232	2/9/00	53447.2	348
Tuvix	140	5/6/96	49655.2	112
Twisted	119	10/2/95	Unknown	52
Unforgettable	190	4/22/98	51813.4	238
Unimatrix Zero, Part I	246	5/24/00	Unknown	382
Unimatrix Zero, Part II	247	10/4/00	54014.4	388
Unity	159	2/12/97	50614.2	164
Virtuoso	234	1/26/00	53556.4	353
Vis a Vis	188	4/8/98	51762.4	234
Void, The	261	2/14/01	54553.4	420
Voyager Conspiracy, The	229	11/24/99	53329	340
Waking Moments	182	1/14/98	51471.3	222
Warhead	219	5/19/99	Unknown	310
Warlord	152	11/20/96	50348.1	144
Workforce, Part I	262	2/21/01	54584.3	422
Workforce, Part II	263	2/28/01	54622.4	424
Worst Case Scenario	167	5/7/97	50953.4	182
Year of Hell, Part I	176	11/5/97	51268.4	208
Year of Hell, Part II	177	11/12/97	51252.3	210